THE FORSAKEN MONARCH

The Chronicle of Maud - Volume II

Amy Mantravadi

Copyright © Amy Mantravadi 2019
All rights reserved. No part of this publication may be reproduced, stored in a retrieval system, or transmitted in any form or by any means, mechanical, photocopying, recording or otherwise, without prior permission in writing of the author.

ISBN: 978-0-9994325-1-8

TABLE OF CONTENTS

Primary Characters — ix

Chapter One — 1
Chapter Two — 25
Chapter Three — 57
Chapter Four — 85
Chapter Five — 110
Chapter Six — 126
Chapter Seven — 160
Chapter Eight — 195
Chapter Nine — 230
Chapter Ten — 258
Chapter Eleven — 279
Chapter Twelve — 309
Chapter Thirteen — 342
Chapter Fourteen — 371
Chapter Fifteen — 402
Chapter Sixteen — 423
Chapter Seventeen — 448
Chapter Eighteen — 475
Chapter Nineteen — 506
Chapter Twenty — 524

Chapter Twenty One	549
Chapter Twenty Two	578
Chapter Twenty Three	605
Chapter Twenty Four	637

Dear Readers,

Thank you for returning for volume two of *The Chronicle of Maud*, or if this is your first introduction to Maud's story, welcome! I hope very much that you enjoy what you are about to read. I truly believe it is a great story.

I say that not from arrogance, but with a good dose of humility. After all, I did not create most of this story. I am simply allowing Maud to pass on her tale to you. In this book, she endures immense challenges, tremendous pain, and circumstances that continually seesaw back and forth. My own experiences from the time when I first started drafting this book until now (2016–19) have not been quite as dramatic as Maud's, but my internal feelings have often seemed equally tumultuous.

It is not my purpose here to dwell on those personal experiences, but simply to say that I felt as if Maud and I walked hand in hand at certain points. Our challenges were different, yet our trajectories were similar. Much like Maud in this novel, I found myself over this period exiting the early days of my life and confronted with a series of very adult challenges. This book does not represent the end of Maud's story, nor is it the end of mine. We are both waiting for the troubled streams of our existence now colliding to move on to a more peaceful confluence.

Much has been learned in this time, not the least of which is that I am (hopefully) a better writer of novels. My goal with this series was always a bit unique: I was not looking to produce books that would please the widest possible audience. I wanted to write the kind of novels that I would appreciate as a reader, and I wanted to do good service to the woman who is at the center of them.

As a result, I have made many decisions which cut against what you might call the books' commercial interests. I have been assured that this novel, like its predecessor *The Girl Empress*, is too long, spends too much time on historical exposition, and has a few scenes that are not critical to the central plot even if they are meant to serve some greater purpose. After initially searching for an agent and/or major publisher for this work, I realized I was never likely to find someone who would embrace this book in the current literary climate. What has been much harder for me to accept is that this does not mean that I am a bad writer.

Self-publishing always felt to me like a kind of defeat: a failure to earn the seal of approval of the literary elite. But when I found out I was pregnant with my first child, I recognized that I did not want to spend the entirety of my pregnancy begging a bunch of strangers in Manhattan to see value in what I already knew had value. After all, I had never expected to make money from writing novels. This book gave me something more precious even before its publication.

You see, I grew along with Maud. I learned from her experiences, and of one thing I am certain: the message of Maud's life is not commercial success at all costs, neither is it seeking the approval of those who are unlikely to give it. In her life, I see the value of family and friends who truly love you, respect you, and are proud of you. Maud did not always have those things, and that has helped me to see once again how important they are.

So I made the decision to drop my pursuit of greater glory and self-publish this book because I felt it was the best thing for myself and my child at the present time. Not only that, but it allows me to release what in film is called "the director's cut": the story I most prefer to tell in the manner I prefer to tell it. I am extremely grateful to Kindle Press for publishing this novel's predecessor, *The Girl Empress*. When Kindle Press decided not to take on new titles, I was initially disappointed, but now I see that it might be a blessing in disguise. They gave me a start in my writing career, and now I can carry on with greater creative control. And most importantly, this time there will be footnotes!

I wish to thank all who assisted me on this project. Kristina McBride performed two in-depth, substantive edits on this novel, resulting in great improvements from the initial draft. She was a real encourager and gave very constructive criticism. Mark Swift served as my copy editor and made sure everything was ready for publication, helpfully pointing out potential Americanisms. I am always grateful for the love and support of my family and friends, most especially my husband, who has given me the opportunity to write even though it does almost nothing to help our bottom line. I love you dear, and I am so happy to dedicate this book to you.

Friends, we live in a confusing and concerning age. We have questions about gender and sexuality, the future of our planet's ecosystem, the prospect of war between nations, etc. People have lost faith in our historic institutions, and many of the bonds that have traditionally held human beings together are breaking. This is not to say that we are all going to hell in a handbasket, but we are certainly living through a time of change, and that is always scary. I worry about the world in which my child will be raised. Will it be less kind than the one I knew as a child? Less hopeful? More hateful?

Empress Maud lived in a time of change as well, standing at the very beginning of what would become the Renaissance. A few generations after her death, the Black Plague swept through the Eurasian continent, consuming 1/3–1/2 of all human life. Yes, these people had problems just like us. They too wondered if their children would have a bright future.

That is why the study of history is absolutely essential: not just the stereotypical, all too easy narratives spoon-fed to us by those with an agenda. I'm talking about the facts laid bare, both good and bad, and analyzed thoughtfully and impartially. This discipline seems lost in our age, but to be fair, human beings have always struggled with it. Myths are much easier to accept than reality. They do not challenge us in the same way, but neither do they provide us with the same kind of hope. Real people facing real challenges and overcoming: that is something from which we can draw real hope.

My grandparents were raised during the Great Depression and my parents during the height of the Cold War. As an old college professor of mine was keen on saying, "The good old days are the result of a bad memory." But there have been good days, and there will be good days again. Our task is to cherish and protect the good.

Grace and peace to you all. Happy reading!
Amy Mantravadi

P.S. In order to maintain a more authentically medieval style, this novel omits most English words with origins after the year 1500 A.D./C.E. At times, this may result in the appearance of a typo when a word like half-brother is given as two separate words. However, this is almost certainly not an editorial error but a case of adherence to earlier grammatical standards.

P.P.S. All scriptural quotations in this novel are taken from the 16th-century Geneva Bible, with occasional alterations to suit a more modern style. This English translation of the Holy Bible is available in the public domain.

PRIMARY CHARACTERS

The Imperial Court

- Henry V, king of Germany, Holy Roman Emperor
- Mathilda, empress consort, also known as Maud
- Frederick, duke of Swabia, nephew of the emperor
- Conrad, duke of Franconia, nephew of the emperor
- Adalbert von Saarbrücken, archbishop of Mainz
- Drogo, knight in the empress' service
- Gertrude, a lady-in-waiting
- Adelaide, a lady-in-waiting

The Norman Court

- Henry I, king of England, duke of Normandy
- Adeliza of Louvain, queen of England
- "The King's Lads":
  - Robert, earl of Gloucester, illegitimate son of the king
  - Brian fitz Count, illegitimate son of the duke of Brittany
  - Stephen of Blois, count of Mortain, nephew of the king
  - Robert Beaumont, earl of Leicester

- William de Warenne, earl of Surrey
- Roger, bishop of Salisbury, *de facto* chief justiciar of England
- Boson, abbot of Bec
- Grimbald, a physician

Others

- William Clito, nephew of King Henry I, claimant to the dukedom of Normandy
- Geoffrey, son of the count of Anjou
- Adela, a novice
- Henry of Blois, abbot of Glastonbury, later bishop of Winchester, brother of Stephen and nephew of the king
- Waleran Beaumont, earl of Meulan

Important Deceased Persons

- Mathilda of Scotland, former queen of England, mother to Empress Mathilda
- William Ætheling, former heir presumptive to the English throne, brother of Empress Mathilda
- Anselm, former archbishop of Canterbury and tutor to Empress Mathilda

For Vijay
A good husband

"Why should she live, to fill the world with words?"

William Shakespeare, *Henry VI: Part Three*

CHAPTER ONE

"William Ætheling is no more."
 Had I really spoken those words, or had some fiend possessed me and harnessed my voice for its own purpose? My brother, dead—the thought of it pierced my soul.

Was it not just yesterday that we ran through the cloisters together with Lady Beatrice in breathless pursuit, children content to play until dawn? No, that was years ago, yet I had only just heard of my brother's elevation to the dukedom. Only a few months hence, his hands were bound with those of Mathilda of Anjou. He had finally achieved the flower of manhood.

"William Ætheling is no more."

Yes, those words proceeded from my own lips. Even worse, they were the truth: a bitter kind that makes one hate truths. There was no power on earth that could bring him back, for the sea had claimed him for its own.

"There is now only one person alive in whom the royal lines of England and Normandy are joined together. I, Mathilda, empress of the Romans: I am the heir."

Here was the second truth. Whatever my life was before the emperor's clerk, Burchard,had rushed into the cathedral of Mainz and pulled us into the small chamber next to the Gotthard Chapel to give us the fateful news, it was now something else entirely. In the innocence of that time, I did not instantly recognize the great burden that was mine. How could I? I knew only that my father was the king of England, and I was his only child through marriage. Therefore, according to all the laws of men, I would inherit what was his.

"Is that possible?"

There they were: the first words of doubt, spoken by my husband, the great Holy Roman Emperor Henry V. I passed but one moment in time before my inheritance was called into question. Even as the news of William's death had changed my destiny, so those three words seemed to mark the dawning of an uncertain future. I had been pacing back and forth in the dark stone room and turned to look at him standing there across from me, hands perched firmly upon his hips. Even as my own chest felt the strain of each breath, weighed down by the grief of the moment, his features showed all the signs of calm. His bearded chin did not quiver. The scars on his face were not joined by wrinkles of worry.

"What do you mean, 'Is it possible?'" I asked him.

"Are there no males in the House of Normandy who are fit to wear the crown?"

"There are men in the House of Normandy, but none who descend from the former kings."

"Even so, surely you don't think…" The emperor hesitated, unwilling to complete the thought.

"Go on, then!" I goaded. "You do not believe a woman can rule?"

"No, I just meant … What of Duke Robert's son?"

"The traitor William Clito?!" The very thought offended me.

"Well, he is a descendant of the Conqueror. He has many supporters."

"He is a traitor and the son of a traitor! He has no right to rule."

"And what of the children of Adela?"

"The House of Blois?"

"Yes, what about them?"

I felt very much as if he was grasping at straws, and it annoyed me greatly.

"Their lineage is no stronger than my own, for it passes through a woman. And their father is not the king, nor do they carry the blood of Wessex!"

"I do not see why you are so perturbed. People will ask these questions."

I gave him a very pointed look. "People, or you?"

The emperor sighed far more deeply than I felt was warranted. What offense had I caused him? No, the offense was entirely on his part.

"I suppose you will make a case now for my half brother Robert," I said, "but for all the love the king bears him, he is a bastard, and a bastard cannot inherit the throne."

"That much I know, my lady, but consider that there are many who would rather be ruled by a man of lower birth than a woman. However"—here he raised a hand to silence my interruption—"it is true that your reign might be accepted were you to act as joint ruler with your husband. Such situations are more common."

"Are you saying that you intend to push me out of the way and take the rule of England and Normandy for yourself?" I asked, casting another glare his way.

"No! Only this: that such a thing might be deemed fitting by the lords and the Church, until we have a son who can succeed to the throne. Just imagine it! The realms of England,

Normandy, and all the lands of the empire, brought together under the rule of our son. Such a thing has never been heard of since the days of ancient Rome!"

Though I still did not like his claim that I would only be accepted as queen if I was under his command, I had to admit that his idea had merit. If we could just have a son, he would indeed be heir to an empire unlike any other. His glory and renown would be unmatched, and as for the king of France, no longer would Normandy pay homage to him, but rather he would surely owe fealty to us! The Lord had not seen fit to grant us children yet, but perhaps by some miracle we might have a son—a son who would one day rule over the greatest empire in Christendom.

Even so, the excitement that threatened to carry my mind into flights of fancy was held in check by the sorrow that filled my heart. Indeed, I felt guilty that I had forgotten William for even a moment. I was in no mood to talk of empires. There was no glory, no comfort to be had. There was only the abyss of death.

"Let us speak no more of this. I must retreat and mourn my brother," I said softly.

Suddenly, I was roused by the sound of a third voice—a person I had forgotten was standing in the shadows near the portal to the cathedral—saying, "Of course, my lady."

It was Burchard: the man who had brought the ill news that first started this conversation. I had been so caught up in my thinking, talking, and pacing that his presence had rather slipped my mind. He had stood silent throughout our discussion, but now sensed his moment to speak.

"Shall I call the ladies and have them take you back to the palace?"

For just a moment, I noticed the distant sound of chanting in the cathedral and business in the market square that stood beyond the stone walls. Outside, men and beasts were enjoying the gifts of the day, free from the knowledge of my pain. I felt that stepping back across the threshold would mean entering the world again, and the news I had received would become doubly real. It frightened me.

"There is no need," the emperor responded. "I will walk with the empress myself."

He took me by the arm and led me first into the nave of the cathedral, then out into the busy streets of Mainz, but my thoughts were not with him. The warmth of his touch lent me no comfort. I felt as if I was stumbling along in some terrible dream. All I knew was the cold embrace of grief. It seemed to invade my form, and the weight was unbearable.

"William …" I whispered. "William … What strange force drew you hence, and what am I without you?"

August 1165
Rouen, Normandy

How strange it seems to think back now on that part of my life, when I was still so young and had most of my days ahead of me! Now I sit alone by the bank of the River Seine. Well, not quite alone. As my life draws to a close, I think more of heaven, and I long to be closer to God. I also long to tell my story to one who is dear before it is too late.

In the first part of my tale, I spoke of my early years, in which I was stripped from my home and sent to live in the empire. Many adventures I had there, and some I must still share. The news of my brother's death changed the course of my life, and it is to that time that I turn now. My faithful clerk, Lawrence, is writing down my words as always. From time to time, I may share something of my daily life now, always noting the date, but this is of less interest. I come nearer the end now. The glorious days are behind me.

I write to you, my daughter—not a daughter in the usual manner, but a daughter nevertheless. I bequeath to you this account of my days. In it, I share the things I have done, whether righteous or not. I pray you, judge me kindly. Have mercy upon an old soul. But most of all, I beg you, remember me. Remember me as I was in the days of glory and the lonely hours. Remember my sufferings and my joys. Remember that I fought, perhaps not always as one to win, but ever as one to try.

Come now, let us return to the past, for in so doing we remember who we are and what we must become.

I struggle to describe just how painful the news of my brother's death was for me to receive. The death of my mother had left a wound in my heart that was still very much open. I felt as if a part of me had died with her. Then with the death of my brother William, it was as if my entire childhood had been destroyed, and I had no home to which I could return. Yes, my father still lived and breathed, but I barely knew him in comparison, and there was no real affection between us. He had never showed any concern for me except in what I could bring him through marriage. My last memory was of him pushing me into the carriage that would take me away from everything I knew. I had hoped one day to return, but with the sinking of the *White Ship*, there was no possibility of fully returning: the life I once knew was gone.

The first hours after I received the news were spent without food or drink. As day passed into night, I cherished the darkness that seemed to match that in my heart. I was thankful to be shut alone in my bed chamber there in the palace of Mainz, where the world would not see the tears it had brought upon me. At some point, I did fall asleep, and upon waking the following morning, I made my first attempt to continue with life: I opened the hours of the blessed Virgin and began to pray.

"*Gloria Patri, et Filio, et Spiritui sancto. Scitu erat in principio, et nunc, et semper, et in saecula saeculorum.* Amen. *Ave Maria …*"

My voice trailed off. The hours lay open on the bed before me as I knelt on the hard wood floor, hands clasped, soul in torment. How does one pray on such a morning? I felt as if I were in my own Gethsemane. At length, I began again.

"*Domine labia mea aperies. Et os meum annunciabit laudem tuam … Deus in adiutorium meum intende! Domine ad adiuvandum me festina!*" I abandoned the Latin and broke into my own language. "God, oh God! Incline unto my aid!" As my eyes wandered to the left, I glanced into the small mirror sitting next to the water basin. I looked utterly dreadful, my eyes red and my hair a mess, but I cared not. Instead, I spoke into it as if to the Lord, "Make haste to help me! Oh God!"

I heard a noise at the door behind me and halted my declaration. It was Gertrude who entered.

"My lady? Is something amiss?"

What a question! Yes, of course, something was amiss! My brother was dead, along with much of the Norman nobility. Did I not have good reason to raise my voice? Yet I found upon further reflection that I preferred not to speak about something that was not only painful, but would escape her understanding in any case.

"All is well, thank you, Gertrude," I lied. "I will just continue with my prayers."

With that, she departed back into the passage and I returned to the Matins.

"Hail Mary, full of grace! Our Lord is with thee. Would that he were with me …"

I continued in that manner until I was forced to rise up and begin the day. My thoughts were so occupied with the news I had received the day before that I seemed to float along, as if in a dream, so much so that when I finally departed my chamber,

I walked straight into one of the imperial guards. He graciously took the blame, but I felt like quite a fool. I descended the stairs and entered the great hall in the lower level of the palace. The large room had a series of windows near the roof that allowed light to stream down to the floor. The walls on all sides were painted with scenes from the battle between Hildebrand and Hadubrand, and great wood doors on either end of the room swung open and shut as people passed through in either direction.

There was a letter waiting for me on one of the four long tables that in the eve would bear food for hungry mouths. By happy chance or divine intent, the light fell on it directly, as if it was a sacred missive. I sat down upon the bench, paying no attention to the members of the court coming and going, and began to devour its words with the vigor of a parched dog.

Here I found a thorough account of the tragedy. It seemed that my brother William and many of his friends had begged the king's permission to sail aboard the *White Ship*, a new vessel of fantastic speed. The prince had arranged for an ample supply of the best wine to be brought along and provided it to all the nobles and the crew. Such foolishness! They had attempted to overtake the king's ship and sight the English shore before him. Manly idiots! With each sentence, my anger increased over this tragedy that might have been prevented. Such a needless waste of life to the detriment of us all!

Two more of my father's children had died that night: Richard of Lincoln and Mathilda fitz Roy, the countess of Perche. Yes, this was the same countess who was so determined to inform us of the inferiority of English manners compared to those on the Continent. I cannot say I was too sad to be rid of her, but it was her cries for help that caused William Ætheling to return to the ship. In this, he was all nobility, and he deserved a better fate than to perish in the attempt. Would that she had drowned herself and spared us all!

The message was composed in haste, without greeting or salutation. I do not remember who wrote it, but he was not much of an author. There was no word of the king, save for the confirmation that he lived and breathed. For myself, there was no instruction. As I found no evidence that any of the king's lads were on board—that is, my half brother Robert, my cousin Stephen, and all the rest—I assumed that they too were among the living. Alas, William Ætheling's young bride was now made a widow! So much for the alliance with Anjou! Her father would surely wish for her to marry again, but to whom?

"Is there any word from King Henry?" a voice asked.

I looked up from my seat and saw the figure of my knight, Drogo, towering over me. Though he had watched over me all my years in the empire, he had still not perfected the art of making an entrance.

"No word and no sign," I answered. "He must be deep in grief, but I wouldn't know it from this letter, which tells too little for my liking. It must have been written by some young clerk who has no sense of what women require. I fear I shall go mad from lack of information. Drogo, the whole world is descending into chaos! My brother is dead, my mother is dead, and my husband is the most hated man from here to … to … Kiev!"

"Have courage, my lady!" he said, taking his seat beside me on the bench. This was a liberty I would not have allowed most servants, but as Drogo and I had ridden together on a horse on more than one occasion, I would have shared anything with him but my bed. "The preacher Norbert once told me that tests are a gift of the Almighty meant to purify us."

"Is that the same Norbert who was once the emperor's chaplain?"

"The very same, and he received the blessing of His Holiness to carry on a reform of the monastic houses. He is gone to France now."

"Yes, I think I heard something about that," I said. As I was not truly interested in discussing Norbert, I returned to the original subject. "Still, I cannot understand why this has happened! What is to become of me now? Everything is changed."

"I beg your pardon, Lady Mathilda, but it does not appear to me that much has changed. You are still the empress and the daughter of King Henry of England. When you and Emperor Henry have a son, he will be heir to two kingdoms instead of one, should the current king fail to produce another heir. That must bring you some cheer."

I laughed bitterly. "Oh, Drogo, do you know me as little as that? How could I ever take comfort in the death of my only brother?"

"I did not mean … Forgive me," he said, the look on his face entirely earnest. "You were close then?"

I looked down at the letter on the table, fingering its edges. "Yes and no. That is, as close as two royal siblings can be at such an age. I don't think I recognized it then, but now that he is passed on, I feel as if there is a void in my soul that can never be filled."

"I know what you mean. I had a brother, but he took a chill one winter and died. Some days, I still miss him."

For a moment, all was silent between us. The court officials continued to pass by, each on his way to some urgent appointment at the other end of the palace, but we took no heed of them even as they took no heed of us. Then I remembered something from long ago.

"The late King Edward once prophesied that a ruler would be raised up who would be able to unite the royal lines of England and Normandy. He spoke the words on his death bed, as the Normans were about to invade and his own royal line was in danger of destruction. Many came to believe that my brother William would fulfill the prophecy and unite the English and the Normans, preserving both the old and the new. He had the blood of both houses in his veins."

"And now that dream dies with him?"

"Perhaps. But then again, prophecies can be most obscure."

Drogo smiled and rose to his feet. "I'd best be off to my duties, but first you must promise me that you have everything you require."

"That and more. Be off, Sir Drogo! The world requires your attention!"

"God bless you, Empress Mathilda," he concluded, then departed through the door to my left even as some servants carried a chest through the one to my right, and from there likely out to the cathedral.

There was a break in all these comings and goings, and I sat for a moment with only my thoughts for company. This moment of solitude allowed me to reach a conclusion.

"King Henry has been robbed of his son. Now he needs a new one."

When William Ætheling still walked this earth, there was little reason for King Henry of England to trouble himself over the succession, but with William lying in his watery grave, the question of who should become the next lord over England and Normandy was of supreme import, and the solution was obvious: the king must acquire another wife who could bear sons. Therefore, he wrote to my husband, Emperor Henry, and asked for his assistance in gaining a bride who would help to strengthen England's position against France.

The emperor informed me of this one day as I was sitting in the upper chamber. Yes, we called it merely the upper chamber, for it had no set purpose, nor any furnishings. It had been used for keeping tapestries not fit for show—that is, until I noticed that its six windows were two more than any other room in the palace and it was terrible to waste such a space. The tapestries were removed and I would often withdraw there in those winter months, for though there was no fire, the sun rays coming through the glass kept it warm enough for comfort. Without the tapestries, the room seemed utterly bare: only dust lay upon the floor boards, and the stone walls looked almost lonely without ornament.

I was sitting on the one chair that had been brought up for me, attempting to distract myself from my grief with the word of God, when the emperor entered through the room's only door and said, "I have received a note from King Henry requesting my assistance in procuring a bride."

"Oh?" I replied simply, closing the book. I felt a sudden pain in my heart to think that the place once held by my mother would be filled by someone else, but as was so often the case, I kept my thoughts to myself. "Did he say whom he hopes to wed?"

"No, but he does wish to strengthen the alliance against—"

"The king of France—of course."

"You are aware that any sons he might have would rank higher than our own in the Norman line?"

"Naturally, but it is better that the succession should be ensured. Who knows what might happen to me?"

The emperor shrugged. "He could always give the crown to one of his nephews."

I was annoyed to find my husband wandering down that path again, for it seemed an offense to my own inheritance.

"Tell me," I replied, "were I not a woman, would you say such things?"

"You are easily offended! Are things really so different in England than they are here? The German nobles would never accept a female ruler. It goes against the laws of God!"

And this from an excommunicate, I thought, but decided yet again to remain silent. After thinking for a moment, I arrived at an answer.

"Adeliza."

"What?"

"Adeliza of Louvain: Duke Godfrey's daughter. She is the best choice."

"For your father, you mean?"

"Yes. She is young and amiable. Her father is duke of Lower Lorraine, which borders Flanders. It is the site of a great rivalry between Normandy and France. What's more, I saw the lady earlier this year, and she is very pretty. I have no doubt that she would please the king and give him a son."

"The idea has merit," he agreed. "I did have some trouble from Godfrey during the former rebellion, and now that he is back on my side, I should like to keep it that way. Such a marriage would bring him power and esteem beyond even his ambition. He would have every reason to show us gratitude."

"If only men could be trusted to show gratitude when it is due!" I said with a laugh.

"Indeed. Now, I shall speak with Duke Godfrey and make the match as soon as I hear from your father that it is his will. The king may be wed by Candlemass."

"To a woman the same age as myself!" I shook my head in wonder. "That is strange to think of. I wonder what she must be ... my lord?"

The emperor had placed a hand on his belly and seemed to be in pain. It was surely the same malady from which he had long suffered—the cancer in his testicle—and I was struck with fear to think that it might be getting worse. As he was standing near me, I reached out to comfort him, but he stepped away, unwilling to be touched. I remembered yet again that though we had been married for several years, ours would never be a particularly physical bond, nor one of the most passionate love. I was only a child when we wed, and the difference in our ages was one of many reasons that we had never experienced such a connection. However, I did respect and care for him as my husband. I therefore chose not to be offended, but instead asked, "What's wrong? Is it the same pain as always?"

"I suppose," he replied, still wincing. "I feel rather tired."

"We must have the doctor examine you again."

"Why? What is there to be done? He can no more help me now than he did before."

"Perhaps, but it might calm my fears. Will you lie down?"

"No!" he cried, his eyes wide. "I do not need to be treated like a child! I cannot afford to lose a single hour. There is too much to be done."

"It might be this belief that has brought you low."

"I think I know what is best," he concluded, and that was the end of the matter.

After agreeing to the match, King Henry was wed on the fourth day before the Kalends of January, just two months after my brother's death. No one was happier than the bride's father, Duke Godfrey, whose position was raised considerably by his daughter's union. We heard that the new queen was favorably received, for in addition to her immense beauty, she had little interest in great affairs of state and did not seek to hinder the king's business. Ah, to be such a woman!

The rising of the sun begets the setting of the moon. A dance of giants needs be won. Even so, the end of one lord is the making of another, for the laws of nature forbid them to stand together. I continued to mourn my brother in the months after his passing, but at the same time I wondered who would benefit from his untimely death. Would it be some child of my father and the new queen, or would other men rise to claim power? What was my own fate to be? I found I could not dwell on such things continually, for there was much work to do in the empire.

During the days of Lent in the year 1121, my husband set out for Regensburg to speak with the duke of Bavaria, and the rest of the court went with him. We had passed about a week there in good company. The imperial chancellor in Italy, Philip Ravenna, with whom I had spent so much time a few years earlier, had been brought north to serve in the kingdom of Germany, and it was wonderful to have his conversation once again. One day, the two of us and the emperor were all enjoying an afternoon ride in one of the imperial ships down the River Donau, which in Latin is called *Danuvius*. It was a hulk with only a single mast, used solely for river travel. The imperial court had three or four that were towed over land wherever we went.

The three of us were all laying back upon cushions, sipping wine from the Palatinate, when the emperor said, "Let us continue down to Konstanz, for I have business there. I promised the monks of Reichenau that I would visit before the year is out, and I should like to meet with my nephew Frederick and discuss several issues of import."

"Konstanz is in the realm of the Archbishop of Mainz," Chancellor Philip noted.

"Konstanz may lie within that archbishopric, but they would be fools to mistake the rule of Adalbert of Mainz for that of their rightful lord," the emperor replied. "A traitor is owed no allegiance."

Perhaps it seems strange that the emperor would call him a traitor, but Archbishop Adalbert of Mainz had been actively opposing him for years and giving no little support to those who rebelled against my husband's will. That is why the emperor said the men of Konstanz ought to support his rule rather than that of Adalbert.

"Is that not the very argument they would use to counter Your Highness?" I asked my husband, sitting up straight. "You still lie under the ban of excommunication, no?"

"Empress Mathilda, you have grown bold since last we met!" said Philip, laughing and spilling a bit of his drink on the deck. He turned his head toward the emperor. "What have you been doing with her? I remember when she was a scared little thing!"

"It's no use, Philip," my husband answered. "There is something of the wild mare about her, but even the wild mare has its uses."

I made no response to this comment, though inside I was secretly pleased to think of myself in such a manner. I suppose the faintest bit of a smile may have passed over my face as I sank back into the cushion and took another drink of the wine. The ship rocked slightly back and forth as it was hit by the waves, and the sun was just peeking out from behind the clouds. It was a most pleasant day.

The emperor continued, "She is right that there are some men who look to the pope for their direction in all things, whether sacred or secular, and I have offended His Holiness."

"You may yet recover his regard. Go to Konstanz and see Bishop Ulrich. Make a grant to the monks of *Peterhausen*. Visit the craftsmen of Reichenau. These will be signs of your good faith. I have ordered the jurists to renew their efforts and produce a solution to this controversy," Philip offered.

The emperor placed his hand on the chancellor's shoulder, perhaps attempting to steady himself as much as anything, for the boat had begun rocking more fiercely. "I thank you for your pains, friend. Lord knows, I wish to see this matter at an end, but if we are to yield anything to Rome, we must also receive our due reward. Lady Mathilda can tell you: I have been in contact with King Henry of England, and I hope that the peace forged in that land between the crown and the Church might be repeated here. We came close before, and I have reason to believe that under the right circumstances, this pope will be more pliable than his predecessors."

"My father has also been explaining to him the *Danegeld*," I added.

"*Danegeld*? What is that?" Philip asked.

"A general tax of the entire kingdom," the emperor replied.

"And you seek to impose it here?" he scoffed. "No man has yet been born who has a love of taxes, save he that collects them."

"Then let them obey the words of Christ: 'Give therefore to Caesar, the things which are Caesar's, and give unto God, those things which are God's.'[1] If only Calixtus could hear me quote the scriptures thus! I might not be an excommunicate after all," the emperor said with a wink.

"Yes, and the devil quotes scripture too," I noted, winking myself.

"So on to Konstanz!" Philip declared, sensing that at last I might have gone too far, and no doubt wishing to avoid an argument.

The next day, we were sailing back up the Donau toward our next destination. We stayed for a brief time at the royal palace in Ulm, which I admit was not my most favored abode on account of its small size. Our time there was made worse because we were fasting from meat, and for all their proclamations about godly manhood, the men in our party did complain about their hunger rather a lot. I was relieved when we finally set that place behind us and continued along the Donau to the small town of Tuttlingen, not far from the river's source. Here we climbed out of the boats and moved south over land.

---

1 The phrase is found in Matthew 22:21, Mark 12:17, and Luke 20:25.

Konstanz sits upon a narrow strip of land that cuts into the *Bodensee*, that most pleasant lake at the foot of the mountains. I had hoped to view those magnificent heights from the northern shore, but alas, I could see naught but small hills covered in pine trees. We did not enter the city itself, but traveled to the nearby island of Reichenau in a new boat that had been procured for the occasion, the hulks having been left to the north. This ship was more like the cogs used in the North, sturdy enough to go out into open sea. In this case, it was needed to carry all the emperor's chests and other treasures. I could feel the ship sink lower into the water as they were brought on board, and I was rather relieved when we made it across without getting wet.

The island is home to that famous community of brothers holding to the order of Saint Benedict. Those monks are skilled in every craft. They produce the most gorgeous texts, but their greatest work is surely the imperial crown itself, wrought by the goldsmiths of old. I was therefore pleased to make their acquaintance after hearing of their deeds for many years.

Once we arrived in our new lodgings, the emperor and all the leading men of court took over the tables in the refectory and began reading through the many letters that had come in over the past day. I left the guest house and made my way through a grove of *Linde* trees—their green leaves still forming—to join my husband and his companions in the refectory, which stood nearer the water. There I found them poring over all the notes from far and wide that had accompanied us to the island: news of the papal court, one or two letters from Archbishop Bruno of Trier, legal matters to be addressed by the jurists, a personal note from the emperor's sister, and a host of others. There were several long tables in the room, and all of them were covered with scattered papers, stacks of parchment, piles of scrolls, leather bags, and naturally tankards and mugs full of beer. My eyes were drawn to the group near my husband, where one piece of business seemed to be particularly urgent.

"Read this," said Chancellor Philip, thrusting the parchment at the emperor, who was seated across the table.

"What is it?" he asked, holding it up. "I can't make out the seal."

"From a canon of Konstanz. He sent it over just now."

The emperor took a moment to read the letter, and I could see the frustration it caused upon his face long before he spoke. "Well, that's it! The birds have all flown!" he declared, throwing the letter down on the table and pounding it with his fist so hard that some beer flew out of his glass and on to the table.

"You mean the bishop of Konstanz is gone?" Philip asked.

"Precisely. I was supposed to meet him here, but he and all his fellows decided now would be a good time to go on pilgrimage."

"Pilgrimage?!" Philip exclaimed, crinkling both his nose and his brow. "To where?"

"Anywhere but here, I presume. It seems they would prefer not to be seen with me."

It was at this moment that several of the men recognized I was standing there and gave polite nods in my direction. However, my husband was so upset by this latest news that he did not acknowledge my presence. I sat at the far end of the table and remained silent, though for myself I was filled with concern that the bishop's open refusal of the emperor's overtures meant the hopes we held for reconciliation with the Church were rather foolish. Being married to someone who is excommunicated by the Church is a daily stress I can hardly describe. Still, I said nothing of this, for I had no desire to be a prophetess of doom.

"Where is Frederick?" the emperor suddenly asked.

"Here, Your Highness," the duke of Swabia replied, striding into the room through the open door behind me. "I just arrived."

"Thank God for that!" the emperor said, standing to embrace his nephew. He patted the younger man on the sides of his face and then gripped his shoulders. "You look well. Did you bring your wife?"

"No, she stayed behind."

There was a knowing smile on the Duke Frederick's face, and it was clear that he had some news he wished to share.

"What is it then?" the emperor demanded. "Tell me what it is that has amused you so."

"Lady Judith is with child," he answered. "She has taken to her bed and demands that none come near her, save for her own ladies. I think it is far too early ... but there it is."

The emperor dropped his hands and touched the duke's chest with his fist. "That is excellent news! Would that I had known when I saw the Duke of Bavaria, for then I might have told him he shall be a grandfather. And you—you are to be a father!"

"Not so hasty!" the duke begged, raising a hand. "These things too oft go awry. Still, I admit that the idea of another Duke Frederick does fill me with pride. Frederick II! How I have longed for a son who might carry on that good name!"

The emperor did not respond, and I could guess his thinking easily enough. In the six years since our marriage, we had brought forth neither son nor daughter. Though the two of us hardly ever discussed the matter, I sensed that it weighed on his heart as much as my own. The poor duke quickly recognized his mistake.

"Forgive me! I did not mean ... that is, I should not have said ... I ..."

"Please! You need not beg my pardon. I am happy for you," my husband replied. His words were fine enough, but I could see the pain in his eyes.

"How can you be so very sure that it will be a boy?" I asked, hoping by this question to bring an end to the tension.

"I cannot be sure," the duke answered, looking my way. "It is too early for the astrologer ... but it must be a boy!"

"Yes, it must, for then the Salian line will continue," the emperor concluded. "Come! I have something to show you."

With that, the two men departed—presumably in order to speak in private—and most of the lords dispersed. I moved down the bench to examine the pile of papers on the table before me. As I sorted through them, I finally saw the one letter that I had sought for months—nay, for years! It bore the mark of the king of England.

I held the letter as if it were a sacred relic, my fingers tracing the outline of the parchment, feeling every fiber. What news might lie inside? At last, I took a small knife, broke the seal, and began to read.

To my daughter, the venerable Empress Mathilda of the Romans, most esteemed lady, King Henry of England, lord over all Normandy, sends this word from Berkeley in Gloucester Shire, upon this Easter Sunday, the fourth before the Ides of April, in the year of our Lord 1121, wishing God's blessings upon you and all those at the imperial court, most particularly his son by law, the Emperor Henry, king of the Germans, in the hope that you are well and in no distress.

We thank you and your excellent husband for the pains you undertook in gaining for us the hand of Lady Adeliza of Louvain, now queen of England. Never have we passed so happy an hour as when we are in her company, and in her youth, we find ourselves renewed. She is to us a healing balm, drawn from the waters of sweet Elysium—a minister unto our very soul. It is our dearest wish that with the coming of a new year, she might clutch a son to her bosom. For we will have an heir of our own flesh and blood, with all the markings of his father and grandfather, who conquered kingdoms and built them from nothing.

But should the Lord delay in fulfilling his promise, we hope that you too shall give birth to children who might serve as a security for us. We heard a rumor that you were barren, but we refuse to believe it, for the women of Normandy have never suffered such a tribulation as this. Therefore, as soon as you are with child, inform us of your condition. We are most eager to see the fruit of your womb.

To this end, we wish to meet with you and speak frankly, for a great many things now depend upon your actions. Remember your duty to this house and to God, for we sent you hence for two purposes: to increase the friendship betwixt England and the empire, and to bring forth children that might provide for the succession in both kingdoms. Do not forget your charge!

The Lord's grace be with you, now and always.
HENRICUS REX

I folded the letter and sat there for a moment, pondering the words I had just read. In my vanity, I had hoped that the king might inquire as to my own thoughts and feelings, but there was no sign of that. Did he care that I still grieved for my brother daily? Did he share my concerns about what path my own future would take? And what was this? He had heard that I was barren! I had long feared that this rumor would reach even the most distant ears. At least my father was happy with his new bride. How could he not be? She was one of the most comely women I had ever seen and far younger than he.

Of course, the possibility that I was barren was a matter of great distress to me, though I also knew something that the common man did not: I knew that Emperor Henry was ill, and that as a result we had not often shared a bed throughout the course of our marriage. There was no question in my mind that the cancer that threatened his manhood had contributed to our distress.

Not that I was desperate to have children for their own sake, mind you. I liked them well enough, but I did not possess that innate longing for offspring which defines so many women. No, I wanted a child because I knew that until I had produced an heir to the throne, I would not be respected in the same way. Every day that my husband and I did not bring forth an heir increased the threat to our reign. This was a concern for my father as well, though I believe he sought his own good and that of England more than mine.

With the letter still in hand, I walked through the side door and into a garden that stood just outside, where I found my ladies Gertrude and Adelaide collecting flowers. I had seldom walked alone since that evil man had assaulted me in Straßburg a year or two earlier, and the memory of that night still haunted my dreams. I therefore desired company in order to move about. The ladies followed at a short distance as I made my way down to the water's edge to take in the view. The sun gleamed upon the surface of the lake, its reflection only disturbed by the birds that swam to and fro.

"Adelaide," I called. "Do you have my satchel?"

"Here it is, my lady," she answered, giving it to me.

I pulled at the string and placed the folded letter inside. As I did, I felt the precious stone that I had carried with me for years: the amber moth given to me as a child by one of the king's lads, Brian fitz Count, a relic of my past. I pulled it out and examined it once again. In the light of the sun, its color was bright orange. The moth was still trapped there, just as it had always been. How strange to think that I might once again see the one who gave it to me, along with the rest of England!

I placed the stone back inside and pulled out my other most sacred object: the *paternoster* handed down to me from my blessed mother and grandmother. Even if I returned, I could not meet with them, for they dwelt with the Lord in heaven. How I missed the land of my childhood: a land which no longer existed, even if England itself remained. As the ladies continued to wait, I closed my eyes and stood there reciting my prayers one bead at a time. I prayed to God that I would be granted a child, the emperor would be reconciled with the pope, my husband would be healed of his pain, I would please him as a wife, and I would one day set foot on the shores of England again.

Suddenly, there was a noise upon the water, and I opened my eyes to see a pair of the most magnificent birds. I was told that the Germans called them *Haubentaucher*, but I thought I remembered seeing such a creature in England with a different name. They were the size of a goose, but far more elegant. Their heads were covered in a plume of orange and black feathers that gave them the appearance of kings. As I watched, the two birds rose out of the water until they met face to face and swayed in a kind of dance. I beheld them in awe, so graceful were their movements.

"What are they doing?" I asked the ladies behind me.

"The male is attempting to woo the female," Gertrude replied. "It is their way. At this time of year, they always act in such a manner, or so I have heard."

"So that is how they express love?"

"I do not know if birds can love, but yes."

"Would that all God's creatures could love," I whispered, not loud enough for the ladies to hear. "Would that we were all as free as the birds of heaven."

CHAPTER TWO

Once I received that letter from my father, I thought it would be joined by others. Indeed, I thought he might call me to Normandy or England to discuss the succession: perhaps even to appoint me officially as his heir, pending the birth of a new son. Instead, I was left to wait in anguish for a year before King Henry finally summoned me home. How happy it made me to think that I would see the shores of England again! Not only that, but I longed to move out of the state of suspended anguish I had experienced since the death of my brother. Was I to be recognized as heir, or was I not?

Alas, though I traveled west for several days—all without the company of my husband—my progress was stopped when Count Charles of Flanders refused to grant me safe passage through his lands. Why would he do such a thing? Because of his alliance with William Clito, my traitor of a cousin. Clito held hopes of gaining the throne of England for himself, either after my father's death or before. Therefore, he set out to ruin everything, including my travels. What a knave!

I therefore returned to Germany with a heavy heart, having gained neither answers nor a chance to see my home again. Instead, I was placed back in the middle of the investiture controversy: the conflict between Emperor Henry and the pope over who had the right to appoint and consecrate bishops. Many years had already passed without any relief from that perpetual controversy. I thought we should never be rid of it! Though the seeds of agreement were always present, neither the emperor nor the Church was able to reap the fruits of peace. However, as we entered the year of our Lord 1122, it seemed that all the parties were in a mood to put this matter behind them and start anew.

An agreement between the emperor and princes had paved the way for further concord. The two sides even released some of the men taken prisoner over the course of those many battles. Pope Calixtus displayed his good faith by sending three cardinals to the German court as his ambassadors. I dearly hoped that they would reach an agreement that not only freed the empire from conflict, but also lifted the ban of excommunication on my husband. I admit that as I watched my husband grow more ill, I feared for his eternal soul, knowing that he stood outside the bounds of the Church. I cared for him truly as a wife, even if I was never to feel for him quite what Brünnhilda felt for Siegfried. The uncertainty of his situation tore at my heart, and I longed for relief.

Moreover, I remembered how, before my great mother passed on to her eternal reward, she bade me do all in my power to reconcile the emperor with the Holy Father. Though she was by that time long gone, her words were ever present in my mind. When I first took on the title of queen, I felt as one thrashing about in the sea, doing my utmost to keep my head above water. There was no thought of progressing toward anything, but merely of staying afloat. I did not know what it meant to leave a legacy for future generations. That summer, I began to wonder what my role might be in the greater drama—the infinite story in which we are all brought together.

Although no physician had declared it, I feared that my legacy, both to the German people and to my own family, would never include children. This grieved me deeply. I had failed in my first duty: whether by my own fault or that of my husband, I could not be certain, but it hardly mattered. I therefore longed to serve some purpose, and as the clerks began to sharpen their quills for the long foreseen council, I was resolved to do all in my power to bring about my mother's dying wish: to aid the reconciliation of the emperor and the Holy Father.

If ever there is a perfect place to endure the hot summer days—when Sirius sets all men ill at ease—and to embrace a higher vision of life, it is the fortress of Trifels. It sits upon that summit as an eagle in her *airie*, and when one ascends her heights, one moves closer to God himself. A castle crowned with the clouds and adorned with the sun, its feet covered in the unending green of the forest. Ah, the forest! Many a wood covers the face of England, but none so ancient and unyielding as the *Pfälzerwald* and its southern brother, the *Schwarzwald*. This is not merely where the people of that land live. It is in their very bones and marrow, even as the rising hills are in their hearts. The longer I remained there, the more it became a part of me. It was in this castle that the emperor chose to reside as he waited for a decision from the bishops.

In the dark of morning, I would rise up and stand upon the battlements, casting my eyes to the East across the endless stretch of forest. No sound of man could be heard—only the gentle wind and song of birds calling to one another. I could see the line of hills just across the valley, naught but dark forms against the sky. Somewhere beyond, the River Rhine flowed through the towns of Germany, born of the mountains and bound to meet its end in the distant sea. Then as I stood there, my body still casting off its slumber, the rising sun set fire to the sky, and I truly believed in that moment that I was witnessing what God must have seen upon the dawning of creation. I felt a desperate longing, somewhere between joy and sorrow: a sense that I was called to something higher.

The emperor would disappear into the woods most mornings with his nephews—Duke Frederick of Swabia and Duke Conrad of Franconia—and only return when they had struck fear into the hearts of every beast within a day's ride. However, if they ever tired of this pattern, they would instead set their birds to the air and let them do the killing. The emperor had many prized falcons, but none he counted so dear as his faithful Blitz. Such a magnificent creature! I watched that falcon hunt many times, rising and diving, ducking and soaring. His eyes darted to and fro searching for prey. His body twisted in perfect motion. His sharp talons could tear through flesh and even crack bone. Some men might have preferred a larger bird—an eagle, perhaps—but in his Blitz the emperor found a companion as fierce as any that flew the skies.

One day, my husband called me out to where the royal falconer kept the birds: both the emperor's own and those of the other nobles. It was further down the hill path from the castle, on a space only a bit too large to be called a ledge. Each bird had its own cage where it could perch. I passed by at least a dozen such dwellings, the ground underneath covered with both feathers and droppings that stunk in the heat of the day, before reaching my husband, who was feeding a small morsel to Blitz through the bars and whispering to the bird in some language of his own making.

"Good day, Blitz! How is your master treating you?" I inquired.

"Very well, I thank you," the emperor replied, though the question was clearly not directed at him. For his part, the bird simply stared at me with his dark eyes.

"Philip said you wanted me to come," I offered.

"Yes, that is correct." He was still feeding the bird, and thus his eyes did not meet me as he continued. "I have a gift for you: something that I think you will like."

"Oh? And what is that?"

"'What is that?'" he repeated, making a rather poor show of copying me, which did not amuse me as much as he might have hoped. "If you wait one moment, you shall see."

I was in no mood for riddles, but I remained still as my husband began stroking the bird's feathers with a level of gentility he seldom displayed.

"You know my birthday was a very long time ago," I finally said.

"Yes, yes. This is not for that."

"Then what is it for?"

At long last, the emperor stopped pampering the falcon and looked at me directly. "Follow me and I will show you."

He led me to another cage farther up the hill. As he began to fiddle with the lock, I fanned myself with my hand, for the sun was beating down upon us, and I was quite warm underneath my veil and several layers of clothing. We often felt a strong wind on top of the hill, but that day it felt as if the air was not moving at all. Finally, the emperor opened the door, retrieving a bird slightly smaller than Blitz. The falcon flapped its wings a few times as if to stretch them; however, it did not move from its position on the emperor's arm.

"There are some gloves over there," he said, pointing to a box on the ground and motioning for me to retrieve them. "Put them on. You will need them to hold the falcon."

"But why must I hold him?" I asked.

"Her. It is a female."

"Ah. Why must I hold her?"

"Because this is your present, of course!"

"What? The bird?" I asked, thoroughly surprised.

"She is not just a bird. She is a prized falcon bred by the duke of Swabia and sent here for you."

"Frederick wanted me to have this?"

I did not wish to offend him by turning down a gift. Indeed, I was pleased that he had thought of me in such a way. However, despite the bird's small stature, I had to admit she looked rather frightful. Her eyes seemed to contain a kind of fire, and her talons were as sharp as razors.

"No, I wanted you to have it," he explained. "It is only right that the empress should have a falcon."

"If you say so."

"I do. I want to see you up on a horse with Helga on your arm!"

"Helga?" Truly, the name sounded very odd to me.

"That is the name we gave to the falcon," he said, smiling proudly.

"That is a terrible name for a bird," I informed him.

"It is a good name for a falcon!"

"Hardly! The only Helga I ever knew was a cook, and a rather poor one at that. Now, if you want me to hold that bird—forgive me, that falcon—you must let me choose a name myself."

He sighed. "Very well then. You take the bird and you can name it."

"Thank you."

I really had no idea what I was doing. I felt rather ashamed that I should be the emperor's wife and yet have no experience with birds of prey. I wanted him to think well of me, so there was no choice but to attempt to do as he said. I took a step toward the creature, and she began flapping her wings again and let out a terrible cry. I leaped backward in fear, convinced that the bird wanted to gouge my eyes out.

"Not so fast," the emperor instructed. "Walk over slowly. That's it—slowly."

I walked as one attempting not to wake a sleeping babe. With all caution, I stretched out my right arm, trying not to make a sound. My heart was pounding with fear. I might have held my breath.

"Now call her, and she will come to you," my husband said.

"Here, falcon!" I tried. "Come here! I promise I won't hurt you."

He laughed and shook his head. "No, use her name!"

"What? Oh. Helga! Come here, Helga!"

Still, the bird made no movement. She did not appear to be impressed by my efforts, but merely tilted her head to one side, her eyes still fixed upon me, as if she sensed that I was no match for her.

"Over there is some food," the emperor said, pointing to the basket sitting on top of Blitz's cage. "Take a piece and hold it in your hand."

"As you wish," I answered, though I was not at all convinced it would work. I was quite thankful no one else was on hand to witness the sad spectacle.

The basket was full of what I could only assume were the entrails of some poor animal. I batted away a few flies and chose the piece that seemed the least repugnant. I then offered the morsel to the bird.

"Here, Helga!" I called. "You like this, remember?"

Still, the falcon was unmoved.

"Try this," the emperor said, making a noise with his tongue.

Although it made me feel an idiot, I repeated the action to the best of my ability, all to no avail.

"Please do not make me keep doing this!" I begged.

"She will come, but you must keep trying."

"Oh, for God's sake! Come here, Brünnhilda!"

As if by magic, the falcon leaped from the emperor's arm, cast herself into the air with a few powerful strokes of her wings, crossed the four or five paces between us, and landed upon my arm, where she began to devour the food from my hand.

"It worked! She came to me! Look!" I cried in delight.

"Yes, I see."

"And she answered to her name!"

"What?"

"Brünnhilda. That is the name I chose for her, and as soon as I used it, she came!"

"Brünnhilda? Like the Valkyrie?" he asked, smiling.

"Exactly like that, yes. Look, she is really holding on to my arm with her talons!"

The falcon finished her meal, and yet she remained there. Although she was a powerful bird, she was not very heavy, and I was surprised that such a frame could bring down large prey. When I saw that she would make no attempt to pluck my eyes out, I no longer found her so frightful. *If this is all I have to do, I might be able to keep her after all!* I thought. I used my free hand to stroke the feathers on her neck, which the bird seemed to enjoy. I was actually beginning to feel happy.

"Let her go then," the emperor instructed.

"Pardon?" I asked, looking back at him.

"Cast her off and let her fly."

"Oh." I had not anticipated this. "But will she come back?"

"Of course," he said. "You have food. Now, raise your arm like this. That is her signal."

I did as he commanded, and Brünnhilda took off into the wind, climbing high above the beech trees. She was an expert flier. Such a pleasure it was to watch something do the very thing it was born to do! As I looked on, she seemed to compress her body and fling herself toward the ground some ten yards down the hill. There was a rustling noise in the brush, and she was clearly struggling with something.

"That will be the day's first kill," the emperor said. "If only all of life was that easy!"

A few weeks later, we were at the *Kaiserpfalz* of Worms—the palace just outside the walls. This was the place where I had celebrated my wedding feast eight years earlier, and it had become our abode once again as we waited for word from the papal camp. Mainz had been the first choice of city, for it was the stronghold of Archbishop Adalbert and the seat of his power. But the emperor favored Worms, a free imperial city that had remained mostly faithful. The inevitable result was that messengers were forced to ride back and forth between the two parties. I remember one particular September day. The rain fell hard, turning the roads to mud, and I could not imagine that the messengers' task was a pleasant one. How fortunate then that I was safe and comfortable in a palace of stone and had only to view the deluge through a small window!

I sat before the hearth in the small chamber that had become my own, with Adelaide seated on the floor before me and Gertrude giving orders to the other ladies, unwilling to allow them one moment's rest. I loved that room, as by some means I know not, a former resident was able to procure several carpets from the East. Their bright colors were somewhat obscured in the general darkness of that day, for there was little light from the window. Instead, the light of the fire seemed to lend a different character to everything it touched: the carpets, the walls of stone, the long red curtains, and the wood trusses above. As I stared blankly into the fire, I considered my desire for purpose: for something—anything—that would live beyond me.

"Read it to me!"

I was drawn away from my thoughts by the sound of Adelaide's voice. She was holding out a worn volume that I had read many times: the *Metamorphoses* by Ovid.

"You know I cannot read it," she said. "Please, if it is not too much trouble, favor us with a passage."

I might have begged leave to busy myself with some pastime, but what pastime was to be had when we remained in that prison throughout the hours of waiting for news, unable even to venture out of doors on account of the foul weather?

"If you wish, but just this once," I replied.

"Oh, thank you, my lady! Gertrude, have the girls come listen!"

Gertrude was not swayed. "We must store the summer clothes and pull out the furs, go fetch new wares from the candle maker, beat the carpets … in truth, you really ought to be helping!"

"Peace, Martha! Let Mary have her joy," I said. "There will likely be weeks of this idleness in which you may clean every last nook of this place."

"With your permission, madam, I would prefer to continue," Gertrude repeated.

"Suit yourself," Adelaide answered on my behalf, then turned expectantly to hear my words.

"Very well," I said, readying myself to both read and translate. I accepted the book from Adelaide's hand and leaned forward in my chair, opening to the correct page. "Here we have it. *Metamorphoses*, by the poet Ovid of ancient Rome. Book the first, page one. The title is 'The Argument.' Appropriate, given that our current situation is naught but arguments. 'My design leads me to speak of forms changed into new bodies. Ye Gods, for you it was who changed them, favor my attempts, and bring down the lengthened narrative from the very beginning of the world, even to my own times.'"[2]

"Wait. Is this Christian?" Adelaide suddenly asked. "Only, he said 'gods,' as in more than one god. That cannot be right."

"The ancient Romans worshipped many deities, both male and female," I explained. "They were pagans."

"But I thought that Jesus Christ was a Roman."

"No, dear. He lived under the Romans, but he was a Jew."

"So what were Peter and Paul?" she asked, tilting her head slightly.

"Also Jews."

"And the Romans were pagans?"

"That about sums it up, yes."

She shook her head in something like dismay. "But Lady Mathilda, if they worshipped all those false gods, then how did they achieve so much? How did they make such great buildings?"

"And *aqueductus* ..." I added, trying hard to stifle a laugh.

"Yes, and those, whatever they are. Should we even be reading this?"

"Fine. Let's have done with it then," I said, leaning back in the chair.

"Wait!" she said, placing her hand upon the book to prevent me from shutting it. "I do not think God would be so very upset if we read it. I mean, you read these things."

"And to date, I have yet to be struck by lightning."

"Good. Continue."

I could not help but be amused by Adelaide, although her lack of knowledge appalled me at times. I was more convinced than ever that women must be taught. *Perhaps that could be my*

---

[2] This translation is by Henry T. Riley, from an edition copyright 1899 by David McKay.

purpose! I thought, but then quickly recognized that it was a fight for which I had no stomach. I could not overturn all the ways of the world in one lifetime. In any case, my greater concerns were the state of my husband's soul and that of my own womb.

"Continuing then," I said, returning to the page. "Ah, the first fable. 'At first, the sea, the earth, and the heaven, which covers all things, were the only face of nature throughout the whole universe, which men have named Chaos; a rude and undigested mass—'"

"My lady!" Gertrude interrupted. "There is someone at the door for you."

Now you see the effect of Ovid's writing upon me, for I had not even heard the noise at the door.

"Oh, now we shall never know what happens!" Adelaide moaned.

"The gods bring order to nature, they fight each other, and eventually humans found the city of Rome," I concluded, shutting the book. "Find out who it is, Gertrude."

"Yes, my lady."

Gertrude vanished through the portal and was gone for what seemed a very long time—long enough that I had just risen out of my chair to investigate, when she opened the door and said, "It is one of the Jews from the city. His name is, oh dear, his name is …"

Here she was forced to turn back toward the visitor and ask him to repeat his name. I could hear only her half of the conversation.

"What was that? Samuel? No, not Samuel. Shmu … Shmuel? Shmuel ben … It … Itshak? No, no—Yitskhak. Did you hear that, my lady?"

"Gertrude, what are you going on about?" I asked, one hand on my hip and the other still clutching the book.

"Perhaps I should let him introduce himself," she admitted, the frustration on her face giving way to surrender.

Through the door stepped a rather short man who nevertheless stood out by virtue of his attire. His robes were long like a priest's, but I had never seen a priest wear such a hat upon his head, nor such a garment around his shoulders. And I had certainly never seen a priest with such a beard! The closest would have been Father Anselm himself. The man's entire appearance was a bit foreign, as if he were one of the many ambassadors that flocked to the emperor's court, and he was still wet from the rain.

"Empress Mathilda!" he said with a bow. "I wish you long life and God's blessing! Thank you for receiving me!"

"And who are you?" I asked, handing the book back to Adelaide and motioning for the ladies to leave.

"Shmuel ben Yitskhak, Your Highness. I have been sent by my father-in-law, Rabbi Ezra ben David, the leader of our *kehillot*—that is, our community."

"You mean to say you are not the leader?"

"No, my lady. I am only a student and a trader, but I speak for all my kin, such as we are."

"Come and sit," I offered, motioning toward the two chairs by the fire. "Your walk could not have been pleasant."

"Sit with you?" he said, his eyes filling with a new light. After another quick bow, he placed his hands together and shook them as he added, "Truly, Your Highness, you honor me. Thank you."

He took a seat opposite me and began rubbing his hands together, holding them before the fire, and blowing on them in turn. I could not help but pity him in his wet condition, so earnest was his manner. As I settled into my own chair across from him, he launched into a further apology.

"I can assure you that our rabbi was most desirous to come visit you himself, and he would have, were he not in poor health and most infirm. You should not interpret his absence as a lack of respect."

"Of course not. I understand. Now, why have you come? And why did you seek an audience with me rather than the emperor?"

"We know the emperor is most occupied at the moment with the great council, but I hoped that Your Highness might be able to spare a few moments. I cannot tell you what a pleasure it is to speak with you. Everyone knows you as 'the good Mathilda,' and they have only love for Your Highness. We well remember your marriage here and what a joyous occasion it was."

"Yes, I think that I did see your rabbi there, though my memory is not perfect. Do people really call me that? 'The good Mathilda'?"

It may seem odd, but given that I spent so little time conversing with the common man, I often had no idea how they viewed me. I feared that they thought ill of me on account of my lack of children, but if this was indeed true and they were calling me "good," then perhaps I was doing something right after all.

"Oh yes! Not only Jews, but everyone in the city. However, if I might say so, our people have a special loyalty to you and your husband, for the emperor has been our greatest advocate during this most difficult time."

"Difficult time?" I asked, quickly recognizing how little I knew about this people.

"Well, since that day of which we do not speak: *di groys tseshterung*, the great destruction."

"Do you mean the killings that took place?" I inquired, seizing on the faintest bit of a memory.

"Yes," he whispered.

For a moment, he closed his eyes and breathed deeply, his features strained. He seemed almost to shudder at the thought of it. Then he continued.

"About twenty-five years ago, it came upon us: the great destruction. We had heard rumors of trouble in Metz and Speyer, but nothing could have …"

He paused again, his voice seemingly choked by sorrow. He was wringing his hands together, his eyes no longer upon me but darting back and forth across the floor.

"Forgive me, it is difficult to speak of it," he finally said. "I was one of the fortunate ones. My brother and I worked in the fields just outside the city. We were very young then. Therefore, we were not present when Count Emicho arrived with his men."

He raised a hand to his brow, and I suspected he was attempting to hide a tear.

"Who was this Count Emicho?" I asked, attempting to help him along.

Shmuel nodded and dropped his hand. "He was what you call a pilgrim, a knight of the cross. He had many hundreds of people with him bound for the East—perhaps it was even thousands. The bishop: he tried to help the Jews. He let them into his own palace, but that is not a fortress that can withstand a siege. My brother and I had been working all day when we heard the distant screams; then we saw smoke rising from the city. What could we do? We hid ourselves in the bushes. We lay like that until nightfall, without moving or even saying a word. I remember … I was so afraid. I was sure I was going to die. Eventually, we both fell asleep there in the field. When we woke the next morning, the crowd was gone. We ran back to the city and looked everywhere for our father, mother, and three sisters. They were not in the house. Everything had been taken or burned. I ran to the bishop's palace, but I was afraid of what I would find. The building was so badly burnt that much of it had crumbled. Everywhere I looked, there were dead bodies. Many of them had been cut down with weapons or beaten to the point of death. Some of the villagers were working to move them for burial, but most were still lying in the open. I remember the lifeless faces: I still see them in my dreams. It was only my desire to find my family that allowed me to continue, or else I would have turned and fled. I began going up to the bodies one by one, turning them over, looking for any familiar faces. I recognized several of them as shopkeepers, fellow students, or friends of my mother, but none were my family. I finally ventured into the building itself. There was still smoke and everything was covered in ash and soot. In one of the rooms, I saw several bodies all together in a corner. A man—I think he was a monk—was about to carry them away. I said to him, 'Wait! Wait!,' only I did not know the German language at that time, so it must have sounded like babble to him. I pressed forward and looked at the bodies. They were among the most badly burnt. It was, forgive me—"

There had been tears forming in his eyes since the beginning of his tale, and now they poured out. I could tell that there was a great weight to his memory—one that he had carried with him for years. I was not sure if I should offer some kind of comfort. Empresses do not often witness such behavior. I was still not certain what this man wanted me to do for him or how it affected the emperor's difficulties with the pope, but for once I attempted to set my own concerns aside and simply listen. At length, he was able to gain control and continue.

"It was only by my father's ring that I knew him. He was a jewel smith, like his father before him. My grandfather began selling such things to wealthy merchants and government officials. He even made some for Emperor Henry IV. But he crafted one ring of the finest gold to be kept in our family, and upon his death it passed to my own father. That was the ring that I saw on my father's finger. I suppose it was a small miracle that the brutes did not take it, as they stole everything else. For that matter, it ought to have melted, but I believe the Lord preserved it. I reached out and removed it, placed it on my own finger—as you can now see—and left. I could not bear to look at their bodies any longer. I should have stayed and made certain that they received a proper burial. In that, I failed them. As I was leaving the place, I noticed a man sitting alone on the steps. I recognized him: he was a *cantor* at the synagogue. He was grasping his legs, rocking back and forth, and muttering to himself. I wanted to know how he was still alive, and to help him. I asked him, 'What is wrong, brother?' I will never forget this: He turned and looked at me, his eyes red from tears, and he said, 'Don't you see? I am a traitor! I let those foul creatures baptize me! That is why I am alive.' Over and over, he kept saying, 'Don't touch me! I am a traitor!' The next day, he killed himself."

This was the end of Shmuel ben Yitskhak's tale, and I could scarcely comprehend its sorrow. I had known loss throughout my life, but never like this man. It seemed strange that soldiers of Christ should act in such a manner. My mind was utterly confounded.

"Why have you told me this?" I finally asked, struck by the power of his tale, but still wishing to arrive at the point.

"Because you are the empress," he answered. "I do not mean simply to burden you, and I would not say such things if I did not believe it was truly necessary. For years, my people have dwelt in the Rhineland. We made our homes here. Of course, there were some disputes with the *goyim*—the native people—but we thought that with time they would lessen. Then, in just a few days, most of us were dead. Those that remained, such as myself—we have been trying to rebuild. But this is difficult work! Not a day goes by when I do not wonder if such a thing might happen again. I have three children, and I want to keep them safe. I want them to live good lives without constant fear. Some of the bishops have tried to defend us, but we now see that it is only the emperor who has the power to keep us from harm. That is why I must ask you ... I must beg you to plead our case to him. In our cemetery, there now lie more of us than those who are left to live and breathe."

"But sir," I finally said, "have you not thought that it might be better to go elsewhere? I am not saying that this violence was deserved, but you must know how it looks when you do not join in with the rest of us—when you remain separate. It leads to all sorts of suspicion, and the people do not understand why you reject the gospel of Jesus Christ."

Looking back on that moment now, I understand that this was the wrong thing to say. I was still quite young at the time and did not know how to properly respond when confronted with such pain. I also knew too little of people unlike myself. He rightly corrected me for my mistake.

"Forgive me, Your Highness, but I must abide by my conscience," he said with conviction. "I must be obedient to God in the way he leads me. Our people are far more ancient than the Germans. Do you think we would have survived this long if we had simply become like everyone else?"

"But even if you are so determined to be separate, why do you remain in a land where you will always face hardship?"

"Do you think that is what we want?!" He said this with some passion, then recognized his mistake. "I beg your pardon, madam. I should not have raised my voice."

"Just tell me what you were going to say," I offered, for I was feeling a bit of guilt for causing him distress.

He smiled and nodded. "You know how every man and woman wants to go to the Holy Land? To Jerusalem?"

"Yes. I too wish to go there one day, though I doubt it will happen."

"Well, that was our home, so many years ago that it is difficult even to remember. We were cast out, and now we are exiles upon the face of the earth, and we cannot go back to the place for which our hearts yearn. Every year, when we celebrate the *pishka*, we say, '*Leshanah haba'ah bi yerushalayim!* Next year in Jerusalem!' That is our hope, but the Almighty has not seen fit to bring it about."

"My lady," Gertrude suddenly said, sticking her head around the door. "You are needed below."

Although I did not know how urgent this request truly was, I was beginning to feel a fool in my conversation with the Jew. I had clearly made things worse rather than better. I therefore seized the opportunity to escape.

"Forgive me, but I must depart," I told my guest. "Thank you for coming."

As our hands met and clasped, I noticed that several of his fingers bore the faded remains of ink stains.

"Are you a scribe?" I asked.

"Yes. I make copies of the *Torah* and the *Talmud*—the sacred writings—along with the commentary of our beloved Rashi." He must have recognized that I had no idea who that person was, for he continued, "Rashi was a great teacher of the last generation. He studied here for some time, and in *Mayants*—that is, Mainz. He still has many followers in Worms."

"I see," I replied, not wishing to delve too deeply in matters I was not likely to understand. Still, I saw an opportunity to make up for my error and show him I did care about the plight of his people. "Tell me, if I had some questions about the Holy Scriptures, would you be able to answer them for me? I know I must gain the full truth from Christian scholars, but it occurs to me that your opinion might be interesting."

Now I had a chance to see upon the face of Shmuel ben Yitskhak the complete opposite of his earlier look of despair. He seemed as if he would burst with joy.

"Empress Mathilda, there is nothing I would love more! But surely, you would prefer someone more learned? As I said, I am still a student."

"I would prefer you," I said, "and I will pass on your sentiments to the emperor."

Thus ended my first discussion with a Jew. At first, I did not know why it should have affected me so, but then I suddenly recognized what it was I had been feeling: the joy of possibly doing something worthwhile. I so longed to do something that would last and to feel that, whether or not I brought children into the world, my time in the empire had some helpful purpose. Perhaps aiding this Shmuel and his people could provide me with a positive occupation. However, no sooner had I reached this epiphany, than I was forced to return my thoughts to that subject which had occupied all of our minds for some time: the controversy with the pope.

"Can the black Moor change his skin? Or the leopard his spots?"

That was the question before us, or very near it. Could a man who had made himself known as one thing, ever striving toward the same end, become suddenly changed? This was the hope in those days of waiting with regard to Adalbert of Saarbrücken, archbishop of Mainz. For many years, he had played the part of a spider spinning us all in his web of rebellion. At one time, he was a true friend to his lord, when the emperor was young and relied on his counsel. But once he was granted the due reward for his fealty, Adalbert transformed into something else entirely.

Could he now affect a different change and become a faithful servant of the emperor? Even the devil may appear as an angel of light, but as I sat in the *Kaiserpfalz*, I worried that Adalbert might be more like the dwarf Fáfnir, whose lust for gold caused him to turn into a hideous dragon. This last tale seemed most proper for our situation, for we were after all in the city of Worms, named for the very *Lindwurm* slain by Sigurd. So would the leopard change his form, or better yet, the dragon?

One morning, about a week after the council had begun, the emperor called me to his private quarters. Based on past experience, I knew there could only be two causes for this: he wished to try again for an heir, or he was in some physical distress that he wished to conceal. If the former, then I supported his desire, but I doubted whether it would do any more good than all the other times. If the latter, then I had great reason for concern, for I had long feared his disease would grow worse. I therefore made my way in haste to the other side of the palace.

Upon reaching the door to his chamber and finding a strange absence of guards, I called to him from beyond the portal. Hearing something like a groan, I determined that it was safe to proceed. I opened the door and quickly closed it behind me.

The emperor was lying on a couch next to the fire, a look of misery on his face. He appeared to have been taken ill suddenly, for only one of his boots lay on the floor, and the other was still firmly on his right foot. The other objects in the room showed very few signs of order, with his bed and a table and chairs being the only things still fairly upright. There were papers lying everywhere, with the largest pile perilously close to the fire. When I had taken all this in, I looked back at my husband's face, on which the light of the fire softly danced. He did not turn his eyes to me, but continued to rub his belly.

"Is it the same pain as always?" I asked, moving toward him.

"Stop!" he uttered, just before I stepped in something that appeared to be vomit.

I strove not to let my face show how repulsed I was by the sight of it. "You are ill! I will fetch the physician."

"No!" he cried earnestly. "Please, stay here with me a while. There is nothing he can do."

"You summoned me just to clean the floor?" I asked in annoyance, still not understanding why he refused to see the physician.

"If you hand me something, I can do it myself," he offered.

He pulled himself upright in a rather feeble manner, wincing in pain as he did so. I felt rather guilty for causing this.

"No, let me do it. Just rest," I ordered.

I bent down and took care of the nasty business, then threw the cloth into the fire.

"Lady Mathilda," he said weakly, "I think not one in a thousand empresses would have consented to do that."

"Well, thank God I chose the proper moment to reveal my special talent," I said with a smile.

I reached out and felt his forehead, which was perfectly cool despite the heat of the fire.

"Have you been like this all day?"

"No, just this once. I was alone reading the day's report," he said, pointing in the direction of the heap of papers just behind me.

"Little wonder you're ill!" I said, taking some of them in hand. "Is there no one who can read these for you?"

"You and I both know it is not the work. The pain—I tried to take more wine for it, but it endures. At times, I think I cannot bear it."

After giving the matter a moment's thought, I set the papers back down and asked, "Will you let me feel it?"

"What?!" he cried, his eyes growing wide. "I am sure I do not know what you mean!"

"Oh, spare me this act! The thing may well be killing you, and you will not let the physician look for fear he might inform the town crier. I am your wife: you can trust me. Now, let me feel it!"

I believe in that moment I was more his mother than his wife, and perhaps it was because of this that he finally relented. He pulled my hand toward him, and what I felt almost caused my heart to stop. More like stone than flesh, the lump had grown so large that I could not imagine how he had remained civil.

"My lord," I said softly. "My lord, you need a surgeon."

"No!" he yelled with such force that I shuddered. "How dare you speak of it?! I am the emperor!"

"My lord," I said again, pulling my hand back as tears formed in my eyes.

"No! You think because I permitted you that liberty, you can speak of such things?! I am the Holy Roman Emperor!"

"Let them remove it," I whispered. "Let them free you of this pain."

He wrenched my arm, a fierce look in his eyes. "I will only say this once, so listen well: no man will make a eunuch out of me!"

I do not know what might have happened next, had there not at that very moment been a rather loud beating upon the door.

"Open up, uncle!" a voice called.

"We know you're in there!" another said.

"That will be your nephews," I whispered to the emperor, who still held me firmly in his grip. "Pray, release me, and I will shoo them away."

By the look on his face, I judged that he would be just as happy for me to shoo myself away, but he let me go, and I made for the door, which was still under assault by the young men's fists. I opened it and saw the faces of Duke Frederick of Swabia and Duke Conrad of Franconia, both of whom were quite surprised to find me there.

"Empress Mathilda!" the elder brother said. "We did not think to see you here."

"That's odd. The midwives said the same thing when they pulled me from my mother's womb and found me lacking a vital member. I seem to revel in the element of surprise."

The brothers remained silent: they either did not see the humor, or were afraid to laugh.

"Oh come, now!" I said. "I merely jest."

"Is the emperor here?" Duke Conrad asked.

"Yes, but he is indisposed."

"Indisposed, how?"

"Never you mind! He is simply disinclined to receive visitors at the present time, however noble."

"Send them in!" the emperor called, and the young men pushed past me and into the chamber. It would seem that my words had fallen on three pairs of deaf ears.

The emperor was able to rise and balance himself against the hearth with one hand, using the other to poke at the fire with an iron rod as if nothing were amiss. Fortunately for him, his nephews did not possess the best skills of observation: they failed to notice how his hand quivered upon the mantle and the muscles in his face were tight, attempting to prevent any sign of pain.

"Lord Emperor—uncle," Frederick began, "we come hither bearing news. As you know, I rode up to Mainz the day before last, and I have spoken with the papal legate."

"You spoke with Adalbert?" the emperor asked with a clear note of incredulity. After all, Adalbert had not been known to speak directly to anyone in the imperial party for some time.

"Yes, I most certainly did, and he assures me that both His Holiness and Bishop Lambert are ready to lift the order of excommunication and make peace with you under the terms we have discussed. They will bestow the *regalia*, it will be a free election, but the bishops must do homage to you for their estates, of course."

The emperor turned his back to his nephews and continued to feed the flames. He looked for a moment as if he might be ill again. I tried to fill the silence.

"Those must have been bitter words for Adalbert to speak. I wonder that he should utter them now."

"Rome is tired of this affair, Pope Calixtus most especially," Conrad said.

"Yes," I replied, "but we have all been quite tired of this affair for the past few years. My concern is that there is always someone a bit less tired than the rest."

"What do you mean?" Frederick asked.

"Tell me, Duke Frederick, do you trust Adalbert? After everything that has happened?"

"He has done all of this to gain the liberty of the Church, which he will achieve through this agreement."

"If he does choose to place his name on such a document, it will only be because His Holiness forced the pen into his hand. How long do you reckon it will take for him to conjure some excuse that will annul what he has written?"

Frederick scoffed. "Truly, my lady, he has shown good faith. Is there nothing he could do that would set your mind at ease?"

He could die, I thought, but decided not to speak the words. As it so happened, the emperor had recovered himself.

"Frederick," he said, turning to face us, "send word to the bishop of Ostia: I will accept their offer, but only if the investitures take place in the presence of the emperor."

"And when they argue that such a request is simply meant to coerce the Church?" Frederick asked.

"There is ample precedent for it," the emperor replied.

"It is true," I said. "In the accord of 1107 set down by my father, King Henry I of England, and Pope Paschal II."

"And the French got such a deal as well," the emperor added. "So will you make my appeal?"

"They will seek consent from Rome, which you may not receive," he answered, a look of concern on his face.

"Yes, I imagine Adalbert will demand it, but the wind is in our favor. Now, leave me to finish my work."

As the three of us turned to leave him in peace, I whispered to Frederick, "Adalbert is false, and you know it. Why would you seek to advise the emperor otherwise?"

"Lady Mathilda, you have much to learn about matters of state. They were friends once: they can be friends again. This is how deals are made."

"Or how fools are made," I concluded, then walked off before he could offer a rejoinder.

As I returned to my own chamber, I was filled with two different sentiments: relief that a deal with the pope might finally be reached that would end the emperor's excommunication, and sorrow that his health, along with our chances of bearing a child, continued to decline.

The ceremony took place in a field just to the north of Worms, upon the banks of the Rhine. Since the agreement had been declared, the conversation had turned from whether the emperor and the Church could settle their differences to what would happen when the emperor and his former chancellor, Adalbert, met face to face. I saw it happen before my very eyes, with each person in attendance straining to catch a glimpse. Apart from myself and a few of the dukes and bishops, the entire crowd was standing, so I cannot imagine those less blessed with height saw anything at all. The emperor and archbishop mounted the dais from either side, with neither man showing any hesitation in his stride. There were no harsh words exchanged when they met—just a shake of the hand and nod of the head.

There was little wind pushing the river along that day, and although summer had by that time faded into autumn, the weather was pleasant. It appeared that the entire town of Worms had been emptied into that field. It was perhaps the greatest assembly of ecclesiastics the kingdom had ever seen, save for my own marriage feast.

First, they read out the two declarations: the *Henricianum* and the *Calixtinum*. The emperor's words were as follows:

In the name of the holy and indivisible Trinity, I, Henry, by the grace of God august emperor of the Romans, for the love of God and of the holy Roman Church and of our master Pope Calixtus, and for the healing of my soul, do remit to God, and to the holy apostles of God, Peter and Paul, and to the holy Catholic Church, all investiture through ring and staff; and do grant that in all the churches that are in my kingdom or empire there may be canonical election and free consecration. All the possessions and regalia of Saint Peter which, from the beginning of this discord unto this day, whether in the time of my father or also in mine, have been abstracted, and which I hold: I restore to that same holy Roman Church. As to those things, moreover, which I do not hold, I will faithfully aid in their restoration. As to the possessions also of all other churches and princes, and of all other lay and clerical persons which have been lost in that war: according to the counsel of the princes, or according to justice, I will restore the things that I hold; and of those things which I do not hold I will faithfully aid in the restoration. And I grant true peace to our master pope Calixtus, and to the holy Roman Church, and to all those who are or have been on its side. And in matters where the holy Roman Church shall demand aid I will grant it; and in matters concerning which it shall make complaint to me I will duly grant to it justice.[3]

---

3   Henderson, Ernest F., ed. *Select Historical Documents of the Middle Ages*, trans. Ernest F. Henderson, Bohn's Antiquarian Library (London: George Bell & Sons, 1892), 409. Edited slightly for stylistic continuity.

And these were the words of the Holy Father:

> *I, Bishop Calixtus, servant of the servants of God, do grant to thee beloved son, Henry—by the grace of God august emperor of the Romans—that the elections of the bishops and abbots of the German kingdom, who belong to the kingdom, shall take place in thy presence, without simony and without any violence; so that if any discord shall arise between the parties concerned, thou, by the counsel or judgment of the metropolitan and the co-provincials, may give consent and aid to the party which has the more right. The one elected, moreover, without any exaction may receive the regalia from thee through the lance, and shall do unto thee for these what he rightfully should. But he who is consecrated in the other parts of the empire shall, within six months, and without any exaction, receive the regalia from thee through the lance, and shall do unto thee for these what he rightfully should. Excepting all things which are known to belong to the Roman Church. Concerning matters, however, in which thou dost make complaint to me, and dost demand aid, according to the duty of my office, will furnish aid to thee. I give unto thee true peace, and to all who are or have been on thy side in the time of this discord.*[4]

Then Bishop Lambert of Ostia announced the removal of the papal excommunication and the restoration of Emperor Henry. He led us all in the Holy Mass, and the emperor stepped forward to receive the host and the kiss of peace. I felt as if a weight had been lifted from my soul, for I had daily made supplication to the Lord that he might spare my husband from the torment of eternal damnation. Not only that, but his rule over Germany would now be assured, for the rebels would have no just cause against him.

---

[4] *Ibid*, 408-9. Edited slightly for stylistic continuity.

At the closing of the service, we sang "*Ubi Caritas.*" It seemed odd to me that the hymn, which was usually reserved for Maundy Thursday, should be employed in such circumstances. Then I considered the words and recognized how clever the bishop's choice was, for it spoke of mutual love and communion.

"*Ubi caritas et amor, Deus ibi est.*
Simul ergo cum in unum congregamur:
Ne nos mente dividamur, caveamus.
Cessent iurgia maligna, cessent lites.
Et in medio nostril sit Christus Deus."[5]

I hoped that this spirit of harmony would remain after the signing of the *concordat*, but experience had taught me to beware the promises of men, particularly when there was something to be gained. Are we not all like Diogenes, wandering the streets of our own Athens, lamp in hand, searching for a true man?

When it was all complete, I lingered for a bit in the midday sun. Although Archbishop Bruno of Trier had been unable to come on account of his ill health, there were still several persons with whom I wished to speak. I quickly found the main object of my search—the archbishop of Mainz—engaged in a conversation with Duke Frederick. Their backs were turned to me, and they seemed to be discussing something of great import.

I heard Frederick say, "It is fortunate that the matter is settled, for I must get back to Waiblingen as soon as possible. I

---

5 "Where charity and love are, God is there. / As we are gathered into one body, / Beware, lest we be divided in mind. / Let evil impulses stop, let controversy cease, / And may Christ our God be in our midst." Translation provided by Michael Martin in "*Thesaurus Precum Latinarum*" ("Treasury of Latin Prayers"), www.preces-latinae.org. Original Latin text from the standard Roman Catholic missal.

have not told the emperor yet, but I received word this morning: my son is born."

"I am delighted to hear it," Adalbert replied, "though I am surprised that you could keep it a secret."

"I know. It has been difficult to contain myself, but I had no desire to take away from this grand occasion. God knows, the birth of a child may prove to be of little note in comparison to the restoration of our beloved emperor."

"Perhaps, but I would not be surprised if your own son lives to be emperor."

"No, no," Frederick said. "I am sure my uncle will soon produce a son of his own, and a great one at that."

"Do not be so sure. Despite what has happened today, the emperor has committed many offenses against our Lord. That is why he has been denied offspring thus far, and I would not be surprised if it continues. In such a case, all of Germany will look to you and yours to unite us."

These words pierced my heart. There was the old slander again: that our lack of a child was caused by the wrath of God. I wanted to deal the archbishop a blow to the head right then and there, but I remained silent to hear the rest of their conversation.

"It is not right for us to speak thus," Frederick replied, "not when the emperor is alive and well."

"Is he well? I admit that it has been several years since I made his regular acquaintance, but he looks rather thin to me. I suspect he is in poor health. If the empress continues to fail in her duty to provide imperial offspring, he will make you heir to the Salian estates. When that time comes, you will find a friend in me."

I could listen no more. I turned and began walking in the direction of my ladies, refusing to heed several calls for my attention. Then came one I could not avoid.

"Empress Mathilda!"

It was Shmuel ben Yitskhak, surrounded by the city's Jewish elders. I had only just met him the week before, when he had come to the palace to make a petition and the emperor was unable to receive him. I quickly took a deep breath—an attempt to keep any tears from falling—and allowed them to approach me. A bishop and a few noble women moved out of the way, striving to remain as far from the men as possible. Shmuel paid them no heed and prompted all of his fellows to bow as one.

"How nice to see you," I said, though in truth I was in no mood to talk. Adalbert's words were still ringing in my ears.

"My lady, this is our beloved rabbi, Ezra ben David," Shmuel said, indicating the oldest one among them. He took the man's arm and guided him closer. "He was so hoping to meet you and thank you for your goodness to us."

"Good day," I replied simply, uncertain how one ought to address a rabbi.

The rabbi's eyes looked just past me, and his left hand groped forward even as his right continued to cling to Shmuel's arm. Looking closely, I could see that his eyes were white in the center, and I concluded that he must be almost completely blind. I reached out and grabbed his left hand so he would know where I was, and this seemed to give him confidence to address me.

"Dear empress," he said, "we have heard of your talk with young Shmuel, and that you are a lover of the sacred word."

I was not sure whether to continue to look him in the eye, for his gaze was pointed slightly away from my face. It made the conversation somewhat awkward, but I persevered.

"Yes, we had a very nice conversation, and I assure you the emperor will see to the matters he raised," I said. "We must leave the city now that the council is completed, but you should receive word from the imperial court very soon. Emperor Henry is committed to ensuring the welfare of your people here in the Palatinate."

I let go of the old man's hand and made a sign to Gertrude, who had come up just behind me.

"Wait!" the old man cried.

He walked forward, feeling the air with both hands, until he was far closer than most men would have dared.

"You carry a heavy burden. I see it in your eyes," he said.

"I am not sure what you mean," I replied, in part because I did not follow his reasoning, and in larger part because I doubted he could see whether I had two eyes or three.

Without saying another word, he reached out his aged hands and touched my belly. Closing his eyes, he breathed in the air and began to whisper words in another language. This made me feel quite uneasy and I could not help but notice the number of German faces staring at us, along with a great deal of murmuring. I was about to ask him to stop, when he opened his eyes again and said, "I have prayed the Lord's blessing upon you. I have asked that he might open your womb and give you sons. I believe he has heard me."

I was deeply moved by his words. How could this man whose eyes could see nothing at all have seen into the depths of my soul and put his finger on the point of pain? Although I was most beholden for his kindness, I had a sudden fear of exposing too much: as if acknowledging my gratitude in front of all those people would betray something that ought to be secret—would make me seem only human. I therefore said a quick word of thanks and set off with my ladies, hoping to avoid any more attention. However, despite this quick departure that was far less than they deserved, I did walk away feeling something I had not known for ages: hope. I sensed it might die before the day was done, but for giving me that feeling for one moment of time, I owed the rabbi a great deal.

CHAPTER THREE

Sometime after I had departed the land of my youth for the Holy Roman Empire, King Henry of England had taken the twins Robert and Waleran de Beaumont into his household. They were the sons of Robert de Beaumont, the first earl of Leicester, and Elizabeth de Vermandois, a relative of French royalty. They therefore had the most noble of noble blood, and they were said to be excellent scholars as well, for they were trained by Godfrey de Bayeux. Yes, this was the same Godfrey who once instructed my brother William and me, only to leave the court of Westminster amid scandal. I am told Master Godfrey ended up becoming a leper and dying in extreme poverty. I would say I felt sorry for him, but that would be a lie.

Upon arriving at the Norman court, the Beaumont twins quickly fell in with the king's lads—my half brother Earl Robert of Gloucester, my cousin Count Stephen of Mortain, Brian fitz Count, and others—and distinguished themselves in the king's household. That is, they distinguished themselves until the year 1123, when Waleran had the very bad idea to throw in his lot with William Clito, the same cousin of mine to whose standard every rebel rallied.

Why would Waleran do such a thing? It was not entirely clear to me at the time, but I tell you with the benefit of years that he hoped in gaining the dukedom of Normandy for William Clito that he would have a new master whom he could control. On account of his bloodline, Waleran thought of himself as something of a king, but as no one would give him a throne of his own, the next best thing was to install a king who harkened to his call.

I remember when I received word of all this. It was during the first days of spring in the year of our Lord 1124, and we were back at the castle of Trifels by then, for the weather was good for sport. Indeed, since I had grown comfortable with the falcon Brünnhilda, I had come to enjoy hunting. However, Emperor Henry's pain was increasing, and there were some days on which he did not feel well enough to ride. I would have liked him to reveal his illness to more people, but he was certain this would lead men to dismiss his authority.

"I swear to you, this is only a passing thing!" he used to declare in those days. "If we tell people that I am nigh unto death, they will never respect me, even when I am well again. I will simply give more of my time to archery, and I will send the nobles away as much as possible. I wish to be alone in any case."

The sad thing was that I had no great hope that my husband's condition would improve. Though he was excellent at hiding his pain, I could tell that it was wearing him down, and I feared for the future of both the empire and myself. Not only would my position be reduced if I lost the husband who had given me standing, and not only would England possibly lose a vital ally, but I would be robbed of the company of a husband I had come to respect. However, I tried as much as possible to put these fears out of my mind, for there was nothing that could be done to improve matters, and when there is nothing to be done, fear is simply a weight without purpose.

On the day I received the sealed message from my father that told of Waleran's betrayal, I read it at once, then ran to inform the emperor, who was out shooting. Whereas the birds had to be kept further down the hill, the targets were mounted on the very summit, right beside the palace itself. When I found my husband, he was practicing with his bow while enjoying the glorious views of the forest below. He had one servant who stood by his side, handing him a new arrow after every shot and retrieving them when requested. In line with his desire, the number of people around him had been greatly reduced.

As I approached them, I said, "My lord, I have received a letter from the king of England."

I had caught my husband as he was about to release his arrow, and judging by the sigh he let out, this caused him no little annoyance. He lowered the bow, turned to face me, and asked, "Has he declared war on us? If not, I see not why my sport should be interrupted."

I was not certain how to respond without angering him, but I said, "No, my lord. He wishes you to go to war with him, or at least to lend him your services in battle."

"King Henry can fend for him—"

"My lord!" I cried, cutting off his words. "Remember your alliance! This was the purpose of our marriage, was it not? To knit together our two kingdoms in bonds of affection."

"I should think it was more like bonds of obligation," he replied with a forced laugh, looking over at his attendant. Why he did this, I cannot imagine, for the man was clearly too scared of both of us to offer an opinion.

"Call it what you will," I said, "but King Henry wishes you to march with such men as you can gather to the border with King Louis' lands."

At this point, the emperor evidently gave up on shooting, for he handed the bow and arrow to his servant, placed his hands on his hips, and asked with some frustration, "Why?"

I moved closer and began to speak more softly. "One of the king's wards—Waleran of Meulan—has risen up against him in Normandy. He hopes to place that false heir William Clito in control, no doubt because he hopes to control him."

"Waleran? Is he the one who descends from the House of Vermandois? From French royalty?"

"Yes, although his natural father was the earl of Leicester. When the earl died, Waleran received lands in Normandy, where he has based his rebellion."

"Why should he rebel against his king?" my husband asked, the look on his face one of honest incredulity. "This makes no sense to me."

"Rebellion never does make sense to one who sits on the throne."

"Careful!" he replied, pointing his finger into my shoulder. "You forget that you belong to that class as well."

"I have not forgotten, my lord," I said, grabbing his finger and lowering it. "I strongly oppose this rebellion and any other action that threatens my right to the throne of England and dukedom of Normandy, or indeed that of my children."

"You mean the children that we don't have."

This seemed like an unnecessary comment. Yes, we both knew that the possibility of having children was becoming less and less likely, but stating it so boldly seemed to have no purpose except to cause pain. I wanted to say something in anger. Indeed, I had formed one or two possible responses in my mind. However, I chose instead to direct him back to the main purpose of our discussion.

"Will you ride to the aid of England or not?" I asked.

"I must understand the purpose before I commit myself. Is he hoping for me to engage the French forces?"

"He does not imagine that it will come to that, but if you are near the French border, then King Louis will be forced to send some of his men in that direction to guard the way to the Ile-de-France. You will not see battle. It will not come to that."

He laughed. "I should hope not, for I have no interest in fighting the French. I tell you this: I will answer the summons of King Henry and aid him in any way I can, for the lord Waleran does not only threaten him. If you are to be your father's heir, then this rebellion is a threat against our interests as well."

"Exactly! I am glad that you see it that way!" I cried, delighted to hear his confirmation that our interests aligned.

Perhaps as a result of this agreement, I felt powerful enough to address the other matter on my mind. I turned to the man servant and said, "Please leave me to speak with the emperor alone."

The poor man seemed uncertain what to do and looked to his master for help.

"Let it be, Bernard," he said. "I wasn't going to hit much today anyway."

The emperor removed his gloves and handed them to Bernard, who quickly gathered the rest of the arrows and carried everything back toward the palace. When he was far enough away that he could not possibly have heard me, I turned back to the emperor and said, "My lord, I wish to discuss something delicate with you."

He had crossed his arms and held his jaw in his hand. I could not determine if this was simply more comfortable, or if he was attempting to distance himself from my words. In any case, he replied, "Delicate how?"

I looked around again, then stepped still closer to him and whispered, "It has been many weeks since last I shared your bed."

"Good God ..." he muttered, moving his hand from his jaw to cover his eyes.

"I do not think this is a subject we should keep avoiding," I said a bit more strongly. "Are you unpleased with me? Have you taken a mistress?"

"You know very well why I have been spending my evenings alone!" he said firmly but quietly. "The pain is ... It does not allow me to ..."

"I understand," I offered, "but you should tell me these things."

"Why do you care?" he scoffed.

"How could you say that?!" I cried, then lowered my voice when his eyes began to look around nervously. "Of course I care what happens to you. I wish you would let me be much more involved. As it is, we still do not speak as often as I would like, and commenting on the food at supper does not count!"

"Be careful what you ask for: you may lose all respect for me if you see all that I have become—all that I am becoming."

"I do not detest weakness," I replied, "only cowardice, and you are no coward."

These words seemed to affect him strongly. He stared into my eyes with a real force that I cannot quite describe. I would say he was rather determined. I was suddenly more aware of myself and everything around me, and I was not sure what would happen. He reached out, touched my face, and said, "I wonder how things might have been if they were—different."

"What do you mean?" I asked, for his words hardly made sense.

He placed his forehead on mine and we both shut our eyes. It was an odd moment: odd because our marriage had never included much physical affection. Perhaps because of that this small touch seemed very powerful to me. I sensed what he meant: that we might have loved each other far more deeply were it not for the manner of our meeting, the years of conflict, and his illness. I understood, but I said nothing, for I suspect he might have wished me to feel far more than I did in that moment. In any case, it seemed far too late to start again.

Finally, he pulled back and said, "Come to my chamber tonight. There may still be hope of a child. After that, I must be away. I must do as your father asks."

"Very well," I whispered.

The next morning, he was riding toward Metz to join forces with Duke Godfrey of Lorraine, father of the new English queen. I found I rued that parting more than any other in the history of our marriage.

It was the express belief among many of the nobility that no man of lesser rank could equal a lord in arms, though the evidence of history proved this to be an outrageous falsehood. King Henry had raised up many men of talent through his generosity, and this caused those of noble birth to murmur. Yet the king believed such common men to be, on the whole, far more true than those born to greatness.

As spring made its first appearance in the year 1124, my father was quite comfortable in his castle at Caen, overseeing the construction of a new line of defenses throughout Normandy that would establish his authority as never before. He sent out several of his household knights to draw the rebels into battle.

Waleran had returned to the forest of Brionne to strengthen his fortress at Vatteville. The king's men waited just to the south, knowing that he would soon be forced to venture out. At length, the traitor showed his face, riding into the vale near Bourgtheroulde with the rest of his rebel companions. They held their heads aloft as men accustomed to win, never sensing the danger in store for them.

The king's guard sprung upon them with a will, led by a team of archers on horseback. Oh, the terror that must have struck the heart of Waleran at that very moment, as he saw his fellows cut down to the right and left! Within the hour, it was over, and he and all his associates were prisoners of the king. Waleran had been bested by those he thought second best.

This victory came none too soon, for Emperor Henry was forced to withdraw to the Rhineland. The city of Worms, the very place that had lately proved its loyalty to the crown, had suddenly become the site of much tumult. The palace in which we had stayed for our wedding was reduced to rubble at the hands of an angry crowd, and all about was chaos. I was still residing at the fortress of Trifels at that time, so I had no direct knowledge of what took place, but I can tell you that it caused an awful rift between the emperor and his nephew, Duke Frederick of Swabia. With each passing year, their bond had come under greater strain, and at that time it became worse than ever.

Finally, I received word that my husband was to join me at Trifels the following day. This filled me with great cheer, not only because it marked the end of those disturbances in Worms, but also because it would be the first time I had seen him in many months, and by that point I truly enjoyed his company as I might that of a friend. More to the point, though I had spoken nothing of it to him for fear of causing offense, I worried about him being under such strain in his condition. As it so happened, the day of his foretold arrival came and went without a sign, and I was filled with dread that some evil fate had befallen him.

Many more hours passed before I heard the beating of hoofs upon stone that announced the emperor's arrival. I believe I actually ran down to the lower level to receive him. He had just entered through the front gate and was still standing in the entry way handing his riding things to the groom when I approached.

"God save you, Emperor Henry!" I cried, bowing low.

After the manner of our last parting, in which we had seemed closer than ever, I had hoped for a pleasant response. However, he merely grunted in a way that did not signal he was pleased to see me. I was a bit hurt by this, and my next words likely reflected it.

"You were meant to arrive two days ago," I said, or rather snapped.

He looked at me with the eyes of one quite beaten down. "No! No inquisition."

This was even odder. I could not account for his anger. Certainly, he was weary from his travels. Indeed, he looked dreadful: his eyes were red, his shoulders were drooping, and he was even thinner than he had been before. I wondered if the pain was torturing him again.

A boy stepped forward with a goblet of wine. The emperor seized it, his hand shaking slightly, and began to drink. Truly, he did not look well at all.

"Was there naught to eat on your travels?" I asked, my concern growing with each passing moment.

"We had plenty," he said, staring at the goblet rather than me.

"Only, you look rather gaunt."

"Battle will do that to you."

"Yes, but you weren't actually in battle."

"A crowd of angry Germans is close enough!" he concluded, finally looking me in the eye. In the end, I might have wished that those angry eyes had remained pointed away.

Sensing that our conversation had failed thus far, I attempted to address the issue directly.

"I know you are vexed about what happened in Worms."

"Is there more of this?"

The emperor turned the goblet over, looking with discontent upon the few solitary drops that met the floor.

"Boy!" he yelled in the direction of the young man who had served him earlier but retreated to a corner when the conversation grew more forceful.

"Yes, my lord!"

"What did you do with the wine?"

"Sadly, that was the last of it, but if you wish for me to go to the cellar, I could—"

"Save it! I'll go myself."

"Really, my lord, it is no—"

"I said, I'll go myself!" he bellowed.

"Yes, my lord. Of course, my lord," the boy said, bowing again and again, or to be more exact, cowering.

The emperor strode off down the passage to my left, which I knew would lead him nowhere near the cellar. As the other servants standing nearby were clearly too afraid to correct his mistake, I made to follow him. He was walking oddly, swaying a bit from side to side. Suddenly, he stumbled and had to catch himself against the wall, dropping the goblet. I ran to his side and attempted to brace him. When he had recovered his balance, I spoke.

"The cellar is in the other direction."

"I know that! Why do you always follow me? Stop following me!" He made a weak attempt to push me aside.

"Good Lord, how much have you had already? You stink of ale."

He turned to face me and raised a finger as he started to say, "I do not ..."

There was nothing to follow that declaration, for he became ill on the spot. I reached to pull his hair back, alarmed by the spectacle I was witnessing. The emperor loved a drink as much as the next man, but he had never been a drunk, and certainly not in the waking hours. I was certain that his present lamentable state was a result of his growing pain, which he could no longer bear in a state of sobriety. Therefore, my pity for him was stronger than my displeasure about his drunkenness. After a moment passed, he was able to stand up and started walking in the opposite direction.

"Where do you think you're going?" I called.

"To look for a new wife. This one begins to annoy me."

"You should be in bed!"

The emperor stopped again and seemed to crumple into one of the niches that held a torch. I ran over and knelt beside him. With no small amount of effort, I was able to turn him over on to his back. His breath was heavy, and there was little color in his face.

"My husband, what is happening to you?" I whispered.

He continued to groan softly as I used the sleeve of my dress to wipe his brow. I placed my fingers on his neck. His heart was beating rather quickly, but there was something else: a small bulge. I felt it, and to my dismay, it was quite hard.

"How long has this been here?" I asked.

"What?" he muttered.

"This lump on your neck. I never noticed it before. Do you have any more like this?"

He made no sign, but closed his eyes and seemed to drift into sleep, or something very like it.

"Help!" I cried back in the direction of the hall.

The boy I had seen earlier came running down the passage. I could see the fear in his eyes as he looked upon the emperor. I could only imagine what he thought as he saw his ruler lying on the filthy stone floor, looking halfway dead. Though I myself was afraid, I could see that it was up to me to be courageous enough for all of us.

"Do you know the physician?" I said very directly, looking him square in the eye.

"Yes, that is ... no, I do not know him personally, but I know what he looks like."

Simply waiting for him to produce these words was torture. I attempted to put the fear of God in him.

"You must find him this instant, boy! The emperor is quite ill."

"Yes, my lady!" he replied, and without another word, he ran off to find the doctor.

I looked back at my husband, who still lay upon the floor. I had never seen him so weak. His disease had clearly grown worse. Though the light was dim, I could see a darkness beneath his eyes, as if he had been robbed of sleep. However, this did not alarm me half as much as the new lump. Was this to be the death of him? How much longer might he have upon this earth?

"Help! Help!" I continued to cry, but there was no answer.

I wondered if I should go look for someone, but I could hardly leave him lying there alone in such a state. Instead, I decided to pray.

"Lord in heaven, hear my prayer. Has he not made peace with you? Make peace with him. Heal him of this. Let him live."

I continued to sit there alone, holding his hand as he slept. There was no telling how long it would take for the doctor to be found, and then for him to arrive. I pushed back the hair from my husband's eyes and felt his forehead. It was not especially warm. How many lines of care were carved upon that face! What strife that mind had undergone!

"Alone with none but thee, my God, I journey on my way," I recited. "What need I fear when thou art near, O king of night and day? Safer am I within thy hand than if a host should round me stand."

The tears streamed from my eyes as I clung to those words of Saint Columba which were taught to me in my youth.

> "My destined time is known to Thee,
> And death will keep his hour;
> Did warriors strong around me throng,
> They could not stay his power:
> No walls of stone can man defend
> When Thou Thy messenger dost send.
> My life I yield to Thy decree,
> And bow to Thy control
> In peaceful calm, for from Thine arm
> No power can wrest my soul.
> Could earthly omens e'er appall
> A man that heeds the heavenly call?
> The child of God can fear no ill,
> His chosen dread no foe;
> We leave our fate with Thee, and wait
> Thy bidding when to go
> 'Tis not from chance our comfort springs.
> Thou art our trust, O King of kings."[6]

The revelation of the emperor's illness spread through the court like wildfire over the next few days. It seemed that in his haste to find the doctor, the boy had mentioned his quest to one or two other persons, who had in turn made it commonly known that the emperor was not well. News of his ill health could only result in rumors. When the emperor did not rise from his bed the following day, the fears of all seemed to be confirmed. When he was in bed three more days, they were

---

6 Saint Columba, "Alone with None but Thee, My God," trans. Anonymous. First appeared in the 1971 version of the *Hymn Book of the Anglican Church of Canada and the United Church of Canada*, but pre-dates that publication significantly.

begging to have the priest speak the rites over him. Yet the emperor did recover, at least well enough to make his way down to the hall and share in a meal. This put some of the talk to rest, but it did little to quiet my soul.

As ill fate would have it, the emperor had called upon Archbishop Adalbert of Mainz to hunt with him that week. This was to be the latest public sign of their reconciliation, but my husband was in no state for such action. Someone made the unhappy suggestion that I should join the archbishop instead. While I was content enough to set Brünnhilda to flight over that forest, the thought of doing so in the company of Adalbert and his retinue was hardly enticing. Then again, I had been asked to do worse.

So there we were, the two of us and the twenty other people who had been deemed necessary to the trip. We had made our way into the wood that lies in the valley just south of the castle. The sound of such a large company surely warned every animal within a mile of our presence, but this was no trouble for the she-falcon. Neither did it present a problem for the archbishop's bird, which was larger and more powerful, but not as fiercely precise as my own. Of course, the hunt was of little importance next to the real matter at hand: the subtle game between myself and Adalbert.

The path through that part of the wood was narrow. Any more than two horses side by side might cause entanglement in the fir trees. I had torn more than one veil riding through there with the emperor, so on this particular day I had taken the rather odd step of leaving my hair braided against my head but uncovered. This earned me a few strange looks, but I reasoned that I would appear even more foolish if my head was suddenly pulled backward by a tree branch, which might even pull me off my mount.

Around this time in our journey, the archbishop and I began riding beside one another in the front of the company, which provided an opportunity for him to address me.

"The weather is fine for our sport today," he said.

"Yes, quite," I replied.

"I have always loved hunting in this wood," he added, "though I admit that not all the memories I have of this place are so comforting."

By this, Adalbert referred to the many months he spent as a prisoner at Trifels because of his opposition to the emperor, a most disagreeable time for us all. I was surprised that he should mention it, and he amazed me further by continuing.

"I would not blame you if you felt some bitterness toward me, Empress Mathilda. I know well the outrage that my actions must have engendered in the imperial household. Yet I believe that you are a woman of profound reason—one who values the sanctity of our holy Church and would do all she could to see it increase. You must know that everything I have done was never for my own benefit, but due to my zeal for the commands of the Lord and my desire to see all things brought into accordance with his will. I live to serve the emperor, and I live to serve Jesus Christ. There have been times when—I'm sorry to say it—the emperor has been a danger to himself and his own rule. I only sought to bring him back into communion with the Church, thus saving his eternal soul."

He ceased speaking for a moment, evidently waiting for my response, but I was not about to give him the satisfaction. When I did not reply, but simply patted my horse on the head, he asked, "Do my words displease you?"

I laughed. "No, archbishop. Your words could never affect me so." This was a lie, but one that I hoped would serve its purpose. "I am simply amused to think that you should come here merely to make such a speech. Surely you had better things to do in Mainz."

"I am not sure what you mean. I am delighted to spend this time with Your Highness."

"Oh, I think we both know the true reason you have come," I said, giving him a pointed look.

We had reached a small clearing, so I alighted from my horse and took up my crossbow. I stopped for a moment and smelled the forest air. It has a particular smell, the forest. The sap of the trees, the decaying leaves covering the ground, the dirt as old as the heavens: all of them give off a smell at once fresh and ancient. No sooner had I begun to enjoy the scent, than I heard the archbishop call behind me, "And what do you believe is the true reason for my visit?"

Sighing, I opened my eyes again and readied the weapon for firing.

"You heard that the emperor was sick, and you had to seek out the truth of it," I answered. "You have come here to glory in your triumph."

"Never, my empress!" he said, alighting himself and chasing after me. "How could you imagine such a thing? The emperor and I have made our peace with one another. I seek only his benefit."

While I had not desired this time with the archbishop, I had at least hoped to use it to determine whether Archbishop Adalbert was true. After his long rebellion against the emperor, I needed to know that I could trust him in the years ahead, but my spirit continued to doubt him, as if something in me sensed that his was the gold of fools. Did he really seek the emperor's benefit alone, or was he still playing the game for his own benefit?

I decided it was best to be honest. I placed an arrow on the string and pulled it back, bracing to shoot. As I did so, I said, "You have made a conquest of the duke of Swabia—I admit it— and you may be able to fool the emperor with this sudden repentance. After all, he is disposed to think well of you. But I see through you, archbishop. You will pour words of honey into my ears, then return to your own lodging to crow in exultation."

The Forsaken Monarch

At that very moment, Brünnhilda dove upon a flock of quail, scattering them in all directions. I spotted one and let an arrow fly, missing it by the smallest of margins.

"Damn it!" I muttered.

"I had heard a rumor that you felt this way, but I prayed it was false," the archbishop continued.

I turned toward him and said, "Yes, well, I have spent many years praying that God would make false men true."

"This is Archbishop Bruno's doing," he said half to himself, looking away. "He has poisoned your thoughts and made you believe me to be a monster."

"You should not speak ill of the dead," I replied, taking another arrow by the sheath and running it between my fingers.

"He is dead then? I had not heard."

"We received word from Trier earlier this week, but with the emperor less than his full self, the news was rather forgotten. I mourned him. He was a good teacher and friend."

"I am sorry to hear of his passing. We did not always agree, but I respected him."

"He was a greater man than you will ever be," I concluded. I turned my back to him and readied my bow to shoot once again. I knew it was wrong to say such things to an archbishop, but I suppose I could not help myself. I imagined the look on his face, had I seen it, would not have been pleasant.

There was rustling in the grass and my muscles tensed. All thoughts of the archbishop ceased as I pulled back the string. I inhaled, then sent the arrow toward the noise at random. Instantly, there was a noise as of a beast in pain.

"The empress has hit something!" Adalbert called, and several of the men ran off in the direction of the noise.

We watched as they circled the region where the arrow had flown, but they found no animal—just a trail of blood leading away from the site.

"Stay here! We will stalk it!" one of them called.

I sighed and placed the weapon back upon my horse. "There will be no need for this as long as they are scaring everything away," I complained.

I walked back into the clearing and whistled for Brünnhilda, who appeared out of the trees and landed upon my arm. I pulled out a small morsel for her to eat. Throughout all of this, the archbishop said nothing. Finally, I decided to break the silence.

"My uncle David is soon to be crowned king of Scotland."

"That is in place of your other uncle?" he asked.

"Yes, Alexander. I never met him, but Prince David was often at the English court."

"I remember your mother well. She was a great queen, and an even greater woman. She would be proud of what you have achieved."

To hear my mother spoken of well always did my heart good. However, I suspected flattery.

"Are you attempting to appeal to my sentiment?" I asked.

"No, I speak the truth! Do you not remember the first time we met? When I traveled to Westminster with Duke Frederick to sign the treaty? You were so small! I think you were afraid at the sight of me."

"Could you blame me? You were come to snatch me away from everything I knew. I didn't know a word of German, and my Latin was dreadful."

It occurred to me that the archbishop might still consider my Latin dreadful, but fortunately, he dared not say so to my face.

"And here you are now, having helped to guide our kingdom through one of its darkest hours. I am not ignorant of all you have done to help bring about peace between the emperor and the Church: how you have influenced him toward the cause of the Lord. You and I are more alike than not. Our methods are different, but our ends the same. And you must know that it was not I who made the emperor sick, nor do I wish him so."

I was unwilling to admit that we were the same, but I could not deny that there was some truth in his words. I placed Brünnhilda back in her cage and turned to face him once again.

"Say that I choose to believe you—that your repentance is real," I offered. "I will still need to see the truth of this in your actions. From now on, you must be the emperor's man through and through. You must strive to follow all his commands. You must do right by this house."

"All this and more, I will do," he answered solemnly.

"So the leopard wishes to change his spots," I mused. "We shall see if your word holds true. Now, on to business. What do you wish to ask me?"

"May I speak plainly?"

"I find it to be best."

"Very well. Is the emperor dying?"

I sighed deeply. "God only knows that." Before he protested, I added, "He has an illness, the exact nature of which remains a mystery. He grows worse by the year—even by the month."

"Then we must make ready for the possibility of a succession. As the chief elector, it will fall to me to guide the rest."

"Why do you think I forgave you?" I asked. "When I first came here as a child, I had no thought but keeping my head above water. I sought merely to survive and convince people that I could be queen of the Romans. But now that I have lived with my husband through many tests, I feel that I have a part in his legacy. If we are not to have children, then I must at least defend what he has built. I have no desire to see everything that my husband has worked for die with him."

"Nor do I. That is why it is essential that you and I work together. Has the emperor said whom he favors to follow after him?"

"Duke Frederick, of course."

"You say 'of course,' but they have not always been on the best terms."

"Common blood covers over a multitude of sins. Surely you know that."

"Duke Frederick is a worthy successor," Adalbert said with a nod of the head. "He has a keen mind and is a friend of the Church."

"And he is of the imperial house, with a son already born," I added.

"I know this is a difficult time for you, made no easier by the controversies surrounding myself, but I have every hope that the kingdom will come through this even stronger. I am only sorry that God has not granted you children of your own."

That phrase, "children of your own," seemed to ring in my mind. For a moment, I imagined myself holding a newborn babe. I felt a swell of pride that I had accomplished this. Yes, I, Empress Mathilda, had ensured the future of my dynasty. I felt something else too. Was it love? I was never a particularly maternal type. After all, the world had forced me to be cold. Yet I felt the stirring of something else within me, as if I was already bound to the child in my arms. But it was nothing real: a vapor, a passing of the wind. Those who dwell on dreams are not fit for this world.

"Never mind that," I finally said. "Do right by the emperor. Do right by this house."

"I shall, my lady. You have my solemn word."

The men finally returned to the clearing, bearing the bloody carcass of a wild boar. My arrow had hit it, but it took a long chase and several more blows to kill it. It seemed that the day had gone well after all, though it remained to be seen whether I had also taken down Archbishop Adalbert.

As the year 1124 wore on, I arranged for several physicians to visit the emperor in secret, but none of them could cure his disease. How the life seemed to drain from him! He was constantly tired, and his appetite had all but disappeared. And the pain—oh, the pain! I have seen few people suffer as he did. We found more of the loathsome bulges beneath his arms, and the one on his neck continued to grow until it could be plainly seen. I was forced to take over many of his duties, and the season of Advent came and went with little joy to be had. We received news of a rather extraordinary papal election in which those two warring families—the Pierleoni and Frangipani—were at each other's throats once again. But what did I care about such things when my husband was dying?

Too late I had come to understand my position as empress. Too late I had found myself able to address him as a wife. I had never been able to relate to him as a girl. Indeed, I hardly saw him in those years! It was only when I became a woman that I was able to have something resembling a marriage, though the odd nature of our union seemed to prevent the deepest levels of affections—or did it? True, I had never burned with passion for him, nor he for me, but in those closing days, I felt my heart torn to such a degree that I concluded, despite all the evidence, that I did care for him deeply: not so much as a lover, but as a partner and family member.

I came to recognize this, but it was too late. He was naught but a shadow of his former self. Everyone at court had guessed it by then. They sensed that the end was nigh, even if they did not dare to say so to the emperor's face. They plotted and schemed, but I was left to hold his hand in the dark of night, when he seethed in pain rather than slept. The passing of my mother and brother had been hidden from me. I mourned them only from afar. The loss of Archbishop Bruno was another blow, for he had taught me much of what I knew. But the slow death of Emperor Henry occurred in front of my very eyes, and it was a torment to endure. His body was broken, and my heart doubly so.

I say everyone knew by this point that the emperor was dying, but he still refused to acknowledge it. Against my advice and his own better judgment, the emperor made ready for a great progress to Utrecht during the New Year. Even in his infirmity, he would brook no talk of surrender, and thus we set off over land from Mainz to Liège for Easter. We then returned to the Rhine by way of Aachen and began sailing north. I remembered the first time I had sailed along that river, as a young girl traveling with my betrothed to my coronation. Now the fates had reversed our course, and we were sailing back to Utrecht, where we first clasped hands and spoke vows to one another. The circle comes back round in the end.

We had only made it as far as Duisburg when the emperor needed to rest for a few days. He had spent the entire time in the boat lying down, but now even the movement of the water seemed too much for him. One evening, I was sitting by his bed, for I was determined to watch over him as much as possible. With great effort, he raised his head and said to me, "Empress Mathilda, see to it that all the lands that I ought to have returned to the Church as part of our agreement make their way to their rightful home. If I do not make right by that accord, the Lord may hold me in contempt, and I shall bear the weight of it eternally."

"You are not dying yet," I said, with far more confidence than I felt. "Get well, and then you can see it done yourself."

He was able to rise the next morning and we traveled on to the palace at Nijmegen. Here again was a repetition of our earlier steps. We stayed there two days while the emperor continued to suffer.

"I pray the good Lord takes him soon," I heard Adelaide whisper. "He has endured this torment long enough."

I was unwilling to admit defeat, for I hoped that the care he would receive upon our arrival in Utrecht might help him in the short term, but I did send word down river to Duke Frederick and bid him make haste toward our position.

"I fear your uncle is not long for this world," I wrote. "He will have need of you before the end."

Finally, the spires of Utrecht came into view. Such a pleasant sight it might have been under other circumstances, but now I saw nothing but a herald of woe. We entered the same palace I had stayed in years before and settled the emperor into his bed: a bed from which I feared he would never rise. It was a dark room without a single window. The only furniture was the bed and two chairs. I requested to put him in a more suitable place, but with what little breath he had, my husband demanded to stay in that dreary chamber. As I did not wish for him to waste what little strength he had fighting this battle, I relented.

There was nothing left to do but sit, wait, and hope. It was very near Whitsunday—the feast in honor of the birth of our Church—but all I could see were the signs of death.

The hours seemed eternal. More than once, I fell asleep in the chair beside my husband, only to wake with a sudden terror. In those hours, I thought back over the many days we had spent together: the first meeting at Liège, the triumph through Rome, the awkward moment in which I discovered his illness. He had never told me he loved me—never said he found me comely—but he was a true husband to me nevertheless. Though I had no desire to be with him in the beginning, I felt at the end that I must remain with him: I must complete the vow I had made to be with him until death. What was more, I had no desire to go elsewhere.

The emperor would struggle to breathe, at times opening his eyes and asking in a faint voice, "Is Frederick here yet?"

"No, my lord, he is not yet come," I would answer.

"Tell him to come quickly," was his only reply.

Frederick did come on the twenty-third day of May. Almost as soon as he arrived, all of the bishops and high officials in attendance were brought into the emperor's chamber. This was no easy task, for the room was quite small. It was rather obscene to see them push to the front, hoping to be in a place of prominence. I had the odd feeling that they were vultures sweeping down upon my husband, willing him to breathe his last so they could get to the business of king making. I wanted to shield him from their prying eyes. I placed one hand on his right shoulder and held his hand with the other, as if to defend him against their intentions.

They were still whispering to one another and paying no heed to the solemnity of the moment when I finally said, "Silence, my lords, I beg you! Let the emperor rest in peace."

The bishop of Utrecht had made his way to the emperor's left side. He was to perform the rite. However, I did not see the emperor's nephew and chosen heir.

"Where is Duke Frederick?" I asked.

I saw a hand go up in the far corner of the room. I was about to say something, but it was the emperor who said, "Frederick! Come to my side."

This small act caused him to gasp for breath. I rubbed his chest. "Be still, my lord emperor! We will take care of things. Just rest."

Once Frederick had worked his way to my side, the bishop said to me, "You may wish to sit on the bed with him, Empress Mathilda. It would be a great comfort to him to have his wife near." I did as he said and again took my husband's hand in both of mine.

The bishop took the holy oil and made the sign of the cross. In the dim light of the candles, I saw it glisten briefly upon his finger tips. He then anointed the emperor's body. My husband could hardly move, but his eyes were open wide as he watched the priest's every action.

"*Per istam sanctan unctionem et suam piissimam misericordiam, indulgeat tibi Dominus quidquid per visum, audtiotum, odorátum, gustum et locutiónem, tactum, gressum deliquisti,*" the bishop said.

He then spoke words in the emperor's own tongue: "Are you truly sorrowful for all the sins you have committed, and do you freely repent of the same and beg the grace of the Lord Jesus Christ?"

The emperor replied without delay, "I do."

Honestly, I do not know how I kept the tears from falling in that moment. They had certainly formed in my eyes. I think it was simply an act of the will, for I thought it might alarm the rest to see female tears. I was calling upon everything within myself to help me through the pain of that moment in which I was being severed from the man to whom I was bound by God.

The Eucharist was administered with some difficulty, for my husband had trouble swallowing. The bishop and I both raised his head to make this possible. The litany continued until at last there was nothing left for the bishop to do.

When his head had been returned to the pillow, the emperor closed his eyes and spoke weakly. "Let all be gone except the empress and Frederick."

At last, the vultures had been ordered away! They filed out silently, leaving only the three of us. When the door had been firmly shut, the emperor said to his nephew, "Do you have the *regalia?*"

"Yes, I placed them in the empress' chamber," he replied. "They will be safe there. I made sure a watch was set."

The emperor was apparently satisfied with this answer and closed his eyes. Frederick and I both looked at each other. He appeared to be quite afraid, whereas I simply felt deeply saddened. At length, my husband made a noise, and we both looked back to see that his eyes were open again.

"What can we do for you?" I asked. "Is there anything you require?"

"Only this," he answered. "Frederick, I place my wife into your care. Treat her as your own flesh and blood. Safeguard her and provide for her welfare."

"I will," he said.

"Mathilda," the emperor continued, turning with some effort to look at me. "To you I give the sacred *regalia* of this kingdom. The man who holds them holds power over the empire. You must get them to Archbishop Adalbert in preparation for the election. He will know what to do with them."

I did not want to receive these words. Each one was bringing him closer to the end. Yet I understood my duty. He wanted to know that all would be well after his death, and I would give him the assurance he craved.

"If that is your will, lord, then of course, I will do it," I said. "Ought I to give Adalbert any instruction? That is, anything regarding who should be elected?"

"It is my firm desire that Frederick becomes emperor after me, and I have full confidence in him," he replied. "Still, it is necessary that all things proceed in order. I have Adalbert's word. He will oversee the election and ensure that everything is done properly. Frederick, you will have the support of the electors."

"I am honored by your confidence, uncle, and I will uphold the honor of this house for all of my days," the duke replied.

The emperor was struggling with each breath, yet he was still determined to speak. He turned to me once again.

"My wife ... my final words are for you. I know ... I know that I have not ... not always been a good husband to you. I have not given you ... all that you deserve."

"That is not true," I responded, unwilling to make his final moments about myself. "I have been happy here—happier than I ever thought I would be."

"Even so," he continued, "with my passing, you will be left with a choice of how to ... live out your days. There are many who will tell you to take the ... take the veil and spend the rest of ... your days in ... devotion to Christ." He looked at me quite firmly. "Do not do it."

"Why ever not?" Frederick asked. "Perhaps she wants that life."

"If she does," the emperor said, "she will not have me ... to get in the way ... but I think that ... she does not."

The emperor was correct about my desires, but I still did not speak. It seemed cruel in that moment to speak of the life I might live after him. I did not wish to keep him from saying anything with what precious time he had left.

"Do not worry about my future, my lord," I begged him. "I am happy enough to be here in the present: to be by your side."

He looked me firmly in the eyes. His face was gaunt. His body was broken. Yet his true strength was displayed in what he said next.

"I see your future, Mathilda. You will be a mother of kings. As for me, I have striven with God and with man. I have had enough ... enough of this world. Say a prayer for me, but do not mourn me. I go to a better place, a place of lasting content."

Both Frederick and I were in tears by that point. I was feeling so many things, I thought I might burst. I raised my husband's hand and kissed it, allowing the tears to touch his skin. I leaned to kiss his brow, my lips pressing softly on to the head that had worn a crown. When I pulled back, his eyes were closed.

"*Heinrich!*" I called to him, but there was no answer.

CHAPTER FOUR

"Oh, how fortune turns upon us all!
Oh, how the mighty are brought low!
One day they rise, another they fall.
A man may reap what he does not sow."

Those words were often sung by Lady Beatrice, the nursery maid of my youth. There was no great skill in that writing—I myself could have composed such a verse without much thought. Yet the words were ever true. Lady Fortuna could be cruel indeed.

How fortune had turned against the emperor! Struck down in the prime of life, when he ought to have been raising sons. I confess that his soul was not always pure, but he sought in his later years to make amends. What justice was there in his too early demise? Such designs he had for the advancement of his people, but they were not to be. Yes, Fortuna was truly *Imperatrix Mundi*: the empress of the world.

The surgeons made quick work of his body, removing the bowels and the heart, which would be buried in the church of

Saint Martin. They cleaned him from head to toe, trimming the hair and beard, which had lately entered a sorry state. They then clothed him in his finest raiment, placing rings upon his fingers and his trusted sword at his waist. The imperial crown would of course be needed for his successor, but another of his diadems was seated on the head. Great chains of gold and jewels were placed around his neck. When all this was accomplished, the body was borne down to the river, where the royal ship was waiting to carry him back to his native land. I could not help but feel that for all their work, they could not erase the awful stain of death.

What an awful journey that was! I had hoped to take some comfort in the soaring heights, the green of spring, and the magnificent buildings—to feel the sun on my face. Instead, we were pelted with rain from beginning to end, an apt symbol of the gloom that filled our souls. When we arrived in Speyer, we found the surrounding heath to be more of a marsh. The streets were filled with slop. The townsmen who came to pay their respects were soaked through and shivering. I rode just behind the bier, and with each step those horses took, the water splashed toward me. For just a moment, I might have envied the dead.

The emperor's body was borne into the cathedral, where it would lie in honor until the funeral. I took up my place in the bishop's palace that had been home to Adalbert's brother, Bruno of Saarbrücken, until his death. The furnishings were not as fine as they had been under Bishop Bruno, but we made due.

A fire was made up in my room, and when I had changed out of my wet things, I sat next to it, attempting to restore some warmth to my bones. Behind me, Adelaide was busy arranging the chests, ensuring that the bed sheets were clean, and lighting the few candles that were set on each of the three tables.

At one point, she offered me a glass of warm spiced wine, and I took it gladly, for even by the fire I still felt cold.

"Would you like one of the furs, my lady?" she asked.

"Yes, please!"

"Wolf, fox, or beaver?"

I did not truly care, but I answered all the same. "Fox."

She placed the fur over my shoulders, and I held the goblet of wine in both hands, sinking further down into the chair cushions.

"I'll leave you then," she said, gathering up the wet clothes to be laundered and departing.

This time alone was welcome. I only had an hour or so before the deluge of people would hit the audience room below, all of them wishing to speak with me. As I stared into the flames, I tried to determine what my purpose was in light of the emperor's death. I had committed myself to help ensure that Duke Frederick was elected: if not directly, then surely by implication. However, I saw no clear path for me in Germany after that. A dowager queen is little good to anyone, and a dowager empress worse still. I had trouble gathering my thoughts in the midst of that grief, and as I sank still further into the chair, I felt myself growing drowsy.

Don't close your eyes! a part of me said.

You need rest! another part said.

You must not miss the reception! the first voice warned.

You are the queen, and they can wait for you! the other replied.

At length, the second voice won out. I set the goblet on the small table beside me, laid my hands on top of my belly, and closed my eyes, allowing my mind to go blank. I was weary beyond weary, worn down by the tears I had shed and the long journey I had endured. Simply to rest felt heavenly. I had almost fallen asleep when there was a knock at the door.

With a heavy sigh, I raised myself up in the chair and said, "Who is it?"

"Sir Drogo, Your Highness," he called back.

If someone had to interrupt my rest, Drogo was a better choice than most. I therefore replied, "Enter!"

He opened the door and ducked slightly as he passed through it, closing it behind him.

"There is another chair there in the corner," I told him, pointing toward it.

"Thank you."

He picked it up as if it were the weight of a feather and placed it next to mine, making himself comfortable in it.

"Is that the spiced wine?" he asked, pointing to my glass.

"Yes," I said, retrieving it. "Did you not get any?"

"I didn't even know they had it."

"Want a drink?" I asked, extending the goblet to him.

"No, thank you," he assured me. "I would hate to taint it in such a manner."

"Suit yourself."

I took a sip, but it suddenly occurred to me that maybe I had dismissed the matter too easily. It was a good moment to say something of import, so I did.

"You know I think of you like an older brother, Drogo. We have been together so long."

"I am truly honored, Your Highness. I am not worthy of such consideration." He bowed his head slightly.

"I also value your opinion," I continued, returning the goblet to the table and turning back to face him. "Tell me, do you wish to remain in my service now that the emperor is deceased?"

"Why would I not?" he asked, his tone a bit sad.

"You once expressed an interest in becoming a minister of the Church."

"But I made a commitment to Your Highness. I could not break that simply because your position changes."

"Your loyalty is honorable, Sir Drogo, and I am so thankful for your service. That is why I am giving you a chance to do what you wish. Do you want to remain a knight in my service or enter the Church?"

"I certainly wish to stay with you, at least until you are safely back in England."

"Is that what you want then? For me to return to England?" I asked, leaning back in the chair. "You do not like it here in the empire?"

"Oh, I like it," he said, "but it is not my home. Cornwall is my home, and I have a better chance of seeing it if I return to England."

"But what of your friends here? I think you are close with several of the men in the imperial household."

"Yes, but I am also old enough to understand that friends come and go, but your home is always your home."

There was a break in our conversation as we both watched the flames dance and spark. Suddenly, it occurred to me that it must be getting rather late.

"My apologies, Drogo, but I must ready myself for our visitors. They will all want to tell me how saddened they are by the emperor's passing. I am not sure how that will make me feel better, but there you have it. The thing must be done."

"How are you doing?" he asked. "You did not speak much while we were sailing back."

"My thoughts were enough to keep me company."

"Do you have no one who can help share the burden of your grief?"

This seemed an odd question to me, perhaps because of the nature of my marriage with the late emperor. I certainly grieved him as I would a beloved brother. Perhaps that was what made me feel guilty: that my love for him, though perfectly real, was not quite the thing of which the minstrels sang. I still had a right to grieve, but I felt it would be difficult for anyone else to enter into that grief with me when the bond I had shared with the emperor was hard to explain.

"Perhaps my grief is not as deep as you suppose," I concluded.

"I do not believe that," he said, shaking his head. "Even if he wasn't the perfect husband, I know you will miss him, even as I miss him. Are there no ladies who hold your confidence that you might speak with them openly?"

"No, I cannot say there are," I replied sadly. It seemed an awful thing to admit.

"Really? That seems most extraordinary."

"Does it?" I asked with a laugh. "I suspect it is a common problem affecting queens. I spend more time with men than women, not by choice but out of necessity. The women I do see often are so far below me in rank and understanding that it is difficult for me to form strong friendships with them. I would like a female companion very much, but God has not seen fit to grant me one as of yet."

"I am sorry to hear that," he concluded.

With that, our conversation ended, and I braced myself to receive people. Scores of mourners lined up that evening to wish me well, though I would rather have been left alone. Their pitying eyes were almost too much to take. The questions seemed to come like a deluge of hail: "What will you do now? Do you intend to remain in the empire? Oh, we hope you do! Have you spoken with Duke Frederick? What will he do? Were you with the emperor at the end?"

Then there were the comments that were well meant, but seemed to miss their target: "How fortunate that you did not have any children to mourn this loss!" "You know, the duke of

Bavaria's son is seeking a wife." "I'm sure you weep all through the night."

Some earnest sisters came from Bingen to express their grief and let me know that, should I be so disposed, they would happily receive me into their number. I smiled, said a word of peace, and sent them on their way. What I truly desired more than anything was sleep, but it was denied me.

Be glad you are not here to suffer through this, husband, I thought, even as I smiled at yet another wife of a local lord who had come to give me her opinion.

The following morning, I awoke before dawn to the sound of Gertrude ordering the other ladies around in the room next door. I sighed and stared up at the painted wood beams above me: one red, one blue, and then back to red again. I had striven in vain to pull myself away early from the crowd, and my slumber had therefore been far too brief to grant me much relief from my weariness. Every muscle in my body felt oddly sore, and a fog lay over my mind. I laid there for a few minutes, not possessing the will to rise. Then there was a knock at the door and Gertrude called, "My mistress, it is time to wake!"

"I'm already awake!" I called back.

She entered the room at once, opened the chest that sat at the foot of the bed, and began to pull things out of it, or so I gathered from the sound. I had to sit up to get a clearer view.

"Gertrude, what on earth are you doing?" I asked.

"Helping you get ready for the funeral," she replied, then called to the younger maids, "Girls! Get in here and help me dress the empress!"

So I was to be made to get out of bed after all, despite my need for more sleep and my utter lack of desire for the grim tasks of the day. I was to bid my final farewell to Emperor

Henry, and though my mind had long perceived that such a thing would occur, some part of me dreaded the finality of it.

I said nothing as the ladies dressed me in my gray mourning clothes, with a black veil covering my face. I was far too consumed in my own thoughts, and they seemed wise enough not to ask. The crown of the queen of Germany was placed upon my head. Here was another thing that I did not foresee happening again.

"Such a grim business," Gertrude said as she fixed it in place, offering her only commentary on the moment.

"We'd best get it over with then," I replied.

I made the short walk across the courtyard beneath a canopy, for the rain was falling still. When I reached the top of the steps, I was greeted by the bishop, who led me into the nave of the cathedral. There were even more people in attendance than when the emperor's father was laid to rest. Where some faces should have been, others had taken their places; still others were there who I might have wished gone. Those at the edge of the nave moved their heads this way and that so that their views of me would not be blocked by the stone columns. I walked past row after row of these figures, all looking appropriately mournful.

And they did not even know him, I thought.

As I neared the front of the nave, where I was to be seated along with those of greatest import, the mourners continued bowing to the left and right. I was fortunate that the veil blocked my own expression, for had they seen into my eyes, they would have known that I was not a mighty queen of lore, but a young woman scared and devastated, with few true friends in the world. At the front were members of the emperor's own family: Duke Frederick of Swabia, his wife Judith, and his mother Margravine Agnes along with several others from her inordinate offspring. It was the emperor's sister who came over to embrace me.

"My dear, how you must have suffered. We grieve this loss with you. Frederick will see that you want for nothing. Know that you are much beloved."

"Thank you," I said simply, and took my place next to them on the left side of the aisle.

To the right was every Church official of note in the kingdom, save those who could not make the journey, and in the place of greatest honor was Archbishop Adalbert of Mainz. I began to wonder what machinations might be working through his mind at that very moment, but then caught myself.

There will be time for that later, I thought. *He can keep for an hour or two.*

The bishop began to recite the words of the *Reqiuem* Mass. Their truth seemed more real to me than ever, or perhaps more urgent. I thought not only of my late husband, but the souls of all those I had lost over the past few years: my mother, my brother, Archbishop Bruno, and all the rest. Those who had peopled the early years of my life were being stripped away from me one by one, and I felt utterly at a loss as to how I could go on without them.

"Grant them eternal rest, Lord," I prayed along with the congregation. "May perpetual light shine upon them."

One of the priests was brought forward for the scripture reading. I found myself uttering the words along with him, only in silence:

"The souls of the righteous are in the hand of God, and there shall no torment touch them.

In the sight of the unwise they seemed to die: and their departure is taken for misery,

And their going from us to be utter destruction: but they are in peace.

For though they be punished in the sight of men, yet is their hope full of immortality.

And having been a little chastised, they shall be greatly rewarded: for God proved them, and found them worthy for himself.

As gold in the furnace hath he tried them, and received them as a burnt offering.

And in the time of their visitation they shall shine, and run to and fro like sparks among the stubble.

They shall judge the nations, and have dominion over the people, and their Lord shall reign for ever."[7]

We continued through the chants one by one, moving ever closer to the moment when the emperor's body would be lowered into the vault directly beside his father. There on the platform before me, just before the high altar, his body was lying in state, but I tried not to look, for fear that it would cause me to break into tears. I was always very conscious that it was not good for a woman to break into tears publicly. We must keep our feelings to ourselves.

But even if I did not look, the words of the Mass forced me to gaze full in the face of death. The specter seemed to rise up before me, and it caused my heart to fear and tremble. I could not help wondering in that moment how many days lay between myself and death, and how long the Lord would choose to spare me. My whole world had moved in orbit around my husband. Now that he was gone, what was I to do? What purpose could my life possibly contain?

Even as I considered these things, the chanting was ended, and the bishop of Speyer beckoned me to come forward. I mounted the steps carefully, some two thousand eyes bearing down upon me. They brought me next to the bier and bid me spend one final moment with my husband. At last, that which

---

[7] Wisdom of Solomon 3:1-8

The Forsaken Monarch

I had feared was upon me, and I looked down on his face for the final time. So peaceful that face seemed in death: it never appeared so in life. He looked as the Roman emperors of old, a lord even in dying, somehow larger and more magnificent than in those last painful days.

"I will miss you, my husband," I said softly, no longer able to keep the tears from falling. "I will miss the days we had together, and even more the days we might have had."

I leaned down and granted him one last kiss, and with it a parting word from Virgil. "*Si quid mea carmina possunt, nulla dies umquam memori vos eximet aevo.*"[8] I looked up at the choir screen and saw the image of Christ upon his throne.

"He is in your hands now," I whispered.

Once the body had been lowered into its final resting place and the service was at an end, I stayed behind for a few minutes to greet those who had come to pay their respects. I was in the middle of a conversation with one of the priests when I was interrupted by Archbishop Adalbert.

"My apologies, empress, but may I speak with you for just a moment?"

"I suppose," I answered, then said to the priest, "Thank you once again. God bless you."

When the other man had departed, Adalbert said, "I will need the duke of Swabia as well."

"I think he is just over there," I replied, pointing to where he stood in conversation with the bishop of Speyer.

---

8 A famous quotation from Virgil's *Aeneid*, Book Nine, Lines 513-14. John Dryden translated it into English as, "If my verse can give immortal life, your fame shall ever live." Robert Fagles renders it thus: "If my song have any power, the day will never dawn that wipes you from the memory of the ages." Latter translation found in Virgil, *The Aeneid*, Penguin Classics Deluxe Edition, trans. Robert Fagles (New York: Penguin Group, 2008).

As soon as Duke Frederick had been collected, we moved into one of the nearby chapels where we would not be overheard.

"The *regalia* have been sent ahead to Trifels, if that is what you wish to know," I said.

"Yes," Adalbert replied. "I was told before the Mass. Thank you. Everything will be in order for the election."

"When is it to take place?" Frederick said.

"In three months' time, upon the feast of Saint Bartholomew," he answered. "I thought it would be simplest to gather in Mainz, if you have no objection."

"None whatsoever," replied Frederick.

"Very good. Empress Mathilda, there will be no need for you to attend. I am sure you have many things to see to."

"Actually, I would like to come," I said. "Is it not common for the emperor's widow to do so?"

"Common, perhaps, but hardly necessary. There may be some debate from the Saxons, but they are accustomed to defeat. The choice seems an obvious one. I see no need to put yourself under strain."

"He is right, dear aunt. You are in mourning. Take as much time as you need," Frederick offered.

"There is no need to call me 'aunt,' for I am far younger than you," I said. "Really, I feel that I should be there."

Indeed, I did feel a strong need to be there, for I felt a loyalty to my dead husband: to ensure that his chosen successor was elected. I had no strong bond with Duke Frederick personally, but I reasoned that as the late emperor's nephew and a member of the same ruling house, he would be the most likely to uphold the things for which my husband had fought and sacrificed. Perhaps it seems odd that I felt bound to my dead husband's wishes, especially given the distant nature of our marriage in its early years, but I did feel bound nevertheless.

"If you must, then let it be so, but there will be little for you to do," Adalbert replied. "It is all up to the electors. As chief elector, I will simply carry out their will. Have you decided which religious house you wish to enter?"

"Actually—" Frederick began, but I helped him.

"Actually, I will not be entering a religious house. I shall remain in the secular realm."

Yes, despite considering the matter a great deal in the days since the emperor's death, there had never been a moment in which the thought of entering a nunnery appealed to me. I had the greatest respect for those women of God, but I simply could not see myself among them. Perhaps I did not feel righteous enough, or perhaps I simply believed there was more for me to do in the wider world. Either way, my will was set.

"Oh! I am most amazed!" said Adalbert. "You have always been so devout. I was sure you would wish for a life of spiritual contemplation."

"May I not think of God and still hold to my duties?" I asked.

"The archbishop means well, my lady," Frederick assured me. "It is just a bit strange to think of a former empress living down the street from the future one."

"I am sure Judith would not mind, but if it becomes a problem, I could always return to England. Indeed, my father may demand it now that my husband is deceased and he still needs an heir."

"But this is your home now!" Frederick protested. "Perhaps we can find a husband for you among the German lords and you may bear offspring who would be heirs to the English throne."

"Perhaps, but there is no certainty that such a good match might be obtained," Adalbert said. "I still feel that a religious house would provide the best opportunity for you."

"That is a question for another day," I answered. "I do not know if the Lord will ever bring me into wedlock again. All I know is that I need rest. Nothing makes one weary like grief. I must return to my lodging. I will leave you to your election."

With that, I left the cathedral and headed back to the palace, where I intended to enjoy a warm bath and attempt to find some morsel of peace in the midst of grief.

Trifels was quiet without its master. There was no loud feasting in the great hall—no clashing of swords in the yard. The only sound was the constant scrubbing of the floors that had taken over life at the castle, for without the master of the house, there was little else for the servants to do.

Although I had gone there with the intention of grieving in peace away from the world, I quickly found this dreary cycle more trying than any amount of company. I had gone through my supply of new books and had my fill of long walks within the fortnight. Worse still was Brünnhilda, who plainly longed for the hunt. As for Blitz, I was not sure if he knew of his master's demise, but I imagined I saw a rather mournful look in his dark eyes. I tried to let them both out for a bit of exercise, but I sensed they felt as restless as myself.

Therefore, when the heat of the summer of 1125 was at its zenith, I welcomed several of the great lords and ladies of the kingdom to Trifels for the feast of Saint John. I desired some merry making that would free our minds from the twin burdens of grief and ambitious plotting, but I was also aware that any martial display might not be seen as keeping with the feeling of the hour. I therefore arranged a quiet festival of Midsummer and the Baptist's nativity, with a small number of minstrels and dancers, and an array of foods from near and far.

Such a transformation the castle underwent! Furnishings and tapestries were brought out of their hiding spots and placed in prominent positions. The amount of chatter seemed to increase threefold. I have seldom seen people so pleased to be given work to do. Though there were many tasks to be accomplished, the general sentiment was one of gratitude that we could finally set our minds to something positive.

There was one visitor whom I particularly longed to see, and a rather small one at that: Frederick Staufer, who at the age of little more than two years was only just able to travel. Too young for any lofty title, he was nevertheless the son of Duke Frederick of Swabia and Lady Judith of the House of Welf. Descended from the two most powerful families in the kingdom, he was bound for greatness.

Before I knew it, I found myself sitting with Master Frederick on my knee and pulling on the chain around my neck as if his life depended on it. Lady Judith had brought him to me almost as soon as they had arrived, and now we were sitting in one of my private chambers, away from the tumult of the servants at their tasks. I liked that room best of all the stone chambers, for it had two large windows that allowed the sun to stream in and warm my heart. Although it was normally the room where I received visiting officials, I had the servants remove all the furniture except for a few simple chairs, a wood table, and a chest full of books and toys. I wanted young Frederick to be able to run free without any worry of him destroying something priceless. I would have had them remove the table as well, for it was a rare master work of carpentry with vines of flowers carved into its legs, but it was constructed of such heavy oak that two men struggled to lift it and I was content to leave it be.

"Who do you think he looks like?" Judith asked, sitting in the chair beside us. "I think there is something of the Welf about him, but perhaps not in the nose."

"I want to know where he gets this hair from," I said. "It looks golden, but neither you nor Frederick have light hair."

"There are some in my family who do," she replied.

I continued to run my hand through the boy's tresses. "Actually, this is almost auburn. It is very like my brother's hair—that is, if he were still alive."

"Really? Was his hair red?"

"A bit, yes. It is a family trait on my mother's side. My father's hair—that is, whatever is left of it at this point—is quite dark. Mine, as you can see, is perfectly plain."

"I think your hair is lovely," she said, though I could tell from her manner that she was being charitable. Her smile was rather forced.

Master Frederick was becoming discontented, thrashing around on my lap, so I let him down. He walked around the room slowly, examining each object he found. He became particularly interested in some letters which I had carelessly left sitting on the table. "No, Frederick!" the boy's mother called as he pulled the one on the bottom of the pile, causing them all to fall to the ground.

The boy was babbling something that I could not understand. He was not old enough for more than scattered words. The two ladies instructed to mind him made quick work of the situation, batting the boy on the hand. He started to cry, and I wondered if it might have been better to simply let him play. He had been quite well behaved up to that moment.

"Here, Frederick!" I said, rising and taking a book from the nearby chest. "I have something I think you will like."

I walked over to him and showed him the volume. "Book! Book!" I said, pointing to it each time. It occurred to me as I did so that an outside observer might find my actions rather odd, but I suppose we all make ourselves odd for children.

He ceased his crying long enough to repeat, "Book?"

"Yes! Come, let us read it together."

I walked back to my chair and sat down, then patted my knee to indicate that he should come. He did not do so at first, but finally decided it might be a good idea and made his way to my position. I raised him up on to my lap and opened the pages of the beloved *bestiarum* that my uncle David had given me as a child. Oh, how I might have loved to read that book to my own child! For just a moment, I experienced the pang of longing, but I determined that I must content myself for the time being. I held young Frederick tightly on my lap.

"This has always been one of my most beloved books," I told him. "It is all about different animals. It has wonderful pictures. Here—here is the lion. See its great mane! Do you know the lion, Frederick?"

I looked down at his face, but the boy merely stared forward.

"Perhaps another one then. Oh, the hare! I'm sure you have seen the hare. We have them here in this very wood. Wait …"

Master Frederick had begun turning through the pages rather quickly, before I had a chance to read them. I waited for him to settle on another animal.

"An ibis … no … a camel. The camel is … ah, I see we are turning the page again."

At last, we came to one page that he was interested in, for he looked at it and declared, "Cat!"

The boy's mother clapped with delight and cried, "Oh, my boy! How intelligent you are!"

"Yes, he is rather intelligent," I said, "although it is actually a dog." I could see the dejection in her face, so I quickly added, "But in truth, they look very much alike in this book, so I understand his confusion. He really is a very smart boy. He helped Gertrude lay out all the silver."

"Yes, people tell me all the time how clever he is. I am sure he gets that from his father."

I was about to protest that she too was intelligent, but it was at that very moment that I suddenly heard the sound of paws running across a wood floor, followed by Drogo yelling,

"Come back, you mad thing!" His cries went unheeded, and a large gray dog with mud trapped in its fur burst into the room with the knight two steps behind. "Apologies, ladies! I'll just get him!" Drogo continued, but no sooner had he said this, than he was forced to avoid the pile of letters, which in turn caused him to trip over one of the table legs. His massive frame came crashing down to the floor.

"What in heaven's name?!" Judith objected.

The ladies who ought to have been minding Frederick were now directing their attention to the fallen knight. I too rose out of my seat to see that he was not hurt. The dog shook its wet fur, sending a shower of drops across the room, pelting Lady Judith. At the sound of her cry, I turned from the earlier calamity to see to the new one.

"Ah! Ah!" she wailed, leaping up and patting her skirt frantically in an effort to remove the drops of water.

"Are you hurt?" I asked.

"That thing—" she wailed, pointing angrily in the direction of the dog, "—just ruined my gown!"

"But it was only water, surely—"

"Ah! Why do these things happen?!" she screamed, casting her eyes to heaven.

"Never fear, empress!" Drogo called from behind me. "But for a few scratches, I am perfectly fine."

"I am glad to hear it, but why is there a dog in my room?" I asked him.

Drogo looked over at the beast, which was happily pacing around the room in circles, as if searching for a suitable explanation. He then turned back to look at me.

"I can see why you would ask that question, my lady. It's one of the hunting dogs. I borrowed her from Ulrich down below. He assured me she is the swiftest dog he has ever raised. Took her out to hunt some hare, but she got covered in dirt.

I thought if I brought her inside and cleaned her up—well, it did not go as well as I hoped."

"I'll say!" cried Judith.

"Where is Frederick?" I asked, suddenly aware that we had not accounted for his presence since Drogo's fall.

"He's over there!" one of the ladies said.

I turned and saw the boy standing directly in front of the dog, repeating the word "no." The dog ceased its whining, sat upon its haunches, and lowered its head as if in submission.

"Not even I can get the dog to do that," said Drogo.

"Incredible," I agreed.

That little boy is now Emperor Frederick *Barbarossa*, the greatest leader his kingdom has ever seen.

The lords of Germany made their way to Trifels over the next few days, as the feast of Saint John moved ever nearer. Upon the eve of Midsummer, I was about to walk down to the great hall, where most of them stood gathered in conversation, when there was a knock at the door of my private chamber. I thought it might have been Adelaide, so I opened the door at once. What I found instead was my old chaplain, Altmann, standing there in a rather simple tunic and outer robe. He evidently was not celebrating the Mass that evening.

"Good evening, my lady," he said in greeting, bowing his head.

"Oh, I thought you were Adelaide."

"Would that I were, for I might bear more favorable news."

"I do not like the sound of that. Here, come in." He made his way inside and I shut the door behind him. "I am sorry that we have not talked much lately. I saw you in Speyer, but there were so many people who wished to speak with me then."

"Never mind it. I understand."

"Now for the matter at hand."

"Yes, the matter at hand," he said, pressing his wrinkled palms together and then rubbing them one on top of the other in turn. "I was not sure if this was the best time to speak of it. I know you must be about to make your way down below."

"No matter. What is it?"

The look on his face was earnest, his gaze direct. "My lady, I have it on very good authority that the bishop of Cologne is gone to Flanders."

"Flanders? What is he doing there? He ought to be here, actually."

"That is what concerns me. He has gone there to speak with Count Charles, and we both know there can only be one reason for that."

I paused for a moment, my eyes searching the floor for an answer. It would be unwise to rush to a conclusion, but though I tried to think of any other reason why the bishop might take on such an errand, there was still only one that came to mind. My heart sank.

"Do you think I am wrong?" Altmann asked, crossing his arms and leaning forward slightly.

"No, I'm sure you are right," I concluded, looking him in the eye. "He hopes to bring him back here for the election. Of course, it is not certain that the count will accept, but it is clear enough what this means."

"Exactly. They are looking for someone other than Duke Frederick."

"The question is, who are 'they'?"

"Well, the archbishop of Mainz, surely. He hates the Salians."

"He hated the late emperor, but he gets on well enough with Duke Frederick."

Altmann raised his brows in suspicion. "Are you certain about that?"

"It would seem that I can be certain of nothing."

I fell silent and began to pace, even as Altmann continued to stand there with his arms crossed. Someone was attempting to introduce a rival to Duke Frederick of Swabia: a man who might win the support of more of the German nobles. Was it Adalbert? I did not doubt that it was in his nature, yet I had little proof. I remembered the last wish of my husband that Frederick should be the next man to wear the crown, and I wished to see it fulfilled, but all around me was shadow.

"Is Adalbert here?" I asked, pausing my steps.

Altmann nodded. "He just arrived. He must have a hundred people waiting to speak with him."

I continued to pace back and forth slowly, considering the matter. Bishop Frederick of Cologne was plainly false. Adalbert was likely false. Yet the duke of Bavaria was father through marriage to Duke Frederick of Swabia, so it seemed impossible that he would stand against him. Likewise, it seemed impossible that the German princes would vote for a foreigner like Count Charles of Flanders to sit upon their throne. That left only one man who could potentially claim enough support to challenge Frederick, though he still seemed weaker. Oh, the thought of it made me ill!

"What have we heard lately about that old rebel, Duke Lothair of Saxony?" I asked.

"Not much," Altmann answered. "He is coming down for the election, but I cannot say whom he will support."

I stopped pacing and turned to face him. "I find it quite likely that he will support himself."

"So you think that Adalbert ..."

"I do."

"And the bishop of Cologne?"

"Lothair cannot defeat Frederick on his own. They might be hoping to divide the vote a third way: present someone other than Frederick who is neither an established traitor nor a northerner."

"That makes sense. So what will you do?"

"Well, there is one difficulty: I cannot be sure that Adalbert is behind it. Perhaps I should do something to make clear to him where his loyalty belongs."

"You will speak with him in private?"

I shook my head. "That would accomplish nothing. He will tell me only what he thinks I wish to hear. No, what he needs is public pressure."

But how was I to apply pressure to Adalbert? As dowager empress, I had little real power. Men were still bound to respect me to a certain degree, but I had no vote in the election and little power with the bishops or the nobles. What I needed was some way to publicly shame Adalbert: not severely, but just enough to let him know to whom his loyalty was due.

Just then, I had a thought of how I might accomplish this. With no words beyond, "I beg your pardon, Father Altmann," I departed the room and made my way down the passage that led to the great hall. As I drew closer, the sound of voices grew louder. I soon arrived at the gallery overlooking the hall of red stone. Below me, the great men and women of Germany were gathered together in discussion, ignorant of my presence. Directly below me, I saw Archbishop Adalbert of Mainz holding court, with a line of people waiting to speak with him.

I descended the stone stairs to the lower level. A few of the guests noticed me and pointed, but the crier was standing by the main entrance and did not see me in time to make an announcement. Perhaps his view was blocked by the collection of hats with feathers sticking this end and that. I simply began walking through the crowd, leaving them to spin around and bow frantically. I turned to the right, walked toward my target with great purpose, and cried out, "Adalbert!"

The Forsaken Monarch

The crowd parted and the archbishop turned to face me, falling instantly to one knee in a deep bow. "Empress Mathilda!" he said, awaiting my response so that he could stand again.

I made no reply, but walked to within a single pace of him and simply stood there as one frozen, staring down at him. After a moment, he lifted his head up to look at me. Uncertain as to what he should do, he began to stand, but I raised my hand up to hold him in position. Without looking, I sensed that every eye in the room was on us. I am not sure how long I made him remain bent over like that—surely not more than the space of a few breaths—but to him it must have seemed a lifetime. I continued looking into his eyes intensely, determined to send a message.

Do not forget who I am, I thought. *Do not forget the respect you owe me. I still have the power to hurt you.* Perhaps I should have said this, but that seemed a good bit too bold.

I have seldom seen a man look so uneasy. When I decided he had had enough, I walked past him and out the back door. Behind me, I could hear a general murmuring of the crowd and someone asking, "My lord archbishop! Are you well?"

I continued out the side gate of the castle and into the yard. There was a large bonfire, and several of the servants were dancing around it, drinking beer and reveling. They were not aware of my presence, and I stood there for a moment watching. The sky was growing dark, and in the light of the fire, their figures seemed almost savage dancing about.

"That was rather bold," a voice behind me suddenly said.

I turned and saw Drogo approaching, bearing a glass in one hand and a leg of meat in the other.

"Oh, it's only you," I said, turning back to look at the fire. "I thought perhaps you were one of the lords, come to tell me off for shaming Adalbert."

"No, he deserved that," the knight replied, his speech muffled as he chewed on the meat. "I dare say it was good for him to feel out of control for once—unable to bend people to his will. If nothing else, he deserved to be shamed for all the trouble he gave your late husband."

"Would that it were only for past grievances, but I fear he is plotting anew."

"To put Duke Lothair on the throne?"

"Why?!" I asked in alarm, turning to face him directly. "What did you hear?"

"Nothing, nothing," he assured me, attempting to raise his grease covered hands in surrender while still holding his food and drink, "but it makes perfect sense. Just look at the last two emperors and how they have dealt with the Church, then consider Adalbert's record. He would probably eat his own leg before he let another member of that family take the throne."

"How very charming," I said. "Let's hope it does not come to that."

"This is much like they do it in Cornwall," the knight said, motioning toward the festivities. "Lighting sacred fires, dancing around them, singing native songs. If they took off their shirts and painted themselves, the picture would be complete."

"Yes, it all seems a bit pagan for my taste, but I suppose we must let the common folk have their revels. It makes them feel alive."

"There's nothing in it. They just rejoice in the season. If they start sacrificing to some idol, then let us be afraid," he concluded, draining the last of his wine.

"So much for your piety! What happened to the man who wanted to be a monk?"

"A priest, actually, but I left that path long ago."

"Perhaps you need not leave it forever. They are still trying to send me away to a nunnery. If they succeed, your services will no longer be needed."

"My lady, if they do try to send you to a nunnery, then that is precisely the hour that my services will be needed," he said, pointing at me with the remains of his leg of meat.

"I agree, but not because I have anything against sacred vows. I simply know that if I take on that life, there will be no marriage, no children—no future, essentially. Unless my father is able to have another child, our family line would die out under such circumstances. More to the point, I do not think myself holy enough for monastic life."

"Which is why I am happy to devote my sword to your service and teach a lesson to anyone who would force you into that life against your will. Now," he said, taking a final bite off the bone and then throwing it to the side, "what do you intend to do about Adalbert?"

"Wait. Let him consider the gravity of his decisions. Let him remember whom he serves."

"Will that work?"

"I don't know, but I have little authority over the situation. I can only hope to shame him into good behavior."

"Let us wait and see then," he concluded.

The two of us stood and watched as the flames continued to leap along with the dancers, sparks reaching to join the stars in the sky. They say it is the brightest day of the year, but I assure you that night felt dark indeed.

CHAPTER FIVE

The week after the feast, I had a messenger from Rouen upon my threshold, come with tidings from King Henry of England. I took the letter from him at once and ran back to my room to read it in private. You will probably not be surprised that the letter was most direct in its message.

> *My daughter, I shall waste no time with fair words. I commend you most urgently to return to your native land. One duty you have fulfilled. Now I bid you take up another. We have need of a son to bring peace to this kingdom, but my wife cannot fulfill this simplest of demands. She is as barren as an old maid. Our name cannot live on but in your progeny. The news of your husband's untimely death has caused me to hope that it was some defect in his person that has left you childless. Therefore, come swiftly to the aid of your kingdom. Make for Normandy with all haste. I shall await you there. By the fruit of your womb, we may ensure the succession. All England calls to you, daughter: 'Come home! Come home!' Heed not the pleas of the Germans, for that is not your path.*

In truth, there was no need for me to return in order to produce children. By the end of that summer, I had received no less than five inquiries with regard to marriage. I suspect you will not judge me too harshly for taking some small pleasure in these attentions, knowing as I did that it is seldom granted to women to oversee their own affairs. Nevertheless, I was hesitant to enter so quickly into another marriage, even if England was in need of an heir. I still felt a duty to my former husband to ensure that Duke Frederick was elected. In truth, there was little I could do to influence the process beyond hoping, but I still felt bound to that task until it was completed.

It helped that the suitors were not exactly tempting. I will not mention their names as some are still living, and I would not wish to shame them. Suffice it to say that one was known to have picked up some disease from his whoring, another was older than my own father, a third was so arrogant that I could not have lived with him for five minutes, and the remaining two had squandered all their wealth to the point that they had no business approaching me.

Still the chief question remained: should I continue to reside in the empire, where I might have greater control over my own destiny but fewer prospects, or should I return to my native land, where my father would make the decisions but I would be among my own folk? It seemed plain that England would call me home at some point, for the king had placed his hopes for an heir in me. I was of no further use to Germany or any of the other imperial lands. The words "come home" echoed in my mind, and I found that my heart knew exactly what to do: I must return.

I am not sure of the day on which I made this decision. I think I simply recognized that the question had never been a question. I was meant to return. But all such thoughts were pushed aside for the moment, for there was an election at hand. I was granted the hospitality of the monastery of Saint

Alban's, just outside of Mainz. I did not attempt to gain quarter in the archbishop's palace, for even if Adalbert had consented for me to sleep under the same roof as himself, my suspicion of him had grown to such an extent that it would have been rather disagreeable. I had no firm proof that he was false: just a feeling that would not go away. However, in the days just before the election, I was given greater reason to doubt him.

Although I held him in low esteem, Duke Charles of Flanders was wise enough to refuse the bidding of Archbishop Frederick of Cologne. He would not allow himself to be considered in the coming debate, fearing the prejudice of the Germans, who were apt to doubt men of foreign birth. In this, the Germans were no different than any other people I have encountered. I was relieved that Duke Charles would not be putting up a challenge to Duke Frederick of Swabia, but I soon had greater cause for alarm.

The monastery of Saint Alban's, which was to be my home for the election, had been a prominent place of instruction in the time of King Charles the Great, the first Holy Roman Emperor. It was perched on a hill overlooking the city of Mainz, which took its name *Albanberg* from the monastery. Its hall was an exceedingly large construction that did not exactly create thoughts of monastic humility. It was divided into thirds, each separated by a row of columns in which were carved vines of flowers, all brightly painted. The roof was made entirely of wood and rose to a superior height in the middle third. But the greatest achievement was three perfectly placed windows that directed beams of light into the center of the hall.

It was in that hall that I received Duke Frederick and his family on the day we received the bad news. A carpet had been brought out at my request, and Lady Judith and I were playing with younger Master Frederick on the ground while his father sat in a nearby chair, reading the day's letters. As we were playing with her son, Judith asked me a question.

"So have you decided whether to stay in the empire or return to your home land?"

"Yes, I have considered the matter a great deal, and I fear I must leave. I will be doing so right after the election."

"Is it because you did not like any of the marriage offers?" she guessed, the look on her face earnest. "I am sure that the duke and I can find you a suitable husband. We will make sure you are well cared for after he is crowned."

"Thank you, but my mind is made up. Apart from Adalbert's very tempting offer of life in a nunnery, I see no good reason for me to stay, though I shall miss seeing the three of you."

She moved a bit closer to me on the carpet and said softly, "I hope you are not doing this on my account. I will not feel threatened by having a former empress still in Germany."

"I know, and I respect you for that," I replied, "but England needs me far more than Germany does, and I find that I miss my home land greatly. I suppose I must have longed for it all this time, but kept my feelings buried deep inside. Now the possibility of a return seems to have awakened them within me. After the grief of the past year, watching my husband suffer and die …"

Here I was forced to pause for a moment as the grief hit me anew. Judith placed a hand on my arm and rubbed it gently.

"I am sorry. Perhaps I should not have said anything."

"No, you did nothing wrong," I assured her, patting her hand with my own. "Actually, the joy of going home has helped me in my grief. I am ready for a new beginning. It is a return to England, but not to the past, for my mother and brother are gone. Yet I look forward to what the future holds for me there."

We embraced and then I returned to the block tower I had been building for the little one, who seemed to be having more fun pounding one block against another. After a few minutes, Duke Frederick suddenly spoke.

"This is interesting."

"What is interesting?" I asked, looking up from my work.

"It is a letter from my groom, Otto," he replied, holding it up as if to prove the point. "He is staying up in Braunschweig."

Hearing a noise, I turned my head back to Master Frederick and saw that he had knocked down the tower I had so carefully constructed. With a sigh, I stood up and walked over to where the duke was sitting, leaving Judith to care for the boy.

"Why is your groom not with you here?" I inquired. "I should think you would want all your servants with you now."

"Actually, as I am not hunting or traveling at the moment, I thought it would be a good time to allow him to visit his father, who is quite ill and near death."

"Oh. I am sorry to hear it. But what does he say in the letter?"

"He was having dinner at a local tavern, when he heard two men at the table behind him discussing the election. He turned around and saw that one was in the employ of Duke Lothair of Saxony and the other was a deacon at the cathedral of Mainz."

"So an acolyte of Adalbert," I concluded, for Mainz was Archbishop Adalbert's see.

"Yes, that is correct. Apparently, Otto returned to staring at his food while still listening to what they were saying. However, they began whispering and he could hear nothing of their discussion. He turned his head again and saw the deacon hand a letter to the other man which bore the seal of Archbishop Adalbert, or at least he was fairly certain that it did. He could not get a perfect look. The servant of Duke Lothair then walked off while the deacon gave Otto a pointed glare and said, 'Mind your own business, dullard! No one likes a lurker.'"

"And that was the extent of their conversation?"

"Yes. Here, you can read it for yourself," he said, shoving the paper in my direction.

"There's no need for that," I said, pushing it back in his direction. "What I want to know is what you think of it?"

He shrugged. "I think it is interesting that they all happened to be in the same tavern."

"Yes, fortunate that we should have a spy in their midst."

"Why should we need a spy?" he asked, the look on his face one of honest confusion.

I began to wonder in that moment if it was not Duke Frederick who was the dullard and not his groom, but I was hardly going to say that—particularly not in front of Judith and the child. Instead, I attempted to explain things kindly.

"You have just told me that a representative of Archbishop Adalbert, who is the chief elector, met with a representative of Duke Lothair of Saxony, the only other person who could make a strong challenge for the throne of Germany and the imperial crown, and handed him a secret letter bearing the seal of the archbishop, all of this taking place in a tavern where they must have been fairly certain that no one would notice them, and when someone did seem to notice, they instantly broke off their meeting and chastised him?"

There was a moment's pause in which Duke Frederick looked off into the distance, his eyes darting back and forth as if he was attempting to process all the information I had just given him. Finally, he looked back at me and shook his head. "I'm sorry. What is your point?"

Keep up, man! Honestly, you're going to be an emperor! I thought.

"My point is that Archbishop Adalbert has secret confidences with Duke Lothair of Saxony, which means that he is likely going to support him in the election, and may even attempt to direct the proceedings so that Lothair is assured of victory," I warned.

"What?! No!" he cried, smiling. "That is incredible, which is to say that I do not believe it. Archbishop Adalbert is a good friend of mine. Even when he was at odds with your late husband, he bore no ill will toward me. Since the emperor's death, he has been in communication with me constantly, helping me through the process and giving every indication that he wishes to see me elected."

"And what do you make of this secret meeting?" I asked, placing my hands on my hips and bending forward.

"I make nothing of it," he said, also bending forward in his chair. "People meet all the time. Everyone is discussing the election. It is not strange that these two men should do so."

"I do not think your servant would have informed you unless he suspected as I did that something treacherous was afoot. I warn you, Frederick, be on your guard against Adalbert!"

"Please!" Lady Judith suddenly said, standing up and holding Master Frederick in her arms. "You two are upsetting the child!"

The lack of tears on young Frederick's face and howls escaping from his throat led me to believe that it was Judith who was truly upset, but we obeyed her in any case. Duke Frederick gathered up all the letters and departed the room, followed soon after by his wife and son. I was left standing there amid the columns, pondering what had just occurred. No matter how much I turned it over in my mind, I still came to the same conclusion: Adalbert would attempt to have Duke Lothair elected, and my husband's dying wish would be betrayed.

As the princes of the realm continued to descend upon Mainz, I was filled with concern that there would be a split between the men of the North and those of the South, in addition to the ever present tensions between the ecclesiastical and secular officials. I feared that Adalbert was also aware of this possibility, and that he would use it to his advantage. Sadly, Duke Frederick paid no heed to my warnings. Although I sent him a letter to the same effect as what I had said to him before, I received no response.

We were advancing quickly toward the election. With each passing day, the men made camp on either side of the Rhine: Bavarians and Saxons to the east, Franconians and Swabians to the west. There were some ten thousand permanent inhabitants of that city, but during the month of August, the number increased six fold. What a boon for those manning the shops and market stalls! Even the monks of Saint Alban's were receiving daily requests to purchase food and drink from their stores: one by one, the messengers prevailed upon the cellarer to provide this sustenance for their noble masters. I was told that the visitors consumed in the space of two weeks a year's worth of wine. Less honorably, we saw carts passing by each day with women from near and far, ready to take part in a rather different trade.

Now, this was how the assembly proceeded. The number of electors, clerks, priests, and the like was so great that no hall could contain them. Therefore, they all met at the cathedral. Duke Lothair of Saxony and Duke Henry of Bavaria were in attendance, but the Salian brothers were both absent, Duke Conrad of Franconia being on pilgrimage and Duke Frederick of Swabia hoping to avoid the appearance of undue meddling in the proceedings. The vote of those four duchies—Saxony, Bavaria, Franconia, and Swabia—would determine who sat upon the throne of Germany.

I was also absent, for Archbishop Adalbert had made a general announcement that it would not be appropriate for women to attend the election. I was beginning to suspect that along with his suggestion that I go to a nunnery, this was simply an effort to keep me from influencing the vote.

Although the election was said to be free, there were certain conditions placed upon it. Only those men of highest birth were considered worthy of the crown of Germany, and it was most typical that the eldest surviving son of the former emperor—or in this case, the eldest surviving male relative—would gain the crown. It may not have been a matter of legal necessity, but it was the strong tradition of that land. Moreover, only those who resided in the kingdom of Germany were allowed to cast a vote. Despite this, the Church of Rome was not content to sit by idly. It seemed best to Pope Calixtus to send two legates to the assembly. Their aim was to ensure that the laymen did not attempt to pervert the election.

Thus it was that on the first day, the assembly met in the great cathedral of Mainz. Although I was not there, I can imagine how the scene must have looked, for it was the same church where I was crowned. They must have filed into the nave sharing the latest rumors in hushed voices. No doubt, the parties of dukes Frederick and Lothair congregated together on opposite sides, with Adalbert and the other high ranking officials seated before the high altar. For the rest, I have my account from the chronicles.

The Saxons and the Swabians each supported their own dukes, making the opinion of Franconia and Bavaria all the more vital. Furthermore, the bishops on the council disapproved of both Duke Frederick and Duke Lothair and nominated another lord, Margrave Leopold of the Eastern March. Wishing to avoid either the greatest supporter or the greatest enemy of the former emperor, this must have seemed to them the choice that would most benefit the Church. However, it placed Margrave Leopold in an ill favored position, for Duke Frederick was the son of his own wife, Margravine Agnes, and thus he felt a debt of loyalty to the Swabian duke. Good man that he was, he refused the crown and withdrew his name from consideration. The next thing I knew, Drogo informed me that Duke Lothair of Saxony had also refused election.

"I cannot think of why he would do such a thing," he told me. "Everyone assumed he wanted to be emperor."

It was indeed strange. I had become certain of Archbishop Adalbert's intent to direct votes toward Duke Lothair, who I was convinced wanted to be elected. However, even as I was wondering how I could have been so wrong, another possibility occurred to me.

"Perhaps he is only feigning humility, as great men are often wont to do," I said. "Make no mistake: he still wants to be emperor. He hopes that the electors will force the crown upon him."

I spoke with more confidence than I actually felt, for there was no way to know exactly what was passing through the minds of those men. Whatever Lothair's true intentions, Duke Frederick was left as the only choice, and he therefore attended the assembly the following day with a large crowd of his supporters. I prayed to God that he would be elected quickly, that any treachery in the heart of Adalbert would be overcome, and that my last duty to my husband would be fulfilled.

As the hours passed, I heard nothing of the proceedings, but given that his adversaries had been forced to back down, I felt assured that the vote would bring forth a happy outcome for Duke Frederick. I spent the early part of the day assembling things for my departure. I had already written to my father the king and informed him that I would be making for Normandy along with my possessions. He had summoned me to join him at the castle of Caen. It was lovely for once to worry less about the election and think more of the happy days that lay ahead.

Late that afternoon, I was sitting under a tree in the garden that looks out over the confluence of the River Main and the

River Rhine. Such a pleasant view! From there I could see the whole city of Mainz, which appeared as a collection of thatched roofs along with the odd stone building. The great cathedral towered over all. I think I might have sat there and enjoyed it for ever. It must have been hot, but I have no memory of that. I remember only the constant hum of the bees as they flitted from one flower to the next. I was as much at peace as I could have been in that moment, reciting the Psalms to myself and praying that all might proceed according to the Lord's providence, although I certainly hoped that the Lord's providence would bend in the direction of my desire and place my husband's relative on the throne.

Hearing the crunching sound of steps upon gravel and the slight clink of metal upon metal, I turned to see the guest master of that house, Hatto, approaching, with the keys to the monastery attached to his belt.

"Attend, Brother Hatto, for I have found the perfect verses to pleasure the ears of the bees," I said. "'The fear of the Lord is clean, and endures for ever: the judgments of the Lord are truth. They are righteous altogether, and more to be desired than gold, yea, than much fine gold: sweeter also than honey, and the honeycomb.' Now, what think you of that?"

"Very good, Your Highness," he replied, arriving near my position. "I see your time among us has not been spent in idleness."

"I do not believe in idleness. Remember, I lived among the monks of Trier."

"Ah, yes! I had forgotten that. You are more accustomed to our ways than most of our visitors. Are you sure you do not mind sitting in the grass? There is a bench just around the corner," he said, pointing to the left.

"I am quite all right, thank you. So what was it you needed to tell me?"

"Oh my! I quite forgot myself when listening to the musical tones of your voice," he declared, clasping his hands behind his back and smiling broadly.

You see, the monk could flatter with ease, which I suspect was how he assumed his position as servant to the monastery's guests.

Still looking rather pleased with himself, he said, "Duke Frederick is here to speak with you."

"What?! You might have begun with that!"

At once, the look on his face was one of fear. "Forgive me, but, the musical tones—"

"Never mind that! Send him over."

The poor monk ran back up the hill toward the monastery and returned a few minutes later with the royal visitor. I rose to greet him, and Hatto departed.

"Good afternoon, Duke Frederick, or is it now good evening?" I asked cheerily.

"What the sky tells us, I cannot say, but in my soul it is blackest night."

These words surprised me greatly. Looking at his face, I could see that he was indeed saddened. His eyes were pointed at the ground, as if he was ashamed to meet my gaze. I instantly grew afraid, but told myself, *Stay calm, Maud. Hear him out before you give him up for dead.*

"What's this?" I said to him, half laughing. "Come and sit with me. I will hear it all."

I motioned in the direction of the stone bench Hatto had mentioned. It was only about fifteen paces away. During the short walk there, I had time enough to consider several different explanations for his mood, each more awful than the next, and all threatening my late husband's wishes.

We sat for a moment side by side as I waited for him to speak, but he seemed too troubled in spirit to form the words.

"What happened?" I finally asked with some unease.

"I'm not sure. We were all gathered there this morning. Everything was set. Then Archbishop Adalbert …"

"Adalbert! I knew it!"

"What do you mean?"

"Nothing. Do continue."

"Very well. Adalbert stood before the assembly. He began to speak about the importance of official neutrality. 'Free choice' he called it. He used those words again and again."

"Oh no …" I muttered, beginning to sense where this story was leading.

Frederick's eyes looked at me, then down at his lap, then back at me, then back at his lap. I was about to command him to continue, but he finally did so of his own accord.

"He said it was in the interest of all that the next king be elected according to the clear conscience of all men. I supposed that he merely hoped to appear considerate, or to please the papal legates. I was just waiting for him to call for the vote. Then he spoke to me directly."

Here he paused yet again. His delays were torturing me, but somehow I found a way to endure. At length, he continued.

"The archbishop said, 'Duke Frederick, your brother lords have acted in accordance with Christian goodness and sought to remove themselves from all possible taint by declining to put themselves forward as contenders. Would you not follow their example and submit yourself to the will of this divinely guided assembly, rather than openly seeking out this office as would a conqueror?' The rest was all confusion to me. He kept speaking along those lines, bidding me to remove myself from consideration. One thing I do remember clearly: he said, 'It is better to be seen as Cincinnatus dragged from the plow than Caesar processing in triumph.' Well, what was I to do? I deferred to the will of the assembly. They will begin again tomorrow as if none of it had happened."

By this point, I was in something close to a rage. I had listened to his account in silence, each sentence provoking me further. Was he an idiot? Could he not see that he had been played? *Calm yourself, Maud!* I thought, but how could I do so in the face of such cowardice? My late husband's nephew had just sacrificed everything for which his uncle had fought. He had let Adalbert win.

I finally stood and began moving to and fro, even as Duke Frederick awaited my response. The tribulations of the past year played over in my mind, and as they did so my pain seemed to multiply into a surge of anger that longed to be set free. The untimely, painful death of Emperor Henry: he had longed to know that the Salian dynasty would continue after he went the way of all flesh. It was one of his few comforts in his dying hours to know that both I and Frederick would do our utmost to make that happen. But Duke Frederick had not heeded my warning about Adalbert. He had trusted him when he ought not to have done so. He had been convinced to take himself out of consideration and start the election process over again. He had given up the chance of certain election for God only knew what.

"I have tried to think of what my uncle might have done in this case," he continued earnestly. "Then I reasoned that I should come here, for you and I knew him best."

"You might have had enough sense to stay away," I muttered, or perhaps it was someone else who said it. My anger seemed to have gained control.

"I'm sorry? Have I offended you in some way?"

For the space of two or three breaths, I had the chance to save myself. I could have declared that he did not understand my meaning. I could have kept my thoughts locked inside myself. Oh, but I had had enough of pleasing powerful men, and so, to my eternal regret, I spoke the truth.

"Only in every way, sir!" I replied. "I have met a great number of fools in my day, but none who are quite so foolish after your manner. Tell me, did Adalbert force you to bend over before he stole away your manhood?"

"How dare you slander me thus!" he said, springing from his seat.

"It is not what I dare, but what you do not dare. Can't you see?! He has been false from the beginning! It was Adalbert who plotted and conspired with Lothair, Adalbert who made the bishops put forth Leopold as a contender in the hope that he might take votes from yourself, Adalbert who has now tricked you into selling away your birth right. At least Esau gained a pint of stew—you have gained nothing! You have covered this house with such dishonor by your damnable uncertainty that I refuse even to pity you. No, I will pity your son, who is now robbed of everything he is owed by his birth."

"I had no choice but to do what I did!" he cried, growing red in the face.

"Even so does the common thief attempt to justify himself. Of course you had a choice! You ought to have gone in there on the first day when you had the advantage and called for a vote. You should never have allowed things to get to this point. And when Adalbert challenged you, you ought to have stood your ground. Now you are left without a leg to stand on. Tell me, Frederick, how will you ever be able to stand by the grave of your uncle knowing you failed to act upon his final wish? How will you be able to look your son in the eye, knowing that you have scorned his inheritance?"

"I will no longer suffer this abuse!" he bellowed. "I thought you were a woman of good sense, but I can see we were all deceived in you. As long as we are speaking of 'oughts,' you ought to leave the city! My moment of triumph is yet before us, and I will not have you here to spoil it."

"Ha! I can come and go as I please." Then I said another thing I really ought not to have said. "You will not be elected, and even if you are, I am no German: you will never be my king, and thank God for that!"

I felt so powerful in uttering those words, but as I did so, I could see that they had cut him too deeply. He pursed his lips and swallowed hard.

"It seems we have nothing left to say to each other," he growled more than spoke. "God grant you safety on your return to England, and may God save the English from your tongue!"

I wish I could tell you I thought the better of what I had said and apologized to him at once, but that would be a lie. It was only several years later that I recognized I had gone too far, allowing my anger to control me. For you see, that was the last I ever saw of Duke Frederick of Swabia. His last memory of me was a horrid one. In my old age, I see the errors of my youth, but I cannot heal the wounds of those who are dead. I had fought for the legacy of Emperor Henry, but too late I saw that one of his legacies ought to have been peace.

CHAPTER SIX

The election quickly became a thing of the past. Duke Henry of Bavaria, father-in-law to Duke Frederick, was made to switch his allegiance to Duke Lothair of Saxony. Lothair offered his own daughter in marriage to Duke Henry's son, an alliance which would create one of the most powerful dynasties in Christendom. Not only this, but Lothair pledged to the Bavarian duke that once he became emperor, the House of Welf would gain control over all the ancestral lands in Saxony as well as the March of Tuscany, for Lothair had no sons of his own. Such a realm many a king would envy, stretching from the northern to the southern sea.

How that name of Welf was advanced! The duke of Bavaria chose to honor his son over his daughter, Judith. He led the Bavarian princes to vote in favor of Duke Lothair, and just that swiftly there was an end of it. Lothair was elected as the new king of Germany and made ready for his coronation in Aachen.

My inability to fulfill my husband's dying wish seemed to stir the grief of his passing anew. At times such as this, there may be only one person with whom it is safe to share one's thoughts and feelings. For most women, this would be a close female companion, but I was not most women. Thus, I was left to speak as I often did with the one man who might understand my predicament.

"I should never have given Adalbert the *regalia*," I said to Drogo as we sat upon the same bench where I had lately accused Duke Frederick, attempting to enjoy the pleasures of the garden, but not entirely succeeding.

"What choice did you have? You were merely the messenger. You did as you were asked," he replied.

"A lack of action is itself an action. In yielding, I gave authority to Adalbert, and he has misused it. He was never the vessel for other men's opinions: he created those opinions. He has played the game with devilish intent, and I gave it to him, Drogo! I gave him the symbols of imperial rule. I sold the *regalia* at too low a price."

I held my head in my hand and let out a deep sigh. Drogo patted me on the back.

"You obeyed the emperor's dying wish. You did exactly what Duke Frederick desired. What could you have done? Hold the *regalia* for ransom? No, you acted rightly and in the only way possible."

"They were too apt to trust him," I said, ignoring his point. "I should have known. 'Oh, empress! You must go to a nunnery, empress! Do not trouble yourself with this affair.' What was that but an attempt to remove me from the situation? Adalbert knew I doubted him, so he wanted me gone."

"If anything, Duke Frederick is the one at fault. He assumed too much and fought too little. You told me you attempted to warn him, but he refused to listen."

"Yes, he was most deceived of all, but I take no comfort in that: not when my husband's greatest enemy sits upon the throne. That is the real outrage. Not only was Frederick denied, but Duke Lothair was the one elected. For Christ's sake! You would think that if Frederick wasn't man enough to claim the throne for himself, he would at least have done so for the sake of his son. That boy has more courage than his father."

"So what will you do now?" Drogo asked, gazing out at the river.

"Return home, as soon as possible. I've had enough of this country."

"You mean you will not even wait for the coronation?" he asked, looking back at me.

"Certainly not, even as I have no wish to be placed on the rack."

"Then I am with you, as sure as the sun rises in the east. We shall make ready to leave at once."

He made to stand, but I placed a hand on his arm.

"One task remains, my friend. As Adalbert has shown himself to be no man of God, we will remove the symbol of his authority. You and I must make a visit to the cathedral."

"Why? So you can shame him again?"

"Not quite."

I fell silent for a moment, attempting to decide how I should proceed. I had an idea—a rather reckless idea. It would certainly make my point, but it would require great stealth and a certain lack of regard for standard morality.

I looked into his eyes and lowered my voice. "Drogo, if I asked you to do something, even if it was against the laws of man, would you do it?"

He leaned back slightly and studied my face, as if attempting to make out my character. "I would assume there was a higher purpose."

"So you would do it?"

"I suppose that we must on occasion sacrifice the laws of man to please God," he said with a nod.

"And common decency, in this case. You are the man I need, Drogo. Come with me, but don't ask questions. All will be revealed in time."

That evening, I expressed a desire to visit the cathedral and to travel not by horse but in a carriage. This became a cause of complaint, for I had no carriage of my own there in Mainz. Thus, one would have to be brought up from town at some expense.

"Are you sure you would not rather ride?" Hatto asked. "The weather is so fine."

Although I understood that my request must have made me seem rather haughty in his eyes, as if I could not deign to have the wind rustle my veil, I knew the carriage was quite necessary, so I objected.

"Dear Master Hatto, do you treat all your royal guests with such disdain, or only myself? I am still an empress, and I wish to travel in comfort!"

Well, that was the end of that. Within the hour, I was being transported through the city by carriage, with Drogo riding behind. No doubt afraid of offending me further, the abbot of Saint Alban's had offered me every form of company, but I refused, claiming it was a matter of private devotion.

We soon arrived in the great market square just north of the red walls of the *Mainzer Dom*. All those gathered in the square turned to look as I climbed out of the carriage. They began to shout and press in very close, so I said to the driver, "We shall take less than half an hour inside the cathedral. Be a good man and wait beside the west entrance, for I have no desire to attract such attention upon our departure."

Now, the imperial cathedral of Mainz is somewhat odd in that it has two chancels. That is, one could perform Mass at either the eastern or western end of the church. I cannot say why it was built in such a manner, but over time the eastern altar had become the site of the standard daily Mass, while the western end was reserved for the princes of the Church, most particularly the archbishop of Mainz. Beyond this, there was the Gotthard Chapel that jutted into the town square. This was Adalbert's special creation, and only the most noble were allowed a place inside. It was there that I had been listening to a sermon with my late husband when we were called out to receive the news of my brother's death.

You may be wondering why I should tell you all this, but it was of great import in that moment. Indeed, I needed to know every point of entry and departure. Because there were two chancels, the main entrance was on the north side of the Church, where my carriage had arrived. However, it was possible to depart through less lofty doors at the western and eastern ends. That is why I told the driver to wait for us on the western end, for it was farthest from the crowds and closest to the object of my visit.

As Drogo and I made our way into the church, my heart began to beat more quickly knowing what we were about to do. If we were to succeed, it was possible that we would become infamous throughout Christendom, but I was willing to place my reputation in that danger for the chance of sending a message to Adalbert that he would never forget. In any case, I had every intention of leaving the empire at once.

As Drogo and I entered through the *Marktportal*, which is the northern gate, we were stopped by a priest whom I did not recognize.

"Fair Empress Mathilda!" he proclaimed. "We only just received the news of your coming. I am afraid we had no time to make ready." His breath was somewhat heavy, as if he had just run from the other end of the cathedral to meet us.

"Peace! I have no intention of upsetting your schedule. What is your name, Father?" I asked.

"Herman, my lady. Herman of Kirchzell," he replied, bowing with each mention of his own name.

"Kirchzell? I'm afraid I never heard of it."

"It has a lovely market."

"I see," I told him, not caring a bit about Kirchzell or its market. "Take me to the chapel of Saint James, Father Herman. I wish to pray in private."

The light in the poor priest's eyes seemed to fade, and I suspect he was rather upset that all his rushing had not gained him a longer audience. Nevertheless, he was nothing if not polite.

"Certainly, madam. Right this way," he replied.

The priest walked a few paces to where a wood box sat and retrieved three candles, for it had grown rather dark. He then used another candle sitting by an image of Saint Martin to light them, and handed one each to Drogo and me.

"It is difficult to see in these shadows," he said, gesturing broadly to indicate the whole cathedral.

All the better for our enterprise, I thought.

As we made our way beneath the first row of columns into the middle nave, Drogo whispered in my ear, "Adalbert is gone. What exactly do you intend to do?"

"Wait and see, Drogo. Wait and see."

The priest then took a turn to the right and led us toward the western altar. This was the space reserved for only the greatest of the great. We climbed the few stairs and saw the table on which the elements were made sacred. Moving behind the altar, we came to the final rotunda. Straight in front of us was the episcopal throne: the seat of Adalbert's power. To the right was the chapel holding the tabernacle of the consecrated host, and to the left was another chapel holding the holy relic for which we had come: the hand of Saint James, just as gray and hideous as always. It looked just as I remembered it from all those years ago, when Bruno first made known to me its secrets.

As I stood there, candle in hand, I felt a lump in my throat and a knot in my stomach. I prayed silently, begging forgiveness for what I was about to do.

"Here we are," Father Herman said. "Sir, if you wish to come with me—"

"My knight will stay," I said, turning quickly to face him.

"Of course, my lady," he replied, bowing his head in submission. "Far be it from me to cause offense. Will you be requiring anything else?"

"Nothing but silence," I told him.

I turned back toward the holy relic and set my candle on the ground, its flame flickering slightly. I knelt on the brightly adorned tiles and closed my eyes as if to pray. When I finally heard the priest's steps moving away from us, I asked quietly, "Is he gone?"

"Yes," Drogo answered.

"Is anyone watching?" I inquired without turning around to face him.

"No."

At this, I opened my eyes and stood up, grabbing my candle once again. "Then quickly, take the relic, and we will leave by the side door."

"Take what?!" he said a bit louder than I would have preferred.

I had never seen such a look of confusion on his face. Clearly, I had pushed him beyond the bounds of belief. I took a few steps forward until we were standing very close.

"Drogo, you said that whatever I asked, you would do it," I said, jabbing my finger into his chest. "There is no time for discussion. Will you help me or not?"

The knight was clearly taken aback by my suggestion. In the dim candle light, it appeared to me that his expression had changed from confusion to indignation. Looking down, he took a small step forward with each foot in turn, either to plant himself more firmly or to buy time for thought, then with a deep sigh, he looked into my eyes.

"Do you want the whole thing, or just the hand?"

"Better make it the whole thing."

He scoffed and shook his head. I could tell that he was angry, but he would do his duty.

"Very well, then, but if anything goes wrong, it's you who will be answering to Saint Peter on the Day of Judgment."

"I shall not forget this, Drogo."

"Yes, well, I don't think God will forget either, and that's what I'm afraid of."

He gave me his candle and attempted to raise the thing up with not a little effort. Indeed, for a moment I was afraid that it might be attached at the base and the whole thing would be for naught. As he continued to strain, I took a quick look behind me to make sure that no one was approaching. At last, he was able to lift the glass container off the stone pedestal.

"Good God, it's heavy!" he whispered, his knees dropping slightly under its weight. "How am I supposed to walk out of here without being stopped?"

"Rule number one, Drogo: act as if you are in command. Second, let me do the talking."

"The things I do for you! There better be a mess of lampreys in it for me, or a new book, or some such thing."

"Gold?" I offered.

He nodded. "That would do it."

I quickly blew out one of the candles and set it on the ground, at which point there was barely enough light to see.

"Follow me," I whispered.

We moved as quickly as possible back past the altar and down the steps. To the right was the door outside which the carriage would be waiting to steal us away. We made it within ten paces of that precious portal when I heard a noise and stopped so quickly that Drogo ran into me from behind. We both struggled to contain a groan, then I looked toward the source of the noise. It was a boy standing in the shadows, although that was a relative term considering the darkness of the entire cathedral. As I squinted, I saw that he was moving toward us and carrying what appeared to be candles. I reasoned that he must be the boy tasked with changing them out after the worshippers had left for the day.

I barely had enough time to note all of this before he was close enough to see us. His eyes grew wide with wonder.

"What are you—" he began to say, but I was not about to let him get the better of us.

"How dare you speak to me before you're spoken to?!" I cried. "Know you not who I am? I am the Empress Mathilda!"

Clearly struck with terror, he pointed at the relic and stammered, "But, but—"

Once again, I did not allow him to finish. "I'll have you know that the archbishop permitted me to keep it in my chambers for my private devotion. Not that I need to explain myself to you, you impertinent—"

"Forgive me!" he cried, bowing low and dropping several of the candles he was holding.

"Now, open the door for us," I commanded, pointing toward the portal to my right.

"Certainly, my lady—that is, my empress!"

He proceeded to drop the rest of the candles and rushed over to open the door, striving to keep his head down all the while. Drogo and I walked through, and my spirit was calmed when I saw the carriage sitting there without a crowd surrounding it.

"Put it in the carriage, Drogo. Quickly!" I whispered.

"What about the driver? He will see me."

"Let me worry about that."

He did as I commanded, and I walked to the front to address the driver. As I had hoped, he only paid attention to me.

"Did you leave that covering inside as I requested?" I asked. "It is grown quite cold."

"Yes, my lady," he replied with a smile. "Do you need any assistance getting in?"

"No, thank you. Sir Drogo will help me."

I walked back to the carriage door, where Drogo was climbing out.

"Is it safely inside?" I whispered.

"Yes, and I covered it with the cloth that was lying there."

"Good thinking. I was about to do that myself."

Within short order, we were back at the monastery, with the driver none the wiser to our theft. As I climbed out, I engaged the few people there in intense conversation so that Drogo had a chance to take the relic and hide it in one of my chests. Apparently, no one thought to ask what he was carrying, or perhaps they were simply too afraid. I had noticed from time to time that people were more hesitant in addressing him, believing him to be some kind of giant still walking the earth.

Now the sign of your authority is taken, Adalbert, I thought in delight. *Now you are truly humbled.*

Long after the monks had gone to bed, Drogo and I sat at the long table in the empty refectory with one of the few bottles of wine that had survived the election. It was wonderful to be alone, just the two of us. The walls were painted with scenes of the different seasons of the year, one of which showed a vineyard harvest. A lone farmer trampled upon the grapes, his feet turned red in the process.

Drogo lifted his goblet toward the man. "Thank you, kind farmer, for supplying us with the last fruits of your labors!"

We both laughed. His jest was nothing special, but we had both achieved that perfect combination of weariness of body and merriness of soul, the latter no doubt brought on by drink. We each took a long draft and then sat in silence, contemplating everything that had occurred in the past few days.

"Let us hope no one checks the chapel until morning," I said, "or that they are too afraid to tell their master."

"I'm amazed that worked," he replied, pouring me another glass. "I feel it shouldn't have."

"I too had my doubts when we were stopped," I agreed, lifting the goblet to my lips.

"Why? You were in complete control. I was a little afraid of you, actually, and I was on your side!"

I stopped drinking but continued to turn the glass round in my hand, watching the red liquid whip inward like a whirlwind. "Well, it may not have been my proudest moment, but it worked. Once our deed is discovered, Adalbert will be out for blood. It is best that we leave as soon as possible."

"Everything is made ready. The men will be here before dawn to receive you."

"I think it best that we take our leave of as few people as possible. The less questions, the better."

"Just tell me one thing: why did you choose to take the hand of Saint James? Why not something else?"

"Because Drogo, the authority of a bishop lies in his cathedral, and the authority of a cathedral comes from the presence of a holy relic. Therefore, since this bishop has made a mockery of authority, we have made a mockery of him. In removing the symbol of his authority, we make known to all men that God has removed his Holy Spirit from Adalbert, even as he did from the evil King Saul."

We both drank deeply from the goblets. Within a few hours, the monks would rise for their morning prayers, and we would be traveling down the Rhine on our winding course toward Normandy. It was strange to think of all that had happened since I arrived in the empire.

"Thank you, Drogo," I said. "You have been with me through it all. I had no one when I came here—not a single soul. Even though we have not always been in one another's company, I am sure I could not have survived it without your encouragement."

"I hope when we arrive in Normandy, we will find lovers each of us," he said, raising his glass to me and drinking.

"Mind what you say, Sir Drogo. I have not given up on making you a priest, and my womb belongs to the king of England to do with as he pleases, barren though it may be."

He laughed. "Very well. But don't forget: you promised me gold, or barring that, some lampreys!"

"Indeed, I did, and as soon as we are in Caen, you will have all this and more."

"I like the sound of that."

So we sat there, two old friends, enjoying the last dregs of our German experience.

This I will say for the Normans: the sea is in our blood. It was the sea that bore us from the lands of ice and snow down to the kingdoms of the South, the green pastures waiting to be settled. There the descendants of Rollo made their home by the white cliffs and the River Seine, and upon that sea my own grandfather William set out to try his fortune on the plains and hills of England.

For some, it may be difficult to imagine such a breadth of water that stretches as far as the eye can see. In all my years in the empire, I had never set out in a ship without being able to see the far shore. Even the endless length of the Rhine is no match for the unknown depths of the sea, which can produce a sense of awe in both the humble and the great. When I first saw those waves again after so many years, it brought tears to my eyes to behold such majesty.

I was to join my father at the royal castle in Caen by mid-autumn, but there was still the trouble of William Clito. Hateful man! He did love to spoil my travels. On account of his quarrel with my father, I was not permitted to travel through the lands of either the count of Flanders or king of France. There was only one path open to us: to travel down the Rhine until it emptied into the northern sea, then to sail through the Channel and down the coast of Normandy. This would add some two weeks to the journey, depending on the weather.

"Think of it this way," offered Drogo, "you will see more of the countryside."

Yes, Drogo was always eager to find the good in any circumstance. I was not born under such a joyous planet, for I saw only pitiable delay. In Normandy, I was to begin my life over again, and I hoped this time I would not be a pawn in the hands of a king or emperor, but an heir with hopes and dreams of my own. Of course, I was also filled with fears. Perhaps my father would find me wanting in some way. Perhaps my long absence had made me a foreigner among my own people. Yes, there was plenty to fear, but at least I felt that I had a purpose: yes, I and not another. I also hoped that the relic hidden among my possessions would help to promote my cause to the king, for he would no doubt covet it for one of his own abbeys.

It took us just a few days to reach the mouth of the Rhine. We then began our course through the Channel, steering none too close to Flanders. Even so, there were plenty of times when I could see the coast line clearly.

"You know, we are very near the city of Boulogne," one of the sailors said to me on a fair afternoon as we gazed at the brown and green coast in the distance.

"Are we?" I replied. "Perhaps young Mathilda is staring back at me, though I should not call her such now, for she is made countess of Boulogne since her father took holy orders. She was wed this year to my other cousin, Stephen of Blois."

"Ah," he said, nodding his head as if he fully understood, but from the empty look in his eyes, I gathered that he did not. "Have you met either of them?"

"Stephen made one trip to Westminster before I left, but I spoke with him very little. Likewise, I only saw the young Mathilda once, though it is burned into my memory."

"Why is that?"

"Because she almost burned the place down. Well, she caused her mother's dress to catch on fire."

"Really?!" he said in surprise, his eyes wide. "That must be some story!"

Indeed, it was quite a story. I laughed softly thinking of it. It was strange that such a terror of a girl was now made countess of the prosperous territory of Boulogne and married to one of the greatest men in King Henry's service. It seemed far better than she deserved, but then again, my opinion of her was based on naught but hearsay and that single meeting. Nevertheless, I struggled to imagine that she had grown into a fine woman of good character.

"Would that she had the ability to turn the count of Flanders toward our side," I said, more to myself than to him. "Then I might think better of her."

Within the hour, the captain was happy to report to me that we had left Flanders behind and entered the waters of Normandy. What joy filled my heart at this news! Strangely, although I was half descended from that land, I had not yet set foot in the duchy of Normandy. I was most eager to see this place I had heard of from my earliest hours.

The sun was already dipping low in the western sky, so we sailed into the bay on which sits the lovely little monastery of Saint Valery, right at the mouth of the River Somme. There we dropped anchor and settled in for the night. The dwellings were not grand, but at least we were able to gain provisions for the rest of our journey and to sleep upon blessed land.

I rose before the sun the following morning, while the monks were still chanting their prayers. I had left Adelaide and Gertrude behind in the empire and was without a maid to help dress me. Indeed, I had changed my garment only once since we left Mainz, and I had not bathed. While the common man may wash as little as he likes, I was accustomed to do so more than once a week. With no one to aid me, there was also no one to stop me, so I took the simplest gown I could find and slipped out of the house.

I set out barefoot on the dirt path, passing first the towering maples and then the willows bent low near the river. The path then disappeared in the brush that formed a final barrier against the sand. I received a few scratches from those small branches, which poked out like hands seeking to grasp any passer by. Thank God they at least were not covered with thorns! I was glad to have made it so far without being noticed, but as I stepped into the open, my reward was not a sandy shore nor even the mess of rocks common in the South of England. Instead, I had walked straight into a fen, and my feet were sinking into the mud.

I muttered a curse under my breath. Had it been lighter out, I would not have made such a mistake, but as it was, I had only two choices: to press on toward the river or run back in defeat. I chose the former.

Finally, I came to the river's edge. The autumn air was cold, and my body seemed to protest against the very idea of that water. However, I was determined to be clean, even though I knew my feet at least would be made filthy again on the return journey. I continued walking until I found a place where the shore dipped down slightly and I might bathe in privacy. The sun had just risen, and I knew the longer I waited, the more likely I was to attract attention. Thus, without deliberating further, I left my clothes behind and walked up to the water's edge.

This is mad—utterly mad, I thought. *This might be the maddest thing I have ever done.* Nevertheless, I waded into the sea.

Oh, such cold! Unbearable cold! I was forced to use all my will to remain under water. It felt as the embrace of death, and that was what caused me to remember that it was in that very sea that my brother William had met his end five years earlier.

Was this what he felt in those last desperate moments, gasping for breath, the heat of the fire and the cold of the water, the fury above and the fury below? Much like myself, he might have never learned to swim. Yet even if he had, there would have been little hope so far from shore.

Even as I considered all this, there was something else gnawing at the fabric of my mind and lending discomfort to my spirit far beyond any I felt in the flesh. It was neither fear nor pain, but rather guilt that seemed to plague me.

"Forgive me, William," I said with trembling lips. "It should have been me in your place. You were the one born to be king. You had everything needed to rule. What am I, William? What am I to England?"

Remembering my original purpose in coming, I rubbed at my arms and legs. The flesh still clung to my bones, but my brother's had become food for the fish of the sea. Denied the dignity of a proper burial, he should have lain with the great kings of old. Instead, he was in a darkness far more ancient: as old as the earth itself. Meanwhile, though my heart continued to beat, I felt as if I had also been stripped, not of flesh, but of every person I loved. William, my mother, my husband—all had succumbed to the icy pull of death. I knew I must begin again, but I feared to do so alone.

I moved to where the water was shallow and fell to my knees on the sea floor. As much as I longed to leave the cold, I felt that in those waters I could be one with my brother again. Somewhere in the channel, his body lay upon the ocean floor. There amid the waves, I was as close to him as I could ever be, save for when we were to meet again in heaven.

I will not fail you, William, I thought rather than spoke. *Stay with me. Lend me your strength. I will fight for what you sought to win. The branches of England and Normandy will be united. Hope will live on.*

My teeth began to chatter and my toes were numb, so I returned to the beach only to find that my clothes had been caught in a wave and drenched. I muttered something unworthy of mention and placed the wet gown over my body, all the while ruing my mistake.

I then moved as quietly as possible back through the woods, at one point tripping over a fallen branch that was hidden beneath the leaves. I must have been quite a sight when I arrived back at the monastery, wet from head to foot, water dripping upon the stone floor. I made it back to my chamber, hid the filthy clothes back in the chest, and slipped into the bed. With any luck, my hair would dry before anyone came to wake me.

"We are one, William, you and me," I whispered into the darkness. "From this moment forward, I carry you with me. I will do all that you could not do. If father has no heir, I shall be heir in your place. I will take up that helm and fight for the honor denied you. I am all that is left of our mother, and all that is left of you; but I shall never be alone, for you are in my very bones."

It was only after I had spent the night there that I learned of the importance of Saint Valery for my own family. Sixty years earlier, on another autumn day, my grandfather William had gathered his forces and crossed over to Hastings to reclaim his crown, even as the chronicler has written:

> "William the earl landed at Hastings, on Saint Michael's Day: and Harold came from the north, and fought against him before all his army had come up: and there he fell, and his two brothers, Girth and Leofwin; and William subdued this land. And he came to Westminster, and Archbishop Aldred consecrated him king, and men paid him tribute, delivered him hostages, and afterwards bought their land."[9]

This knowledge brought some cheer to my heart—to think that I was repeating the very steps of my forebear. But it was not to England that the ship would take me, but along the alabaster coast of Normandy, past the great towns of Dieppe and Fécamp, rounding the corner into the bay of Honfleur and then rowing the last few miles to the mouth of the River Orne.

What a sense of prospect seized me! We had only the last length of river before we would come to the city of Caen and I would see my father once again. Our last parting was unhappy: he had pushed me into the carriage with little regard as my mother shed many tears. There was a violence about it that had remained somewhere in my heart all those years: a ripping, a tearing. I had barely known him. I feared him. But at that moment, as the castle walls came into view, I was disposed to forgive him, for I was now returned from the empire with little

---

[9] Anonymous. *The Anglo-Saxon Chronicle*, ed. J.A. Giles, Bohn's Antiquarian Library (London: George Bell & Sons, 1914), 141. Based on the translation by Rev. James Ingram circa 1823.

harm done, grown older and a bit wiser. Though I would always carry that experience with me, I felt somewhat renewed. I would place those days of death and doubt behind me. I would hope for the best when it came to my father. Perhaps the years had changed him even as they had changed me.

"Drogo!" I called, as I looked out from the bow. "I can see the castle, there on top of the hill, and that must be the abbey of Saint Étienne, and over there is the women's abbey."

"Yes, I see it all too," he replied, walking up to join me. "I guess this is it then: a new country, a new life. I doubt you will have need of me now."

"What utter drivel is this? Of course I will need you! We are friends, Drogo, and always will be."

"I am glad to hear you say so, but who is that?" he asked with a nod.

"Who is who?" I asked, my eyes searching.

He pointed ahead. "That man there at the landing, about a furlong yonder."

Sure enough, I was able to make out a man standing beside two horses, waving to our captain.

"He must have been sent down to wait for us," I said. "They cannot have known the hour of our arrival. The rest will be waiting up at the castle."

"Yes, but who is he?"

I bent down slightly and strained my eyes to make out the figure. He was of middle height and build, and looked to be not much older than myself. His attire was rather fine, so he was a lord of some sort. He had a beard and some rather long brown hair that made it difficult to see his features. Then as we drew closer, the sun hit his face and I recognized him beyond a doubt.

"That is my cousin, Stephen of Blois."

"Really?" Drogo asked, squinting in the sun light. "I never saw him before, so I cannot say one way or the other."

"It's a bit hard to tell under that beard, but yes, I am sure it is him. My father will have sent him down to fetch us."

He looked at me and smiled. "You'd best ready yourself to be fetched then."

"Well said."

I had put on a blue silk dress and the finest fur mantle I possessed for this occasion, draping my neck in several chains. During the months of mourning in the empire, I had covered myself in layers of gray, black, and brown, but it was time to put such things behind me. I was, after all, a woman of only three and twenty years—a widow, but not an aged one. It was essential that I look my best, for this would be the first time any of them would see me as Empress Mathilda, and I intended to prove it to them.

"How does my hair look, Drogo?" I asked, tending to a few stray bits. "Is it all still in place? Is my veil crooked?"

"How should I know?" he asked, looking at me with no more interest than one might grant to a turnip.

"Oh, come now! You are not blind yet. Do I have any dirt on my face? How do I look?!"

I held my hands up as if to present myself for show and turned first to the right and then to the left.

"I don't know. You look very nice." He spoke the latter sentence almost with the air of a question, clearly seeking to end the conversation as soon as possible.

"'Very nice.' That is what you get from a man," I concluded, throwing up my hands.

We had reached the pier. The ship was being tied up and the plank lowered. My heart, which had been beating firmly for the past hour or so, quickened still further.

Breathe, Maud. Just breathe, I told myself.

As I turned and made to alight from the boat, cousin Stephen was standing there waiting, holding out a hand to support me.

"Empress Mathilda!" he said, bowing once I had set foot on land. "The king has sent me to welcome you home."

Your home, but not mine, I thought.

"Count Stephen, isn't it?" I asked, although I knew the answer. "It has been too long! It was good of you to come."

I took his hand and stepped down on to shore. How strange it was to speak to him after so many years! Then again, we had never spoken much in the past. During his two visits to England, I had been too young to converse much with my elders.

"I hear you are wed to my cousin Mathilda, lately made countess of Boulogne," I said, as he began to lead me toward the two horses, who I now saw were tied to a pole.

"Yes, we have been married a few months now," he replied with a smile.

"Will the countess be joining us here in Caen?"

"No, I traveled here at the king's pleasure, but she preferred to stay behind."

I wondered if I should ask him about the trouble with William Clito and the count of Flanders, but I thought the better of it. After all, I hardly knew him.

"This is the horse that will take you up to the castle. He is quite gentle," Stephen explained, untying the handsome white stallion from the pole.

As he did so, I turned back to see what the others were doing. The men were passing the chests down the plank in a line, while Drogo stood at the end examining each one for damage.

"Sir Drogo!" I called.

When he turned and saw that I was ready to ride, he came over at once and helped me on to the animal, while Stephen mounted his own black horse, which was slightly taller than my own. With my knight's help, I sat in the usual womanly manner.

"Not quite like when we escaped from Goslar, is it?" Drogo whispered, a twinkle in his eye.

"Yes, with any luck, I will never have to share a horse with you again," I replied.

I rode with my cousin the short distance—about half a mile—from the river up the hill to the fortress established by the first King William. We passed by the rows of timber houses and shops on narrow, winding streets, and as we rose higher, I caught a brief glimpse down one of the roads to the abbey church off to the west.

"Is that where our grandfather is buried? At the abbey?" I asked, pointing.

"Yes, and his wife sleeps at the nunnery. You must have seen it when you came in."

"Yes."

The conversation stopped there, and I struggled to withhold the thousands of questions in my mind. The stone walls of the castle had risen up before us, but it was necessary to ride around to the northern side to enter. Apparently, grandfather William had hoped to avoid an assault from the river.

"It is rather large, isn't it?" I said, as we galloped past yard after yard of stone piled upon stone.

"You will find it in a state of construction," Stephen replied. "The keep is completed now, but the king is building a new hall far grander than the current one."

That sounds like him, I mused.

Above us, I could hear the guards yelling to one another, "Count Stephen and the empress have returned! Inform the royal court!"

After we had ridden for at least another furlong, we came at last to the stone tower where a tall wood gate swung open before us, giving way to a sight I had long imagined. It was not the stone keep to the left that caught my eye, but the crowd standing in the courtyard beside it. There must have been a hundred people gathered there, but one stood out among them: King Henry of England, my father. His hair was gray, and there was far less of it than I remembered, to say nothing of his expanded waist. There were trumpets playing, and the crowd let out a great cheer as we rode through the gate. "All hail, Empress Mathilda!" they cried. I brought the horse to a halt and the king himself stepped forward to help me down.

"My own daughter!" he proclaimed. "What joy it brings me to see you here among us!"

It was one of those odd moments when one finds it difficult to accept the sight before one's eyes. To look upon my father again after all those years stirred up such feelings within me. I was pleased to see that he was smiling, and I was tempted to believe that he really was joyful at my return. He reached up his hand, and as I placed my own in his I could feel the firmness of his skin—the callouses gathered over years of battle. In that kingly grip, I might be saved or crushed if he had a will. But for just that moment in time, I had only one thought. *This is my father, bone of my bone and flesh of my flesh.*

My feet touched the ground and he let go of my hand.

"Your Highness," I said, bowing my head. "Thank you for sending Count Stephen to welcome us."

"Here, there is someone I wish for you to meet," he said. "My queen, Adeliza."

He stepped back to reveal a rather small woman who was nevertheless just as lovely as I remembered, even if her crown rather overwhelmed her little head. It had likely been made for my mother, and though she wore it in great state, it may have been a bit heavy for her.

"Empress Mathilda," she said, stepping forward with her hands clasped together. "Welcome to Normandy. How was your journey?"

"Rather longer than I had hoped, but we survived. It is good to see you again! I believe we only met the one time."

She smiled a bit meekly. It seemed she was not entirely comfortable with the situation. No wonder, for she must have felt the weight of comparison with the former queen, my beloved mother. If she doubted that she would match the greatness of her predecessor, I knew she could not, but not one in a hundred queens could do so. Indeed, I myself knew that I was unlikely to ever enjoy the love of the people as my mother had, nor to match her level of piety. Therefore, as much as it pained me to be meeting Queen Adeliza upon my return rather than my own mother, I felt compassion for this young woman who, like me, had been brought far from home to marry a much older man.

"*Es gibt keinen Grund zur Sorge,*" I said to her. "*Ich weiß, woher Sie kommen—Ihre große Familie. England hat das Glück, Sie als seine Königin zu haben.*"

Her eyes lit up at these words. I had guessed that she might be more at ease with the German tongue, and I was correct.

"*Sie sind zu freundlich, Kaiserin Mathilda!*" she said. "*Ich kenne alle gut Sie für das Reich getan haben. Ich hoffe, dass wir Freunde sein können.*"

"*Ich würde das mögen!*" I agreed.

"What is this?" the king asked. "I send you off for a few years, and now you are speaking in code with my wife!"

"There is nothing to fear," I assured him. "I was merely thanking the queen for all the good she has done for England."

My father bent close and whispered in my ear, "Would that she were doing a bit more good in bed!" Then, so that all might hear, he said, "Here is the steward of this fortress, Raymond, and Bishop Richard of Bayeux, and the abbot of Saint Étienne …"

He continued down the line of officials as I acknowledged each of them in turn. Then he came to someone who meant a bit more to me.

"And this handsome man right here is my son Robert, earl of Gloucester!" the king declared, patting him on the back.

"Of course!" I said. "Brother Robert!"

It was indeed my elder half brother. When last we had met, he was already a full man and I was still a girl. He could have avoided me and William, but instead he had doted on us. The only trouble was that we were not often in the same place. Seeing his bright green eyes and easy smile again brought back feelings I had almost forgotten, and I hoped with all my heart that I would have a chance to spend more time with him and feel that we were truly family.

"Empress Mathilda," he said, removing himself from the grip of the king and bowing low. "You will find that many things have changed here, but I have not. I'm just as much trouble as ever."

"But who is this?" I asked, looking at the young boy standing next to him.

"This, I am proud to say, is my eldest son, William. He has two more brothers back in England, and one sister." He brought the boy forward, placed his hands on his shoulders, and commanded, "Say 'good morrow' to your aunt, William!"

The lad's head hit just above his father's waist, with dark curls reaching down to below his chin and topped by a red cap. I did not remember his father's hair ever being quite that extraordinary, and as Robert's hair was rather short at the moment, it would have been hard to believe he was the boy's father had they not shared the same eyes. How small he seemed in the shadow of the great warrior!

"Good morrow," William said meekly. "Are you the empress then?"

"Yes, I suppose I am," I answered, bending down ever so slightly to meet his gaze.

"So are you more powerful than Grandfather?" the boy asked.

"Ha!" the king scoffed. "This boy has some cheek, Robert. Mind you teach him what is right!"

I, on the other hand, was most pleased with my nephew's question and might have handed him a bag of gold for his effort had it not seemed imprudent.

"Nephew William," I told him, "I think we will get along just fine."

"Empress Maud," a voice called.

Even before I turned to look at the speaker, I knew who it was. The sight of his dark hair and hazel eyes only confirmed it: this was Brian fitz Count.

"No one has called me that in a very long time," I said.

"Well, that is your name, is it not? Do you remember mine?" he asked, smiling.

"I could not forget you, Lord Brian. I still have the stone you gave me when I was young. I treasured it during my time in Germany. It always called me home."

"Oh? Forgive me. I do not remember that," he said.

I wondered if I had said too much, but he was most certainly the one who gave me the amber moth.

"Here, meet another of my lads, Robert Beaumont," my father said, directing me down the line.

"Yes, of course," I replied, shaking the next man's hand.

My mind was still caught up in the last conversation, for as foolish as it might seem, I was slightly hurt that Lord Brian did not remember giving me the stone that had become so precious. It was only after my fingers were clasped within those of the burly Robert Beaumont that I suddenly remembered it was his brother Waleran who had mounted a rebellion against the king, and I wondered if I should have embraced that hand after all.

"Robert is the most faithful of subjects, and a good friend of Stephen and the other young men," the king said, evidently guessing my suspicion.

"So do we call you Empress Mathilda or Empress Maud?" the young William interrupted.

I turned back to him and smiled. "You may call me aunt if you wish, but I answer to either name. Maud was what my mother and brother used to call me. It is just the English way of speaking."

Once I had finished meeting everyone, the king declared that we should all move to the hall, where a feast was made ready. I walked just behind him as he led his queen toward the new hall that had been built close to the northern wall of the castle. It was a magnificent stone building, though it stood separate from all the other structures: the kitchen was in another building just to the side. Above the main door of the hall were carved jagged lines in the shape of a half arch with rows of stars above and below. There was one window just above it and then a row of windows on each of the long sides of the building, with the wood roof inclined toward a point in the center.

Upon entering the hall, I saw that it was far grander inside. All the walls were hung with tapestries displaying a unicorn hunt, a merry fire was lit in the center of the room, long tables on either side were covered with both food and the late flowers of autumn, and the high table on the dais was draped in cloth of gold. A herald trumpeter near the door announced the king and queen's arrival, while four musicians stood near the dais ready to entertain us with voice, flute, lyre, and drum.

I was seated with the king and queen on one side and brother Robert and cousin Stephen on the other. When they brought out the platters full of lampreys, I cast a smile down to Drogo, who was clearly as happy as a fox among hens.

"Ah, I know I shouldn't eat these, but damn it, I love them!" the king declared. "I suppose I will pay for it in the morning."

"Father, I brought back something to enrich the abbey of Reading," I said, changing the subject.

"Oh? What's that?"

"The hand of Saint James the apostle."

"Really?! You astound me!" he cried, and I believed him, for he actually dropped the piece of meat he was holding on to the table. "Was that not the prize of the cathedral of Mainz? I suppose they gave it to you as a parting gift."

"In a manner of speaking, yes," I said, quickly looking down at the plate in front of me.

"Well, I shall let the monks know that they are to receive this mighty relic, and tomorrow, if you wish, we shall go to the abbey of Saint Étienne, and you can pay your respects at the tomb of King William."

"I should like that very much," I said quite honestly. I had always desired to visit the grave of my great forebear.

"So, Maud, what did you make of the Germans?" Earl Robert asked. "Are they really as dour as everyone says?"

"No, they love humor as much as the next man, though I cannot say I left in a happy hour. The election did not go as I had hoped."

"That is why you do not have elections," the king replied, hitting the base of his knife on the table. "They are simply an opportunity for men of little sense to pervert the divine order of things. I tell you, he who holds elections will end up with chaos: that is God's honest truth."

"There is some merit in the process," I argued, "but in this case, the archbishop bent it to his own advantage."

"Well, that is no surprise! How many times did Archbishop Anselm attempt to usurp me? He was hungry for power, that one."

My memories of Father Anselm were slightly different, but I felt it would not be wise to gainsay the king.

"Tell me of your wife, Robert," I said. "What is she like?"

"Lady Mabel? She's as good a wife as any man could hope for," he replied. "She asks just enough questions but not too many, she handles all our affairs as a woman should, she has given me four wonderful children with more to come, she knows her place, she follows God, and she has brought me most of the West for my descendants."

"I am glad to hear it," I said. "It is a rare marriage that brings such contentment."

"Stephen here made out even better than I did, didn't you, lad?" brother Robert teased. Dropping his voice a bit lower, he added, "That woman is so desperate for children, she never leaves his bed. I'm amazed she let you come here."

"It would not be proper to speak of my private affairs in public," my cousin whispered just loud enough for us to hear, "but since you have already done so, yes, the woman is insatiable."

I did not enjoy them talking like that about a lady, even if I was not entirely convinced that she deserved the title. However, if there was one thing I had learned about men in my twenty-three years, it was that they could always be relied upon to make coarse jests.

"Well, I hope I can meet Mabel some day and see the rest of my nephews and nieces," I said, attempting to divert the conversation. "I have been without family for so long that I truly crave it. That is, I had my husband the late emperor, but no one else. Even the pleasure of letters from my mother was taken from me. So yes, I do hope to enjoy the blessings of family now."

"Then you must meet our brother Reginald," said Robert, stealing some bread off of Stephen's plate and earning an evil look in the process. "He is almost a full man. He has excellent aim."

I laughed. "Thank the Lord, for that is the one thing I desire in a brother: good aim!"

"Do not dismiss it so easily." Here he consented to place half the bread back in Stephen's waiting hand. "You never know when you might need such a man on your side."

"Oh, that is too true!" I said. "The emperor was always having to defend his rightful place. If I take any comfort in his passing, it is that he finally has some peace from all of this."

Suddenly, one of the minstrels hired by the king stood up and declared, "Good lords and ladies—their Highnesses King Henry, Queen Adeliza, and Empress Mathilda—if you wish to dance, we will now favor you with some music!"

The four men began to play a jolly tune, and several people started dancing in a circle around the fire. They looked so merry that, had I any confidence in my ability, I should have joined them at once. But alas, while my time in the empire had taught me many things, it had done nothing to improve my lightness of foot. Thus, I was afraid to test myself before the royal court when my reputation was yet to be established.

"Dance with me, sister!" Robert said, and I was faced with a choice: agree and face humiliation, or remain seated and possibly offend him.

"All right," I answered, taking his hand and walking out among the others.

I suppose I am an empress, so no one can laugh at me aloud, I thought.

We joined the other dancers and stepped in a circle this way and that. I struggled to remember everything I had learned in my youth. My only comfort was that some of the others appeared as confounded as I was. As the pattern continued, Robert moved further and further away from me, and I was passed from one stranger to another in quick succession.

"Robert!" I called out, but he could not hear me over the sound of music and cheering.

I continued to perform the steps as best I could, whirling around the room from here to there, my degree of stress ever increasing. It was already warm near the fire, and with so much exercise I was growing positively hot and hoping that no one would see me sweat, for such a thing is hardly fit for a royal lady. I became stuck with one man who clearly had no idea what he was doing and seemed to push me toward a rather large woman. I moved to avoid her, but began whirling out of control. It was at that moment that someone caught me from behind and before I knew it, I was face to face with Brian fitz Count.

"Shame on Robert for abandoning you," he said, pulling me aside.

"Thank you. I'm afraid I almost crashed," I told him, feeling rather ashamed.

"It wasn't your fault. I saw what happened. You can dance with me if you wish."

"Thank God! I have no idea what I'm doing." I hated to admit this, but thought it best to be honest.

"You seem to be doing fine. When you get to the end of the line, you just turn like this," he said, demonstrating. "See, it's simple."

I laughed. "Not so simple for me. This is nothing like the dances we had in Germany."

"Well, it looks like Lady Fortuna is on your side, because the music is changing."

The minstrels began playing a lovely tune that was more in line with what I knew, though I could not understand the words. It was intended for each pair to dance on their own, so we took our place in the circle and began moving through the steps, weaving back and forth and occasionally joining hands.

"You seem to like this one better," Brian said, as he stepped around me.

"Thank you for helping me. I'm afraid this is not my greatest talent."

"Oh? What is your greatest talent?"

I laughed. "I'm not sure I have any—at least not any that are particularly helpful for a woman in my position."

We both clapped in time with the music, turned our backs to one another, stepped forward then back, turned around again, and joined hands.

"I don't know about that. You were able to bring a smile to the queen's face. Even the king struggles to do that."

"I know something of what she is going through," I said, changing hands. "It is no small thing to be sent away to marry a king. Everyone is looking for her to be England's salvation."

He looked into my eyes earnestly. "Maybe you could be England's salvation."

I laughed at the audacity of his words. Of course, a part of me certainly hoped that I could save England from an uncertain future, but I had no idea if I could do so. It was such a heavy burden to bear! I therefore thought it best to laugh off the matter.

"Well, if the queen goes much longer without providing an heir, you can bet the king will marry me off to the highest bidder, and then may God and the angels help me!" I said, smiling at him.

We clapped and repeated the process of turning and stepping until we joined hands again.

"You should not doubt yourself, not after everything you have already accomplished," he told me. "I heard the Germans were loath to part with you. That shows what you meant to them."

I continued to hold his hand as I spun around.

"Yes, but I don't have a child, do I?"

Just as I finished speaking those words, I turned to face him again and saw the look on his face. He seemed quite surprised by my comment, and for the second time that day I worried that I had said too much. Speaking with him seemed so natural that I had forgotten to check myself: I had said what I really thought. I dropped my hand and stopped moving for a moment. When he did the same, I spoke again.

"Forgive me, I should not say such things, at least not to you."

He looked as if he was about to reply, but I decided to ask about something else.

"What is this song? I cannot understand it."

He smiled, taking my hand once again. "It is the language of Aquitaine: a poem of Duke William."

"I did not know that the duke was a poet."

"Oh yes, and a great one at that! This is one of his famous ones, I think."

"Do you speak their tongue?" I asked.

"Not very well, but I can give you the words in our own language, if you wish."

"Really?" I said, somewhat surprised. "All right, then. Impress me."

He smiled broadly. "From such a lady, I will always accept the chance to prove myself."

As we joined hands again, he looked at me with a very firm gaze and recited the words of the poem.

"I'll make a little song that's new,
Before wind, frost, and rain come too;
My lady tests me, and would prove
How, and in just what way, I am
In love, yet despite all she may do
I'd rather be stuck here in this jam.
I'd rather deliver myself and render
Whatever will write me in her charter,
No, don't think I'm under the weather,
If in love with my fine lady I am,
Since it seems I can't live without her,
So great the hunger of sire for dam.
For she is whiter than ivory,
So there can be no other for me.

The Forsaken Monarch

If there's no help for this, and swiftly,
And my fine lady love me, goddamn,
I'll die, by the head of Saint Gregory,
If she'll not kiss me, wherever I am!
What good will it be to you, sweet lady,
If your love keeps you distant from me?
Are you hankering after a nunnery?
Know this then: so in love I am,
I'm fearful lest pure sadness claim me,
If you don't right my wrongs, madam."[10]

I quite enjoyed his recitation and was even a bit in awe. "I have never heard men speak of love thus."

"Have you not?" he said. "It is quite common now. All the minstrels write songs like that."

"But such love is hardly common. I have never witnessed it."

He smiled. "Perhaps you have not lived long enough."

The song finally ended and we ceased our dance. I returned to the dais, where a large pie awaited me.

---

10 Guillaume of Poitiers. "Farai chansoneta nueva," *From Dawn to Dawn: Troubadour Poetry*, trans. A.S. Kline (Poetry in Translation, 2009), 31–2.

CHAPTER SEVEN

It is often said of the Normans that they eat their own young, a reputation no doubt built upon the legacy of those early pagans who wreaked havoc among the Christian peoples. So wild and strange they must have seemed! The duchy they built upon the coast was to become a testament to the workings of their minds as well as their arms, but it was that same warlike spirit that often set them against one another. Into this world my grandfather was born, an heir to discord and child of conflict. History was to know him as *Le Conquérant*, "The Conqueror"; but before he became lord of England, he was known by another name: William the Bastard.

My grandfather was the child of Duke Robert of Normandy and a woman of no consequence. He might have been forgotten had his father produced any legitimate sons, but it was the will of God that William should sit upon the throne. Duke Robert departed this life when his son was still a youth, and owing to the circumstances of his birth, the new Duke William was forced to defend his seat from the very beginning. He had not a moment to spend on pleasant affairs, but devoted his entire being to the study of warfare. In so doing, he became one of the greatest commanders the world has ever seen, but at some cost to himself. And ever did that scorn ring in his ears: "William the Bastard! Descendant of a tanner! Child of iniquity! Bastard! Bastard!"

Therefore, my grandfather had no choice but to find some other means of defining himself that was an honor rather than a source of shame. When it came time to choose a bride, he aimed for the heavens and sought the daughter of the count of Flanders, descendant of the French kings. For any other duke of Normandy, such a conquest might have been swift, but it was not at all certain that Mathilda of Flanders would accept one born outside the bonds of wedlock. By the strength of his person, William gained her father's blessing, but he still had to face the obstacle of consanguinity.

Despite William's pleas, the Holy Father refused to grant the dispensation that would have allowed them to wed. Here it is necessary to remember that old saying of Bruno of Trier: "At times, you must simply wait for someone to die." Such was the case with Duke William, for once Pope Nicholas II was installed, the duke received his dispensation straight away. As the price of his consent, the new pope bid William build an abbey for the furtherance of God's work in the city of Caen.

Although he himself was not taught after the manner of scholars, Duke William embraced his new role as patron of learning. He built not one but two houses—the *Abbaye aux Hommes* and the *Abbaye aux Dames*—endowing them with all the wealth of his duchy. It is sad to think that for all the texts they produced, my grandfather could read none of them, but he knew his role was at the head of an army rather than behind a lectern. Nevertheless, as his earthly life drew to a close, Duke William chose to be laid to rest not in Falaise, the town of his birth, nor in Rouen, the capital of his duchy. He sought to be buried in the abbey he had founded: the church of Saint Étienne.

All this history weighed upon my mind as I arose the next morning and made ready to depart for that very abbey to stand before the grave of my forefather. A new crop of ladies had been given to me, most of them wives of the men at court. It seemed strange to hear them all buzzing around me, speaking the Norman tongue that had been absent from my life for so long. Had I not kept up my conversation with Drogo, I might have forgotten most of it.

"Do you want anything to eat before setting out, madam?" one of them asked.

"Just some sop in wine, please."

"Right away."

She ran off and returned within moments with the remnants of the last day's bread and a glass of wine. I had a few bites, then left to join the others already gathered outside.

My lodging was in one of the timber dwellings on the southern end of the courtyard, near the chapel of Saint George. These were set aside for the greatest nobles who were in the king's party. The king himself and his queen were housed in a stone building next to the hall. The space in between included some tents set up near one wall and the stables and other animals' stalls on the far opposite side. In the middle was a vast stretch of bare earth, and it was here that the men engaged in sport, the bottoms of their boots making a scratching noise on the ground with every step.

As I walked out into the yard, the sun was shining wonderfully, and it was so warm that I barely needed the cloak I was wearing. Alas, I could already feel my feet growing moist in my shoes! I saw that the king and queen had not yet arrived, but the king's lads were already hard at work hurling a ball back and forth. I continued toward them until I was close enough to hear them talk.

"Throw it nice and hard, William!" Robert yelled to his son.

The boy sent the ball into the air with as much force as he could muster. It bounced once in the dirt, causing a bit more dust to fly into the air, then landed in the arms of cousin Stephen.

"Good, but this time turn your shoulders as you throw. You'll put more force behind it," Stephen said, giving the ball back.

Young William went to throw again, but this time shouted, "Brian!" He aimed it toward the other man and let it fly, this time reaching his target.

"Excellent, William! Excellent!" Robert said. The pride of fatherhood was evident in his eyes. "What do you think, cousin? Can he join our team for Allhallows?"

"Not if we are playing *La Soule* again. His mother won't thank you if he comes home without half his teeth," Stephen replied.

"Rubbish! That only happened once! Herbert doesn't even need those teeth. He just chews his meat on the other side."

"Gentlemen!" I said, choosing to make my presence known.

"Good morrow, empress!" William called. "Do you want to play with us?"

I would have liked to join them, but I suddenly remembered the last time I had attempted to share in such a game. It was when my brother William and I were just children, and he was kicking a ball around with Robert, Stephen, and Brian. My efforts to take part had ended in ruin when I sent the ball flying into the chicken coop. Ever since that day, I had been too ashamed to play such games. I therefore demurred.

"I wish I could, but I think it would be rather unseemly," I told the boy. "Have you ever seen a woman throw?"

He shrugged. "My sister throws things all the time."

"Yes, but she doesn't know any better, does she?" Robert said, tousling the boy's hair until he broke into a fit of laughter and started punching his father's belly.

Seeing the two of them together, I found myself suddenly struck with sadness. As a young woman, I had not thought myself particularly fond of children—that is, I would not have gone out of my way to seek their company. I accepted that all men and women must begin as children, but I could not imagine that any sane person would want them to stay that way. Perhaps this was because I myself had been denied a proper childhood. I had been forced to play the adult from the time I could speak. Therefore, childhood was something I could hardly comprehend. But seeing my brother together with his son, the two of them made so happy by one another, I suddenly recognized that at some point along the line, I had begun liking children for their own value and not just for the security they provided. Too late I had developed this feeling, when I might never have any children of my own.

"How did you sleep on your first night back, sister?" Robert asked, pulling me out of my thoughts.

"It's not exactly 'back,'" I replied. "I never came to Normandy in my youth."

"Ah, right. I forgot."

"But I slept well, thank you for asking. Have you heard naught from the king this morning?"

"He's waiting for the queen," Stephen said, "so he will probably be waiting a while." The look on his face betokened his disdain.

I took a few steps in his direction to relay a message of some import. "Count Stephen, you men might be able to pick yourselves up off the floor and head out at a moment's notice, but if you want us to look a certain way, it takes time," I assured him. "You have a wife now. You will find out."

Stephen simply laughed, and the men continued to throw the ball for several minutes until we heard the trumpets signaling the king and queen's arrival. They walked toward the gate hand in hand under a special canopy made of red silk with gold tassels, surrounded by four servants carrying the poles. The rest of us moved to join them near the gate, until at last the entire party was ready for departure.

"Let's be off then!" the king said, and we started the short walk to the abbey of Saint Étienne.

As we departed through the north gate and made our way down the gravel path, I walked ahead of the pack, leaving them all to their conversations. Instead, I delighted in the morning calls of the birds and the feel of the wind upon my face. It was only about a mile to the abbey by the path north of the town, and I intended to put it to good use. We were far enough inland that I could no longer smell the sea—pity that! I closed my eyes for just a moment and began to silently recite the Lord's Prayer. Even as I enjoyed this brief moment of serenity, I suddenly heard the sound of quickened footsteps on the gravel behind me. I turned around and saw that it was Lord Brian fitz Count.

"Empress Mathilda! You're a hard woman to catch up with," he called, a bit out of breath. "You need not walk alone."

"Perhaps I wished to walk alone, and you have now spoiled my pleasure." I had intended this to be clever, but it came out sounding rude.

"If that is the case, then I will happily go back," he replied, beginning to turn around.

"No, stay! Tell me how you are these days."

As I said this, I made sure to smile so that he would know I really did not mind his company, and we began walking side by side.

"I've been busy," he answered. "Too busy, really, for the king charges me with more duties all the time. I don't mind though. I live for it."

"From what I hear, you live to read as well."

"Yes, I do as much of it as I can. Were I not a knight in the king's service, I should have been happy to spend all my days writing charters."

"Better you than me. I would much rather spend my day reflecting upon the law of God than the common law, not that I am such a saint, but I find legal texts to be very—"

"Tedious?" he asked, a smile on his face.

"And overly wordy, yes."

"Well, I can hardly fault you there, but were you to study the writings of the ancients—Cicero, for example—you would see the passion with which they worked their craft."

"Perhaps, but I would rather have Ovid any day."

"Fair enough. There are few as great as Ovid."

"I do love his work! I think I must have read the *Metamorphoses* at least once a year while in the empire. It helped get me through some particularly trying moments."

"I can imagine you must have had a lot of those. We heard how you traveled with the emperor to Rome and faced down all the cardinals—how you were at times driven away by those who sought your life. We all feared for you."

"I'm just amazed that anyone remembered me after I was gone so long."

Just as I said this, he held his hand in front of me, not actually touching me but causing me to cease my progress. He looked me in the eye.

"You sell yourself at too low a price, empress," he spoke softly.

"Yes, I tend to do that on occasion," I replied with a laugh. "But perhaps that is because so many others have sold me at an even lower price."

He began walking again, and I followed him, both of us looking ahead.

"Anyone who would sell an empress at a low price is a great fool, and no mistake," he said. "I do not know what they told you in the empire, but here we see you as you truly are: a great royal lady. You are the king's daughter, for God's sake!"

"You are kind," I concluded. While I was thankful for his words, I feared that he did not understand: it was not the Germans so much as my own father whom I feared would sell me at a low price.

As we continued along, he kicked a stone out of the path, then looked behind us.

"Is it true that you are to marry the lady of Wallingford, Mathilda D'Oyly?" I asked.

He looked back at me, then down at his feet. "I have heard that rumor, yes."

"Such an honor the king bestows upon you! Wallingford is a great estate."

He smiled, but in a way that signaled he was not entirely happy.

"What's wrong?" I asked. "She's not hideous, is she?"

"I wouldn't know. She's never been at court."

"Then what is it? Too old? Too young?" I dropped my voice a bit further and asked, "Too mad?"

He laughed. "None of that. It's just—I prefer not to be taken away from the king. The closer I am, the better."

"And to Robert: the two of you are close. And to cousin Stephen, of course."

"Stephen I am not sure about. He's changed since he was younger. Things are not as easy between us all as they once were."

"Why should that be?" I asked, surprised.

He looked behind us again, and when he had ensured that no one was able to hear us, he spoke rather quietly. "I cannot be sure, but if you want my opinion, he sees a need to confirm himself in the position of greatest favor. For all that your father has given us, Robert and I can never be equal in birth to Stephen. If the legitimate and illegitimate are allowed an equal share, then the very foundations of our kingdom would be shaken."

"But are we not on the way to King William's abbey, he who was always known as William the Bastard? It is the king's choice which men he raises up and which he puts down! Let each man be measured by the measure of his character—by the nature of his deeds."

As if to make my point further, I too kicked a stone into the grass.

"Well, I hardly think you need to worry, you who are first among us by every measure," he replied.

"Yes, all except one. Tell me, is Stephen really so vile to you?"

"Oh no! He is perfectly noble. He would never say anything. I just sense it."

We walked a few paces in silence, drawing ever nearer to the abbey. I finally worked up the courage to ask the question that had been on my mind.

"Lord Brian," I asked, "do you really not remember giving me that piece of amber?"

"The moth? Yes, I remember. It was a most strange object."

"Then why did you deny it yesterday?" I inquired, annoyed that he had lied to me.

"I don't know. I suppose I thought it would be impertinent."

"Impertinent, how?"

"Maud and Brian, hold there!" the king bellowed at us. "You ought not go ahead of us, unless you have secret confidences, in which case I shall have you hung up as traitors!"

While I knew him to be jesting, my father's reputation was such that one could never be too careful, so we fell back with the rest of the party. Soon, we arrived at the abbey and entered in line behind my father and Queen Adeliza.

It was a magnificent church, built entirely out of stone from the town's own quarries. I had seen many lovely churches in my life, but it brought me a special joy to see such a work of art produced by my own countrymen. The ceiling was unlike any I had seen in my youth: a vault made up of ribs, or so they called them. It was a superior design. The abbot led us all forward to the grave itself, which was before the high altar. An *effigia* had been placed over the black marble slab, a later addition from what I was told.

The king was first to kneel before the altar and pay his respects at the tomb of his father. He then beckoned for me to come and join him while the others looked on. I stood beside him and marveled at the stone face before me, wondering if it bore any resemblance to the real King William. If the likeness was correct, then he must have been very tall. No wonder men fell in line behind him!

In that moment, I longed to speak with him and discover the secret of his greatness. Surely I who might be called upon to uphold the kingdom he built was worthy of one moment's quarter with this giant among men! Was there some part of him that resided within myself, even as the spirit of the Northmen had guided him?

"What was he like?" I whispered to my father.

"The Conqueror? He was a lion, the greatest of the great. He gave me all I have and bid me defend it."

"Did he ever doubt?" I asked, still staring down at the stone figure.

"A king has no room for doubt. Where is the doubter on the field of battle? Lying dead in a pool of blood. My father was a mighty warrior because he did not waver. That is why men will always remember him."

And yet, he delayed in crossing the Channel, and because he did so, Harald Hardrada invaded first and diminished King Harold's forces, leaving the Normans an easier task. I only thought these words, for it did not seem the proper time to speak them.

"Father, should we not call over the Conqueror's other descendants?" I asked. "Stephen and Robert and young William?"

"If you wish."

He signaled to the other three to come join us, and we formed a circle around the tomb, linking our hands together.

"Father William, help us remember you," the king said. "Here we stand, we five of your children. Let us carry on your legacy."

"Wisely spoken," said Robert. "William, have you anything to say?"

"Rest in peace, Grandfather," the boy whispered. "Your turn, cousin Stephen."

"Very well. I speak for all my kin when I say we will defend this kingdom you built. We will never give in. It shall last for a thousand years and more!" Stephen declared.

It was my turn to speak. I wanted to say something of great import: something that would leave an impression on the living more than the dead.

"And I speak for William Ætheling," I added, looking at each of the men in turn. "As we are one in blood, let us be one in spirit. Let us stand together."

"Amen," we all concluded.

"Left, left, right! Left, left, right! Good! Left, left, right!" Drogo bellowed.

We were back in my private chamber in the castle—that is to say, not my bed chamber, but the small reception space next to it. Most of the furnishings had been removed from the room so that Drogo could teach me how to hand fight. He might as well have been teaching a pigeon, as I was a rather poor student.

"Honestly, how long must I keep this up?" I asked, rather out of breath.

"Until it becomes natural," he said, still holding up the pillow for me to hit. "Block once, block twice, then punch."

Suddenly, I had a thought that might allow me to have another rest. "What if my enemy is left-handed?"

Sadly for me, he dismissed the question easily. "No man of good sense is left-handed. Come now—keep it up. Left, left, right! Left, left, right! Now each time you hit, I want you to yell out, 'No!' as if your life depended on it."

"I doubt that will scare anyone," I muttered, but took my stand once again.

"Now yell it out," he repeated. "No!"

"No!"

"Louder!"

"No!"

"Still louder!"

"No, no, no!"

"That's right. Keep saying it."

"No, no, no! No, no, no! No, no, no!" I said, hitting the target again and again with my fists.

"What is this?" a voice asked.

We both turned and saw that brother Robert had entered the room. He was leaning on the door frame, arms crossed, a partially eaten apple in his hand.

"I am just training the empress to fight," Drogo explained.

"I gathered that, but do we imagine that she will need to fight?" he scoffed more than asked, taking another bite of the apple.

Drogo looked at me and I gave him a very stern look in return, as if to say, *Don't you dare tell him what happened!* Alas, this glare did not accomplish its task.

"There was an incident when we were in Germany," he told Robert.

"Drogo!" I cried. "You promised never to speak of it!"

"Speak of what?" Robert asked, his eyes growing wider.

The knight had been chastised far too much to speak again, so it was left to me to provide an explanation. I walked a bit closer to where my brother was standing, wiping a trace of sweat from my brow.

"A few years ago, there was an evil man who tried to steal my virtue."

"What?!"

"It's true! I was saved by a priest with a *krug*."

"What is a *krug*?" Robert asked, though I hardly thought that was the most pressing question.

"It's for beer. The Germans like a lot of it," Drogo answered, setting down the pillow and coming over to join us.

"Thank you once again, Drogo," I said. "My knight demands that now that I no longer have the duties of an empress to concern me, I practice these simple methods of defending myself. You're not going to tell the king, are you?"

"No, I think it wise," Robert admitted, throwing the apple core behind him into the courtyard and wiping his hands on his tunic. He then stepped fully inside the room and closed the door behind him. "Out of curiosity, do you fear the king would be offended that you are taking up a manly pursuit, that you are dressed in simple clothes, or that you are alone with a man?" he asked, a twinkle in his eye.

I could see that my brother was just as eager to cause trouble as ever, and I was unwilling to indulge him. "What did you come here to tell me?" I asked, changing the subject.

"Nothing of great importance. Merely to share the latest rumor spreading abroad."

"Oh? Well then, by all means, sit down and tell us everything!" I declared, suddenly eager to hear who was stealing from whom or sleeping with whom.

The only furniture remaining in the room was a table and four chairs that sat in the far corner. A pitcher of wine had been left there for us. Robert walked over and poured us each a glass, then we all took a seat, Drogo and I being still quite hot from our exercise. While their attention was diverted, I patted my forehead with a cloth from my pocket, ashamed at my appearance. I ceased this just in time for the conversation to resume.

"I just received word from England: as you know, the papal legate, Bishop John of Crema, concluded his great spiritual tour and held his synod in London," Robert began. "He stopped in Rouen just before we came down to meet you."

"John of Crema? I remember him. He often spoke against the emperor," I said.

"Well, he has been quite helpful to King Henry with regard to that rascal who is always trying to steal the throne, William Clito. It was he who pushed for Clito's marriage with Sibylla of Anjou to be annulled on the ground of consanguinity. This came none too soon, for their alliance would have threatened Normandy for sure. As payment, the king allowed the bishop to travel to England and collect the Peter's Pence tax from every lord and monastery, as far north as Scotland. Then he returned to London and held a council in which they passed no less than seventeen acts of canon law, prohibiting simony and the like. Now Bishop John is off to Rome with the archbishop of York."

"Oh, the archbishop of Canterbury will not like that!" I said. "He considers his seat to be superior to that of York."

"Yes, but that is not the best part," Robert continued, setting down his glass and leaning forward. "You see, on the final day of the council, Bishop John rose before the assembly and commanded them all, as he had in his journeys throughout England, to 'put aside their wives and concubines and embrace the divine call to chastity, which is most proper in the eyes of the Lord, being a higher form of righteousness,' or something of that sort. Well, the bishops of England found it rather presumptuous for this man, who is truly no more than a mere priest raised up by the current pope, to be tramping around to every abbey and parish church, telling them how to conduct their business. Therefore, they must have all been quite pleased when the papal legate was discovered that very night in the arms of a whore."

"What?! You are making that up!" I cried, pounding my glass down on the table with such force that some of the wine spilled out.

Robert threw up his hands. "I swear by the Virgin Mary, this is what I heard from my man who was at the synod, and he should know."

"Might his enemies have crafted this tale to suit their own ends?" Drogo asked.

Here Robert laughed knowingly. "Yes, in truth, I think that is likely, but it still makes for a good story."

"So you do not think he is guilty?" I said.

"I think he is guilty of nothing more than shearing the flock of England to the point of bleeding, for his pockets were so full upon leaving, it's a wonder the ship didn't sink," he jested.

"So which is worse then: fornication or avarice?" Drogo asked.

I considered the question for a moment and arrived at what I thought was a good answer. "The real crime in both is hypocrisy. He is no friend of Christ who disobeys his commands."

"Well, that was all I came to say. I thought you might enjoy it," Robert said, standing and making for the door.

"Wait, Robert!" I called, standing as well. "Let me speak with you in private."

We stepped into a small passage on the opposite side of the chamber that connected to the rooms of my attendants, then closed the door. I had looked both ways to make sure no one was listening, then spoke softly.

"Tell me, brother, does the king intend to offer me up in marriage, and if so, who does he have in mind?"

"You're worried about that already? Good God, your husband's only been in the ground a few months!"

"Indeed, I've only just finished the weeks of mourning, but unless Queen Adeliza is hiding something from us all, there is no male coming forth from the royal line. If the king is to ensure the succession, he must marry me off soon. Even so, I fear his choice."

"He chose well for you the first time, did he not?"

"If you mean that he chose the man who would best suit his own ends, then yes, he chose very well. I suspect he will do so again. It is true that I did end up enjoying my time there, but he had no way of knowing that: he acted only for his own advantage. So tell me, which way does the wind blow? France? Or to the empire again? I know he would never marry me to one of my own countrymen. That gains him nothing."

Robert patted me on the shoulder. "Calm yourself, sister. All shall be revealed in time."

"I am calm!" I said a bit too loudly, drawing a laugh from my brother. I then lowered my voice and continued. "It is easy enough for you to tell me to be calm. It's not your future we're talking about."

"No, it is the future of us all—the future of England and Normandy. We are just one generation away from the Conquest, and the wounds of those battles are still fresh. Each of us must do our part to ensure peace and stability." Here he touched my shoulder once again as if to stress our common blood.

"So I have been told since my youth, but it is much easier to say than do. I often feel torn between the duty I owe to the world and the duty I owe to myself. If only I already had ten sons! Then I might be allowed some choice as to whom I marry. But as it is, I still feel like a pawn in the king's game. You men live in a perfect world: you can marry one woman and carry on with as many others as you like. A lady could never do that without attracting public scorn and the wrath of God. Yes, that's right, I said it! You men are hypocrites."

"Who do you want to marry then?" he asked, overlooking my accusation.

In truth, I was still so caught up in adjusting to my new situation, and indeed still so raw from the long suffering and death of my first husband, that I had no wish to enter another marriage immediately. Nevertheless, I knew it must happen sooner or later in order for the royal line to continue. As for whom I hoped to marry, I had no idea.

"Well, there's no point discussing it, as I shall have no choice in the matter, but should the king ask your opinion, beg him stay away from men of foul morals and fouler odors," I concluded.

"Your wish is my command," he said with a smile, and we took our leave of one another.

Just one day's march south of Caen—or two, if you travel with the king—is the city of Falaise, birth place of William the Conqueror. It was there that King Henry chose to spend his Christmas feast in the year of our Lord 1125, in the new keep he had built. By that time, I had spent several weeks in Normandy and come to know the members of the royal court quite well. The sense of grief I felt over my final years in the empire had faded, and I was able to think of the future with hope. I was very much looking forward to celebrating the Lord's birth with them all in Falaise, most especially my brother and Lord Brian, who had become dear friends.

Sadly, the fortress had but one private quarter within the keep, and that was reserved for the king, so I found myself caught between Scylla and Charybdis: I could either sleep with the men in the hall or stay in one of the outer buildings. Needless to say, I chose the latter. When I arrived at the castle, I was led to my new chamber, which was little more than a hovel. Instead of a true bed, there was only a pallet to sleep on and a pit instead of a hearth. A stack of rather sad little logs sat in a corner.

"Will this do?" the servant asked me.

"I suppose it will have to," I replied.

He left me alone in the small room. The wind whistled and the boards creaked. The cold air slipped in through every crack. It was fortunate that I had brought several furs with me from Caen. Suddenly, I felt something rush past my feet. I let out a scream, only to see that it was a poor mouse hoping to escape the cold.

"I do not mind you seeking warmth, but I have no desire to share my bed with you," I said, shooing it away.

I set my things down and squinted through one of the larger cracks in the wall. The yard was packed with hundreds of men gathered around fires, some knights and others humble servants. They rubbed their hands together and blew on them, no doubt imagining the heat of summer.

"What a sorry sight," I murmured.

It was Christmas Eve, so I had no time to dally. I called in the ladies and made ready for supper. As fate would have it, snow began to fall, and ere I departed, the hardened mud had been covered by an inch or two of frozen slop.

"Should we try to clear a path, madam?" one of them asked.

"It's no use," I moaned.

We made the best of it, but by the time I reached the keep, I was soaked through from toes to knees, having been splashed with every step.

The hall lay within the great stone keep. In order to enter, one first had to pass through the entry building, which contained nothing more than a set of stairs. This led directly to the doors of the great hall. I stomped my feet on each of the stone steps in an effort to dry them. The doors then opened before me, and I looked into an entirely different land of light and color.

To the left was a row of brightly painted columns backed by bright red curtains. Each column had been wrapped in boughs of green, with dried flowers and bits of cloth of gold placed in them just so. On the far end of the hall was the king's table, upon which sat every manner of food. The great crest of the royal House of Normandy was hung behind it. To the right were windows to the outside, in which sat rows of candles. From the ceiling beams were hung shining stars, lit from below by the two small cauldrons of fire that provided warmth for the gathering.

"The Lord Himself could not have wished for a better reception upon the day of his birth," I said to myself.

There were two long tables on either end of the room with room for dancing in between. I walked in the space just beyond the columns to avoid all the merry makers. Very soon I reached the high table. As I lifted my skirt and climbed the two steps up to the dais, I saw that the queen was not in her usual seat next to the king. I left her chair open and sat two down from the king's chair. Once he was also seated, I turned and asked him, "Where is Queen Adeliza?"

"She claims to have some malady, though I cannot think how she got it," the king replied, not meeting my eyes.

If her lodgings are anything like mine, it's a wonder she's not dead already, I thought.

"Stephen!" the king cried, for my cousin had just entered. "Come sit beside me!"

Count Stephen then took the place between myself and my father, and the king patted him on the back. I wondered that my father had not asked Robert to sit there, being the king's son, but my brother sat just across the table, along with my nephew. Since my return, I had noticed that King Henry had a special affection for my cousin. Perhaps it was because Stephen received every word the king gave him as if it were a drop of gold from the sun.

"Robert, William, Maud, Stephen, Beaumont... all are here except Brian. Where is he?" the king asked.

"He went to bid the servants get more wood for the fire," Stephen said.

As there was no one seated to my right, I offered, "Lord Brian can sit here when he returns."

"Very well. Let's eat!" my father said.

This was fortunate, for I knew that I would have the best conversation of all with Lord Brian. Ever since my return, we had enjoyed many pleasant discussions on an array of subjects, and it seemed that we were very much of the same mind in regard to many of the pressing issues of the day. What was even better, while most men either knew less than me about the world or knew more and held themselves superior, Brian was gracious in the way he explained things, and he listened intently when I spoke of my experiences in the empire. Actually, that was his greatest strength: he was an excellent listener.

After the food had been placed on our table and everyone had a chance to devour a few bites, the king spoke again. "Now, just so you all know, I've sent word to Bishop Roger of Salisbury, and he is taking all the false moneyers into custody and dealing with them in a manner that most befits their crimes."

"And what manner would that be?" Stephen asked.

"With their hands, they have struck the coins unjustly, mixing them with lesser metals, and thus defrauding the public. They offend us greatly, and therefore I have chosen to follow the words of Christ himself: 'If thy right hand make thee to offend, cut if off, and cast it from thee.'"

Those of us who had been eating ceased doing so and looked at one another. I believe none of us were certain if he was jesting, and I for one was too afraid to ask. The king gave us no sign and continued to tear the flesh off the goose in front of him.

"Do you mean to say you're having their hands cut off?" Robert Beaumont finally asked.

"Ha! That is not the half of it," the king said. "I'm also having their privy parts removed."

"Really?!" young William asked, rising a bit out of his seat. He seemed rather more delighted than the situation warranted.

"Please tell me you're not serious," I begged.

"When am I anything but serious?" the king replied, ripping one of the legs off the goose. "If men will not act as they ought, then we shall take their manhood from them. They are not worthy of it," the king concluded, tapping the leg on the table with each of the last few words.

"Well, a Merry Christmas to us all!" Robert said. "Except the moneyers, of course, who are in for a rather nasty surprise."

"What surprise is that?" Brian asked, having just arrived at the table.

We all turned and looked at him in surprise, for we had been so caught up in our conversation that no one saw him approach.

"King Henry is making all the moneyers into eunuchs, just in time for the New Year," I replied. "Tell us, Lord Brian, where is that in the common law?"

"This is no time for a discussion of ethics!" the king said. He leaned across Stephen, perching himself on the table with his arm, and pointing at me with the half eaten goose leg in his right hand. "My daughter, I will place upon you the same burden that the Lord placed upon Abraham. Find me ten men, whether English or Norman, who disapprove of my decision, and I shall revoke it."

"What do you think, Stephen?" I asked, knowing that if my cousin supported me, the king would be forced to listen.

Stephen took one look at me, then another at the king who was mere inches from his face, glaring at him.

"I think this is a matter for King Henry's good judgment," he answered, sinking down a bit in his chair.

I sighed and accepted the cut of partridge that was handed to me, though I had rather lost my appetite after our discussion.

"Have you heard anything from the countess?" the king asked Stephen, returning fully to his own chair.

"My wife is well. She is visiting her father for the holiday. However, my lord, I think I had best return soon and see her. You know how the women get when we are away too long."

"Well, if you must leave me, then you must, but I shall be sorry to see you go," my father declared. "You are the best of us, Stephen. You do us proud. Tell me, how is your younger brother coming along? I know your mother intends him for the Church."

"Only if that is what Your Highness desires."

"I do desire it. The sooner we can get him to England the better. I have a place in mind for him, but I shall not announce it yet. Suffice it to say, I trust both your mother and brother will be pleased."

"Thank you, my lord. I shall inform them of these blessings soon to come from your hand. You are most gracious, as always."

What a sycophanta *you are,* I thought, *and what a glorious language is Latin to call you so!*

"Father, you should see what William can do," brother Robert said, breaking into the conversation. "Show him, William."

The boy took a knife from the table and balanced it upright on the palm of his hand.

"Very good! Here, try it with my dagger," the king replied, pulling the weapon from its sheath.

"I really don't think that's a good idea—" I began to say, but the boy had already taken it in hand and performed the same feat with ease.

"Try my sword!" Robert Beaumont cried, but there even my brother drew a line.

"I think he had better get back to eating," the boy's father said. "Here, have some turnips."

He set a whole plate of them in front of William, who let out a groan, covered his eyes, and sunk down in his chair as if he wanted the floor to devour him.

I finished my meal before the others and had no desire to dance or remain in conversation, so the king permitted me to leave.

"Brian!" he called. "Accompany my daughter back to her room!"

"Certainly, my lord," he replied.

"There is no need," I said. "Where is Drogo? He can accompany me."

I looked around the room quickly, but for all his height, I could not see my knight anywhere.

"He seems to be in the middle of something," Brian told me, pointing over to the one corner I had not yet checked, where Drogo stood hunched over in conversation with a lady whose name I did not know, but who was clearly far too pretty for him to willingly desert any time soon.

"Oh, very well. Let's walk together," I concluded, then muttered, "Go with God, Drogo."

The two of us descended to the main floor and made our way around the tables of feasters, stepping this way and that to avoid those who had imbibed too much.

"You and your knight seem to be rather good friends," Brian said.

"Yes, we have been through it all together," I replied over my shoulder, moving to the left to avoid a man carrying several bowls of mead.

"He is very devoted to you."

I suddenly sensed that the conversation was going in a bad direction. I had made it to the door, and once I was in the quiet of the entry way, I stopped to let him catch up. As soon as he did, I said to him in private, "I wouldn't want you to get the wrong idea."

"What do you mean?" he asked, his look earnest.

"When I was in the empire, I had no real family. Drogo was like an older brother to me: an older brother I could laugh with and even cry with. It is true that we are very familiar in our speech, but I assure you, it is nothing more than friendship."

"You don't need to convince me," he replied, moving toward the door.

I stepped in front of him, for I was intent on removing any shadow of a doubt. "It's just—I would hate for anyone to get the wrong impression, because actually, I do not think of him that way at all. I mean that honestly."

"I believe you, truly," he said with a smile. "Are you ready to brave the cold?"

"I doubt I'll ever be ready, but I suppose we must," I concluded.

He opened the door, and I was instantly hit by the winter cold. The yard of Falaise Castle is rather small, for it is perched on top of a crag and thus limited by the size of the hill. It should have been an easy walk, but alas, while we had been enjoying our feast, the puddles of slop had turned to ice. I was completely ignorant of this, and a few steps into the yard, without warning, I slipped and fell to the ground. I caught myself with both hands, thus saving my head but causing my palms to become bloodied and raw. I wanted to scream, but was able to suppress it. I had no desire to draw even more attention to myself.

"Are you hurt?" Brian asked, reaching down to help me up.

"I think my pride is hurt more than anything."

"Your dress is torn."

"What? Where?" I replied in alarm.

"Just on the arm there," he said, pointing.

Sure enough, the sleeve was torn near the elbow, and the skin beneath was bloody.

"I thought I had just hit it. I didn't know it was bleeding," I said quietly, feeling rather awkward.

"No need to fear. Truly, it was my fault for not helping you properly. Here—let's get you back and tend to your wounds. You can lean on me."

"No, really, I promise I will not fall again," I assured him. I had no desire for him to put himself out on my account.

"Please," he said quietly, looking into my eyes, "I already have a lot to answer for."

I was still a bit uncertain about this idea, but I relented.

"Very well ..."

I placed my arm around him and he did the same to me so that we walked as one. It was a good thing too, because we both slid at one point or another. The walk to my lodging—if indeed you could call it a lodging—was not a long one, but our slow pace made it seem so. We both laughed a bit as we clung together, and I can only imagine what the few guards looking on must have thought.

"Almost there," he said. "We'll get you by the fire and you can warm up."

Was it cold? I had quite forgotten. Something far stranger had come over me, and it seemed to increase with every sound of his voice and touch of his hand. My heart was beating quickly and I felt lit by an inner flame.

We arrived at the door and I walked inside. I then turned to say farewell, but saw that he had come in after me.

"You've naught but embers left. Let me get it started again," he said, grabbing a pair of logs from the stack in the corner and using them to build up the fire. Some sparks leaped and it began to glow more brightly.

"Please, I can call one of the ladies to do that."

"You cannot think that I would let you walk back out there on your own, or do you want me to hang?" he said with a smile.

For one of the few times in my life, I seemed utterly unable to speak. The fire inside me—I felt bold, as if I had never been more alive. I knew exactly what I wanted to say, and yet I was far too afraid to utter the words. I was at war with myself.

"Is something the matter?" he asked, lowering the rod and looking back up at me.

I pulled myself out of my daze and said quickly, "I am tired—that's all."

"Of course. Let me see your hands."

As he grabbed them, I felt my heart leap. He examined each one carefully, turning them over. He then looked up and I recognized that I had been staring at him. I quickly looked away.

"Forgive me, I am making you nervous, the two of us here alone," he said. "I should leave."

Leaving was the opposite of what I wanted him to do. At least, I thought it was. I felt a powerful longing to be with him, and yet this longing filled me with fear. I could hardly speak what I felt, so I simply nodded and gave him some word of thanks.

"I will send the ladies over. They can clean those for you. A merry and blessed Christmas to you!"

He turned and departed out the door quickly so as not to let too much of the cold air in, although given the poor construction of the dwelling, there was not much hope of that. At last, I was left standing there alone, my heart still pounding. I ran over to the wall and looked out the crack to watch him walk away, then caught myself.

"Stop this, Maud! What on earth do you think you're doing?" I chided.

I actually hit myself on the head, but it was no use, for I knew most assuredly what I must have suspected for some time: that I did not desire to be around Brian merely for his good conversation. It seemed I had become quite partial to him.

"No," I whispered. "That is not all. I love him. I must! I want to be with him. Why else do I feel this way?"

Even as I said this, I hit my head again. "Idiot! What are you thinking? All those years, you're married to someone and you never feel like this. Now you're friends with someone for a few weeks and—"

I did not finish speaking but began to cry. I sat down on the pallet and pulled my knees against my body, burying my face. The more I thought about it, the more I wept, for at the very moment I had recognized my love for him, I also sensed that my love would never be fulfilled. If no man had loved me that way before, why should this one be any different? Yet I suddenly felt the need for that kind of love urgently, and not just from anyone, but from him. The more tears I cried, the more I came to see that I had fooled myself for a very long time. There was a part of me that had always longed to be alive, and now that it was, I knew not what to do.

The heat within me had died down. The icy wind was pouring in through the cracks. I continued to wipe the tears from my face.

Well, this can hardly end well, I thought. *It is already a tragedy.*

Through the watches of the night, I lay awake remembering every conversation, every glance, every smile. I turned over in bed, pulling the only fur I had been given against my body, needing sleep and yet unable to gain comfort of mind. I longed for some assurance that I was not alone: that he felt as I did. Yet I was not fool enough to allow myself hope.

"You're a hard woman to catch up with," he had said to me.

What was the meaning of that? Did he truly desire my company? Or did he merely pity me? Or had they drawn lots to see who would speak with me and he came out the loser?

"I thought it would be impertinent," he had told me.

Impertinent because it revealed his love for me? Or impertinent because he was my inferior? Did it warm his heart to know that I treasured his gift? Or did it make no difference? And when he held me, was the ice his true concern, or was it something else? Did he feel what I felt in that moment? No, he couldn't love me. He barely knew me. I was seeing only what I wanted to see. And what did it matter anyway? He could not love me and I could not love him, for I was the king's daughter, and he was a simple noble man. But oh, if he did love me, even to know that—what ecstasy! But surely he did not. No, that was a foolish way to think.

Before I knew it, Christmas morn had arrived. The interrogation had carried me through to the sun's rise with naught but a wink of sleep. This weariness did nothing to lessen my mental distress. I did not understand how I could have passed through years of marriage without this feeling, or why it had taken hold of me at such a time. I had enjoyed pleasant conversation with many men over the years, and had even felt strong bonds of friendship. Near the end of my marriage, I had loved my husband as a family member, even as he had me. That is, we respected one another and wished the best for one another, but we did not drip with passionate longing.

This was something different. It overwhelmed my thoughts, and the more I thought about Brian, the more sick I was with desire. Rather than filling me with joy, it scared me. Having long been starved for affection, I had contented myself in the knowledge that it was not all that essential. However, I felt suddenly—indeed, rather urgently—that it was the most essential thing of all. I feared this would ruin me.

I would be married to someone, but it would not be Brian fitz Count. He was not a foreign lord. There was nothing for the king to gain through such an alliance. And even if it was allowed, which I knew most certainly it would not be, it would do me no good if he did not love me as much as I loved him. That's the thing about love: you want the other person to utterly rejoice in you, as if your very bones and marrow were the same and your hearts beat as one.

By the time I formally arose, I had reached the conclusion that I must adopt the most practical course. I could not assume that he was anything but indifferent. Therefore, I needed to make myself equally indifferent, and the surest way I saw to achieve this was to simply avoid him. The trouble, of course, was that the very nearness that had caused such feelings to grow was now my chief enemy. Was it possible to make one's self indifferent after having become devoted? It seemed nigh on impossible. Nevertheless, I intended to try. I did not see that I had any choice.

A storm had come through during the night and left even more snow on top of what was already there. I tried to imagine as I left my room and walked through that cold, my toes half frozen, that I was back at the Doge's Palace in Venice, the summer air coming in from the sea and warming my bones. This did not work as well as I might have hoped, but it at least distracted me from my thoughts about a certain person.

As soon as I entered the hall, my first task was to find the man whom I was seeking to avoid, that I might therefore avoid him. Fortunately, he was at the opposite end of the room in conversation with one of the local barons.

How handsome he looks today! I thought, then chided myself. I was not off to a good start.

"Handsome, isn't it?" someone behind me said.

"Yes. Wait ... what?"

I turned around and saw that my brother Robert had walked up next to me.

"The hall—the way it looks today," he said.

"Oh, yes," I agreed, glad that I had not given myself away.

Indeed, it did look like something out of a dream. The tables had been pulled back, and the king sat upon his throne on the dais, which was draped in all sorts of green boughs and dried flowers. There were candles lit on every wall and in every window. A great gold star had been hung from the ceiling, and it guided us to the celebration, even as the Magi were led to the Christ child.

"You looked a bit lost in thought," Robert said.

"I couldn't sleep last night."

"Oh, I know! I slept in here beside the fire, but it was still too cold. I can only imagine what it must have been like out where you were."

Of course, the cold was not the reason for my lack of sleep, but I saw no need to correct him.

"Where is the queen?" I asked. "Is she feeling any better today?"

"She's over there," he said, pointing. "You can ask her yourself."

Sure enough, Queen Adeliza was standing in the corner—alone.

"Thank you, brother. I think I should go speak with her."

"Good luck with that. I can't get two words out of her."

"Yes, it is truly amazing that anyone would not want to talk with you," I mocked.

"It's Christmas Day! Have some heart!" he protested.

I left him to his murmuring and walked over to grab some spiced apple juice. This had been made as a special treat for the Christmas feast. I dipped one goblet into the large silver bowl, causing the apples floating on top to bob up and down. After I had filled a second goblet, I walked over to where the queen stood.

"Merry Christmas, Queen Adeliza!" I said, extending one of the goblets toward her. "May I stand beside you? I am in need of some good female conversation. These men do wear me out exceedingly."

"Of course," she replied rather quietly, accepting the drink.

After we had both sipped for a moment, I continued, "The king told me you were ill. I hope it is nothing serious."

For a moment, she said nothing, but looked rather uneasy. Although she was already a small woman, she seemed even smaller than usual, as if fear had shrunk her down to nothing. Her pretty face and golden hair were entirely hidden under an overly large head covering. Perhaps her attire was chosen on account of the feast, but it almost seemed as if she was hiding.

"Forgive me. Did I say the wrong thing?" I asked.

"No, no," she assured me. "It's just that I often become nervous at such gatherings."

"You mean, on feast days?"

"At any great occasion of state, when the court is all together. I must admit, I feel a bit lost. Customs here are very different than they were in the empire."

I found it somewhat curious that the queen was willing to admit this to me, and I decided to tread lightly.

"From what I can see, you have been doing just fine. Everyone here likes you."

"Do they?" she asked, with a clear note of doubt. "You have only arrived here of late, so perhaps they have not included you yet, but I am certain that they speak ill of me when I am not around."

This surprised me greatly. I would not have thought Queen Adeliza bold enough to gain anyone's true ire, unlike myself.

"Speak ill of you how?" I asked, leaning in slightly. "Your conduct seems blameless."

Until this point, she had mostly stared ahead, but she looked directly into my eyes, and I saw that there were tears forming in hers.

"Empress Mathilda," she whispered more than spoke, "you and I both know that a queen who cannot produce a child is never blameless."

Here was the root of the matter. I knew too well the pain of which she spoke, for I had felt myself rather useless during my time in the empire when I saw that I could not fulfill my first duty. I had also endured the pain of hearing false rumors about why I did not have children. Every day, I still wondered if I was barren. But what could I possibly say to put her at ease?

"I know what you mean. When I was at the German court, I always feared what people said about me behind my back. They would never denounce me to my face, but we women can sense things," I offered.

"Exactly! And what is more, I am not as natural in these situations as you are. I do not possess the same easy wit as you. When I was with my friends, I could converse without a problem. But this—this is beyond me."

I laughed. "Perhaps you mistake my abilities. I can speak, yes, but as often as not I say the wrong thing. It has gotten me into trouble time and again. But I know what you mean about feeling nervous, for I too have felt that pang even today."

"Yes, but I think you feel it for a different reason," she said, smiling.

"What do you mean?" I asked, suddenly worried.

The queen moved a bit nearer. "When one stands alone, one makes a study of everyone else in the room. I have watched each person who comes through that door. When you entered, you seemed to be looking for someone. Then you found him, and I spied on your face the same thing I have detected there before: you have a special affection for Lord Brian fitz Count, but you are afraid for anyone to know."

The ease with which she had reached this conclusion struck me with fear. Were my feelings really so plain? Were they plain even to Brian himself, or worst of all, to my father? My first instinct was to deny, but I quickly sensed that would be useless.

"How ... how did you do that?" I stammered.

"I told you. I have no skill in speech, but I have a great power of observation. It's how I know that that lady there—the one in the green dress—is with child. And that man there, Robert Beaumont, has been carrying on an affair with one of my ladies."

"Truly, you amaze me," I said, shaking my head in wonder.

Sensing my fear, she stroked my arm. "Do not worry! I have no intention of sharing your secret. It's rather sweet, actually. He is a good man. He always asks after my welfare, and I think he truly seeks to know. Has he spoken of his love for you?"

I let my eyes trail across the room until they found Brian playing dice with my brother while several others looked on. He was smiling broadly, and while I wished very much that smile could be for me, I knew it was not.

"You mistake me, madam," I said, looking down at my goblet as if it was a compelling object of study. "There is nothing between us but friendship. It is true that, of late, I have grown rather fond of him—too fond. I have done myself a great injustice by allowing things to get to this point." Here I looked back up at her and said, "I have no reason to suspect that he has any particular love for myself beyond that which is owed by convention."

"So he does not return your affection then? He is a fool."

"I hardly think that makes him foolish! Even if he did care for me, how would such a thing work? He is to marry the lady of Wallingford, and I am to marry God only knows whom. He is the illegitimate son of the former duke of Brittany, while I am currently the heir to the throne of England. My father would never—no, it is wrong for me to even speak in this way. Whatever silly hopes I entertain must be done away with."

"I suppose that is wise," she agreed. "It would not do for us all to become love lorn, and to what purpose? Even so, you are a passionate person. There is a fire inside you."

"Perhaps, but it may one day destroy me, or else be snuffed out by the will of others."

We continued to stand there together, listening to the tunes of the minstrels and sipping. Before we spoke, I had never considered how alike our situations were.

"Did you ever love anyone?" I asked.

"Once, when I was fifteen," she said with a smile. "He was the son of a local lord. He was all wrong in every way. Perhaps that is why I liked him so much. I suppose it was not love in the mature sense, but it was close enough."

"What happened to him?"

"He died of dysentery. It was awful. I cried for weeks. My poor mother had no idea what was wrong with me. My father was sure I was going mad. Then I got better, and they sent me here to marry the king. Such an honor for our family!"

"Only now you are married to a man you hardly know, who scares you at times, and you cannot have a child."

I thought I saw a tear trail down her cheek and felt guilty for what I had said. I had allowed our common experience to cause me to speak when I ought to have remained silent.

"I beg your pardon, my lady. I should not have said that."

"No, it's true!" she said, then let out a great sigh. "I wish it was not, but it is. I do not know where to turn or whom to talk to."

"Well, for what it's worth, you can always speak with me. My advice may be worth little or nothing, but you'll find I give it quite freely."

This brought a small smile to her face. I placed my hand on her arm and said to her, "Child or no, you are a comfort to my father: I am sure of it. You bring honor to this house, and I am very glad to have you here."

"Oh, thank you, Empress Mathilda! You are a good friend. I only wish I could do better."

"Don't we all," I agreed. "Don't we all."

CHAPTER EIGHT

October 1165
Rouen, Normandy

Forgive me, daughter, for I cannot continue our tale today. My mind is o'er consumed with this controversy of late—that is, the matter of Archbishop Thomas Becket. God knows I am too old for this! Would that he had spared me from such things in my present condition, but the thing must be done with and quickly, or it may threaten all we have achieved.

Perhaps it is wrong of me to speak thus: all is not yet lost. And why should I trouble you—you who are not yet in being and are patient enough to endure all I have written up to the present time? Yet I must trust you with my story, for no one else will listen.

Here, then, is an account of the day's proceedings. I awoke to the sound of rain for the seventh day in a row: weather fit for Noah himself. My bones ached and I turned over in bed, heeding not the song of the monks. I stared up at the wood beams above me. There was no fire in the hearth, so the only light came in through the window to my left, and a rather pitiful light it was, leaving shadows. My eyes moved to the wall opposite, where a spider was attempting to make its way from floor to ceiling. I wanted to crush it, but that would have required the effort of rising from my bed. I sighed and turned over again, watching the water drops pelt the glass panes.

Suddenly, I heard the door swing open and turned back to see Adela standing at the threshold, looking so wet that I might have believed she had swum to the monastery. It is less than a mile from her home—where she resides with her husband and three boys—to the guest house where I am staying, so this is a testament to how hard the rain was falling. In her hands, she held a bundle of some sort wrapped in cloth.

"Good morning my—oh, pardon, are you still asleep?" she asked.

"I might have been but for your presence," I said.

This was a bit uncharitable, I admit, but I was not feeling my best. My arms and legs felt stiff as they so often do at break of day, and my hands ached.

"Are you still feeling ill then? I could fetch the doctor."

"Not ill—just old. I shall be like this until I die, which God knows is likely to be soon."

"Don't say that!" she scolded, concern written on her face. "I am sure you have many years left!"

"What is that you have in your hands?" I asked, finally rising and sitting on the edge of the bed.

"These are your letters. I did not want them to get wet."

She set the bundle down on the small table beside the hearth and unwrapped it with care, as if it were the Holyrood. She then untied the letters and began to sort them. I stood up, grabbed the blanket that lay on my bed, and wrapped it around myself. There was a chill in the air, and I very much wanted Adela to finish sorting my correspondence and light the fire.

"I am sure they are of little value," I said.

"I think you'll find that this one is," she replied, turning toward me and holding it up for me to see. She was smiling and seemed very pleased with herself, much like a cat when it puts a dead mouse on display.

The letter bore a red seal. I had to move closer to read it, for my eyes are not as good as they were in my youth. I squinted and was finally able to make out the letters. The mark was impossible to mistake.

"From Pope Alexander?!" I said, truly surprised.

"Yes, now you get it! But I suppose you have no wish to read it, as it is of little value."

"Very well, I repent. Now let me see it!"

She handed it to me, and allowed me to read its contents.

"So what does His Holiness want?" she asked, when I had finished.

"He wishes me to work a miracle," I replied, still staring at the parchment, hardly able to believe what I was reading.

"Is there a leper needs healing?"

"I wish that was all. No, he asks me to heal a kingdom."

"This one, or another one?"

"This one, of course!" I said, setting the letter back on the table.

"Sorry, I thought I might lighten the mood. This has to do with the archbishop of Canterbury, I presume?"

"Yes, everything has to do with the archbishop these days, but I have no intention of allowing him to steal all the pleasure from my few remaining days on this earth."

I was still staring at the letter on the table as I said all this, but I heard a slight noise behind me and turned to see that Adela was stifling a laugh.

"What? Why are you laughing?" I asked.

"I was only smiling!" she declared, biting her lower lip.

"Neither seems appropriate under the circumstances."

"It's just—you are still you. Still fighting the old battles, never willing to surrender. I do not know why it makes me smile. Perhaps to think of everything you have been through—every time life has tried to take you down. You are still standing. You are still Empress Mathilda through and through."

It was my turn to smile. "Thank you, Adela," I said, embracing her. "Your friendship is so dear to me. Now fetch Lawrence, will you? The Holy Father asks me to reconcile these two of his sheep—King Henry II and the Archbishop Thomas—for the remission of my sins. He actually said that: 'the remission of your sins.' Well, I love the Holy Father, and God knows I am a child of iniquity, but it seems to me in this case the one who needs forgiveness is Thomas Becket and possibly a few others, not myself. Even when there was much I could say and many accusations I could level against him, I kept my mouth shut and submitted to the Lord's will. Now I must bring about peace between two men who do not desire it. Such an evil day!"

"I will let the archdeacon know you have need of him," she said, turning to leave.

"Quickly!" I called behind her. "I'm not getting any younger!"

While I waited for her to return, I looked over the remaining letters and found one from Queen Eleanor's clerk.

Here, perhaps, is some good news, I thought, for I knew the queen was to give birth any day.

My eyes quickly moved over the parchment, searching for the vital words. There they were: "The queen is delivered of a daughter." A daughter? The queen's astrologer had been wrong after all. He had sworn it would be a fourth boy.

"That is why I do not place my trust in soothsayers," I told myself.

So a girl then: not what we had been hoping for, but any hale child is surely not a calamity. With three sons already among us, gracious Eleanor has little to fear. She can afford to give birth to a daughter. Whether the king will see things the same way, I cannot say. I am certain he dreams of having twelve sons, though what lands he should give to them all I hardly know.

Here was a note near the bottom: "The queen hopes to welcome you in Angers that you might see the new princess." Oh, that I could, but my health would not permit such a journey!

I laid the blanket back on the small bed and walked over to the chest that sat in the corner. Inside were the few clothes I keep at the monastery guest house, the rest being back at my own home, which lies to the west, closer to the river bend. I lifted the lid of the chest, causing some dust to fly into the air.

After turning my head aside to sneeze, I reached in and grabbed the ermine coat that lay on top, nicely folded. It is one of the more costly things I still own, being made of the brown summer fur rather than the white of winter. It was a special gift from the king upon his coronation, but on this day it was to be used simply for warmth. I took out the simple white gown with gray trim that lay below it. I put the gown on first, then the coat. I then searched for a pin to keep my braid against my head. Alas, I could not find one anywhere.

"I swear, there were ten of them the other day!" I complained aloud.

Even as I was standing there pitying myself, there was a knock at the door. I took two steps toward it and pulled it open, revealing the figure of Archdeacon Lawrence, my clerk.

"Archdeacon, thank you for coming! I must send a letter to Archbishop Thomas, and my hands are too sore for the task. You know I prefer to write my own correspondence, but—"

"I shall be happy to aid you. I see you have everything here from last time," he said, pointing to the parchment and ink on the table.

"Yes, have a seat." I waited for him to settle in, and for my part I simply sat on the bed. Once he had the quill in his hand, I continued, "Now, how shall we begin? Simple is best, I think. '*To Thomas, archbishop of Canterbury, Empress Mathilda.*' Do you have that?"

"Yes," he said, scribbling on the parchment. "Then what?"

"Well, now we come to the delicate part. I must make it appear as if I have a great deal more respect for him than I truly possess, or else we shall make no progress."

"Perhaps you should begin by stating your reason for writing," he prompted.

"Because the king did not heed my warning, and he put in place a man not fit for the office."

He laughed. "You know what I—"

"Yes, I know what you mean. How about this then: 'The lord pope charged and enjoined me for the remission of my sins'— make sure you include that bit—'to intervene to reestablish peace between the king and you and attempt to reconcile you with him. Then, as you know, you also asked me, as much for the honor of God as for the honor of the Church, I took pains to sort out the matter.'"

I had been looking over at the far wall, but when I heard the scratching stop, I turned and saw that Lawrence had indeed ceased writing.

"What is it?" I asked, standing up and walking toward him.

"Your Highness, might I offer a slight change?"

"My, my! And I'm not even paying you!" I said, placing my hand on the back of his chair.

"'Sort out' sounds as if you took all the action yourself. It could seem overly …"

"Overly what?"

His face looked almost in pain and he cast his eyes down toward the table. "Arrogant, my lady."

"How is that arrogant?!" I cried. "He is the one that begged me to take the matter in hand! Lawrence, look at me when I speak to you."

He looked up toward me slowly, as a young child fearing discipline.

"Forgive me, my lady. I do not think it is arrogant. Notice that I said 'seem.' If we are to win over the archbishop, we must condescend to his point of view," he explained, pushing the air downward with the palms of his hands as if to illustrate his point.

I laughed softly, shaking my head, then replied.

"Oh, Lawrence, you do vex me at times, but I am sure you are right. Very well. What would you have me write instead?" I asked, turning to walk back to the bed.

"'I took pains to begin and manage the matter'?"

"Fine," I replied, sitting down. "Let us continue. 'It seemed very grave to the king and his barons and council, since he asserts that though he loved and honored you and made you lord of his whole kingdom and all his lands, and raised you to greater honor than anyone in his land, so that he should believe more securely in you than in any other ...' Is this sentence too long?"

"No, keep going," he said, dipping his quill in the ink again.

"Where was I? Oh, right. 'You disturbed his whole kingdom against him as much as you could so that little was left for you to do but to disinherit him by force.'"

He ceased his scribbling again and said, "That is rather strong, my lady. What of reconciliation?"

"There can be no reconciliation without truth, Lawrence. He has abused the laws of this kingdom. He must be called to account if we are to achieve anything."

"Very well," he said with a nod. "What next?"

"'Because of that, I send you our faithful retainer archdeacon Lawrence …'"

"You want me to carry this to him in person?" he said, turning his entire body in the chair to face me.

"Of course. Who else?"

"Does it not concern you how that might look?"

Here I laughed again. "Everything concerns me, but it must be done. Now write!" When he had taken up his position, I dictated, "'I send you our faithful retainer archdeacon Lawrence so that I may learn your will about these things and what feelings you have toward the king and how you would wish to act if it happened that he wished to hear fully my petition and prayer about you.' See, that makes it seem as if I am on his side. Now, this is essential, Lawrence: 'One thing more I tell you truly, that you cannot recover the grace of the king except by great humility and most evident moderation. Let me know what you wish to do about this through my messenger and your letters.' As if the man could show humility! I think that's it."

He scribbled a bit longer, then ceased. "That's all?"

"Yes, that ought to do it."

"In that case, I will add a few final touches and set off with this directly."

He laid aside the quill and placed a cover over the ink, rolled up the piece of parchment, and stood to depart.

"I would tell you to give him my love, but then you would be going empty handed," I told him with a sly smile.

"Is there nothing in the archbishop of which you approve?" he asked, shaking his head.

I considered the question for a moment. "He has a rather nice dog. I met him once: huge gray thing, slobbered on everything, but she was quite jolly."

"Really, I know he has caused you a great deal of trouble, but from whence springs this hatred?" Here he seemed to gesture with the roll of parchment.

"I do not hate him, Lawrence. I simply believe him to be devoid of godly character, which is most displeasing in an archbishop."

"Plenty of men are like that, and yet you find a way to work with them. There is something else there. I know it. One day, I will get it out of you."

"You may try if you wish."

The rest of the day, I am sorry to say, was spent writing further letters, save for one brief pause for dinner. I cannot abide supper most days, but keep the monk's schedule. 'Twas not always so, but now that I am grown old, my appetite is less. I did bid Lawrence write down these few lines for you, as a record of my present thoughts, but now I must let him depart on his urgent errand. What mood he shall find the archbishop in, I can only imagine. Upon his return, I shall take up our tale once again.

Oh, Rouen! How you fill my heart! How you are in my very being! I gave you a bridge, but you gave me far more. I never spent a happier hour than I did within your walls.

The first time I visited the city was during Lent in 1126, when my father wished to spend the season at the castle. Following the feast of Epiphany, I had returned to Caen with Queen Adeliza while the men sojourned to the north. It was foul weather for the hunt, so I am not certain what they hoped to achieve. We women were happy enough to have a decent roof over our heads and a proper fire. Most of all, I hoped in that relative solitude to chase from my mind any thoughts of Brian fitz Count.

However, the more I endeavored to remove him, the more the thought of him seemed to cling to every fiber of my being.

I would see a book he had mentioned, and I thought of him. A food he enjoyed would be served at supper, and again I thought of him. I had made a habit of keeping the satchel with the amber moth with me at most times, but now I hid it at the bottom of one of my chests so it would not enter my mind. Yet I still saw the chest, so I was no better off than before. Always the thought entered my mind, *How wonderful it would be if he loved me as well and we could share that love together!* And always that thought would be followed with, *Only the lovely can be loved.*

By the time the snow melted and the hunt was improved, we had reached the days when meat was forbidden. Therefore, it seemed right to the king to travel to the one place where he was sure to find the best catch of fish. It is just as Lady Beatrice used to say when she wanted William and me to eat: "A man can only go where his stomach will take him." Thus, our stomachs took us to Rouen just in time for Ash Wednesday.

This was the first time I had laid eyes on Lord Brian in many weeks, and I had every hope that upon doing so, my spirit would remain untroubled and we could resume that easy friendship of old. I say I hoped this, but in truth I knew better. I often had dreams where I would see him with other women, then would wake in a state of discontent, wishing never to sleep again. Was it not enough that I should be tormented by day, but that the devils should see fit to haunt me at night with such visions?

We had only just arrived in town and settled into our quarters when we were called to the abbey of Saint Ouen for Mass. It was a short ride along the main northern road, but a grim one, for we were dressed all in black, in mourning for our Savior. Upon our arrival, we were met by the abbot, William, and Archbishop Geoffrey "*le Breton*" of Rouen. They stood just in front of the western door to the abbey church, its lone tower rising toward the sky and catching the midday sun. The king alighted first, then helped the queen and myself down in turn. He then took the hand of his wife and left me to follow behind.

The abbot and archbishop stepped forward to welcome us, the former in his simple black cowl and the latter in his white tunic and cope made of cloth of gold, with a grand red miter on his head embellished with jewels. Although both were dressed according to custom, only one of these garments was in keeping with the mood of the day.

"King Henry, we are honored that you should choose to lodge within our city walls, and to attend this humble house today," the abbot said, as both men bowed.

"Where better to spend a day of mourning than the site where my own father passed from this world?" the king replied. "Archbishop, I am happy to see you once again."

"A pleasure as always, my king," he replied with a nod. "But let me meet this daughter of yours whom I have heard so much about." Here he looked at me with a smile.

"Only good things, I trust," I said, stepping forward to be better seen.

"Naturally!" he assured me, then took my hand and kissed it. I felt this gesture was a bit much, but I said nothing. "Tell me, how do you find our city?"

"As fine as any I have yet seen. Such a great number of ships upon the river!"

"Yes, they all come from Paris, the realm of the French king."

"Who speaks of the French king?" my father asked, the look on his face revealing that he was incensed. "I should hate to see this day ruined with talk of him!"

"Forgive me, my liege," the archbishop quickly replied, "but where is my countryman: your knight, Lord Brian?"

Now, as may be guessed from his title, *le Breton,* the archbishop was from the duchy of Brittany, the very place where Brian fitz Count was born to Duke Alan.

"I am here, sir!" Brian answered.

I almost leaped in surprise when he said this and turned to see he was standing right behind me, along with cousin Stephen and Earl Robert.

"Come forward. Let me see you," said the archbishop.

Brian walked right past me, brushing my right arm as he did so. The older man embraced him, then placed a hand on either side of his face. "They have not removed the *Breton* from you yet, have they? I know you never return."

"It is not for lack of affection that I do not return, but due to that immense loyalty I hold toward King Henry and his dominions," he replied.

"Well, that is as it should be, I suppose. Come, one and all! Let us enter the church!"

I wanted to avoid speaking with Brian, for I was afraid that if I did so, I might say something that would give away my feelings. Were I a normal woman and he a normal man, I likely would have simply spoken my mind and been done with it, but there was nothing normal about the situation. If Brian knew, he might want nothing to do with me, and if the king knew, he would surely chastise me for thinking to give my heart to anyone he did not personally choose. Therefore, as we moved toward the doors, I looked down at the ground. I was too afraid to speak to him, and yet as it turned out I could not avoid it, for he addressed me directly. Indeed, he seemed to have waited for me to pass so that he could join me.

"Empress Maud, it is good to see you once again!" he called.

A tremor of excitement and fear swept through my body as he spoke these words, and I tore my eyes from the ground to look at him. There was a broad smile on his face that warmed my heart. He was wearing a gray tunic and an even darker cloak on account of the day. This was too bad, for I thought he looked best in blue or green, but in truth he looked quite fine to my eyes in any attire. Indeed, I thought in that moment he might look rather nice without any attire at all, and for this I instantly chastised myself and begged God's forgiveness. His dark curls had grown longer since last time we met, falling all the way to his shoulders. And his eyes—oh, his eyes captivated me as ever! I could have made a study of that face all day, but it occurred to me that a response was necessary.

"I ... that is—thank you. How was your hunt?" I asked, as we entered the church.

"Not so good. It was not the proper time of year for sport, but we did our best. I am sorry you did not choose to join us."

"I was happy to remain with the queen. The lodgings in Caen are far superior," I said quickly, my eyes trained on the altar at the far end of the nave.

"You will hear no argument from me there, but even so, I missed our conversation."

We had by this point passed the first row of columns and were nearing the congregation, so I took the opportunity to depart.

"I am sorry, but I really must join the others up front," I whispered.

"Of course," he replied, and we went our separate ways.

I looked over quickly and saw his face one last time before his back was turned to me and he had made his way to the back of the crowd. Had I glimpsed a tinge of sadness in those eyes when I took my leave? Surely not—I must have imagined it. Too oft we see only that which we desire. I took my place at the front standing next to the king and queen, but my mind was very much with the man toward the back of the room. I bowed my head and clasped my hands, as if by doing so I could crush what I felt.

The abbot began the service with the words of the Psalmist. "'Have mercy upon us, O God, according to your lovingkindness: according to the multitude of your compassions put away our iniquities. Wash us thoroughly from our iniquity, and cleanse us from our sin.'"[11]

"Lord, have mercy," we all replied.

He continued, "'For we know our iniquities, and our sin is ever before us. Against you, against you only have we sinned, and done evil in your sight. Behold, we were born in iniquity, and in sin have our mothers conceived us.'"

"Lord, have mercy," we replied again.

"'Behold, you love truth in the inward affections: therefore have you taught us wisdom in the secrets of our hearts …'"

Secrets of hearts—I knew something of those. I could scarcely remember a time when my heart was not filled to overflowing with secrets. And now, I held an even deeper secret: one that was gnawing at me from the inside. Even as the abbot lifted his hands in prayer, I struggled to hold in the tears that threatened to flow.

"Create in us a clean heart, O God, and renew a right spirit within us," he recited. "Cast us not away from your presence, and take not your Holy Spirit from us. Restore to us the joy of your salvation, and establish us with your free Spirit.'"

"Lord, have mercy," I prayed along with the others.

We passed through the readings and came to the deposition of ashes. The abbot stood at the front of the nave with a small metal dish whose contents would shortly be on our foreheads. Each of us went up in turn and formed a line: the king first, then his queen, followed by myself and Stephen, who moved in very close behind me. As the abbot began the ceremony, I turned and saw that Stephen had stepped in front of Robert.

---

11 This quote and the ones that follow are excerpts from Psalm 51.

It is wrong for the king's son to stand behind his nephew, I thought, and I might have said something to my cousin had I not arrived in front of the abbot.

"Remember: you are dust, and to dust shall you return," the abbot said, lifting his fingers and making the sign of the cross on my forehead.

It was not as if I had forgotten. The whole day served to make us aware of our mortality. Nevertheless, as I returned to my position and the others had the ashes placed upon them, I considered that in comparison with the sacrifice of our Lord, my own cares were as dust.

You must stop this. Truly, you must, I told myself. *You got yourself into this mess. You can get yourself out of it.*

Yes, I told myself that, but even so, my thoughts continued to turn back to my problem. I chided myself to no end.

Why do you seek something you know you can never have? You know the king would forbid it, and more than that, you have no reason to suppose that Lord Brian desires it. Who do you think you are? They may respect you for your crown, but they will never love you. If the emperor never had a passion for you, and he was your husband, then why would anyone else? You must find your contentment in God alone.

Once the service was mercifully complete, we made our way out of the church and were about to return home when young William made a declaration.

"Father, we must show the empress our new game!" he cried.

"New game? What is that?" I asked.

"The monks call it 'hand ball,' but I think it an ill name," brother Robert replied, then looked down at his son. "We can show her the court, but I do not think we should play today, given the occasion. This is the day of Christ's death, after all."

As the king and queen remained behind to speak with the archbishop, the king's lads led me to the cloister just to the south of the church. A covered stone walk in the shape of a square was separated from the main stretch of grass by a row of columns and a low stone fence that connected each one. The grass courtyard was surrounded by a gravel path just inside the fence, and in the middle a rope was hung up between two posts.

"I don't understand. Do you have to hop over it?" I asked, as we stepped on to the grass.

They all laughed at these words, and I felt rather foolish.

"No, one person stands on each side and they throw or hit the ball back and forth," Stephen explained.

"And if the ball hits the ground, you lose the point," William added, clutching the rope.

"So you just hit it with your hand?" I inquired.

"Yes, hence the name," said Robert.

"Actually, you're wrong," Brian told them, reaching down to remove some stray pebbles from the grass. "That is the way the monks used to play, but now they hit the ball with a stick—well, it's more of a paddle really."

"So why do they still call it hand ball?" Robert Beaumont asked.

"Last I heard, they were calling it 'palm game,'" he replied, throwing the pebbles back in the gravel path, "for you still throw or hit it with the palm at times."

Even as he said this, a door at the far end of the cloister opened and shut, and one of the monks entered the courtyard where we had assembled, his hands evidently clasped together inside his long sleeves.

"My lords, may I help you?" he asked, bowing his head in deference.

"Yes. We want to play!" William cried, leaping up and down for good measure.

"Son, I told you no," his father said, grasping the boy's shoulders firmly as if to plant his feet to the ground.

"But father, the empress wants to see!" William whined.

"We can show her another time."

"It is not a problem," the monk said. "I can pull the balls out if you wish."

With this, brother Robert finally relented and allowed them to set up the game.

"Two on each side," Brian said.

"My son and I shall take this side. Stephen, you go with Robert," brother Robert instructed.

As the monk retrieved the chest holding the balls and paddles, I took a spot within the square passage, leaning on the low stone fence with my arms crossed. All was made ready and Stephen began the game by throwing the ball off the roof and on to the other side of the court. My brother then hit it back toward Robert Beaumont, who was not quick enough and let it drop to the ground.

"Yes! One point for us!" William rejoiced.

Out of the corner of my eye, I saw Brian rounding the corner of the passage and coming in my direction. I stood up a bit straighter but did not look at him directly until he took his place right next to me.

"So what do you think of our game?" he asked.

"Very nice, I suppose," I replied, looking back at the players.

"You suppose?"

"Well, I am sure it is fun to play."

"But ... what?"

I turned my head to face him again. "What do you wish me to say? It is four men—well, three men and one boy—hitting a ball back and forth." Here I moved my hand as if to demonstrate the path of the ball. "This may not be the greatest excitement I have ever received, but I admit the game has merit."

"Very well, I accept your answer," he said with a smile, leaning on the fence and looking forward.

I tried my best to pay attention to the game, but his very presence was distracting. Of course, I enjoyed being near him. Every part of me seemed to be more alive around him. However, I was held back as always by the fear of how my father would respond, along with my fear of rejection by Brian himself. I valued his friendship and did not want to lose it on account of some foolish whim. I wondered if there was anything I could do that might diminish what I felt. Alas, that did not seem likely.

"I hear your father receives many new offers for your hand," he said. "You must be flattered."

I had not heard anything of the sort and learning of it from Brian seemed doubly painful. Yes, I knew that the king would not allow me to remain a widow for ever, but the idea of being married to some stranger was awful when I was standing right next to someone I loved. More to the point, it was terrible to hear the news from his lips. Had he actually felt drawn to me as I did to him, it seemed unlikely that he would speak of me being flattered by other suitors, and no matter how much I tried, some small part of me had still held out hope that I was wrong and he actually did like me—yes, even love me. Thus, my heart felt very torn, and I simply said the first thing that came to mind.

"It is my standing they desire and not myself."

"Don't be so sure," he told me earnestly. "I am certain that, were they to meet you—"

"It would make no difference. My first husband liked me well enough. If I achieve that a second time, I shall count myself fortunate."

"But you must believe that—"

"Please!" I said with some authority. "I do not think we should be discussing this. It is a private affair."

He made no reply, but I suspected he was a bit wounded, for his countenance was clearly fallen. *Maybe that sounded too harsh*, I worried, but I did not dare to speak further and make the damage even worse. He looked back at the players, and I did the same.

As we stood in silence, my eyes glanced down at his hands, which were perched very near mine on the stone rail. There was so little space between us, and yet it seemed like an eternal abyss. I imagined myself reaching out, crossing those few inches of space, and taking his hand. My heart leaped even as I thought about it. Yet no sooner had I done so than the scene in my mind changed and he was pulling his hand back and crying, "Why would you do that?!" I shook my head slightly and pulled my mind back into the present, where the ball continued to bounce back and forth.

Another minute must have passed before Brian suddenly turned and spoke rather bluntly, "Have I done something to offend you?"

"No," I replied quickly.

"You're certain?" he asked, his eyes searching my face.

"Yes."

He planted his hand on the rail, leaning closer to address me. "On Christmas Eve, I walked you back to your room. We were alone for a moment, and it seemed to concern you. Ever since then, we've hardly spoken."

He was very close to guessing my secret, or so it seemed. I certainly did not want to be rude, but I was quite afraid that acknowledging how I enjoyed being around him would give the game away. Uncertain what else to do, I decided to turn the game around on him.

"If you find me poor company, then there are plenty of others with whom you may converse. Why do you feel such a need to speak with me?"

"Because …"

The features in his face were strained, as if he was searching for the words.

Oh, please say you desire my company above all others! I thought.

But he did not say it, nor did he say anything else. He simply hit the railing with his hand and walked off without another word. My eyes followed him as he walked swiftly down the passage and departed the cloister without stopping to inform the others. I was quite stunned and stood there for a moment, uncertain as to what I should do.

That was odd, I said to myself. *Very odd. I have never seen him act that way.*

My mind raced back through our conversation, attempting to discover the point where things had gone wrong. I had asked him why he desired my company, and then he had stormed off, unwilling to answer. Was it possible that he enjoyed being around me and yet felt ashamed to say so? But why would he feel ashamed by that? No, it couldn't be. It made no sense.

The more I considered the matter, the more I recognized that I must have wounded his sense of honor with my question. I was not sure how, but that was what usually made men forsake a conversation. I was still watching the game, but all I could think was, *Well, now you've done it, Maud! He hates you!*

I count myself fortunate that, from my earliest days, I was taught to read the written word. When I think of the poor souls who must stare at those letters in stark ignorance, unable to gain the knowledge they provide, I pity them most truly. For when life becomes a sore cross to bear, some easy occupation is needed to bring a measure of comfort, and a good book can be the perfect remedy.

I was blessed with many volumes, some of which I have already mentioned. There were few I loved as much as the *Metamorphoses*, that ancient tale of the pagan gods. While I remained in the palace of Rouen upon the banks of the Seine, provided the weather was fair, I would walk out and take my repose in the shade of an apple tree near the water's edge, where I might read without interruption. Thus, upon Easter Monday in the year of our Lord 1126, I set out with my volume of Ovid in hand. As I desired some exercise, I left the palace by way of the main tower and made my way into the gardens, each of which was surrounded by a hedge. I began walking amid the rows of herbs in the first garden, knowing I would come to the tree eventually.

"What shall it be today?" I asked myself. "Perhaps the story of Icarus: there is a tale that would induce caution."

Even as I continued walking, I turned to the eighth book and began to read, the words of Ovid bringing delight to each step.

"'Along the middle runs a twine of flax, the bottom stems are joined by pliant wax. Thus, well compact, a hollow bending brings the fine composure into real wings.' Hmm ... I wonder if anyone has tried this? It seems simple enough."

I entered the garden for the infirm and continued walking toward the largest garden near the castle wall. It was delightfully sunny, and there were butterflies here and there. I smiled and returned to reading.

"'My boy, take care to wing your course along the middle air; if low, the surges wet your flagging plumes; if high the sun the melting wax consumes.' Well, this father is negligent! Of course the boy will go too high!"

At that very moment, I heard the voice of Brian fitz Count. "Empress Maud?"

My first thought was that I might have imagined his voice, but as I looked to my right, I saw that it was indeed Brian walking toward me, and he had evidently seen me making a fool of myself by speaking my thoughts aloud. *Oh dear! Oh dear!* I thought. Yes, even though I knew my cause was hopeless, some part of me was still trying to impress him.

"Good day, sir," I said, shutting the book quickly.

"Good day, Your Highness," he replied with a bow.

"I seem to have wandered too far. I had best get back."

I started to retreat toward the infirmary garden, when he said, "Come into the garden, if you will. I have something to show you."

I turned back to look at him. He seemed honestly pleased to see me, a smile upon his face. Perhaps he did not hate me then. Nevertheless, I briefly considered denying his request, but a voice in my head seemed to say, *Have courage, Maud. Speak with him. It won't kill you. How will you make it through life if you cannot talk to people?* Therefore, despite how awkward I felt, I approached.

I walked to within a single pace of him, quickly tucking a loose piece of hair behind my ear. I looked in his eyes meekly but saw nothing there to make me think he was the least bit angry. Indeed, those eyes almost seemed to beckon me. Then again, I could be seeing what I desired yet again.

"So what is this thing you have to show me?" I asked.

"Over here," he replied, pointing to the right. "Some of the roses are starting to bloom."

I followed him toward the outer wall of the castle, where a line of rose bushes was planted. "Over here!" he called, beckoning with his hand even as he bent down and pulled one of the branches toward us. Sure enough, a few pink flowers had opened.

"Usually they don't bloom for a few more weeks," he said. "Here, smell one!"

As he continued to hold the branch, I set my book down on the ground, leaned forward carefully, and placed my nose near the bloom. I closed my eyes and took in its fragrance. It was indeed wonderful. I had gone for months without smelling a flower in bloom. Its scent seemed to call to mind everything wonderful in the world. I then opened my eyes and noticed that my face was very close to Brian's. My heart leaped and I straightened up at once.

"What accounts for these early blooms?" I asked, reasoning that this was a fairly safe subject of conversation. I was unlikely to slip up as long as we were discussing plants.

"It has been rather hot for the season, which has caused them to grow more quickly," he replied, letting go of the branch and standing up himself. "The only danger is that it may yet freeze, and then the buds will die."

"Well, I hope that they continue to grow without a problem. Now, I really must be getting back."

"Wait!" he said, taking hold of my arm.

In an instant, I felt heat pass through my body. It was rare for anyone to touch me in such a manner, and to have the man I loved do so seemed to heighten every desire within me, even if he only did it to get my attention. I strove to reclaim my thoughts and direct the situation. I looked at his face again. His eyes were wide. Indeed, they looked almost desperate, searching my face. All this happened within the space of two breaths, and yet it seemed to be moving slowly.

"Did you come here because you knew I would be taking my walk?" I asked.

He let go of my arm and raised his hands as if in apology. "Yes, I am sorry," he said softly. "I just knew it was the only way I could speak with you."

He wanted to speak with me? I could see that this conversation was about to go one of two directions, and I was exceedingly interested in which one it would be. I waited for a moment to see if he would continue. His lips began to form a word, and then he stopped. Finally, I spoke instead.

"I do not understand you, Sir Brian. Why are you always so desperate to speak with me? Is there some favor you require?"

I had no desire to be rude, but I very much wanted to find out the truth of the situation.

"No, that isn't it," he said definitively.

"Then what?"

"Why are you always avoiding me?" he asked, his tone direct but not rude. "For the past few months, every time I try to speak to you, I feel there is a wall between us, and it saddens me. Your friendship means a great deal. I must know the answer to this riddle, for you claim I have never offended you. So why do you withdraw?"

He almost had me there. He had clearly recognized that I was avoiding him, or at least avoiding the kind of open conversations we used to have. Well, that was no surprise. He was one of the cleverest men I had ever known. Sadly, were I to answer his question honestly, I would be forced to admit that I loved him. I feared that rejection would be only one step behind, so I was determined to give nothing away.

"It is not for me to tell you what I think or do not think about anyone," I told him.

He shook his head slightly. "I do not seek to command you. I am asking you as a friend, for I hope that is what we are. Please tell me what I have done wrong."

"Why does it matter?" I asked, afraid to know the answer, and yet longing to know it.

"Of course it matters!" he cried.

"No, you didn't answer my question."

"You didn't answer mine."

So there we stood, staring at one another, both breathing heavily, neither of us willing to admit what was on our mind—neither willing to cross the Rubicon that stood between us. I did not want to lie to him, and yet I feared what might happen if I told him the truth.

"I cannot answer your question," I finally said, "not truly, so I shall not answer at all."

I attempted to leave once again, but he stepped in front of me and blocked my path.

"Please, you can tell me anything, even if it is to assail me. Even if you wish to send me into exile and never see my face again. I should hate it, but I will hear it."

My heart was feeling so much in that moment that I was on the verge of tears. I held my eyes shut and whispered, "That is the last thing I want."

"If you seek to be near me, then why do you avoid me?"

"Because I cannot be near you!" I cried, opening my eyes again.

"Why not?"

The look on his face was so earnest, so determined that my defenses were breaking down.

"You really want to know the answer?"

He nodded firmly. "I do."

I could see there was nothing for it. I summoned every ounce of boldness I possessed, looked him in the eye and said, "I love you, Brian. That is the answer to the riddle. Now let me go."

"What?" he asked, looking as if he'd been stunned.

"I said, let me go!"

He did as I asked, stepping out of the way. I turned to leave as fast as possible, for I could no longer remain calm. The boldness I had felt for a moment in time had disappeared, and the fear was again exposed. I walked swiftly toward the infirmary garden, lifting my skirt slightly so I could move faster.

Oh, good God! What have I done?! Why did I have to say that?! I thought. *I've striven not to say anything for so long, and now I cannot take it back. What will he think? What will my father think if he finds out?!*

I could hear Brian calling out my name behind me, begging me to stop, but I continued walking. There was nothing more to be gained from conversation. I had made it back to the herbs when he caught me from behind.

"Maud, there is nothing to be afraid of," he said, his hands moving to hold my face. "Breathe. Please breathe."

As I looked into his eyes, it was as if the scales began to drop from my own and I was seeing the truth for the first time, or rather I allowed myself to trust it for the first time. I did as he said, breathing deeply, and continued gazing at him in wonder. I had tried so hard not to look at that face, even though all I wanted was to stare at it. Every inch of it seemed perfect to me, and what was truly amazing—his smile told me that he just might feel the same way about mine. I could hardly believe it, and yet there it was in front of me.

"Come here," he said, and pulled me close, until my face was resting against his chest.

For a moment, he simply held me in his arms as I closed my eyes and savored his embrace. I could feel his heart beating strongly, and it seemed entirely possible that it was doing so for me. I dearly hoped this meant he felt as I did, but some small part of me still held back, waiting for the words.

"I am sorry I ran away," I said softly. "I've wanted to tell you for so long, but I was afraid of what you would say. I suppose I was overcome."

He pulled back slightly so that he could see my face again.

"That's the strange thing, you see," he said, his hand tracing the outline of my chin. "I've been afraid as well."

"Afraid?"

"Afraid of losing something I never had. That is, of never having something I don't deserve." He let out a sigh and shook his head. "Do you really love me, Maud? Truly? Because I love you more than anything on this earth. I feel drawn to you like a gull to the sea, and yet I thought I was alone."

And there they were: the words I had so longed to hear, the truth I had wanted to believe. "I love you more than anything on this earth." At last, I could believe it fully and completely, and it brought me such joy—such incredible, immense joy.

"I thought I was alone!" I said, smiling.

"God must love me if you do," he replied, pulling me closer until our faces touched.

There are many other things I probably should have said in that moment, but as we rubbed noses and I felt the warmth of his breath upon my face, I was so overcome—so wholly and perfectly content—that everything else faded away.

When we kissed, it was such blessed relief! I finally knew what it was to love a man passionately and be adored by him in return. What was more, he did not smell foul like most men: trust me, that is of great value. I do not know how long we might have stayed there, but we heard the gardener's voice just beyond the hedge and were forced to break off our tryst. As I smiled and waved farewell, I was pleased to see that he was as happy as ever I knew him.

When I entered the tower again, I happened across one of the king's stewards, who asked quite innocently, "How are you this afternoon, madam?"

"Fantastic!" I cried, giving a rather more ardent reply than he must have foreseen.

Poor Ovid! I had left him in the garden.

Brian's declaration that he loved me seemed to produce an instant change in how I viewed myself. To confess your love for someone is, in a way, to bind yourself to them in spirit. Yes, there are many forms of love: love between a mother and her child, love between friends, love between brothers, and highest of all, the love of God. But the love of a man and woman for one another, not merely as friends, but as objects of desire, provides its own form of definition. Brian belonged to me, not because I was his master, but because I was the object of his love. Even so, I belonged to him, and what a blessing that was! It was enough for that one moment in my life to simply treasure that love.

However, the elation I felt upon that most blessed revelation of his affection quickly abated, for I saw that I had merely been transferred from the fire into the flame. Brian fitz Count was to be married to another Mathilda, the lady of Wallingford, thereby obtaining his fortune. The king intended him for that high honor; I suspected it was to be carried out as soon as we all returned to England. Some might even have said that he was bound to her by law, though such bonds could be broken easily enough by those with means. Yet there was no denying that this was a difficulty that might never be overcome.

Then there was the far greater matter of my own future. The king would never countenance a union between the bastard son of a duke and his own daughter. I had sense enough to see that. Thus, my joy quickly gave way to despair, and I knew what I must do, though I hated it with the utmost hatred. I had but one small comfort: that Brian surely knew as well as myself the impossibility of such a union, and thus he was not seeking his own advancement.

A few hours after our meeting in the garden, when the sun had only just set, I made my way down from the private chambers to the great hall, where I intended to inform him that we could not be bound together in any formal sense of that word, even if our hearts were bound. What a loathsome charge to be given! I prayed the Lord would give me strength.

Once I arrived, I was briefly distracted by the spectacle before me. The hall was arranged as usual, with the high table on the eastern side of the room and a longer one on the opposite side for the rest of the court. There was no proper hearth, but only a pit in the middle of the room. Two of the king's men were wrestling with all the others gathered around and cheering. Their bodies twisted and turned, coming dangerously close to the fire.

"What madness is this?" I asked no one in particular, still standing in the door way.

I then recognized that, given the intense distraction in the room, I might be able to steal away with Brian, if only I could find him in the crowd. My eyes began to examine each face without any luck until I saw him standing to my right near the barrels of wine, beckoning for me to come over.

Be strong, Maud, I told myself again, and walked in his direction, unseen by the raging mass.

Brian held out a glass of wine, and I took it gladly, for I needed something to calm myself. Without saying a word, he led me behind a large tapestry and opened a side portal, which we then entered. I had never walked through this door before and had no idea what it contained. As it turned out, it was the space just below the great stair that traveled up the tower. The room was used for storing things, with only a small window to the outside for light. As it was evening, I could see all this only faintly, even as I could barely see Brian closing the door and turning to face me.

"Brian," I said, hoping to seize the conversation before he had a chance, "I am glad to have the chance to speak with you, for—"

"You're extraordinary, do you know that?"

"Thank you, but—"

"Everything about you. Your beauty, your cleverness, your grace—everything," he said, kissing me again and again.

"Take care you do not lie," I commanded, pulling my face back. "Everyone knows I am no great beauty and I talk far too much for my own good or anyone else's."

"Everyone is wrong then."

"Brian …"

He was making it rather impossible for me to speak, what with the number of kisses he was planting on my mouth, and the sad thing was that I had no desire for him to stop, so I gave way. Then I hit something behind me and there was a sound of metal striking the floor. A surge of fear ran through me and both of us fell silent, so that the only sound was the cheering in the hall. After enough time had passed to convince me that no one had heard the noise and would be opening the door, I spoke again.

"Brian, what do they keep in here?"

"All the serving implements."

"Ah, so that is what I felt poking me in the back!"

"It is hard to see in here, but I didn't know where else to go."

"What if they need something and come to fetch it?"

"Then I hope you will vouch for me at the inquisition."

I could barely make out his face, but I sensed that he must be smiling.

"I do not find that comical," I said, hitting him on the arm hard enough to make my point, but not hard enough to cause pain.

"No one is coming!" he assured me. "They have all they need for tonight."

Brian moved his face closer to mine again until I could at least smell him, even if I could hardly see him. He did smell quite nice.

"I see you are playing the part of the devil now," I whispered.

He laughed and attempted to kiss me again, but I held him in place.

"Stop, I really must tell you something."

"Let me guess: your father will never approve, so we should stop this right now. And perhaps you are also going to mention Lady Wallingford."

"You disagree with me?" I asked, uncertain how something that was causing me such great concern could be of little matter to him.

"No, I too see the difficulty."

"Then you know that it doesn't matter if I hold you in high esteem."

"'High esteem'?" he said, pulling back. "It seems I have been relegated. Earlier today, you led me to believe that you felt something more than 'esteem.' Was that a lie?"

I sighed. "No, it was God's honest truth."

Here he moved to embrace me again, holding me tightly, even as I held him.

"Maud, I never thought I would hear you say those words to me. Ever! Do you think I can simply forget them?"

I moved my head back and reached up to touch his face, or at least the dark object I knew to be his face. "I think you should put that mind of yours to work and recognize that there is no future for us. We are like two travelers whose paths may cross for a moment, but who are headed for different destinations."

Even as I said this, I began moving my fingers through his hair, not so much because it added anything to the conversation, but because I had simply wanted to do so for months.

"Do you like this?" I asked. It was a very silly thing to say, but I had never really touched a man's hair before, and I had no idea how he would feel about it.

"I think you are attempting to distract me," he said.

"Oh … Forgive me."

"No, by all means continue," he replied, laughing. "I enjoyed it."

"But do you agree with me?" I asked, returning to the subject at hand. "Are we simply setting ourselves up to be crushed? We cannot continue like this for ever."

"But that is why we must embrace it! We may only have a few weeks, a few months, a few pleasant hours before the world calls us to part ways. If I didn't at least try to make something of that time, I would regret it. Wouldn't you? You have seen even more of this world than I have. It is cold and empty and heartless. How common do you think real love is? This may be the only chance we ever have. But my love does not respond—that is not like you."

Hearing him call me his love made my heart beat faster again, and not for the first time that day, I gave in to what I felt.

"What can I say? Your study of the law has clearly improved your argumentation," I told him. "Do you really love me, then?"

"Yes, of course I do! That is why I made a fool of myself when you first came back to us."

"What? In Caen?"

He wrapped his arms around me again. I felt so safe there, as if nothing in the world could hurt me.

"I saw you come through the castle gate. You were a wonder to behold."

"But you only remembered me as a small girl."

"Before that moment, yes, but it all changed when I saw you as—"

"Rich?"

"No! You twist my meaning!" he objected, pulling back.

"I do not think you could have loved me then."

"But I did! That is why I was always trying to get close to you—to speak with you."

"Because you thought you had a chance with me? What presumption!" Here I hit him again playfully so he would remember his place.

"No, because I wanted to bask, as it were, in the glow of your light. I never dreamed you might return my affection until today."

"You know what I think?" I asked, kissing him on one cheek and then moving to kiss the other.

"What?"

I whispered, "I think you're full of ..."

Before I could finish, he kissed my mouth again, and after that point neither of us had much interest in talking until we finally decided that any further absence from supper would be deemed suspicious.

I was first to leave the room and peek out from behind the tapestry. Instead of wrestling, some of the men were now sparring with their fists, so I was once again able to move around without being seen. All the men and some of the women were gathered in a circle around the combatants, while the rest paid me no attention. I made my way up to the high table and took a place beside the queen.

"Men are such brutes, aren't they? See how they carry on!" I said to her.

She made no reply, and I looked over to see the beginnings of tears in her eyes.

"Oh dear! What is the matter?" I asked.

Once again, she said nothing, but stared forward into the fire that burned in the middle of the hall, biting her lip in what seemed to be an effort not to weep openly. In the light of those flames, I caught a glimpse of something on the side of her face. Her veil almost covered it, but there was a shadow of some kind.

"Forgive me, my queen, but it looks like you have some dirt on your face. Here, you can use my kerchief," I said, retrieving the square of silk fabric from my pocket.

"No, thank you," she replied quietly.

"But it might help—"

"I said, no thank you! There is nothing that can help me. Now, stop being such a nuisance!" she said, her eyes cutting like daggers.

Her harsh words took me completely by surprise, and I could not account for them at all. I had gone from one of the loveliest moments of my life to being scolded by the least likely person in the room. I sat there for a moment and said nothing, my mind hard at work. My eyes wandered over and rested on my father, who was staggering across the room and laughing fiercely, clearly drunk. Suddenly, I remembered something from my youth: a faint whisper that I had tried to forget. I was standing next to my mother while she was working a loom. Her sleeve fell back and I saw dark marks on her arm.

"What are those, mother?"

A shadow passed over her face, and she quickly moved her sleeve back in place.

"Nothing, my child," she said, stroking my chin with her other hand. "It's nothing."

It was such a small thing that I had nearly forgotten it, but for the first time I understood what my mother had refused to tell me then, and I found myself nearly robbed of breath. A sudden dread of the possible fell over me. I knew I had to find out the truth, and that the woman beside me was unlikely to surrender it. Just when Queen Adeliza must have felt the storm had passed and I would trouble her with no more questions, I pulled back her veil and saw the large bruise just to the right of her eye.

"How dare you?!" she cried. It was loud for her, but not loud enough to be heard over the noise of the crowd.

"Who did this to you?" I demanded. "Was it the king?"

"I have had about enough of your questions, empress. Good night!" she concluded. She rose at once from her seat and marched around the cheering crowd, eventually making her way out the door and back toward the private chambers.

I continued sitting there alone and studied the figures lit by the fire. Brian had found his way back among the king's lads.

We would not be discovered this night. To the left and right, men were pulling money out of their pockets and placing bets on the next fight. Then I saw my father, ale in hand. Was that the hand that had struck the queen, and for what? No wonder the woman lived in terror of us all!

I had long heard stories of the king's cruelty to his enemies, though I seldom witnessed it. Now, I had the evidence of his wrath laid out before me, and what was even worse, I was courting that wrath with my behavior. Would he end up wounding me as he had my mother and the new queen?

Perhaps I mistook the parable of Icarus, I thought. *Maybe the father wished him to burn.*

CHAPTER NINE

Many years ago, my brother Robert gifted me a copy of the *Historia Regum Britanniae* by Geoffrey of Monmouth, one of the many scholars in Oxford who has since passed from this life. Earl Robert served as patron to many such works of history, but this was easily one of the best. It is now read in every school and treated as gospel by our friend, Robert *du Monte*, whom I hope to see again soon.

There is a tale in this book of the ancient King Leir, after whom the city of Leicester was named. The Lord did not see fit to grant him any sons, but only three daughters. Thus, the old king chose to divide his inheritance among them according to who loved him best. Now, the first two daughters were flatterers and swore they loved him more than all others—even more than life itself. But the third was honest above all else, and she bid him, "Look how much you have, so much is your value, and so much do I love you." The king was furious and gave her no portion with the other two. It was only later that he saw that only this daughter truly loved him.

This Leir is not unlike all his royal brothers, for a king seldom knows what to do with a daughter. A son may be a successor, a foe, a treasure above all else. But a daughter: what is she? At times a tool, at times a burden. She is the last hope if all else should fail, and such was I to my own father, who was bereaved of his prize son, the boy who was born to be king.

In those days, I waited upon whatever destiny the king saw fit to bestow. A thousand fathers may seek to better their own lot by giving their daughter in marriage, but my father sought to better the lot of a kingdom. And I who felt as distant from him as London is from Jerusalem—I would have to find some way to influence his choice on my behalf. But how could such a thing be done? Who can stem the fury of a Leir?

Such questions filled my mind continually that spring—that is, when I was not devising some means of speaking with Brian, which was more difficult than you might suppose. We could not even send each other letters or give each other gifts, for those might be discovered. I simply treasured the few moments we had alone together and the amber moth he had granted me in my youth.

In the week leading up to Saint George's Day, the court was consumed with preparations for the tournament that would take place in the yard of the palace of Rouen, and all else was thrown aside in pursuit of this one object. Therefore, when upon the morning of the feast I received a knock on the door of my private chamber, I was most pleased to hear one of the ladies declare, "Sir Brian is come to speak with you, my lady."

My heart leaped at this announcement, but I attempted to remain calm and not reveal my feelings.

"Send him in," I instructed.

The three other ladies in the room were all seated on the floor stitching flowers on the bottom of a new silk gown the king had allowed me to have made for the feast at no little expense. Meanwhile, I had been sitting on the ledge of one of the two windows in the room, reading some of the poetry of William of Aquitaine to which Brian had first introduced me. I quickly set the book aside and felt my veil to make sure nothing was out of place. As the servant who had originally informed me of his presence entered the room with Brian, I stood and pressed my palms together in the hope of appearing more formal than familiar, not wanting to give the game away. He bowed deeply and we exchanged a smile, though for my part I might have preferred far more.

"It is good to see you, Sir Brian," I said.

"Likewise, Empress Mathilda," he replied, stepping carefully around the four ladies and their project until he was closer to my position.

I observed that he was wearing his blue mantle. This was my favorite, both because it gave his appearance a great advantage and because he had worn it the very first evening we danced together in Caen. I might have liked to simply stare at him for a while, but as that would have seemed exceedingly odd to the ladies in the room, I spoke instead.

"What message do you have for us on this fine day?" I asked him.

"The king has summoned you."

"Oh? To what?"

"To a meeting—just the two of you. He bids you come now, before the games begin."

"I am the king's servant," I replied. "Now, if you think it proper, I would speak with you in private, for I have a surprise for the king that I prefer to keep secret."

"Certainly," he said, his face breaking into a smile.

"Perfect. Ladies, be about your business."

To my great relief, none of the four women so much as looked up from their work as Brian opened the door for me and we stepped out into the hall. As soon as the door was shut behind us, I instructed, "Follow me." We made our way down the stairs in the main tower and out the back door of the palace that led toward the stables, animal pens, and armory. There was a cistern right next to the palace wall, hidden on all but one side by a stone curtain. When I had looked around and ensured that no one was watching, I took his hand in mine and led him to this chosen hiding place.

"We shouldn't be seen here as long as we keep our eyes and ears open," I told him.

"Thank God for that! I have missed you so!" he said, leaning in to kiss me.

I placed a hand on his chest to hold him back. "Not half as much as I have missed you, but that is not why we are here."

"It's not? Pity."

Poor man! He pulled back a bit, and I could read in his features that he was badly let down.

I took each of his hands in mine. "I actually wanted to ask you about the king. Do you have any sense of what he wishes to discuss?"

"I repeated every word he told me. There was nothing more."

I considered the matter for a moment. "Brian, can I tell you something in confidence?"

"Of course."

"I have reason to suspect that the queen was struck by someone."

"Someone? Meaning the king?" he asked, raising his brows.

"That is my fear, yes."

I had clearly surprised him, but as always, he adopted a careful approach. "What evidence do you have?"

"The last day of the Easter feast, I saw a bruise on her face. She had attempted to hide it and became quite angry when I looked. She left the room and has avoided me ever since."

For a moment, he stared at nothing in particular, as if deep in thought. He then seemed to snap out of it and looked back at me. "Might she have had some accident?"

"I think not. She would have no reason to hide that."

"And you really think it was the king?"

"Who else could do such a thing without being skinned alive?"

"But why should he treat her so?"

"Because she has disappointed him, and he is not the most forgiving of men."

"Hmm. It does seem unlikely that anyone else could have wounded her without reprisal," he said thoughtfully. "Do you believe the queen is in any kind of danger?"

"Some danger, certainly—how urgent, I cannot say. Should I raise this matter with the king?"

"Oh, I think that is a bad idea," he said with conviction. "If his temper is truly as violent as you say, then charging him with his misdeed might only increase his anger and direct it toward yourself." His grip on my hands seemed to increase just a bit as he said this.

"It would give him a chance to deny it, if it is not true," I offered.

He raised his right hand and ran his fingers through the bits of hair that peeked out from under my veil. I closed my eyes for just a moment, allowing the feeling to sink into my bones.

"Well, if you seek my advice," he said, stroking my cheek, "I say let the matter rest for now, until more evidence comes to light."

"I suppose that is most prudent. My spirit is troubled though. If he tells me that I am to be sent away from you now, I do not think I could bear it."

His brow furrowed a bit as I said this, and he shook his head slightly, as if he refused to accept it. "You would find a way to bear it. I am certain you would."

"I just wish …" I began, but found it too difficult to continue. I simply reached out and held him, allowing my thoughts to churn.

"What is it, my love?" he whispered.

"I wish that I had the strength to overcome my fear of him: to make known my desires and see them done. When I was a little girl, I simply did as he said. I had no choice. Now even though I am a woman who has ruled in my own right, I doubt he has any regard for my opinions. Add to that his apparent abuse of his own wife, and I cannot help but feel concern. Despite my position, there is little I can do to oppose his will. I do not wish to think ill of my own father. Truly, I do not! He has never caused me physical pain: only pain of the soul. Even so, were I to tell him my desires, I fear what he would say or do."

"And what are your desires?" Brian asked, pulling back slightly so he could see my face.

I might have answered him, but there was a noise and we let go of each other.

"There you two are!" Earl Robert called out.

He had evidently seen us as he was walking back into the palace. For a moment, he looked at me and then at Brian, and I greatly feared that he was about to accuse us of something entirely true. However, he did not.

"Father sent me to find you, Maud. He says that if you choose to follow the example of Queen Vashti and reject his summons, he shall make you share in her fate."

"Tell him I am coming," I replied.

He then left as quickly as he had come, and Brian and I were once again alone.

"Do you think he saw anything?" I asked.

"No, but we ought to be more careful in the future. Come! Let's get you to the king."

"Wait! Before we go, I just—"

"Just what?"

Unable to come up with anything better to say, I uttered, "I love you, Brian. You're the best man I've ever known."

"That is the greatest gift anyone has ever given me," he replied, kissing my forehead. "And you may rest assured that I will love you until I die. Your beauty dazzles me. My soul delights in you. You bring me to life."

It seemed terrible to end our conversation there, but we had no choice. He led me out to the stables by the northern wall, where the king was surveying the horses that were to be used in the games. There were ten stalls on either side of an open path, with a wood roof overhead. When we arrived, I thanked Brian and made my way over to the third stall on the right, where my father stood feeding parsnips to one of the beasts. Upon hearing my approach, he looked up from his work.

"There you are, prodigal daughter!" he said in a rather rough manner, not moving from his work and returning his eyes to the beast instantly. "I thought you might have gotten lost, but then I reasoned that no child of mine could have done such a thing."

"You think me free of error?" I asked, stopping a good two paces from where he stood.

"You have it in you to commit venial sins, but nothing truly heinous: it is not in the nature of noble women, at least not any of our stock."

I wondered to myself if he would consider my dalliance with Brian to be truly heinous, but decided not to pursue the idea. In any case, I was happy to accept any praise he might lend me, even if it did flow from ignorance.

"So what is the horse's name?" I asked, moving a bit closer.

"Hal, for he is my other self, the spirit of a king in the king of beasts."

"Whatever happened to Merlin?"

"Merlin?!" he cried with a laugh. "Dead. Stone-dead! That must have happened ten years ago."

"Pity! I liked him. I remember Herbert would let me stroke his mane when you were at Westminster."

My father shoved two parsnips into the horse's mouth at once, and the animal seemed to inhale them. "Herbert: there's another name from the past, and just as dead as the horse! Indeed, it was on account of his profession that he died, for he fell while riding and broke his neck. That about did him in."

"Oh no! Did he have any family?"

My father looked off into the distance for a moment, as if deep in thought, then shrugged and returned to feeding the horse. "Never thought to ask. I cannot keep track of these things! I have a kingdom to maintain."

"Very right," I replied, though I was somewhat appalled that he had failed to note whether this man who had served him for years had anything else in his life. Perhaps the king did not believe there was such a thing as existence outside of his presence.

"Now, you must be wondering why I called you here," he stated, interrupting my thoughts.

I had done more than wonder. I had been afraid since the moment he called me over. I watched as he patted the horse's nose and then rubbed his hands on his cloak to remove any dirt. My stomach seemed to be forming a knot. Was he about to speak of some possible marriage?

"I have about given up on my queen," he said, "if indeed she is a queen, for she has failed in the only duty I ever bestowed upon her, and I could hardly blame someone for thinking that I had not even bedded her, for where is the proof? Yet I have bedded her every chance I have had—unceasingly, with vigor! But though she seemed fair to me at first, now I find her small and weak, as barren as a corpse. And how she cries when we are together! Such weeping, it puts me off my work! As if everything she has was not given to her from my hand! I tell you, daughter, I have begotten as many children as any man I know. I must have one in every county of England and Normandy, so let no man claim that I am impotent!"

The noise of this declaration was so great that even the resting horses were beginning to stir, the sound of their breathing and neighing adding to the tension of the moment.

"I truly doubt that anyone is claiming that," I replied, praying to God that I would not have to hear him discuss this part of his life any longer.

"Well, if he does, then let him rot, I say!" he declared, gesturing wildly with his hands. "Any woman would count herself blessed to receive my generosity. Except for Queen Adeliza. I have no hope of an annulment, so I must simply endure her. I place my trust in you, my daughter. Swear to me that your womb is fertile!"

What a demand! Even as he said it, he pointed his finger directly at me, the look on his face utterly serious, although the absurdity of his words made me want to laugh. But I dared not laugh at the king. Having little choice, I said the best thing that came to mind.

"As fertile as I can make it and as God intends."

"Hmm …" he muttered, placing his hands on his hips. "That is not much of an oath, but it will have to do. Now comes the matter of choosing a husband."

The dreaded moment had arrived. I held my breath, waiting for my doom to be announced. He began pacing in a small circle, hands clasped behind his back.

"I have received inquiries from every corner of Christendom. Never you mind who!" Here he shot me a glare as if I had said something particularly rebellious rather than standing there in silence. "Most are of little merit, but a few could prove beneficial. But I will not accept their word on its face—oh no! I have sent forth my ambassadors to seek out the truth of their claims." He ceased his pacing directly in front of me, placed his left hand firmly on my right shoulder, and said, "Rest easy, Maud! Soon enough, I'll have you wedded and bedded."

Perhaps it seems odd that a man would act in this manner—jesting one moment and blustering the next—but that was my father. He never did anything halfway. There was a recklessness to every aspect of him, which allowed him to speak freely and even absurdly while striking at his enemies in an equally free manner. I certainly did not want to become his enemy: I could endure crude talk, but his aggression would likely be my undoing. Thus, I attempted to arrive at a reply that would achieve what I desired without angering him.

"There is no need to rush," I said. "Such matters call for careful consideration, and you will surely wish to take counsel from all the lords of England as well as those here in Normandy."

"Yes, and we shall not return until Michaelmas. Therefore, have patience, my daughter!"

Good, that gives me a bit of time, I thought. My aim was to delay things as long as possible, for that would give me more days with Brian—at least, the few moments of those days that might be afforded us. I say it was my aim, but actually another had been forming in my mind: one that spoke to my very deepest desire. I had been too afraid to mention it before, nor even to acknowledge it fully to myself, but as the king turned his back to me and picked up the bucket to feed Hal again, I summoned as much courage as I could.

"I wonder, my lord, will you be considering men from our own kingdom?" I asked, taking great care not to betray any particular longing in my tone.

"Certainly not!" he cried, turning his head toward me even as the horse stuck its nose into the bucket. "What is to be gained from that? You were not born yesterday, so you know that the purpose of marriage is to create alliances with those who might do us good."

"Yes, of course, my king, but is it not also true that the greatest alliances and those of most lasting value are built upon shared aims and principles rather than the convenience of the moment?"

In desperation, I had actually hit upon a good line of argument. I could see it in my father's face: he looked slightly confounded, as if it was the first time he had ever heard good sense from a woman. Either that or he had no idea what I was referencing.

"What is this?" he sputtered. "Something they taught you in the empire?"

"It is merely my own observation, my king," I continued, attempting to remain as deferential as possible. "Consider that our great father, Rollo, was wed with a lady of France and gifted the duchy of Normandy in the hope that he would be faithful to Paris, but he was not content to remain a vassal and contended with his former ally on more than one occasion. Therefore, marriage alone does not preserve alliances if there is not that mutual desire that can sustain the union."

"I hardly think I need to be taught the rules of government! As I said, leave this matter with me, and I will see to it that we have an alliance that lasts." Having contented himself that his reason had prevailed over mine, he looked back down at the bucket, which by that point was empty. "Ah, I see there are no more parsnips for Hal. Bid one of the grooms bring me some, then make yourself ready for the tournament."

"As you wish, my lord."

As I left, I knew that unlike Saint George, I had not slain the dragon, but I hoped I had laid the seeds that might create a change of heart in my father.

"Give me the strength of Siegfried, and the cunning of Brünnhilda," I prayed.

For years I had treasured the amber moth that Brian gave me as a symbol of home, but in my twenty-fourth year of life, it took on a new meaning. It became a symbol of love: a pure affection that I had only ever received from the woman who bore me, and now I found in a man. How I craved that love! I felt I should become drunk of it and still not be full. When I saw myself through those eyes, I was bolder than ever before, and I believed I might take on the world and win—yes, even my father.

Perhaps it was this belief that caused me to hope as I had never dared hope. It might be possible, I thought, to devise an argument by which even the king would be forced to acknowledge that I should marry Brian and no other. This proves how my mind had grown dependent on him, for I had been willing to accept defeat a few months earlier, but now my desire for victory overwhelmed my senses, or at least my good sense.

The perfect argument came to me one day when I was in conversation with the king's physician, Grimbald, the same who was present at my birth. It was one night during supper in the great hall. I remember the moment well.

"I hear the king is considering many offers for your hand," he said.

"Yes, that is true, though he must work with the English nobles. They will want to have some say in the matter."

"Of course! They will seek to prevent foreign influence. Forgive me, my lady, but I am sure they will assume that whomever you marry will be the true ruler."

There it was: my hope of salvation. Grimbald had unwittingly provided me the perfect weapon for my dispute, for he was right that all men hate to be ruled by foreigners, and a female could never rule by her power alone, so a foreign husband would amount to a foreign ruler. Of course, I had more hope than the average person that a woman could rule: after all, I had served as regent for the emperor in Italy, and that had gone well enough. I at least had confidence that a woman could govern with the help of counselors until her son came of age, but the concerns of nobles surely had some merit, for any husband of a queen would attempt to do half or more of the ruling. As these concerns worked to my advantage at that moment in time, I saw every reason to embrace them. Indeed, I was made so glad by the good doctor's words, that I might have kissed him had I not possessed some sense of propriety.

The second bit of good fortune came when the entire court was taking part in the hunt. We had ridden about two hours east of Rouen into the forest of Lyons, but not quite as far as the king's lodge at Lyons-la-Forêt. This was the best hunting ground in that region of Normandy, with a wealth of small animals to chase and even the occasional stag. As the company made its way along the dirt path, which was less visible on account of the many leaves that had fallen upon it, I thought I saw a doe running off into the thicket.

"Oh, I saw one over there!" I declared, pulling on the reins to stop my horse and pointing to the right.

The king himself did not stop, but the king's lads all looked in the direction I had indicated. Robert Beaumont seemed to speak for them all. "I see nothing. Are you sure you're not imagining things?"

"I certainly am not," I replied. "I will not delay to debate the point. I must chase after it, even if you all refuse to come."

Drogo had been riding beside me. "I will come with you, my lady! You must not ride alone."

"I am beholden to you, Sir Drogo, but I need you to stay with the king," I said.

In truth, I had no good reason for him to do so, and I dearly hoped he would not press the matter further. The whole purpose of this ruse was to get me to my next question.

"If you insist," Drogo muttered, his eyes rather downcast.

Poor man! I had refused his services more than once of late for the same reason, and I began to suspect that it was having an ill effect on our friendship. Nevertheless, I did not feel I could tell him or anyone else about my secret affairs without great hazard. I would make sure he received some extra lampreys that evening.

"Is there no one else who is willing to break off from the company?" I called out.

Perhaps you can guess which knight was willing to leave the main party and follow me deep into the forest, far from curious eyes.

"Would you permit me to accompany you, my lady?" Brian asked. "I know this wood very well, having accompanied the king here many times. I will ensure that we return safely."

This answer was deemed satisfactory to all. The two of us left the main path and rode deeper into the forest, until we were far enough away not to fear being discovered. Brian led me to a grassy meadow, where the sun was not blocked by the tall beech trees. He set out his cloak on the ground and we lay down side by side, holding hands.

After we had remained there for several minutes with hardly a word passing between us, he asked, "How long do you suppose we have?"

"This is a stubborn deer. I think I had better stalk it for a while."

"Fine by me. Here, I picked these for you," he told me, holding out some pretty purple blooms he had kept hidden beneath the cloak.

"How lovely!" I said, clutching them in my free hand and smelling them. "Did you find these in the woods somewhere?"

"Sadly, no. I took them from the garden before we left."

I gasped in mock outrage and swatted him. "Thief! I ought to tell on you, only I should get myself in trouble as well."

"Very wise. Now, let me ask you this, though I hate to say anything that might take away from this moment. How long do you think we have ... ever?"

"What do you mean?"

"How long before the king finds you a husband?"

This was a most unpleasing line of inquiry. I could see the sadness in his eyes as he asked it.

"I hope never! But I am sure he will decide on someone in time," I answered quietly.

He turned his eyes toward the heavens and I did the same. The only sounds were the wind running through the grass and the distant songs of the birds.

"So where does that leave us?" he asked, after a moment had passed. "I mean, as far as anyone knows, there is no 'us.'"

"Oh, there is certainly an 'us'!"

"I doubt the king will see it that way, and I owe him everything. He is the closest thing to a father I've ever had, given that my own father forsook me."

I did not remember hearing Brian speak of his father before, and no wonder, for he hardly knew the man. I had not recognized that he was carrying around that pain. I touched his face and he closed his eyes, seeming to savor it. I then leaned in and rubbed my nose on his cheek gently.

"He did not forsake you," I said firmly, pulling back and looking into his eyes. "He sent you where he knew you would have the best chance."

"Well, he was right. The king has given me everything, though I am afraid that the one thing I want most is the one he would be most loath to part with."

He rubbed my hand with his own. I saw the sadness in his eyes again, even as his mouth formed into a smile.

"Brian …" I whispered.

"Maud?"

"I am not sure how to say this, so I will just say it." I took a deep breath, gathering my courage. "I wish to be your wife."

He did not respond at once, but raised my hand and kissed it. He then looked deeply into my eyes. "My love, you know that is not possible, as much as we might long for it."

I had anticipated this answer. However, I had devised a response that I thought would allow him to overcome his concerns, and I was eager to tell him about it.

"It may be possible. I thought of how it would work. You are the son of the former duke of Brittany. I am sure you could be given estates as great as most men who would pursue me. But more than that, the king knows you and trusts you."

"He may trust me less when he knows our secret."

"What have you done that is so ignoble?"

"Well, the lady of Wallingford would likely be unhappy if she knew what we've been up to, though that matter is not settled. The king has made his will known—"

"You never entered an agreement with her, Brian. Even the king cannot take a vow for you. We have no reason to feel ashamed!" I said quite firmly, for I was not about to be overcome by false guilt. "But here is the most essential point: the lords of England and Normandy do not want me to marry a foreigner who will strive to rule by himself. If I marry you, then they will be ruled by one of their own, and someone who is not a tyrant. I see many points in your favor!"

"You really are serious, aren't you?" he said, the look on his face one of concern more than anything.

"The king already used me once to make an alliance. He owes me this. So what do you think?"

He sighed deeply. "I think it will not work, and it will get me banished from court."

I was somewhat hurt that he was opposing me on this matter. I had thought that Brian of all people would support me in the pursuit of my desires, for they were our desires—at least, I thought they were. Instead, he seemed to be placing his own position at court ahead of any chance the two of us might have to be together.

"Oh, so that is all you care about, then?" I snapped, pulling my hand back from his.

"No! That is not what I meant."

"Honestly, Brian! Do you love me or not, because if you really care for me as much as you say, then I do not understand why you are unwilling to put up any kind of fight."

This answer was a bit too much to the point, but my frustration in the moment prevented me from seeing it.

"I have no concern for myself, but for you," he said, his voice growing louder along with mine. "What if he decides to deprive you of your rightful inheritance?"

This question stung. Would my father really do such a thing? Deny his own flesh and blood? I had to admit that he might, but what then? Might he send me into exile and give the crown to one of my cousins? What kind of life would I have then? Perhaps it might be worth it. Oh, but what kind of future would England have?! No, it was too awful to consider further. I would not allow myself to be drawn in to such thoughts.

"He can't do that!" I declared. "I am the only one descended from the line of Wessex."

"Except for your cousin, Lady Mathilda of Boulogne, who has just married Count Stephen, and we all know how fond the king is of Stephen."

I stood up, for I was getting quite upset. "Why will you not support me in this?"

"Because it is madness!" he replied, springing to his feet as well.

"Why?! Why is it madness?"

"For all the reasons we have discussed."

"But I know that you would be a better husband to me than any man who walks this earth!"

"And I know that you are the king's daughter—his only heir. You must marry someone high and mighty with whom you can give birth to a dynasty. I know this. Everyone knows this! I dare say, you know it too, though your generosity toward me makes you wish to deny it. But neither of us can change what we are. However much I might desire—no, it is best not to speak the words. It cannot be!"

A thousand thoughts were filling my mind, but it was my heart that called attention to itself. For weeks, we had existed in near perfect bliss, and all for the sole reason that we did not address the question of our future. Now that the issue had been raised and I had spoken my desire, I felt hurt that he was seemingly opposing me. I knew I would have difficulty in convincing my father, but I had assumed that Brian would be on my side, walking with me no matter where the road led. His claim to be serving my interests seemed rather hollow: indeed, it felt like cowardice. My interest was to be with him. I truly did not understand. What had he been playing at?

"Then what is the purpose of this?!" I cried. "To what end did you decide to woo me if not to have me for yourself?"

He sighed and shook his head. "I admit that I have been reckless. It is not my usual habit, but you have somehow bewitched me."

I found this argument very weak and let him know it. "Oh, so you kissed me because I placed a spell on you? What rubbish!"

"I kissed you," he said, putting his hands on my face, "because my entire being compelled me to do so. I could not deny you when I learned that you shared my love."

"And yet you would deny me this?" I asked, pushing his hands away.

I was beginning to cry again. I shed far too many tears in those days. He pulled me close to himself and rubbed my back slowly.

"Breathe, Maud," he said softly. "Perhaps you have good reason to be angry with me, but do not allow it to bring you low. A creature as lovely as you is meant to fly, and you will fly: I know you will."

The anger seemed to slowly diminish. My breath was coming more easily again. I stepped back and took each of his hands in one of mine. I rubbed each one with my thumbs, making a study of them with my eyes and then lifting those eyes to meet those of my love.

"Brian, I know the king. He has nothing but respect for you, his faithful servant. The succession is now of first importance. The king needs me to provide an heir, and in order to do so, I believe he will be more considerate of my wishes. You measure yourself far too harshly. When we return to England, I will make my address unto the king, and I will not rest until I have gained his consent. I simply need you to be with me, Brian. Will you fight for me?"

His eyes seemed to search my face, and then a smile formed on his lips. "I swear to you now, there is nothing I would not do to ensure your contentment and the peace of this kingdom."

"Thank you," I whispered. "I knew you would not fail me."

In the days just before Michaelmas in the year 1126, when the autumn leaves were just beginning to change their colors and the summer heat had left us behind, I saw something which I had thought I might never see again, a sight so dear to my heart that it brought a tear to my eye: the white cliffs of England. Sixteen years! That is how long it had been since I sat upon those cliffs with Drogo and cast my gaze in the opposite direction, pondering what the future might hold. Now they rose up to welcome me to my heart's content, for I was come to my true home and the place of my birth.

We were not to make port in Dover, but rather to sail up the Thames until we reached the city of London and its sister, Westminster, where we would finally drop anchor. That was not the most pleasant voyage, for we had with us two infamous traitors: Waleran Beaumont of Meulan and his fellow, Hugh the son of Gervase. Since their defeat at the hands of the king's men two years earlier, they had been rotting in the prison of Rouen, a just punishment for their treason. Now, the king saw fit to bring them to England, the better to keep them under his watch.

I remember well the day we set off. We had all made our way down to the pier at the southern gate of the castle of Rouen, where the king's fleet of ships were waiting for us to board. It was a rather chill morning, so I was bundled up in my best fur cloak. The servants had almost finished moving a vast number of possessions from the palace down to the boats. I moved this way and that to avoid men carrying tables or leading horses. I had made it through the south gate and was about to board the king's ship when I heard a voice calling, "Halt! Everyone make way!"

Along with the servants, knights, and nobles who were standing nearby, I moved back to clear a path between the gate and the boats. I saw the warder walking in front of a gang of four prisoners all chained together. They had come from the dungeon that was attached to the north wall of the castle, a place where I had not set foot once during my time there, for I was far more interested in other endeavors, and in any case, noble ladies are not frequent visitors to dungeons. Now I saw the four men with my own eyes. They wore fine clothing, but it was so filthy and tattered that it gave no appearance of nobility. Their heads had all been shorn, either to keep out the lice or to shame them.

"Behold, traitors of the king's majesty!" the warder cried. "Look upon them and beware!"

Several of those standing by hurled abuse and even spat at them as the guards worked to load them on to one of the ships for transport to other prisons in England. As they were passing, one of the men gazed directly at me. The look on his face was so stern, I was convinced that he loathed me. It sent a shiver through my bones.

When they had all been placed within the hold of their ship and the warder was making his way back up the slope toward the gate, I approached him and gained his attention.

"Tell me, who was the last of the prisoners: the one with the light hair wearing the green cloak?" I asked.

"That was Waleran of Meulan, my lady," he replied. "He is being brought back to England to answer for his treasons."

"What will happen to him? Is he to be put to death?"

The warder took a deep breath as if bracing himself to say something of great import.

"He is subject to the king's justice now, whatever that may be," he replied firmly.

His words made me feel uneasy. I had a sudden vision of axes dropping and bones cracking.

As the warder made to leave again, I touched his arm and asked him the question I most feared.

"Please tell me, sir, is there any particular reason why this man should hate me?"

"That I know not," he answered, "but the men under my watch are not what you might call gentle souls."

This conversation was on my mind as we set off down the River Seine. I felt the icy stare of Waleran burned into my mind. It made me ill to be joined by traitors on our voyage, although I do not think it would have disturbed me half as much had those eyes not pierced into my soul and left a mark.

For all their betrayals, Waleran and Hugh would hardly be the most well-known prisoners kept in an English castle. That honor—if you can call it that—was held by my uncle Robert, eldest son of the Conqueror. Since his defeat at Tinchebray in 1106, he had spent twenty years at Devises, chief castle of Bishop Roger of Salisbury. There he must have had ample time to consider the height from which he had fallen, even as his son William Clito was a continual thorn in the side of us all.

Though I never met my uncle, I had it on good authority that he was as poor of a general as he was a ruler. His attempted invasion of England after my father came to the throne was swiftly put down, for even the common people would not approve of his disloyalty. It was only a few years before he lost Normandy as well, leaving his son to carry the banner while he lived out his days in prison. I might have pitied him were he not such a fiend.

Despite his defeat on the field of battle and long imprisonment, Duke Robert's cause was not altogether dead, hence the rebellion of Waleran of Meulan. And as long as William Clito lived and breathed, and the French king had cause to support him, King Henry could not rest easy in his rule of Normandy. Thus were the two traitors brought to England to fulfill those words I often hear: "It is best to keep your enemies where you can see them."

We sailed two days from Honfleur to Ramsgate, where we gathered fresh provisions. We then made a further stop in Gravesend at the mouth of the Thames before moving along the sacred way to Westminster. I remained in the same boat as my father, but as a measure of caution introduced following the tragedy of the *White Ship,* the rest of the king's lads and members of the nobility were divided between the ships to ensure that if one sunk, it would not take all of England down with it. Thus, the only three persons I could truly converse with on our ship were my father, his chancellor Geoffrey, and the physician Grimbald. Drogo was there too, but he was often occupied with duties. Needless to say, I spent much of the time reading.

However, on that final day, the king called me over to himself and spoke with me at great length, telling of all the changes England had undergone. Most of it was of little interest to myself, concerning matters legal and ecclesiastical that were unlikely to affect me. Even so, I was impressed to see the degree of concern he showed for every corner of his kingdom, which naturally led me to wonder why he showed not a bit of concern for some of those closest to him. But that is a king, I suppose.

"Look, Mathilda!" he said to me, as we were standing upon the bow. "The great Tower of London! See how we have made improvements to the walls?"

I looked to the northern bank of the river, where the high walls of the fortress begun by my grandfather stood watch over the city. They did appear more fearful than I had remembered, with further layers of stone added here and there.

"Yes, it is even grander than I remembered, but I see they are still hard at work on Saint Paul's Cathedral," I said, looking farther to the west at where the tower of the church was still being finished. "I think they were repairing that roof when I left."

"Less money, less speed," he concluded.

We were coming very close to the heart of the city, and I suddenly smelled an odor that I had not experienced since the days of my youth: filth and rubbish flowing into the river, the stinking rot of fish laying out in the sun, and pigs being slaughtered.

"Oh my!" I said. "It still smells just the same."

He placed his hands on his hips and breathed in deeply, seeming to bask in the odor. "What of it? That is the smell of good business."

"It smells like dung," I countered, placing my hands over my nose and mouth.

"Yes, the manure that makes our kingdom grow!"

"That is not what I meant."

"You had best improve your opinion of our chief city!" he said, shooting an evil glare at me.

"I like the city well enough. Just not all the rotting fish."

"Never fear! We are making the turn, and then we will come to Westminster. Your dainty nose will be spared."

"Thank God for that," I muttered.

Within minutes, we reached the pier of Westminster, and there as he had always been was the second most powerful man in the kingdom: Bishop Roger of Salisbury, grown more gray and wrinkled but still as well clothed as ever. His gold crucifix caught a sun ray and threatened to blind me. The bishop stood right next to the pier, with a host of other officials gathered behind him. Above, the palace of Westminster stood gleaming in the midday sun.

"Home," I whispered.

The king was first to set foot on land. "Bishop Roger!" he cried. "How has England been in our absence?"

"As fair as ever, and even fairer now that you have returned!" he shouted, smiling quite eagerly. Indeed, I thought it was almost too eager.

"Excellent, excellent!" the king replied, embracing the much shorter man with a firm pat on the back.

I had followed the king on to land and was standing just behind him. After the two men exchanged a few words I could not make out, my father stepped to the side and Bishop Roger looked at me, recognition appearing on his face.

"But this must be your daughter!" he said, stepping toward me and bowing low. "I should not have recognized her but for the marks of royalty she carries. Tell me, fair empress, how do you find our island?"

"Much the same as when I left, only it seems sweeter to me now, for I have missed it so!"

"Well spoken!" he replied. "I thought you might like to stay in the same room where you resided as a child. It is not quite the same, for it has been new furnished, but you will find it somewhat familiar."

"You mean the room I shared with William?"

"Yes," he said with a nod. "That is not a problem, is it?"

A flood of memories entered my mind. I saw my brother and me playing together, teasing one another, or simply ignoring each other in those rooms. I felt a surge of joy at the thought of it, followed directly by a pang of loneliness, for I knew I would never again have a full sibling on earth. I was not about to reveal these personal thoughts to the bishop.

"No, I am sure it will be fine," I replied simply.

"Right," the king said. "Now, while the others are still arriving, there is a matter we must attend to, Roger. I have brought over the traitors Hugh and Waleran."

"Do you wish them to be kept at Devises?" he asked, referring to his own castle.

"No, three traitors under one roof would be two too many. I will send Waleran up to Bridgnorth and keep the other at Windsor."

"Quite right, Your Highness."

There was a slight pause in which the king looked at the ground and laughed slightly: not a hearty laugh, but a forced one, as if he wasn't sure what to do with his thoughts. I could guess the reason easily enough. My uncle, the king's brother, was kept at Devises. Given that they had gone to war with one another, there was little in the way of filial affection left, if any. My father had shut his brother up where he need never see him again. He had left him to rot, and yet they were still brothers, and he could not change that.

"How is the former duke these days?" the king finally asked Bishop Roger.

"Your brother?"

"The former duke—he is no brother of mine," my father replied with some conviction.

"He is as well as any man could be after spending two decades in a cell. He is well fed and does not complain as much as he did in the early days. He knows his fate is sealed. Why?" he asked, turning his head slightly. "Do you have some reason to worry?"

"No, that man could never concern me!" my father declared. Then he said a bit more softly, "I do wonder though if we shouldn't transfer him to some place more remote."

There it was: the fear of rebellion. More than anything else, King Henry wished to safeguard his dynasty. He was desperate for control over the future. Any man who stood in the way, whether William Clito or Waleran of Meulan, would feel the king's wrath.

"Where, my lord?" the bishop asked.

Here I decided to force my way into the conversation, as I had been excluded for some time. "You could send him to Wales with Earl Robert," I offered. "That is most remote."

"A fair point," the king said.

Oh my. He actually approved of something I had to say, I thought. *I must treasure this moment, for it may be a long time until it comes again.*

My suggestion did not seem to please Bishop Roger. The look on his face was suddenly one of deep concern. "But, my lord, have I not kept him in security all these years?" he asked, leaning forward to beseech, almost as one begging for his life. "There is no fortress stronger than Devises. You have no need to fear."

The king appeared to consider the matter for a moment, then reached a conclusion. "I know what I shall do. I will discuss it with my brother when he comes."

"I thought you just forbade us to call him that," I said.

"No, I mean the king of Scotland, your mother's brother."

"King David?!" I asked, feeling a sudden excitement at the mention of my beloved uncle. "Do you mean to say that he is coming here? Oh, I would love to see him!"

"Yes, he will be here just after Michaelmas. It has all been arranged."

"Will he be staying at court for some time?" the bishop asked.

"Possibly as much as a year," the king replied.

This revelation was a bit of very good news. As a young girl, I treasured my uncle's visits. He had always taken a great interest in William and me, and since the death of my uncle Alexander, he was the final living link with my late mother. He had liked me far better than my own father did, though it remained to be seen whether the passage of years had changed that.

"I can't believe I will see Uncle David again—that is, King David! I don't mind saying that I have always favored him more than all my uncles," I said.

The king laughed. "Yes, but that is not saying much, given that your other living uncle does not even warrant the name, being a traitor to this house."

My father had made a good point, but he was not about to lessen my joy at this news. I had intended to speak with the king about Brian soon after our arrival, but chose to wait until after our royal visitor had come. If there was anyone who, by the strength of his person, could lend credence to my case, it would be King David. Therefore, I waited for the opportune moment.

CHAPTER TEN

The isle of Westminster, formerly Thorney Isle, is by no means large. It can hold the palace of Westminster with its great hall, the abbey church and grounds, and a few roads of shops and taverns. From all else it is cut off by water, and it is therefore a world unto itself, despite being so close to the city of London.

In that time, the palace included the hall built by my uncle, King William II, and three levels of rooms closer to the river. The kitchens and cellar were on the lowest level, the official rooms just above that, and the private chambers at the very summit. As always, it was of greatest import for the king's palace to send the message that he was on top. From the second and third levels, one could enter the great hall on the ground level or the upper walk, a great convenience in my childhood when I had wished to secretly gaze down at the revelers. The first level was further down the slope—very near the water's edge. Here goods could be received at the pier and brought directly into the storerooms.

In addition to the main building, there were several wood structures nearby for the keeping of animals, weapons and armor, and the like. But the main business on the island often occurred in the yards. The new yard lay to the north of the palace, very near where the carts came in from London, having traveled down the Strand. The old yard stood between the palace and the abbey, and this is where visitors were typically received.

It was in this outer yard that we gathered three weeks later to welcome the king of Scotland, his queen, and their son Henry, the latter named for the king to whom David owed his advancement: my own father. I had longed for this moment ever since I heard of my uncle's coming. It had been a difficult period for me, for though I loved being back in the place of my childhood, I had been granted few opportunities to speak with Brian. Even as I readied myself to address the king with my supplication, I felt distant from the man for whom I was doing it all. In the months since I returned to the Norman court, my thoughts of having children and becoming queen had not disappeared, but rather had become combined with my desire to marry Brian fitz Count. I felt that I no longer had those dreams for myself alone, but for both of us. Mad dreams, yes, but what dreams aren't a bit mad?

These thoughts filled my mind as the company from the North arrived to the sound of trumpets. My father and I stood in front of the others, who formed something like a line. Queen Adeliza was not with us, having declared yet again that she was ill.

We watched as the first riders came into view. The court of Scotland was not as large as that of England, but its composition was much the same, for my uncle had surrounded himself with men from the South, as I plainly saw upon their arrival. Only a few rustics accompanied them, most of lower rank. The rest were dressed as Norman nobles, even wearing their hair the same way.

At the front, riding upon a great black steed, was my uncle in all his splendor. The Scottish king looked just as I had remembered him, apart from the new crown on his head and the lines of care upon his face. Surely you have noticed how kings tend to show their age faster than the rest of us, and King David of Scotland was not immune, as I plainly saw when he drew near and alighted from his horse. Yet I could tell that his spirit had lost none of its vigor as he spun around to help his queen. Next was young Henry, who in truth was not so young, for he refused his father's aid and stepped down of his own accord.

"Hail, King David of Scotland!" my father called out.

"And all hail, King Henry of England!" he replied, not bowing but dipping his head slightly. "And all hail, Empress Maud, if it is indeed you: I cannot call you my 'wee niece' any more, I see."

I did not hesitate to walk up and embrace him, nor did I hesitate to call his speech into question.

"I hope you are not implying that I have grown fat, Uncle," I said.

He laughed heartily. "No, only tall and graceful, just like your late mother, may she rest in peace."

How apt that he should speak these words, for I had just been thinking of how much he resembled the late queen himself. His hair was not so red, but his eyes were just as green, and there was a great likeness in their features.

"Let me see my name twin then," King Henry said, commanding the attention of all. "Henry, how you have grown! I see you are a man now and not a boy." Here he pushed his first two fingers into the young man's chest, as if to test his strength. "How many years have you on this earth?"

"Twelve, lord uncle," he answered, beaming with pride.

"Twelve—that is a good age. Indeed, you are not unlike my William when he was that age. He was a fine knight, and you shall be too, provided you receive the proper training up north."

"We are not so distant," King David said. "Were you to visit, you would find a great many improvements, I dare say. Scotland is coming into the new age. I make sure of it."

"Lovely to see you, Queen Mathilda," my father said, taking her hand and raising it with a bow of the head. "Why, here is a Mathilda, there a Mathilda—everywhere a Mathilda!"

"That is because it is the best name: don't you agree, Queen Mathilda?" I asked.

"Yes, naturally," she answered. "I am honored to share it with you."

"Earl Robert! How are you?" King David called.

I turned to see my brother had walked up from the line behind us. He stepped forward and embraced the Scottish king.

"Very well," he replied. "I have my own son with me."

Here he beckoned for my nephew to come forward. The boy had been held back by cousin Stephen, who now pushed him toward his father. When young William had made his way to us, his father commanded, "William, greet your uncle the king."

"Good day, Your Highness," the boy said rather meekly.

"And good day to you, young William!" said King David. "You look to be a few years younger than your cousin Henry, but I am sure the two of you will make good friends."

"Here you will find the rest," my father said.

We all turned and made our way to the line, where the other nobles and officials were standing. The king began introducing them one by one.

"We have Count Stephen, son of my sister, and Bishop Roger, who hardly needs introduction. And there is Brian fitz

Count and Robert Beaumont, and my chancellor, Geoffrey, and the butler William …"

On he continued down the line, with the Scottish king stopping to shake each hand as the roll was called. I stood back a bit with Queen Mathilda and took the opportunity to seek out her conversation.

"So how was your journey?" I asked. "Not too long, I hope."

"It was most miraculous, actually. It did not rain once."

"Really? That is fortunate."

"Yes, when you consider that we might have received a deluge this time of year."

Here she looked up toward the sky as if she thought the rain would fall at any moment.

"It sounds as if you intend to stay here a while," I said hopefully.

She nodded. "As long as we can. Things are more stable in the North than they were in the early days. We have had some trouble from the false king—Máel Coluim mac Alaxandair—and King David has been working to bring all the lands under his control, but we have reason to hope."

Although my uncle had officially been king of Scotland for some time, he had faced some difficulties from this false claim to his throne. Naturally, I supported King David entirely.

"I am glad to hear it," I said. "You are always welcome at court."

"Thank you, that means a great deal. But tell me, where is Queen Adeliza? She is not still in Normandy, is she?"

I dropped my voice slightly. "No, she came, but she has been unwell ever since. Indeed, I have not seen her for the past week, not that we talk much anyway."

There was some pain in my heart as I uttered these words, for I feared that I had offended Queen Adeliza greatly by bringing up the subject of her injury. I was only thinking to help her—to discover the truth. However, she seemed to view me as more hurtful than helpful.

"Such a shame!" the Scottish queen commented earnestly. "I would dearly like to meet her."

"Perhaps she will join us tonight."

"Empress Mathilda!" Drogo called.

I looked to my right and saw him approaching.

"Yes, Sir Drogo, what is it?" I inquired.

"The king ... that is, the kings are going inside now."

I had been so caught up in my conversation with the queen that I had not noticed this change.

"Ah, we had best join them," I replied. "It is so good to see you, Queen Mathilda!"

"Likewise, Empress Mathilda!" she said with a smile.

We then moved into that greatest of halls, the pride and joy of Westminster Palace. How many times in my early days had I longed to take part in the feasts the king would hold every evening? The wood beams that held up the ceiling had been painted with red and blue designs since I last saw them, and banners with the king's emblem were hung from the upper walk. Other than that, it was little changed from the hall of my youth. However, instead of being consigned to the private chambers that were out of sight, I was seated in the place of honor next to the two kings and their queens. When we had finished the meal, the men left us females sitting at the table while they attended to their games. That put me in conversation with Queen Adeliza, Queen Mathilda, and the countess of Surrey, Elizabeth Vermandois.

Now, Lady Elizabeth was one of the most prominent women at court, being not only a descendant of French kings, but also the widow of the second earl of Leicester. By him she was mother to the Beaumont twins—the traitor Waleran and the rather forgettable Robert—and a few other children, including a daughter who was once my father's mistress. The countess had since been wed a second time to William de Warenne, count of Surrey, and given birth to five more children, for a total of more than a dozen, only one of whom had committed treason to date. She was so fruitful that I felt as if she was mocking me.

Some said her second marriage was too impetuous, coming as it did right after the death of the old earl, and this in turn gave rise to rumors that she may have had good reason to marry in haste, for her son William was born rather soon. What the good lady did in her spare time was truly none of my business, and I did not find it half as repugnant as her compulsion to chatter on and on about this and that, to the point of inducing slumber in the hearer. Thus, when I saw my chance to break away, I seized it and left the two queens to their sad fate.

I walked toward the far end of the hall, where several of the men were crowded around a small table at which Stephen and Brian were playing at checks.

"Well met, sister!" brother Robert said, placing his arm around me. "Come to join the men, then?"

"You all left me over there alone," I complained.

"You were not alone! You were with the queens and, oh—"

Here he caught sight of the queens Mathilda and Adeliza still locked in conversation with Countess Elizabeth, looking very much as if they hoped an invading army would save them.

"Yes—oh!" I said.

"Sorry about that."

"It only took me about ten minutes to get out of it this time. That might be a record. The queens were not much help. They're far too polite. So who is winning?" I asked, looking back at the two men bent over the table.

"Brian can usually beat him, but I think Stephen is doing better this time," he said, even as the crowd cheered the seizure of Brian's rook from the board.

"Why aren't you playing?" I asked, turning my head toward my brother.

"I was, but I lost to Stephen in the first round."

"Oh—pity."

"Ah, that's my girl!" he said, embracing me again.

"Come, Brian! We don't have all night for me to beat you!" Stephen mocked.

Brian did not respond but continued to study the board. We had hardly spoken since arriving in England, and a part of me hoped he would lose so I could invent some reason for us to talk. Then again, I would certainly enjoy watching him beat my cousin.

"Sir Brian!" I called. "Move your knight to threaten the queen."

"Cheaters!" Stephen protested, looking at each of us in turn even though Brian had not asked for my help.

"Fine, you can seek my advice on your next turn," I replied.

"I don't need advice, especially from a woman!" he said, returning his gaze to the board. His tone was one of mockery, but I sensed there was something real to it. He looked rather angry.

"That's where you're wrong, friend," Brian said, moving his knight as I proposed. "Your move."

Stephen took little time to consider, moving his queen to seize Brian's knight.

"There: that is what you get for listening to a woman," he said, leaning back and taking a drink from his goblet.

Brian simply looked at me and smiled. He moved his own queen to the side, struck his palm on the edge of the table, and declared, "Checkmate!"

Stephen was so taken by surprise that he actually coughed up some of the wine he was drinking. His eyes darted from one side of the board to the other, desperately seeking anything that would belie Brian's words, but there was nothing to be done. There before him, plain as day, was the sad tale of his defeat.

"Lay down your king, cousin!" Robert cried.

Stephen continued to stare at the board for a moment longer, searching for something Brian might have missed. At last, he did lay down his king and stood up. "You have bested me today, Sir Brian, but do not think to receive such charity tomorrow!" Here he pointed at him fiercely as if slicing the air, the better to make his point.

"I am sure it was merely the good fortune of the moment," Brian offered, standing up himself. "Now, who is next?"

"Why not the two kings?" I asked.

This seemed to draw the support of the crowd, and a representative was sent to retrieve the two rulers. After stopping to talk to six or seven more people, they finally sat down and began to arrange the board for play.

"Now, King David, you know that as my vassal, it is your duty to let me win," King Henry said, as he arranged his pawns.

"Vassal?" King David replied. "What is this you speak of?"

"Why, that I made you into what you are today! No man would deny it."

"I think you will find that it was my sister who made you into what you are," the Scottish king contended, placing the last of his pieces. "And that was only because she rejected both your brother and Count William here," he added, pointing to William de Warenne.

I looked at the count's face and noticed that it was rather more red than normal.

"You aren't still sore about that, William?" King Henry asked, not even turning to look at the man as he addressed him.

"No, of course not, my lord," he answered faithfully. "I could never compare myself with you."

"Right you are. Very well, let's begin!" my father declared. "Your move, brother."

King David moved a pawn forward and King Henry did the same. Back and forth they moved in quick succession, taking little time to consider.

"I meant to ask your advice about something, brother," my father said.

"Does it have to be now?" my uncle asked, moving one of his bishops.

"Yes, or how else shall I distract you from the game? As you know, I have the traitor Robert Curthose in custody."

"What else is new?" King David replied.

"I am considering sending him off to Cardiff Castle."

"That is one of yours, Robert?" David asked, looking at my brother.

"Yes," Earl Robert replied.

"And what does the lord of Salisbury think of that?" my uncle inquired, looking over at Bishop Roger, who was speaking in the opposite corner with the bishop of London.

"He is my man. He will think whatever I wish him to think," King Henry said with conviction.

"Well, it would move the traitor farther away, but is that really something you want to take on, Robert?" the Scottish king asked.

"I am perfectly content," brother Robert replied.

"Then I see no problem," said King David.

"It's settled then! Robert, you will return home by way of Devises and transfer the prisoner to Cardiff," King Henry announced. "Now, where were we? Ah yes! Check, brother."

About this time, I looked over and saw that Brian was standing alone by the far wall, so I walked over to him. I offered him a smile, which he returned.

"You have been rather distant," I whispered. "Is something wrong?"

"Not at all. The king has me looking over his accounts."

"His accounts?"

"Yes, he wishes your brother and me to do a full audit of the royal treasury in the New Year."

"That is excellent news!" I said. "He treats you as if you were his own son."

Of course, I very much wanted to see Brian rise as high as possible in the king's opinion, for that could only aid my efforts to gain him as my husband. However, my excitement did not seem to be shared by my love. He let out a sigh, and there was a frown on his face.

"Take care, Empress Maud," he warned, guessing my thoughts. "You know the king intends me to marry Mathilda D'Oyly—very soon, I think."

It was then my turn to frown. Dropping my voice, I beseeched him. "Brian, you must delay as long as you can until I have a chance to speak with him."

"I don't think you should," he told me, a sadness in his eyes.

I could not understand why he was opposing me yet again. Did he not want the same thing that I wanted? I was afraid—yes, afraid of what it might mean.

"But it is not your decision whether to address the king, is it?" I asked, becoming quite passionate. "It is mine! Do not worry: I will just tell him that I prefer you, not that you have been pursuing me in any way. That way, you remain innocent if he denies my request. There is no need for you to speak with him at all."

He sighed, then moved a few inches closer to me and spoke even more softly. "I am afraid for you, my love. Very afraid. What you are suggesting—the consequences for you could be …" His voice trailed off and he seemed to shudder. "Is there nothing I could say that might make you—"

"Change my mind? Only that you do not love me. Is that the case?"

He paused for a moment. I suddenly feared that I had erred in judgment. I had assumed the answer to my question would be obvious, but maybe things had changed, at least from his point of view. Had he stopped loving me? The idea was simply too terrible. My heart began to race. Thankfully, he put me out of my misery.

"No, I could never say that. Forgive me, the situation is difficult. The king is a severe man, and I would hate myself if anything bad happened to you."

"Happened to us," I said.

I wanted so badly to take his hands in that moment—to make him see that I was strong—but there were far too many people who might see it.

"We are in this together, Brian," I told him. "Perhaps you are afraid—so am I. But we must not let that fear keep us apart! Please, I have been longing for you! I have never known love like this. It is something I must do. I will never forgive myself if I do not try."

"Very well, then," he concluded. "I am with you."

The following week, the king's lads all dispersed on their own errands, and my moment arrived. The king called me into his throne room to speak with him alone. This was on the second level, near the other official chambers. How nervous I was! As I descended the stairs, my heart seemed to pound like a drum, my palms were sweaty, and each breath came hard and fast. Yet my mind was fully committed, and as I approached the great double doors there was nothing on earth that could have prevented me from taking my stand.

Those heavy wood doors, bound to the stone with iron, were little different than the iron will I was about to face. I had but one small hope—one thing that caused me to hazard it all: he was my father, and as such, I prayed that within his soul there was some tiny speck of paternal devotion to which I could appeal. I had never quite seen it before, but I chose to believe it was there—that even if he was a severe and violent man, he would not seek to destroy one who was flesh of his flesh.

God in heaven, hear me now, I prayed. *The desires of my heart, I present to you. I place myself in your hands. Lord Jesus and all the saints, look upon me as a frail child, or as David before Goliath. Grant me courage. Make me strong for the fight. Reach down and touch the heart of my father. Turn the stone to flesh.*

I took one last deep breath and knocked on the right door with the ring of iron that hung there. From inside, I heard my father's deep voice say, "Admit her." The doors then swung open before me, pulled by guards I could not see. Before me was the long wood floor, and at the end of it the king upon his throne, which was set upon a platform covered in red carpet. To the right, a pair of windows provided a view of the river. To the left were tapestries of the great Battle at Hastings, where my grandfather William had triumphed over Harold Godwinson and won dominion over the English.

"Come forward," the king instructed.

As I crossed the room, I continued to look at the tapestries. There was William the Conqueror on his great white horse, his spear planted in the helmet of an Englishman. His companions followed him in the charge, cutting down their enemies, who lay bleeding upon the ground. The second tapestry showed the defeated captains kneeling before the triumphant William, their hands held aloft, some even clasped, all begging for mercy.

I had made it about halfway to the dais. The king sat with his hands gripping the arms of the chair, his head bearing the royal crown: a circlet of gold adorned with jewels of every color. To his right stood the chancellor, Geoffrey, whom I barely knew on account of having only met him a few weeks earlier. A clerk sat off to the side, ready to record anything of importance. The only other persons in the room were the two guards who had admitted me.

I bowed lower than was strictly necessary, allowing one of my knees to touch the floor, in the hope that this would increase the king's regard for me. Rising again, I addressed him.

"Lord king, gracious father—you summoned me."

"Come hither," he said, beckoning with his hand. The look on his face betrayed none of his thoughts.

I moved a few steps closer. "And how may I be of service, Your Highness?"

He stared at me for a moment, as if deep in thought, fingering the end of his beard with his hands. "I suppose there's no sense delaying it. You know, daughter, that in the interest of ensuring the succession—that is, of preserving this house, the house that was built by your grandfather, King William—you must be wed again to a worthy lord. It was for this reason that I called you back to our kingdom rather than allowing you to take the veil."

"Yes, my king," I said, my heart beating even harder.

"And you are ready to enter into wedlock once again, having observed the days of mourning and then some."

I nodded. "Yes."

"Excellent. It will then please you to know that I have entered into discussions with the count of Anjou—"

"Anjou?" I asked in surprise.

"Yes, that's it—the better to make our alliance against—"

"King Henry, I beg you, wait a moment," I interrupted, hoping to prevent him from continuing along that line. "Give leave for me to speak."

The king let out a great sigh, as if I had ruined a speech he had been making ready for some time. He bit his lower lip slightly, grinding his fist into his knee. "Very well, then. Let's have it."

I took a deep breath in and out, striving to calm myself. I sensed that the words I was about to speak might alter the course of my life. In my mind, I sent a final prayer to the Virgin, then I spoke.

"Gracious king, I know that you are a great ruler, always bestowing goodness upon your subjects, and on none so much as I. You are truly most excellent, most esteemed. I know that in all things you seek my advancement and that of England."

"Even so, but get to the point."

"That I shall."

Having sufficiently flattered him, I had to stop for a moment to summon the courage for what I intended to say next. Only when he raised his right brow to signal his annoyance did I continue.

"My lord, I know you seek for me the best alliance possible, with a man who is fit to be my husband. It therefore pleases me to tell you that I have formed a most decided attachment to a man of noble standing and one whom I know you hold in the highest regard: Brian fitz Count."

"Pray, continue no further," he commanded, raising his hand.

"But—" I sputtered.

"I said, continue no further! Men, leave us!"

They did as they were told, departing the room one by one, until at last it was only my father and I in the room. I feared this change, but tried to calm myself and hope for the best. King Henry rose from his chair and began to walk down the steps in my direction. The sound of his feet hitting the wood boards seemed to beat against the silence. I clasped my hands in front of me, pressing them together. He took his stand about two paces in front of me.

"Mathilda …"

"Yes, father," I replied quickly, hoping to call to his mind the bond we shared by blood.

"I have no doubt that these men—the king's lads, as I hear them called—being most gallant and accomplished, and showing due fealty to the House of Normandy, have made themselves quite worthy of your regard. But take care that you do not speak unwisely. You must know that I have already chosen a match for you."

"With the boy from Anjou?!"

The very thought of it offended me. Not only did I know him to be far inferior to me in age, such as to make any union between us almost obscene, but he was equally inferior to me in rank—nay, more so! And he belonged to the hated enemy of England!

The king took my objection in his stride and attempted to counter it. "Count Geoffrey of Anjou, as he shall be when his father makes for Jerusalem. He is reported to be a handsome youth, which should please you."

How little my father knew me that he thought such a consideration would be at the fore of my mind!

"But I declare to you now that I wish to be wed to Brian fitz Count!" I answered him, shaking my head and pressing my hands so tightly together that it must have left a mark. "You speak to me of young Geoffrey's standing, but he is the mere son of a count and not fit to wed an empress! Brian is the natural son of the duke of Brittany, and you have raised him to your right hand, treating him as your own son and crowning him with honor. After all I have already accomplished by marriage for the sake of this kingdom, and for all the love you bear me, I beg you: do not force me to bind myself with this foreigner who is so far beneath me! Do not allow the blood of England to be thus sullied!"

The king had advanced very close to my person, hands clenched behind his back. I could mark the signs of strain in his features. He was gritting his teeth. I had pushed him to the point of frustration.

"You speak as one with knowledge, but I have far more," he said to me, his tone the same as one might take with a young and very disobedient child. "Allow me to inform you, daughter, about the one you claim to adore. He was wed two days hence to Mathilda D'Oyly near the lady's home, with her family present. With this marriage, he has attained the Honor of Wallingford. Now what say you to that, you who know so much? Everything here has taken place according to my will. So what have you to say?"

I was utterly stung by these words: so much so that I could barely process them. Brian was married?! He was married without telling me?! I was about to despair when I recognized that my father might have conjured a ruse merely for effect.

"I say that you hope to play me for a fool, and through these lies to compel my submission—nay, my humiliation! As I live, I will not suffer it!" I cried.

"Foolish girl! Do you take me for a common jester?" he asked, his face red with anger. "I assure you, they are joined even now in the bonds of matrimony! I have my witnesses to prove it. The papers are signed—the deed is done. They are joined before God. Did you really think that a man of noble standing would defy his king in this manner? I spoke with your beloved Brian, and he declared that while he had no wish to deny you the respect you are due by rank, he had grown weary of these attentions and believed that such behavior was not merited. He loves you but as a brother and repented of anything he might have said that led you to believe otherwise. This, my daughter, is the end of the matter, and you must accept it."

"Accept it?! I can scarce believe it! When did he speak with you?" I cried, clinging to the hope that it was a lie.

"The day before he left, when you and the ladies were detained. He informed me of his concerns, and I bid him wed his betrothed forthwith. This he did without delay, and now you have the proof of it."

With the addition of so much detail, I began to suspect that he was telling the truth, and it grieved me deeply. Indeed, I felt as if a knife had been plunged into my frame. I had foreseen that he might refuse, but I had never foreseen this. In that moment, I felt anger such as I had never felt before in my life. Something fierce was rising up inside of me, and it aimed to counter each of his verbal blows with one of my own.

"If what you say is true—though I struggle to accept it, so loathsome is this news to my ears—then I must conclude that you have used me quite ill, for I suspect you knew of my regard for him, and fearing that your own designs would come to ruin, you purchased his submission with villainous threats!" I said, almost spitting out the words.

"I have used you ill?!" He stopped to laugh: a savage sound that made me cringe. "No, look you to your beloved, for it is he who used you ill! It would seem he has all the constancy of a cat in heat! And who could blame him? Did you really think he would sacrifice his fortune on your behalf? Your face is barely pleasant enough to tempt a toad! Your value to men is in your dowry: nothing more. Without that, no man would pursue you."

The news that I had lost Brian was terrible, and the announcement that the king would marry me to the Angevine imp equally terrible, but these words cut to the core of my being and confirmed the deepest fears I had always held about myself: that I was loathsome and unworthy of love. I truly believe that if I had been pierced with a knife, it would have hurt less, but having lost both the man I loved and the love of my father, I was determined to fight for the one thing I had left: my future marriage.

"No, I cannot accept it!" I cried.

"Oh, but you must, dear daughter," he answered, his seemingly kind words belied by the evil glint in his eyes. "Dearest, dearest Maud. You are to be wed into Anjou, and there will be no debate on this point, for I declare there is not a royal woman from the queen of Sheba down to the present day who would stand where you are now and hurl such abuse at her king. As God is my witness, you shall learn obedience!"

"If obedience means joining myself to someone so inferior in every way, then the Lord condemn me if I should obey!"

I had hardly spoken these words, when he grabbed on to my garment and pulled me so close that I could feel his breath upon my face. There was a fury in his eyes, and though I was determined to endure it, he was unwilling to allow me the luxury of rebellion.

"You do not struggle against me, but against the Lord Almighty. How dare you speak to me in such a manner! What has possessed you?" He let up his grip and turned to walk back to his throne. "You will marry him, I say!" he yelled.

Without stopping to think, I moved as if by instinct to my knees and raised my hands into the air. I was pleading to both my earthly father and my father in heaven.

"No, no, no! I will not marry the boy count! That is my word, and I shall not be moved."

He turned again to face me. For a second, I felt as if my very life was perched upon the brink, ready to fall one way or the other: freedom or enslavement, heaven or hell, England or Anjou. Then came the judgment.

"If you will not move," he said, "then I will move you."

He came toward me at once, raised me up with his strong arms, and struck me so hard across the face that I fell to the ground, my weight crashing into the wood boards. There was a taste of blood in my mouth and all about me seemed to spin, but I was determined to return to my feet. No sooner had I risen, than he struck me again in the same manner. I caught myself this time with my hands and looked back up at the figure who seemed now a beast rather than a man.

"Get up!" he bellowed, spit flying from his mouth. "I command you: get up!"

I rose slowly this time, using one arm to guard my face. I started to say something, but before the words left my mouth, he struck me thrice and pushed me over. I was unable to catch myself, and my whole body met the floor again. My mouth was by this point filled with blood, and I could not see for all the tears.

Then something possessed me. In my head, all I could hear were the words of Drogo: "Left, left, right! Left, left, right!" The pain in my heart and my body was so great that it had nearly overwhelmed my anger. Even so, I stood one final time. I hardly knew what I was doing. I was acting on instinct.

The next thing I knew was that my fist had struck my father's chest. There was such a look of surprise in his eyes! I had not hurt him in the slightest, but nevertheless, we had both seen what happened. With a fury I had never known before, and which I dearly hope never to witness again, he grabbed me around the neck, choking me. He then moved one hand down and grabbed me between my thighs.

"I own you!" he yelled at me, his spit flying on to my face.

He then thrust me to the ground and kicked me again and again. I had no more strength to fight back. I was simply waiting to die ... but I did not die, as much as I might have wished to do so.

After waiting to ensure that I would not challenge him further, the king finally said, "Let that be a lesson to you! You will be wed to Count Geoffrey if I have to latch that tongue to a horse's arse and drag you bleeding all the way there! Would that God had denied you the power of speech, such trouble has it brought me. Your mother would be filled with shame to see you now."

As he departed, I was just able to raise my head and utter one last reply. "Do not suppose that I will ever forgive you."

He did not stop to listen to the words, but left me there upon the floor.

CHAPTER ELEVEN

"How did this happen?" Grimbald asked me.
Yes, that was the proper question for the hour. How did I allow myself to be so blind? How were my affections able to rule me? How could I have believed those empty promises, I who had ever trusted in the practical?

But that is not what Grimbald meant: he simply wished to know how I came by the scrapes on my hands, the bruises on my arms, and the red marks on my face. He wanted to know why I was too sore to leave my bed. It was not necessary for him to hear the details of what had taken place a few hours earlier. He was a physician, after all, not a confessor.

"I tripped on the stairs, just out there," I lied. "I fell headlong."

"Was no one with you?" he asked. "I thought you did not walk alone."

"I was in haste. I admit it was foolish," I replied softly.

Grimbald seemed to accept this explanation and continued with his work. I was sitting on the edge of my bed in my private chamber, and he knelt before me on the ground, a bowl of water and some cloths sitting on the floor beside him, along with a leather pouch containing tools of his trade, a flask of wine, and a small wood chest filled with herbs, bottles of this and that, and a few other objects I could not see. He poured some wine over each of the cuts, the sting of which might have made a bee envious. Once he was satisfied that he had caused a sufficient amount of pain, he dabbed at the wounds with a cloth and then pulled back to survey his work.

"You should not need stitching," he said.

There, at least, was a small blessing, for the few stitched wounds I had ever seen looked truly monstrous. He cleansed each spot again with water, then wrapped the worst one. Next, he opened the lower drawer of the chest and pulled out another object.

"Here is a *pultes* you can hold against the bruises. It may help," he added, with less certainty than one might prefer from a physician.

I simply nodded, and he began wrapping it to my arm. As he did so, my eyes wandered without aim across the stone walls of the room until they came to one of the two windows. The sun was sinking low in the sky, and the auburn rays were drifting through the panes of glass, creating a pattern on the wood floor. It seemed that the sun was giving up on the day even as I was giving up on everything. The pain in my heart was so great and my despair so extreme that I had utterly lost my sense of purpose. I had no idea what I would live for or why I was living, beyond serving as a pawn in my father's game. Oh, my father! Merely thinking of him filled me with terror, and I had no wish to call him father.

There was a knock at the door on the far side of the room, and Grimbald spun around. "Who goes there?" he called out.

The door opened, and I was rather stunned to see Queen Adeliza standing there with a most serious look on her face.

The physician stood and bowed. I was about to stand as well, but she requested, "Please, stay where you are. What is this, Grimbald?"

"I am just tending to Empress Mathilda's wounds," he replied. "She fell down the stairs."

She raised her brows. "Is that so?"

"Yes, and she has some rather nasty bruises."

I could sense that the queen did not accept the story she had been given, but she did not intend to reveal this to Grimbald.

"Good doctor, pray, let me speak with your patient," she requested with a nod toward myself.

"Of course, if she wishes it."

He looked at me, and I nodded my head in affirmation.

"Very well. I shall depart," he said, moving to collect all his things. When he had gathered everything but the flask, he held it out to me. "I will leave this wine with you. Pour some on that cut once per hour and have one of your ladies change the binding. It will prevent infection."

"Thank you, Grimbald," I said, and just like that, he was gone.

Queen Adeliza stood in front of the closed door, simply staring at me. I did not move from my place, but simply returned her gaze. She seemed to make a study of me with her eyes as I rubbed my left shoulder, attempting to ease the pain.

"May I sit beside you, empress?" the queen finally asked.

Once again, I simply nodded, and she took her seat beside me, just to my left. There was another moment of silence. She placed her right hand on my knee and patted it gently.

"I think you and I both know that you did not fall down the stairs," she began.

"You're one to talk!" I replied. "Hiding away from us all day and night."

"So the king has made liars of us both then," she stated.

I looked down at my lap, uncertain of what to say.

"Tell me, why did he strike you?" she asked quietly.

"Queen Adeliza, perhaps you mistake my manner," I told her, looking her in the eye once again. "I have no wish to discuss this further."

"Then you give him what he wants! Do you not see that? He depends upon our silence!"

I admit that in my state of despair, I took offense at this. She seemed to accuse me of being complicit in my father's actions, but if that was true—which I would not own—then she was even more complicit, having remained silent for God only knew how long. Her words angered me, but my spirit did not have the strength to truly push back against them.

"What goes on between you and the king is your own affair," I said. "As for me, it hardly matters what I say: there is nothing that can be done."

"So this is about Sir Brian then?"

"The king told you?" I asked, truly surprised.

"There was no need for him to tell me. News of the marriage is spread throughout the court."

I turned my face in the opposite direction so as not to reveal how much this distressed me. Queen Adeliza was not my enemy, but I had so little trust in humanity at that moment that I did not want to let anyone see how deeply I was hurting.

"I see," I replied. "Well, now my folly is made clear to me. Why does everyone else see what I cannot?"

"Why? Did you speak to the king about him?"

"Yes, because that is the kind of fool I am! I went right in there, said my peace, and I have been harshly punished for my candor. Did you know he wants me to marry the boy from Anjou?" I asked, turning my face back toward her.

"That would be Count Fulk's son?"

"The very one."

She pulled back her head slightly and had a look of judgment upon her face. "Isn't he barely of age?"

"Yes."

"And very far beneath you …"

"Yes! What is more, the lords of England will hate him. It will cast doubt on the succession."

She nodded in agreement. "So you refused to consider him?"

"Yes, though I think now I may as well submit my neck to the yoke."

"You must do nothing of the sort!" she said with some real passion. She placed her hand firmly on my shoulder. "Trust me, for I have also borne your father's wrath. He must not win! Fight him, Mathilda! Fight to the death!"

"That is exactly the kind of thinking that bought me this black eye."

My breath was coming in harsh bursts. I could feel the tears forming again in my eyes.

"I thought he was going to kill me," I whispered more than said. "I knew he never loved me as he did William, but such hate was in his eyes. With every blow he struck, I felt my will for life ebbing away. I felt everything just gone."

Another moment of silence passed in which my tears grew heavy and fell. I thought the queen might reach out to comfort me, but to my surprise, she did not. Indeed, she almost seemed to berate me.

"So that is all, then?" she asked. "You are giving up?"

I laughed. "There is no giving up about it. There is no choice of any kind on my part. I have been beaten in more ways than one, and I think I may be seeing reason for the first time in months."

Now she did grab my arm, causing me no little pain as I had a large bruise there. With a shake of her head, she beseeched me.

"Please, Empress Mathilda! I told you, I know people, and this spirit of defeat is not like you. You may be deeply hurt by what has taken place, and you are longing to give in, but you must not! You owe it to your descendants."

My descendants who did not even exist were the least of my worries at that particular moment. How did she know I would have any, and why did she think their lives could be any better than mine?

"Perhaps what I owe them is a world at peace, which might be achieved by marrying with Anjou," I concluded.

"But you just said that the lords of England will not accept him as your husband."

"Maybe—maybe not. Only time will tell. Honestly, if I cannot marry the person I desire, then it hardly matters whom the king chooses. They may all be equally bad, so there's nothing for it. If I reject this Geoffrey, then tomorrow it will be another, and all the while I stir up the king's wrath against me."

"No!" she said firmly, the creases in her brow increasing along with her determination. "Anything is better than Anjou!"

"He could send me off to the Rus—the ends of the earth. That would be worse."

"You may have a point there," she admitted.

We sat in silence for a moment, and by the sound of her breathing, I gathered that Adeliza was growing calmer. My head still throbbed with the pain. I reached up and held it, but this did little to help.

"Queen Adeliza," I said, "it occurs to me that virtually every misery in this world is brought about by men. I wonder if we should just remove them from the face of the earth?"

"That would be the ending of humanity."

"Yes, but imagine what content we women would experience during those final years before we turned things over to the beasts!"

"Hmm, that is probably true." Her tone now grew merry and her eyes sparkled. "So how shall we go about our work then? Dagger, bow, or cannon?"

I considered for a moment. "Dagger. I want to see them bleed and hear them squeal."

"Oh, but we cannot!" she objected. "For then we would have no bishops or knights…or lawyers!"

"And that would be a bad thing?"

"See, you have your old spirit back already!" she said with glee, wrapping me in an embrace.

"Well, it is not a death, but it is still an end. I shall not recover from this for some time."

"That is as it should be after your heart has been sorely wounded."

"But I don't understand: what made him do it?"

"He wanted to remove anyone who might tempt you from the Anjou boy: anyone he felt was unworthy."

"No, not the king—Brian!" I had hit now upon one of the sorest points in my soul, and it filled me with passion. "I swear to you, we were soul companions! At least, I thought we were. Now I wonder if I ever knew him at all. Was he lying every time he declared his love for me?"

"I wish I had an answer for you, but perhaps all will be made clear in time. I should mention: he is to come to court with his new wife."

"What?!" I cried, breaking out of her embrace and standing to my feet.

"Do you wish to speak with him?" she asked, far more calmly than I thought the situation warranted.

"Certainly not! I do not even want to see his face."

Here I turned my back to her, crossed my arms, and let out a powerful sigh of frustration. I stared out the window, but my mind was completely elsewhere. I could not bear to see him—ever! And yet, I would plainly have to sooner or later. How awful. How utterly, utterly awful.

"Very well, then," said Adeliza. I heard her stand and her footsteps near me. "I will do what I can to make that possible. But you know you will have to see him at some point."

"Perhaps at some point, but not today," I stated with my back still turned to her. "I am in no fit state for company, let alone for that."

"I should let you rest," she said, patting my knee in a kindly manner. "You know, when I am sad, I go to the one place that might bring me solace. Whatever that place is for you, go there, and perhaps you will be made whole again."

"But I have no such place," I whispered.

"I suspect you do," she concluded. She then departed the room, leaving me at last as I was meant to be: alone.

I walked back over to where the flask Grimbald had left me was sitting on the floor. I bent down and picked it up, then took a smell. It must have been the poorest of the king's wine.

"*Extremis malis ... extrema remedia*," I sighed, and drank my fill.

I gave some thought to the queen's words and determined that there was one place I should go, though I did not know if it would grant me the succor I required. I arose early in the morning, while those in the hall still slept, and made the short walk across the yard to the abbey, still quite sore from head to toe.

Now, I have seen many churches in my day, but this one is of special worth because it preserves the work of my uncle four generations earlier, King Edward the Confessor. When the Normans came to England, they improved most of the major structures, but they let this one be, for it was the best of the old English way. Its tower rises up to catch the morning sun, and its wood roof is a thing of beauty, with the spine flanked on either end by carvings that draw the eye and have just a touch of the Northmen about them. It is not as large as the great cathedrals, but it does not need to be.

I entered the abbey church upon that morn not to pray at the tomb of King Edward, as so many are apt to do, nor to behold the relics of Saint John. This was to be a time of personal reflection.

"Good morrow, Empress Mathilda!" said Abbot Herbert, when I arrived at the door. "Right this way."

I had made sure to come when the monks would not be at their prayers, just between *Prime* and *Terce*. Therefore, the church was rather quiet when I entered. The high vault and stone arches gave off no sound, and had my eyes been closed, I might have believed I had entered a crypt. How appropriate that seemed, given that I had come to visit the dead.

The abbot led me down the nave and halted before the altar to show me what I had come to see.

"Here is the final resting place of the late Queen Mathilda. You may find it less grand than she deserved."

This was certainly true, for the grave was quite simple. However, had she been granted the grandest shrine in Christendom, my dear mother still would have been cheated.

"No, if I knew her, she would have preferred simplicity," I offered.

"Yes, that was the case, though I am sure the people of this kingdom might have given their last penny to see her properly honored."

"Perhaps that bestows more honor than the work of any mason."

"Of course, you are right," he said, bowing his head in deference. "Is there anything else you require?"

"No, thank you."

"Then I shall leave you to your thoughts."

There was a dangerous proposition! Leave me to my thoughts? It was those thoughts that threatened to pull me into the abyss. Indeed, that was why I had come. I looked at the grave: a simple crypt crowned with black marble and no adornments. She really did deserve more. I had come with a great sense of purpose, but in that moment, I knew not what to say.

I knelt down and ran my fingers over the carving at the base: "*REGINA MATHILDE ANGLORUM DOMINAE DILECTISSIMAE SERVUS DEI.*" Could such words contain an entire life?

"I am here, mother. I have come," I whispered.

I had never heard the tale of the queen's final hours, and in truth I had no wish to find out, for I feared that they must have been lonely. Had she suffered? Was there much pain? Yes, it was better not to know. My late observations of my father's behavior led me to doubt that he would have shown her great devotion. After all, he never had in earlier years. I could not help feeling that I ought to have been there, and I would have been, were it not for the king's edict that sent me hence. I wanted to believe she had been at peace at the end. I wanted to believe it, but I struggled to do so.

I leaned over the tomb and spoke to her in a whisper.

"Mother, I know you cannot hear me. Well, perhaps you can. The scholars disagree. In any case, I need to speak with you whether you can hear me or not. I need my mother."

My voice seemed to catch in my throat, holding back the words. I breathed deeply and continued.

"You always used to tell me that it was only in Christ that we are made content, but I wonder, were you ever content? How many women has the king had? You watched them all come and go. After he had moved heaven and earth to win you! What must that have done to you? I wonder. I came here because I had nowhere else to go. I did everything you said.

I was brave. I performed my duty. I spoke the truth, even at great cost—incredible, unbearable cost! And what am I now? Abandoned. Ashamed."

I was still bent over the tomb, clutching at the edge, much as I had seen my first husband do at the tomb of his own father. Was he searching then for the same thing I now craved? I closed my eyes and allowed the pain to wash over me in waves. Never in my life had I felt so much anger: at the king, at Brian, at myself, at the world. But I had come for a reason, and I would fulfill it. I opened my eyes, took another deep breath, and continued.

"Never mind that. The choice now lies before me, so what must I do? Should I go to Anjou? Is that my path? Tell me, for the future of our kingdom depends on it! Can you give me some sign? Cause a bird to sing, cause the wind to blow? Anything would do, really."

I stopped for a moment to see if my request might be granted. Alas, there was nothing but silence.

"Ah, the sound of silence! So pleasing to the ear! Sweeter than any other I hear, except for now. So you will be silent then. I suppose I must try to think of what you would have said, were you here. What would you have done?"

I looked up at the altar screen, on which the coronation of the Virgin was painted. Something in her face made me think of my mother. They did not have the same auburn hair, but the eyes were equally kind. As I no longer had the face of my mother to address, I delivered my next words to the Virgin, as if they were one and the same. Somehow, looking into those eyes, I sensed the answer.

"You would have tried to reason with the king—nay, to bargain with him. Very well, that is what I will try to do, though I fear to even enter his presence. I might be sick for fear of it, but I must overcome my fear. If that is the wrong choice, then remember that I gave you a chance to oppose me!"

I stayed there for another moment, looking back down at the grave. There is no rush when one converses with the dead, for they have naught else to do. Such an odd discussion, but I felt it had done me some good.

"Do you remember, mother? Do you remember the first hymn you taught me? 'Now we must honor the guardian of heaven, the might of the architect and his purpose …' But I cannot see his purpose! I may not know the will of the creator, but this much I do know: I love you now and always. You were the best of us, and that is how I will always remember you. Be with me now, for there is hard work needs doing, and I may well break before the end."

As I stood there praying, a memory entered my mind. It was not clear: indeed, I could not place it in time. Perhaps it had never happened at all or was merely the product of my soul's desire. My mother and I were seated on a bench in a rose garden—I had no idea where. She was holding me and rocking back and forth, singing softly in her native tongue. I felt so safe, so whole.

"Remember, Maud," she whispered. "I love you. You are my treasure. Remember. I love you. I always will."

With that the memory seemed to fade, and I was still looking down at the dark stone. The tears were falling from my eyes and hitting it one by one.

"Come back!" I cried from the deepest part of my soul. "Come back!"

But there was no answer. There was nothing.

About an hour later, I walked out near the stables in the new yard, where I found Drogo bent over a wood block playing at dice with one of his fellows. He was evidently doing well, for he had a broad smile on his face and pumped his fist in the air.

"Sir Drogo!" I called, when I was within a few steps.

He looked up from his game and the other knight, whose name I forget—perhaps Gerard or Bernard—turned his head. Both stood and removed their felt caps, offering greetings of, "Good day, Your Highness," and so forth.

"Yes, very good," I replied. "I will only be needing Sir Drogo, but thank you."

The other knight then returned his gaze to the dice, as if hoping to discover a way to bend them to his will, while Drogo and I met about five yards hence.

"How have you been feeling, my lady?" my knight asked, bending down slightly to get a better view of my face. "I have not seen you since I heard of your fall. I have been most distraught. I had it in mind to come visit your chamber, but Queen Adeliza met me in the passage and said you needed to rest."

"I thank you for your concern, but I am feeling much better. I shall take better care in the future to lift the hem of my gown so I do not trip over it."

"How did you get such a bruise by your eye though? I do not understand," he continued, examining me with wide eyes as if I were one of a band of jesters, with teeth pushing out of my mouth or ears hanging down to my knees.

I wanted very much to avoid the subject of my wounds, so I said the first thing I could think of to distract him.

"As long as we are on the subject of appearance, you're going bald, you know."

"What?!" he stammered, standing up straight and pressing his cap back on to his head. "You cannot even see the top of my head!"

"When you are down on the lower level in the great hall and I am up above, I have noticed that there is rather less hair there than in former days," I replied, goading him. "You have been keeping it longer to hide the fact, but women notice these things."

His cheeks were turning red. "Well, I do not see why you have to mention it! I may look like a lumbering giant, but I have a heart. Why did you call me over here in any case? To laugh at me?"

"No, I wish you to accompany me to a meeting with the king."

"Oh?" he replied, the look of annoyance on his face fading quickly.

"Yes, indeed. So if you feel like doing your duty today, by all means accompany me, but if you wish to stand out here and complain, suit yourself."

This ended the conversation, and I could tell by his manner that Drogo had not been too deeply hurt by my words, despite his protest to the contrary. At the very least, he had not gone as far as Elisha and called down the bears on me. His vanity was not my chief concern at that moment, for I had decided I must speak with my father, and the thought filled me with great anxiety. I hoped that in bringing along another observer—one who I knew would protect me against all threats—I would avoid any repeat of the great evil that had occurred the day before. Had it only been one day? It seemed like a lifetime of pain.

We entered through the north door of the great hall, and I approached Chancellor Geoffrey to request an audience with the king.

"He is out on the green shooting," he replied. "Do you wish me to take you to him?"

There was an odd question. Yes, I knew he must take me to the king. Indeed, I had requested it, but the last thing on earth I wanted was to see my father again. The mere thought of it made me feel the need to vomit, but I attempted to work up something like courage.

"Yes, and I should like to bring along my knight, Drogo," I answered, pointing to him.

The three of us made our way down the stairs and out to the gardens by the river bank, where targets had been set up for the knights to practice on a stretch of grass. Of course, we had no true archers upon Westminster isle, and it was unlikely that the king should use such a weapon for anything but the hunt. Even so, the noblest persons often find joy in common pursuits.

I saw that the king was thankfully not alone—he was joined by the earl of Surrey, William de Warenne. This did not keep me from shuddering at the sight of my father. I think Drogo must have noticed that I looked less than well, for he whispered, "Are you all right, my lady?"

I nodded quickly, and he said no more, though I noticed that he took a step closer to me, perhaps sensing something was amiss, though he knew not what.

On a table next to the two shooters lay bows of every description, both short and long, and even two crossbows. The king was taking his turn to shoot. He pulled back the string and let the arrow fly. It hit near the edge of the target.

"This confounded wind!" he cried, throwing the bow down in anger and breaking it. "It makes a mess of my aim. Damn it!"

"My shot, sire?" the earl asked.

"Yes, have at it," he replied, waving off a servant and stooping to recover the weapon himself.

The earl was using a longer bow, and it took some real strength to control the string, or so I surmised from the way he seemed to strain and his hand shook slightly. His arrow hit very near the center.

"See, the wind was less there," the king concluded.

"My lord King Henry!" the chancellor called.

The king turned to see the three of us standing there. Another chill of fear passed through me as our eyes met.

"Whatever this is, it can wait until we've finished," he replied. "I think I'll swap, William. Do you mind?"

"Of course not," he said.

My father walked over to the table and set down his weapon, exchanging it for a crossbow. He examined it carefully, testing the lever and the string. I gazed out at the river, where ships passed by heading toward the distant sea. How I wished I could step on to one of them and never be seen again!

"This should do it," the king declared, interrupting my thoughts.

He then took up his position and let the arrow fly. It was a better shot, but still not as good as the earl's. I thought I heard my father curse under his breath. They each took a few more shots, until the target was sufficiently covered. I was beginning to wonder if he would ever stop to talk to me.

"Retrieve the king's arrows!" the earl called to the servants, and they did so accordingly.

"You may have bested me that time, but I'm just getting started," the king said to his friend. "How about another round? Let me win my honor back?"

"The honor would be all mine, but I should hate to make the empress wait any longer," the earl replied meekly, looking in my direction.

The king did not seem pleased. He let out a sigh so loud that it was almost a groan. Having registered his annoyance, he turned to me. "What is it, then? I see you have chosen to gift us with your presence again."

I felt a knot in my stomach and the chill remained in my bones, but I was able to reply.

"Yes, my king, I wished to speak with you regarding what we discussed last week."

"I did not think there was a discussion to be had," he began, but after seeing the perplexed looks on the other men's faces, he tempered his words. "Very well then. Men, you had best be off."

"Actually, I would like Drogo to stay with me, if you would permit it," I said, fearing my father's wrath.

The king and I both looked at the knight, who was standing at attention but seemed to have a fire in his eyes as if to say, "Do as she requests." Perhaps I only imagined that he intended this, but either the look in the knight's eyes or his immense size caused the king to reply, "Oh, fine! Take a walk with me."

The three of us—the king, Drogo, and I—then set off along the river, with the knight walking slightly behind us. The king was still wearing the golden bracers that he always used for shooting, and it gave him a rather more martial appearance than I might have preferred for that conversation. I could feel the tension inside me merely from being so near him, even as one might feel upon the edge of a cliff. Silently, I prayed to God and the saints to help me speak.

"So what is it?" he asked. "I see you are somewhat recovered from your fall. I was sorry to hear of it."

The conceit of these words was most extreme, for both he and I were entirely aware of why I had remained in my room. He was evidently attempting to make a show of being a proper man. I had no desire to play along with him, so I simply moved past it.

"Lord king, I wanted to say how very sorry I am for any act of defiance. You took me by surprise, and I was not certain how to act. It seems that I chose poorly."

"I'll say!" he scoffed.

In truth, my choice of actions was only poor because of how I was treated and not because I committed any moral wrong. No, I was entirely in the right. Yet, if I was to have any chance of averting the Angevin marriage I detested, I needed to somehow reclaim the king's good favor. And if I was to do that, I needed to allow him to feel superior, even if it meant apologizing when I alone was righteous.

"I hope that you can find it in your heart to forgive me, because I truly desire the benefit of this kingdom and your rule," I continued. "You are, after all, not only my king but my father, and I respect you on both accounts." My insides seemed to protest against these words, for I no longer respected him on either count. "Please know that you have my loyalty."

"I pardon you," he said, making the sign of the cross in the air. "Now get to the point."

There was the first hurdle cleared, no doubt with the aid of some guilt on his part, but another awaited. I worked up my courage once again.

"I have given much thought to your demand that I marry the count of Anjou's son," I said. "In many ways, it makes sense. Indeed, I can see why you should favor it. And I would not balk at any match that might help to ensure the future of this house. However, my concern arises because some of the lords might object to the idea of an Angevin ruler."

"Yes, that was Robert's concern."

"You spoke of this with Earl Robert?" I asked, somewhat surprised.

"Just yesterday, yes."

"And he was opposed to the idea?"

"He had some reservations."

"I see," I said, hoping to disguise my pleasure at this revelation. If my brother was with me, then perhaps I had a fighting chance after all, for he had the king's love.

"Yes, you ought to erect a monument in his honor for the good service he has done you, for after speaking with him, I am less certain of how to proceed. Don't be too happy!" he commanded, perhaps having seen a hint of a smile on my face. "I still favor Anjou, but I think it best that we have all the lords and magnates swear to you first. Let them pledge their fealty to our line. Then we will decide how to act."

I was a bit surprised to hear that despite how he had treated me just a few days earlier, my father still intended to make me his heir. I had not thought it safe to assume that this would be the case. While I was still quite afraid of my father, I allowed this news to grant me just a bit of boldness: enough to ask another question.

"But my lord, if they are to pledge loyalty to me in the case of your demise, might they not demand to have some say in whom I wed? I have no children at the present, and it is those descendants to whom they will make their pledge as much as to myself."

"Yes, I thought of that, but if you are betrothed now and then they take the oath, after which point the marriage falls through, then they will claim that they are no longer duty bound. Worse yet, they may reject the oath entirely. Therefore, we must make the case for your person—let them be faithful to you alone. And if any refuse, we shall know how to deal with them."

"So they would pledge fealty to me? But I am—"

"A woman? Yes, but you are still the true heir, and in your sons the throne will be vested. These are extraordinary times, and you know what they say: *extremis malis extrema remedia*. Of course, I will require sons from you. Should you fail in that, all our efforts come to nothing."

At this point, my heart was somewhat torn. On the one hand, I was pleased that my father was willing to have the lords of the kingdom swear to me, his daughter. On the other, I knew that this decision was not on account of any perceived merit in myself. Rather, he was placing his hope in a son that I may or may not have—one who would be an altogether more proper human being. His opinion of me had not changed, but merely his perception of my utility. He had declared his true belief when he said that he owned me, and he believed that I would surely acknowledge that at some point. It was a grim situation, and one in which I took no pleasure. I was still reeling, uncertain of my purpose. The one thing of which I was sure was that I had no interest in marrying the Angevine imp. I therefore continued to play his game in the hope that I might one day be free.

"Thank you, my lord, for the faith you have placed in me," I said, with all the gentility I could muster.

"You might consider yourself fortunate if you end up in Anjou," he replied. "They say this Geoffrey is the fairest youth man ever did see."

"Who says that?" I asked, still amazed that he would think I only cared about appearance and not character.

"I don't know. This kind of thing gets around."

"How old is he, my lord?" I asked, afraid to know the answer.

"What does it matter how old he is?"

"I am simply curious."

"Twelve? Thirteen? Old enough to do the deed, I should think."

"Ah …" I said, but inside I was screaming.

Twelve years of age? He was a boy, not a man! How could I be bound to such a person: I who had seen far more of life than was usually fit into two dozen years? I had been an empress! Indeed, I still bore that title. The idea of being joined for ever to someone who was in no way my equal was truly dreadful. Not that many people believed that even the greatest woman was equal to a man, but the very laws of nature seemed to testify that Geoffrey of Anjou was my inferior. What was I to do? I kept my anger to myself yet again, hoping that by appearing docile I might escape that awful future.

We had made our way back to the green, where the earl of Surrey had continued his game with the chancellor.

"Get your hands off my bow!" my father bellowed, and with that he left us.

"Come, Drogo," I said. "Let's head back."

We started to make our way back up the hill toward the palace, and I was relieved to at least be out of my father's presence.

"Thirteen?" Drogo asked, when we were far enough away to not be heard. "At that age, he would be lucky to even find … well, you know."

"Watch yourself, Drogo," I said, glaring at him.

"Are you sure nothing is wrong?" he asked, his features growing soft. "That is, nothing besides your father's plot to marry you to that child?"

"You are sweet, Drogo," I said, touching him on the arm. "What would I do without you?" With that, the conversation dropped.

As we approached the entrance, I allowed myself to feel a very small sense of accomplishment, although the greater part of me still despaired. I had been sorely afraid to return to the company of the man who treated me like an ant to be crushed. I was forced to suppress my own sense of justice in order to speak with him in such a manner. Even so, I had passed the test, and thanks to the apparent intervention of my brother, there was a chance that I might at least be spared the very worst outcome.

We climbed the main stair on to the second level and entered the great hall. I had almost forgotten my troubles, when I saw Brian fitz Count standing there in the middle of the vast room, plain as day, with his new wife, both of them surrounded by members of court.

"Oh, Drogo! Let's go back the way we came!" I whispered.

Fortunately, he did not ask why, but simply turned on the spot along with me. Perhaps he really did guess more than I let on to him. We had almost made it back to the double doors that led into the newer part of the palace, when brother Robert burst through them. Both Drogo and I instantly halted to avoid colliding with him.

"There you are!" Robert said, a smile on his face. "I heard about your fall. Are you on the mend now?"

"I've felt better," I answered, desperately hoping to avoid a long conversation.

"Look! Sir Brian is here with the lady of Wallingford, and I am sure you want to meet her," my brother declared.

How wrong you are! I thought, but there was nothing that could be done. He had already grabbed my arm and pulled me toward a conversation I wished desperately to avoid. For the life of me, I could not think of an excuse that would free me from what was about to take place. *Lord, give me strength, and keep me from slaughtering someone!* I prayed.

"Lady Mathilda," Robert called out, "here is my sister, the Empress Mathilda!"

As she turned, I received my first good look at the lady of Wallingford's face. To my eternal dismay, she was far more comely than myself. Nevertheless, I chose to look at her rather than Brian, who was standing just to the side.

"How wonderful!" the lady said. "Empress Mathilda, I have heard nothing but your praises since I arrived here. How magnificent that you are back at court again!"

"Yes, most magnificent," I replied.

Actually, it was anything but magnificent. It was hell—pure hell. I strove to look into her beaming eyes, even as I longed to cast my gaze on the man who had rejected me. Or did I? I could not decide. I feared seeing him, and yet I struggled to look away.

"Your father, the king—he is so good to us," she continued, oblivious to the misery she was causing. "I never thought to have a husband who is so caring, so honorable—"

"Well, that's the king," I agreed, hoping to put an end to it. But no, she would continue.

"You know, he has given us such a position of honor here at court. I never would have dreamed!" she said, clinging to her new husband's arm. "You must feel fortunate to have a father who is not only royal by birth, but also royal in spirit."

"Indeed, there are few people with such fortune as I," I said, with no little irony.

"Perhaps we should let the empress be about her business. She must have many things to attend to," Brian said.

That led me to look at him directly for the first time. To my surprise, his beard was completely gone. Was this something his new wife had demanded? It made him seem almost alien to me. He was wearing blue again. That had been my favorite color, but now he was wearing it for someone else. Maybe he had never really worn it for me at all. I looked into his eyes and hoped to see some sign of remorse—something that would explain the tumult of the past week—but I saw nothing. He simply stared back at me blankly.

I pulled my eyes away from him and looked back at the lady of Wallingford, her fair skin so perfect, her lovely golden locks peeking out, her blue eyes radiant. *What a bitch*, I thought. *What an utterly perfect bitch.*

"It is good to have you both at court," I concluded quickly, then turned to leave.

I walked past the others, ignoring some poor lord who was seeking to gain my attention. I sought only the double doors that would safeguard me from my pain. Not waiting for Drogo, I opened them and stepped through, rushing into the passage to the right, where no one else was standing. I leaned back against the wall and rubbed my left side, which was still in pain from all the times I had been kicked—or perhaps the pain was inside me. I knew not. I was simply praising God that I had survived without saying something truly worthy of regret, when Robert walked through the doors to my left.

"Maud! Where are you?" he called.

For just a moment, I remained silent, hoping I would not be visible. However, he quickly saw me, and I was forced to say something.

"Honestly, what now?" I replied, a bit lacking in courtesy.

"I know that was awkward, but it was necessary," he said, walking toward me.

"What are you talking about?"

"When you saw Brian just now."

"Why would that be awkward for me?" I asked, suddenly afraid of what he might have discovered and repeated to everyone at court.

"Forgive me, but I saw something once or twice that implied a bit more than friendship between you."

So Robert apparently knew as well. Did everyone know of my shame? I made one last attempt to avoid it.

"Honestly, brother, you are imagining things—"

"I saw you kissing!"

There was little point in denying at that point, but I had a question. "Fine, there was something between us. If you knew that to be the case, then why did you have to be so cruel?!"

"Because you will have to be around him day and night, and the sooner you get this first pain behind you, the better. That is why you have been hiding, no?"

I had not guessed that my brother gave so much thought to my situation, not because I thought him a man without compassion, but because I had not imagined he knew of it.

"Robert, is this why you advised the king against Geoffrey of Anjou?" I asked.

"No, I honestly think him a bad choice, but it helped, didn't it?"

Surprising even myself, I smiled. "Yes, I must admit that it did."

"You are my sister," he said, grasping my shoulders lightly and then patting the sides of my face. "I actually do want what is best for you."

"And I for you," I said, "but is that the same as what is best for the kingdom?"

"One question too many," he concluded with a wag of his finger.

"Very well," I said with a nod. "I thank you for your efforts on my behalf. Nevertheless, I must beg you, brother, do not speak of this to anyone! What's done is done. There is no point in repeating what ought to remain in the past."

"You have my solemn oath: not a word!" he assured me.

Then he surprised me yet again: he reached out and embraced me for a good minute. Again, I had not doubted that Robert cared for me, but he was a man of war, and while he may have shown all manner of affection to his brothers in arms, he had not held me since I was a little girl. It felt wonderful. It felt like ... family.

Later that same day, I was notified by one of my ladies that Brian had requested an audience. I was not quite ready for that, so I had her return with a letter.

> *Sir Brian, it has been brought to my attention that you wish to speak with me. Sadly, I am not at my leisure today, but if you have some message to remit, you may do so through my knight, Drogo. Yours faithfully,*
> *MATHILDA IMPERATRIX*

Those final words were most proper, as it was his lack of faith that had created our predicament. The next day, I received a reply.

> *Gracious Empress Mathilda, I thank you for your magnanimity. You were no doubt surprised to hear of my marriage, which has taken place in accordance with the king's command.*

Though I acted out of necessity, I regret any pain this has caused you and beg your pardon. I remain as ever your servant—Brian fitz Count

I was standing at the time in the room connected to my bed chamber, which simply had a table for eating and a few chairs placed by the hearth for receiving guests. Drogo alone was with me as I read the words over a few times, my frustration increasing with every line.

"Drogo, what is this?" I finally asked, holding up the piece of parchment.

"A letter." He had a knack for stating the obvious.

"No," I said, shaking my head. "What was Sir Brian's mood when he gave it to you?"

"Serious, I suppose. Why?"

I looked back at the words on the page. There was much that Brian had not said. How could he have sent such a letter without any feeling, as if we were merely discussing the weather? No, I would not allow him to get away without explaining his behavior: without telling me why my hopes had been destroyed.

"Bring him here at once," I said to Drogo.

"But I thought you said—"

"Never mind what I said!" I snapped. "I am saying: bring him here."

"Yes, my lady," he replied, leaving the room quickly.

He departed and I spent the next few minutes pacing back and forth on the floor boards, trying to control my anger. At one point, I picked up the iron poker sitting by the hearth and began stirring up the fire, allowing the sparks to fly even as the fire burned inside me. How could he offer up such a reply? I could see that I must address him, but what should I say? I was still trying to make up my mind when Drogo opened the door, and in stepped the object of my discontent.

"Lord Brian of Wallingford," the knight announced.

I threw the poker to the side. Although Brian bowed, I said nothing in acknowledgement. I simply pushed aside the chest of treasured objects that was sitting near the edge of the table and leaned back against it with crossed arms, as if doing so could block him out.

"I'll leave you then?" Drogo asked, or rather pleaded, for he was gritting his teeth a bit and looked very much as if he longed to be anywhere but there. He recognized I was in a fury and Lord Brian was the subject of my wrath, even if he did not know why. Whatever respect he may have had for Brian, he was not about to get between a lioness and her prey.

"Yes, thank you," I replied quietly.

As my knight made to leave the room, I locked eyes with Brian. He took a deep breath in, no doubt in preparation for the onslaught he knew was coming. He had broken faith with me, and he would be made to feel it. I suppose I desired to transfer some of the shame within myself to him: to place it on the rejecter rather than I who was rejected. Either that or I was simply so angry that I had to berate someone, and I could hardly say such things to the king.

We continued to stare at one another until I heard the thud of the door and click of the bolt.

"Coward!" I yelled.

"Maud," he began, taking a step toward me.

"Don't you dare!" I cried, pointing my finger at him. "Don't you dare pretend to be what you are not! I am your superior, sir. You have no right to use the name given to me by my mother!"

He froze in place and his shoulders dropped ever so slightly. "Forgive me, Empress Mathilda. You received my note?"

"I received a beating."

"What?!" he stammered, his expression changed to one of shock. "What do you mean? They said you fell down the stairs."

"Help me understand," I continued, avoiding his question. "Had you been plotting to betray me all those months, or was it a sudden decision?"

He may have wanted to ask me more about my injuries, but he was forced to answer the question at hand.

"I can see why it might seem like a betrayal to you," he said with a nod, "but I acted in your best interests and for the benefit of us all."

I laughed perversely. "And I suppose you gave no thought to what you might achieve by this marriage!"

"That is not why—"

"Yes, why sacrifice your fortune for the woman you claimed to love when you could be perfectly rich and content with someone else, all without losing the love of your king? It makes sense!"

I could see that my words were starting to wound him. His eyes had the glassy look of one who is trying not to cry. His lips were parted slightly, straining for air, as if he had been punched. I was not at all sorry. He deserved it.

He began to speak slowly, as if trying to calm us both. "I cannot say all that I wish to say, but this had nothing to do with gaining a fortune." When I scoffed, he cried, "It's true! I was not lying when I said I loved you, but you must see that there was no other way!"

"Oh, spare me your complaints! History is nothing but a long line of men claiming, 'There was no other way!' There is always another way for those who are bold enough to take it, but that is not who you are. You are a coward!"

He seemed to wince at the sound of my words, and for a moment, I thought he was going to make some angry reply.

Instead, he took another deep breath and responded more calmly—almost tenderly.

"You are upset. You have a right to be. For that, I am sorry. But what did you mean about a beating? Did the king harm you?" He squinted a bit, as if looking for any sign, but I had made sure to hide my wounds as well as possible behind my veil.

I abandoned my perch against the table and stepped toward him. "Please, let's not pretend that you suddenly care: not when you left me to the wolves! How can you stand there and declare that what you did was noble? God save us from such nobility!"

"But—"

"No!" I cried.

We were standing by this point very near to each other, studying each other's faces, breathing deeply. That space between us was, after all, an eternal abyss that could never be crossed. I had given my love to him, and he had set it aside for something else. He had acted without informing me, and thus made me his fool. Oh, how it hurt! The longing within myself for something more—something higher—was never to be fulfilled. I feared I would never feast again at the table of joy, and all that was left was to fight for the scraps that fell.

"This is the way it will be," I said softly. "What's done is done. We may have to be around one another, but you are only to address me in company, do you understand?"

He sighed. "Yes."

"We will just continue on as if none of this ever happened."

"Agreed."

"And you will never speak of this—to anyone!"

His eyes squinted again, as if he was surprised that I would have to command it. "Of course. You will have my silence."

"Good. Leave me now. I have no desire to speak any longer."

Brian nodded slowly, his face still tinged with sadness and his shoulders still drooping. He truly looked completely defeated. I remained standing there with my arms folded as he turned and walked toward the door. He placed his hand on the knob, then paused for a moment, turning his head back toward me.

"What now?" I asked. "Are you going to claim that you dream of me when you lie with her?"

"I'm sorry," he whispered. "There is much that I cannot say, but please know how deeply sorry I am for any pain you have experienced. I hope someday you find it possible to forgive me."

With that, he took his leave. I stood there for a moment breathing heavily, finally allowing the tears to fall. My eyes wandered over to the fire, which continued to burn with vigor. The anger within me burned with equal force. I had made Brian share some of my pain, but I felt as if I had to do something more to put that part of my life behind me: to destroy any love I still had for him, if such a thing was possible.

Suddenly, I had a thought. I walked back to the table, on which sat the chest that held my most prized objects. I lifted the lid and saw the amber moth sitting there. In anger, I picked it up and made to throw it on the fire. I stood there, the flames dancing before my eyes, my arm held aloft. I wanted to be done with it, but something held me back.

"Do it, Maud!" I said aloud. "Do it or you will never be free!"

I looked again at the amber moth, holding it up and turning it over. The light of the fire made it glow brightly, as if the stone itself was a thing of flame. The moth was eternally trapped within, always burning but never consumed, even as it would never be free. Here was the perfect symbol for myself, yet I could not destroy this thing that meant so much to me. It almost seemed profane to do so. Instead, I dropped it on the floor, even as I began to weep.

"Now who's the coward?" I said to myself.

CHAPTER TWELVE

A woman must have a purpose or she cannot live. Without meaning, without hope, she drifts aimlessly like a twig in a river, until she is pulled under with the current. Darkness—such darkness I felt, gasping for air, longing for light, but at a loss as to what I should do. I had not recognized until after the fall how high I had climbed above the earth: how far my dreams had reached beyond what was possible.

Having been seized by the harsh grip of the truth, I had no choice but to acknowledge it: I might never know joy in marriage, I might never give birth to children, and my name might never be remembered by anyone. What was my heart feeling? The only thing I was certain I felt was pain. Though I hated it, I cherished that hurt, for it told me that I existed and had thoughts and feelings of my own. I had become numb to much that ought to tempt a human to joy.

Every part of me hurt—yes, every part felt sore, as if the smallest word would undo me, or a single look would bring me back to the darkness in which I had dwelt, or in which I continued to dwell. I knew it should not be. I was a royal and must be ruler of my own heart, forcing it into line. But was that not the very problem? Does a woman need permission to feel pain?

We flee from it. Yes, we shun it. But is pain not a gift of God: the very thing that assures us we are alive? I knew not. Indeed, I know not. All I knew for certain was that I had been utterly consumed by that pain, and though it had dulled from its original sharpness, the memory of it remained.

At such times, a young woman needs her mother, or at least a faithful friend of her own sex. I had none. Any consolation from my father was certainly out of the question, and having hidden the whole affair from Drogo, I could not even discuss it with him. No, there was only one person who knew it all and was on my side—one soul to whom I might disclose the secrets of my heart. In that hour, I needed my brother. I needed Robert.

The month of December arrived and brought with it an unusually bitter cold. All the ponds around London froze, and even the Thames began to fill with pieces of ice, though its constant flow prevented it from freezing over completely. Such things did not usually take place until well into January, but it did not seem out of place to me. After all, the warmth and light had long since departed my own world.

I had taken to remaining in my room certain evenings while the rest of the king's court was feasting in the hall. I would complain of a cough and then spend the night in my mother's old audience chamber, reading a book by the hearth and trying not to think of what was taking place below: the king enjoying a life without judgment and Lord Brian dancing with his lovely wife, who might already be with child for all I knew.

On one such eve, I was sitting in my chair near the fire as usual, reading the prophet Jeremiah or something else appropriately mournful and clutching a fur around my shoulders to keep out the cold that came in around the windows. Suddenly, I heard someone beating on the door and the sound of my brother's voice.

"Maud, are you in there? Open up! I have an offer to make you."

I set my book on the floor but did not rise. "I have no intention of coming down, if that's what you're asking. I am far too ill." I forced a cough to make my point.

"You're no more ill than I am. Now get over here and open this door!"

I was at a loss as to what he could possibly want, and it perturbed me that he would not accept my lie. Nevertheless, I rose and made my way to the portal slowly, still holding the fur around me for warmth. I placed my hand on the bolt and pulled it free, then opened the door to see my brother standing there, a smile on his face, holding a glass in each hand.

"If that's beer, I'm not interested," I told him.

"No, mine is beer, but this is wine—the king's best, from Burgundy."

He held out the goblet in his left hand and lifted it upward a few times as if to say, "Take it! Take it!" Well, I was not one to refuse spirits when my own spirit was positively gloomy. I took it from him straight away and had a draft. It slipped down my throat with a slight burn, then ran into my insides, lending my body a bit of warmth.

"This is very good. Where in Burgundy do they make it?" I asked, looking down at the liquid as if I might discern the answer in its depths.

"Cluny Abbey."

"Oh, of course. That explains why it is so rich." The monks of Cluny were, after all, the lords of the monastic world, with no lack of provision.

"Actually, I did not come here to talk wine."

I took another drink and exhaled. "That is very well, because I know too little about it for a woman of my standing. I thank you for the drink, brother." Here I lifted the goblet as if to toast him.

"Have you ever been skating?" he suddenly asked.

I looked at him in confusion. He might as well have been speaking Greek. However, the look on my face did not provoke a reply. He simply stood there leaning against the door frame, sipping his beer and staring at me.

"What on earth is skating?" I finally inquired, not sure if he was having me on.

"It is sort of like sliding on ice, but upright. You wear shoes with pieces of bones on the bottom. They allow you to move about."

"That sounds terrible."

"Oh, it's quite enjoyable! The Londoners do it every winter on the moor just north of the wall. I wondered if you might like to try it."

"You don't think I will fall straight away?"

He laughed. "Yes, probably. Indeed, I dare say assuredly, but I will be there to catch you, or if necessary to pull you back up."

"And what happens when you fall down as well? Or do you think yourself immune to the forces of nature?"

His goblet was empty by this point, and he dropped it to the floor rather carelessly. I looked down and watched it roll for a good three feet before stopping, then lifted my gaze to meet his face again.

"What on earth was that for?" I asked. "This is not the king's hall! You can't just throw things wherever you wish."

"Ah! But look—it didn't break!"

I was beginning to wonder if he might be drunk, so odd were his words. "It's made of firm metal. Of course it didn't break."

He leaned toward me slightly. "And you are made of stronger stuff than that! Now, are you coming with me, or are you a coward?"

"What, now?!" I asked, convinced he had taken leave of his senses. "It's December—December in England. The sun has been down since mid-afternoon. It is cold enough to freeze the moor, and it is a long way out there."

"Which means no one else will be there! There will be no one to see us falling on our arses."

I gave him a very stern look, as if he was a young child who had been caught with his fingers in the pudding. "Robert—"

"Honestly, sister, are you going to sit in here moping until kingdom come, or are you going to come and hazard your life for a few minutes' entertainment?" Here he leaned in still further and whispered, "I'm sure the king would hate it if he knew what we were doing."

Oh, you know just how to play me, I thought. I was not sure how much my father would truly hate it, but the gleam in my brother's eyes was simply too much for me to withstand. "Fine then, you devil! I'll be dead or delighted."

"That's the spirit!" he cried.

Within the half hour, we had collected two horses from the king's stables and crossed the bridge toward London town, our bodies covered in so many layers of cloth and fur that even if we did hit the ice, our bones would likely be safe. The isle of Westminster itself was well lit by torches, as were the city walls of London, but as we made our way down the Strand between the two, we entered a portion that was very dark indeed, with only the soft glow of the moon to light our way. The hot breath of the horses could barely be seen lingering in the air, but the sound of their hoofs in the snow was clear enough. I was riding along just behind Robert, and my brother's horse would occasionally send snow flying so high that it caught me in the face. Even under all those layers, I was very cold. I cried to my brother, "God curse you for bringing me out here! We will both die, and then England will be ruined!"

"No, I shall do the honorable thing and die first. You can eat me to survive the night," he called back.

How could one respond to such a comment? I saw only one way.

"Exactly how many times has someone hit you on the head in battle?" I asked.

He paid no heed to my question. "We turn to the left here, up to Watling Street. We'll use it to cross the Fleet."

Within a few minutes, we were close to the city walls on our right, and thus enjoyed a bit more light. Sadly, this did nothing to warm my toes. I could see a few of the watchmen upon the battlements, keeping to their nightly labor. There were gatherings of huts by each of the gates that likely belonged to either merchants hoping to sell wares to travelers or hermits hoping to collect tolls. Some still sat outside around fires, singing and drinking. They made an odd sort of choir, gathered not under the vault of a cathedral but the greatest ceiling of all: the night sky filled with stars.

We had made our way round to the northern side of the city, and Robert led me further from the wall toward a dark, open field. Up until this point, we had been passing either trees or farmers' fields on our left, but here the grass grew taller, and there was no sign that the earth had ever been worked.

"This is the place," Robert announced. He alighted from his horse, then still holding on to the reins, he lifted his free hand to help me down.

"It looks like a bog," I said, though in truth I could see little for lack of light, so this was mostly my bad mood talking.

"Just wait here," he instructed.

I gathered that he was tying the horses to a shrub, or perhaps a small tree. Again, the darkness obscured everything. I could hear him rustling around in his saddle bag. I turned and looked back at the city glowing in the distance. What time was it? It must have been two hours since Robert had first come to my room—perhaps more. Could it be midnight already? I looked up and tried to judge the position of the moon, but it was of little use to me. I was never able to tell time by it as well as I could by the sun.

Suddenly, I saw a glow coming from the other direction, its light touching the ground. I turned back and saw that Robert had been able to start a small fire.

"Come help me!" he called.

I moved as quickly as I could across the snowy ground toward the flame. We both crouched down and began to blow on it in turn and fan it with our hands, but not so hard as to snuff it out. How fortunate that there was little wind that night! When the flames had increased in size, Robert handed me a few sticks with wax on the end that he had brought from the palace. I held two in each hand as he lighted them each in turn. I then helped him to light four of his own.

"Follow me," he instructed.

We walked a few paces and then Robert stopped so suddenly that I was lucky not to run into him with those fiery torches. By the light of the fires, I could see him take one step forward with his right foot, resting it carefully upon the ground. He then took another step with his left in the same manner and I heard the clear sound of ice straining under weight: something between a crack and a groan.

He turned his head back toward me. "I will test it. Stay where you are. If I should be pulled under, then find a branch and hold it out to me. Do not walk on the ice yourself."

I held my breath as he took two more steps forward, placing his full weight on the ice. He hopped up and down slightly, but it did not break. He then walked around on it a bit. It continued to hold his weight.

"It's good and solid," he concluded, walking back in my direction.

We then spent the next few minutes carefully planting the torches around the edge of the frozen pond. It was quite large, so we did not circle the entire thing: just enough to provide room to skate. Next came the difficult task of placing the special shoes on our feet, which I had brought along in my saddle bag. They were not at all comfortable, and I wondered once again why anyone had thought this sport a good idea. Nevertheless, I pressed on, for we had come so far, and happily the cold and my general fear of what I was about to do distracted me from my sorrows.

Robert was a good bit steadier on his feet than me, having walked in skates before. I had to cling to him as we made our way to the ice. How afraid I was as I took my first step on to it! You must remember, I was not a good swimmer. I took a second step just as carefully, but again I remained upright.

"See! You're doing fine!" my brother said. "Now, take a few steps on your own."

"No, Robert, I—"

"Just do it."

Before I could protest further, he let go of my hand and I was standing there alone on pieces of bone, on top of ice, with the watery depths below. I wobbled a bit and moved my left foot to the side to recover my balance. When I felt stable again, I slid my right foot forward, then my left. Actually, I was not truly sliding, but stepping. Even so, I felt the slightest bit of confidence.

"Now try to glide on them," Robert said, demonstrating. His blades cut through the ice as he slid forward. He hardly even seemed to be making an effort.

Well, he may have been my older brother, and he may have had far more experience than I did, but I was not about to let Robert best me. Throwing caution to the wind, I pushed forward and my skates glided across the ice. Oh, it was perfect! It was magic! I was doing it! Then I recognized that my feet were not sliding on the ice so much as they were sliding out from under me.

Before I even had time to scream, I was flat on my back. My whole body felt at once very cold and very sore.

"Ow!" I cried. "God Almighty, ow!"

I could feel the pain surging through my body. Then I heard the sound of Robert's blades, and soon he was hovering over me, asking, "Are you hurt?"

I carefully moved each of my limbs and determined that they were in good working order. "Nothing seems to be broken."

"See, I told you. Now, come on! Get back up!"

"Actually, I feel quite safe laying here. I think maybe I'll remain until morning."

"Very well. You'll take a chill and die, but who am I to stop you?"

A terrible question occurred to me. "Would it be so bad if I died? I mean, would anyone miss me?"

Frowning, he bent down and pulled me back on to my feet.

"There you are, Empress Despair" he said. "Now, I'll have no more talk of dying, or misery, or anything like it. This spirit of defeat is not helpful."

"Easy for you to say," I muttered.

"What was that?"

"Easy for you to say!" I repeated more forcefully. "You're not the one who's been through it and then some these past few months."

He smiled and took hold of each of my arms at the elbow. "Hold on to me tight," he instructed, and I did as he said. He began to skate backward, pulling me along.

"Not so fast!" I cried.

He paid no attention to me but continued to move in a circle. Slowly, I grew more comfortable. Indeed, I was almost enjoying myself. It was something between dancing and flying: a kind of movement I had never experienced.

"Keep holding tight," he said, stopping in place and swinging me around.

We were spinning on the ice. It felt terrible and wonderful all at once. For the space of a breath, I leaned my head back and looked up at the stars as they spun above me. It was like something out of a dream. I looked back at Robert and we laughed.

"See, I told you this would be fun!" he said.

"Yes, but I'm getting rather diz—"

Then it happened again. I fell hard on to the ice, only this time it was not my own fault. I had been pulled down by my brother, or rather he had fallen down and I fell on top of him.

"Sorry!" he told me, as we both sat back up, holding on to the most painful spots on our bodies. "I must have caught a rough patch."

I did not reply, but simply rubbed my shoulder, which had taken the worst of it. I could only imagine the bruises I would have the next day.

"It hurts," said Robert. "It must hurt fiercely."

"I dare say I'll recover," I remarked, attempting to stand under my own power.

"It hurts to fall: to try so hard, and then have your legs taken out from under you."

I sensed that we were no longer talking about skating. I watched as he pulled himself up from the ice and brushed himself off. We looked each other in the eye, our faces illuminated only slightly by the torches.

"Was this meant to be a parable of some kind?" I asked.

"No, mostly it was for fun. You've been locked in a prison of misery for weeks, and I thought something new might do you good. If a point is made as a result, so much the better."

"Because you could have taught me about falling and getting back up without putting me through all this."

"Maybe," he said softly, "but you're more likely to remember it this way, aren't you?"

"I don't think my body will let me forget it for at least a week," I muttered, rubbing my shoulder again.

He placed his hands on my arms and rubbed them to warm me. "Just remember this: everyone falls at times, but you must not stay down. Staying down is death."

"Peace, Socrates! My bones can bear no more of your lessons. Now, can we return to the palace?"

"Very well. Your wish is my command."

We hobbled more than skated off the ice, then exchanged the painful shoes for our original ones. Oh, how wonderful they felt! As we gathered up the torches and snuffed them out in the snow, Robert spoke again.

"They don't have any power over you unless you allow them to."

"What do you mean?" I asked, thrusting one of the flames into the snow.

"The king is powerful—that much is certain—but he is not all-powerful. He does not control your thoughts or your feelings. Neither does Lord Brian. Yet you have been allowing them to control you. You have been withdrawing out of fear of them, when you ought to be striding out as a conqueror."

I had snuffed out all my sticks and was standing in place, waiting to hand them to my brother. He was busy placing his own back in the bag.

"Robert, what exactly would you have me do?" I asked. "I am little more than a pawn in this situation. I have no control over my own destiny. More to the point, I do not see how you can argue that my feelings are exempt from the actions of others, when our father has gone to great lengths to make me fear him, and the love I felt—that I still feel—for Lord Brian is not something that simply goes away overnight."

"Nor would I think it would," he said, taking the sticks from my hands.

"Then I ask again, what would you have me do? I cannot forget the past. It is a part of me. Nor can I do much about the future."

"That is where you are wrong!"

He finished placing the last of the sticks in the bag and turned to face me again, grasping each of my arms. I struggled to make out his face in the dark, but his voice I could hear well enough.

"You know why I have always liked you, Maud?"

This seemed to me a very odd question. "Because I am your sister?"

"No!" he said firmly. "Plenty of people hate their blood relations. I like you because you are like a man."

"Oh. Well, now I feel wonderful!" I cried with derision.

"Hear me out!" he begged. "You are a woman, sure enough, but you are strong, intelligent, and you have a will."

"Do you mean to say that other women do not have these qualities? That they are not given to us by God? I should spit on you! Truly, I should!"

He laughed. "See, this is what I mean! You can sense foolishness a mile away, and you are stubborn as an ox. You are not afraid to speak your mind when necessary. Had you been born a man, they would have gladly made you a king."

"Is there a point to this, or do you simply intend to go on comparing me to beasts?" I asked, speaking as much on account of my frozen toes as anything else.

"That you have been through difficulties, I do not deny," he continued, "but there is much about your future that you still control. You can choose who to live for—what to live for. Other people may have their own aims for you, but you can set your own, even if it is known only to yourself. You say you have been miserable, but you can seize joy! You can create it within yourself. Every day, when you wake up, say, 'I am not living for the king today. I am living for myself. If I obey him, it is only to achieve my own ends.'"

"Are you implying that I can simply produce joy within myself just by wishing it to be there?" I asked. The suggestion seemed truly absurd.

"No. You produce it by pursuing your desires to the utmost whenever you can: by milking as much pleasure out of this life as possible!"

I shook my head. "I will not win if I fight the king."

"You don't have to fight him. You just have to wait him out. You are the heir to the throne of England! One day, he will die, and you will be able to set your own destiny. Start working for that now!"

My brother was saying a lot of things, some of which seemed wise, but for whatever reason, I did not feel I could fully adopt his method. For one thing, I did not possess as much confidence in myself as he apparently did.

"All of this is well and good," I said, "but I do not think I could stop loving Brian. When you give your heart to someone as I did to him, it leaves a mark on you. I think he will always have a hold on me."

"You can share his bed for all I care, but that doesn't mean he has to rule over you. He cannot be your final goal."

"I know that well enough," I whispered. "Whatever hopes I had for him are long dead, and there is no question of me sharing his bed. Even if I had no respect for the laws of scripture, he does not think of me in that way any more, if he ever truly did. I just—I miss him, Robert. I miss what we had. He used to tell me what he was reading: some play of Seneca, a bard of Aquitaine, an astronomer of Cordoba, or the book of King William. Even if it was simply the royal charters, I loved when he would tell me about them. I loved to hear his mind at work. He would teach me things—tell me stories. He always told me I was just as intelligent as him, but I knew better. At least I was wise enough to value such a mind, but it has left a hole for me now. I may never find its equal again. I miss our conversations. I miss him."

I had cast my eyes down toward my right foot, which was digging into the snow. I was not entirely comfortable discussing this subject, even with my brother.

"Look at me, Maud," he said, and I did. "Let him go. He no longer has a claim on your heart, so don't give it to him."

I closed my eyes and took a deep breath in and out. "I am letting him go," I said.

"Yes, good. Keep telling yourself that."

"I am letting him go!" I cried. Yes, I was crying tears as well as words.

We stood there embracing for a minute or so, then mounted the horses and began the long ride back to Westminster, where I hoped very much to climb straight into bed and sleep until noon the next day.

"The people that walked in darkness, have seen a great light: they that dwelled in the land of the shadow of death, upon them has the light shined."[12]

The prophet Isaiah wrote those words about the coming of our Savior, but he may as well have been speaking of England around the anniversary of Christ's birth. No one knows darkness until they step outside mid afternoon and find the sun already set. Ah, England in winter! The jolliest soul might be driven to despair by that eternal gloom. That is why, even before they saw the light of Christ, the peoples of these lands held great feasts in the middle of winter, for though we may be without harvest, we are not without hearth.

Our Savior came to earth at its darkest hour, all the better for his light to shine. That Christmas may not have been my darkest hour, but it was certainly among the worst. I had striven to follow Robert's advice, but try as I might, I found it difficult to seize joy, nor did I see how merely seeking pleasure was a worthy life pursuit. When I obeyed the king's call to Windsor, it was with a heavy heart. I did not foresee a joyous season.

Since the ruinous incidents of that autumn, I had employed every means possible to distract myself. I began by sewing—never a particular skill of mine in my youth, and as it turned out, nothing had changed. I made pilgrimages to Waltham, Saint Albans, and the new abbey in Reading, where the hand of Saint James had been sent. I must have played one hundred games of checks with brother Robert. How kind he was to humor me! And of course, I read.

It was in those hours of reading that I particularly came to enjoy the poetry of Archbishop Hildebert of Tours, an old friend to our family. Such a blessing I received from his verses!

---

12   Isaiah 9:2

"Alpha et Omega, magne Deus!
Heli! Heli! Deus meus,
Cujus virtus totum posse,
Cujus sensus totum nosse,
Cujus esse summum bonum;
Cujus opus, quidquid bonum."

Thus on and so forth read the lyrics of his most famous hymn, a testament to the Holy Trinity. I was so impressed that I wrote to him of my admiration for his work. A few weeks passed before we received a reply. I was making ready to leave for Windsor when Drogo entered my private chamber bearing a chest that despite its medium size seemed rather heavy, if the bend in his knees was any evidence.

"What on earth is that?" I asked.

"From Tours—it just arrived," the knight replied.

"From Tours? That must be from the archbishop. Open it!"

He placed it on the table near the door, opened the latch, and lifted the lid. For a moment, he simply examined the contents as I looked on, eagerly awaiting an explanation.

"I think you will like this," he said, looking up once again.

"What is it?"

He smiled broadly and raised his brows. "Wine: lots of it."

"Really?" I said, with some surprise.

"See for yourself."

He stepped back, allowing me to move forward and look into the chest, which certainly did include eight bottles of the finest wine the Loire Valley had to offer, along with a sealed letter. I lifted one of the bottles and turned it around in my hand, examining every side.

"This is a kingly gift," I said. "Here, Drogo: for your service."

I extended my arm to hand him the bottle, but he stepped back and raised his hands.

"I couldn't, my lady!"

"Oh, yes you could. Happy Christmas!"

He finally gave in and accepted the gift. As he continued to examine his treasure, I broke the seal on the letter and spent a moment reading it.

"What does it say?" Drogo asked.

I turned to see that he had set the bottle aside and was looking over my shoulder. "It is a poem made out to me by the archbishop."

"A poem? About what?"

"About myself."

"Oh ... good or bad?"

"Good, I think. I haven't read it all yet."

"Well, go on then."

"Very well. Let's see ..." I looked back down at the piece of parchment in my hand. "It's in Latin. Let me try to translate it: 'Born to august parents, Mathilda is more august still, in whatever praises'—No, forgive me—'You evoke praises from skilled mouths, but in vain, for no one can render praise unto you which your birth and customs and beauty demand.' Ha! The man has never laid eyes on me! 'A tongue may make utterance about you, but you alone provide the matter of highest praise to all tongues. Your queenly face is fragrant like juniper, serious in gait, a beauty not fashioned by art. Learning did not lend sacred customs, a virgin modesty: each flowed from your ancestors.' Virgin modesty? There are some who might disagree with that! Now, where was I? 'You have it all from your mother who, closed in the tomb, gives light to the English kingdom with her merits, and lest the glory of the female sex should decline, she gave birth to you, fully reborn in your birth. Not born only once, the parent lies in the urn, rules in the court, here beside men, above beside God.' Well, that is nice that he should speak of my mother. I wonder how well he knew her?"

"Are we near the end?" Drogo whined.

"Yes, yes—I am getting there. 'Beside God, she sees how all that is left is nothing, how her daughter holding the scepter is … poor.' Can that be right? Hmm … 'Herself secure, I think she watches over you, and beseeches her maker thus …' Ah, I think this is supposed to be my mother speaking now. 'I have not yet been admitted fully to the heavenly see, great God, I enjoy only somewhat blessed rest.'"

"Is he saying she is in purgatory?" he asked, sounding as if he took offense.

"No, here we go: 'A part lies in the tomb, a part governs the English kingdom—the court, the tomb, and heaven hold me divided. Help the one in the court, reform the one in the tomb, hear the one in heaven, and be a crown to all three.'"

"Well … that was certainly strange," Drogo concluded.

I set the letter back in the chest and took a moment to think. It was certainly nice to hear anyone speak of my mother. It made me think of a happier time in my life, but more than that, it caused me to remember what kind of a woman my mother was. She had sacrificed her own desires so many times on behalf of others. Her love was not selfish, but deep and pure. I recognized that I wanted to be that sort of person, but I didn't know if it was possible for me. After all, my mother was so good. She seemed to live closer to God than the rest of us. Did she have something to teach me about purpose? In the end, I could not decide, and I recognized that Drogo was still standing there, waiting for me to say something. I therefore obliged him.

"I liked it, how it spoke of my mother looking down on me."

"Hmm … maybe. I think I shall never enjoy poetry though."

"That is why you are a knight, Drogo, though these days even knights are fond of verses. I must write to Archbishop Hildebert and thank him for these lovely words."

"Thank him for the wine. The words, eh," he said with a shrug.

"I do wish my mother was here now. I would ask her what I should do about the Anjou boy."

"Why don't you ask your friend the archbishop? Is he not in the lands of the Angevins?"

My knight had hit on something truly helpful, and it improved my mood. "Yes, he is. Excellent, Drogo! Now, let me just gather my things together and then you can take them down to the cart." I walked around the bed with its high posts and looked at the objects I had been gathering on the other side of the room, pointing at each in turn. "We have the gifts for the king and queen, Bishop Salisbury—Heaven help us!—Lady Elizabeth, Beaumont, Beaumont ... Drogo, are you paying attention?"

I turned around to see him testing the wine, which is to say taking a long drink straight out of the bottle.

"You couldn't wait until I was done?" I asked.

He closed his eyes to savor the drink, a look of contentment on his face.

"Drogo?"

He opened his eyes. "I think you should marry the Anjou boy."

"What?! Why?"

"I want to drink this until I die."

With that completed, we made the trip up river to Windsor, prized hunting ground of the king. It was a pleasant enough holiday, though I might have enjoyed it more were I not forced to watch the lord and lady of Wallingford taking part in the carol dancing night after night, with everyone observing how wonderful they were together, how they were sure to have lovely children, *et cetera*. "What a comely face she has!" they would say of Lady Mathilda, though I noticed they made no mention of her intelligence. Alas, though I strove to keep Lord Brian from having power over me—even as my brother had instructed—I did feel jealousy springing up inside me, and I found that for no fault of her own, I loathed the lady of Wallingford.

Shortly after Christmas Day, the two kings—Henry of England and David of Scotland—set out for London, heading there to speak with Archbishop Thurstan of York regarding the matter of Scottish bishops. This matter is surely of little interest, except that it brought me within the walls of London for the first time in my life. Now, I have often found that no matter which day one decides to travel—whether it be in winter, spring, summer, or autumn—the weather is sure to be far worse than normal. Such was the case then, for we had made it through late December without snow, until that day when we were forced to travel. Happily, it did not fall heavily, and the worst of it was the cold.

We chose to travel by road on this occasion, hoping to avoid the ice upon the river. Along the western road, the journey can be made in one rather long day, passing north of Brentford until reaching that street called the Strand, or also Fleet Street after the river of that name. In truth, "river" may be too lofty a term for the Fleet. When we crossed, it was full of two things: barges carrying materials for the construction of Saint Paul's Cathedral, and the refuse of all London. I imagined I saw a cat being carried along on a board, but perhaps this was merely the product of weariness.

"Here is King Lud's gate. Follow close!" my father called.

We crossed over the ditch and through the wall, which was less thick than some I had seen, but still wide enough for two men to lie down end to end. Now came the crowds to greet us, standing ten and twenty deep on either side as we passed the cathedral and made our way on to Watling Street. Those homes were piled one on top of the other, so that I thought they might fall to the ground. A flock of geese was forced to abandon our path near Walbrook, and a careless shop keeper let out a bucket from high above, almost hitting the bishop of Lincoln. Recognizing his mistake, he ran from the window with the look of death in his eyes. All about us cried, "Long live King Henry! Long live King Henry!"

Having finally moved east of London Bridge, we came with some effort to the fortress begun by my grandfather, known to all simply as the Tower. The late bishop of Rochester, Gundulf, oversaw its construction, making use of the walls to the east and south and surrounding the rest with a vast ditch and a ring of pales. The men of England stood in awe as the Tower first rose above the buildings of London, an eternal watchman upon the river.

As magnificent as it was, I could not help but wish that we might have spent those days at the palace of Westminster instead, for the rooms at the Tower were inferior in every way. They were created primarily to hold men at arms rather than ladies of the court, and as such they were smaller in size and had few adornments. I was fortunate to find a place within the stone walls, just above the chapel of Saint John. Many poor men were forced to freeze in the tents. The bishops, of course, found lodgings within the city that were more to their liking.

Upon our arrival, King Henry made his intention known to all: they must swear an oath that upon the hour of his death, whenever that might be, if he had not begotten a son, they would accept me as queen, being the only legitimate child of the king. This oath he required from the least to the greatest of them, the lords both secular and ecclesiastical. Of course, there was murmuring about this, with some saying it was too soon to require such a pledge, for Queen Adeliza was not yet at an age when we ought to despair of her fertility.

Though they were unwilling to own it, there were others who would have preferred that the king name his nephew as his heir—that is, William Clito. Thus he might have done, were it not for my cousin's continual rebellion against the crown, by which he forfeited any right he might have possessed. So the date was set, and the oath would be taken as soon as the king's business was completed. I suppose I was happy that I was to be made the king's heir, but every other feeling at that time was still clouded by the pain and fear I felt. My sense of purpose was floating in the wind, and I could not foresee how things would turn. I knew I did not want to marry the Anjou boy, or anyone else unworthy. I knew that I wanted to carry on the royal line of my fathers and mothers. Beyond that, I was at a loss. I felt numb.

There were ten earls at the time who held the greatest power in England, and it was to these lords that the lesser nobles would look for their lead. It was therefore essential that they be won over to the king's cause. As the king's chief justiciar and one of the richest men in England, Bishop Roger of Salisbury's support was also of particular import. The Church would likely follow in his steps, and thus I did everything I could to please him.

No woman had ever succeeded to the throne of all England in her own right. The very laws of nature seemed to forbid it, to say nothing of the laws of God. Yet there was no man linked by blood who was not either a traitor to the House of Normandy or descended through a woman. Thus, my father aimed to impress upon them all the righteousness of my cause and make them swear fealty before Almighty God. Such an oath would bind them upon pain of death and the damnation of their soul.

As the day drew nearer, the lords seemed to make their peace with this new situation, knowing that any other choice would lead to war either before or after the king's death. I had good reason for confidence, yet I could still hear the voice of Godfrey de Bayeux, the tutor of my youth, quoting from Saint Paul: "I permit not a woman to teach, neither to usurp authority over the man, but to be in silence. For Adam was first formed, then Eve." These words seemed to haunt me, and I therefore remained on my guard. Like Thomas, I would not believe until I had seen.

Finally, the day came on which everything depended. What does one wear on such an occasion? What does one say? After some consideration, I resolved to wear the finest raiment I possessed and speak as little as possible. This had at least the semblance of wisdom.

We gathered on the main floor of the Tower, which is to say the middle level, for one does not enter from the ground. At the time, there was a single open space surrounded on two sides by curtains and on the other two by the Tower walls. There was a dais at the north end with two thrones. The only other furnishings were a set of iron lamp stands in which fires were lit every eve.

As the lords gathered, I waited just to the side, peeking through the curtains. There must have been over one hundred persons in there. I reached up to adjust the crown on my head, which had been loaned to me by Queen Adeliza for the occasion. It was not the official crown of the queen of England, but a special one set with rubies and emeralds that the king had given to her as a token when they were betrothed. In most cases, I hated to wear such an object of discomfort, preferring a simpler adornment, but it seemed necessary to enhance my authority. The gown I wore was from my time as empress, crafted from materials I had purchased in Venice. It may well have been the most costly thing I owned, composed of purple silk and cloth of gold. I wore the same crucifix that had borne me through the streets of Rome, my mother's rosary, the pearl ring that Emperor Henry had given me on our wedding day—anything that might bring good fortune. I was sure to need it. I still struggled to believe that it could be so easy: that I, a woman, could walk in there and have all great lords swear to honor me and make me queen. Could it really be so?

My insides seemed to churn, and I thought I might be sick. But there was no time for such things, for my father the king had walked up next to me quite suddenly, and almost before I knew what was happening, he had put his arm inside mine without a word and pulled back the curtain. I squinted slightly as the brighter light hit my face. The herald announced our arrival and the trumpets played. We walked in—or rather boldly strode, as my father was wont to do—mounted the dais, and sat upon the two thrones that were meant for the king and queen. On this occasion, I was the one sitting beside my father.

Bishop Roger of Salisbury was set to begin the proceedings. He mounted the two steps with his head held high, holding the scroll in his hands that contained the words of the oath and a roll of all the lords, bishops, and abbots in the kingdom. My heart was by this time beating quite quickly. I saw many pairs of eyes fastened upon me and searched for my few true friends, hoping to gain strength from their smiles. Despite having been back in the land of my birth for more than a year, I still did not feel entirely comfortable with the vast array of persons at court, let alone those who had arrived from further afield. I was something of a stranger in my own home, and therefore my eyes sought the ones whom I could trust. Before I could find any of them, Bishop Salisbury had turned to face the crowd and began his proclamation.

"My lords, your king has called you here today to declare your obedience to his chosen successor: his rightful daughter, the Empress Mathilda."

Here there were some calls of support from the crowd, which did my heart good, but I could not help but notice a few faces that looked less than pleased. *Mother Mary and all the saints, let this go well!* I begged.

"I need hardly inform you of her pedigree," the bishop continued. "Daughter of King Henry, granddaughter of King William the Conqueror, in whose debt we all stand, niece of the second King William called Rufus. Through her mother, the late beloved queen, she is descended also from the ancient line of kings—Edward the Confessor, Alfred the Great, and thus on back to the time of the Romans. In her are the houses of England and Normandy united, and in no other."

That is not strictly true, I thought to myself. *Countess Mathilda of Boulogne also possesses such blood, though she is not daughter to a king or queen. Oh well. No need to mention that.*

The bishop continued, speaking loud enough for those in the back to hear. "Through her offspring, that line which has built this kingdom may be preserved, and its greatness will continue. Therefore, your king bids you stand and take the oath of obedience to her and her descendants, that you will remain faithful and true in your service, and that peace will be maintained in this land. It is his absolute will that she should inherit upon his death."

My eyes continued to scan the crowd. I saw Queen Adeliza standing near the front, a broad smile upon her face. The Beaumont contingent was not smiling, but they seemed peaceable enough. Brother Robert winked at me—God bless him! Another brother might have challenged my right, but not him. Then I saw Brian, who was clearly pondering the bishop's words in all seriousness.

I hope you are more faithful to me in this, I thought.

King Henry then stood and spoke in his deep, bellowing voice that sent a shudder through my bones. "I trust that every man of you knows his duty and will take the oath without faltering. If you love me, you will do so without delay and hold to it. Remember, the king does not bear the sword for naught. Now, Bishop Salisbury, call them forth."

Bishop Roger obliged him, unrolling the scroll and holding it open with both hands. "The archbishop of Canterbury!"

Archbishop William de Corbeil stepped forward with some effort, as he suffered from gout. As he did so, Bishop Roger motioned to one of the servants standing off to the side, who also came forward bearing a small wood box. The younger man beat the archbishop up the steps and stood next to Bishop Roger, lifting the lid on the box to reveal a small piece of wood—a splinter, really—resting upon a bed of silk the color of wine. This I knew to be a piece of the Holy Rood of our Lord Jesus Christ: a precious relic that the bishop of Salisbury had acquired with his wealth and brought to London just for the occasion.

"Are you willing to take the oath?" Bishop Roger asked, when Archbishop William had finally made his way on to the dais.

"I am willing," the archbishop replied.

"Very well. I bid you kneel and place your hand upon this piece of the Holy Rood, knowing that the very blood of Christ holds you to your oath."

He did so, kneeling with no little effort, then repeating the words.

"By the Lord before whom this relic is holy, I shall to the Empress Mathilda be true and faithful, taking her as my lady, loving all she loves and shunning all she shuns, according to the laws of God, the kingdom of England, and the duchy of Normandy. I pledge this day that I will not offend in word or in deed, nor shrink from due obedience, nor deny her service, submitting myself to her rule and that of her descendants without deceit. And should I fail to keep this oath, I shall receive the due punishment for my actions. May she live and reign."

The first oath was taken, and as the archbishop came over and kissed my hand, I felt a great sense of relief. Indeed, I may have even let out a sigh. Surely, the other lords of the Church would follow, and they did: first Archbishop Thurstan of York and then all the others, including poor William Warelwast of Exeter, who had to be led by the hand as he was completely blind. I had just enough time to marvel at the ease with which this was all taking place, when we reached our first obstacle. Once the bishops had all sworn, Bishop Roger of Salisbury glanced again at his scroll.

"His Highness, King David of Scotland!" he called out.

"Brother Roger, wait a moment!" someone interrupted.

Oh no, I thought. *It's happening!*

I looked at once to see which of the earls was fool enough to betray me openly, but it was only Abbot Anselm of Bury Saint Edmunds. He was a rather short man, and perhaps because of this he had made his way to the front to see the action. Along with his words, he had raised up a finger to register his comment.

Bishop Roger lowered the scroll slightly and glanced over it at the diminutive abbot. Although the difference in height between them was not so great, the bishop's position on the dais made him appear rather a force of nature in comparison to the poor abbot, not to mention the humility of the abbot's monastic garments in relation to the bishop's sumptuous attire, which certainly cost no less than my own.

"What is it?" Bishop Roger asked rather slowly, putting so much stress on each word that one could not help concluding that he must be annoyed.

"Should not the abbots swear first?" Abbot Anselm asked. "It seems that that should be the way of things."

Oh, thank God! I thought. *It is simply a matter of precedent, not an outright rebellion.*

"You will have your turn," Bishop Roger assured him. "Now, King David, please come forward."

As the abbot crossed his arms and frowned, my uncle climbed the steps and knelt down, placing his hand on the relic. As he did so, he smiled at me with those eyes so like my mother's, and I thought of her for a moment—of all she had endured to make my position possible. What would she have thought to see me then? Would she have been proud to know that the line of Wessex might have a future even though my brother had perished? Or did she fear even as I did that my womb might never produce a child to carry on the dynasty? I hardly knew, but as my uncle David knelt before me and kissed my hand, he whispered something to me.

"I believe your mother, my sister, smiles down on us all today."

Had he been reading my thoughts and sought to allay my fears? I did not know, but I felt gratitude all the same. This happy feeling was not to last for long. The Scottish king had only just made his way back down the stairs, when Abbot Anselm once again interrupted.

"Lord king, such a thing cannot be allowed! The secular lords must not be given precedence over the clergy! All my brother abbots agree!"

Things were getting out of hand fast, and my father was in no mood for such debate. He rose from his seat.

"Every man is to hold his peace! What has been done cannot be undone. I don't care which of you goes first or last, and neither should you. All that matters is that you show proper fealty to your lords, and last I checked, I was lord of England. Now stand back, brother Anselm, and shut your mouth, or I will have you removed from this assembly and thrown to the dogs ... or worse!"

Well, that was the end of that. It may seem rather absurd: why should it matter who went first or last? Because there was more than one game being played that day. Yes, everyone had gathered to swear fealty to me as King Henry's heir—that much was true. But the lords secular and ecclesiastical had as much interest in advancing their own authority as they did in supporting that of the throne. They knew that whoever swore first would be perceived as greater in rank and therefore greater in power. My own concern was not so much that the order be strictly followed, but that the occasion would not descend into rancor, for that would surely reflect poorly on me.

Bishop Roger began calling out the roll again. "Stephen, count of Mortain and Boulogne!"

The king's nephew before the king's son? That did not seem right to me, and by the look on Robert's face, he clearly agreed.

"I think I should go first, being the empress' brother," brother Robert said, as Stephen took a few steps forward.

Bishop Roger did not answer but turned instead to the king. On this occasion, my father seemed a bit at a loss, which gave Stephen time to speak.

"Earl Robert, he has already called me."

"Yes, but I am sure you would not begrudge me this," Robert replied.

Stephen smiled a bit perversely. "Yes, cousin, but the manner of your birth ..."

There was a marked change upon my brother's face: such anger in those eyes! It looked as if the two men might come to blows. I did not blame Robert for being offended, for I felt offended on his behalf. Yes, it was true that my brother was born outside the bounds of wedlock, but what an awful thing to bring up in front of everyone, and only to shame him! Robert was still the king's son, an earl, and a great warrior. He did not deserve to be treated so by Stephen, but I suppose it should not have surprised me. I had seen since my return how Stephen had latched himself on to the king like a leech, sucking good will from him day by day. He had risen high in the king's regard, so much so that he clearly felt himself superior to the king's natural born son. *Might he even feel superior to me?* I wondered. *Will he refuse to swear? Will he break faith with all of us?* These thoughts passed through my head so quickly I barely had time to know them. Just then, the king spoke.

"Never mind that! Just swear, Stephen. It doesn't matter."

I took a deep breath as my cousin climbed the stairs and Bishop Roger asked, "Are you willing to take the oath?"

"I am willing," he said without delay, a smile upon his face. Behind him, brother Robert still looked rather furious.

"I bid you kneel and place your hand upon this holy relic," the bishop continued. "Repeat after me: By the Lord before whom this relic is holy ..."

"By the Lord before whom this relic is holy ..." Stephen repeated.

"I shall to the Empress Mathilda be true and faithful ..."

"I shall to the Empress Mathilda be true and faithful ..."

"Taking her as my lady ..."

"Taking her as my lady ..."

They completed the sequence, and Stephen walked toward me, knelt, and kissed my hand. I was still feeling quite perturbed over how he had treated Robert just a moment earlier, but I attempted to set these feelings aside. After all, it was a victory for me to have even the king's beloved Stephen swear fealty to me. This was not the time for anger. My brief fear had been allayed.

"I accept your oath, and will hold you to it," I said, looking firmly into his eyes.

He simply nodded and returned to the crowd.

"Earl Robert of Gloucester!" Bishop Roger called.

"It's about time," he muttered, and took his position.

"Are you willing to take the oath?"

"I am more than willing," he replied, or rather almost growled. He was still sore over the wound that had been dealt to his pride.

"Very good. I bid you kneel and place your hand upon this holy relic …"

Robert took the oath, and after he kissed my hand, I leaned forward and whispered in his ear, "Thank you, brother. I am sorry about all of that."

"He's a right cockscomb," he replied, and I had to stifle a laugh.

We continued with the rest of the earls. Even Queen Adeliza took the oath, and I am sure she felt some pain in doing so, for it was her inability to produce a son that had led to this day. However, if she was at all bitter, she did not show it.

"I am happy for you," she whispered to me.

Among the last of the nobles to swear was Lord Brian fitz Count of Wallingford, for he was not one to put himself forward in such a situation. I struggled to hide any lingering feelings when he made his pledge, but as he spoke, I was transported back to that evening when he led me across the ice and I first felt the pang of love for him. Had it only been a year since that night? In the present, he kissed my hand and offered up a smile, which I did not return. Receiving such false affection galled me.

The abbots finally had their turn to swear, and once every man had been called to account, the king stood up and surveyed the room with his eyes, as if to put the fear of God in all of them.

"Not only I, but God will hold you to the oath you have made today!" he cried. "Loyalty will be rewarded—treachery will be punished. The future of our kingdom is set in stone. Now, the empress will say a few words."

I had not been informed of this obligation and was taken by surprise. My father turned back to look at me, but I could only stare at him in fear. I was no orator! Nevertheless, I could tell from the look on his face that there was no avoiding it: I must speak, and it must be good. After all, I was to rule over all of them. I therefore stood and strained to come up with the right words.

"My lords, I thank you for the trust you have placed in me and any sons I might have, and for your pledges of fealty," I began.

"Speak up! We cannot hear you!" someone called from the back of the room.

I took a deep breath and attempted to project my voice. "I know this is most unusual, but I also know that, with your help, we can make this kingdom even stronger for our mutual descendants, and ..."

Oh no! My mind was a blank. A hundred faces were staring at me, bidding me to continue.

Think, Maud! something inside me cried. *Think!*

"And your loyalty will not be forgotten! God save England! God save the House of Normandy!" I concluded.

To my great delight, several people began to clap, and a few even cried, "God save Empress Mathilda!" I felt a burst of confidence: enough to utter a command.

"Come! Let us join hands!" I said, descending the stairs and taking the hand of Queen Adeliza. "We will sing a hymn of the season. It is proper that we should be joined in unity!"

Unity was what the kingdom needed. I knew well enough that though they had all sworn to me, there was not much desire for the reign of a female. I was therefore determined to set a good tone. Their smiles gave me strength to believe that

I might be able to accomplish the task ahead, if only the Lord and the lords were on my side.

They did as I asked and joined hands—even my father. We then walked in a circle and sang those famous words of Saint Hilary.

"Jesus refulsit omnium
Pius redemptor gentium
Totum genus fidelium
Laudes celebret dramatum"[13]

---

13 Translation from *The Book of Hours: In which are Contained Offices for the Seven Canonical Hours, Litanies, and Other Devotions* (New York: Hurd and Hougton, 1866). "Jesus hath shone benignly forth / Redeemer of the tribes of the earth; / Let all the faithful far and near / The praises of his deeds declare."

CHAPTER THIRTEEN

"But anxious cares already seized the queen:
She fed within her a flame unseen;
The hero's valor, acts, and birth inspire
Her soul with love, and fan the secret fire.
His words, his looks, imprinted in her heart,
Improve the passion, and increase the smart"[14]

Thus Virgil wrote of Dido, the queen of Carthage strung up by an evil fate, who for the love of Aeneas set herself alight. She never burned without ere she burned within, betrayed by the one she loved. When he set sail upon the Middle Sea, she hurled forth a curse upon his line, that there should never be peace between their two peoples. And indeed, history proved this to be true, for the Romans and the Carthaginians were sworn enemies through and through.

How the Romans must have rued their father's disloyalty when the hordes of Hannibal visited their threshold! How

---

14 Virgil. *Virgil's Æneid*, trans. John Dryden (London: George Routledge and Sons, 1884), 80.

Carthage was made to feel that betrayal again when the Romans salted their fields! And what did this hate yield? Naught but suffering. Therefore, we may conclude either that the Romans received the just punishment for Aeneas' betrayal, or that in her cursing Dido brought about the end of her kingdom, or that all of life is chaos and there is little purpose to it all.

But I took a different lesson from Dido: namely, that Brian fitz Count was a most fortunate man. When he forsook me, I did fall into despair for a time, but I never sought to curse him or anyone else after the manner of Dido. Within the space of a few weeks, I had been forced to accept my state of being. There would be no fiery bier for Empress Maud.

So how did I avoid the fate of Dido and make myself instead as one of the Stoics? I owed it all to the knowledge that Anjou was a less certain possibility than it had been before. The idea of that marriage had seemed to me no less fearful than marriage with Gunnar must have appeared to Brünnhilda, a fate unworthy for an empress. I lived in hope that some other match might find favor with the king. It was not much of a hope, but it allowed me to continue with life for the time being.

About a month after the nobles all swore to make me queen upon my father's death, we traveled by way of Winchester toward the hunting lodge at Woodstock, near the city of Oxford. It was the first time I had visited that part of the country since I was born just up river, and as I had no memory of those early years, it was essentially my first visit. Woodstock was a fine manor and easily twice the size of the other hunting lodges in the kingdom. Some complained that it could not have been built without the destruction of the peasants' homes nearby, but the king was always ready with a reply: "It's hardly my fault that they chose to live next to the choicest wood in England!" The beasts must have known they were not safe when the king's party came to Woodstock, despite the fasting for Lent. I suspect some of them fled as far as the River Avon to avoid us. There were a few creatures, however, who had nothing to fear from the king and his knights: namely, those kept within the bower.

The king had for some time been collecting certain animals at Woodstock, most of them sent as gifts from the far corners of the world. He received them happily, then handed them off to the poor man who was forced to care for them, often without any proper knowledge of their origins or habits. By this lack of knowledge, more than one of the beasts became supper for another, while others could not bear the climate.

Being around the animals helped to raise my spirits and create some of the pleasure my brother had instructed me to pursue. I therefore made the trip down to the garden to visit them almost daily, usually going alone. However, about a fortnight into our stay, Queen Adeliza asked if she might walk out with me, and I was more than happy to oblige. We went in the morning, when I had found most of the creatures to be awake. When we arrived at the entrance to the bower, we were greeted by Edward, keeper of the king's animals.

"Good morning, my queen, my empress," he said, nodding to each of us in turn.

"Good morning, Sir Edward!" I answered. "The queen wishes to see your charges."

"Certainly. We have all sorts."

Some of the animals were kept in wood pens or metal cages, while others were simply allowed to roam free. The arbor itself bore all the signs of careful attention: not a branch or leaf out of place or anything less than perfectly green. We had not walked four steps with Sir Edward when he had something to tell us.

"This fellow here is our most beauteous," he said, motioning toward a rather curious peacock that dared to approach us. "We only have the one male but three hens. What a life he must live!"

I bent down and stroked the bird's neck with the backs of my fingers, but the queen had her eyes on something else.

"Is that a camel?" she asked, pointing to the large brown animal chained to a stake and nibbling on the grass. "I have only seen drawings."

The keeper turned to look and then nodded in agreement. "Yes, some knight brought it back from the Holy Land, around the time of the great pilgrimage. He might have ridden it all that way. I'm not sure. No one foresaw that it would live this long, but by God, it keeps on living!"

"Maybe it is glad to be out of the desert," I said, standing back up as the peacock departed.

I made my way over to where the camel was standing but did not get nearer than a few paces. Its great frame seemed to tower over everything else as it raised its long neck and continued to chew. Perhaps there were some who rode such beasts, but for my part, I was fearful of anything larger than a horse.

"What is that?" Queen Adeliza suddenly asked.

"What is what?" I inquired, too occupied with the camel to turn around.

"What is that?!" she repeated, tapping my shoulder to get my attention and then pointing at one of the animals.

This time, I looked in the proper direction and saw the animal walking around in its cage. "Oh, that! It's a thorny pig, and a big one too."

"What in God's name is a thorny pig?!" the queen asked.

"Well, a porcupine, properly. I remember seeing one in Tuscany."

The two of us started to walk in this new animal's direction while the keeper hung slightly back. It was a magnificent dark creature covered in what appeared to be spines that looked as if they might be proper for knitting.

"Those spines grow from its flesh?" Adeliza asked me, evidently confounded.

"I believe so, yes."

"Why?"

"For defense, I should think."

"You think right," Edward said, coming up to meet us, his hands clasped behind his back. "One of my dogs got too close and ended up with a face full of spines. The poor brute! Next thing you know, the wounds got infected and he died. Now, that's a hard way to learn!"

"Poor dog!" the queen said. "Why should you keep such a hideous thing about?"

"It was a gift from King Roger of Sicily. I can't exactly let it die now, can I? If word got back, it might provoke a crisis."

"It has a kind enough face, I suppose, but those spines!" the queen responded, not yet won over by the animal's charms.

As she said this, I caught something in the corner of my vision and turned to see Stephen of Blois approaching the bower at great speed, the features on his face strained as if under great stress.

"Empress Mathilda!" he called out to me.

"Excuse me, Queen Adeliza," I said, tapping her on the back. "Cousin Stephen is asking for me, and he does not look in any mood for delay."

"Very well. Have at him."

I left the two of them behind with the beasts and walked over to meet my cousin just outside the bower.

"What is it?" I called out, as he made the final few strides in my direction.

"The count of Flanders. He's been murdered!"

"Murdered?!" I cried, my mind struggling to process this new information. "Where? When?"

"In Bruges, two days ago."

A rush of terror ran through my body. What did this mean? Was it the beginning of war? Who was in danger? These and other thoughts flooded my mind so quickly that I could barely register any of them. It was simply a mess of fear and confusion.

I shook my head and let out a sigh. "I cannot believe it! Who would do such a thing?"

"That is what we would all like to know. As near as we can tell, it was someone local."

My mind continued to work furiously, attempting to put the pieces together and determine what it all meant.

"I suppose that's a small blessing, but they might still attempt to blame it on us," I replied. "The king of France and the traitor Clito are always looking for some *casus belli* to seize the duchy of Normandy from us, and men have gone to war over far less."

He nodded his head in agreement. "That is indeed a concern. The countess thinks they may seek to invade."

"The countess? Do you mean your wife?"

"Yes. She is the one who sent us this dreadful news. Of course, she is worried sick."

"That does not surprise me," I said, a response that may have struck too close to the truth of my actual opinion of the countess, despite its apparent compassion.

I was already imagining the French king and his allies riding along the banks of the Seine and pillaging the Norman country. I saw my father and brother Robert fall in battle and the false heir William Clito being crowned in Rouen Cathedral, then racing across the channel to slit my throat and take the crown of England for himself. It was dreadful. The only thing I had left was my claim to the throne of England and duchy of Normandy, and the hope that it might grant me some measure of authority over my own life. Even though the nobles of the kingdom had just sworn to me, I knew many of them had not done so happily, and were they to have a conqueror—nay, a conquering man to rule over them, why would they not choose him over me?

"William Clito!" I said, almost spitting the name out, for to me it was as loathsome as any curse. I was very angry, and yet I recognized that I had a chance to make common cause with my cousin. "He is a threat to us all: to your lands, to my inheritance. We must work together to counter this threat. But what of the murderers? What is to be done with them?"

"Oh, they are still holed up somewhere in Bruges. I cannot imagine they'll survive long. We may not even know their names until their heads are perched upon the city walls. From what my wife tells me, the whole of Flanders has descended into terror. Men are afraid to leave their homes—to trust their neighbors. There is suspicion upon the very air."

"Little wonder there! You must go to her, Stephen. Go to your wife. Safeguard Boulogne for our side!"

"I await the king's command. He is already making inquiries abroad."

Even in that terrible moment, I was somewhat pleased to have something—anything really—through which I could unite with my cousin in purpose. We had never been particularly close, and his behavior toward Robert had frustrated me of late, but he nevertheless had the king's love, and were I to make him my ally, I might just depend on him to sway the opinion of the king regarding my marriage.

"Tell me, cousin, where is the king?" I asked.

"Back at the lodge, with his council."

"Very good. Take me there without delay."

We made our way to the king's chambers inside the lodge and entered a small room with naught but two windows and a large table holding several maps. A meeting of the king and his advisors had clearly just ended. Several of the lords were making their way out of the room, and brother Robert was rolling up the maps on the table. The king stood at the opposite end from myself.

"Empress Mathilda!" he called.

By the harsh tone in his voice, I gathered that my father was under a great deal of stress and prone to anger. I therefore endeavored to remain as pleasant as possible.

"I came as soon as I heard, my lord. Where do we stand?"

"On the edge of a cliff, more or less. We must press to ensure that the new count of Flanders favors our cause."

"I wholly agree," I said, glad that I could do so for once.

"Stephen, you sent word to the countess of Boulogne?" the king asked, walking round the table to where Robert was standing.

"Yes. I should hear back by the end of the week."

"We must get in front of this thing," my father continued, speaking rather forcefully. "Have Brian come up from Wallingford. Go send word, now!"

"Certainly," Stephen replied.

My cousin then departed to undertake his charge, leaving only myself, the king, and brother Robert in the room. I recognized that I needed to make my next moves carefully, looking for common cause. For the moment, my father's anger was aimed at William Clito and the French king, and I wanted to keep it there. I had barely survived his wrath before, and if I came under it again, there was no telling what the king might do: marry me to the Angevine imp or someone even worse, rob me of my inheritance, or have me strung up by the thumbs. Perhaps he would not stoop to the thumbs, but I had no desire to find out.

"Such awful news!" I said, walking toward them slowly. "To think that a man of such high birth should be cut down by his own countrymen!"

"He was no true friend of ours, though I admit he was better than the last count," Robert replied.

"Even so, such a fearful example! How did this happen?"

"Charles was never the great ruler that men claimed," the king said. "He had plenty of enemies."

"Wasn't his father also murdered?" I asked.

"Yes, when he was king of Denmark," said Robert. "But the son, Count Charles—he was a poor administrator. Their crops failed, so they sent the Jews away. Little good it did them! When men began hoarding, he tried to stop it, all to no avail. He reduced some of the lords until they were little more than common peasants. One of these families took special offense and killed him while he was at prayer."

"Yes, it's all a very sad tale, but we are not going the way of Count Charles!" the king declared. "Every man will look to his own gain now. We have no choice. Mathilda, you must be married to Geoffrey of Anjou as soon as possible. It is the only way to ensure that they remain in our camp."

My heart sank. Here was the very thing I had hoped to avoid! Indeed, avoiding this thing was all that had impelled me for the past few months. It was the reason I had made a kind of peace with my father, even though I had never forgiven him in my heart. It was the reason I had borne his presence and spoken to him with kindness, when my true desire was to curse him and never stand beside him again. For the right to marry a better man, to sit on the throne as his heir, to have some power over my own life—in short, to be free—I had sacrificed my freedom to protest abuse: the right that is given to every man and woman by God.

In that moment, I saw it slipping through my fingers. I had to stop it! He wanted Anjou as an ally. Might Anjou prove to be of no use to us as an ally? No, that seemed unlikely. However, it was possible that they could prove a false ally. This was my only hope: the only form of reason that might save me.

"They did not remain in our camp when Prince William married an Angevin. Why should they do so now?" I objected.

"It will be different when you marry the male heir. A daughter is nothing," the king said. "A son is everything: I should know."

Here he looked at me very directly and glared, and I knew there was nothing I could say to change his mind. He would marry me to the Angevine imp, not only to save Normandy, but to make a point. I had stood against him, and I must be punished. I must learn my place. Yes, there was nothing that I could say to alter his opinion, so I turned to the one person who had been able to influence him on this matter.

"Robert!" I entreated, my words desperate, my soul overwhelmed. "Tell him that I cannot do this! I know you do not support it."

But there was no light in my brother's eyes. They were sad and downcast.

"That may have been the case, but all is changed now. The king is right. I'm sorry, Maud," he said quietly.

If my heart had sunk before, now it sunk doubly. I could hardly believe that things had changed so suddenly. Half an hour earlier, I had hoped that the king would be talked out of the Angevin marriage—that if I was on my best behavior, my brother could bring him round. The murder of Count Charles had changed everything, so that even Robert was unable to help me.

Think, Maud, think! I commanded myself. *Think of something else! Quick, before the death knell sounds!*

"What of the lords? What do your counselors have to say?" I asked, looking to them each in turn.

"The king has not spoken of this with anyone but myself," Robert replied.

This truly surprised me. How could the king proceed with such an enormous decision without discussing the matter with his advisors? I couldn't decide whether to laugh, cry, or scream.

"Not Bishop Roger of Salisbury?" I asked in surprise. "Not Chancellor Geoffrey? Not his precious Stephen?!"

Robert began to open his mouth to speak, but the king beat him to it. "It would not do to tell the lords. They all have their own opinions, and I will not have them gainsaying mine!"

"But this will only lead to calamity!" I argued. "Remember the lesson of Count Charles! When they find out, they will rise up against you."

"Is that what you think of me? I cannot defend my own throne?!" the king asked, clearly perturbed. He had that look in his eyes again: a look of fire, with which I was playing a dangerous game. He had pressed his right hand down on to the table and leaned in closer to me. His manner was such that I would not have been surprised if the table broke under the pressure of his grip. My only comfort was that the two of us were not alone.

Be bold, Maud, I told myself. *This is your last chance!*

"I think you are desperate men seizing at a desperate chance. Pray, have some patience! God only knows what is to come," I begged.

"I have made my decision, and it is final!" my father declared, pounding the table with his palm.

"No!" I cried. I stood up as straight as I could, breathing in deeply to keep the tears from falling. "You cannot force me to marry him. You can drag me there, but you cannot pull the words from my mouth."

"Sister!" Robert said. "Consider what you are hazarding by your obstinacy! Is it really worth sacrificing the king's love?"

I turned my eyes toward him and finally allowed the tears to drop. "As if I ever had it," I whispered.

"Enough!" the king cried, placing one hand on his hip and using the other to point at me. "You forsake your duty to this kingdom and place your own contentment above that of the commonwealth. History will not judge you kindly!"

"I love England, but this is folly!" I contended. "It will not save her!"

"Maud, you must see reason!" my brother argued. "Perhaps if you took some time—"

"I could take all the time in the world, but it would never change my opinion that this is a travesty. My mind is set."

The king was in a rage and wished me to feel it. He moved his head from side to side in frustration, and he slowly curled his fingers into his palms until they became a pair of fists.

"God cursed me on the day of your birth!" he bellowed. "Were you not all that is left of my line, I would say that we should have thrown you out with the rubbish!"

That was surely one of the most awful things anyone had said to me in my life, and it came from my own father. I wanted to throw his curse back at him, but the pain he had caused was so great that I could hardly breathe. I had lost not only my chance at freedom, but any chance I ever had at gaining the love of my father. There was nothing I could do or say to change things. Taking a deep breath, I whispered, "I am very sorry to disappoint you, my lord. Now, if you please, I must be going."

I turned to leave before the fall of tears became a flood. I would not grant him that satisfaction. As I departed, I could hear Robert say, "You did not have to be so harsh."

The king's response was as one might assume. "Quiet! Fetch me some strong drink! I'll have done with that bitch."

Five steps, ten steps. I ran down the stairs to the lower level, my skirt flowing behind me. I fled from that place as quickly as I could, but not quickly enough, for as I approached the front gate, Brian made his way in, having just arrived from Wallingford. Apparently, he had no need of Stephen's summons. I halted at once in the middle of the foyer, a thousand thoughts and feelings passing through me. My face was still covered in tears, and the man who had made a fool of me—whom I still loved, despite all my efforts to the contrary—was standing there in front of the threshold, staring at me with a look of concern. He had evidently noticed that I was upset.

Why, God, why?! I prayed. *Why now of all times, after I have tried to avoid him for weeks?! Why when my heart is broken anew and I simply want to run—to hide far from the watchful eyes of men?!*

He was standing between me and the way of escape, and I had to consider whether it was better to go back the way I had come and possibly face another conversation with my father. Before I had time to decide, Brian bowed and addressed me.

"Empress Mathilda!"

"Lord Brian," I replied none too cheerfully, quickly wiping the tears from my eyes and striving to gain control of myself.

"I beg your pardon, Your Highness," he began. "My wife wished me to tell you that she was sorry she could not speak to you more at Wallingford when you passed through, for she had looked forward to making your acquaintance more fully. She invites you back to our home to enjoy the use of our estate for as long as you like. She would very much like to become friends."

I had never known the word "wife" to be so repugnant. I hated the very sound of it from his lips. I might not have hated it so much had I not been scorned by the king moments before, but such is life. My anger was shifting from my father to Brian.

"She told you to say that, did she?" I replied. "Well, please inform Lady Mathilda that I have no idea when I might travel near Wallingford, for that is not my usual path, but if I am in the neighborhood, you will be the first to know. Does that satisfy you?"

"Not quite, my lady. I wanted to ask you: is all well? I heard about the count of Flanders, and I feared for you."

"Why should you do that?" I snapped.

He shook his head slightly in confusion. "Simply because this has caused such tumult, and I know it might affect your future."

"As far as it concerns you, I am perfectly content. Things will work themselves out soon enough."

Inside, I was screaming. *Can't you see that I'm dying?! I still love you, and I'm being sent to marry someone unworthy while you are married to the Lady of Everything Perfect, and I hate it! I loathe it! You will never love me again, and I cannot bear it!* But I remembered Robert's words to me, and I refused to let Brian feel he had power over me: not after everything that had taken place.

He approached me slowly. "My lady—"

"I'm not your lady!" I cried, stopping him in his tracks.

"Your Highness, then. Are you still so angry at me that you must remove yourself from my home?"

"Ha! You would like that, wouldn't you? You must take special pleasure in the thought of me pining after you."

"Not at all!"

"What does that mean?" I asked, suddenly hurt. Why was I hurt? Because of course, a part of me hoped that he still cared for me as well, although I was unwilling to admit it to myself, for that would have also meant he had power over me.

"I mean that my dearest wish is to see you happy, not miserable," he explained.

"Don't make me laugh!"

"You may not believe me, but it is true."

"You made your choice, Lord Brian. You cannot have it both ways. When you married that woman, you forsook my love. Now you shall never feel it again. Also, I am not afraid to set foot in your house, or any house for that matter, but I have better things to do! I am an empress, after all," I said, as if he did not remember.

"I hope in time to earn your forgiveness," he told me earnestly.

"Ah, so you have hope yet. Beware! That is no blessing, but the last of Pandora's curses! Now, if you will excuse me, I must go devise some means of avoiding marriage to the Anjou boy, though I begin to despair that such a thing exists."

"Geoffrey of Anjou?" he asked, the look on his face one of clear surprise. "But he is still a boy and far below you in rank! That is the king's choice?!"

"Yes, and I intend to fight it by tooth and by claw, not that it's any of your business."

"If I can make the king change his mind, will you forgive me?" he asked almost desperately.

"If forgiveness is what you seek, then I recommend you find yourself a priest. I have no time for this. My God! Why do you always have to be so … so … incessant?!"

With that, I stormed off to my chamber, where I hoped to shut myself off from all men.

Over the next few days, the news grew worse. The French king had entered Flanders and summoned all the barons to himself. William Clito—the traitor to whom he had already gifted the Vexin, the phantom kept alive daily through their mutual plotting—was his man of choice. No one could have been ignorant of this. King Louis would force that choice upon the barons, even if Clito's claim was weaker than some of the others.

The Forsaken Monarch

And what could we do about all of this? Next to nothing! Our position was not to be favored. King Louis was there on the ground, even as we struggled to influence matters from afar. Never cease to respect the importance of being on the ground! I have seen this time and again to my own hardship.

Even so, King Henry used every weapon at his command. He paid a pretty sum to Count William of Ypres and Duke Thierry of Alsace, two men he hoped could win support. He bribed the local lords, flattered their wives, and praised their children. He even attempted to stake his own claim to the county through his mother, the late Mathilda of Flanders.

By this time, I had made several efforts to gain an audience with my father and protest the Anjou marriage again, but I was always refused. Hardly a word passed between my father and me in those days. Once, I tried to address him at dinner, but he replied, "Not tonight!" and rose to get another glass of mead. It was a sorry state of affairs. I walked by him in the passage one day, and he pretended not to see or hear me. That is the game of a small child!

I dearly hoped—yes, I hoped and prayed—that someone other than Clito would be made count of Flanders, and that this would change things on the Continent in such a way that a different marriage would be sought by my father. In truth, this was the only way his will could be changed: not by any words of mine. His will was harder to breach than the highest bulwark. So after a week or so, I stopped seeking an audience. I simply waited and hoped.

One day, the king went off hunting with the lords and Queen Adeliza, while I stayed behind in the lodge with only a few members of the household. Around midday, I became quite hungry and decided to walk down to the kitchen to see what was left from the feast the night before. I descended a small spiral stair to the lowest level, which was partially buried in the earth. Here I entered the kitchen through a door so small that I felt the need to duck, although I am not an especially tall person.

The room was large and open, with the hearth almost covering the east wall. The great spits sat mostly idle, waiting for the lords to deliver their latest kills. Only a poor old goose was making the rounds for supper. The western wall was covered with an array of pans and knives hung with care. There was a large water basin for cleaning the dishes on the far wall, and two long tables placed beside one another. On one, a cook was grinding grain for bread, and on the other a servant was slicing garlic and leeks. I noticed the remnants of a cheese wheel at the end of the table nearest me.

"Excuse me, but may I take some of this?" I asked the cook.

The woman had been so intent upon her work that she evidently had not heard me enter the room. When she looked up, her head snapped back slightly in surprise.

"Empress!" she said, bowing, wiping her hands frantically on her apron, and adjusting her cap. "We happy sees you."

This was a very odd comment, but I quickly recognized that the woman must have little knowledge of the Norman tongue. Upon hearing her words, the other servant, a young man, recognized what was happening and appeared to fumble his knife as he moved quickly to remove his cap and bow his head. He opened his mouth but seemed to struggle to form any words. I could almost see his mind straining to remember any bit of Norman he had been taught. I wanted to spare them both the trouble, so I reached back into my own memory for some words of the native tongue my mother had taught me in my youth. It had been so long since I made regular use of the language, but I was determined to try.

"*Wesap hale!*" I said in greeting. "*Forgiefe mec. Bidde—*" Here I pointed to the cheese and then myself.

"*Gea! Gea!*" the woman said, picking it up and handing it to me.

"*Ic þancie þē!*" I said, thanking her.

I then moved through the small door to my right, next to all the pans. I knew this led to the cellar. The only light in the room came from a small window near the ceiling that was so covered in grime that it hardly deserved the name. I could see at least that the center of the room was full of barrels, while the bottles rested on wood shelves along the walls.

"Where in God's name are the candles?" I muttered.

I had only just spoken the words when I heard the noise of approaching steps behind me and turned to see that it was the young man from the kitchen come with not merely a candle, but a torch.

"Thank you!" I said, without thinking.

Fortunately, he seemed to understand at least that much, for he bowed his head in acknowledgment.

With torch in hand, I was able to move into the cellar and examine the bottles. I was hoping to find more of the wine from Cluny, but no matter how many hastily written labels I read, I did not find the object of my search. I did, however, breathe in quite a bit of dust, which caused me to sneeze. I then heard the pounding of boots upon the wood floor and turned back to see Drogo's form in the glow of the fire.

"Good afternoon, my lady," he said.

"Good afternoon, Sir Drogo," I replied. "Do you happen to know if they keep any of that stock from Cluny here?"

He did not respond, which concerned me. I moved closer to him and held up the torch so I could clearly make out his features. All the marks of concern were written upon his face.

"Oh God," I whispered. "Is someone hurt? Did someone die? Tell me, Drogo! I command you!"

"This has nothing to do with the king's company," he assured me. "The news is from Flanders."

His visage had told me the news before his lips could. I knew what he was about to say. I knew it and I feared it.

"I am afraid that William Clito has been chosen as the new count of Flanders."

I let out a great sigh. "Of course he has."

With the torch still held aloft in my hand, I closed my eyes and allowed the pain to waft over me. If Clito was count of Flanders, then my last hope of changing the king's mind was gone. Indeed, I had as much hope of escape as a corpse from the grave. He would want—indeed, he would need—the alliance with Anjou to keep the French out of Normandy. Even I could see that marrying Geoffrey of Anjou made the most sense. But oh, how I hated the idea! My closed eyelids and my cheeks pressed together as I once again began to cry. I'm afraid I shed many tears during that part of my life.

"Empress Mathilda, what can I do? How can I help you?" Drogo asked, taking the torch from me with one hand and placing the other on my shoulder.

"There is nothing—nothing anyone can do to help me," I told him, my voice quivering.

"You are worried about marrying Geoffrey of Anjou?"

I never did understand why Drogo felt it necessary to state things that were well known to all. I could only imagine that someone in his childhood had been impossible to understand.

I opened my eyes again. "Well, yes! Wouldn't you be?"

"Perhaps it will not be so very bad," he offered. "He is only a young man now, but he may grow into a mighty warrior. Many marriages are begun under odd circumstances, but they become strong."

Was Drogo really that thick? Surely not! He did not know how to ease my pain, so he was resorting to empty phrases. I could see it in his eyes.

"It's not only that. I know that most of the Norman lords hate the Angevins, and now I am to become one of them!" I shook my head in frustration. "All this to preserve a dynasty, and I don't even know if there will be children to whom I can hand the throne."

I covered my face in my hands and wept. Without asking, Drogo reached out and embraced me with his free arm. It was not ordinary behavior for a knight, but I was too upset to concern myself with such things. In any case, we were family in all but name, and nothing about my life was ordinary. After a minute or so, my crying slowed, and I was able to speak again.

"I admit that my anger at the king has poisoned everything. I do not think I would have preferred an alliance with Anjou under any circumstances, but it is even worse given how it has come about."

"What do you mean?" he asked, looking down at me. "Did something happen?"

For a moment, I considered telling him everything that had taken place over the past year, but I thought better of it. What good would come from awakening that tale of woe when my fate was already certain? I simply buried my face in his chest again and remained silent.

"Well, there is one thing I can tell you that might grant your spirit some peace—at least, I hope it will."

"Oh?" I said, looking up. "Is there any good news left in this wretched world?"

"If you will have me, I intend to come with you to Anjou, or even to Africa if need be. You are the best mistress a knight could have, and I will follow you until the end, which I hope is not any time soon."

What wonderful words! Truly, what had I done to be blessed with such a friend?

"That does help," I said, nodding my head. "Indeed, knowing I will have one friend at least is a boon."

"Come," he said, releasing me and grabbing one of the bottles from the shelf. "Let us return to the upper level and drown our sorrows."

As he turned to leave, I cried, "Wait!" I then picked up another bottle with each hand, holding the cheese underneath my arm.

"I like the way you think!" he said with a wink.

It was around this time that I received another note from Bishop Hildebert of Tours. Since he lent me that flattering lyric, our correspondence had yielded fewer results than I had hoped. My request for information about the young Geoffrey of Anjou was met only with the usual empty praise—nothing that might help me discern the young man's character. Now he sent me the following letter:

> *Your page fulfills my desire to know about you more richly than others' accounts. For whatever I get from you about yourself will be more certain to me than what common rumor might bring to my ears. Therefore, when I learned that winds blew in your service favorable to sending a message across the Channel, I immediately sent letters to you about what had been conveyed from England revealing the will of the king and what the father's breast was feeling about the offense of the daughter. I claim from you what I deserve to know through you. I claim, indeed, but as your friend in the Lord, as your servant in Christ, as one who puts your honor at the forefront of my happiness. What you know, therefore, about the king and yourself that should be told to a friend, I ask you to tell me.*

There was a message I liked not! "The offense of the daughter." The only offense I could think of was my objection to Geoffrey of Anjou, so I concluded that word must have reached him that

I was opposed to the marriage—a true surprise, given that only a few people knew of my father's intention. Perhaps the good bishop had merely sensed in my inquiry the shade of rebellion. So here he was, searching out secrets, but hiding it in the language of a spiritual guide. No, thank you! I would not be discussing this matter with him!

As for my father, he continued to aid any person who could be seen to pose a challenge to the new Count William of Flanders. With one hand, he sent Stephen to negotiate with the enemy in Bruges, and with the other he raised support for William of Ypres and Thierry of Alsace. "Just wait for it!" he declared. "The usurper will make a mistake. These fools always do. He will turn the people against him."

Yes, when my father wasn't crushing my hopes and showing contempt for my person, he was able to pass on some of the benefits of his experience. Just as he had said, Count William did anger the Flemings when he and the French king executed twenty-eight accused murderers of the former count without having them properly tried, paying no heed to the codes of justice. The citizens of Bruges had welcomed their new count with open arms, but after they saw all those men thrown from the summit of the tower without any regard for their own laws, they began to have serious doubts. Those doubts were confirmed when the traitor Clito imposed a new tax on the movement of goods. He was driven out of much of his own county, with several of the major towns in open rebellion. With his great ally, the king of France, no longer by his side, his weakness was made clear.

Even as all of this was taking place, King Henry traveled to Westminster during the Rogation days for a legatine council called by Archbishop William of Canterbury. I believe this meeting had something to do with Archbishop William's dispute with Archbishop Thurstan of York, but that is not the chief thing I remember about it. I was naturally in attendance, along with all the lords and bishops of England. Not in attendance were three delegates sent by Count Fulk of Anjou: they were staying at the abbey across the way, putting out the story that they were simple pilgrims. In truth, they were there to negotiate a marriage on behalf of their master's son. I did not approve of the king's decision to keep this matter secret, as I knew how such things tend to find the public ear, and when they do it is best not to appear deceitful. However, it was clear what the king thought of my opinion.

Let him get shouted down by the lords when they find out. He deserves it! I mused. *Perhaps he will make such a mess of things that the marriage will fall through!*

Yet no sooner had I thought this than I recognized that such a thing was not possible. Once my father had set his mind on something, the whole world could not make him change course. He would find some way to get his way, as he always did. If anyone was to feel the pain of the lords, it would be me.

We were gathered in Westminster Hall: the same place where I had spent so much time a few months earlier. As usual, the dais was set up at the eastern end of the massive hall, and on it sat my father and me, along with the archbishop of Canterbury, as he was the one who had called the council. About a hundred men stood on the stone floor in front of us, and on the walk high above that wrapped around the entire room, men at arms were standing guard. I was braced for a most tiresome afternoon of lords and bishops babbling on about this and that, for such is the life of a royal lady.

The opening words had been completed, the archbishop had said his peace, and there was a call for any other business.

"I have a question!" said Bishop William Giffard of Winchester. He was standing near the front of the crowd, raising his right hand and lifting himself on his toes.

"Pray, speak it now," the archbishop of Canterbury replied.

"My question is for the king," he continued, returning to his normal height and folding his hands together. "I have it on good authority that there are currently three men from Anjou staying as guests of the abbot of Westminster. I was just there on a visit yesterday. Abbot Herbert declared that they were there on pilgrimage, but when I spoke to one of the men—Renaud something or other—he said they were called here by the king. I pressed him, but he would speak no further. His fellows entreated him to silence. So with all due respect, lord king, why are they here?"

Here was the moment I had both longed for and feared in turn. As far as I knew, there were only four people in the room who were aware of the king's intention to marry me to Geoffrey of Anjou and therefore understood the purpose of the Angevins' visit: the king himself, Earl Robert of Gloucester, Brian fitz Count, and me. By the look of complete surprise on the face of Bishop Roger of Salisbury, who as always was standing in front of everyone else, I received confirmation that he had not been told. Neither, it seemed, had the archbishop of Canterbury or the earl of Surrey, for they both looked positively at a loss for answers. I then turned along with every other person in the room to look at my father, who had not yet responded.

"My king," the archbishop of Canterbury asked, walking a step closer to his master and speaking in a low voice, "what are we to make of this report?"

"Everyone will please settle down!" the king said in a firm tone of voice, though I noted that no one had done anything particularly uncouth as of yet. "Thank you, Bishop William, for making the ambassadors feel so welcome. You see, both stories are true. They are here to view the holy relics and to see our magnificent country, and also to speak with myself."

"Speak about what?" Bishop Roger inquired, stepping as close as he could to the dais without actually mounting it.

My father turned to look at me. I cannot think why, for I had no intention of raising a finger to help him after he rejected my advice. Chatter began to grow, and he looked back at the crowd.

"Very well!" he declared, none too happily. "For reasons of necessity, I had not declared their purpose until now, but they are here …" He paused for just a moment and looked at me again. Was that regret I saw in his eyes? Perhaps not. "They are here to discuss the marriage between my daughter, the Empress Mathilda, and Geoffrey of Anjou, son of the count," he continued.

In my memory of that moment, I always hear a gasp from the crowd, but that may just be the product of years. Whatever the case, they were clearly both surprised and offended. All at once, several of them began to speak, so that the king was forced to raise his hand for silence.

"One at a time! One at a time!" he ordered.

Bishop Roger of Salisbury was in no mood to wait his turn. "My lord, my king, you know I love you more than the woman who bore me, but this is an outrage! I was never once asked for my opinion!"

"You are not the lord of England, no matter what men say!" the king cried, stepping very close to the edge of the dais and pointing down at the man below. "I sought the counsel of exactly those persons whose counsel I required."

"And who was that?" Bishop Roger demanded. He looked up at the archbishop of Canterbury, who was standing off to the side of the dais. "Did you know about this?"

"I must own that I did not," he replied, careful to temper his words.

"We know the bishop of Winchester was left out," Bishop Roger continued. "What about you, or you, or you?" he asked, pointing at some of the lords in turn. "Did he seek your advice?"

They shook their heads, and Bishop Roger turned back to face the king.

"I demand to know who counseled you!" he cried.

Even in the middle of that horrible argument, I was rather impressed to see Bishop Roger, for once in his life, refraining from flattering the king and instead speaking his own mind. What a pity it had to come at such a time! There was only one thing worse than having to marry Geoffrey of Anjou: having to marry him against the objections of the nobles and bishops. I needed them to support me whenever my father went to his eternal reward—or damnation. They would be unlikely to do so if they detested my husband. I understood the bishop's anger, for I had long been angry myself. Yet I also feared his anger, for I knew him to be an exceedingly powerful man. What was more, there was a very faint hope within me that the objections of the lords might just be enough to make my father change his course. I was torn within, uncertain what to wish for.

"Shut your mouth, or I will be more than happy to shut it for you!" the king responded, and not a very clever response at that.

But Bishop Roger would not be silent. It was as if his apparent loss of influence over the king had caused him to lose his fear as well. "Wait! I think I can say with some confidence that the three people you spoke with were ... oh, let's see ... Robert of Gloucester, Stephen of Blois, and Brian fitz Count! And, if she was fortunate, the empress."

A few people actually clapped, no doubt displaying the jealousy they all felt toward these younger men who had earned the king's favor. There was only one problem, of course.

"I was never told!" cousin Stephen shouted, pushing his way to the front of the crowd. "I swear to God, I was just as ignorant as the rest of you! You think this offends your honor? Anjou is the sworn enemy of the House of Blois! If anyone has reason to take offense, it is me and mine!"

So evidently Stephen had not been told, and by his declaration, the reason was made quite apparent: the king feared he would oppose the match. Yes, I had hoped that the opposition of these men would lead my father to repent of the Angevin marriage, but it seemed it was a false hope. If he had not sought the counsel of Bishop Roger or even Count Stephen, it was because he had decided not to let their opinions influence him. Therefore, I feared the clash of wills I was witnessing. Indeed, I felt so ill at ease that I wished for the floor to open and swallow me whole. I was gripping the arms of my chair, my whole body straining.

"Enough!" my father bellowed. "Perhaps you have all forgotten who sits on the throne! I do! I, the son of William the Conqueror: I sit on the throne! Now, I have borne your complaints up until this point, but if anyone speaks another word against me, I will hold it as treason! It matters not who advised me, for I am the one who decides! Yes, I am the one who decides! Not you, not you, and not you!" Here he pointed his finger at different persons in turn, as if attempting to put the fear of God in them. "The death of Count Charles and elevation of the infamous traitor William Clito has left our realms in danger, and an alliance with Anjou is the only way to ensure the peace and prosperity of both Normandy and England. I will hear no more debate on this matter! Geoffrey of Anjou is a descendant of Emperor Charles the Great, a proper husband for our daughter. You will respect him as your lord, even as you have respected me all these years, though I am beginning to doubt it. Now, I have heard quite enough for one morning. We will suspend until further notice!"

He then descended the steps and marched out the main door to my right at a furious pace, with brother Robert and a few others chasing after him. I remained in my seat, too stunned by what had just happened to move, though my mind was very much at work. The whole room broke into conversation. Several men went up to praise Bishop Roger for his words, patting him on the back, while others seemed to fume in silence. No one dared to speak with me, though I received more than one look of disdain.

They all hate me! I thought. *And I did not even want this awful marriage! The king should have listened to me. Why did he keep this secret?*

I finally stood up and walked down the stairs, pushing my way past a few bishops and lords. I was quite angry, primarily with my father, but I dared not speak to anyone and utter something I would come to regret. I had made it through most of the crowd on my way to the same door through which the king had lately departed, when I heard Stephen's voice behind me.

"Empress Mathilda!"

I had not the slightest hint of desire to speak with him, but to shun him would place me in greater danger. I therefore turned to face him.

"Yes, Count Stephen?"

"The Anjou marriage cannot take place. It would degrade the lords of Normandy—especially my own house," he said angrily, his hands on his hips.

"Cousin, I think you mis—"

"You have been pushing for this, have you not?"

"What?!" I cried, for I could not help myself, his accusation was so absurd. "I have been opposing it at every turn!"

"Well, you have not done very well at that, now have you?!" he bellowed, red in the face.

"Honestly, cousin, do you think I control the king? Do you think that anyone in this room cares what I have to say? The king is far more likely to seek your advice."

"And yet he has not done so on this occasion. I have been left in the dark. Do you have any idea how much of a fool that makes me appear before men? It is a humiliation!"

For a moment, I stood there staring into my cousin's eyes. I had never seen him so enraged. His eyes were wide—his lower lip quivering slightly. I felt for a moment as if I was looking into his soul. With that one word, "humiliation," he seemed to have betrayed something about himself. At least, that was my suspicion. Yet I had little time to consider the matter, for the archbishop of Canterbury was tugging on Stephen's tunic, bidding him to let me go.

"The Empress Mathilda is not to blame. She is a servant of the king's will, even as we all are."

"Thank you, archbishop," I replied softly, then said to my cousin, "Do you want to know what humiliation is? Humiliation is for a woman of royal blood, the former wife of an emperor, crowned by the Holy Father himself, beloved by a kingdom, to be sent away to marry a child of little rank like some cheap toy to be played with today and thrown away tomorrow. To be a woman, cousin: that is the humiliation of humiliations. You will never understand."

With that, I turned, threw back the train of my gown, and departed the hall. Things had not gotten off to a particularly good start. Yet for all the complaints made by the bishops, it was Stephen's words that caused me the greatest concern.

CHAPTER FOURTEEN

Having stirred up the ire of the lords, the king of England knew he must move with all speed to ensure that I was, in his immortal words, "wedded and bedded." Less than a fortnight after the council at Westminster, we were putting in at Southampton waters on our way to Honfleur, and thenceforth on to Rouen: the king, myself, Earl Robert, Drogo, the crew, and in a final act of ill humor on the part of the king, Brian fitz Count. These were the men who would accompany me to my first meeting with the man—nay, the boy—I was to marry.

For several months, I had been on a journey of sorts from complete opposition to the Angevin marriage to grudging acceptance—extremely grudging. I had finally reached the point where I was forced to accept defeat for the good of the kingdom, only to have it thrown in my face when the lord and the bishops voiced their objections. I hoped for only two things from my second marriage: that it would produce children and keep the peace.

I had always been rather uncertain about the first, and now the second seemed unlikely as well. There had been no formal rebellion due to the announcement of the marriage agreement, but neither did anyone seem to be very happy about it. Thus, I was filled with fear upon that journey, and my mood was made worse because Brian was often nearby. This kept the wound in my heart fresh as I was forced to think of the love I had lost hour by hour.

The day before our departure from England, we were all staying at Southampton Castle, with most of us sitting in the large wood hall, eating and drinking by the fire. There were a few tables at which the others played games, but I was reclining in a chair by the hearth, reading the daily hours. A teller of fortunes knocked at the front gate of the castle, hoping to benefit from our largess. He was allowed to come in and approach those of us in the hall. Were it up to me, he would not have made it past the threshold, but the men who were to sail with us were given to superstition. How they hung on his every word! He worked his way through the company, winning over the lot of them, before coming at last to his primary object.

He approached me quietly, the smile on his face appearing somewhat savage given that half his teeth were missing. He had very long hair pulled back in a tie and an equally long beard. I suspected he was either too much of a sluggard to use scissors or too poor to own them. He wore a plain tunic with several holes. His hands were wrapped in cloths, as was his neck, and I could only hope that this was not because he was a leper. There was dirt on his face, and he had hair pushing out from his nose. The only thing he carried was a small purse, filled with coins by the sound of it. He looked as if he could use a bath: yes, his entire appearance was most unpleasing. There was another chair just across from mine, and he sat in it without asking permission.

"Gracious empress, before you set sail for parts unknown, would you have me proclaim your future?" he asked in a voice much like that of a toad, smiling again with his few dark teeth.

"I know my future. I am to marry the imp from Anjou," I replied, looking back down at my book.

"Ah, but perhaps you wish to know if your marriage will produce any children! I can look into the nether world—"

"No need. A rabbi already told me I will have sons."

"I beg your pardon, my lady. What was that?"

"A rabbi—you know, a Jew. He put his hands on my belly and swore that I would have sons. That's assurance enough for me."

"Yes, but you can hardly trust a Jew, can you?" he said with a cackle.

I thought it quite likely that I could trust the Jews more than the man in front of me, but I saw it was no use attempting to avoid a conversation. I closed my book and set it on the floor.

"Let me guess: you won't leave until I pay you," I said, finally looking him in the eye.

"I wouldn't put it that way. I would simply say that I would hate to rob you of a wondrous opportunity." Here he rubbed his hands together in glee.

Wanting nothing more than to get him out of my sight as soon as possible, I reached into the purse attached to my belt and pulled out a small coin, placing it in his filthy palm.

"The tall one gave me more than this!" he objected, gesturing toward Drogo.

With a deep sigh, I gave him two more coins.

"Thank you muchly!" he said. "Now, give me your hands."

I hated the idea of him touching any part of me. "Is that really necessary?"

"Most necessary! The magic will not work otherwise!"

"Yes, but there is no magic, is there? You will devise something so general that it could be applied to anything."

"I am no fraud!" he declared, placing his hand on his chest as if he was taking a solemn vow. "Fine. I will simply look into your eyes. That will tell me all I need to know."

"If you must ..."

He leaned very far forward and stared into my eyes. His smell was like cat piss. Indeed, I thought he must sleep in a puddle of it. I moved back slightly, attempting to spare my nose. His eyes were deep and dark, and they were searching mine as one who looks for a gold coin in the hay.

"I can see that you are a person who has experienced great loss," he concluded.

"The deaths of my mother, brother, and husband are common knowledge."

"It is not death I speak of! Something else is eating away at your soul. You were wounded by someone close to you."

He seemed very near the mark, but then again, half the people in the world could have found some meaning in those words. I therefore pressed him further to prove his powers.

"Who?" I asked.

He cackled again. "Surely you already know!"

"Yes, but if you really have the gift of sight, then you can tell me who it was."

"That is not how it works!" he protested. "I only see shadows."

"I figured as much," I said, making to leave my seat.

"Wait! Wait a minute!" he cried, holding up his hands. "There is something else: something strong! Only, I do not understand it."

"Well, if you do not understand it, then how should I?" I asked, standing up completely.

"I see a lion, the king of beasts, stalking the earth."

"Are you saying I will be eaten by a lion? There is but one of those beasts in England, and I just left it behind at Woodstock."

"No, I think it is a person—that is, the lion is the symbol of a person."

"Oh, that must be my grandfather you're thinking of: the first King William. The lion was his symbol. He must be watching over me," I said, hoping to speed the process along.

"No, that's not it," the soothsayer replied, turning his head as if to hear some whispering voice. "No, it's something else. Something in the future—I can feel it!"

"Well, thank you, this has been most helpful!" I concluded. "Now, I have a long journey tomorrow, and I must take some rest. Sir Drogo will see you out."

Thus ended a particularly odd conversation, with Drogo essentially picking the man up and carrying him out of the hall despite his protestations. By no means did I actually think the man saw a lion, but if he had, it may have been the beasts of Anjou circling to devour my hopes.

When we arrived at last in Rouen, we remained there for the next year, in part to allow the king's ambassadors time to work out a treaty with Anjou, but mainly because of what was taking place in Flanders. This was an unhappy period of waiting for me in which I often visited the monastery of Bec for weeks at a time, both for the sake of my soul, which was continually troubled, and to escape the presence of my father and Brian. I first developed a strong affection for that house during that period.

By that summer of 1127, the county of Flanders was at war. William of Ypres, my father's favored contender, had already been taken prisoner. Never one to give up easily, King Henry had turned his attentions to Duke Thierry of Alsace, whose strongest support lay in the northern merchant cities.

My father's intention was simple: he would work along with Queen Adeliza's father—Duke Godfrey of Louvain—and Count Stephen of Boulogne to place a siege upon the whole of Flanders, not through armed might, but by the power of the purse. They imposed a block on trade, placing the entire Flemish market under severe duress. Their aim was to rob William Clito of money and set the people against his rule. It was a harsh method, but one that was likely to yield results. Of course, my father also continued to bribe as many of the castellans as he could. One can never be too careful about such things.

The traitor Clito then set his sights upon the county of Boulogne, cousin Stephen's realm. He hoped by invading to cut himself out of King Henry's noose, securing one of the vital sea ports in Flanders and destroying Stephen's forces in the process. Though he met with some victories at first, Count Stephen had the experience of many battles and was keen to defend his wife's ancestral lands. They fought for about a month before Clito was forced to return to Flanders, where the rebellion against his rule was growing by the day. He concluded a truce with Stephen, and thus the blockade held.

I was quite proud of my cousin in that hour. I would receive regular reports from Flanders while I was at the monastery of Bec. Clito's alliance with the French king was the reason I was being made to marry Geoffrey of Anjou, so naturally I wished ill on them both. I also wanted to see the duchy of Normandy held, for it was the inheritance granted to me by my ancestor Rollo, the Northman who had first won it from the Franks. Although my heart was more with England than Normandy—which put me at odds with many in the king's company—I certainly saw its value and did not want it diminished. However, I had no part in the battles in Flanders. I spent my days reading scripture and attempting to resign myself to the marriage I knew must come. I supposed the one good thing about the delay was that young Geoffrey would have the chance to mature slightly. Every time I thought about how young he was, it made me cringe.

In the meantime, Thierry of Alsace won the support of the northern Flemish cities with strong trade links to England. With only the southern lords still true to him, the traitor Clito was forced to make a desperate choice: he released William of Ypres from prison on the condition that he fight along with his own men. He also rode south to meet King Louis, but even as he did so, Thierry gained control of Lille.

The French king knew he had no choice but to ride to his vassal's defense. He sent William Clito back to the North to wreak destruction upon the cities there, then rode to meet Thierry's forces at Lille. Of course, we all feared upon hearing this intelligence that it might spell the end of Duke Thierry's efforts, but little did we know how God smiled on him. His men defeated the French army and sent them fleeing back to the South. It would be the last time the French fought on Clito's behalf, for King Henry's forces were by then moving into Louis' own lands, and the French king had no choice but to direct his efforts toward that quarter.

Things were going rather well, and we all thought the reign of Clito would be over by summer's end. I therefore made my return to Rouen, there to fulfill my duty. King Henry finally felt it was safe enough to summon Geoffrey of Anjou to Rouen, and he intended to make him a knight after the manner of the Normans.

I remember one night around that time, when we were all feasting in the hall of Rouen Castle, for it shows how high the king's spirits were at that time. He was leaning back in his tall chair, feet resting on the table, not caring one bit if the mud on his boots landed in the soup. He had already thrown back three pints of ale and was savoring a fourth.

"I cannot wait to see this boy with my own eyes!" he proclaimed. "In his face, I hope to glimpse the future of my dynasty!"

"Let us pray then that it is not covered with pock marks," Robert jested.

"I should think not! Everyone says that he is—"

"The fairest youth in the land? Yes, you may have mentioned it."

We soon received word that the party from Anjou was staying at the abbey of Bec and would be with us presently. Along with Archbishop Geoffrey of Rouen, we made ready to welcome the foreigners. The king would be relying on both the archbishop and Earl Robert to complete the marriage agreement.

When the terrible day arrived, I made my way to the outer yard near the gardens. There most of the king's court was already standing at the ready upon the gravel, talking among themselves. I moved past the household servants, the king's lads, and the rest of the knights without addressing any of them. All I could think of was how scared I was of whatever might come through that gate in the castle wall, for I knew it would determine my future. I dearly hoped it would not be as bad as I suspected.

I greeted the archbishop and Abbot Rainfroy of Saint Ouen, who were already waiting by the king's side at the head of the reception party. Queen Adeliza was not there, for reasons I cannot remember.

"Good morning, most excellent Empress Mathilda!" the archbishop called as I approached. "What a pleasant day for us to receive your future husband!"

"Thank you for coming," I said with rather less ardor, a knot in both my stomach and my throat. "Any word on when they are to arrive?"

"Less than an hour out," he assured me.

I nodded gently. I was in that odd position where half of me wished to delay the painful revelation as long as possible, and half of me wished it to come instantly that it might be over and done with. I took a deep breath to calm myself and attempted to produce a smile.

"Abbot Rainfroy, good morrow!" I said, shifting down the line.

"And to you, my lady," he replied with a bow.

"So I suppose there is nothing left to do but wait," I mused, turning my gaze toward the broad wood gate in front of us. It seemed almost a gate of doom.

Oh, cease your complaining, Maud! I chided myself. *Many people live far worse lives than you. At least you have food to eat and a bed in which to sleep. What man or woman alive wouldn't gladly trade places with you, no matter how bad your new husband might be?*

I tried to tell myself this. I had been attempting to believe it for more than a year, and yet the words seemed hollow. Something inside me could not be stilled, and I suddenly felt the need to flee from the sight of that gate until the last possible moment.

"I think I shall return to the hall for now. Have someone come and retrieve me when they arrive," I said.

As I turned, I saw that my brother had come up behind me and must have heard the last part of my conversation.

"You will not have to wait long. They are here already!" he proclaimed, pointing ahead.

Sure enough, the gates were opening, and a party of riders entered: eight men in all. One I knew to be the abbot of Bec. Two appeared to be bishops. The rest were knights, save for one man in plain clothes and another younger man whom I took to be Geoffrey.

I will never forget how he looked in that first moment, when I saw him riding in on that white horse. He was a good bit shorter than the rest, being not yet fifteen years old. What he lacked in height, he more than made up for in his manner of dress. Good Lord! I had never seen a young man dress in that manner before, nor a grown man for that matter!

His tunic was made entirely of purple silk with gold thread. It was clothing meant less for purpose than for show. Most of all, I remember the hat, which was far larger than necessary and adorned with flowers. Beneath it was a long trail of red curls—so long that I had no doubt that he spent far more time caring for his tresses than I did mine. Perhaps this was meant to distract from the absence of hair on his face, but to me it seemed rather vain. Even the king of England did not wear silk for riding! The scriptures tell us not to judge based on outward appearance, but in my experience, it can reveal something about the inner man, especially when it comes to nobles attempting to promote themselves through extravagant dress.

He alighted with ease and began to walk toward us. The sword at his side was clearly meant for a much larger man, for it hung almost to his ankles. Why he needed a sword under such circumstances, I was not certain. Even his boots seemed from another world entirely, for they were painted with pink roses! I had observed him for less than a minute, and already an impression had formed in my mind of a boy so full of conceit, so arrogant, so pompous … well, I need hardly go on, for you sense my mind. I lived in fear of what might spring forth once he opened his mouth. Did I see merely what I wanted to see, or rather what I feared? Perhaps, but I am only human after all.

"Kill me, Robert. Kill me quickly!" I whispered to my brother, who was standing just beside me.

"Sorry, I should hate to hang," he replied, barely stifling a laugh.

The young Geoffrey came within two paces of us and removed his great hat, bowing so low that the red curls draped over his shoulders came close to the ground.

He then returned to his usual upright position and placed his hat back on his head, adjusting one of the flowers, and for the first time I heard him speak.

"God save King Henry!" he proclaimed, with the same manner of voice I had often heard among men from Anjou or Aquitaine. The tone was neither high nor low, strong nor weak. It betrayed nothing of his feelings.

"You must be Lord Geoffrey!" said the archbishop of Rouen. "Let me bid you welcome to Rouen and to Normandy!"

"Thank you," the young man said, with a slight smile that was almost a smirk. "Your duchy is very ... nice. Very proper."

I thought this reply a bit odd, but then again, I was disposed to think ill of him. I also noted that at no point since he had arrived had he given me more than a passing glance, while I seemed unable to look away from the spectacle before me, almost as if I were at a bloody joust.

The archbishop continued, "Allow me to introduce his grace King Henry of England, Abbot Rainfroy of the monastery of Saint Ouen, Earl Robert of Gloucester, and of course, Her Royal Highness, Empress Mathilda."

"Well met, Lord Geoffrey! We are glad to have you among us at last!" the king said, stepping forward.

The young man clasped arms with the king. I was a bit surprised to see my father raise his right hand and pull the younger man's face toward himself until their foreheads touched. It was a rather intimate gesture for two people who had just met, and I wondered if the king saw it as a mark of fatherly affinity, as if he hoped that Geoffrey could take the place of William. Perhaps he merely thought it the usual custom in Anjou, but given the look of slight confusion on Geoffrey's face, I guessed it was not common there either.

"Tell me, how is your father, Count Fulk?" King Henry asked, as the two men—if indeed they both deserved the title—let go of each other.

"As well as always," young Geoffrey replied. "He sends his greeting."

"Here is my daughter, your future bride," my father said, stepping back so he could have a clear view.

Geoffrey looked me up and down, rather as one might a horse for sale. He took a step closer to me, and his eyes examined my face. However, he said nothing, nor did he smile. I sensed that he was not impressed.

"Well met, Lord Geoffrey," I finally said, hoping to break the silence.

Three of the men with young Geoffrey had by that point walked up behind him, and he turned and whispered something to them. All three nodded with vigor.

"Thank you, Empress Mathilda," he finally said to me with a bow of the head. "Thank you, lords of Normandy. We have come to you as soon as we could. This is the bishop of Angers and the bishop of Le Mans."

I felt compelled to engage him further. After all, this young man was to be my husband. I chose a subject that seemed in line with custom.

"Did you have a pleasant journey?" I asked.

Young Geoffrey made no answer, but simply shrugged his shoulders. The man in secular garb behind him then stepped forward and spoke.

"Our journey was most pleasant, Your Highness. You must forgive Lord Geoffrey. We have ridden many miles, and he is tired."

"And who are you?" I asked.

"Hugh of Durtal, my lady. I serve as chancellor. Count Fulk was most sorry that he could not be with us today, but he is just completing his affairs in Anjou, and will be present for your wedding day in the next few weeks—that is, before he departs for his own."

"Yes, we can discuss that inside. Come, we have plenty of food made ready!" the king said.

As we all turned and entered the palace, I muttered to myself in the English tongue in order to avoid being understood. All I knew of it I learned from my mother, and she never used the words that might have been most helpful in that moment. How fortunate then that I remembered my German!

"What are you saying, sister?" Robert asked.

"Never you mind," I replied.

Young Geoffrey was walking beside the king, shaking his hair back and forth like a fool.

God damn you, William Clito! I thought. *This is no lion! He is half cock and half ass!*

Ever since the *White Ship* went down along with all our fortunes, King Henry of England had desired three things above all else. First, he wished to have the marriage alliance with Anjou restored to Normandy. Second, he wished to have a son restored to himself. The king was now to have both his wishes granted through my marriage to Geoffrey of Anjou. Not only would it ensure the Norman union with that county, but my father would once again have a son to mold after his own image.

This is how things might have appeared, but the truth was less clear. To start with, Geoffrey of Anjou was no William Ætheling. He was not of the same flesh and blood, nor was he likely to share the Norman view of the world. He would have the interests of his own house to defend. Second, it was not certain how much of a son Geoffrey would be, for there was some debate even in those early days over whether he was a true heir of King Henry.

That Geoffrey and I were to be joint rulers upon my father's death, no one disputed, but as is so often the case with legal matters, there was much disagreement as to what that actually meant. You need not doubt my opinion: the lords of England and Normandy had sworn to me before the marriage was ever announced. They were not asked to make such an oath to young Geoffrey when we were betrothed. Therefore, although my future husband would likely play some role, authority would lie with myself and our children, if indeed we were able to have children. Needless to say, the Angevins always saw things differently, and in the interest of ensuring the match, King Henry did his utmost to avoid lending clarity to the matter.

Thus, as the day drew near for young Geoffrey to be made a knight, to be quickly followed by our wedding, there was as much unknown as known. This is all without mentioning the war that continued in Flanders, which filled our thoughts daily. On account of the fighting, neither Count Stephen of Boulogne nor Countess Mathilda would be in attendance. I am sure that pleased them both, for they despised the Anjou alliance. I only wished that I could be absent as well.

On the eve before the knighthood ceremony, we were all packed into the small chapel of Saint Romain within the palace walls for a vigil led by the king's chaplain, Adalulf. The young Geoffrey was then left alone to spend the night fasting and praying. The rest of us did exactly the opposite, engaging in much feasting and mirth. Of course, there was little mirth on my part, for I had still found nothing to love in young Geoffrey, his charms with the ladies notwithstanding. The only good thing I could say for him was that he seemed to be a good rider. The rest of the women at court, on the other hand, were quite taken with him, and were he not ensured a marriage with myself, I am certain he might have had his pick. I cared less about his appearance and more about his inner person: would he be a good husband and father? Of this I was less certain.

The following morning, after young Geoffrey had purified himself and been clothed in his knightly garments, he set out for the cathedral of Rouen accompanied by his two sponsors: William de Warenne, earl of Surrey, and Earl Robert of

Gloucester. I had gone ahead to the cathedral before him in the company of the king and queen, but I could still hear the cheers of the crowd as they made their way to the front gate. I stood at the front of the nave with the queen, while the king stood next to the archbishop just above the altar steps. We all turned to watch Geoffrey's entrance.

The great doors at the opposite end of the nave were opened, and Geoffrey of Anjou made the long walk toward the altar, where his vestments stood ready to receive him. He was a rather magnificent figure that day with his red robe and locks of the same color. On this occasion, it was appropriate for him to look so grand, but I could not help but think that Father Adalulf, whom I had once heard deliver a passionate sermon against the long hair favored by some noble men, might have loved to take the knight's sword and offer that hair as a sacrifice to the Almighty. That might have amused me; however, it was not to be. The procession stopped at the end of the aisle, just in front of the altar, which is to say directly next to us. The two patrons stood in front of young Geoffrey, with two other nobles carrying the train of his robe.

"My lords," the earl of Surrey called out, "we present to you His Excellency, Geoffrey of Anjou, son of Count Fulk V of Maine and Anjou, descendant of Emperor Charles the Great, who has come this day to be knighted."

"Lord Geoffrey," the archbishop asked, from his position near the altar, "are you willing to take your vows this day as a knight in the service of King Henry of England, duke of Normandy?"

"I am," he replied softly but with conviction.

The young Geoffrey then climbed the three stairs carefully and knelt before the altar as his sword and shield were blessed by the archbishop of Rouen. The vestments were then handed to the king and the oath was recited.

"I swear before Almighty God that I will faithfully serve King Henry of England, lord of all Normandy, giving due obedience to the same, that I will not keep company with traitors, nor commit evil in word or deed, but safeguard the helpless, observing all the commands of our Lord Jesus Christ, and doing justice by the oppressed. I make this pledge of my own free will."

Something then happened that neither Geoffrey nor any of the Angevins foresaw. It is the tradition in many parts of this world for the lord to tap the knight on the cheek with the flat of his sword, or perhaps on the shoulder. But the Norman lords never do things halfway, and as I watched my father step forward, I remembered the story of what my grandfather William had done when he knighted his son, and I was certain that King Henry was about to do the same. Sure enough, the king lifted his hand and struck the knight on the side of the face, hard enough that the sound could be clearly heard. I was seated in just the right position to see the expression on Geoffrey's face when this happened, and to say he was displeased would be putting it mildly. His face was turned away from the king because of the blow, and his eyes were wide, nostrils flaring, lips almost clenched together. After a few seconds, he seemed to gain control again, and made to continue with the ceremony.

Fortunately, the rest of it went well, and for the first time I had a small amount of respect for Geoffrey, who despite his plain frustration continued on as if nothing odd had happened. He was given his spurs, sword, and shield by the two earls, and was then proclaimed to be Sir Geoffrey, knight in the king's service. It occurred to me that the two of us were in the same position: we were both being forced to go through with a marriage although we were not entirely happy with the choice of spouse. More than that, we were both forced to act happy about it. It was not much to have in common, but it was something.

Once the ceremony was completed, we all moved back to the palace yard for the tournament. Stands had been built on either side of a course for tilting, and they were covered in bright banners bearing the symbols of Normandy and Anjou. A chain of tents was set up around the course for the preparation of the riders, while the horses were lodged in the stables north of the palace.

At the queen's suggestion, I walked back to where the knights were gathering to wish young Geoffrey good luck. Whether or not I actually wished him to have good luck was perhaps an open question, for were he to fall and break his neck, I might escape the marriage yet. However, I knew that as much as I may have loathed that young man, I needed to make the best of the situation. If we could learn to be allies, then at least we might produce heirs to the throne and thus provide for the security of England and Normandy. Were I to give birth, I might finally gain the respect of my father, or at least have a greater sense of purpose for myself. In any case, it was all I had left to hope for after those I loved were taken from me along with my freedom. But oh, the thought of having to lie with him! I would have as soon bedded a hog, which I suppose makes sense, since my new husband had something of that nature about him.

I made my way to the tents that were set up near the gardens. The largest and grandest of these was being used to dress my future husband in armor for the tournament. When I arrived near the entrance of the tent, I was surprised to see that I was not the first person to wish the knight well. In addition to his squire and groom, Sir Geoffrey was joined by a lady, the daughter of some minor lord. Geoffrey was already clothed in armor save for his helm, and the two of them were conversing while the other men were busy putting things away. Rather than making my presence known, I remained out of sight just outside the tent so that I might hear their conversation, for I was curious to see how the young man would act when the lords of the kingdom were not about to set the fear of God in him.

"What is that on your shield?" the fawning maiden asked.

"Three lions. It was the symbol chosen for me by the king," he responded.

"How magnificent! Is that real gold?"

"The very finest," the boy crowed.

I do believe that I rolled my eyes at that remark. I wanted very much to see what was happening as well as hear it, but I was afraid that if I peeked, I might give myself away.

"My lord, shall I go with William to tend to your horse?" one of the men asked.

"Yes, tell the beast I look forward to riding him!" young Geoffrey replied.

I suddenly recognized that they were coming my way and I would need to hide, but there was no good place to go. Fortunately, as the men walked out of the tent, they threw open the flap. It hit me in the face, stunning me but also concealing me for the space of a moment. As soon as they were gone and I had recovered from the sudden blow, I heard the maiden say, "You know, my lord, if you wished it, you could ride me."

Oh! Apart from being utterly repugnant, that was not even close to clever! I had it in mind to storm in and beat that whore to the ground, but I was more interested in hearing the response of the man I was to marry. As it turned out, he said nothing—at least, nothing I could hear. Well, that silence was enough to drive me mad! I pulled back the cloth just enough to peek inside, and what I saw rather alarmed me: she was kissing him all over, as if she were some wild beast.

"Stop this!" he said, pushing her back.

"But why? Do you not like my kisses?" she whined.

"I have to joust," he told her.

"But sir, will you not wear my colors?" she pleaded. "My love will bring you good fortune!"

"Madam, please, go and watch the tournament."

"Will I see you tonight?" she asked.

Say no, you fool! I thought.

"Speak with my man. He will take care of you," he said, then left the tent so fast that I was forced to run around the corner to be out of sight. I glanced back carefully, just in time to see him begin a new conversation.

"Who was that?" the squire asked him, having just returned from his duties.

"Some local of little significance," young Geoffrey said. "She begs to share my bed, but I'll not have her. She lacks a thing or two, if you take my meaning."

Even as they walked off laughing, I turned the other way and saw the lady slipping out the back. I was not so very wounded by the possibility that I did not have the love of Geoffrey of Anjou. After all, he certainly did not have mine. It was the utter lack of respect that so deeply offended me, both on his part and on hers. Without giving the matter much consideration, I rounded the corner and caught her off guard.

"Stop right there!" I called.

She turned and looked at me, then quickly bowed upon recognizing who I was.

"Empress Mathilda!" she cried. "I did not see you there!"

"Yes, you will find that I am often where you least suppose," I said. "What's your name, girl?"

"Margaret, daughter of the lord of—"

"Really, you must forgive me, Margaret. I don't actually care who you are, for I know what you are: a rotting whore! You are not to see Lord Geoffrey again. Do you understand?"

"But my lady, what if he wishes to speak with me?"

I honestly could not believe that she would ask such a question. Who did she think she was speaking to? I was not about to advise her on how to proposition the man to whom I was betrothed! I took a step closer to her and looked down at her with a firmness of will. She was shorter than me, and indeed she seemed to become shorter with every second she spent under my gaze.

"How old are you?" I asked.

"Fifteen."

"Then if you wish to make it to sixteen, do as I command. From this moment on, you are to stay where you belong: far below my notice or that of anyone else. I will not have you corrupting Sir Geoffrey, but more to the point, I will not allow you to dishonor me in such a way! I am an empress and the daughter of a king! You do not dishonor me! Do you understand?"

"Yes, my lady," she said quietly, her eyes by that point wide with fear.

"Now, get out of my sight!"

"Yes, my lady!"

Once she had run off, I turned and made my way back to the lists, taking my seat on the platform next to Queen Adeliza. She looked at me and smiled.

"How did it go? Did you give your colors to Lord Geoffrey?"

"I would have, but it turned out someone else beat me," I replied.

"What?! Who would dare do such a thing?"

"Oh, she did far more than that!" I replied with a laugh. "She offered him her body as well."

"And what did he do?"

"He refused."

"Well, at least there's that!" she said, the expression on her face oddly hopeful.

I shook my head and cast my eyes forward. "He only refused because she was common, plain, or both. I have little doubt that he would have taken her to bed were she more to his liking."

"You cannot know that for sure. Take care that you do not poison this marriage before it begins."

"How is this my fault?" I objected, snapping my head back in her direction. I am sorry to say that I glared at her.

She cast her eyes down and raised her hands with palms downward, as if hoping to temper my fury. "I am not saying that it is your fault, but if he denied her attentions, then he did as much as he could have."

"He should not have been speaking with her in the first place. It shows a lack of respect for me. At the very least, he is careless."

"Well, that is perhaps a lesser sin. Come, let us watch the games and speak no more about it."

I did as she asked, but I assure you it was not the tournament that occupied my mind.

So my father gifted the imp with lions, I thought to myself. *It must have been a curse after all.*

Having made a knight out of young Geoffrey, there was naught to do but proceed with the marriage. The very next morning, we moved south with some real speed, for the wedding was to take place in just a week's time. We made a brief stop at the abbey in Bernay and another to collect Bishop John of Sées. Between that and the endless forest, it was all we could do to get to Le Mans with a day to spare.

It may seem odd that the marriage was to take place in Le Mans, for it was not a Norman town. However, it was precisely for this reason that it was chosen, for Le Mans was the chief city of the county of Maine, which had been the subject of dispute between Normandy and Anjou far longer than anyone living could remember. The marriage would bring this

Angevin possession within the sphere of Normandy, and thus of England. What better place for King Henry to celebrate his triumph?

For the extent of our journey, my father aimed to speak with young Geoffrey as much as possible, which made it rather difficult for me to have anything like a private conversation with the man I was to marry. I wished very much to make a better study of his character and establish some affinity with him before we were to enter the bonds of wedlock. Even on the eve of our wedding, as we all sat feasting in the hall of the comital palace in Le Mans, my attempts to speak with Geoffrey were constantly repelled. Every man hoped to curry favor with his future lord, or at least to determine whether he was worthy of respect. To make matters worse, we had been joined by young Geoffrey's father, Count Fulk of Anjou, soon to depart for the Holy Land. I say it was worse, because whatever moments might have been left to us after the nobles were through with him, Geoffrey was forced to spend in discussion with the father who was about to depart for ever. All of this made me rather uneasy.

Having failed on that front, I chose instead to make the acquaintance of my cousin, Count Theobald of Blois, properly count of Blois, Chartres, Champagne, and Brie. He was the older brother of cousin Stephen, though not the eldest: that was the pitiable Count William of Sully, who for want of good behavior was denied his birth right by my aunt, Lady Adela of Blois. One can only imagine what that family was like in private! I hoped very much that Count Theobald could provide me with some news from Boulogne, his own opinion of my marriage in comparison with Stephen's, and perhaps a few other things as well.

I approached Theobald as he was standing on the far side of the hall, near the high walk that led to the palatine chapel. He was bending down to fill his goblet from one of the wine barrels. As I approached him, he stood back up to his full height, which I observed was considerably taller than his brother, Stephen. Although the hair on his head was brown, much like mine, his beard was as red as my uncle David's. This was rather strange to me, as Stephen's hair was far darker, whether on his head or his face. Even so, there was no mistaking the connection between them: their noses were the same shape, and they both had bright green eyes. Those eyes were now looking directly at me, and he bowed his head in respect.

"So you are the famous Count Theobald," I said. "It is good to finally meet after hearing so much about you."

"Empress Mathilda, I too am honored to speak with you," he replied. "Would you like a drink?"

"No, but you are kind. I hate to get to the point so quickly, but have you heard anything from your brother?" I asked.

"Which one?"

This was a good point, for as I noted, there were four brothers of Blois in total.

"Ah, right you are. I should have said, have you heard anything from Boulogne? I am most eager for news of the action in Flanders."

"No more than you must have heard," he replied, after taking a drink from his goblet. "Count William is hoping to draw Thierry into battle. He has laid siege to Bruges in the hope of drawing him out. Last I heard, they were somewhere near Ypres."

"Yes, that is what I heard as well," I said, feeling a bit let down. "What a shame that we are no longer in Rouen, for we should have received the news faster there!"

"Perhaps they lie in wait for news from Maine."

"I doubt that. Everyone knows what will happen here. But you must be glad to come to Maine, being a member of the

House of Blois. You have been trying to get here for years, have you not?"

He did not laugh at this jest about his family's ambitions, and I wondered if I had gone too far in bringing up old history.

"I am sorry, my lord. Have I offended you?" I asked, leaning a bit closer and lowering my voice.

"Oh, no! I am sure if you really hoped to wound me, you could mention my brother William's misdeeds."

"I hope you do not think I would stoop to that level! In any case, you can hardly control your brother."

"In truth, he is not as bad as everyone says," Theobald explained, moving the goblet around with his hand as if to support his point, "but he is a source of some discomfort to our dear mother, Lady Adela."

"How is she?" I asked. "Still at the abbey?"

"Yes, she loves it there. The life suits her, and she can keep a watch on her sons from afar."

"And your younger brother, Henry—she must desire great things from him. What a pity that he could not join us either!"

"Well, he could hardly abandon the monks of Glastonbury."

"It is a great honor for him to be made abbot of that house at such a young age," I agreed, nodding my head. "I am sure the king intends to raise him even higher."

"That would certainly please our mother!" he said with a laugh.

I paused for a moment to consider my next words carefully. I had not seen my cousin Stephen in more than a year, and we had not parted on good terms. He had declared the objection of the House of Blois to my marriage with Geoffrey of Anjou. Theobald's presence seemed to signal that not all the family was opposed, but appearances can be deceiving. I therefore proceeded carefully.

"Count Theobald," I began, "when last I saw your brother, we were at Westminster Hall. I believe he was very sore not to have been approached by King Henry about the alliance with Anjou, as he has normally been kept in confidence these past few years."

"Yes, he mentioned something about that to me, but I wouldn't lose sleep over it," said Theobald. "He has a temper on him. That much I will admit. But at the end of the day, he seldom acts unless provoked. No one in the House of Blois wishes to see a division over this issue, I assure you."

"It's just—the support of both your brother and you, not to mention Lady Adela, is of great import to me, not only in terms of kings and kingdoms, but also personally. I would hate to think that any of you felt cheated by King Henry or myself."

"No one feels that way, I promise. But since you have been asking about all of us, what about you, Lady Mathilda? Are you ready for the wedding tomorrow?" he said, motioning toward the dais, where young Geoffrey still held court.

"As ready as I am ever likely to be. I have been trying to talk to him for the past week, if only to learn if we have some common interest, but without any luck. It worries me. I knew my first husband for four years before we formally took vows, but I still feel like this one is a stranger."

"There will be plenty of time to talk after the wedding," he offered.

This was an answer I liked not, so I decided to change the subject. There was a final reason I had hoped to speak with my cousin, and it involved one of the chief subjects of gossip in Christendom. The barrels of wine were all sitting on a table, with a collection of goblets beside them. I picked one up and lifted a lever to release the precious liquid.

"I hear that you have provided sanctuary to Pierre Abélard in Champagne," I said, my eyes still fixed on the pouring wine.

"I wouldn't say that. He founded a monastic house, yes, but he intends to turn it over to the Lady Héloïse."

I ceased what I was doing and turned around to face him again, my eyes wide with surprise.

"Not the one he was caught with?!" I cried. "The one who bore his child? The scandal of all Christendom?!"

"She's not as bad as all that."

Ah! Here was some real news. Abélard and Héloïse were the most famous lovers of the day, and their tale was hardly one of righteousness. I longed to hear about this woman who was spoken of by everyone.

"So you've met her then? What is she like?" I asked, taking a drink from the half full goblet.

"Very normal, actually, except that she is most intelligent for a woman. She will make a fine abbess."

"What a strange love they have! Do you believe what people say: were they married?"

"Oh yes! That is true," he said with a nod.

There was something else I wished to ask, but I was almost ashamed to do so. I decided to whisper it to him.

"And is it true that Master Pierre is … you know?" I asked quietly.

"Without his manhood? Yes, that is also true. He says it ensures that his mind belongs to the work of the Lord."

I laughed. "I suppose that is one way to look at it. I admire him in a way. There is not one in a thousand men who would hazard that kind of wrath for the love of a woman."

"I should think not!" Theobald scoffed. "What good is a man without his manhood? He hardly deserves the name!"

I glanced back at young Geoffrey and sighed. "There are many things that make a man, cousin. I have met few true men in my day. Far too few …"

I went to bed a bit early that night, hoping to get plenty of rest before the day ahead. How different it felt from my first wedding! Then I was still a girl, ignorant in the ways of love, afraid that I could never match my husband in stature. Now I was a woman, all too aware of love's painful sting, and certain that my husband could never match me in stature. Upon our marriage, Geoffrey would be made count of Anjou, and I his countess. What a trifle to offer an empress! I had no intention of ever using that title. This much I could say, though: as much pain as the marriage was likely to cause me, it was as nothing compared to the marriage of Pierre Abélard.

I was awoken quite early by the ladies and placed in a bath of rose water. Under other circumstances, this would have been lovely, but I was in a rather poor mood. Lord Geoffrey may have earned the praises of everyone else at court, but I felt I did not know him at all. More than that, I feared he would never truly know me. Was it wrong of me to want a husband with whom I felt some kind of bond of the soul? It is all well and good to say that a thing is one's duty, but duty does not warm the heart. It does not give hope to the person who is about to make a sacrifice of themselves.

When I was dry and a comb had been dragged through my hair at least a hundred times, they began the process of braiding, placing my tresses in knots from top to bottom. So many memories passed through my mind as they did this: Lady Beatrice attempting to make me presentable in my youth, the thousand pins that had been used at my first wedding to create a perfect holder for the royal crown, Lord Brian stroking my hair as he kissed me. A tunic of white cloth was pulled over my body, followed by a red gown. Neither of these were of particular import, for they were to be covered. My white veil was held in place with a gold band. These were lovely garments, but then again, prisons often appear lovely from the outside.

After I had been properly covered in jewels, they brought forth the last element: a great robe of many colors which had been produced by a weaver in Bayeux and his many apprentices. It was a thing of beauty, covering me in warmth and letting off a kind of glow on account of the gold thread woven into the fabric. It had a high collar that came up behind my neck and made me look entirely royal. However, as I glanced at myself in a mirror, I wished for all the world that I could trade places with someone common and not be forced to marry into Anjou. What did I know of Anjou? What did I care for it? This was the will of the king.

"How lovely you look!" one of my ladies said.

"Yes, I thought it only fitting that I should look my best for the funeral," I jested.

"Oh, my lady! I know you meant to say 'wedding,' but you've gone and said 'funeral.' You must have so many things on your mind!"

"I meant what I said," I replied, leaving her rather perplexed.

When I stood before the door to the cathedral, waiting to enter at the sound of the trumpets, I thought of my mother. Had she been alive, I believe she might have attempted to prevent the marriage, or at the very least to spare me from my father's wrath. Had William lived, the marriage never would have been necessary. Had my first husband never had cancer, I might have still been living happily in the empire. Had I been a mere peasant girl, I might have been able to wed the man I loved. All of these wounds were still within me, some less healed than others. The last thing I remember thinking about before the doors opened was how I had sworn to my father that I would never marry Geoffrey of Anjou. I had taken a beating for it, and still I had gained nothing.

I will never forgive him for that, and I will never forgive him for this, I thought.

Within the hour, I had allowed my hand to be taken by Geoffrey of Anjou and pledged to remain faithful to him until death. I really see no need to mention much else about the ceremony: suffice it to say, the deed was done. I kept my eyes on the bishop the whole time and did my best not to glance at Brian fitz Count when I walked down the aisle. For his part, the new Count Geoffrey of Anjou spoke his vows with conviction, but there was no sign of actual affection: a smile, a word, a touch. Sadly, I could not help but see the smile on my father's face. He clearly wished to make up for the lack of joy on the faces of the bride and groom. When the priest declared us to be husband and wife, and bid us kneel for the Mass, I closed my eyes and allowed myself to shed a few tears—silently, of course.

I do not think I said ten words at the wedding feast. I performed my duty, and that was all. When they said "dance," I danced. When they bid me raise a glass, I did so. But if they wanted me to be happy about it, well, that was something I simply could not do. When the eve was at its close, I made for my chamber in the upper level of the palace to brace myself for the work that lay ahead. The prospect of spending the night with young Geoffrey might have excited most of the ladies in the county, but I was not most ladies.

At least I know what is coming this time, I thought.

My father was determined that there be some proof of consummation, thus removing the possibility of annulment if things should go ill. Some poor woman named Emma was selected to serve as witness to the deed. How she came by that awful task, I can only imagine. I suspect they drew lots. So in the end, I am not sure who wished to be there least: myself, Count Geoffrey, or the unhappy Emma.

There was a small ceremony in which we were all seen to the bed chamber at the end of the passage and the lords and bishops bid us good night. I assure you that every moment was misery. Then it was only the three of us locked in that room with two pieces of furniture: a large bed covered in rose petals and perfumes, and a chair for Emma. Perhaps the door was not actually locked, but it might as well have been. The first night I spent with Emperor Henry ended with me fleeing into the darkness to retrieve the physician. I could only hope and pray that things would go rather differently the second time around, for as much as I loathed the marriage, I desperately wanted children. The things we women must do that our kind might live on!

So as it happened, the first private conversation I held with my second husband—that is, as private as a conversation can be when there is a mute observer sitting in the room—came at a time when prudence might have dictated that one should say nothing at all. We were standing a few feet apart from each other, each dressed in a simple cloth sleeping tunic blessed by the bishop of Le Mans.

"So, just the two of us then," he said, pointing his finger back and forth.

"Surely you mean the three of us?" I noted, pointing to poor Emma sitting in her chair in the corner.

"I'm not here," she whispered, rather against the laws of reason.

"I don't mind," young Geoffrey said, moving a step closer. "Do you need anything before we begin?"

"You are brimming with confidence for one so young," I observed. "May I ask you something?"

"Of course," he replied, his face breaking into a smile.

"Have you ever done this before?"

He laughed. "Yes. Why? Have you?"

I was taken aback by his question. "I assume you know this is my second marriage," I said, beginning to doubt his intelligence.

"Yes, but you do not have any children, so—"

"So you thought I was still a maid?!" I scoffed.

His eyes shifted quickly away from me and then back again. He was evidently attempting to devise a response that would justify his question. Finally, he smiled.

"I only meant that I should hate to make assumptions about a lady's affairs."

"It was not that kind of marriage, I promise you! He was sick—very sick toward the end. It made things difficult."

"Well, rest assured: the women I've been with have all sung my praises."

What a thing to say! I could hardly believe my ears.

"If that is an example of the type of humor you intend to bring to this enterprise, then I recommend you think again!" I declared, crossing my arms in front of me.

"Please! I only meant to say that whatever it is you like, I am more than happy to oblige."

"Oh, for God's sake!" I wailed.

"So what is it you like?"

There was a question I had never been asked. Indeed, I had never really thought about it, but when it came to Count Geoffrey, I knew the answer as if by instinct.

"Brevity."

"Very well," he replied. "Brevity it is."

CHAPTER FIFTEEN

Having achieved his desired end of marrying me into the House of Anjou, King Henry left the very next day with all the Norman lords and marched northeast into the county of Blois, having gained permission from Count Theobald. I watched them go with a heavy heart, for I was once again left as a stranger in a strange land. They passed through Chartres, and by the end of the week they were within the realm of the king of France, not two days' march from the gates of Paris. I dearly hoped that they could make an end of the alliance between Clito and the French king, which threatened both my position and my inheritance.

My father's intention was not to conquer the lands of King Louis, nor even to engage him in open battle. Rather, he hoped by means of skirmishes to draw the French forces to the south and thus prevent them from coming to the aid of William Clito in Flanders. In that at least, he succeeded, but the fates were not so kind to Thierry of Alsace.

On the eleventh day before the Kalends of July, just south of Ypres, the forces of Thierry and William Clito met in battle. When the traitor Clito's men saw that they were far fewer in number, there were some who begged to call off the charge, but he would have none of it. He bid them cast off all the vanities of this world and pray to God for remission of their sins. And so they did cast off their noble clothes and even the very hair on their heads, and rode into battle as if they were monks. Whether or not this appeased the Almighty, I cannot rightly say, but they did achieve the unlikely victory against Thierry.

What a blow this dealt to all of us who believed the traitor's downfall to be near at hand! I was filled with dismay when I heard the news, for we had lost our best ally in Flanders. A great disagreement broke out between King Henry and his own father-in-law, Duke Godfrey, with each blaming the other for the defeat. Here the game was badly played, for their dispute led Godfrey, who by right should have been on our side, to throw in his lot with William Clito. Well, it should be clear by now that my father did not always treat people as they deserved, and on that occasion, he reaped his ill reward. It was bad news upon bad news.

Those were stressful days for me as I awaited news of the fighting to the north. Along with my new husband, I had traveled back to Angers, home of the counts of Anjou, and had quickly set to work forming my household. Though I took no joy in it and may have preferred to delay the task as long as possible, I knew there was no point fighting what could not be fought: Anjou would have to become my home.

I was angry with my father for pushing the marriage, angry at the world for requiring it of me, and angry at myself for breaking my pledge to never marry Geoffrey of Anjou. As much as I hated to admit it, my spirit had indeed been broken. I had lost the will to resist, for I felt there was no hope of succeeding. I tried to convince myself that it was the noble thing to do: to sacrifice my desires for the good of the kingdom. In any case, the deed was done. I hoped that the assurances of others were correct, and that something good might come from my marriage, however small. If by some miracle I could have a child, perhaps it would be worth it after all.

The former Count Fulk had departed for Jerusalem, along with his daughter Sibylla. I would like to think that it was fraternal devotion that led her to the Holy Land, but the rumor was that she did not wish to be within fifty miles of me. The reason was simple enough: she had once been wed to William Clito, but my father had convinced Pope Honorius to annul the marriage, thus leaving her out in the cold. Well, Godspeed, Sibylla! I had no wish to be friends with her either.

My husband's other sister, Mathilda, was the widow of my own brother, William Ætheling. She had lately taken the veil at Fontevrault Abbey, and the only other sibling was young Elias, who was studying under a tutor in Le Mans. That left the two of us—Count Geoffrey and I—to man the family estate. I hoped this might finally provide a chance for us to have some long discussions, but as it turned out, Geoffrey was not much for long discussions with anyone. He was a restless type, always intent upon action. Even on the occasions where we would engage in marital relations, it was a rather brief affair, but I could hardly blame him for that, since I had requested brevity.

Count Geoffrey had many young friends with whom he spent his time, jousting during the day and feasting late into the night. Every elegant lady in the county wished to be seen at those gatherings. I, on the other hand, merely wished to get some sleep. I had never thought myself among the aged, but I certainly felt old in their company.

On one such night, I had returned to my room in the hope of getting some rest, even as the noise continued below. It was rather late: indeed, it must have been near midnight when I received a knock at the door of my bed chamber, which was tucked away in the corner of the upper level of the castle.

"Who is it?" I called from where I was seated on the bed, brushing out my hair before slumber time.

"It's only me—Agnes," she replied.

Lady Agnes was one of the chief women in my household. She had arrived at the same time as myself and proven rather helpful, if a little dull.

"Come in," I said, setting the brush on the small table next to my bed.

She entered, but the room was so dark that I had to reach back over to the table and hold up the candle to make out her face.

"What is it?" I asked. "I was about to go to sleep, or at least attempt it."

"I am sorry to disturb, my lady, but they just received some news down below, and I thought I should make you aware of it."

"News? What kind of news?" I stood up from the bed and moved toward her, holding up the candle to shine on her face.

"There's been a message from Flanders. Count William was wounded in the fighting. He is very near death."

Now there was a piece of news! I felt somewhat guilty, for upon hearing that a man was near death, I experienced joy. Perhaps it is not proper to rejoice in the torment of another, but given what trouble I had suffered because of that man and the threat he posed to my future, I believed my response was justified.

"Near death?!" I cried. "But this news must have taken most of a week to reach us. He may already be dead!"

"That is what we are hoping to find out. They sent someone to look for Count Geoffrey so that he could send out a messenger—"

"Wait! Count Geoffrey is not at the feast?" This surprised me, as he had been feasting every time I left for the night, and I had been led to believe that he continued to do so long after I went to sleep.

"No, he left about half an hour ago. I thought perhaps he was with you," Agnes explained.

"Well, as you can see, he is not."

"Ah ..." she uttered with great pause, as if she was not at all certain what she should say next. "Right. Should I go and look for him?"

"No. Let me go look in his private chambers. The way he drinks, he may have taken ill and gone straight to bed. I can see it will be up to me to be both his mother and his wife."

"Very well, my lady. I shall return to the hall."

"Thank you, Agnes."

As soon as she was gone, I quickly put on a robe and set off down the passage toward my new husband's room, the stone floor cold upon my bare feet. It was strange to think that I was making my first trip there under such circumstances, for we had always met in my room before. William Clito dead? It was hard to believe. Knowing him, he had probably found a way to cheat death as he had a hundred times before. His good fortune had always done me ill, and it was hard to believe that his luck had finally ended. Either way, my husband would need to know, for the death of Clito was likely to shape all our fortunes.

I soon arrived at his door and was about to knock when I heard a noise from inside, as if someone was moving around furniture rather carelessly and allowing it to hit the wall. I could not think why my husband should be doing such a thing, and thus I became exceedingly suspicious. I listened a moment longer and heard the same sound of something hitting the wall, only this time it was joined by a human voice—no, more than one human voice. My suspicion seemed confirmed.

I flung open the door and held the candle aloft. The light fell upon the bed, on which the naked bodies of my husband and two women were ... well, perhaps I can say they were seated. What followed next were screams, flailing limbs, and a mess of red hair.

"Who is it?" one of the two women called out, for she had fallen on the floor in the tumult.

"*Ich bin die Göttin des Todes, kommen Sie zu zerstören!*" I yelled.

This meant roughly, *I am the goddess of death come to destroy you!*, although in truth I could have said anything in the German tongue, and it would have had the desired effect.

"Ah! Good evening, my wife," said Count Geoffrey, who was standing there stark naked, a look of complete surprise on his face, even as his two lovers frantically sought to cover themselves.

Oh, you bastard, I thought. Indeed, there were several other curses that ran through my mind.

"Choose your next words very carefully," I warned him.

He turned around to look at the two ladies behind him, perhaps attempting to decide if he could explain them away. He then turned back to face me.

"Care to join us?" he asked with a shrug.

I quickly scanned the room and saw a small table just to my right with a clay pitcher sitting on it. I picked it up and threw it in his direction, not truly hoping to wound him, but merely to put the fear of God in his heart. It hit a bed post and shattered, causing the ladies—if they truly deserved that title—to scream again.

"Go to hell, you fiend!" I cried, and left the room, throwing the door closed behind me.

I began to walk, or rather stomp, back to my chamber, muttering under my breath.

I hated him the moment I saw him. I should have trusted myself about him. I should have known he would never respect me, even if he respects my father.

On and on my thoughts continued in that vein. His behavior not only showed a lack of respect and loyalty toward me: it proved his lack of regard for the laws of God. So caught up was I in these angry thoughts, that when I turned the corner toward my own room, I almost ran into Agnes.

"There you are, my lady!" she said. "There is still no sign of Count Geoffrey. Were you able to find him?"

"Oh, I certainly found him," I assured her.

She smiled. "I am relieved to hear it! How did he take the news?"

"Never mind that. Tell me, Agnes: how long has Count Geoffrey been at it with every lady in the county?"

Her eyes grew large like a dog caught doing something rather naughty. There had been little time for the two of us to become familiar, and judging by the look on her face, I think she was afraid that I might eat her alive.

"What? I'm not sure what you mean," she stammered.

"Don't play coy with me!" I cried. "I know you all know."

Her replies came out quickly and with passion. "But I am new here, my lady! I know nothing! Please, I only joined the household just before your marriage!"

"Is that so?" I asked, feeling a bit bad for yelling at her. "Well, now you know."

I left her behind, entered my room, and locked the door. I was not particularly surprised by what I had discovered, but that did nothing to blunt the sense of betrayal. All I could think was that, had William Clito decided to die a few weeks earlier, I might have been saved from marrying Count Geoffrey. As always, the traitor had proven his ability to ruin everything, even in death.

"Farewell, William Clito!" I said. "I have a new enemy now."

As it turned out, William Clito really did die. He had gone to relieve Duke Godfrey at Aalst, and in the midst of fighting with some common peasant, he received a cut on his arm. Such a small thing, but for him it proved to be everything. The wound became putrid and the infection spread throughout his body. He lingered on in agony for most of a week before giving up the ghost. They bore his body to Saint Omer and declared him a monk *post mortem*, no doubt in the hope of moving his soul closer to heaven. Never mind that his proper place was next to Judas Iscariot!

Before his death, the traitor had written to King Henry begging forgiveness for both himself and his supporters. Though he had no love for his errant nephew, my father decided there was no point holding a grudge when the end of their feud was near. He offered his pardon and allowed my cousin to die in peace. At least the king was content. I did not see how I ever could be. I would not forgive the role Clito played in forcing my second marriage, nor would I forgive my father for offering more mercy to a traitor than his own daughter.

The poet Walo wrote an epitaph for Count William. I am not sure he truly deserved it, but it was a thing of beauty nevertheless.

> "Mars has died on earth, a star has fallen down,
> The gods lament a god, honor mourns honor's demise
> A new thing this, that gods can die
> And immortals know they are mortal.
> The hero of heroes is fallen, he who never fled,
> Turned not from the fray, from arrow or danger,

First to the foe, in battle the foremost,
Thundering as the thunder.
Flanders cradles his tomb, Normandy rocked his cradle;
The bright star rose in one, in the other it has set."[15]

Would that a more worthy person should receive such a worthy epitaph, but that is life, I suppose. The truly valiant die without honor. The brave are chastised, and talent goes to waste. He who has a good name may triumph where others fail, but once that good name is gone, it is gone beyond repair. The best men and women I ever knew were hardly deemed worthy of remembrance, and the brigands play us all for fools!

On the subject of being played for a fool, there was my marriage to Count Geoffrey. It had been hard enough for me to bear him at the beginning, but once his true character was revealed, I truly loathed him. You may find my opinion on adultery to be rather absolute, given that so many men of noble birth engage in the practice. But it is all well and good to pardon another's indiscretion when it has no bearing upon one's self: to claim that love is a thing of mystery that cannot be controlled. But what of fidelity? What of honor? It was not even love that my husband felt for those harlots, but simple lust. Must we applaud him for giving in to his base desires at the expense of those around him? I think not.

For two weeks, I refused to see him. He sent me a note in which he pledged never to commit such an offense again. He claimed to be suffering from the ignorance of youth. What rubbish! A boy of five knows not to do what my husband did! I put the paper straight upon the fire. He sent me another letter and

---

15 This translation is found in the following source: Lack, Katharine. *Conqueror's Son: Duke Robert Curthose, Thwarted King* (Stroud, UK: Sutton Publishing, 2007), pg. 186. The original Latin text has been included as an appendix in translations of Henry of Huntingdon's *Historia Anglorum*.

begged me to come to his bed. I wrote back and vowed I would never share the bed of a whore.

Of course, I knew that only by returning to his bed could I ever have children, but my anger had taken control at that point. As I lay in bed at night, I would dream of leaving him: running far away, perhaps to the ends of the earth, where no one knew my name or cared what I did. It was only a fantasy, of course. In truth, I did not see any way of escape that would not be utterly ruinous. Therefore, I simply passed the days with my disdain for Count Geoffrey increasing every hour. I was forced to see him at supper, but that was all.

In August, we received a visitor: Archbishop Hildebert of Tours. I was glad to have such an esteemed person among us, though I well remembered how he had attempted to sway me toward Anjou. Given all that had taken place that summer, my opinion of the archbishop was hardly at its zenith, but I still intended to receive him with all due hospitality.

I asked him to walk with me in the rose garden beside the River Maine. We strode down the grassy lanes in and around the sweet smelling blooms, our conversation just as sweet. Oh, the tales he could tell! I had quite forgotten that the archbishop was once taken prisoner by my own uncle, King William II. He had thus spent a year in England, and heaped much praise upon the place—this despite the nature of his stay there. Perhaps he was hoping to regain my goodwill. We spoke of our experiences in Rome, our frustration with King Louis of France, and our love of Ovid. We continued on in this manner for the better part of an hour despite the summer heat, he with his hands clasped behind his back and I using a silk fan to cool myself a bit. Then the archbishop came to the true purpose of his visit.

"My lady, I have spoken with Count Geoffrey, and he is most upset over the state of your young marriage. He says the two of you hardly speak. Can that be true?"

I sighed at this change in the conversation, though I had known it was coming. "Yes, it is true," I admitted. "Am I in trouble, then?" Here I cast a glance to the side so I could see his face.

"Not at all! He took the blame for it. He said you caught him doing something rather impertinent."

"Was that how he put it?" I asked with a laugh. "That would not have been the word I might have chosen."

"My lady," the archbishop continued, "Count Geoffrey is young and bound to falter at times. He seemed truly repentant when we spoke. He fears he has lost your love."

At this point, I was not sure if the archbishop was that easily deceived or if he and my husband had devised such an obviously specious account together.

"He never had my love, but he has lost my respect, such as it was," I replied.

It was his turn to laugh softly. "I see you have no fear of speaking your mind. Perhaps that is good. These things must be addressed openly if there is to be healing."

I stopped in my tracks and lowered my fan. "Archbishop Hildebert, I know you mean well—"

"Please!" he said, raising his hands as if in surrender. "I do not come here for myself, nor for your husband, but upon an order from the Almighty to bring peace to this house."

"I was not the one who broke the peace," I argued. "Let his sin be on his own head."

"Everyone falls into sin from time to time, my lady—even archbishops." Here he winked, amusing me greatly.

"You can say that again, with all due respect. I mean, you seem a very decent fellow, but I have known too many archbishops."

"Granted. But if the houses of Normandy and Anjou are to survive, your union must live on as well. Consider that no marriage is perfect. Can you not give him a chance to redeem himself?"

He did have a point. Forgiveness was the Christian way, and my best path toward having children and a real future was still through Count Geoffrey. However, I had to somehow ensure that our marriage would at least be tolerable—that my husband would not bring shame on me at every turn.

"And what will keep him from falling into error in the future?" I asked, as we both began to walk forward again.

"The very knowledge that by doing so, he will endanger all you have worked to build."

"I still don't know," I said. "Archbishop, I respect your loyalty, but these are not my people. I am not sure that Count Geoffrey even knows where England is, let alone cares about it. He only cares for the dukedom of Normandy. I fear that all he sees in this marriage is the chance to better himself at my expense."

"Use caution, my lady!" he entreated. "I would sooner say that Count Geoffrey cares too much than that he does not care enough. He knows you are in this together, and he wants the same thing you do: for your children to rule over both Normandy and England."

I was forced to admit to myself that he had a point. I did at least believe that my husband wanted children who would rule, though I still felt he was too locked into the Angevin way of thinking to value England as it deserved.

"Well, if I do give him another chance, and it goes ill, I hope you will return here so I can say I told you so!" I declared.

"I pray there will be no need for that, Your Highness, but should the time come, I shall be willing to receive your censure. Even so, I will vouch for your husband that he has a good heart. Give him a chance to show it."

I hoped the archbishop was right: truly, I did. But at the same time, I doubted that there was much goodness within the heart of Count Geoffrey of Anjou. He seemed to care about himself far more than anything or anyone else.

"Tell me, archbishop: did you bring any wine with you from Tours?" I asked, changing the subject.

"I have one case, and will happily leave it behind if you desire it."

"Oh, it's not for me. It's for my knight."

"Sir Drogo? Yes, I met him. I was surprised to hear that he carries on a regular correspondence with the archbishop of Magdeburg."

"Archbishop Norbert? Yes, they met in Germany. I believe he made quite an impression on Drogo."

"How marvelous that he has stayed with you all these years! I wish I could keep a clerk for that long!"

"Yes, but that is just the thing, archbishop: I have known great loyalty in men, so when it is absent, it offends me greatly."

"Understood," he concluded.

At the archbishop's request, I did make an effort to forgive. Not that I wanted to, of course. It was a matter of cold necessity. I may have wished as Brünnhilda to plunge the world into flames and take the gods down with me, but there is a reason such tales only appear in mythology. We are not the gods and goddesses. We are frail creatures of dust, and we must make a life of it if we can. I needed a son to ensure my position: to earn me respect and grant me the authority to control my own affairs. And as terrible fate would have it, the only way for me to even have a chance of achieving that goal was to attempt to make something positive of my marriage—or at least to make it fruitful.

So I went to my husband and we made amends, and everything continued on as it should have at the start. I had my doubts, certainly, but he did his best to assuage them. There was no repeat of the incident I had witnessed the past summer, and I was determined to at least bear with him, even if I could not like him. The months came and went, passing from autumn into winter and then back into spring. In time, my husband's behavior was no longer my chief concern. Nor was I that worried about having to sleep with him, for I had learned when I was still young how to play the right tricks with my mind that would allow me to endure: I used to imagine that I was wandering through a field of lavender, my hair flowing freely in the wind, gazing upon mountains like the ones I had seen years before in Bavaria, with no one in the world to trouble me.

Rather, I was saddened that I was not with child. A whole year, and no offspring to show for it! I wondered if the rumors were true: if I really was barren after all. My father left Normandy and returned to England, and I could not help but wonder if he had given up waiting for an heir to be born. I prayed it was not the case. If my father became convinced that I was barren, then not only would I be an object of ridicule, but he might change his mind and appoint someone else as heir: someone who had already demonstrated the ability to produce offspring. All I had endured for the sake of my marriage would come to nothing. These grim possibilities were a torment for my mind.

The one person who was a good support, as always, was Drogo. He helped to introduce me to the other household knights, and when the weather was properly warm, we had an archery tournament: nothing official, but enough to raise the spirits. Count Geoffrey took part as well, as did Lady Agnes and others of the ladies in waiting. I do not remember who won, but the preparation allowed me to improve my shooting to the point where I gained a bit of confidence.

In August 1129, my husband announced that he would be making a journey to Fontevrault Abbey to visit his sister. I thought nothing of it at the time, even when he did not ask me to accompany him, for the counts of Anjou have long favored that establishment. As it so happened, he had not been gone a day when I decided I might like to join him and instructed Lady Agnes and Drogo to ready my things for travel. It had occurred to me that accompanying my husband on official visits was probably the sort of thing I ought to do if I hoped to have a good marriage. It was less than two days before we reached the abbey, and we quite surprised them all when my carriage arrived in the courtyard along with six knights on horses.

As we had not sent a messenger ahead, there was no one in the yard in front of the church save for a company of nuns, perhaps on their way to prayer, who paused for a moment to observe our arrival but then carried on with their task.

"Not much of a welcoming party," Drogo noted, as I climbed out of the carriage. "I should have sent someone ahead. I am sorry, my lady."

"Think nothing of it," I assured him.

In front of us stood the church. There was a building to the right, which judging from the smoke rising from a chimney likely contained the kitchens and refectory. Connected to that was one of what I assumed were a pair of cloisters holding the rooms of the monks and nuns, for Fontevrault was a joint community.

"Perhaps we should just enter the church and see if we can find Abbess Pétronille," I said to Drogo, then turned and told the rest of the knights, "Take the horses to the stable, but leave two here for a moment in case there is a need to fetch anything in the village."

As the rest of them busied themselves with my commands, Drogo and I walked forward into the abbey church, then departed to the right into the first cloister that was attached to the kitchens. We had just entered the square walk when we saw Abbess Pétronille rushing toward us from the left. She had evidently been informed of our presence.

"Countess Mathilda!" she cried, attempting to catch her breath. "We did not know you were coming as well!" Here she clasped her hands together and bowed.

"Forgive me, dear abbess, but I got it in my head to visit your fine halls, and we came so quickly that I saw no point in sending a herald. Also, if you do not mind, it's Empress Mathilda."

"No, I do not mind—either the title or the surprise," she assured me. "Indeed, it is a lovely surprise. Allow me to show you to our guest rooms."

She placed her right hand upon my left shoulder, while her left hand gestured toward the passage that led down to the refectory.

"First, where is Count Geoffrey?" I asked. "I should let him know I am here."

"We can send someone for you. There is no need for that," she said hastily.

"But my ladies will take my things—"

"Really, madam, he cannot see you right now."

These words were more direct: almost forceful. The abbess still had a smile on her face, but it had grown rather strained.

"Why ever not?" I asked, growing annoyed.

She paused for a moment. "He is at confession."

Now, I had no doubt in my mind that Count Geoffrey had done many things worth confessing, but the amount of time it took her to come up with that answer was nothing short of suspicious. I cast my eyes to the left, in the direction from which the abbess had come, and noticed the fear that appeared in her eyes.

"Sir Drogo, come with me," I commanded.

"But my lady, I really must protest!" the abbess called after us, as we took off down the passage.

"What are we looking for?" Drogo asked me.

"I'm not sure, but they will be most unhappy to see us," I replied.

We made it to the other side of the cloister and entered what seemed to be the infirmary wing. Sure enough, as we turned the corner, we almost crashed into a rather startled nun carrying some bloody cloths.

"Countess!" she cried, not stopping to bow. "Surely you do not want to go down there! Are you lost?"

I took one look at the cloths in her hands and made up my mind.

"No, that is precisely where I want to go, and it's Empress Mathilda!" I declared. I then turned back to face Drogo. "He's in the infirmary for sure."

"Are you sure you want to see what is in there, my lady?" he asked.

I scoffed. "Honestly, Drogo, how long have we known each other?!"

At this, he nodded his head. "Very well, lead on! Let's catch the bastard at it!"

We passed by a few more people who begged us to turn back, which confirmed my suspicion. Then I heard a familiar voice, and opened a door behind which I assumed I would find my husband deflowering an entire flock of sisters. What I found instead was far worse. Upon the bed lay a young woman whom I had never seen before, having clearly just given birth. Beside the bed stood my husband, with a babe in his arms.

In that moment, I felt as if I had been pierced with a dagger. Truly, if my husband had been intending to wound me, he could hardly have picked a better way to do it. He had hit me at precisely the point of pain. For more than a decade, I had longed to have a child. I had felt the shame of not producing one. I had resigned myself to a marriage I never wanted all in the hope that I could at least have a child. And there my husband was, standing there holding a child, but it was not mine. I wanted to scream, weep, flee, fight. There was a fury inside me that wanted to wound as I had been wounded.

"What is this?!" Drogo cried, his eyes filled with anger even as my own.

There was no need for the question, for the answer was plain enough. The young woman rolled over weakly. "Are you the empress?"

"Are you the whore?!" I replied, though in truth that was less than gracious. She had at least called me empress.

"Is that your child?!" Drogo yelled at my husband.

"Yes, it is my son," he replied.

Count Geoffrey looked afraid: more afraid than he had been the night I caught him with the two strumpets. He must have seen the fire in my eyes—either that or he was rightly afraid of Drogo's fists. He handed the babe to its mother and stepped between them and us. He need not have worried: I had but one target.

"How could you?!" I cried as loud as I could, not caring who heard. "After I forgave you—after everything I have done! How could you do this?!"

"I did warn you not to come," said the abbess, who I saw had found her way into the room and was standing behind me.

"Yes, thank you, Mother Pétronille. I am pleased to see that the nuns of Fontevrault have nothing better to do with their time than provide harbor to adulterers!" I replied with contempt.

"That is not fair. I sent her here so that she would be cared for, and they showed her great mercy, even as they have shown to me," Count Geoffrey argued.

I looked back at him again. His lips were pursed and he was breathing heavily, as was I. Here was a boy who could barely grow a beard, and yet he had hurt me so deeply that I felt as if I would explode. I hated him. I hated that he was able to hurt me, but most of all I hated that I was bound to him. He had violated his vow to be faithful to me. He had broken the covenant of our marriage, so much so that I despaired of it entirely.

"Such a strange word, *mercy*," I said. "How many times have I pleaded to God for mercy, only to be denied? How many times did I beg him for a son? How many times did I beg him to spare me from this hateful marriage? I granted you mercy, and you have returned it with treachery. Now that you have your son, you clearly have no need of me, so I will be going. Take a good look as I walk away, for this is the last time you shall ever set eyes on me!"

"What do you mean?!" he cried.

"I will write to Pope Honorius and demand a divorce!"

"God forbid!" the abbess protested.

"You wouldn't dare!" Count Geoffrey said.

"Oh, yes I would!" I declared. "Come, Drogo! We are leaving."

It is a testament to Drogo's character that despite everything that had just happened and the extreme nature of my proclamation, he did not hesitate to follow me out of the room. He never thought for a moment about abandoning me in that dark moment. Yes, it was his duty, but in contrast to the behavior of my husband, it meant something. We both departed the room and began walking back the way we had come, surprising several nuns who were folding cloths.

He leaned down and whispered in my ear, "Will you really seek a divorce?"

"As God is my witness! This marriage never should have happened. It is a tragedy. No, a humiliation!"

"Yes, but will the pope grant it to you?" he asked, as we made the turn into the cloister.

"If there is any justice in this world. But even if he will not, I would rather rot than come back here again!"

Nuns continued to pass us, their eyes wide, but I could not care less what they thought. The business would be public soon enough.

"But where will we go?" Drogo asked, as we entered the church once again.

"To Normandy: Argentan first, then perhaps to Rouen. I need to get out of Anjou and return to the land of my fathers. If I stay here, they will try to control me."

"I fear your father will not approve," he said, perhaps attempting to warn me that there was another who sought to control me.

"He never approves of anything I do, but enough is enough! The worst he can do is choose another heir. I admit that would be terrible, but nothing is worse than this!"

We had made it back to the yard and were approached by another one of my knights. "We put everything away, my lady, just as you asked!" he announced with a smile on his face.

"Bring my personal items back!" I declared. "We are leaving this instant."

"All of us?" he stammered.

"No, Sir Drogo and myself, on those two horses there."

Yes, happily the two animals were still standing in the yard, just as I had commanded.

"Are you sure about this, my lady?" Drogo asked.

"Yes, and if you don't stop asking questions, I will go on my own!"

It was one of the few times I had seen fear in Drogo's eyes, for like me he had no idea how things would turn out.

"Do you wish to stay?" I inquired.

"No, my lady," he replied. "I would follow you into the fires of hell. I just hope I am fit for the task."

Within minutes, we left that place and set out to the north. It would take a few days to reach Argentan, and after that nothing was certain.

"Mercy," I muttered to myself. "Mercy is for the humble."

CHAPTER SIXTEEN

When I departed from the abbey of Fontevrault in great haste, with only Drogo at my side, I was in such a state of anger that I had not given much thought to how my departure would be perceived or what threats there might be to my safety. All I knew was that I had to leave Anjou, and I had to do so at once.

My first thought was to ride for Alençon, the most southern of the castles in Normandy. However, this would require us to pass through the whole of the county of Maine, that region which had been so often contested by the houses of Anjou and Blois. Even were we to go at a full run, stopping only to sleep each night, it might take us three days to get there. My primary concern was to flee the Angevin lands before news of my departure did, for once it was told far and wide that the heir of the king of England and duke of Normandy had left her husband and was riding abroad without a proper guard, a host of persons with ill intentions might find reason to pursue me: either to force me back to my husband or kidnap me for ransom.

It was therefore necessary for us to escape the notice of others as much as possible until we were out of the Angevin lands, and to move at a quick pace that would keep us ahead of any messengers. Fortunately, among the few items we had grabbed to take with us before our flight were a few spare clothes and a pouch of gold. We stopped to change in a wood after about two hours' ride, and then used the gold that eve to rent a pair of rooms at a small inn. Our hosts were no doubt curious as to why a noble woman should be traveling alone with a single guard, but I told them I was a lady of Dieppe who had made a pilgrimage to the cathedral of Tours.

We continued on in that manner, not stopping at the royal palace of Le Mans. I might have sought the refuge of an abbey, but there were none along our route. After some bad weather, we came into the duchy of Normandy on the fourth day and begged the hospitality of the castellan of Alençon. I told him I had been so eager to see my home land again—indeed, sick with longing to the point of weeping—that I had taken off without any preparation. I do not know if he truly believed me, but he feared me enough to offer a dozen of his own men to accompany me to Argentan, where I finally stopped to properly rest.

The first night, I was so weary that I slept through until afternoon the next day, stayed awake long enough to eat a few morsels, then promptly returned to bed. Therefore, it was only on the third day that I made it down to the private dining room of Wigan Marshal and his wife, Agnes, the lord and lady of the castle. It was a small chamber near the great hall, with a single long table and about ten chairs. I understood that the five young children of the home were allowed to join at times, but on this night it was only Lord Wigan seated at the head, with Lady Agnes to his left and me to his right. A stew had been poured for our nourishment and we were all sipping from our goblets of wine when Lord Wigan began to speak in earnest.

"My lady, I must apologize for the state of the place. We never thought to have a guest of your stature. Had I known, I would have hired more servants for the length of your stay."

"Have no fear, sir. I know the manner of my coming is most unusual," I assured him. "Simply to have a bed to sleep in and a hearty meal is all I ask at this time. Your generosity will not be forgotten."

"It is not generous to give what is due," he replied, reaching forward to fill my glass once again from the pitcher. "And how long do you think you will be staying?"

"Please, husband!" said Lady Agnes, her tone quite direct. She turned her gaze toward me. "The empress is welcome to stay as long as she wishes."

I smiled at them both. "There is no harm in the question. It is entirely fair. I hope to be able to tell you how long I will stay by the end of this week. I have some matters of great import to consider."

Lady Agnes and I both placed our spoons back in our stew and raised them to our lips. As I placed mine in my mouth, I looked over again at Lord Wigan, who was sitting back in his seat, looking rather pensive.

"What is it, Lord Wigan?" I asked. "Do you have no stomach for food tonight?"

He let out a small sigh and bit his lip, as if considering whether or not he should speak. I placed my spoon aside and turned in my chair to face him more directly.

"Sir, I do not know what thoughts are passing through that mind of yours, but you need not fear telling me whatever it is you have to say."

"Is that so?" he replied softly, leaning forward. "Empress Mathilda, I have received a letter today from Anjou."

"Anjou?" I asked, bidding myself remain calm.

"Yes. From Count Geoffrey of Anjou, to be precise. I have it here."

He reached down into his lap, produced a piece of parchment with the seal broken, and held it up for me to see. It was covered with only a few lines of ink drawn in a rather careless manner.

"What does it say, dear?" asked Lady Agnes.

Her husband did not answer but addressed me alone. "Do you want me to read this, my lady?"

"If you wish," I said softly, very much fearing what it might reveal, but attempting to maintain the impression that I had everything in hand.

He let out a laugh, or rather a kind of snort. He then turned the letter back toward himself and recited. "To Wigan the Marshal, castellan of Argentan, Count Geoffrey of Anjou sends greeting. I wish to inform you that on the day before last, my wife the countess abandoned her proper place at my side without seeking my permission and has not been seen since. She has forsaken her duty to her people, who already grieve her loss most sorely. Even so, I am grieved. I cannot think but that Lucifer himself has blinded her eyes and tricked her into leaving her natural lord. I am most eager for her return, that she may be restored to the way of righteousness. Anyone who is found to be harboring her will be seen as a traitor to Anjou, and I will have no choice but to come and claim my wife from him, by force if necessary. Therefore, if you have any knowledge of the countess' whereabouts, please inform me at once. Grace and peace to you and yours."

With this, he ceased speaking and set the parchment on the table. I had been staring down into my bowl throughout. I lifted my eyes and looked across at Lady Agnes, who appeared rather confounded. Indeed, she seemed most afraid and reached forward to take another long drink from her glass. I looked again at her husband. He had leaned back in his chair and was resting his chin on his left hand.

"Lord Wigan, I have no doubt that after what you have read, you must think me a terrible sinner, but please know that there is more to this story than appears at first glance," I told him. "I am guilty of bringing trouble on your house by coming here, but not of that which he accuses me."

"Do not worry about this house, my lady," he said. "Just tell me what happened."

I nodded my head and glanced down again at my stew. I did not think to get help from my food, but it gave me a moment to collect my thoughts. I looked up again, and found that he was still sitting in the same position, looking completely at ease. This gave me just enough courage to speak.

"Lord Wigan, Lady Agnes—my husband Count Geoffrey is not a good man, if indeed the title of man can be properly applied to one so childish. I was forced to marry him by circumstance and the will of the king, though I had made known my deep concerns. He does not respect me as he should. Not long after we were wed, I discovered he was sharing his bed with many other women, even though he was most fortunate to marry a great lady such as myself. He preferred the fleeting pleasures of sin to the bounty he stood to gain through his rightful alliance. He made a show of repentance, and I forgave him, all in the hope that we might have a child together. However, he never ceased from his whoring, and about a week ago, I discovered that he had a son with another woman. He has denied me the honor I am due time and again. He is a man without heart who makes a mockery of the gifts he has been given. Well, I did not know what to do. I returned to the land of my ancestors so I could consider how to respond."

I did not tell them that I hoped to seek a divorce from the pope. I feared it might be one piece of information too many. However, I was very surprised in my host's response.

"So Count Geoffrey is a dastard—well, a dastard and a bastard. It does not surprise me," he said, leaning back in his chair and joining his hands together on his chest. "We have heard stories about the Angevins for years. They have made rather an art of lechery, and their tempers are a thing of legend. When I was told you were to be married to that boy, I admit I pitied you. He is not worthy of a woman such as yourself. I was not sorry to see greater peace between Normandy and Anjou, living as I do rather near the border, but I also know that the count is likely to come calling one day and demand control of these castles. I would much rather serve you, my lady. At least you are of the old stock of Normandy—a descendant of Rollo. I do not trust the Angevins, and I am sorry to hear how they have treated you. As if the dignity of their house can compare to that of Normandy! Well, he can come here if he likes, but he will not be satisfied. I do not believe he has the men to prosecute a victorious siege. These walls are strong."

"Sir," I began, stammering slightly in my relief, "I cannot tell you how glad it makes me to hear these words! For some time now, I have gone from trouble to trouble. I have had nothing but bad fortune. Your kindness to me is great indeed. But to be honest, I fear more the choices of my father. He has no special love for me, and it was he who pushed for the alliance with Anjou. If he feels that I have broken it through selfishness, there is no telling what he might do. He may punish you for giving me aid. Therefore, I think it best that I leave in the morning. It is too bad, for I have enjoyed your food. The Angevin fare does not always agree with me."

"*Ira principis mors est*," he said. "The anger of the king means death. Ah, but it will not be our death, my lady! The king would never harm his only child, nor would he call me a traitor for aiding her."

"You have such respect for the House of Normandy, but if there is anything I know about us, Lord Wigan, it is that we treat our enemies with cruelty, and especially those among our own kin. That is what they say, isn't it? 'The Normans eat their own young.'"

He leaned forward and placed his right hand on my left. "Empress Mathilda, you are a great lady. I do not believe you will share in that fate."

"And yet I must fly," I whispered.

He nodded and sighed. "Yes, you must, but I will send my men with you. No more of this running around alone. If you were to fall prey to danger on the road, then the king would most certainly hold me guilty of treason, and he would be right to do so!"

"But where will she go?!" Lady Agnes inquired. She looked at me earnestly. "My lady, if you truly fear your father's wrath, then perhaps you should go to the lands of your kin to the east: to the county of Blois. I am sure Count Theobald would receive you."

I laughed softly. "I am afraid the House of Blois is not entirely happy with me since I married into Anjou."

"Then they would have something to gain if you seek an annulment," she said. "Is that what you intend to do?"

I looked toward her husband and then back at her. "If you must know, yes, I seek the dissolution of this marriage. It should never have happened. However, I do not have much hope for an annulment. We are not related too closely, the marriage contract was perfectly legal, and despite the absence of offspring, I assure you we have shared in marital relations. No, it would have to be a divorce for cause. The Lord permitted divorce for adultery."

Even as I said these words, I did not feel at all comfortable. They sounded strange coming from my lips.

"You know, I never thought it would be like this," I said, shaking my head. "If you had told me when I was young that I would end up seeking divorce, I would have said you were out of your mind. My mother would have been truly dismayed to hear of it. Nevertheless, I'm afraid it has come to that. I am sorry if you do not approve."

"It is none of our business what you decide," replied Lord Wigan. "But my wife is right. You should choose a place to go."

I looked back at my bowl of stew again, which by that point had surely gone cold. I needed to get myself further from Anjou and out of the danger of an incursion from that corner, but going north would take me further into the lands of my father and the danger that presented. The idea of going to Blois seemed to have merit, but I doubted that cousin Theobald would endure the fury of the king to grant me safe haven, and in any case, I felt most uneasy about that family, with or without good reason. Finally, I arrived at a decision.

"I will make for Rouen: for the city of my fathers. There I will decide what to do next. It will take a week for this news to reach my father in England, and then perhaps another week for his command to reach Rouen. That is enough time for me to consider possible paths. Yes, I will make for Rouen, and God help me."

Lady Agnes rose from her chair, walked around to my side of the table, and embraced me.

"God speed to you, my lady," she whispered in my ear. "Feel free to take some of the food with you. There's no telling what they'll serve you up there."

A week later, I was back in the palace of Rouen, having stopped briefly at the abbey of Bec, where I was offered hospitality by

Abbot Boson. This time, I had sent word ahead of my arrival, and Rouen was made ready for my stay. In the days since leaving Argentan, I had decided it was best to write and inform my father of the reason I had left Anjou, as well as my intention to petition the Holy Father. I hoped that in expressing honesty, I would be deemed worthy enough of his trust that he would simply scold me rather than punishing me in some manner. This was perhaps wishful thinking, but it seemed worth a try.

As the new archbishop of Rouen had not yet been consecrated at that time, I discussed my desire for a divorce with the abbot of Saint Ouen, Rainfroy, who was rather offended by the suggestion and bid me return to my husband like a good Christian wife. He even offered to come with me and help me gain the forgiveness of Count Geoffrey. This seemed utterly absurd to me, since it was my husband who had committed sin on so many occasions. I politely refused his admonition.

I waited upon news from England, but I did not wait idly. I needed to know what to do should the worst happen: if my father came over from England, gathered an army, and attempted to bring me back to Anjou by force. I well remembered the time he had threatened to drag me there by the tongue. The words still haunted me. Perhaps my father might beat me until I bled once again. Ever since that day, I believed he might do almost anything cruel. I would not feel safe until I had somewhere to flee.

But who would shield me from the wrath of the king of England? Any house of God might be bound to safeguard one fleeing harm, but I did not have enough faith in my father's character to believe he would respect the sanctity of the Church. In any case, were I to go to the abbey of Bec or another such house, it would simply become my prison. I would not be able to step foot outside its walls without falling under the king's rule again. Therefore, it was necessary to find a land that was not only free of my father's control, but was under the control of someone who would not simply turn me over to him.

I had come up with three possibilities, one of which was so unthinkable that I prayed to God I would never have to use it. The monastery of Prémontré, founded by Norbert of Xanten, was northeast of Rouen near the city of Laon. Drogo's friendship with Norbert would help me to gain sanctuary there, and it was close enough to Rouen that I could flee there quickly. However, it was also close enough that my father might dare to invade. The second choice was the monastery of Clairvaux, whose abbot Bernard was already famous in those days. It was far beyond the reach of any Norman army, and I hoped Bernard might be able to aid me in my communication with the Roman see.

The final possibility was to run to someone with his own army—someone who had no love for my father and would not lift a finger to help him. Yes, I am speaking of King Louis of France. I hated the idea of casting my lot with him, but as he was a natural enemy of both England and Anjou, he would surely support my desire for a divorce. He was the obvious choice, and yet I feared that allying myself with Paris would ruin me in the eyes of my countrymen. Not only that, but it would cause me to lose respect for myself. It was therefore the last and worst option, to be taken only if all others failed and I was in fear for my life.

One morning, after I had been in Rouen for about a fortnight, I was standing in the queen's chambers on the upper level of the palace, looking out across the yard and the gardens to the River Seine. As the queen was not in residence, I had been allowed to use these grand rooms rather than the smaller chamber at the end of the hall that had been my home in times past. I therefore had a perfect place from which to view the falling rain as it struck the ground, leaving large puddles in the dirt.

It was in that courtyard that I had first beheld Geoffrey of Anjou. True, I had hated him from the start. Perhaps I had no right to hate him then, as I knew barely anything about him, but having had ample time since to make out his character, I felt that my first judgment was right on the mark. To my left were the gardens, which held a very different kind of memory. It was there that I had told Brian I loved him. These two moments seemed to bring together everything that had happened since I returned from the empire: every painful bit of it.

With a sigh, I looked back at the room behind me. The hearth on the left held the fire that warmed me. The rest of the room was filled with two tables and chairs, as well as a desk to my right. My eyes were trained on that desk as I walked toward it slowly. Three letters, all fixed with my royal seal, sat upon it. I walked around the desk and sat in the small wood chair, my gaze still centered on the letters. I reached forward with my right hand and ran my fingers over each of the seals. Perhaps my future lay inside them.

I heard a knock at the door and turned my head. "Who is it? State your purpose."

"It is your knight, Drogo, here with some messages," came the reply.

He entered at my command and walked over to where I sat, peeking over my shoulder.

"What are those?" he asked, pointing to the letters.

"This one goes to Norbert in Magdeburg, this one to Bernard in Clairvaux," I said, indicating each one in turn. I then set my finger on the final piece of parchment and said, "This is the fearful one."

"For the king of France?"

I closed my eyes, nodded, and gave a slight shudder.

"Are you sending them out now?" he asked.

I began running my fingers over the seals again. "I cannot decide if I should. Once these letters are sent, there will be no turning back. Yes, I am only asking for assistance in case I need it, but even if it never comes to that, they will still know that I asked. I am not worried about the monks so much as King Louis. How it would thrill him to open this letter and find out that there is division within the House of Normandy! Perhaps I should just send the other two and wait on his. After all, he is the closest by far. A letter would not take as long to reach him."

"Before you make any decisions, you should read the day's correspondence," Drogo offered. He had been holding it at his side with his left hand and now raised it for me to see.

"Why? Is there something from England?"

He reached into the pile and picked out a single letter that bore the seal of the chancellor, Bishop Roger of Salisbury. Given my concern about its contents, the red seal took on a rather fearful appearance, as if it had been stamped in the blood of my father's enemies.

"Oh, Drogo," I whispered, "I cannot open it. Will you read it to me?"

He set the rest of the pile on the desk and broke the seal on the bishop's letter. My heart began beating faster as he opened each fold in turn. He looked me in the eye, perhaps trying to gauge my mood. I nodded to indicate that he should start, and thus he did.

"'To the Empress Mathilda, countess of Anjou, daughter of King Henry of England, duke of Normandy, I Roger, bishop of Salisbury, send greetings and my best wishes for your continued good health. I will not waste words but get straight to the point.'"

I folded my hands together and pressed them against my lips, closing my eyes. *Lord Jesus and all the saints, make haste to help me*, I prayed silently.

"'Your father the king has received the letter you sent him explaining your decision to depart Anjou and reside for a time in Normandy. He is also made aware of your desire to petition His Holiness Pope Honorius for a divorce from your rightful husband, Count Geoffrey of Anjou, with whom you were joined in the bonds of wedlock more than a year hence. This news came as a terrible surprise to all of us at court, who had wished the best for your marriage and looked to you to provide an heir for the House of Normandy.'"

Drogo stopped reading for a moment and looked down at me. "Are you all right, my lady?"

"It is just as bad as I feared," I whispered, my eyes growing moist. "What will become of me?"

"Perhaps I should finish reading the letter before we declare that all is lost." He smiled slightly as he said this, not I think to mock me, but to grant me courage.

"Very well," I said, with a wave of my hand. "Continue."

Drogo's eyes returned to the paper and suddenly his expression changed. "This is interesting."

"What is interesting?" I asked, pressing down on the arms of the chair and raising myself slightly, as if doing so would draw out the answer quicker.

"'We were quite ready to make a reply to you on this score, when the king received a most unwelcome letter from the hand of the count, which accused him in the foulest terms. Among the crimes that my lord is said to have committed are breaching the marriage contract, refusing to turn over castles in Normandy, and failing to command the Norman nobles to pledge fealty to Anjou. He even had the gall to command the king to do fealty to him for the Angevin estates!'"

"Good Lord!" I cried. "He is an even greater fool than I took him for! I cannot remember the last time someone threatened my father and it turned out well for them."

Drogo nodded in agreement. "Allow me to read on. 'Well, I need not tell you that this has caused great offense throughout England and Normandy, and with no one so much as our beloved sovereign, King Henry. He sees now the weakness of character in this young count. Fear not! My master pledges that he will not rest until the honor of Normandy is restored. He will travel to you in Rouen and discuss this matter. Therefore, be without fear, for all will be set right.'"

I was overjoyed at this news. I could hardly believe that for the first time in almost two years, my father and I seemed to be on the same side. It was too good—truly, too wonderful!

"Drogo," I stammered, so filled was I with excitement, "do you know what this means?! It means I am safe! I have hope! Of course, it is due to my husband's presumption rather than his disloyalty to myself that the king has undergone this change of temper. Nevertheless, I shall take it, and gladly! But what about my request for a divorce? Does the letter say anything about that?"

"One moment," Drogo replied, his eyes scanning further down the letter. "Ah, here we are! 'The king and I are both determined to safeguard the alliance with Anjou at all costs, for it is the key to defending Normandy. For this reason, we bid you wait before making any petition to Rome. Divorce is a most severe path with grievous penalties in this life and the next. Therefore, your father commands you to wait until he is in Normandy, that the matter may be discussed further.'"

"He will safeguard the alliance at all costs?" I scoffed. "He means at all costs to me. He would never take on a cost himself."

"I regret to say that is all the bishop writes on the matter," Drogo concluded. "There is something else about your cousin, Henry of Blois, being named bishop of Winchester—"

"Oh, that will please Lady Adela! She is ever so eager to advance her sons in any way possible."

"Yes, and here I see that the king has forgiven the traitor Waleran Beaumont and returned most of his possessions. Well, that seems like an awful chance to take."

"Indeed," I said, standing up and taking the letter in hand to examine it myself. "I remember when my first husband pardoned Archbishop Adalbert: that proved to be a poor decision. I hope we will not have a repeat of that treachery."

Even as I spoke these words, an image passed through my mind. I remembered the way Waleran had looked at me that day he was being led off in fetters. His eyes burned like fire and sent a chill through my bones. I truly hoped he was a better man.

"I suppose only time will tell," replied Drogo. "Now, I shall leave you to read the rest of your messages alone." He took two steps toward the door, then turned back. "Do you still intend to send out those other letters?"

"No, thank God, they are no longer necessary!"

With that, he departed the room and left me there to ponder just what had been given to me: it was hope, yes, and more than I had thought to receive. Yet it was not hope of the highest kind. It seemed my father was still quite determined to keep me married to Geoffrey of Anjou. He wanted his heirs, and so did I, but I also wanted respect.

"What am I to do?" I whispered. "What cost am I to pay?"

I received a few letters from Anjou during this time begging me to return and take up my place as countess. Sadly for them, I was much happier living alone in Normandy than I ever had been with Count Geoffrey in Anjou. In addition, my desire to be free of him had, at least for the moment, exceeded my desire to produce children. Perhaps that sounds selfish, and perhaps it was, but my own interests had been considered so little throughout my life that something inside me had finally rebelled and demanded its due. I wanted the respect of the world that came from having children, yes, but not at the expense of being treated without respect by my husband.

As the year came to a close, I continued to discuss with the scholars how I might remove myself from that marriage. My father was still against the idea of sending a petition to Pope Honorius. He preferred to use the situation to his own advantage and force a compromise out of his son-in-law. For him, the alliance with Anjou was always sacred. I, on the other hand, was not convinced that the alliance would last even if I did remain married, and thus it did nothing to change my mind.

However, the point became moot, for Pope Honorius died that winter, and all of Christendom descended into chaos. While the poor man drew his final breaths, the papal chancellor and some of his fellows were already plotting to install Gregory Papareschi in the throne of Saint Peter. Less than ten men chose Gregory as pope, and they had him consecrated the day after Honorius' death, without the advice of their brother cardinals. This did not sit well with anyone, least of all the powerful Pierleoni family: the same clan that caused so much trouble for my late husband. Under their influence, a separate meeting of cardinals within Rome chose Peter Pierleoni as Holy Father, and he went by the name Anacletus. The other pope, who took the name Innocent II, was chased out of the city.

All of Europe was greatly upset by this, and not without good cause. Most of those on this side of the Alps supported Anacletus, including the Holy Roman Emperor Lothair, King Louis of France, and my own father. Others, notably Abbot Bernard of Clairvaux and the Italians, favored Innocent. I knew not whom the lords of Christendom would choose in the end, and even less what God willed. What I did know for certain is that there was no way that the issue of my marriage was likely to come before the papal court. As long as the rivals fought with one another, I had no chance of obtaining a divorce, and I had no hope that they would reach a peace within the year. This was a blow, and no mistake.

"What are we to do now?" Drogo asked one evening, as the two of us sat alone by the fire in the great hall of the palace in Rouen. "It seems that the Church itself is nearing divorce."

"Were you a better student of history, Drogo, you would know that such things happen in every age," I replied, pulling my shawl tighter for warmth. "The churches of the East have still not reconciled with Rome after some seventy years, though I dearly hope they shall one day. In time, either Anacletus or Innocent will come out victorious, or else the Lord may call one of them to heaven and spare us all the trouble. But I heard that Count Geoffrey is facing a rebellion in Anjou. We must wait until my father the king arrives in Normandy. Then he will play upon that boy's weakness."

I was still feeling cold, so I pulled my chair closer to the hearth. Our chairs were very large with high backs, so I was able to pull my legs up near my body and lean against the left arm. I once again wrapped the shawl around my shoulders and rubbed my hands together nearer the fire. From his chair across from me, Drogo reached with his long arm and grabbed an iron poker, then used it to provoke the flames back to life. He returned the instrument to its place, leaned back and crossed his legs, and broke into a smile.

"What is it?" I asked, still attempting to warm my fingers. "I know that look. You have heard something."

"Your husband is ready to depart on pilgrimage to Compostela," he answered.

"What an idea! Why should he leave his kingdom at such a time? And since when does Count Geoffrey care about the things of the Lord?!" I cried.

Here the knight's expression became more serious. "He is a knight, my lady. We too take sacred vows."

"I think yours were a bit more sacred than his, Drogo. Speaking of vows, did you know King Henry gives one hundred pounds a year to Fontevrault and Abbess Pétronilla?"

This, of course, was the house that had sheltered my husband's whore.

"It is still a good house, my lady," Drogo argued. "They had no choice but to help that woman when she came begging for aid, even if she was of ill repute."

He had a point there, but I was still inclined to dislike both Fontevrault and its abbess for harboring such sin, even if it was done out of mercy.

"You know, they have given the child a name," I said, with contempt in my voice. "Hamelin."

"Hamelin? Wasn't there a town in Germany by that name?"

I examined my memory and determined that he was correct. "Yes, in Saxony. So you see, the Saxons are out to destroy me again!"

"They were never out to destroy you—just your husband," he noted with a smile.

"I wish they would destroy my present husband. He intends to acknowledge the boy openly. Well, he is a bastard."

"Wait—Do you mean Hamelin is a bastard or Count Geoffrey?"

I laughed. "By happy chance, it works both ways."

King Henry did arrive in Normandy in early September 1130, along with Hugh, the abbot of Reading. Archbishop Geoffrey of Rouen had died more than a year earlier, and it was the king's intention to install Hugh as the new archbishop before Michaelmas. However, before doing so, the king wished to visit the abbey of Bec to confirm his authority. There had been a dispute with the new abbot, Boson, who was loath to swear a personal oath of loyalty to the king, preferring to remain faithful to the Church alone. They had reached some agreement, but my father nevertheless wished to visit the place and look the man in the eye, therefore putting the fear of God in him. If the king goes to Bec, all must go to Bec. Therefore, I set out to meet him.

It is a short journey from Rouen to Bec: about a day's ride. The country is pleasant and full of wheat farms. When the sun hits them just so, you might mistake them for fields of gold. As we approached the monastery, we saw some of the monks still at the harvest, gathering the grain for their winter bread.

Only a monk could use the same breath to lower a scythe and chant a hymn, I thought.

We entered the outer court, part of which was paved in stone. What a nice change from the dirt and gravel! Abbot Boson was standing in front of the main collection of buildings—the church, refectory, dormitory, infirmary—with a broad smile on his face.

"Welcome back, Empress Mathilda!" he called out. "Your father and his companions have only just arrived."

"Thank you, abbot," I said, patting my horse on its head and then alighting. "Is the king inside?"

"You will find them all in the refectory," he answered. "Allow me to guide you."

We made the short walk over to the hall, where the weary travelers were enjoying a hearty supper. It was a stone building with a lovely roof, its beams carved so that it appeared that they were rows of leaves born out of the wood itself. Few churches were decorated with such excellence, but that was not the primary subject on my mind. This would be the first time I had seen any members of the Norman court since the wedding, which already seemed a lifetime ago. So much had changed since then: the very earth seemed to have shifted beneath me. Yet there they all were feasting and drinking, as if nothing odd had taken place.

I followed the abbot through the front doors, which were painted bright green. The scene inside was jovial, with both of the long wood tables full of men merry with wine. A few of their dogs were wandering about the room, and a bright fire burned in a pit at the center.

"Empress Mathilda!" a voice called.

I turned to the left and saw that it was Robert Beaumont walking toward me.

"Well met, kind lord," I said, extending my hand for him to kiss. "It is good to see you again."

He straightened back up and looked at me with a face that was all confusion. "Again? I did not think we had ever properly met."

Now I was the one thrown into confusion. "What do you mean? We were in each other's company all the time not two years ago."

"Oh, you must mean my brother!" he said with a laugh. "Forgive me. I am Earl Waleran, his twin." Here he bowed deeply.

The moment he spoke his name, I was filled with fear. Could this be the same man who had once given me such a look of hatred that it shook me to my core? His appearance was altogether different. For one thing, he had a mess of brown hair on his head, though his face was still bare. He was no longer gaunt, but once again had the same rosy cheeks as his twin brother. His clothes showed no signs of dirt or holes, and by the manner of his greeting, I would have thought him a decent fellow.

"You are Waleran, truly?" I asked nervously. "You are not trying to trick me?"

"No, we are quite alike. Our own mother used to mistake us."

"Ah, right! How fortunate for her to be twice blessed!" I replied.

I could still hardly believe that I was speaking with an established traitor only just forgiven by the king. The same man who had been brought so low that he was willing to cast an evil look my way was now standing before me clad in gold chains. I was beginning to regret having shaken his hand, but I tried to put such thoughts behind me.

"Tell me, cousin, where is the king?" I asked.

"Just over there," he replied, pointing at the far table.

"Thank you," I concluded, and walked over to where the king sat next to the fire with the earl of Surrey, brother Robert, Count Theobald of Blois, and Brian fitz Count.

As I approached, I began to doubt if it would really be best to speak with them all together, and I was about to turn around when the king caught sight of me and waved his hand. "Get over here, prodigal daughter!"

The sound of his voice alone seemed to tie my stomach in knots. I took a few uncertain steps toward his position and bowed. "Yes, my lord, I have come."

"Do you want to discuss your knave of a husband now, or later?" my father asked, taking a swig of wine.

"Perhaps you could first tell me how you've been," I offered.

Here the look on his face grew more somber and he set down his goblet with some real force. "If you must know, I've been rather singed."

"What? I think I mistook your meaning."

"No, we really were singed, or very near it," Robert said.

"How did this happen?" I asked, looking over at my brother on the right and then back at the king.

"When we were in Rochester, back in May," the king explained. "Half the town burned to the ground."

"Oh no!" I cried. "Was anyone hurt?"

"Not seriously," Brian answered. "Some of the animals perished, but no human deaths."

Up until that point in the conversation, I had been standing behind Brian and he was facing away from me, but at that moment he turned to face me and I looked once again into his eyes. I took it he had either been away from Wallingford for some time or his wife had given in, because he had a beard again and his hair was a good bit longer. Why I should have made this observation, I am not sure. It was just odd to see him again. It had been a good three years since that time when we were in love, or at least when I was in love. Ever since he had forsaken me, I looked back on that period uncertain of where Brian had truly stood. All I knew was that it seemed like an eternity had gone by, or that no time had passed at all.

"Well, that is a relief," I said, quickly returning my gaze to the other side of the table, "but still, how dreadful that you should have been there when this happened, or that it should have happened at all!"

"Sit down, my daughter," the king ordered.

There was an open spot next to Brian, but instead I walked down to the end of the table and rounded the corner, moving to take a seat to my father's right. Truly, it was a choice between hell and Hades. I sensed that he was about to scold me about Count Geoffrey, so I spoke first.

"Have you heard anything regarding the papal schism?" I asked, motioning to one of the servants for a glass of wine.

"The monk Bernard has written to me, begging me to accept this Innocent as pope," the king explained. "Well, he's not so innocent, if you ask me. I have yet to meet a man in this part of the world who supports him, save for a few monks. Bernard, the abbot of Clairvaux—he writes to me constantly in the most pleading terms, bidding me for the benefit of my soul to remove my support from Anacletus. But that's just what they say, isn't it? 'Innocent possesses Rome, but Anacletus the whole world.' Now this Bernard wishes to meet with me, but he is within the realm of King Louis, and that concerns me: I doubt his motives." Here he seemed to squint, as if spying out some criminal act.

"Perhaps his only motive is to promote Christian unity," Count Theobald said from across the table. "This monk is well known to us. If you wish to meet him in Chartres, it is about half way."

"I would rather meet Count Geoffrey and give him a piece of my mind!" the king replied, hitting his palm on the table.

I took a deep breath. We had made it back to the subject I feared, and yet I knew it must be discussed. Fortunately, the man had returned with my wine, and I was able to take a quick drink as the king launched into his argument.

"He is a fool if he thinks he can force my hand!" my father bellowed. "Nevertheless, you know you will have to go back to him, daughter. This separation is not proper. You promised me heirs!" Here he pointed at me directly.

"But my lord, you know what he is like!" I argued. "If I return to Anjou, he will find some new way to make a mockery of this house."

"I think you only fear that he makes a mockery of you, for you care not for this house," my father concluded. I was about to object strongly, but he continued, "Divorce is out of the question. You must devise some other solution. I will have heirs!"

I thought of a few things to reply in that moment, none of which would have been genteel. At the very least, I wished to say that I could have children with someone else, but I noted how my father's eyes seemed to be cutting into my flesh. I felt a shudder of fear, and it was that fear rather than any deeply held principle that caused me to seek a brief retreat.

"Thank you," I said quietly, "for making your position so clear. I am sure there will be plenty of time to discuss this later. But tell me, where is cousin Stephen?"

"At home with his wife and son," Theobald replied.

"Stephen has a son?" I asked, turning to face him. "I had not heard of this. What is his name?"

"Eustace," Robert answered. "He cannot be more than a month old."

My eyes quickly scanned the persons at the table. Brian was staring off into the distance, while the king still appeared annoyed, if not completely angry. The combination of my distress over seeing Brian again and hearing the king's words, along with the news that Stephen too was made a father, combined to push me over the edge.

"So everyone is having sons but me," I concluded. "Well, isn't that just ... wonderful. Pardon me, my lords, but I think I need a bit more to drink."

I gulped down what remained in my goblet, then got up and walked over to the barrel on the far side of the room. More than anything, I wanted to be alone and free from the comments of others. I came to the barrel and reached out to pull the lever, but another hand slid in and I saw that it was Brian's.

"Here," he said, taking the goblet from my hand. "An empress should not have to fetch her own drinks."

"Is that so?" I asked. "What else is an empress not meant to do?"

"I think she is not meant to frown as much as you do," he said, handing it back to me full.

I looked down at the liquid and swirled it around a bit, playing for time as much as anything. "If I am in ill humor, it is because life has made me so," I concluded softly, not meeting his eyes.

"I was sorry to hear about everything that has happened," Brian said. I was then quite surprised that he reached out and touched my arm lightly to pull my eyes back to himself. "He is a fool to treat you like this," he said with conviction.

You're one to talk! I thought, trying very hard not to allow myself to dwell on this very small touch, for I knew it meant nothing. "How is your wife?" I asked instead.

"Last I saw her, she was well, but that has been quite some time now."

"She is not with child, then?"

"No, God has not seen fit to bless us with children—at least, not yet."

There was a sadness in his eyes that I understood, for I felt it in my own heart. However, my feelings were rather mixed given the history of our friendship. Well, I was not so vengeful as to wish both him and his wife bereft of offspring.

"I am sorry to hear that," I said in all honesty.

"Never mind it," he replied. "Perhaps things will improve with Count Geoffrey. He has had plenty of time to rue your absence."

"Perhaps, but I think not," I concluded, for I suspected that on a personal level Count Geoffrey was glad to be free of me. "Thank you for the wine, Lord Brian."

As I moved to leave, he took one step after me to reclaim my attention. "Is there anything I can do for you? Anything at all?"

I looked into his eyes for a moment. Several possible answers entered my mind. *Tell me you still love me. Tell me this was all a terrible mistake. Wake me up from this nightmare. Make it all undone. Run away with me far from here, where no one can hurt us.* But I could say none of this. It was a dream. It was wrong. It was impossible. It broke my heart.

"Nothing," I answered, then returned to the others.

CHAPTER SEVENTEEN

I have made mention of Bernard, abbot of Clairvaux, defender of the faith. It was in those days that we first came to recognize his genius. He was called upon by King Louis of France to judge between the two popes, Innocent and Anacletus, only one of whom could be the true one. He not only chose Innocent, but he caused all the kings to do so as well: quite a feat when one considers that they seldom agreed on anything! I had not foreseen an end to the dispute any time in the near future, but thanks to the efforts of Bernard, I again had hope that my case might be brought before a pope recognized by all.

During Advent, King Henry sent word through Abbot Bernard to Pope Innocent informing him that he wished to honor the Holy Father in person and express his devotion to him. This request was granted, and they agreed to meet in the cathedral city of Chartres, which lay within the lands of my cousin, Count Theobald of Blois. When I heard the news, I was filled with joy that I might have the chance to make my case to Pope Innocent face to face. After all, correspondence might go astray or be passed through unfriendly hands, but if I could simply tell the Holy Father directly of my husband's continual adultery without any sign of repentance, he might allow the marriage to be declared null without any punishment for myself.

Without the consent of the Church for the breaking of our marriage, I would be cut off from its grace and declared excommunicate, stripped of the means of salvation. Apart from my personal terror at the destruction this would bring to my soul, I had seen what excommunication did to my first husband, and I knew I would never be accepted as a ruler of the smallest hamlet if I was seen to be rejected by God. That is why I was so desperate for papal consent, for if the pope declared my actions righteous, then no bishop or abbot below him could reasonably object, nor could any king who wished to remain faithful to Rome. Yes, even my father would have to accept it.

Sadly, the king was away at his hunting lodge of Lyons-la-Forêt for much of December, and I was therefore denied a meeting with him to discuss these matters. I told my ladies to make ready for travel, but I knew it was vital that I be of one mind with my father before we set out. After all, he had been firmly opposed to a divorce. Therefore, when I heard that the king was likely to return upon the Ides of that month, I sat next to the window in my chamber from the early morning so that I might be among the first to observe his arrival. I hoped to catch him before he became involved in other matters of state.

It was a rather long wait, for by the time the king's company came pouring through the gate and into the courtyard, the sun had sunk low in the sky. I made my way down to the lower level as fast as I could without running and entered the yard just as my father was alighting from his horse. I rushed forward to meet him as he removed his gloves.

"All hail, Henry king of the English!" I cried, bowing low before him. "Rouen welcomes your return!"

There were about a dozen servants and officials gathered there, along with the party of fifteen or twenty men that had returned with the king. It must have seemed a bit odd to them for me to approach the king in such a manner, for I usually hung back with the others on such occasions. But I cared not what they thought, for I had an urgent task.

I raised my eyes to look into those of my father. He was smiling, which was good, but I could not discern his thoughts. Fortunately, he informed me of them rather quickly.

"I know what it is you desire, and the answer is no," he said firmly, then began to walk past me toward the palace.

I straightened up quickly and walked beside him. "What do you mean, my king? Surely you cannot answer without knowing my query."

He stopped near the entrance and handed his gloves to one of the grooms who was standing there. He then proceeded to remove his helm, bracers, hilt, and cloak, placing them all within the poor man's arms until he seemed to bend under their weight.

"You want to accompany me to Chartres and speak with Pope Innocent, no?" he asked, as he handed off these items.

My heart sank. Was he really intending to refuse me this—even a simple opportunity to speak with the pope? I pressed on in hope.

"Naturally, my lord, I seek to meet the Holy Father of our beloved Church—"

"And to discuss your desire to abandon your husband."

"I am not abandoning anyone," I argued, stepping in front of him so he would be forced to look at me. "It is Count Geoffrey who has behaved deceitfully and broken the marriage covenant. He abandoned me!"

"There will be no more debate on this point."

The king pushed me aside and entered the palace. Inside, I was trembling in fear, but I was not going to give up this time. No, I followed him into the entry way and continued to speak to him as he stopped to wash his hands in a bowl held by the steward.

"You know I am right on the moral point. There is no reason that I, a faithful Christian, should not be allowed to approach the representative of Christ on earth and make my concerns known, as a daughter to her father." Here the thought passed through my mind that I had never had such a bond with my father by the flesh, but I set it aside. "I am aware of how greatly you treasure the Angevin alliance, but now that the danger from France has passed, perhaps you may wish to marry me to another lord in any case: one who shows respect for you and your throne."

"Oh, I will have it out with young Geoffrey—have no fear!" the king assured me, drying his hands on his tunic. "But if we break the alliance with Anjou, there will be more danger from France. Make no mistake! King Louis and Count Geoffrey will be the best of friends just like that." Here he snapped his fingers. "You fancy that you know something about governing, but truly, you know nothing. How could you?"

The king moved on to the butler who was standing about two paces away, holding a silver tray on which sat a goblet full of wine.

"He has dishonored me! He has dishonored you! He has dishonored this house!" I cried. "Does that count for nothing? Where is your pride, my lord?! Even if he goes over to the king of France, you always love an excuse to slaughter their kind. Perhaps you could gain dominion over the Île-de-France, even as our father Rollo attempted!"

He took a long drink from his goblet, his eyes studying me the whole time. Having drained it, he set it back on the tray with real force, startling the poor butler.

"Do not think to win me over with flattering words!" he yelled, pointing his finger in my face. "When I decide a thing, it is final. The greater problem here is not Count Geoffrey's arrogance, but yours. You refuse to take any man as your lord. You are disobedient to the last. Perhaps that is why he tired of you!"

Both the servants had scattered by this point, along with anyone near enough to hear the king's bellows. It was just the two of us standing there at the base of the stairs to the upper level, locked once again in a battle of wills: one that I seemed to be losing as always. I could see that the king's mind was unlikely to be changed, so I tried a new approach.

"You cannot keep me from going," I said more quietly. "I am free to go to Chartres of my own accord. I am a married woman, and thus under the authority of my husband, not my father."

"You are in my duchy and subject to my rule!" he cried, the fire burning in his eyes.

"I think you will find that I am not. I am a visiting official from the county of Anjou. You have offered me your hospitality, and I thank you for that, but you cannot bar me from leaving. To do so would present Count Geoffrey with *casus belli*."

"Don't be a fool! Count Geoffrey no more wants you in Chartres than I do!"

"Oh really?" I said, folding my arms and smiling. "Shall we bring him out and ask his opinion?" I began looking around the room. "Come out, Count Geoffrey! Come out and tell us what you think!"

I glanced back at my father, whose face had grown red, even as his brow had been folded so firmly that it looked as if he was trying to push his eyes into his chin.

"My husband has not given his opinion," I continued in a pleasant tone of voice. "When the ruler is away, his consort is seen to have the prerogative. I have decided: I shall make a pilgrimage to Chartres for the benefit of my soul."

"Enough!" the king cried, dropping his hands and forming them into two fists. "Stop this ruse!"

He moved very close to me and held up his right fist near my chin. For a moment, I was quite afraid that he would strike me in the jaw, and by instinct I looked back through the open door to the yard to see if anyone was watching. Alas, they were not, but in the end all my father wished to do was yell.

"You have played the game as well as you could, but you forget that I hold the winning piece! I can choose my own successor. The lords and bishops will swear as I tell them. I made you into an heir." Here he thrust his finger near my face again. "I can unmake you!"

"You wouldn't dare!" I said quietly, but with a real force of conviction. "If you cast me aside, you will never have descendants on the throne of England! Your line will be broken!"

"I don't have descendants now!" he cried, his hot breath hitting my face, his eyes wide with anger. "You have failed me, Maud! I sent you to Anjou for one purpose: to make babes! But have you? No! What good, I ask, is a girl? I knew it from the moment you were born! You are of no use to me! Your womb is as dry as a desert, as barren as the moor!"

The more he spoke, the more I shrank into myself. I had fought to overcome my fear, but it was all coming back to me with the force of a cannon. I took a step back to be further away from him, but I was up against the stone stairs. I felt trapped. He moved in and pressed his hand against my belly.

"What good is this?" he seethed, each word coming out like a fiery arrow. "What good are you?"

I mustered all the strength I had to speak. "Don't touch me," I whispered. "Get your hands off me."

"Get your arse back to Anjou," he commanded, then to my great relief, he granted my request.

As he turned to walk away, I placed my hands over my stomach and closed my eyes, breathing deeply, trying to endure the waves of fear.

"You are not going to Chartres, and that is final! I swear to you, I will cast you away if you do so! And don't even think about writing to the pope!" he called back over his shoulder.

"This isn't over!" I cried, causing him to pause for just a moment, though he refused to look at me. "This is my choice, and I will make it, so help me God!"

To my great surprise, he attempted no reply. He simply departed into the yard. I may not have won his approval, but with this final declaration, it seemed possible that, for once, I had won the war of words.

As soon as I was certain he was gone and would not return, I ran up the stairs, down the passage, and into my bed chamber, where I threw the door shut behind me. For a moment, I simply leaned back against the door, still breathing heavily. I was naturally upset that I had become the subject of my father's anger yet again, but I lauded myself that I had not simply given in to his reproach. I had at least tried to stand up to him. Even so, it had cost me. My spirit was trembling.

I looked over at the bed and saw the book I had been reading earlier in the day still lying there. It was a new collection of writings by Bernard of Clairvaux, the very man who had arranged the meeting with the pope. Hoping for some word of wisdom, I walked over and picked it up, opening it at random. I came to a page where I had made a mark to note its import.

"Help me, Bernard," I whispered, and began to read:

"Ah, if you wish to attain to the consummation of all desire, so that nothing unfulfilled will be left, why weary yourself with fruitless efforts, running hither and thither, only to die long before the goal is reached? It is so that these impious ones wander in a circle, longing after something to gratify their yearnings, yet madly rejecting that which alone can bring them to their desired end, not by exhaustion but by attainment. And if their utmost longing were realized so that they should have all the world for their own, yet without possessing Him who is the Author of all being, then the same law of their desire would make them contemn what they had, and restlessly seek Him whom they still lacked, that is God Himself. Rest in Him alone. Man knows no peace in the world; but he has no disturbance when he is with God."[16]

I stood there in silence for a moment, the book still open in my hands, pondering the words silently. I took one breath after another, in and out, in and out. I closed my eyes and addressed myself to my Creator.

"Help me, Lord. I am restless—nay, I am furious! How my heart aches! I have been ... forsaken. Utterly forsaken! Save me from the wolves of Anjou. Let me rest in you."

King Henry attended the meeting in Chartres without me, and I passed the rest of that winter with a renewed sense of despair. I was running out of options. How could I preserve my right to the throne while also escaping my marriage? I dared not write to the Holy Father immediately after what the king had threatened. However, I had not ruled out such an appeal in the future, nor had I given up on the possibility of divorce. I simply battled each day within myself. Which would grant me greater

---

16 Hastings, James, ed. *The Great Texts of the Bible: II Corinthians and Galatians* (New York: Charles Scribner's Sons, 1914), 135. Excerpted from *On Loving God* by Bernard of Clairvaux.

joy and control over my own affairs: remaining with Count Geoffrey and keeping the king's favor, or departing from him and suffering the wrath of both the king and the Church? I could not decide, but I knew for certain that whatever I did, I did not want it to be because the king had commanded it. I wanted it to be my own choice.

With the papal dispute all but settled, King Henry was eager to return to England in the summer of 1131, and he wished me to accompany him to a great council in Northampton. The purpose of this council was plain enough: he would have all the nobles and bishops pressure me into returning to Anjou. Well, they were welcome to attempt it. All I knew was that my anger at what I had been forced to endure had consumed me. It was not merely Count Geoffrey with whom I was angry, but all the men who had ever denied me my due.

A large company came over with us from Normandy, for it was to be one of the greatest gatherings in the reign of King Henry. Strange as it may seem, I never traveled any farther north than the city of Northampton, much as I might have desired it. Circumstances always had a way of preventing this. We resided at the castle, which by then had reverted to the control of King David of Scotland through his marriage to the former countess, Mathilda.

While the site was perfect for such a meeting, we could not have come at a worse time, for upon our arrival we learned of the sudden death of the Scottish queen. What a terrible loss this was for my uncle, who had loved her most truly! She was laid to rest at the abbey of Scone, and it is said that he often went there alone to pray at her tomb. Queen Mathilda had left her husband with two living children: their son Henry, who was ever his father's pride and joy, and a daughter named Claricia. This was not much progeny to speak of, but King David nevertheless refused to marry again. I asked him about this once and he told me, "She was not only my queen, but my very heart and soul. I was so content in her that I needed no other."

The greatest women on earth might have paid all their riches to hear a man make such a proclamation. I had certainly never heard such a thing spoken by either of my husbands. Even so, it seemed a rather poor decision for a king to make: that is, to bet his kingdom on one son. But perhaps he knew what he was doing, for though Henry did not make it to old age, he did leave behind many descendants who still sit upon the throne of Scotland.

So the council began at Northampton without the presence of King David, which felt strange given that he spent half his life in England. I was greatly discouraged, for I had very much hoped to have the support of my uncle in my bid for a divorce. Nevertheless, we all made due the best we could without his company. On the first day, the king held a court of pleas and the archbishops of Canterbury and York tore into each other once again, neither of them wishing to surrender influence to the other. The following day, the council was to discuss the chief matter at hand: my unhappy marriage to Count Geoffrey.

That evening, I was sitting with the queen in the room she had chosen to be her audience chamber for the length of our stay. It was perfectly square, with tapestries on the walls and a fire in the hearth. The two of us sat in chairs across from one another, each reading a book by the light of the fire. I confess that I spent less time reading and more simply staring at the pages while I attempted to decide how to make my case to the great lords of the land. We had been at this for about half an hour when we received a visit from Abbot Boson of Bec.

"Empress Mathilda, may I have a moment of your time?" he asked, poking his head through the door across the room that had been left ajar. "Begging your pardon, Queen Adeliza."

"Of course," I said, setting my book upon the floor and beginning to stand.

"There is no need, Empress Mathilda," the queen said, raising her hand and causing me to freeze in place, half sitting and half standing. "This is a good room for a private conversation. I will make my way down to the hall."

"But this is your room, and I do not intend to steal it from you," I countered, standing to my full height.

However, the queen had done me one better. She had already stood herself and walked over to grab my hands and clasp them in her own.

"I command it then," she said with a smile. "May God bless your fellowship."

Protesting further at that point would have caused things to turn sour, so I submitted to her request and returned to my chair. The queen nodded politely to Abbot Boson and departed by the same door through which he had lately entered. The bolt clicked and then all was silent except for the soft crackle of the fire. I looked at the abbot, who was standing there with his hands clasped, all calmness and serenity.

"Have a seat," I said, motioning to the chair across from me.

"Thank you, gracious lady. I am sure you know why I have come," he replied, crossing the space between us, pulling his robe forward slightly, and settling into the seat.

"Of course. You wish me to return to my husband by law."

He folded his fingers together and smiled at me. "He is not merely your husband in the eyes of the law, but by God's holy ordinance. My lady, why will you not go to him?"

"Because he is a swine. You know I know this, and I know you know it. The world does not hold as many secrets as men suppose."

"Even so, are you to live apart for all eternity?"

"We've kept it up for almost two years thus far," I said with a shrug.

"My lady—"

"Abbot Boson," I interrupted, growing rather annoyed, "I know what the world demands of me. They wish me to trample upon my own spirit and suffer that which ought not be suffered. Let us be honest now: no one was very happy about this marriage when it started. They all hated the idea of an Angevin husband. Now when I have the chance to rid myself of him, they forbid me to do so. Do you have any idea what it is like to be bound in life to a man you do not respect and who does not respect you—a man who hardly warrants the name? Do you have any idea what it is like to break into tears upon seeing a child, knowing that your husband would rather make babes with a whore? Please, I beg you! You must see that I cannot do this. Nothing you could say would convince me to take back Count Geoffrey."

"Perhaps not. I am only a poor monk," he admitted, bowing his head. "Yet I must say, my lady, with all due respect, that you are thinking about this the wrong way."

I had been pressing on with my argument at full speed, and his quiet words, uttered with all courtesy, caused me to stop in my tracks.

"What do you mean?" I asked.

"This question does not touch yourself only. It is not even a matter for the living."

"Well, I hardly think the dead should care what I do."

"That is not what I mean either."

"Then pray, get to the point, for you confound me utterly!" I begged.

He nodded and took a deep breath. "Empress Mathilda, you must think not in terms of one lifetime. You must think in terms of a thousand years."

"A thousand years?" I whispered, overcome with a sense of awe. To even imagine such an amount of time was difficult.

"Yes, quite. Do not think of yourself at all. Think of the children who might be born. Think of the kings and queens that might reign. Think of this kingdom and what it might accomplish." His voice grew stronger with each sentence, carrying an excitement that touched both our souls. "A thousand years from now, I dare say no one shall remember my name, and even yours may be forgotten. Yet your descendants will live and inhabit the earth! Through them, you may live on for ever! Your dream must be larger than yourself. It must live for a thousand years! Consider this island, my lady. They have only just made peace with the new order of things. As the apostle says, they do not yet know what they shall be. But search your heart: you know the greatness for which this land is bound. That is your destiny, and you must see it done!"

He had made a good point—a very good point. Any possible retort seemed quite selfish, but I was not going to acknowledge defeat that quickly. I had come too far and suffered too much.

"Truly, good abbot, you amaze me. Your words have such power, yet I have spent my entire life sacrificing my own contentment for that of others. Will it never end?"

"Once again, I entreat you to think not of what you are losing, but of what you might gain," he argued. "Count Geoffrey may well be a disagreeable fellow, but he is the only man living who can give you sons."

Here I opened my mouth to interrupt, but he boldly held up a hand to stop me.

"No, my lady! Do not speak the word divorce. Whatever right you may have to such a thing, we both know that we do not live in such a world. He is the only one who can give you sons. Would you for hatred of him throw away your own fortune, turn the king against you, and live out your days in misery? Or will you return to him, bring forth an heir, and sit upon Saint Edward's throne? We are not merely the contents of our days. We are the authors of the future, for that which we create lives on to become either the hope or the bane of future generations. Only in your blood can the greatness of the past—the kings of old—be passed on to enrich England for years to come. Does that not stir your heart and cause you to see the passing sorrows of this age as the birth pangs of a brighter future?"

By this point, there were tears in my eyes. No one had ever presented my duty to me in such terms. Indeed, it seemed no longer a mere duty, but a privilege, albeit one that was filled with sacrifice. He allowed me to sit and absorb these words for a moment, then I wiped the tears on my sleeve and continued.

"I know that you speak wisely, good Boson. Yet a part of me does not want to accept it. I have suffered greatly, not only at the hands of my husband, but also those of my father. I cannot simply forget that."

"Granted," he said, with a nod of the head.

Again, I wiped my eyes with my sleeve and sniveled. "Do you really suppose my descendants might reign for a thousand years?"

"If they have any of your blood in them, I should say their odds are as good as any that walk this earth," he replied, leaning forward and smiling.

I laughed. "You are too kind."

"No, my lady. You are the kind one. You have borne my words with great patience."

Many thoughts were floating through my mind. His words had struck me as true, and if that was so, then I must return to my husband. Oh, how I despised the thought! Yet the abbot had played me to perfection. He had presented me with something I loved even more than I hated my sorrows—even more than I hated Count Geoffrey!

"Patience is precisely what I shall need if I am to return to Anjou," I whispered.

"Never fear, empress! The Lord himself goes before thee. He will give you strength."

I cast my eyes toward the ground and spoke quietly. "My father would think it was his doing. He would think he had conquered me once again."

"Let him think what he will!" the abbot said. "You and I know the truth. We know you serve a higher purpose. He cannot control your mind, my lady. He cannot bend your heart."

That night, I went to the church of the Holy Sepulchre and prayed for hours both upon my knees and lying on the floor. Tears flowed from my eyes and supplications from my heart. I was at war with the Almighty. I despised the very thought of Anjou, but hour by hour, my heart seemed to soften, and by morning, I knew what I must do.

I walked into the hall of Northampton Castle, and pledged before them all that I would take back my idiot husband, for the good of England and Normandy. The king could not have been more pleased with my decision, and he promised me that he would extract from Count Geoffrey everything that was possible. He pledged to turn over the castles in southern Normandy to myself and my descendants, as soon as they were born. King Henry also made all the nobles swear fealty to me once again, for there were some who complained that they had been tricked the first time, not being aware of the king's intent to marry me into Anjou. By forcing them to take the oath a second time, my father removed any such doubts.

So it was settled then: I was to return to Anjou. I could only hope and pray that Abbot Boson's charge to me was as wise as it seemed. Not for the first time, I was about to do what I had sworn not to do. I was going to surrender the desires of the moment for desires that would last a thousand years. Indeed, I think they were eternal desires. Would it be worth it? Only if I had children, and there was no guarantee of that. Yet I wanted it—I desired it so strongly. Having heard the words of the abbot and seen where my place might be in history, I could think of little else. Yes, I hoped. I hoped and I prayed, for I was sorely afraid.

By the time the council was completed, the weather had taken a turn for the worse. I was forced to wait until November 1131 to make the crossing, and then I remained in Rouen well into the next year before returning to Anjou in time for Midsummer. I can well remember the day we rode through the north gate of Angers Castle, a place where I had vowed I would never again set foot. How life makes hypocrites of us all! We made our way into the inner court, and standing there to greet me was my husband, Count Geoffrey of Anjou, who had finally been able to grow a slight beard. I had imagined this meeting for months—ever since I had made the difficult decision to return—but I was not entirely certain how he would react or what I myself would feel in that moment. As it turned out, he acted as if nothing out of the ordinary had taken place.

"Good day, my wife!" he said, reaching up to help me off my horse.

I settled on to the ground and patted my gown back into place. I then looked up and observed that Count Geoffrey must have grown in my absence, for while he had only been a bit taller than me before, he had now passed me by a good half foot. I quickly took an account in my mind and determined that he must be eighteen years of age. Well, he may have grown in stature, but I was not about to give him any marks for growing in character: not until I observed such a change.

"Good morrow," I replied, with some degree of loathing.

It was not much of a beginning. After I had been received by all the lords, ladies, and bishops, my husband held out his arm and I took it. We walked together into the castle as if nothing out of the ordinary had happened and I had not been gone for almost two years. He led me up the main stair and down the hall to his private room in the castle. A fire had already been made up in the hearth and a small table was set with a bottle of wine and glasses. Most of the room was taken up by the very large bed with its high canopy. The only other item of note was a desk by the lone window, on which sat a few small boxes.

I had never spent much time in this room before, and I could only guess that he had brought me there to speak without being heard. I let go of him and he moved to close the door behind us. He then turned to face me.

"You came back to us. I admit, I did not know if you would."

"You have only yourself to blame for my absence," I replied, crossing my arms.

He laughed. "What did you think this was? We were forced together, you and me. We were made to wed. This was not some kind of love match, as if we were common peasants. You can't have been too surprised. You are too clever for that."

"Are you saying we don't have to like each other?" I asked.

"I am saying we were brought together for one purpose, and we must see it done."

"Then I suppose that is the difference between you and me, because I always wanted a real marriage, where I would not have to wonder whose bed you might share on any given night. It shows a lack of respect for my person, not to mention making it very difficult for me to respect you."

"Such things are permitted for princes. Just look at your father!" he argued, gesturing with his hands as if the king was standing off to the side.

"He may be my father, but he is a poor Christian, and so, I think, are you."

Neither of us spoke for a moment. I looked him over even as he did me, each of us no doubt seeking some advantage over the other. I saw a face that so many women had come to love, but which to me seemed more foul than fair. The glow from the flames gave it a somewhat different character, though I was not sure how. Perhaps he seemed a bit older, which he most certainly was.

"God does not command us all to be saints," he said quietly but with authority. "There may be some who are called to a higher righteousness, but we are not among them."

I shook my head in censure. "Well, there we will have to disagree. The commands of the Lord are meant for everyone, including you! But just look at you: a grown man who walks around with flowers in his hat, hair that is longer than mine, garments that I can only describe as eccentric. 'Oh, I adore that *planta genista*! How handsome he is! If I see him again, I may faint!' Yes, I hear how they fawn over you and lust after you, young women without a brain between them. It makes me sick!"

"So you would prefer me to look like an Englishman?" he jeered, moving closer to me.

"Not an Englishman—just a regular person. I would not mind if it wasn't done to increase the desire of those who ought not give it, and we both know perfectly well that is your aim. You look as if you're putting yourself out there as bait to be swallowed by every maid in Anjou!"

"You would judge me based on my appearance?" he complained, moving closer still.

"No, I find your deeds wanting as well."

Here he turned and walked toward the fire, laughing as he went. I did not see any humor in the situation, but he evidently took some pleasure from it. He grabbed a poker that was sitting beside the hearth and used it to move a log back on the fire. Then he turned to face me and pointed his instrument in my direction.

"You know what I think? I think you never liked me from the moment you saw me," he charged, pointing the poker at me. "I swear to God, you are the most stubborn woman I have ever met! It's no wonder the Normans sent you back!"

Better stubborn than a libertine, I thought. I remembered why I had come back—for a dynasty and not Count Geoffrey—but I nevertheless struggled to contain my anger.

"They sent me back because we have to make this marriage work, but I truly doubt whether you are willing to do so!" I cried.

"Oh really?!" he shouted in response. "See what I am willing to do!"

With a great flourish, he ripped off his hat, flowers and all, and threw it upon the fire.

I screamed and ran toward the fire to recover it, but he grabbed me by the waist and held me back. I watched as the flames began to consume it, turning it black. He then released me and I moved to the far side of the room, hoping to put as much distance between him and myself as possible.

"There was no need for that!" I protested. "I seek moderation, not destruction. I am not hateful."

"Oh no! Don't be so shy, wife," he mocked. "I will give you what you demand!"

He then began removing his outer clothes, pulling on each lace in turn.

"Are you mad?" I asked. "Truly, have you lost your mind since I left? Those must have cost a fortune!"

He made no reply, but continued taking off his clothes. I threw up my hands and laughed.

"Well, don't think I'm going to try to stop you again, because I won't!" I cried, though in truth I had no idea where things would end or what I would do.

"For you, my dear!" he replied, then threw them into the flames as well.

"You know very well this is not what I meant for you to do. Now stop it already!" I yelled.

Again, he made no reply, but walked across the room to the desk, clothed in nothing but his pants. He opened one of the boxes and began looking through it.

"Wait! What are you doing?" I asked, for his bold actions had filled me with concern.

"Exactly what you want," he replied.

He turned and held up some scissors that he had retrieved, and I guessed what he was about to do, though I could hardly believe it.

"No! Stop! I didn't mean it!" I cried, running across the room to stop him.

I attempted to move around the bed so quickly that I hit my big toe upon one of the wood legs and cried out in pain. Indeed, it was so bad that I fell to my knees and grabbed my foot, wincing and groaning. The pain continued to come in waves. About the time I was able to open my eyes again, I was lifted up from behind by Count Geoffrey and heard him ask, "Should I call the physician?"

I turned to look at him and saw that his hair no longer fell down the length of his back but ceased somewhere near his shoulders. I was in such a state of shock that all I could utter was, "Good Lord!"

"I hope you see now that, as you say, I am willing to do anything to make this work," he declared.

"I can see that you are a great fool! Honestly, who does something like that?!"

"Fool or no," he replied, "I hope my actions prove that I am serious."

"What you have done doesn't matter," I said. "Do you have any idea the kind of sacrifice that is required to truly honor someone? The price you have paid is a pittance in comparison with that. No, it doesn't matter. I know you will be back to whoring tomorrow."

He laughed. "Lady England forget about tomorrow. This is today."

He grabbed my face and pressed his lips on mine with such force that I could hardly breathe. I suppose some women might have loved it, but a kiss without real affection or even respect meant nothing to me. He pulled back and looked into my eyes.

"Tell me you didn't enjoy that," he dared.

"Even so the traitor Judas kissed his Lord," I whispered, "and I will say to you what Christ said to him: do what you must, and do it quickly."

It would hardly be proper for me to tell you what happened next, but suffice it to say, our marriage was thoroughly renewed. His vanity demanded that I heap praise upon him, yet he had no idea how to win me. I may have let him into my person for the sake of a child, but I would never let him into my heart.

The worst part of returning to Anjou, apart from having to spend time with Count Geoffrey, was having to eat the Angevin food. I was not sure why, but it often sent me into an ill humor. However, it seemed to get worse a few weeks after my return. For several days in a row, my stomach became sick and I was forced to spend hours in bed, and after about a week my bowels settled into a permanent knot. When this continued for most of a month without relief, I was filled with concern. This condition was plain to the women around me, and one day in late summer, Lady Agnes decided to ask me about it as she tended to me in bed.

"This has gone on so long, my lady. Have you come any closer to discovering which foods upset you?"

"Actually, my entire body has been ill at ease," I replied. "Not only is my appetite all but gone, but I also feel constantly tired—so very, very tired."

"That's it! I'll get the physician for you," she declared.

"Why? He will just tell me the meat has gone bad again."

My experience with the Angevin physicians had not been good. That was perhaps the third thing I hated most about the county.

"Have you been eating much meat?" Agnes asked, pressing her hand on my forehead to check for fever.

"No, come to think of it, and especially not any fish. Last time I tried fish, I couldn't keep it down."

She stepped back and continued examining me with her eyes. "Perhaps you have a worm."

"Wouldn't that make me more hungry and not less?"

"Who knows how these things work? My cousin had a worm for God only knows how long, and we only found out when it came out the other end."

"Lovely," I groaned, fearing that this story would only make my stomach feel worse.

"There is a new physician here in Angers: a student of the schools in Italy," she said. "Please let me fetch him for you."

I closed my eyes and breathed in deeply. "Very well. Send for him."

So Agnes went to retrieve our physician, Master Odo. This gave me a few minutes to worry in equal measures about what my condition could be and how this Odo might attempt to treat me. I never did decide which was more fearful. When he arrived and Agnes left the two of us alone, I sat up on the side of the bed, bringing on more discomfort.

"I am very sorry to hear you have been in ill health," the physician said.

"Let's just get this over with," I muttered.

He began by conducting a simple physical examination, poking me here and there, then pulled up a chair by the bed. He set his hands in his lap and looked at me directly. It seemed to me that he showed too little fear for someone of his age. He was a thin young man with short light hair, and his clothing was very simple, but he bore himself as one with authority.

"You said you have been tired. Are you sleeping through the night?" he asked.

"Some nights yes, some nights no. It depends on how loud the feasting is below."

"Is it possible that you could have suffered an injury in your abdomen?"

"No. At least, nothing that I can remember."

He smiled and nodded. "And you say your appetite has changed."

"Yes, though I suppose that could be due to the different food in this part of the world. It has always disagreed with me."

"To the point of sending you to bed?" he asked, raising his brows.

"No, I suppose not."

"Are there any foods in particular that seem to trouble you?"

"It depends on the day, but I can hardly stand the sight of fish."

"I see."

He closed his eyes as if deep in thought. This left me feeling rather awkward just sitting there, but it did at least give me a chance to observe that I was feeling slightly better—almost as if I could eat some sop and bread.

"Forgive me, my lady, but are you sore anywhere?" he said, opening his eyes and interrupting my thoughts.

The multitude of questions proceeding from his lips started to concern me. *What on earth does he think is wrong with me? Is it something deadly? Or could it be—no, surely not. I have wondered that before, but it has never been the case. The blood always returns. No, I must have some disease.*

"Sore?" I asked, breaking out of my thoughts. "Yes, my belly is quite sore from all the times I've been ill, and then ... well ..."

"Well what? Is there somewhere else that is hurting?" he inquired.

"If you must know, my breasts have also been ... tender."

I would have felt more comfortable discussing this subject with another female, but there was nothing for it. I simply had to trust in the physician's discretion. Fortunately, it did not seem to concern him. Indeed, he pressed into even more dangerous territory.

"How often have you and your husband had intimate relations?" he asked.

This was such a strange question to receive, even from a physician, and I could not help but laugh for just a moment. "You don't hesitate, do you?"

"You may tell me. There is no need to be afraid."

"I am not exactly afraid," I explained. "We were together several nights a week, until a few weeks ago when I began feeling more sick."

"And when was the last time you passed any blood?"

"That's rather personal, is it not?" I said, growing offended.

"It could be pertinent," he maintained.

I let out a sigh. "Very well. I suppose it was about two or three months ago now. That is not so strange, is it? I have had such things happen in the past when I was under stress, and returning here has certainly been a cause of stress."

"It is not so very strange on its own, no, but along with your other symptoms, I think I can say with some degree of certainty that you are with child."

I stared forward at the physician, blinking quickly. His words were so odd, almost as if he was speaking in another tongue.

"Forgive me. I'm not sure I heard you correctly," I said.

He leaned forward and patted my hand, a smile on his face. "Empress Mathilda, countess of Anjou, in about seven or eight months' time, you are going to give birth to a child."

This was such strange news. Of course, his questions had led me to hope, but I had hoped before. Ever since I was fifteen, whenever I noticed that my blood was late, I had hoped, but it never came to anything. As odd as it may seem, the doctor could not have surprised me more if he had told me I was sprouting cabbage from my ears. Simple reason proved his words to be true, but fear had long held me back.

"What? Me—with child? How?" I stammered.

"Surely a woman of your standing knows how babes are made!" he said, laughing.

"Yes, I know that, thank you! What I meant is, I have been doing that thing that makes babes for a long time, but it has never produced a result. Of course, I have hoped ever since I returned, but I hoped as one wandering in the dark. Everyone thought I was barren! Are you quite sure?"

He leaned back in his chair, his overall manner far more casual than mine, which was quickly reaching a state of complete excitement. "Well, there is nothing certain about these things, but from what I can tell, it appears that you are going to be a mother. Indeed, you already are, in a manner of speaking. Yes, I think I would bet my right hand that you will have a child."

I was so overwhelmed by this news that I began to weep openly, even with the doctor sitting right there. It was as if many years of longing were suddenly released in a torrent. I placed a hand on the bed post for support as I gasped for breath.

"Forgive me, Your Highness," he said, reaching out to brace me himself. "Have I made you cry? You are not unhappy, are you?"

I wiped the tears from my eyes and looked into his. "No, not at all! I just, I was not sure if this would happen for me. Now that it has, I feel ... I feel ..."

"What do you feel, my lady?"

I shook my head in wonder. "Proud. Afraid. Overjoyed—everything! I feel it all. I feel as if I will burst!"

"As well you should. Now, let us pray that you may be safely delivered of this child."

He stood up and made to leave the room, but I reached out and grabbed on to his robe.

"Please! What must I do now?" I asked, rather foolishly.

"Eat what you can, get plenty of rest, and wait for the winter," he answered.

"Is there any way of knowing if it is a boy or a girl?" I asked again, equally foolishly. Even as the words escaped my lips, I knew they were worthless.

"Apart from seeing an astrologer, I should think not. I have heard that you set no store by superstitions, so I will not trouble you with those. If it is a girl, you can take comfort in the knowledge that the ability to have one child means you are likely to have more."

"Yes, I suppose you are right. Thank you."

The doctor packed up his things and left me there in the room alone. I began to cry again, mostly out of joy, but also because I was so afraid that I hardly knew what to do. I placed my hands on my belly. Could there really be a child growing in there? Would it survive to enter this world? Would it survive its first year of life? I knew not what to do. I had been so eager to reach that point for so long—to simply become pregnant—that I had given little thought to the potential dangers that lay beyond. Uncertain of what else to do, I knelt beside the bed and pressed the crucifix I wore around my neck between my folded hands.

"Thank you, Lord God. Thank you for hearing my prayers. You are truly most merciful, most gracious," I prayed. "Please, I beg you, let this child be strong. Let him live … or her. Let them live, whoever they may be."

I continued to rub my belly, as if by doing so I could transfer some form of maternal defense.

"My child, we do not even know each other yet, but everything depends on you," I whispered. "We are on a journey now, you and me. We must make it safely to the end. God be with us."

CHAPTER EIGHTEEN

February 1166
Rouen, Normandy

I awake daily to the sound of two choirs: the monks singing their morning hymns, and the birds chanting the praise of their creator. More than once, I have mistaken this for heaven itself, being half in a dream. Recovering my senses, I am sad to find myself still trapped within this helpless frame, growing weaker by the day, for there can be no heaven on earth. Even so, I woke today to clear evidence of my mortal state when Adela burst through the door of my bed chamber carrying a basket full of rosemary.

"Do you know what today is?" she asked me, in her ever cheerful voice.

I blinked a few times, my eyes still adjusting to the light, then raised myself up with my right arm until I was sitting upright.

"Five days after the feast of Candlemas," I muttered in reply, rubbing my eyes.

"Yes, but also—"

"The seventh before the Ides of February."

"Which means?"

"It is time for this snow to melt!" I offered, wishing to avoid the answer she desired.

She laughed softly as she began scattering the herb on the floor, the better to improve the smell. "Yes, that too, but of far greater import, you have now been on this earth four and sixty years!"

Four and sixty years? That hardly seemed like cause for rejoicing.

"Lord have mercy! Has it really been that long?" I asked, or rather groaned.

"Were you not born in the year of our Lord 1102?" she asked, setting the empty basket on the floor and removing her outer cloak.

"So they tell me. I have no memory of the day."

"That is quite an accomplishment. I have known a good many people who never made it to sixty-four."

I swung my legs over the side of the bed and allowed her to sit beside me.

"An inability to die is not necessarily an accomplishment, Adela, especially when one feels half dead already."

"Oh, I do not believe that!" she said, and indeed Adela is loath to accept anything but the best of news. "You have many years left in you: I am sure of it!" Here she patted my left knee. "Come, what should we do to celebrate?"

I suddenly had a rather wicked thought and gave a sly smile.

"What is it?" she asked, leaning in slightly.

"Perhaps we can roast the archbishop of Canterbury on a spit."

"My lady!" she objected, rising to her feet.

"Oh, calm down, Adela! You know I don't mean it. But why can we not celebrate something better? Let us celebrate our friendship!" I motioned for her to sit beside me again. "How long have we known each other?"

She smiled and perched beside me, fixing the folds in her skirt. "Well, I was about seventeen when we met. What is that? Thirty some years?"

"A good long time," I agreed. "We have seen each other through many hardships. Let us celebrate that instead. I'll have none of this getting old."

"Shall I tell Lawrence to cancel the feast tonight then? The brothers have a special song ready, and the cook is making that food you love most."

"And what, pray tell, is the food that I love most?" I asked, hoping to test her.

"Venison stew?" she asked more than stated. Indeed, she seemed about as certain as a young man attempting to behead a criminal for the first time.

"I think you will find that is not the food I love most, but if the cook has already made it, and the monks have been practicing as long as I suspect they have, then it would be best not to disappoint them. I can pretend as well as anyone."

"Very good, my lady," she concluded. With this, she rose and walked over to the hearth to start the fire. "I was wondering, have you heard anything from the king of late?" she inquired.

"He writes that he will come over by next month, but not to Rouen. He has business in the South."

"Oh, pity that!" she said, ceasing from her work long enough to give me a sorrowful glance. "I know you would have loved to see him."

Still seated, I turned behind me to gaze out the window at nothing in particular.

"I do miss him greatly at times—I admit it—and I worry about him. Then again, I have been worrying about him since before he was born. This business with his imperial highness, Thomas Becket ..." I turned back to look at her. "I love the king, Adela, but when he gets something in his mind, that's an end of it. He is as restless and determined as anyone I have ever known, and that is saying something."

She had provoked the logs into flame and moved to retrieve an ivory comb from a box that sat on my desk.

"Well, he was always like that, wasn't he? Even as a boy?" she said, sitting beside me once again and beginning to take apart my braids.

"Yes, quite. He could keep himself busy for the longest time, unlike his brothers. He would hold all his thoughts inside; then suddenly, they would burst forth like blood from a wound. I thought he might change with time, but it never came to pass. Do you remember how he used to trick us all? Once, he caught some frogs down by the river and set them loose in the kitchen."

"Really? I do not remember that. Were the servants very upset?"

"How could they be? He was their master even then. Then there was the time with the snake—"

"Oh, I hate snakes!" Adela cried. She had just started running the comb through my tresses, and as she uttered these words, she pulled with real force and I struggled not to cry out.

"He always loved them: dreadful creatures! He knew well enough not to leave them in my chambers though. Henry always saved his more harmless tricks for me, for fear of punishment."

"He has always been a jester—the king."

"Yes, now that there is no man who can tell him no, he gets away with murder."

"Except for the archbishop."

"Pardon?" I asked, turning to face her.

She swallowed hard, perhaps struggling to come up with an answer that would not cause offense. "The archbishop can tell him no; at least, he tries to."

Adela had hit very near the mark with that comment. "Time will tell what is to become of the king. I do fear what would happen if I was not here to pray for him," I responded.

I turned back and allowed her to finish her task.

"We do not have to worry about that for a good long time," she concluded, applying the final strokes. "Come! Let us get you dressed and enjoy this day on which the Lord blessed us all with your birth ... for on the day of your birth, there must be mirth! That is a pleasant rhyme, is it not?"

"Not half as pleasant as you," I said, thus flattering her without admitting that she was no minstrel.

As she set to work gathering my clothes for the day, I found myself thinking not of my own birth, but of another: a story I will now share with you.

In the waning days of February, in the year of our Lord 1133, I stood heavy with child before the door of the birth chamber, ready to be shut in. We had just completed the service of thanks giving in the castle of Le Mans, and it was there that I would complete the required days until the child within me sprung forth, either to life or to death. The door stood open before me, and inside was the small room, its walls covered with dark linen and the window blocked by wood boards. Many candles shone brightly upon their golden poles, and there was incense burning on a small table in the corner to ward away bad humors. Then there was the bed in which I would be forced to spend my days. At least the red sheets and the pillows looked comfortable.

With me stood the four women who would be my constant companions for the next few weeks—the midwife Bertha and her fellows—along with the bishop of Le Mans, the seneschal, and my husband, Count Geoffrey.

"Do not fear, my lady," the bishop said, patting me on the back. "The very angels of heaven watch over you. Along with all the prayers of the monks, I shall daily add my own supplications to the Almighty that you may be brought through this without distress."

"Thank you, Bishop Guy," I replied, thankful for any assistance I could gain, divine or otherwise. "You cannot know how thankful I am for all the prayers made on my behalf—that is, on our behalf," I added, pointing to my enlarged belly.

Although I had been with child for many months, I still felt overcome with wonder whenever I glanced down or felt the kick of the child. Indeed, the first kick was a source of great hope for me, for having waited so long to become pregnant, I had greatly feared that I might miscarry. I had lived every day on the edge of a knife, and now I had come to the greatest test of all: one out of which many mothers and children were not delivered. Yes, the sight of the bed before me was a subject of fear as much as anything, for I recognized that the most dangerous moment was near at hand. All my hopes hung in the balance.

"Take this blessed image of Saint Margaret," the bishop continued, handing it to the midwife. "Place it by your bed and, should you have any cause for alarm, look to it for comfort. She is watching over you."

"Again, I thank you," I said. "Now, if you all please, I would like a moment alone with my husband."

They obliged and left us there for a moment, the last that we would spend together until after the babe arrived. Since learning that I was with child, Count Geoffrey had been somewhat more kindly disposed toward me, and I in turn was more forebearing with him, but it was not what one would call affection. We had simply made a truce of sorts. It was a source of some pain to me that my beloved child should be the result of a union with an unworthy man who would likely try to make the babe like himself, but there was nothing for it. The child bound us together more truly than even our marriage vows.

Geoffrey stood in front of me, his hands clasped behind his back, a smile upon his face. This was not to be his first child, but perhaps it was the first one he truly wanted. For all the disdain I had felt toward him, I did not doubt his genuine love for the child I hoped to bear.

"Have you written to my father?" I asked him, rubbing my belly.

"Yes, I sent word earlier today that you were to begin your lying in."

"Is there any chance that he will come for the birth?"

"In the last letter I received from him, he mentioned a host of ecclesiastical disputes and said he should be detained for some time. However, he stated in the most passionate terms how eager he was to meet this new child, how his dearest wish was about to be fulfilled, and how he could not think of anything more pleasing."

"That at least is something, I suppose," I said softly.

For a moment, I thought of everything that had taken place between my father and me since my return from the empire. I remembered how he had cast words at me like vitriol and seen no worth in anything but my womb. Now that my womb held a child, I was of some value to him. He might finally receive what he desired. But what was I to him or to the world? Still nothing—still without love. But oh, how I was ready to give love! I would shower love on my child. I would do what my father had not.

"How are you feeling?" he asked.

This is a nice change of manner, I thought, my face breaking into a small smile. "Not too bad. It is just as well that I should lie down, for I can hardly walk as it is."

"And the child? Does he feel strong?"

"I wish you would not say 'he,' for it may be a girl."

"What harm is there in hoping?"

"Only this: that you may well have your hopes crushed, and we should all hate to see that."

He shook his head. "I can never satisfy you. But he—that is, the child—is strong?"

"Well, my belly has been kicked so much it is likely to burst," I remarked with a sigh. "I am not sure if that tells you what you wish to know."

"It's just, I am so eager, so very eager for everything to go well."

Now, I have told you that our marriage had improved slightly while I was with child, but we had still not spent much time together, for I dared not travel in my condition. I had also naturally eschewed all physical relations, and as I was already pregnant, my husband had no reason to pursue them. I suspected he had gotten his fill elsewhere. Nevertheless, in this moment, I felt that I was seeing the best of him. He was not an entirely changed man, but perhaps he deserved to be closer to his son.

"Here," I said. "Feel for yourself."

I took his right hand and placed it upon my belly. It did not take long for the child to move, and Count Geoffrey's eyes grew to twice their usual size.

"By God! I can feel him! He is strong indeed!"

"Or she."

"Yes, or she. Oh, but it must be a boy!" he declared joyfully. "That was the kick of a warrior—at least, a very small one."

For a moment, we stood silent while he continued to feel the child's movements. He was looking down at my belly, but I was looking at his eyes, wondering what he was thinking. Finally, he raised those eyes to meet my own.

"Thank you," he whispered.

"For what?" I asked.

"For coming back. For giving me a son."

Had I wished to cause injury, I could have pointed out that he already had a son born out of the bonds of wedlock, but that hardly seemed right.

"I am ready now," I said. "Call the ladies. I shall withdraw."

I then entered the chamber in which I would meet my destiny, whatever that might be.

For almost a month, I remained in that dark room, waiting for the day I both longed for and dreaded. My first aim, of course, was to deliver a hale child. My second was to survive the experience, not only because I desired life, but because I hated to leave my child to the Angevins. I assure you that, by the time I did feel the quickening of my heart and the contraction of my bowels, I was so tired of seeing those same four people that I might have reached in and pulled that child out with my bare hands just to make an end of it!

The midwife Bertha stood beside the bed where I lay, clutching my hand, bidding me breathe in and out. When she determined that the child was indeed coming, she said to one of the girls, "Quickly! Go inform the steward that the countess is in labor."

"It's the emp—" I started to say, but was unable to continue on account of a new pain in my belly.

"Would you like me to rub more oil on your legs?" one of the ladies asked.

I had it in mind to tell her what she could do with her oils, but I was too weak to protest and allowed her to lather me. I was already drenched with sweat, so I am not sure what she intended to accomplish. I looked to my left at the image of Saint Margaret that sat on a table in the corner, but it lent me no strength. I thought instead of she who had borne me into the world: a world full of suffering and darkness, where a single flame of hope still burned. I clung to that hope and to her memory. I prayed to her as if she were a saint. *Help me, mother. Help me to do well.*

"Here, let's take your hair down," Bertha said. "It may help to ease the pain."

"How?" I asked, in between breaths.

Rather than answering, she continued with her work, knowing full well that I would soon be robbed of speech again.

"How do you feel now?" she asked, once my tresses had been released.

"Like my entrails are being pulled out of me one by one and my back is on fire," I groaned with some difficulty.

"Oh good! Not long now!"

It was a few more hours before I was being held up near the edge of the bed while the midwife squatted below with a pile of cloths in her lap, ready to receive the child.

"Let us say one last prayer to Saint Margaret," one of the ladies offered.

"No time for that: the child is coming!" Bertha cried. "Now, push again for me, my lady! Push with everything you have!"

"Please, Lord, let us live!" I prayed aloud, no longer caring the least bit what any of the ladies thought of me. "Let us live to sing your praises!"

I drew upon every ounce of power in my being. My poor body was so tired, I do not know where I found the strength, but somehow I was able to push just enough so that the midwife's skillful hands could pull the child out. I was overcome with the pain of many years just as much as the pain of the moment. My eyes were so filled with tears that I could hardly see. Then suddenly, I was not the only one crying.

"There you go, love. That's perfect," I could hear the midwife say.

The women laid me on my back and did their best to soothe me, wiping my forehead with a damp rag and rubbing my legs. The babe was still crying, which I took to be a good sign. There were so many questions that I wanted to ask, but I was too tired to form the words. Fortunately, there was no need.

"Empress Mathilda," Bertha said, walking over to me with the child wrapped in her arms. "This is your son."

"My son? Truly? I have a son?" I asked.

"A most hearty son," she replied, her face beaming.

She leaned down and pulled back the cloth a bit to reveal the very rosy head of a tiny boy, his eyes closed tight and the entire face looking as if someone had pressed against it, which of course was the case. He was a strange looking, alien creature, and yet he was perfect—so very perfect that I was filled with a delight far beyond all the words I knew in Norman, English, Latin, and German. There are no words sufficient for perfect joy.

"Can I hold him?" I asked, desperate to touch this miracle that had come into my life.

"I should think so, yes."

The ladies helped me to sit up and then, with the greatest of care, Bertha placed my son within my arms. He was so light! Yet already I felt the weight of the world was on him, even as it was on me.

"He has red hair," I observed, stroking it with care.

"Just like his father!" one of the ladies said.

"Just like my mother," I quickly added, for I much preferred this comparison.

"What will his name be?" Bertha asked.

Much as I hated to do so, I tore my eyes from my child and looked up at her. "His name?"

"Yes, at the christening: what will he be called?"

It may seem strange to think that I had given this question little consideration. After all, royal names are a matter of great import. I had simply been so intent on delivering a child—any child, male or female—that little else had passed my mind over the last seven months.

"I will have to speak with Count Geoffrey," I said, but then looking back down at that precious face, I answered, "Henry. His name is Henry."

"After your father?"

"And my husband—that is, my first husband." I said this because I had respected the emperor far more than I did my father in that moment.

They all agreed that it was a most excellent name, then at my request they left me alone with my son. When the door had closed, I leaned down and touched my lips to his warm forehead. He smelled like—well, not like anything I knew, but it was a wonderful smell. I suppose it was the smell of Henry.

"I love you, my son," I whispered. "I love you more than anything in this world."

He made no response, but I was willing to forgive him for that. I continued to stroke his head as he shifted to the side and his breathing became more even. He seemed to be just as weary as I was.

"Go to sleep, little one. I don't mind," I said.

As if he understood my words, he proceeded to fall asleep in my arms. How sweet was that face! I felt I could gaze upon it for the rest of my days.

"Just so you know, Henry," I whispered, "from this day forward, everyone on earth will try to claim you, for you belong to all of your people. Very soon, they will take you from me and make you into a knight, a scholar, a king—and that is what I want you to be. But remember always: you are my son. You have the blood of the Normans, the Angevins, and the royal house of England, but you are my son, through and through, and no matter what happens, that will never change."

The news of my son's birth was treated almost as the second coming of our Savior. The people took to the streets with great rejoicing and the church bells rang throughout the evening. Drogo had somehow been able to purchase a box full of fruit from the South and presented it to me as a special winter treat in honor of the occasion. In the hall below, there was such a feast as had never been seen in Le Mans. I heard there were some people weeping with pleasure, which I might have deemed rather foolish were I not so overwhelmed with joy myself.

I was forced to remain in that room for another week, right up until the christening, but it was more pleasant as I had two daily visits with Henry. The ladies were so intent on keeping him free of disease that the first time Count Geoffrey saw the boy was when we were about to take him to the cathedral of Saint Julian. He demanded to hold little Henry throughout the procession, much to the midwife's dismay, and when the boy was raised from the font, it was his father who cried, "Behold, the future ruler of England, Normandy, and Anjou!"

Those were happy days, and for once my husband and I were on good terms, united in our joy at Henry's arrival. I had received warnings that things would not be as smooth after the birth as I supposed, but it did not come to pass. I had the nurse and Lady Agnes to help me, and there was little else to occupy my time unless I desired it. My spirits were as high as they had ever been. I treasured the moments I had with my son, and I must admit, I loved how people seemed to treat me with a good deal more respect after I had done the one thing women ought to do.

I soon received word from King Henry that he wished me to ride north as soon as possible, for he was most eager to see the child with his own eyes. Therefore, I consented to make my stay in Normandy for a time, and along with a small company led by Sir Drogo, I arrived in Rouen before Michaelmas. Because I had the child with me, I spent the whole time in a carriage with Lady Agnes and the wet nurse, Joselyn. I had enjoyed no private moment to myself for a fortnight, so when I saw the streets of Rouen passing by out the window, I said a silent prayer of thanksgiving to God.

The carriage entered through the castle gate and pulled into the courtyard, along with the knights who had accompanied us. I clutched young Henry in my arms. He was dressed in white linen and had by that point filled out a bit and taken on a more normal color. I was also able to see the green of his eyes.

"Here we are, little one," I whispered. "You are about to meet your grandfather, the king of England. He will love you far more than he has ever loved me. One look at you and he will seek to give you all he possesses. You are my good fortune today."

I stepped out of the carriage with Henry in my arms. Though both of the other ladies had attempted to convince me to let them hold the child, I was unwilling to surrender him on such a great occasion. I had finally fulfilled my father's desire, and while I did not foresee that he would treasure me for it, I at least wanted to see the look on his face.

For once, he did not disappoint me. The king was standing there eagerly, bouncing slightly on his toes. When first he had us in his sights, he proclaimed, "Let me see him! Let me see the boy who is to succeed me!" He then walked toward us quickly with his arms extended, his face alight with joy.

"Greetings, father," I said, hoping in vain to receive some small amount of attention.

"Yes, yes—very good. Now hand him over!" he demanded.

I took the boy and placed him gently into the arms of the king. Though my father had not been a young man for many years, he was still mighty, with broad shoulders and arms like iron. The contrast of such a warrior holding a small child struck me as rather odd, but in a nice way. For my own part, I was still afraid of the king and felt ill at ease in his presence, but I did not believe he would raise a finger against Henry, the blessed child for whom he had longed.

"Ah, he has the light of Jupiter in his eyes!" my father declared. "I see thee, good Henry: you will be a lion among men. How like myself you are! See how he grasps my finger? There is real strength in that grasp, be it ever so weak! Men will bow before you, Henry—that is, when I have left this earth, and let us hope that is not too soon!"

As my father continued to stare down at Henry, Agnes tapped me on the shoulder and handed me a toy for the young boy.

"Here is his poppet," I said to the king, holding it out for him. "He is rather fond of it."

"Poppet?!" my father cried, furrowing his brow. "Why should he have a poppet? Put a sword in that hand and see what he does!"

"Ah, yes. The perfect gift for a nursing infant: a sword," I muttered to myself.

"I hope you are looking forward to the feast tonight," my father continued. "We have a fine catch of perch, halibut, crabs—"

"Is the entire meal to come from the sea?" I asked, with some apprehension.

"Yes, for that is the time of year."

"Oh dear."

"What? You have no stomach for fish?" The very thought seemed to offend him, judging by the look on his face.

"Not at the present, no."

"But I had it made especially for you, to welcome you back to your native land!" he objected.

"And I thank you for that," I said, touching his arm lightly to show my concern, "but were I to eat of the sea on this night, I am afraid it would end poorly."

"Why? Is something wrong?"

"Well, I cannot know for sure, but the last time I felt this way was when I was first bearing little Henry here."

Yes, it was true. Every royal lady needs more than one legitimate son to avoid the sort of disaster that had befallen England when my brother, William Ætheling, perished at sea. Therefore, very soon after the birth of Henry, Count Geoffrey and I had renewed our relations, for given the effort it took to bring our first offspring into the world, we feared it might be years before I was with child again. It was hardly my favorite way to pass the time, but it seemed more pleasant once I had seen the beautiful boy who was the result. I therefore assumed that this was the reason I could not stand the sight of fish.

"So you are with child again?" the king asked, his mouth breaking into a smile.

"As I said, I cannot know for sure," I began, hoping to stem the tide of his excitement, but it was too late.

"You are with child! God be praised that he should send us another heir!"

"Please, keep your voice down!" I beseeched. "I do not want anyone to know. It is far too early!"

"Of course, but you must know how pleased I am," he said, moving closer to me. "By God, I have not been this happy since the day I crushed your deceitful uncle at Tinchebray! Look, even young Henry is smiling that he should have a brother!" Here he pointed to the infant, his eyes gleaming.

"It may well be a sister."

He shook his head as if my words defied common sense. "Bah! Sisters have their uses, true enough, but you have delivered a boy once. I am sure you can do so again. And what a fine boy he is: my grand son! The fortunes of England and Normandy are restored in you! Now, if you are with child, we must get you to Grimbald straight away. There can be no mishaps."

"The midwives in Anjou are quite able. They did well with little Henry here," I said, tickling the boy's toes.

"Even so, one can never be too careful," he argued. "He is out on business now, but I will call him back directly. You can see him first thing tomorrow."

"As you wish, my lord."

I was not opposed to receiving advice from the greatest physician in the king's employ, but I had so little trouble with Henry, that I had no reason to suspect that this new child would be any different, if indeed there was a new child. But to satisfy the king, I was more than willing to meet with the good doctor.

By the season of Advent, it was confirmed that Henry was to be a brother, and I was almost past the period in which I was made ill by the very smell or sight of fish. I wrote to Count Geoffrey informing him that he was to be a father once again, and everything seemed to be proceeding according to the proper course. What a blessing to be with child again so soon! I began to pray in earnest that even as Henry and I had been spared death, my new son or daughter and I would be delivered from our hard labor.

Throughout those months, my sole regret was that I did not have more time alone with my son, who was usually kept away from the rest of us by the nurses. More than once, I begged them to let me take him out into the garden, but was told it might make him infirm. *How am I to know my son if I cannot see him?* I wondered. My brother and I were not so imprisoned in our early years, but we had my mother as an advocate. When I begged the king to make them see reason, I found him in agreement with the rest. So I was forced to content myself with brief interludes here and there, even as he began to walk and speak a few words.

You knew this would happen, I often thought to myself. *Stay the course. All will be well once the new child comes.*

With the arrival of spring came the time for my lying in. Oh, how I loathed it! It had been bad enough with my own chosen ladies, but in Rouen I was forced to make due with such midwives and attendants as were under the direction of Grimbald. It was most odd that a man should be involved at all, but King Henry placed his full trust in the physician's abilities.

Rather than setting aside a special room for me as had been the case in Le Mans, the same bed chamber I had often used in Rouen was made fit for my final weeks. I was laid on the bed with its high canopy, and tables were set on either side to hold candles and instruments. There were two windows behind me to the right and left, and one on the far wall. All three were covered with curtains. It was decided that a fire should remain burning in the hearth, for there was still a chill on the air, but a screen was placed in front of it.

As in Anjou, the idea was to keep the room as dark as possible. I always thought it was foolish to do so, but that was not a battle I chose to fight. Besides all of this, there were a few chairs scattered about the room and one more rather large table. Anything else I have forgotten, but I did spend quite a long time staring at the same objects, so that I knew every inch of their surfaces.

A few days before Whitsuntide in the year of our Lord 1134, I felt the first pangs of labor and readied my mind for the ordeal to come. The midwives were named Eleanor and Sybil, and they did all they could to lend ease.

"Do not worry, my lady: the second delivery is always easier than the first!" they assured me, and I took some comfort in their years of experience.

Yet while my Henry had taken not more than twelve hours to enter this world, my second child seemed intent on delay. Before long, I was into my second day of labor, and in the eyes of my ladies I saw the first signs of fear. So tired was I from the endless string of pain, I might have prayed every prayer in the book, but that is the funny thing about it: when your body is in enough distress, it becomes rather impossible to form any clear thoughts. Toward the end of the second day, I truly began to fear for my life.

"It's not getting any better!" Sybil said to her fellow as they bent over me.

"I think the child will come soon," Eleanor replied.

"Yes, but what if it doesn't? She cannot keep this up!"

Of course, hearing such an argument from the alleged experts in the room was less than encouraging. I tried my best to put it out of my mind, but the situation was becoming quite desperate. Like everyone else, I had heard the stories of mothers whose children became trapped inside them. Almost always one or the other seemed to die, and I feared the same fate.

As the sun dawned on day three, Eleanor spoke to me again. "Empress Mathilda, we do hope that this child will be delivered soon, but we are fast approaching the time when we may have to—"

"Cut out the child?" I asked, a new wave of fear rushing through my veins.

"I'm afraid so, or neither of you will survive," she said solemnly.

I pinched my eyes shut and considered her words. If I agreed, it would be the end for me. There would be no options left. It would be everything I had dreaded for months coming true all at once. I was not ready for that.

"No!" I cried. "No, I will not let you do it! It will kill us both! Please, just give it a little longer."

The look on her face was all compassion, but she struck me to the core. "My lady, I have attended at many births, and I do not see any way that this child will come naturally."

My despair was great upon hearing these words. If I continued to allow the child to linger within me, it was likely that we would both die. Were I to allow them to call forth the surgeon and cut the child out, there was a small possibility that it might live, but I would surely die. Was it selfish for me to continue in the same manner? I did not know, but the specter of death had overwhelmed me. I felt absolute terror, which may seem odd, as I had often found little joy in my time on earth. Yet I feared that my children might need me at some point in the future, and more than that I was afraid to meet my maker. I knew who I was and what I had done, and I doubted there was room in heaven for such a sinner.

"My lady, what do you want us to do?" Sybil asked, interrupting my thoughts.

"Give me three more hours," I concluded. "If the babe is not free in that time, then I will assume that God has chosen against me. I beg you, have the archbishop and all the monks say a prayer for our souls."

Thus began three hours of hell on earth. Up until that point, I had been almost too weary to go on, but the prospect of death placed before me seemed to awaken something fierce. I struggled with all my might to push the child out. After about an hour had passed, I heard the blessed words: "I can see the head!" At last, a bit of hope! However, another half hour and we were no closer to the goal.

"I do not like to do this, my lady, but I have no choice: I shall have to reach in as far as I can and pull this child out by force," Sybil told me, wiping the sweat from my brow and then her own.

It was not a very good option, but it was far better than the one I had faced two hours earlier.

"Do what you must, only do it quickly," I replied, closing my eyes.

Here the midwife showed her skill. She reached in with all care and pulled the babe out by the shoulders. I cried out in pain as she did it, for my very flesh seemed to rend. Nevertheless, it worked. The child sprung free and was taken to be cleaned.

They had held me up for the last hour, and I found that upon completing my task, my legs would no longer hold my weight.

"Lay me down!" I commanded weakly.

As they did so, I could hear someone commenting, "That is a lot of blood. Fetch some towels! We must stop it."

I was beginning to feel quite faint despite lying on my back. The whole room seemed to spin and then go dark. The last words I heard were, "Another boy! God be praised!"

Someone was hitting me, but why? Where on earth was I?

"Mathilda! Empress Mathilda!"

What was the last thing I remembered? I had been in pain. No, I was still in pain.

"Raise her legs. Place them on the pillows."

"I want to sleep," I muttered.

"What was that, empress? Empress?"

The room was spinning again. I felt another strike on the cheek and opened my eyes to see the face of Grimbald looking down at me, his blue eyes open wide and his gray beard almost brushing my face.

"She's back!" he cried.

"Master Grimbald? Why are you here?" I asked. "Is something wrong?"

"You lost a good deal of blood, but it has stopped now. How do you feel?"

How did I feel? I was still only half among the living, but I was fairly certain—yes, I was sure—that I was in pain. I also felt weak, but that was no surprise.

"I … I feel sore all over, and weary beyond weariness."

"You have had a hard labor, but fear not! We will do everything in our power to make you well. In a few days' time, you will be back to your old self. Lady Sybil, help me lift up her head."

I was still lying back on the bed, and though at first I felt as if I had been gone for a week, I gathered from Grimbald's manner that it had only been a few minutes at most. With one of them on either side of the bed, they pulled me up and leaned my head back against the wall, but I began to feel as if I would vomit, so they were forced to lay me down again.

"The empress needs more rest," Sybil declared, chiding the physician. "Leave it with us. This is women's work."

"Wait!" I said rather weakly. "What about the child? What about my son?"

"He is well. He is in good health," Sybil assured me.

"I will go inform the king that he has another male heir," Grimbald said, and with that, he left the room.

"I will just sleep then …" I mumbled, as I fell back into slumber.

The next time I awoke, I was far more aware of my pain. I looked over toward the far window and saw Eleanor asleep in a chair, with Sybil apparently gone. There was only one other girl in the room—a young novice by the look of it—tending to the fire in the hearth off to the left.

"You there," I whispered. "What time is it?"

She turned around to look at me, clearly surprised that I had addressed her.

"Did you mean me, my lady?" she asked quietly.

"Yes, you. What time is it? I cannot tell since they covered the windows."

She set down the poker and stepped closer to me. "I should think it's the third watch now."

"So it is night then. I have missed supper."

"Would you like something to eat, my lady? I would be more than happy to get it for you."

I shook my head. "I just wondered if I might have some wine. This pain is not to be born."

"Is it very bad, my lady? Should I wake the midwife?"

"No, there is no need for that. Just bring me a glass, and maybe a little bread."

A few minutes later, the girl had returned from the kitchen with the items I requested. I had little appetite, but was able to drink the wine without a problem. She set down both the plate of bread and the goblet on the table to my left, which had been cleared of the midwives' tools.

"Thank you, sister," I whispered, not wishing to wake Eleanor, who was still sound asleep in her chair. "What did you say your name was?"

"I didn't say."

"What is it then?"

"Adela, from the abbey of Saint Catherine, up on the hill."

"Thank you, Adela."

She departed and left me lying there, feeling awfully sore in both my belly and my loins. After consuming the few morsels, I slipped back into sleep for no longer than an hour before I woke again. This time, I was covered in sweat from head to toe. The fear was rising in me, for I sensed that something was very wrong.

I turned my head to the right and saw that Eleanor was awake and standing at the side of my bed.

"My lady?" Eleanor said. "My lady, are you warm?"

"I feel like I'm burning," I moaned.

She placed her hand over my brow. "You do feel quite hot."

"That's bad, isn't it?" I said. "It means—infection."

"It is too soon to say that," she told me, but I could sense that she was nervous. "Are you still in pain?"

I closed my eyes and nodded. "Yes. My nether regions—"

"Say no more. I shall fetch the doctor."

"Please don't leave me alone!" I begged, for my fear was beginning to take control.

"You are not alone, Empress Mathilda. I am here!" a voice said.

I turned my head in the opposite direction and saw that it was the same young woman I had spoken with before, carrying a pitcher of water.

"It was Adela, right?" I inquired.

She nodded and smiled. "Yes, my lady."

"Good. Stay with me."

She set the pitcher of water on the table next to the remainder of the bread and wine, then perched on the edge of the bed next to me. Even without looking, I could sense that Eleanor's brow must have been raised to see this young woman being so familiar, but given my state, I suppose she chose to bite her tongue.

"Would you like it if I held your hand?" Adela asked earnestly.

"Actually, yes, I would like that," I said, oddly relieved that someone had asked. "I am ever so afraid."

She continued to sit beside me and pat my hands in silence for a moment. I winced as the pain surged through my body. I thought about asking for the fire to be quenched, but I knew it would not help much if I was burning due to a fever.

In my mind, I imagined a coffin being led into the cathedral of Rouen with four mourners behind it: my father carrying my first son and my husband carrying the second. My body was committed to the ground, and the men walked away with smiles on their faces. I could bear it no longer and attempted to pull my mind back to the present.

"Are they coming?" I asked.

"Very soon," she replied.

It was indeed very soon after that that the door to the room was opened and Grimbald strode in clothed in his dark robes and cap, with Eleanor following close behind him.

"I am sorry to wake you, Master Grimbald," I said.

"No matter," he replied.

Grimbald was not one given to displaying his feelings, but I was beginning to see great concern in his eyes, and this as much as anything caused me to fear. He looked me over, feeling both my pulse and my forehead, and determined that I did have a fever, just as I had feared. He bid the ladies place cold cloths upon my body.

"Is it very dangerous?" Adela asked.

"It might be. It is too early to tell," he concluded, though again I could see that his countenance was grim.

Oh Lord, what is happening? I prayed. *I beg you, think of my boys! I cannot leave them alone! They are innocent. Spare my life for their sakes!*

As the hours wore on, the fever grew worse. My whole body began to shake, and no matter how many coverings they placed on me, I felt as cold as death. My heart pounded with such a force, I might have been running a race. Slowly, my spirit began to despair. I knew what became of new mothers who experienced such things.

"Eleanor," I said weakly.

"I am here," she replied, hovering over me.

"I bid you send for a priest."

"My lady?"

"I said," I continued, gasping for breath, "send for a priest."

"Of course," she consented.

What evil spirit had invaded my body and sent a chill through my very soul? Was this to be the end of me? Such tremors racked me from head to toe! I had not completely given up hope, but I was very near. I needed someone to speak to God for me, for I felt as unworthy as a snail. I needed to confess my sins whether or not it was a sickness unto death, and death seemed more likely by the minute.

I have no idea how long it took Eleanor to return with the archbishop: perhaps an hour, or perhaps a day. Time no longer had any meaning. I was not entirely aware.

"What is it, my daughter?" a man seemed to ask.

"She is ill—very ill," someone replied.

"Let us anoint her with oil," he said. "Empress Mathilda, can you hear me?"

"Yes," I muttered.

"There is no need to talk, child. Do you wish me to administer the holy sacrament?"

I attempted to speak, but a very high buzz seemed to rattle my brain, and for whatever reason it held me silent.

"Best do it, just to be certain," another voice said.

I sensed that Archbishop Hugh was speaking the words over me, but I could no longer remain awake.

"Oh God, my God," I whispered, and then there was nothing.

"Maud! My precious Maud! Awaken!"

"Is that you, mother?" I asked.

"Yes, it is I. Wake up, I say, wake up!"

I opened my eyes to see my mother standing there beside my bed, her hand stroking my wet hair. She looked the same as she had when last I saw her: young and full of life, and far more comely than myself.

"Mother!" I cried, great tears in my eyes. "Mother, I am sick."

"I know, my love," she said, her voice as smooth and pleasant as the flow of a stream. "You have suffered greatly."

"Thank God you are here! I am ever so distraught."

"Peace, child! I will comfort you."

"Where are the others?" I asked, though the reason was not clear to myself.

"What others?"

"Father Anselm, William—where are they?"

"I am here," said Archbishop Anselm. "I am just at your feet."

Sure enough, I saw before me the tutor of my youth, still smiling behind his great white beard.

"Yes, I see you there," I replied. "But where is William?"

"Here, sister!" he called, stepping out from the darkness. He was not as I remembered him in our youth, but a young man tall and strong, as he must have been at the end. "Have no fear! We will stay with you."

"My love," my mother said. "Very soon, a man will come to the door. He will ask you a question that you may fear to answer."

"What question is that?" I asked.

"Where you wish to take your eternal repose," Anselm said.

"Eternal repose? Am I to die then? Is that why I can see you all?"

They did not answer, but looked upon me with downcast faces. I could feel the terror rising within me.

"So I am dying then," I concluded. "I will be with you all within hours."

"You must not fear death!" Anselm declared. "It is the passing into life."

"But what of my sons?!" I cried. "What of young Henry and his brother?"

"There are others who will care for them," my mother said. "They will grow into strong men."

"They will be raised by Angevins," I assured her, my heart filling with anger. "They will know nothing of me or of England."

"Trust in the Lord," William urged me. "He will provide for them. Soon, you will see him face to face."

Tears flooded my eyes as I spoke my last and greatest fear.

"I am not ready to face the Almighty!" I argued. "He will send me to purgatory on account of my sins! I am sure of it!"

"No! He will fetch you to heaven," said Anselm.

"You do not know what I have done. I am plagued by sin! I am not like you all. I am selfish, proud, angry—yes, I am filled with passions!"

"So make your confession," William told me. "Make it in full."

The figures began to darken, and I cried out in deepest despair.

"No! Please, do not leave me! Do not leave me here to die alone!"

My mother and brother disappeared, and all that was left was the dark figure of Archbishop Anselm. I looked upon him intently, my eyes begging him to stay. Then I saw a change in his visage: something most strange. He stepped closer to me and held out his hand, his face set like stone. He spoke with authority. "Maud!"

"Yes!" I answered. "Tell me what I must do!"

He looked deep into my eyes and spoke a single word. "Rise." Then all was darkness.

Suddenly, I felt someone shaking me: it was Adela.

"My lady! My lady!"

"Yes," I murmured, opening my eyes.

"Oh, thank God!" she said. "I was afraid you were gone. You seemed to cry out, and then you stopped breathing."

There was a knock at the door, and she moved to answer it, racing across the floor and swinging it open.

"Abbot Boson!" she called, as he walked into the room. "Thank you for coming."

"Where are the midwives?" he asked, looking in both directions.

"Out tending to the child Geoffrey."

He walked nearer the bed and looked down on me. "Where does she stand?"

"I think she is having delusions."

"That is the final stage," he said quietly. "She may not be long for this world."

"I am awake at this moment," I stated, causing both of them to turn and look in my direction.

The abbot sat on the bed beside me.

"Empress Mathilda," he said, "I have been sent by your great father, King Henry of England, to ask—"

"Where I want to be buried," I whispered.

"Yes, that is correct. How did you know that?"

"My mother—she told me."

"Ah, well, of course, we all trust that you shall recover very soon, but in case you do not, we must discuss the disposition of your estates."

"Must you really burden her with that at a time such as this?" Adela asked, looking over his shoulder.

"No, the abbot is right," I said. "Please, sir, I wish to leave the bulk of my estate to your monastery: the monastery of Bec."

"Truly?" he replied. "We would be most honored if you should—"

"And I want to be buried there," I stated, as firmly as I could in my condition.

He paused for a moment, then said, "My lady, you should know that the king is most intent that you should be buried here in Rouen, in the great cathedral beside your ancestors."

"I don't give a—I do not care about that," I replied, struggling with each word. "Your abbey holds a special place in my heart, for you were the one who caused me to place my hope in a greater purpose. This is my desire. Please, promise me that you will see it done."

"I am sure it will not come to that, my lady," Adela said, taking hold of my hand. "You will rise from this bed within days: I promise you that!"

"I will inform the king of your decision," Abbot Boson concluded. "I am sure he will not deny your dying wish."

Without warning, someone burst through the door. It was the physician Grimbald.

"Let me see her!" he demanded, and the others moved out of the way.

He placed his hand upon my neck to feel the beat of my heart.

"Your breathing is very quick," the doctor said. "We may only have a few hours left."

He then pulled a bottle out of a small purse that he had been carrying. When he removed the top, it smelled worse than sulfur and not unlike a pig's sty. Even in my state, with my sensesall amiss, there was no mistaking how awful it was.

"What is that?" the abbot asked, covering his nose.

"It is an old remedy I found in one of my books," replied Grimbald. "It may be our last chance to stop the infection. My lady, do you think you could swallow this?"

"I don't know," I whispered. There was no food on earth that sounded appealing to me in that moment, and the contents of that phial least of all. But if there was ever a time when the phrase "*extremis malis, extremis remedia*" applied, it was that one.

"What is in it?" Adela asked, a look of dismay upon her face.

"Garlic, onion, wine, leek, and one other thing I do not care to mention."

"If you are to put that in her body, you should at least tell her what it is!" the abbot demanded.

"Very well—the dung of a cow."

"And you actually think that will work?" he objected.

"Good abbot, I pray you perform your task and I will do mine!" Grimbald cried. He lifted the phial to my lips. "Drink it! This is the best chance we have."

Who was I to argue when I was upon death's door? Of course, I could hardly have put up a good argument in my state. With some difficulty, I was able to swallow it. It was so utterly vile, that were I not to be killed by the infection, I was sure that the medicine would have the same result. I leaned back my head and sighed. The buzzing in my ears was increasing again and the room was growing dark.

"What now?" Adela asked.

"We wait," Grimbald replied. "We wait and we pray."

CHAPTER NINETEEN

"*Per istam sanctan unctionem et suam piissimam misericordiam, indulgeat tibi Dominus quidquid per visum, audtiotum, odorátum, gustum et locutiónem, tactum, gressum deliquisti.*"

Those were the words I hoped never to hear: the words that come just before death. Yet the archbishop was speaking them over me, praying that I might be accepted into heaven.

"Do you repent of all your sins?" he asked, bending over me.

"I do, most truly," I murmured.

"Do you make contrition for the same?"

"Yes."

"Then speak the words: *Mea culpa, mea culpa, mea maxima culpa* ..."

"*Mea culpa, mea culpa, mea maxima culpa.*"

He again made the sign of the cross upon my forehead with holy oil.

"*Ad deum, soror mea,*" he whispered.

Archbishop Hugh then stepped aside and I was joined by both Eleanor and Sybil.

"How is my boy?" I asked. "How is Geoffrey?"

"He is well, my lady," Sybil replied. "He was christened yesterday."

"I wish to see him before I die," I pleaded. "Please. Send for him."

The two women looked at each other with concern, then Eleanor spoke. "Forgive me, my lady, but that might place him in danger to be so near disease."

I sighed. "Yes, of course, you are right. It's just—I never saw him properly."

"But you will!" Adela said, stepping in front of the midwives. "You will live to be a mother to your sons. You will rise from this bed! Do not give up hope!"

"Sister Adela, that is quite enough!" Sybil ordered.

"We must wait to see if the medicine will work," the younger woman argued. "It is too soon to tell. Besides, her fever seems to be dropping. Perhaps it is the medicine!"

"We ought not set store by some pagan witchcraft," Eleanor chided. "I hear Grimbald receives his knowledge from the Moors, those enemies of Christ!"

"No, it is from the English! He told me as much," Adela said.

The young woman rushed to my side and again took my hand within her own.

"You must not lose faith, my lady," she entreated. "The Lord walks even in the valley of the shadow of death."

"Enough!" Eleanor cried. "Sister Adela, kindly remove yourself from this room at once!"

"Do not send her away," I commanded. "She is to stay with me. If you have nothing further to add, then it is you two who should leave."

That took them very much by surprise. Though they left the chamber without another word, I could sense their minds furiously at work, devising some slander they might have hoped to throw at me.

"You are a good girl, Adela," I said. "Sit here. I must sleep."

I did sleep for quite some time before I was visited again by Grimbald. He felt my pulse, examined my breathing, placed his hand upon my brow, and looked over my extremities. A smile appeared on his face.

"Empress Mathilda, I am pleased to report that your fever seems to have improved and your breathing is more regular. Have you experienced any more delusions?"

"No, sir," I said. "I do feel a bit better. I can see everything clearly and speak freely, though I am still exceedingly weary and have no appetite at all."

"Is it the medicine?" Adela asked. "Is it working?"

"Quite possibly," the physician answered. "I will administer it again this evening—with your permission, my lady."

"Foul as it is, if it can make me well, I shall drink a barrel of it," I replied.

"Excellent. I will have the apothecary make another batch."

"Can we please open a window?" I asked, as he rose from the bed. "I have such a need of fresh air and sunlight."

"Certainly," he replied.

He threw back the curtain on the window at the far end of the room, and sunlight poured into the room. It was glorious, although my eyes had been in the dark for so long that I was forced to close them in view of that brilliance. As they slowly adjusted, I looked out and saw that the sky was blue and birds were flying hither and thither. The world was still alive, and so it seemed was I.

From that point on, I seemed to improve with each new day. I was able to sit up and take food, and on Midsummer Day, I walked out of that place under my own power into the waiting arms of my young son, Henry, who was waiting for me in the passage.

"*Mama!*" he cried, a broad smile upon his little face.

"Oh, my son! My son!" I said, through tears of joy, kneeling down and pulling him into my arms, running my fingers through his red curls and kissing him.

My trusted Lady Agnes was standing there with the babe in her arms, and when I had finished embracing my eldest, she handed over my youngest son. I stood there as he murmured softly in my arms. Unlike his brother, he had brown hair very like my own. He looked up at me as if to say, *Where have you been, mother, and what was all that strange business about?*

"We meet at last, Geoffrey," I whispered close to him. "I did not know if this day would ever come, but I am glad of it. I fought my way back to life, and I will never stop fighting for you both and for England."

"Are you pleased that they named him after his father?" Agnes asked.

"Why, of course!" I replied, not breaking my gaze. "It is a most proper name, for like his father, he almost made an end of me. But do not think that I shall hold a grudge, Geoffrey. You too are my beloved son, even if you did try to kill me."

I remained in Rouen for some time along with my sons. King Henry was eager to enjoy their company, and he was filled with pride to think that our line would be ensured twice over. It ought to have been the happiest time of my life, but ever since I had come back from the brink, a cloud had hung over my mind, and I could not escape it. While my body was restored, my spirit seemed to be still upon that death bed. I took little joy in the moments I shared with my boys. Indeed, I took little joy in anything.

Have you ever sat to read a book, and found you could not do so without great effort? Have you ever awoken in the morning to the fierce beating of your heart? Have you ever felt numb to the touch of water, the heat of the midday sun, or the cries of a child? Have you ever found yourself in such a plague of darkness, that you despaired of ever seeing the light again?

Such was my state at that time, and I could not seem to free myself from it. Grimbald advised me to take more exercise, yet this did little to calm me. He recommended a change in diet, but all to no avail. Even Drogo's jesting failed to break me out of the stupor. In truth, I was loath to admit the full extent of my torment, for it seemed to me utterly shameful.

"Your body has suffered a terrible blow," he would say. "It may take some time to recover."

Oh, happy Grimbald! He could not know what I felt. My suffering was as much a mystery to him as it was to myself. For any pain of the body, he might have devised some remedy, but he was no match for the torments of the soul.

I had experienced despair, apathy, and fear throughout my life in equal measures, yet there always seemed to be a direct cause for these things. The difference that year was that there was no clear reason for my malaise. I finally had two sons, my father was pleased with me for once, and I was not forced to spend time with my husband. It made no sense to me. All I knew was that the darkness I had felt in those moments when I was near death had continued to hang over me even though I was in perfect health.

One afternoon, Lady Agnes and I took the boys out to the rose garden to play on the grass. In truth, Henry was still a rather poor walker, and Geoffrey merely rested in my arms, but that sufficed for their age. The sun was beating down, but there was a nice wind, and the flow of the River Seine was a vision as always. Sadly, none of this had a positive effect on me. I felt thoroughly empty inside, as if I might break into tears at the slightest provocation.

"Are you well, my lady?" Agnes asked.

I turned to look at her, for up to that point I had been staring into space. "Quite well, I thank you."

"You do not seem very well. It appears that you are lost in thoughts that are not altogether pleasant."

"Forgive me. I did not mean to rain on our sunny day. There are just many things for me to consider, given my position."

This was an answer meant to distract from the true reason for my melancholy, and the maid sensed it.

"My lady, I know I am a good bit older than you, and that I do not care for the things that interest you—books and the like. You have never warmed to me." Here I attempted to object, but she raised her free hand while holding young Henry with the other. "Please, Your Highness, I am not offended. Not every two people feel a natural affinity. I would say that is what ails you: a lack of true friends who can comfort you."

"Oh, but I do have friends!" I argued. "I have my brother, Robert, and Abbot Boson, and the physician Grimbald, and of course my knight, Drogo—"

"Yes, but they are all men," she interrupted, "and what's more, men who are often gone. None but Drogo will return with you to Anjou."

"It is not my fault that most of my friends are male," I said, feeling suddenly defensive. "The nature of who I am requires me to converse with men, and perhaps I have more in common with them. My brother once said something to that effect—that I was like a man in certain ways. I was not sure how to take it at the time—indeed, I am not sure how to take it now, but perhaps there is something in it."

Geoffrey began to wrench in my arms, breaking out of his cloths. I set him down and rubbed his chest, whispering as I did so. "Do not fear, Geoffrey. *Mama* is here. Be calm. Be at peace." I then wrapped him again, pulling each fold over him in turn.

"My lady," Agnes began, "I am not implying that there is anything wrong with you, and by no means do I think you are too much like a man. You are just a special kind of woman. Do not despair of finding female friends. I am sure there is someone who can be a good companion for you—perhaps someone closer in age to yourself and not old and gray like me."

Even as she said this, I thought of those long hours I had spent sick in bed, and how the novice Adela had been such a good friend to me at that time, never hesitating to encourage and support me in my darkest hour.

"Have you had a thought?" Agnes asked, a smile breaking on her face. "It looks as if the wheels of your mind are turning."

"Maybe, maybe not," I replied, lifting the babe back into my arms. "I am still not sure that a new friend will solve all my problems either."

"Oh, good Lord, no!" she said with a laugh. "Friends don't solve our problems. They merely help us to bear them, for some burdens are too great for one."

I was indebted to Lady Agnes for her words, which made a great deal of sense. The next day, I decided to do something about it. I called Adela over from her home at the abbey of Saint Catherine so that we might speak with one another. She was quite surprised to receive such a summons, and made a great show of bowing and displaying true reverence when she entered the great hall of the castle, where I sat near the hearth stitching a pattern. As soon as I saw her, I set down the cloth, needle, and thread and bid the servants depart.

How exactly did one make a friend? Most of the friends I had ever enjoyed were persons who happened to be around me rather than ones I had sought out on purpose. I did not think it was something that could be forced. I waited for the door to close before I began speaking, and dearly hoped that it would not be too awkward.

"Sister Adela, I am glad to see you again," I said.

"And I you, my lady, though I cannot account for this honor."

It was a bit strange to see her in the full light. I could see that she was a lovely young woman, probably less than twenty years of age, with golden hair that just peaked out from beneath her white veil.

"I have a few questions for you," I said. "Tell me: how long until you take your vows before God?"

"Not long now, my lady—before the end of this year," she replied, bowing her head slightly and smiling.

"And how came you to the monastery of Saint Catherine? Are you from a noble family?"

"No, my lady. My family was poor, and I had little hope of marrying well."

"And the nuns took you in?"

"Yes, my lady."

I could see that it would be necessary to make her feel more at ease. After all, friends are meant to be equals to a certain degree.

"You need not always say 'my lady,'" I offered. "It becomes tedious after a while."

"Forgive me, my—that is, forgive me, Empress Mathilda."

I motioned toward the seat opposite me. "What is your commission at the abbey?"

"I care for the infirm," she replied, sitting down. "Sister Agatha is given oversight, and I help her."

"And that is why Grimbald brought you over for the birth?"

"Yes, Your Highness."

Her hands were folded tightly in her lap, and her head nodded with each response to show her respect. She seemed very much like the kind of nice girl who would feel it was her duty to continue serving God at the monastery, so if we were to be friends, I would need to present her with something even more appealing.

"Do you read, Adela?" I inquired.

"Not a word," she replied, her eyes sad.

"What a pity they did not teach you!"

"I suppose they thought I had no need of it."

Not for the first time, I questioned why any woman, or any living person for that matter, should have no need of reading, but I kept the thought to myself.

"Would you like to learn?" I asked.

"Yes, I should, but it is not likely at my age."

"We can teach you here, or at my court in Anjou."

"You honor me, my lady, but surely I cannot leave the cloister."

Here was the answer I had feared, and I would have to counter it if I was serious about gaining a friend.

"Adela, there are two types of people in any abbey: those who are there because they have answered the divine call, and those who are there of necessity. I gather that you are the second type. Is that correct?"

Her eyes grew wider and she tilted her head. "Are you saying that I should leave the sisters?"

"Not if that life is your desire, but if the will of the Lord is somewhat more ... open when it comes to you, I think you could be of real value to me as one of my ladies."

"I am honored that you should think so," she said, smiling and bowing her head yet again, "but I am afraid I have few of the skills that are needed for such a position."

I had foreseen this reply and had an answer ready. "On the contrary, I have already witnessed traits in you that could be quite helpful: discretion, courage, a quick wit, cheerfulness."

"But my lady, I have no knowledge of royal life. Surely your friends would laugh to think you had taken on such a maid!"

I could see that a change of approach was needed.

"Do you question my judgment?" I asked, rather firmly.

"No, but—"

"For that is the problem, you see. It matters little what my friends think, because I am short on friends. I have been passing through a great darkness with hardly anyone beside me for comfort, especially given how busy my knight, Drogo, has been. What I need, Adela, is a helper and a friend. I already have women who understand wine, fine dress, and the art of court gossip. But in all my years, I have never had a lady with whom I felt a connection as I felt with you when you took hold of my hand and willed me back to health—that is, apart from my mother. I am not sure why I have struggled so to find female friends. Perhaps it is because of the nature of my position, or perhaps I have not tried hard enough. Either way, I am loath to pass up an opportunity when it presents itself. I will not tell you to forsake the calling of the Lord, but perhaps he brought you to the monastery that you might be brought to my side. So what say you, Adela?"

She did not reply instantly, but turned her head to the right and stared at the fire burning in the hearth. She then closed her eyes and I thought she might be praying. I was not accustomed to waiting so long for a response, but this was a matter concerning devotion to God, so I allowed her more time. Of course, I hoped very much that God would lead her to the answer I desired. Finally, she opened her eyes and looked back at me.

"Empress Mathilda, I could no sooner deny such an offer of love than I could deny my own name!" she proclaimed. "I may never see myself as a fit companion for Your Highness, but if this be your will, then who am I to refuse? God knows, I have not been content among the sisters. I have longed at times for another life, but I did not think to receive such a blessing at my door. I accept your offer with much gladness, and hope to confirm your faith in me."

I smiled and clapped my hands. "Then I shall speak with your abbess and arrange it all. We can have you here within the week. You have made me happy, Adela, truly!"

Thus began one of the greatest friendships of my life, and one that would not disappoint.

As much as I might have preferred to remain in Normandy, the arrival of autumn forced me to return to the land of the Angevins before the weather became too ill for travel. Count Geoffrey was eager to meet his new son, and it hardly seemed right for a wife to be so long absent from her husband—at least, it hardly seemed right to those around me. Therefore, we perforce made ready to depart by Michaelmas. Although I was not eager to forsake Normandy, where for once I was being treated well, for the company of my husband, I received some good cheer from the knowledge that Adela would be going with me. It would be nice to have someone in addition to Drogo who was, if you will, my person and not my husband's.

The day before I was to leave, I made one final visit to the abbey of Saint Ouen to pray, accompanied by the king. I hated being alone with him, but I had little choice on this occasion. They set aside the chapel of Saint Peter for our private devotion, a small room just off the main nave with a lovely blue ceiling and a golden statue of the apostle perched in a niche behind the prayer rail. We knelt side by side with our folded hands perched on the stone ledge. I was reciting the blessed hours to myself when I was interrupted by my father.

"There is something that we need to discuss."

"Must it be now, my lord?" I asked, turning my head to face him. "Could we not leave it until we have returned?"

"There must be no one else present, for it is a delicate matter," he argued in a low voice.

Why he could not have arranged for such a discussion at the palace was a mystery to me, but I sensed there was no point arguing. With some frustration, I shut the book and granted him my attention.

"What is it?"

"I have received a message from Count Geoffrey—your husband," he said, as if I might have forgotten to whom I was wed.

"What of it?"

"He wishes me to turn over the fortresses in the south of Normandy to his control."

Somewhat to my surprise, I failed to see the problem with my husband's request. "Well, you did pledge to do so, and now that we have two heirs born, it seems right and proper to confirm their inheritance. If Henry and I are to carry on your legacy, we will need the right instruments for the job."

"That is not the point. Your husband," he said, as if to blame me by connection, "seeks to make himself duke of Normandy in all but name within my own lifetime. He sees no need to submit to me, though I am his liege lord."

Perhaps it was because he seemed to accuse me that I found it difficult to accept what my father was saying. After all, he had made me his heir, and Count Geoffrey was only asking for what would make it possible for me to control my inheritance after the king's death. And again, my father had promised to turn over the castles.

"Forgive me, my lord, but I do not think it can be true that Count Geoffrey is seriously attempting to take over Normandy, for he does not possess the strength or arms for that," I said, keeping my tone as calm as possible. "He simply seeks some proof that the inheritance will pass to our line. The lords of England and Normandy must be left with no doubt as to who will rule when you are gone."

"So you would defend him then?" the king responded, his voice growing louder.

I could see that the conversation was becoming rather dangerous and attempted to proceed with caution. "I do not defend his methods, but I think his argument is correct."

"I have gone to great lengths to ensure the succession!" he cried, striking the rail with his hand. "Have I not made all the lords swear to you, not once, but twice?"

"Yes, my king, but as you said, this is a delicate matter. You must give Count Geoffrey something real, or he will only slide into discontent. What harm does it do to let him control a few castles?"

"It makes it appear that I am not in control of my own duchy!" he said, his face beginning to turn red. "He is the vassal here, not I."

"I understand, but he may accuse you of breaching the marriage agreement," I warned, my frustration increasing. "This is a matter of great import to Anjou."

Even as I was speaking these words, it seemed very odd indeed that I was defending the Angevins. However, I had two Angevin sons and felt a need to defend their interests.

"I beg you not to make such accusations! I am a man of my word!" he cried. "I cannot believe that you who hated him from the beginning are now taking his side against your own father."

"Yes, but it is not just about Count Geoffrey, is it? It concerns my sons. I must do everything in my power to promote their cause."

"Not if it means violating the command of your king!"

I had come to that point I always seemed to reach in these discussions with my father. I had stated the desire for which I intended to fight, and he had balked at it. Were I to press on, he would no doubt fall back upon the same old threats: he would disinherit me, he would make me pay, and so on and so forth. It was not possible to win an argument with a man who could never admit that he was in the wrong. My only hope was either to wait for circumstances to change or to hope that Count Geoffrey could force sense upon him. Pressing him to the point of extreme anger would only place me in danger. If I had to provoke him, it was best to do so from the safety of Anjou.

"I can see that we shall have no agreement on this," I said, standing up, "and it hardly seems fitting to continue such a discussion in a house of God. I think we ought to leave."

"You cannot run from me!" he yelled.

Nevertheless, I did not run but walked away from him, returning on my own to the palace. Although my father did see us off the next day, I believe it was only on account of the two boys. To me, he said hardly a word. The brief period of respect I had enjoyed was over. I had no desire to part on bad terms, but how could I surrender such a point? For once, I agreed entirely with my husband. The castles had been promised, and they must be granted. Little did I know how vital this issue would become or what calamity it would release upon all our destinies.

The journey back to Anjou was rather more difficult with two little boys, so I was quite thankful to have Adela's help in keeping them as happy and quiet as possible. On occasion, my sons would both fall asleep at the same time and Adela and I were able to rest a bit ourselves, but these moments never seemed to last long. Still, I was grateful, for I had seldom enjoyed so much time with either son in my presence. It was lovely to hold Henry in my lap and point out interesting sights through the window of the carriage. In truth, he could not have understood much of what I was teaching him, but as his mother, I was certain he was the cleverest little boy who ever lived.

Count Geoffrey rode to Le Mans to meet us, and when we were safely within the castle yard, he ran up to the carriage where both Henry and Geoffrey were still deep in slumber.

"Where are they?" I could hear him call. "Where are my boys?"

The curtains were drawn on either side of the carriage to help the boys sleep. Henry was lying next to me with his head in my lap, while Geoffrey was sound asleep in a basket on the seat across from me, which was held in place by Adela.

"Henry," I said, patting him gently. "We are home. Adela, can you wake Geoffrey?"

Henry was not yet speaking much, for he was only a year and a half old, but his face told the tale. He looked at me with eyes still half shut, very much in the land of slumber.

"We are going to see your *papa* now," I told him. "Do you remember your *papa*? You were quite young when we left."

He looked at me with a rather blank expression, rubbing his eyes. Poor thing, the long journey had made his little body quite weary.

"Here, just you come to *mama*," I said, taking him in my arms.

I looked over to Adela, who had roused a very cross Geoffrey. His little cries filled the carriage.

"Everything is fine, Geoffrey. Your father is waiting for you," Adela told him, but it was no use. The cries continued apace.

I heard the call of my husband outside. "I hope you do not intend to make me wait for ever to see my sons!"

Suddenly, little Henry pointed toward the curtain and said, "Mean!"

"What did he say?" Adela asked, desperately patting her charge on the back.

"He thinks his *papa* is mean," I said, trying hard not to smile. "Your *papa* loves you very much, Henry," I assured him. "Let us go see him!"

The four of us finally stepped out of the carriage, and Count Geoffrey cried with delight.

"Henry! Come to me!" he called, bending down and throwing his arms open.

I set my firstborn on the ground and he tottered more than walked to his father, who swept him up in an embrace.

"How big you have grown!" Count Geoffrey declared. "Do you know who I am?"

For just a moment, I was afraid that he might answer "mean," but fortunately young Henry answered, "*Papa.*"

"Hand me the baby, Adela," I instructed, and she placed him in my arms. I waited until my husband had released our first son, then approached. "Here is your other self, my lord: the new Geoffrey of Anjou."

"And how very like myself are his looks," he replied, taking hold of the child.

He looked down on little Geoffrey with far more affection than he had ever granted me, but I was not jealous, for I wanted my boys to have a more positive bond with their father than I had with mine, even if he was not one of the better men in the world.

"What a happy day this is for Anjou that two such princely lads now rest within the bosom of our love!" my husband proclaimed. It was only after he had marveled at the babe for some time that he noticed the other person standing there. "Who is this?" he asked, nodding his head to indicate Adela. "And where are Lady Agnes and Joscelyn?"

"This is Adela, my new lady," I explained. "I found her in Rouen. The other ladies are with us, but they stopped in town to collect some things for the boys."

"Of what family are you, Adela?" Count Geoffrey asked, looking at her, turning up his nose slightly.

"No family of note, my lord," she replied with a bow. "I was lately with the nuns of Saint Catherine, but left before taking my vows."

"Do you mean to say you stole her from an abbey?" the count said to me with a laugh, raising his brows.

"I did not steal her!" I declared. "She came of her own free will, and with the permission of her superior."

He shook his head, still laughing. "It seems an odd way to acquire a royal servant."

"She helped to save my life, and that of your son," I noted, pointing to the babe in his arms.

This seemed to change his mood. The look on his face became more serious and respectful.

"Then I suppose we must welcome her with open arms," he admitted. "Well met, Adela, and welcome to our county!" He tipped his head.

"Thank you, sir," she replied.

"Come, let us feast!" Count Geoffrey proclaimed.

We all turned and began walking toward the entrance of the great hall, Adela holding Henry and big Geoffrey still carrying little Geoffrey.

"Has your father consented to grant us the castles?" my husband whispered to me.

"I attempted to reason with him, but he would not see sense. He continues to refuse them," I said quietly, being careful not to make any show of anger that could be guessed by those around us.

"What?!" Count Geoffrey cried, stopping in his tracks. "What on God's earth does he think he's playing at?! Those are mine by right of marriage! They are to go to our sons!"

So much for keeping this conversation secret, I thought. I looked around and saw that not only those walking near us, but even the guards on the bulwarks were paying attention.

I took a step nearer my husband. "My lord, please lower your voice. We do not want all the servants knowing our business."

"Everyone should know of this treachery!" he argued. "You and the rest of the Normans have done nothing but scorn Anjou since this marriage started."

"Me!" I cried. "I defended you to the king, and believe you me, that was not an easy thing to do when I was feeling his wrath!"

"I do not mean that," he said. "I mean when you abandoned me."

"Oh, so we are bringing up ancient history today?" I scoffed. "I came back to Anjou. I came back and I am committed. I have borne you two sons now. What more must I do to convince you of my resolve?"

He looked at me for a moment, the breath flowing strongly in and out of his nostrils. I thought he might devise some new affront against me, but he did not.

"Very well," he said. "I am—" Here he seemed to bite his tongue, as if struggling with the words.

"Do you mean you are—sorry?" I asked, truly astounded.

"Let us go inside," he concluded, moving on quickly toward the door.

I stood there for a moment smiling and laughing softly. *Not much of an apology, but I'll call it a victory!*

CHAPTER TWENTY

Ah, what anger was awoken in my husband when I informed him of the king's words! The joy he felt in his new son was quickly turned to bitterness. Before the day was done, he sent a new letter to King Henry, demanding that he surrender all the castles along the frontier, from Pontorson in the West to Conches in the East. I need hardly tell you the response he received, but perhaps I will relay some of my father's choicest words.

> *Geoffrey, who ought to have been a true son to us, but I find you now as the prodigal son of scripture, coveting your father's fortune while still he lives and breathes. Shall I then consent to this base demand and bend the knee to him who is by right my sworn vassal? The Lord himself would not have advised such a course.*

What our Lord Jesus might have advised, God only knows, but this reply only served to harden Count Geoffrey's resolve.

For myself, I was bound to side with him, for we needed those castles to ensure the inheritance of my sons. If and when my father passed from this earth, it would be difficult to control Normandy if the castles were held against us, and even more difficult to press on to England. Why my father could not see this was a mystery to me.

There were great stirrings throughout the land and rumors spread abroad. Men looked upon my ascension as the ancient Israelites did the coming of Jezebel. I knew full well how I looked in comparison to others: Count Theobald of Blois, Count Stephen of Boulogne, and even brother Robert. Any one of those men seemed more fit for the royal office, or so the masses said. I knew the danger, and my husband saw it as well.

"We must press to have the nobles swear to you again, now that you have two children," he said to me at one point, "or better yet, let them swear also to young Henry."

"You know not the mind of the king," I replied. "The years have taught me that I never had his love, I who was from the beginning despised, loathsome, not fit for great affairs of men—I who was in my mother's womb deformed, born not of the noble breed of Adam, but with the sinful taint of Eve! Were he to be given the keys of the kingdom of heaven, even as Saint Peter, King Henry would spring Prince William from his eternal sleep and send me off to my reward!"

"Even so, it is all the more vital that he should make them swear to you again, that no man may claim that he did so without knowledge or under threat of force," Geoffrey concluded.

Although I did not particularly care for the man, Count Geoffrey did hit upon the truth occasionally. His argument won the day, and I wrote to King Henry and made the request, which was promptly denied. The matter then rested for the remainder of the year, and I was able to devote my time to watching my sons grow and learn. Oh, how I adored them! Even though I was a royal lady, I wanted to spend time with them whenever possible. They were my pride and joy. I could see already the types of people they were becoming: Henry brave and active, Geoffrey more cautious and meek, but both equally beloved.

Around this time, we received word that my only living uncle, Robert the former duke of Normandy, had at last died in Cardiff Castle. For twenty-five years he had languished in prison, forced to endure the scorn of men and the death of his son, William Clito. Not that I pitied him, for treason must have its just reward. In truth, it removed one more person to whom men might flock upon my father's death, and thus I had no cause to rue it. Although my sons ought not have suffered any challenge to their right by blood, evil and rebellious men will find any false standard to follow.

The New Year brought with it a return to our controversy, with King Henry swearing that while he lived and breathed, Count Geoffrey would never be lord over a Norman castle. But the king made an error of sorts when he denied the inheritance of the sometime rebel William Talvas, count of Ponthieu, one of the most powerful lords in southern Normandy. The count banded with Robert Stafford, castellan of Conches, and together they rose against the king's authority.

I remember the day we received the news. Our little family was sitting by the fire in the hall, which had been otherwise deserted to give us privacy. I was helping the boys—who must have been ages two and one—build something with their blocks. Actually, I was helping Henry build, and Geoffrey was knocking all our creations down on the wood floor. Count Geoffrey was seated on a bench by one of the long tables, reading over his letters and paying little attention to our endeavors. Suddenly, he rose from his seat, filled with a new vigor.

"Now we have caught the king and can force his hand!" Count Geoffrey declared. "These men—William Talvas and

Robert Stafford—control the very lands we hope to gain. Let us ride to their aid!"

While I understood why he should desire to ride out and claim the castles, I was filled with fear at my husband's declaration. The Norman rulers had a habit of going to war against their kind—that much was true. However, I feared King Henry far more than Count Geoffrey did, whether because I had felt his wrath personally, I was older and wiser, or I had a lesser opinion of my husband's skill in battle. Indeed, Count Geoffrey had never undergone a real test of arms: not against someone like the king. He was only about twenty-one years of age! Would he gain King Henry's respect by riding out against him, or would he merely be goading the dragon? What if he did something so rash that it caused the king to forsake my sons?

"Have a care, husband," I cautioned, rising to address him. "It is a fearful thing to take up arms against the king. If you wish to have one of my cousins on the throne, by all means proceed."

"You do not think I can do this?" he asked, anger in his voice. "Do you think me so weak?"

I shook my head. "No, I think the king is strong—strong and prone to great cruelty and wrath. My father may be old and less powerful on a horse than he used to be, but my brother Robert is as good as any commander on earth. He loves me, but he also loves our father, and he will fight for him. Trust me, husband: you do not want to face Earl Robert of Gloucester in battle. And if you are thinking of appealing to France, you can forget that too. Just remember when William Clito tried that in Flanders!"

My husband still had a glare on his face, but he let out a great sigh, and I sensed that his spirit had given way. "Let us do it from afar then," he said. "We shall lend them our support without lending them our presence. We will send aid to the count of Ponthieu, but I will not ride out."

He collected his papers and made to leave, but turned suddenly to utter one last comment, which seemed rather like a threat. "I hope you are right, Lady England, for the sake of our sons."

What was I to do? It pained me to think that in the space of less than a year we had descended into such rancor that it cast doubt upon my inheritance. It was the king who began it by denying me what was my due, yet were I to reach out and seize it, an even greater inheritance would be denied. I consented to Count Geoffrey's design, but forbid him to set foot in Normandy. King Henry then rode south and crushed the rebellion with all swiftness, even as I had foreseen. We were accused of treachery, and for what?

Lord, preserve the life of the king for long enough that I might recover his regard! I prayed. *Let the inheritance pass to me and my sons!*

Many years earlier, on the second day of August in the year of our Lord 1100, a hunting party had set out into the wood that men call the New Forest, though in truth it is no more new than the earth on which we stand. At the head of the company was King William II of England, and with him was his brother Henry, my own father. The king went out that day to hunt, but little did he know that he would be fortune's prey. An arrow pierced his chest and the life ebbed from him even as his blood. Some said it was murder—others an act of God, for the king's pleasures were not as they ought to have been. My father rode with all haste to Winchester and laid claim to the royal treasury, ere some lesser men might take advantage of the king's death for their own devices. He then proceeded to Westminster, where he was crowned king of England.

William II was not the only one of my uncles to meet his end in the New Forest. Some thirty years earlier, Prince Richard, son of the Conqueror, had suffered an accident of equal severity, but as he was not king at the time, the story did not pass into legend. My brother Robert's bastard son also perished in that very same wood. It is no wonder that men counted it accursed!

Yet even a devil's spell would not have kept King Henry from the hunt. He simply sought out a happier forest. In Normandy, my father's best hunting ground was near Lyons-la-Forêt and the castle of Saint Denis. It was there that his thoughts turned once he had put down our ally the count of Ponthieu, and in the waning days of autumn 1135, he pursued the beasts of Normandy to his heart's content.

Meanwhile, those of us in Anjou were filled with concern over the count's defeat, and none more so than I. We had lent support to rebels against King Henry's authority, but they had been crushed easily. We therefore gained nothing but my father's anger. While the king was off stalking, I was left to wonder what the future held for myself and my dear sons. So far, the king had not seen fit to revoke my inheritance, nor to cast doubt upon the succession, but I could well imagine how some noble might whisper in his ear and cause him to forsake that allegiance of blood that is more sacred than any on this earth.

As the season of Advent began, I sought out something to distract myself, and I found it in my sons. Little Henry was growing apace, his mess of red curls duly increasing, and every day he learned a new word. He no longer toddled but ran, and his frame was more lean and less like an infant. Meanwhile, Geoffrey was beginning to walk on his own, but he could not yet form words. He was particularly taken with Adela and could often be seen tugging on her skirt, wanting to be held.

One evening, I asked Lady Agnes to bring the boys to me in my bed chamber before they were sent to bed. They were already in their night shirts when she presented them. Geoffrey's was far too large: the maids had given up sewing him a new one every other month and made something to suit him for a year. The result was that it trailed on the floor even as the arms absorbed his hands, and I was tempted to laugh at the sight.

"Young Geoffrey, young Henry," I said, kneeling down and kissing them each in turn. "Were you good today?"

"Yes, *mama*," Henry replied, but his brother was mute.

I looked into the eyes of my younger son. Even as the lids drooped farther down, he made a valiant effort to open them further.

"Geoffrey, I know there is some great discourse forming itself in your mind, waiting to be released," I mused.

The boy babbled something, which I took to be a sign of agreement.

"We shall be counting the days before you are able to speak it. Now, off to bed with you!" I concluded, embracing them both.

"*Mama*," Henry asked, "where is King Henry?"

"Why, he is in Normandy, watching over his kingdom," I replied, taking his two little hands in mine. "Do not think that he has forgotten you! He loves you most in all the world."

In truth, I was somewhat surprised that the boy even remembered the king, for he was less than two years old when last they met. Yet for all the sadness in those little eyes, they might have been the best of friends. *Perhaps he has simply heard us speaking about him a lot*, I thought.

"I will write to the king and ask him if we can visit," I told him. "Would you like that?"

"Yes," he answered with a smile.

"Very well. Follow your brother to bed, and make sure to say your prayers."

I embraced him again, and the three of them departed. I walked over to my desk of cherry wood next to the far window. It had been a gift to me from my husband after the birth of our second son. As I sat upon the soft cushion in my chair, I observed that while Count Geoffrey had many flaws and no great love for myself, he at least had an eye for fine things and knew how to reward those who did him a good turn.

I straightened the stack of parchment in front of me and dipped my quill in the ink. It was made from the feather of some strange African bird that my husband had acquired, the very sort of thing he enjoyed wearing. I could not help but shake my head and laugh softly. I then considered how I might make my request of the king for my sons to visit him, which in effect was a request for a truce of sorts. It must be written in my own hand: that much was certain. I would appeal to his love for my boys, and in so doing, hope for reconciliation. I had only just begun to set ink to parchment when there was a knock at the door.

"Come in if you wish me well!" I called over my shoulder.

Count Geoffrey swung the door open and entered the room with great purpose, striding toward me and brandishing a paper in his hand.

"What is that?" I asked.

"A message from the archbishop of Rouen. King Henry has been taken ill at Lyons."

I felt a twinge in my stomach. "How ill? Is it serious?"

"All the lords have gathered around him," he said, still evidently catching his breath from running up the stairs. He then bent down slightly, placing one hand on the desk, and spoke earnestly, "They say he is likely to die."

"What?!" I cried, pushing back the chair and standing up, my heart suddenly beating fiercely.

"My wife, do not make yourself uneasy," he urged, raising his hand.

What an odd thing to say at such a time! I had just received a piece of news that might change my life and affect the destinies of us all, most especially our sons.

"I think we have good reason to be uneasy!" I cried. "The last time I saw the king, we parted badly. This past year ..."

My words trailed off, for already my mind was calculating the cost of our support for the rebels. What might the king decide in his final hours? Had he lost faith in me? So many thoughts were passing through my mind, it was a wonder steam did not flow from my ears!

"What must I do?!" I finally asked, uncertain which of a hundred paths my thoughts should take.

"You could travel to Rouen to be by his side, but you would not get there in time if he is truly dying. It is better that we should move to take hold of Normandy from the south." He then began pacing around the room, or rather stomping. In anger, he kicked the frame of my bed and cried, "Oh, would that your father had granted us those castles before now! We are forced to begin with nothing!"

I saw that it was my turn to attempt to calm him. "Not nothing. We have the oaths of the lords made twice over."

"And you believe they will keep their word?" he asked, the look on his face almost desperate.

I certainly could not prove to him that they would remain true, so I offered the only comfort I could. "We must hope that they will, for what have we in this life but hope?"

"I will tell my men to make themselves ready. We ride at my command!" he concluded, then stormed out of the room, shutting the door behind him.

I remained standing in the same position, my breath coming quickly, considering what had just happened. For years, I had dreamed of my father's death. A few times I might have even wished for it. One cannot help thinking of such things when it comes to a king, for the future must be won before his death creates it. I was not sure if I should feel happy or sad, but one cannot always go by what should be when it comes to feelings.

I felt a sense of grief that my last parent might be dying, and an even greater sense of grief that he was hardly a father to me. I felt happy that I might have a chance to wield authority for once in my life, but afraid that I would not be up to the task. More than anything, I felt a pressure to do the right thing and make the right choices for myself and my sons, but I feared that circumstances might spin out of my control.

I also had a secret: one I had not yet revealed even to Count Geoffrey or Adela. I placed my hand on my belly, in which I suspected that another child was growing. I could not be completely certain, but I had gone without passing blood again, and this had been the first sign with my sons. The feeling of possibly being connected to a child by flesh once again only increased my desire to fight for all the heirs to the throne: all the ones who could bring order and stability to England and Normandy. I had never coveted that throne for myself apart from wanting the power to make my own decisions, but I knew I must fight for it on behalf of my sons, no matter what happened. It was my fate—my purpose on earth.

"Oh, mother Mary and all the saints, make haste to help me now, for I must be England's queen," I prayed. "Let him not deny me at the end!"

I hardly slept that night. My mind was sore oppressed with worry, and I longed for news from the North. Just when I ought to have been at the king's side, receiving his final blessing, I was fifty leagues away. Before the breaking of the dawn, I was at my desk again, this time writing to my brother.

> *To Earl Robert of Gloucester, the Empress Mathilda sends greeting and bids you remember the bond of love between us. I have heard that our most gracious sovereign and mutual father, King Henry of England, is nigh unto death, and this news*

has caused me to tremble. I would be with you at this time, but fate has kept me away. Therefore, do what you can to ensure the support of all the nobles for our succession. Bid them remember the oaths they made to us, and write to assure us of your continued affection.
MATHILDA IMPERATRIX

I then wrote letters to the archbishop of Rouen, the count of Surrey, and Bishop Roger of Salisbury. Still in my robes, I walked down to the front gate where the messenger Pierre was sitting.

"Pierre!" I said. "Take these to Argentan and have the king's men deliver them. Quickly now!"

"Yes, my lady!" he replied.

I stood there for a moment in the courtyard, breathing in the winter air. The sun was just starting to rise, and the sky was a hue of red. "A red sky bodes ill for this day," I whispered to myself. "Horace was right. '*Pulvis et umbra sumus.*' Dust and shadows. All we are is dust and shadows."[17]

I made my way back into the palace and was about to mount the stairs when I passed by the new chaplain, Philip. He had been installed that very month, but already I had found three occasions to confess to him. I was a bit ashamed to see him with my hair uncovered and still in my night things, but I attempted not to show it as he bowed to me.

"Good morrow, Empress Mathilda," he said softly, for there were many who still slept.

"Good morrow, father. Tell me, what is today's date?"

He raised his eyes to the ceiling as if in deep thought, then looked at me again. "It must be the Kalends of December."

---

17 Horace, *Odes*, Book IV, Ode vii, Line 16.

"A fearful day—" I said quietly, half speaking to the chaplain and half lost in my own thoughts.

"Why should it be fearful, my lady?" he asked, pulling my attention back to himself.

"King Henry lies this day upon his sick bed and is never likely to rise again. Pray for me, father. Pray that God will grant me strength."

"Of course," he promised, his eyes filled with concern. "These are sad tidings indeed. I will ask the monks of Fontevrault to say a Mass for his soul."

"Yes, well, very good."

In truth, I did not require prayers so much for my father, whose soul I was certain would be forced to endure either a thousand years of purgation or the fires of hell itself. Neither did I need strength to endure my grief at his passing, for I was not sad to lose his company as I had been upon the death of my mother and brother. No, I required strength to face down the wolves of the Norman court who would be looking to gain an advantage. I knew the hatred for Anjou ran deep among the Norman nobility, and I knew that they hardly yearned for a female ruler. Those were two strikes against me. I needed every bit of divine aid the prayers of the saints could muster.

I locked myself in my bed chamber and was about to ponder my next steps when there was a knock at the door.

"Who is it?" I called, annoyed that I should be interrupted so soon.

"Your husband," came the reply.

With a great sigh, I walked back over to the door. As soon as I had pulled back the bolt and allowed him to enter, I asked, "What now? Is there some news?"

"I'm afraid not. I came to say that I have considered the matter, and perhaps you should ride to Rouen after all. I can send my men with you. Even if he is dead when you arrive—"

"Please, speak no more of this," I pleaded, closing the door.

He placed his hands on his hips and glared. "Why ever not? Don't tell me you have changed your mind since last night!"

"Not changed my mind exactly. I have merely considered something I did not take into account before. You see, I cannot go to Rouen. It is too dangerous."

He laughed. "Lady England, you may have enemies in Normandy, but I am sure none of them would think to murder you upon the road!"

"That is not what I mean! I do not suppose that anyone would try to murder me, though they might attempt an abduction. I am sure that if Sir Drogo and the rest of the knights were to accompany me … But that is not the point. There is something else."

"Then out with it, wife, for I grow weary of this discussion!" he ordered a bit more forcefully than I thought was warranted.

I looked down at the ground and then back up at him. "I am with child again."

Well, if I had wanted to surprise him, I could not have picked a better means of doing so. Of course, Count Geoffrey knew full well that we had been in the marital way of late, attempting as always to produce more heirs to the throne. He had also seen me have two children before, so I am not sure why it took him by surprise. Nevertheless, he acted as if I had just informed him of the second coming of the Lord.

"What?!" he cried. "Are you … how can you … how sure are you?"

I chose to respond to his third attempt at a question. "Quite sure, and I fear the journey might prove too much for the babe that grows inside me."

Count Geoffrey placed his head in his hands and began to pace around the room. You would think I had told him a child of his had died rather than was about to be born.

"This timing could not be more ill, but if you are certain, then I suppose there is nothing we can do," he complained. "We will just have to wait and hope, as you say." He then moved within an arm's length of me. "But that had better be another son in there, for if I find out that we have placed everything in doubt for a girl, I shall be most displeased."

Ever since I had returned and given the count two legitimate sons, he had been disposed to treat me with a bit more respect. We had found a way to be civil for the sake of our children. However, every once in a while, he would say something that caused me to remember why I hated him in the first place: because he was not a proper man, but an arrogant arse. This was one such moment.

"You are all charm as ever, my lord," I replied.

One day, two days, three days passed, and still no news of the king. I thought I would go mad with waiting. My ladies bid me be calm so as not to harm the child, but how could I be calm at such a time? Finally, a lone rider was sighted upon the morning of the Nones riding down the road by the river and approaching the castle gate. He bore the standard of the Normans.

"Let him in!" Count Geoffrey called. "Let us hear what he has to say!"

The man was brought into the great hall, which had up until that moment been in the middle of preparations for a feast that evening. The tables were decorated with green boughs brought in from the nearby woods, and all the candles sat ready to be lit. I stood in front of the fire pit flanked by Agnes on one side and Adela on the other. Count Geoffrey stood just to the side, his hands folded together so tightly it was a wonder they did not crack. My heart seemed to pound, and I thought I might be ill, though that could have been on account of the child in my belly.

"Empress Mathilda," the man said with a bow, "I come with a message from Archbishop Hugh of Rouen."

"Read it," I said quietly.

"Very well."

He broke the seal and opened the scroll. I grasped the hands of my ladies on either side and breathed deeply. I had guessed that I was about to receive news either of my father's recovery or his death. If the latter, I would likely be informed of whether or not the Norman lords were submitting to my rule. In my heart, I said a prayer to the Virgin, to my mother, to anyone who might listen. Then the messenger began to read.

"'Be it known that this day, the second of the month of December, in the year of our Lord 1135, I have delivered into the keeping of Earl Robert of Gloucester the mortal remains of King Henry I of England, duke of Normandy. He passed from this world at Lyons-la-Forêt, on account of a malady in his bowels, as the physician Grimbald assures me. We shall bury his inner parts here in the city, then send his body on to Caen and thenceforth to England, for he sought to be buried at the abbey of Reading. We offer up our prayers for you in this time of great mourning, for there never was a king of England such as King Henry, last son of the Conqueror. The lords must now consider the matter of the succession, and we have already among us Count Theobald of Blois and Champagne, who many of the nobles hail as king, being the eldest male descendant of the first King William. However, it is not yet known if Earl Robert shall support him.' Thus ends the letter."

Within the space of a few seconds, I had gone from absorbing the news of my father's death, to being enraged at the news that the men of Normandy were already plotting to deny me my inheritance. However, I remembered how I had spent the last few days praying that I would act wisely rather than rashly,

The Forsaken Monarch

and I knew I needed more information. I wanted very much to say something, but Count Geoffrey was able to speak first.

"What is the meaning of this?!" he cried, his voice shrill and his fists clenched. "Have they so quickly forgotten the oath they swore before God? Damn them! Damn them to hell!"

"Pray, hold your tongue, Count Geoffrey," I said, then turned to the messenger. "Tell me, do you have any other message? Anything from Earl Robert?"

"No, my lady," he replied. "Perhaps something will come later today."

"Not likely. I am sure he means to take the crown for himself!" Count Geoffrey cried.

I was not about to throw my beloved brother overboard so easily. "You do not know my brother," I argued. "He would never put himself forward."

"But he may choose to support Count Theobald, or perhaps even Count Stephen. You allow your judgment to be clouded by sentiment!"

"Robert and Stephen have been at odds for some time," I replied, "and in any case, Stephen is not the eldest son of Lady Adela. You need not fear that he will gain Robert's support."

"Well, this puts an end to our debate," he declared. "I will make now for Normandy and ensure the support of the castellans: Domfront, Argenteuil, the whole lot of them! I will not sit back and watch my sons' inheritance be stolen!"

"I hope you are not implying that is what I intend to do!" I objected, filling with anger.

"What do you intend then?" he asked.

What I wanted to do was punch him in the face and then ride off to Normandy to set things right, but that did not seem likely to produce good results. I closed my eyes and attempted to consider all the players, all the obstacles, all the possible outcomes. Unable to arrive at a firm decision, I opened my eyes again.

"I need time to think," I told him.

Even to myself, this sounded rather weak. In truth, I wanted to strike, but I knew not what my target should be or how I could go about it.

"Come, my lady," Adela said, touching my arm. "You have had a blow. You must rest."

"And I shall make for Normandy!" Geoffrey concluded, turning to leave.

Suddenly, I had a moment of clarity. Yes, I needed to take care of the babe growing inside me, but I knew that if I did not go—if I allowed others to fight for my children's inheritance rather than myself, I would regret it. If I did not do all I reasonably could, they would never forgive me, nor should they. I had to take the chance. In any case, I could not bet everything on an Angevin when it was the association with Anjou that had caused the nobles to doubt me in the first place.

"No!" I cried, with such force that my husband instantly froze. "This is my inheritance, my people, my land. The only way to ensure it is to go myself."

"But I thought you said—" Count Geoffrey began.

"Never mind what I said! This is war and no mistake. Lady Agnes, tell Sir Drogo to gather the Bohun brothers and whatever knights Count Geoffrey can spare, and we will make for Alençon."

"Surely I should come with you!" my husband objected.

"Surely not!" I replied. "Why do you think the lords have failed to grant me their due fealty? Because they want nothing to do with Anjou!"

The red in Count Geoffrey's face threatened to match the red in his hair.

"I thought it was because you are a woman," he said scornfully.

I laughed perversely. "Oh, they may well fear me for that! The fiercest man cannot out run the mother keen to defend her sons!"

Frozen ground passing beneath us, sky of gray gazing down upon us, warm breath meeting the cold air: even so we moved across the earth as the falcon dives upon its prey, intent upon our urgent purpose. The endless ground trailed beneath us, with each beat of the hoof surrendering its length. Thus we pressed on hour by hour for the fortress of Argentan.

"Not long now," Drogo breathed. "We shall claim what is yours."

Would that I had his confidence. I traveled with a small band of knights—two dozen at most—led by one Alexander de Bohun and his brother Engelger. These were not my men, but my husband's. I had spent too little time in Anjou to expand my household. But while I left the ladies with my sons, I would never have surrendered Drogo. I had seen less of him since the children entered my life, but I still depended on him as ever.

"Will they open the gate for us?" I asked him, as we rode side by side.

"You know Wigan, my lady. He helped you before in an hour of need. He will not let us down."

I was not of such good cheer as my knight. Wigan the Marshal had certainly stuck out his neck for me when I left Count Geoffrey and returned to Normandy, but much had changed since then. It was also possible that the fortress had been seized by someone else. The land itself seemed more hostile to my aims, and the loyalty of all was in doubt. *O tempora! O mores!* Who was to be trusted when all honor was thrown aside? Fools trust, but the wise man carries a knife.

"If they refuse to open the gate, then this will be a rather short invasion," I said. "It could be days before Count Geoffrey collects his fighting men."

"Have faith, my lady!" he urged me.

We had passed around Alençon without trouble, making for our chief aim of Argentan. With every mile we traveled, I feared that we might be set upon by enemies. With every brief night we passed, I feared for the child inside of me. Yet if anyone did see us, they evidently decided not to try the strength of that band of knights, for we were never stopped. We simply continued mile after mile, moving ever farther north.

By the time we reached Argentan, snow was falling quite heavily, and our presence could not have been concealed from any who sought to follow us—at least, not until the snow filled in our tracks. I was more eager than ever to be safely within the castle walls, but such access was hardly certain. So much time had passed that the fortress may well have been seized and archers placed behind every crack. Therefore, when we came within about a furlong of the city walls on the western side of the River Orne, the company stayed back and Drogo rode across the bridge to the gate along with two others. The castle itself lay within a second wall inside the city.

I watched as they moved forward, praying to God they would not be cut down. They did make it to the gate and conversed with someone through a small window in the door. My horse stamped its hoof in the snow as I pulled my cloak tight around me. It was not a long wait at all, but on account of the cold and my fear, it seemed eternal. Finally, the men returned the way they had come. As soon as they were within range, I cried out, "So what did they say?"

"The castle is still controlled by Wigan," Drogo replied. "The guards had been instructed to watch for us. They will open the gates on his order."

The Forsaken Monarch

What relief swept over us all at these words! Within moments, we had passed beneath the portcullis of the castle itself, and I was seated before a fire in the same dining room where I had spent time about four years earlier, a glass of warm mead in my hands. One of the men brought a blanket to warm me, and I was almost thawed when Wigan, viscount of Exmes, made his appearance.

"Empress Mathilda!" he said, clasping my hands in his own. "It is an honor to welcome you again, though I wish we could meet under better circumstances. We have been waiting for you ever since the king died."

"I am a bit surprised that you have done so. I did not know who would remain true to their oath once the king no longer lived."

"The count of Ponthieu and I have remained true at the very least," he said, pulling over a chair from the table and sitting next to me. "He is holding Domfront for you, while I have this castle and my home at Exmes. I thought it likely you would come here first, being on the road from Le Mans. I must say, it did take you rather a long time."

"We had to start in Angers, and the weather was poor," I explained, taking another drink of the mead.

"Ah, that would do it."

"What news is there?"

He sighed and placed his hands on his knees. "Only that the lords are all in Caen: Earl Robert, Earl William, Count Routrou, and of course, Count Theobald. Last we heard, they wanted to hand the throne to Theobald, but you should know, my lady, that none of us here support that idea. You will find you have many friends in the South, and we hold you as our rightful lady."

He said this last bit with great conviction, which did my heart good, but I knew Wigan the Marshal was a far better man than most of those gathered in Caen.

"That is rather charitable of you, for the rest of the world seems to hate the very air I breathe," I told him. "But I suppose William Talvas wishes to have his family lands returned to him, and Count Geoffrey has always supported him in that."

William Talvas, the count of Ponthieu, was the very same man we had helped in his rebellion against King Henry the year before, so he would have been a knave and a half if he turned against us.

"Will Count Geoffrey be joining us?" Wigan asked.

"He is gathering his men as we speak and will ride for the North at the first opportunity, but given the suspicion that many hold toward Anjou, I thought it best to come alone first."

He nodded in agreement. "That may be wise, though for myself I rely on the trade with Anjou, whereas from the late king I had more trouble than not. But I should not speak ill of the dead, nor of your father. Forgive me."

"Why not? I have plenty ill to say about him, but I take your meaning. It is good and noble for a man to respect his sovereign, even after he has gone the way of all flesh."

I had not properly mourned the death of my father. Since I first heard he was sick, my only thoughts were of what to do next and how to obtain my inheritance. So steadfast had I been in this pursuit, that I had never truly acknowledged that my father—the man who at times had made my life a living hell, but who was nevertheless an inseparable part of myself—was gone. I was quite happy to be free of both him and his wrath. Indeed, I was experiencing great relief, and it seemed somehow wrong that I should feel such in response to the death of my own father. But how could I feel otherwise after all that had taken place? Perhaps it was the guilt this created that led me to put such things out of my mind.

"Well, he certainly left you in a bad spot!" the viscount said, interrupting my thoughts. "How are we to go about it then?"

He folded his hands together and leaned forward, waiting intently for my judgment.

"Do you have anyone who can carry a message?" I asked, draining the last of the mead and setting the cup on the floor.

"Most of them are already out, but we have one rider still here, yes."

"I need him to go to my brother, the earl of Gloucester."

"Certainly, my lady, but perhaps you wish to go yourself? I have some men I could spare, and you can take all your knights."

"I think it best that I remain here for the present."

I could tell by the look on the marshal's face that I had perplexed him.

"Why would you not want to go?" he asked. "Surely, it is best for you to travel to Caen in person and promote your claim. I do not mean to worry you, my lady, but a ruler who is not seen is not always feared."

He was right, and I could see I had no choice but to tell him the truth. "I did not intend to announce this until much later, but I am with child, and I must take care not to harm it, whether it be a him or her. My body has already endured much just to come this far. I fear what might happen if I marched all the way to Caen."

"I see," he said with a nod, his eyes grown wider. "Naturally, you can rely on my discretion. Are you to give birth soon?"

"No, not for many months."

"I am surprised you can be so sure then. You don't look it."

"Well, not that it is anyone's business, but I often felt ill with my two boys, and that is how I feel now."

It was strange to be speaking of this with a man whom I did not know well, but the marshal had such an easy way about him that I felt comfortable sharing.

"To tell you the truth, I ought to be more fearful," I added. "The birth of my second son almost killed me. I suppose it is a bit dangerous for me to be pregnant again, and at such a time as this. Yet for some reason, I have a peace about it. If God wished me dead, he could have taken me already. I believe he will keep me alive for as long as it takes to ensure that my children receive their inheritance. The child in my womb may be another matter though. I have often heard of women miscarrying when placed under great stress."

"I am certain you are right that it is your destiny to fight for your sons, and I believe that the child in your womb will be safe, but nevertheless we must take care. Should I send for someone? A physician? A midwife?" he asked.

"No, this must remain our secret for now. Just tell your man to make himself ready. There is nothing a doctor could do at this point in any case."

Within the hour, the rider was heading north to Caen with my letter in his bag. What would he find when he arrived? My thoughts were half with him and half with the sons I had left behind. Yes, I had only been away from them for a short time, but it was the first occasion on which we had been separated for more than a few hours. Already, it gnawed at my heart.

I was not to enjoy that merry season, sitting alone in Argentan Castle without family or friends, save of course for Drogo. The messenger I had sent to Caen never returned: an ill sign if ever there was one. Instead, I was forced to feed upon rumors. I did finally receive a letter from Count Geoffrey, who had joined with William Talvas to make an assault upon the fortress of Sées. I wished they would make for Honfleur and prevent any ship from leaving the port, but that was outside the realm of possibility. If Theobald was to be the nobles' choice, then our best hope was to keep the holy oil from touching his brow, or there would be little chance of overcoming him. A king once anointed is second only to God.

Finally, on the day after Christmas, some three weeks after I had arrived in Argentan, a message came from the North. I had been sitting alone in my outer chamber—a small room with naught but a couch by the fire for me to rest—seeking out every possible means of distraction when Drogo entered without even stopping to knock. He stood there silent, all six and a half feet of him, his eyes wide and his lower lip quivering, as if he had just seen a ghost.

"What is it?!" I demanded, sitting up straight. "Something bad?"

His face said more than his tongue could speak, and when he still remained silent, I imagined the worst.

"Has Count Geoffrey been slain?! Has Count Theobald been accepted?!" I cried, standing up and walking toward him. "Tell me, Drogo! Tell me now!"

For a moment, our eyes were locked, and I sensed that when he spoke, the die would be cast. Destiny would be set in motion.

"No, my lady," he said quietly. "The news is not from Normandy, but from England. Your cousin, Count Stephen of Boulogne—he made for London as soon as he received news of the king's death. He won the support of all the men there, and of the treasurer, William Pont de L'Arche. But most of all, he had the support of his brother, Bishop Henry of Winchester, and of the former chancellor, Bishop Roger of Salisbury. Together, they pressed his case, and won over the archbishop of Canterbury."

"What are you saying?" I asked desperately. "Drogo, what are you saying?!"

"He was crowned in Westminster Abbey. Already, he holds his royal court in London. My lady—he is made king."

I felt in that moment much as Lot's wife must have felt when she was turned into a pillar of salt. The sheer weight of his news seemed to crush my spirit. I could feel anger coursing through my veins, bitterness filling my very breath, and wrath as of the Almighty beating the drum of my heart.

"Are you … quite sure?" I asked slowly.

He nodded sadly. "Very sure. The nobles in Caen were ready to lend their support to Theobald, but when they heard that his brother was crowned, the count removed himself from consideration."

"And what of my brother? What of Earl Robert? Did this message come from him?"

"No, my lady. From him, we have nothing."

I looked down at the stone floor, so hard and unfeeling—cold and bereft of life. That was the world I lived in: a world with neither compassion nor any trace of loyalty.

"What do you wish me to do?" the knight asked.

I looked back up at him, tears in my eyes.

"Tell me this, Drogo: For what did I surrender my youth? For what did I come to Anjou and make an end of my own content? For the benefit of whom, I know not. I sacrificed my very dignity for the House of Normandy, and see now how I am rejected, cast aside like so much rubbish! I swear, were he not already safe in Abraham's Bosom, I should have made my father pay for this. I will make the lords of England pay for it!"

"You will fight him then?" Drogo said. "You will make war upon Stephen? For if that is your intent, my lady, I am with you until the end!"

I reached forth my hands and gripped both of his shoulders. "I have suffered many betrayals in my life, but none as foul as this! I swear to you, Drogo, that usurper will live to rue the day he forsook me. How he kissed me and sent me forth unto the wolves, even as Judas Iscariot! Yes, we will make war upon him, and all those who support him. Those cursed traitors shall not enjoy a peaceful night ere I make amends! Lock up your babes, England, for the Empress Mathilda is coming to you!"

CHAPTER TWENTY ONE

This was how Stephen of Blois was declared to be king of England, though he never deserved that title. For some time before the king's death, he had set his aim upon the crown, acquiring wealth and lands as the common man gathers timber, the better to build his house. He made friends of the merchants and promised them liberties. Through his mother and brother, he earned the respect of the sons of Cluny Abbey, the most powerful of the spiritual lords. In all of this, he was unwittingly helped by my father, King Henry, who gifted him Countess Mathilda of Boulogne as his wife, one of the few remaining descendants of the old line of kings. By her, Count Stephen already had a son and two daughters living when his great benefactor, the king, gave up the ghost.

The speed with which Stephen acted revealed his firm intention. As soon as the news of the king's death reached him in Boulogne, he made no attempt to speak with the other lords, but set sail for Dover with a band of armed men. Upon their arrival, they were denied entrance to the castle, which was under the control of Earl Robert of Gloucester. My brother must have ordered them not to open the gates for anyone but the true sovereign. Here I salute them for recognizing a fraud when they saw it. Stephen was, however, allowed to continue north into Kent, where he attempted to enter Canterbury, but was once again turned away by my brother's men.

Count Stephen was not one to take "no" for his answer. He pressed on to the one place where he was sure to find supporters: the streets of London. Here were men ruled by the ledger rather than the law, who would have sold their very souls for a reduction in their taxes. So presumptuous were the Londoners that they set themselves up as the jury for all England, claiming to elect Stephen as their king. How very like them to believe that theirs is the only opinion that matters! Might we also assume that they hoped by making Stephen their ruler to ensure favorable trade with the Flemings? Yes, when they ask what the throne of England is worth, I may answer, "All the wool in Flanders!"

Having won London, Count Stephen rode to Winchester, where his younger brother Henry was bishop—again, my father's doing. Naturally, Bishop Henry lent his support to his brother, but only at a high cost, for he forced him to make such pledges to the Church as my father would have surely rejected. No one knew the full extent of what was promised, but it surely made Bishop Henry even more powerful than he already was.

Winchester was not only the home of the bishop, but also of the royal treasury, being the old English capital. There most of the gold laid up by King Henry was in the keeping of William Pont de L'Arche, lord of Portchester Castle. It is said that the brothers coerced him to part with the treasure, though he does not seem to have offered up much of a fight.

Next, that old devil, Bishop Roger of Salisbury, made common cause with Count Stephen, no doubt helped on by the younger Bishop Henry of Winchester. They had a common grievance: namely, that their advice was not sought regarding my marriage to Count Geoffrey, which was yet again my father's doing. Both had much to lose should the Angevins be granted power, yet both had also sworn their allegiance, without regard to any possible marriage, as had all the lords and bishops. And as for the alleged honor of Bishop Roger, who knew not that he had a son whom he hoped would be given the office of chancellor? A bishop with a bastard: now there's a mark of honor!

The very first man to swear his allegiance to me had been Archbishop William of Canterbury, and if they were to convince him to crown Stephen, they would need to present some just cause by which the oath might be declared null. Here they found just the man they needed: Hugh Bigod, constable of Norwich Castle and a man without honor. He repeated a tale to Archbishop William that upon his death bed, King Henry in his anger had released all the nobles from their former oath and bid them offer fealty to Count Stephen, his true heir.

Such a very convenient story it was, and it had the appearance of truth, for my father was disputing with myself and my husband at the time of his death. Based on this story, the archbishop crowned Stephen at Westminster on the eleventh day before the Kalends of January, without the presence of a single earl or abbot. I imagine that the ceremony was rather hollow.

Now, you must not fault me when I call Hugh Bigod a perjurer, for though the archbishop of Canterbury did not know it and many men sought to deny it, Sir Hugh was not with the king in those final hours. I have this on the testimony of at least a dozen persons who had reason to know. Moreover, those who were at the king's side never brought forth such a claim of his reversal—rather the opposite. Thus, Count Stephen bought the crown of England with a damnable lie, playing upon a man who had become foolish in his old age. Perhaps it was fitting that the Lord called the archbishop home later that year.

Oh, how those ill tidings worked upon my mind with each passing hour! Stephen's betrayal created a storm of wrath inside me. That wrath drove me on and gave me purpose. It consumed me and made me stronger: more present, more alive. Yet my wrath was not as that of the Almighty against human iniquity. The wrath of the Lord is perfect and unfailing. It does not ebb and flow like the wrath of man, but tends toward holiness. Can the fire that lives so freely within the heart of God reside in a man without causing his destruction? Beware of that flame!

The news from England grew worse by the day. Count Stephen had gained the support of Miles of Gloucester and Pain fitz John, who between them were sheriffs over all the western counties along the border with Wales. They transferred their allegiance so quickly that they clearly had something to gain, and here we come to it, for Earl Robert of Gloucester was lord over much of that land. Indeed, this Miles had held Gloucester Castle on behalf of Earl Robert, but now the usurper offered it to him as a direct grant of the crown, making Miles faithful to Stephen alone. What a pretty piece of work! There was not one game being played, but many, and I feared that I was not aware of all of them.

The dead king's body finally arrived in England just after New Year's Day, without most of the lords who had accompanied it on its progress through Normandy. It was laid to rest at Reading Abbey with Count Stephen and his allies in attendance. As enraged as I was to think of those traitors surrounding my father's grave when they were so clearly in violation of his wishes, I took some small comfort in the knowledge that Earl Robert remained in Normandy and did not announce his support one way or the other. My best hope was that he would remain true and take up arms against Stephen, for unlike Count Geoffrey, he had many lands and supporters in England itself.

By the end of January 1136, I had sent for Adela, bidding Lady Agnes remain with the boys in Anjou. As much as I longed to see my sons again, I knew they would be far safer to the south. I had to be where I was for their sake, and it was not uncommon for royal mothers to be separated from their sons, but it still brought me sorrow. Sometimes when I was alone in my room, I would begin crying for no other reason than that I missed them so much.

At least when Adela arrived, I had another friend with me. It was she who was with me when I received a rather interesting letter from across the Channel. We were sitting on the couch in that same room where Drogo had first informed me of Stephen's treachery, enjoying the warm afternoon rays that passed through the two windows on either side of the hearth, when one of the servants came in and delivered a letter bearing a rather large seal.

"What is it, my lady?" Adela asked, after the servant had left.

I squinted and read the letters, which had been somewhat smeared. "It is from my uncle, the king of Scotland. I assume it is rather old, for they must have taken it the long way round to avoid Stephen's men."

"Maybe it is good news!" she offered.

I had my doubts, but as I broke the seal, I found that I could not dash that small morsel of hope that was raised within my soul. I opened the parchment and read in silence.

> *To my dearest niece, Empress Maud, true heir of King Henry of England—King David of Scotland, earl of Huntingdon sends his greeting and hopes this letter will find you in good health and among better men than have falsely claimed power in London.*

Allow me to set your mind at ease, for I have every intention of fulfilling the oath I made to you. Already, we have invaded the north of England and seized the castles of Norham, Alnwick, Wark, Carlisle, and Newcastle without much resistance. I have with me my son, Prince Henry, and have seen to it that all the local barons swear fealty to Your Highness. We are currently camped north of Durham, though I dare not name the town, for there are spies throughout the land who wish us ill. I heard that the lords are slow to acknowledge Stephen as king, and that he is left without an army. Therefore, do not fear, for by spring we may well feast in London. May the grace of our Lord be with you always.

"Well, that is good news indeed!" I concluded. "King David has taken much of the north of England and will march south before long. He seems to think that the lords will not lend their soldiers to Stephen, though with the amount of gold he stole, he can no doubt purchase a large force."

"My lady," Adela said, "I know nothing of battle, but can an army of mercenaries truly contend with a faithful force? Might they not flee at the first sign of trouble?"

"Not if they hope to be paid, but they may well have trouble against an army of Scotsmen. King David controls the earldom of Huntingdon by right of his late wife, and thus much of England is his already. Count Stephen will find him an able foe. If Earl Robert was to follow our uncle's lead, then we might have a real chance! But we must not get ahead of ourselves: there is nothing certain in battle. Let us hope Count Geoffrey can get through to him, for all my messages to Robert seem to go astray. I suspect that my enemies ensure it."

"Very good, my lady. See, there is hope still!" she concluded, patting me on the arm.

Sadly, our hopes for King David were to be disappointed, for only a few days after we received his letter, Drogo informed me that Stephen was gathering men from Brittany to Flanders. They met in the South of England and marched north to Durham, paying more men to join them at each stop. It is said that ten thousand men flocked to his banner.

King David had not foreseen this, and he was forced to meet with Count Stephen and beg a truce. This peace was dearly bought, for Stephen made the king surrender the earldom of Huntingdon to his son and heir, Prince Henry. Though my uncle refused to do homage of his own accord, he was forced to allow his son to return with Stephen to York and there join his court. My poor cousin had thus become a hostage.

The usurper did allow King David to keep the castles of Doncaster and Carlisle, but it was clearly a defeat. No one, myself included, thought that Stephen could summon so great an army so quickly. In those first months of his accursed reign, the traitor had shown a greater natural talent than he ever had in his four decades of life. I had no doubt that he was driven to it by his wife, the Countess Mathilda. She always made mischief as a child, and both she and her mother had coveted the throne. It made me ill to think that the crown that ought to have been placed on the heads of myself and my descendants would soon adorn her raven tresses.

Perhaps she has nothing but gray hairs now, I hoped.

So the month of February began badly, and it ended even worse. Between the two of them, Count Geoffrey of Anjou and Count William of Ponthieu had apparently made enemies of anyone and everyone. They were accused of behaving like brutes by the people of Normandy, who saw them as naught but foreign invaders. They achieved little by moving north, and then were forced to retreat anyway when a rebellion sprung up in Anjou, no doubt in response to the count's absence.

Thus, by the beginning of Lent, Stephen was in control of England, Earl Robert was silent, my husband was unable to control either the Normans or his own people, and I was still trapped in Argentan. With Stephen's victory in the North, it seemed only a matter of time until the lords made their way to bow at his feet. I was angry for myself, yes, but for my sons my heart ached. The only good news was that my pregnancy was going well, a small bit of relief. In the night, I would lay awake feeling the movements of the child inside me and whisper into the darkness, "Robert, my brother: do not forget us!"

The first day of spring warmth draws many a man outside, even if the remnants of winter are still clearly present. Shortly after Easter, one such day arrived in Argentan, and Adela begged me to experience it.

"You have been staring at these same dark walls for far too long!" she declared one morning, as she pulled a gown over my growing belly. "I suspect that is the reason for your melancholy."

"Might it be because the lords have lately deserted me and traveled to the traitor's Easter court, there to kiss the sinful ground on which he walks?" I asked.

"Perhaps, but my mother always used to say, a change of weather will do you good, and so it shall!"

She spoke these words so earnestly and with such a nice smile that I was willing to agree, but only within a certain limit.

"I have no intention of stepping beyond the castle gate," I declared.

"No matter. There is always the yard."

The yard that she referred to was the inner ward of the castle, where there was neither a blade of grass nor a single shrub, but simply a mess of gravel with carts and booths sitting here and there, along with the remnants of fires. A few last bits of ice still clung to the pavement, not to mention the refuse of horses and men alike, for the stables sat next to the southern wall. Even so, Adela was determined to take me there, and after I had been sufficiently wrapped in two different robes, we made our way outside. She set down two wood chairs and her bag of things in one of the cleaner spots and we sat side by side.

"What a pleasant day it is!" Adela said, raising her face to bask in the sun. "The bird song is sweet to the ear."

"This wind is less sweet to my skin," I complained, sinking beneath my fur. "I thought you said it was warm."

"The sun is out."

"Yes, but that hardly means it is warm, now does it?"

"Would you like me to take you back inside?" she said, with a tilt of the head and rise of the brows.

"No, we are here now, and in my state I move nowhere quickly. We must simply suffer through it."

Adela laughed and closed her eyes, laying her head back. I too closed my eyes for a moment and breathed in the air, which was perhaps not as cold as I had made it out to be. I tried not to notice the sounds of all around me—the blacksmith, the barking dog, the chattering crows—but rather to consider my predicament. The babe inside me would remain there well into the summer, or so the midwife had told me. Count Geoffrey was forced to stay in Anjou for the time being. Earl Robert remained mute, no doubt for some reason of his own. The usurper grew in strength by the day, and it was said that the Holy Father had granted his support to that traitor. I had not seen my sons in months.

"Try to relax," Adela entreated. "Feel the sun upon your face. Think of something peaceful. Now, if you hold still, I will fix your hair."

"Why? What is wrong with it?" I asked, opening my eyes.

"Nothing! It just needs to be combed," she explained, walking toward me and drawing a comb from the bag.

"Out here? With everyone watching?!" I said, turning my head left and right as if to catch someone making a drawing.

"Oh, no one is watching."

"I do not like this."

"Close your eyes and tilt your head back," she instructed with a smile.

I did as she said, though I was not happy about it. Adela began to take down my braids and place the comb through them. It did not hurt as much as I had feared, and I actually found myself relaxing for just a moment when I heard footsteps fast approaching. I opened my eyes again to see Drogo standing before me. He was clearly surprised to find me in such a position, and though I waited, he said nothing.

"Yes?" I finally prompted him.

"Should I come back later?" he asked. "Only, I did not know you would be—"

"Just tell me, Drogo."

"As you wish. I regret to confirm that Earl Robert has traveled to England and met with King Stephen—"

"Do not call him that!" I snapped.

"Forgive me—Count Stephen of Boulogne!" he said, his head dropping not unlike a dog who has just been scolded. "They met in Oxford, and Earl Robert offered him fealty. I thought I should tell you."

Adela stopped her work. "What? Are they not sworn enemies?"

"Close to it," Drogo replied, "but he may well have felt there was no choice. His lands would be forfeit had he continued to demur, and in any case, all the barons have gone over to Stephen now."

"All of them?!" she cried, stepping in front of me with the comb still in her hand. "Not a single one stayed true? These are dark days indeed!"

"What about Lord Brian of Wallingford?" I asked, pushing her to the side gently. "Brian fitz Count—has he declared himself?"

"Forgive me, my lady, but he was also at Stephen's court and did homage to him. Is he of particular import?"

My heart sank. "No, I just hoped that one of my old friends would see fit to keep their vows, but it seems I am surrounded by traitors. This is a tragedy and no mistake. Earl Robert was our last hope. Without him, our cause is doomed. Not in Normandy—here we have a chance—but I fear England is lost to me. Even so, thank you for telling me, Sir Drogo. Adela, I think it is time we returned to the warmth."

"I am very sorry, my lady," Drogo said softly. "So very, very—"

"Please," I interrupted, raising my hand, "there is no point. We need not speak when no words will suffice. There are some things in life that defy our efforts of expression. God knows I can think of no lyric worthy of this betrayal."

Drogo nodded sadly and walked away, leaving the two of us there in the cold. Adela returned to her work, once again pinning the braids against my head. Very soon, she was finished.

"What is this, my lady?" she asked, as I rose to leave.

I turned my head. "What is what?"

"Here in the bag. I was putting the comb back and I found this."

She pulled out the amber stone that I had quite forgotten, so long had it languished at the bottom of that pouch. Seeing it in that moment when I had just learned of Brian's support for the usurper seemed to awaken the old pain all over again.

"It is an ornament given to me in my youth," I answered quietly, very much hoping the conversation would end there.

"It looks like a moth," she said, holding it up to examine it in the sunlight. "Why do you carry this around?"

"I don't really—not any more. I forgot it was in there."

"Does it bring good fortune?" she asked, a new light in her eyes.

I laughed. "When I consider my life so far, I would have to say no."

"Who gave it to you?"

There was the question I had hoped to avoid. I feared an honest answer might bring me too close to confessing the true significance of the object. I had never spoken to anyone of my former love for Brian, and it hardly seemed the right time to start.

"My mother gave it to me before I left for Germany," I lied.

"How sweet!" she said. "You must keep it as a sign of your love for her."

"Something like that," I muttered.

As we walked back to the front door of the palace, hand in hand, I almost wished that the stone had been from my mother, for she at least had remained faithful to me. I knew in that moment it would take many weeks or months for me to recover from my brother's betrayal, if indeed I ever recovered from it. Some wounds are too deep to ever heal. And as for Lord Brian—I doubted once again if he had ever loved me at all.

As it turned out, Drogo's claim that all the nobles had gone over to Stephen was not quite true. There was one lord who had refrained from offering fealty: Baldwin de Redvers, baron of Devon and lord of the Isle of Wight. As his family had received all they had from the former King Henry, Baldwin did not have the personal strength of the great earls of long standing, but he was more faithful to the late king's wishes. He had failed to attend the Easter court, and it was only after Earl Robert of Gloucester announced his support for the false king that Baldwin sent a message to the usurper saying he would do homage in exchange for being confirmed in all his possessions.

But Baldwin had waited too long, and Stephen suspected him of treachery. He refused the offer and ordered that Baldwin's lands be seized.

Lord Baldwin knew it was only a matter of time before his enemies would come for him, so he set about his preparations at once. He rode east and took control of the castle of Exeter, which was a stronger fortress than his seat in Plympton. He had perhaps a week to fortify the town before Count Stephen arrived along with most of the nobles of England: a massive force. Some men were sent west to take Plympton, thus cutting off Baldwin's escape, and the rest set to work on the main castle of Exeter.

The usurper was determined to make an example of Baldwin. The poor residents of Devon felt the brunt of his wrath, as the soldiers moved about the region, slaughtering their cattle and burning their crops. The siege continued for weeks until Lady de Redvers finally came out the front gate barefoot, her hair hanging limp and her face covered in dirt. She fell upon her knees before Count Stephen, begging him to show mercy. It was said that his brother, Bishop Henry of Winchester, noticed the signs upon her face, and declared that those inside the castle must have been without water for some time. The poor woman was sent back into that hell house to die of thirst. In the end, they chose to surrender rather than suffer that unhappy end.

Of course, I did not hear all of this at the time. I simply knew that Baldwin had rebelled and Stephen had placed Exeter under siege, finally taking the castle. I then heard that Baldwin had fled to his fortress of Carisbrooke on the Isle of Wight, and that Stephen meant to pursue him there. The full tale was only revealed to me when, on the first day of June, Baldwin de Redvers arrived at the gates of Argentan with only a single servant for company. I had him brought in and agreed to meet with him, for I had not yet begun my lying in. However, as I did not know the man, I required that we meet in the hall on the lower level rather than my private chamber, and that Drogo should join us.

The hall in the castle of Argentan was not as great as those in Rouen, Caen, or Le Mans. It could only hold about fifty persons comfortably. This was of little matter, for as I have mentioned before, the family of Wigan normally took their meals in the private dining chamber and did not hold many lavish feasts. Indeed, the hall had been in a state of disuse for so long that all the furniture had been moved elsewhere and three chairs had to be brought in for our meeting. As the summer air was hot, there was no need to light a fire: the windows near the ceiling let in enough light. We sat in a circle to view one another better. I folded my hands on top of my belly and rubbed it gently, while Drogo leaned back in his chair and crossed his legs. For his part, Lord Baldwin looked the worse for wear. His outer tunic had holes in it that were likely the result of scrapes with tree branches. The sole on one of his shoes was breaking off from the rest, and he bore what looked like a rather fresh cut on his left cheek.

"Empress Mathilda, I must thank you for your hospitality," he said. "I have passed through many dangers to come here."

"Why are you here?" I asked, with some suspicion. "Last I heard, you were shut up in Carisbrooke and not likely to come out, but how did you get there in the first place?"

"Ah, yes," he said, nodding his head. "I was at Exeter in the early days of that siege, and bloody days they were. We were surrounded on all sides, and through my window I could see Stephen standing there, with Earl Robert beside him. I suppose he wanted to keep him close by, for fear that he might cause mischief. Some of my own men came with them—without revealing their true intent, of course. They made like they would assault the front gate, but we opened it to them, recognizing their faces." Here he let out a hearty laugh. "What a fool they made of Stephen! I can only imagine what he must have been thinking. Not all those within his camp are true: I promise you that! In any case, it soon became clear that we could not win, so I slipped out the postern."

"What, out the back door?" Drogo asked. "Surely someone had their eye on it!"

"You would think so, but no," he replied. "A siege is always chaos. I was dressed the same as the rest of them. I knew I had to make it to the isle, but Stephen's spies were all about the country, and the nearby ports were closed. I had to walk all the way to Wareham, not knowing what had become of my poor wife and my men." Here he shook his head as if the matter was beyond belief. "I was able to bribe some fishers to stow me below deck and transport me to Wight. It was there that I learned that Exeter had fallen, and that Stephen intended to put to death all the souls inside—that is, until Earl Robert made clear his opposition. When they saw that I was not there, they must have known I fled to Carisbrooke, for it did not take long for the navy to arrive. I would have held out, but we had so little rain this spring that there were naught but a few bottles of wine to drink. What could I do? I went out to meet Stephen, and he sent me into exile. I am an outlaw now. That is why I came to you, my lady. Of course, I did not know for sure that you would be here. We only hear rumors of your whereabouts. I cannot tell you how glad I am to see your face!"

The last few months had caused me to doubt everything and everyone, but as I listened to Baldwin de Redvers describe what it had cost him to stand against Stephen, I felt that here at least was one Norman lord who knew something of loyalty. It did my heart good.

"I am glad to receive you, Lord Baldwin," I told him. "You are one of the few men who has kept your oath, and at great cost to yourself and your house. Where are your people now?"

"Stephen said they were free to go," he explained, sighing in relief. "He declared they were innocent, as they were simply obeying their lesser lord. To myself, he was not so merciful, of course. I have written for them to come to me when they are able."

"There is one thing I do not understand," said Drogo. "Why should Earl Robert entreat Count Stephen on behalf of your household? What did he hope to gain by that?"

In my excitement to hear of Lord Baldwin's escape and faithfulness to myself, I had forgotten this detail, but Drogo was right: it did seem a bit odd. My brother was not a cruel person, but he was a man of war as well.

"I assumed that he must be working on behalf of Your Highness," Baldwin replied, looking at me. "Surely you have been in contact with him?"

"I wish that was the case, but I have heard nothing," I said, feeling the pain of his betrayal once again. "Whatever game Earl Robert is playing, it does not involve me."

"Perhaps he is afraid of Stephen's men," Baldwin offered. "He has been watching Earl Robert from the very beginning, placing spies around him."

"And yet he bowed the knee to Stephen, and he continues to do so," I replied, unwilling to let him off easily. "Trust me, Lord Baldwin, if my brother was on my side, I would know it. He has gone over to the enemy, along with the rest of my kin."

For a moment, I stared down at the floor and neither of them spoke. What could they have said in response to such betrayal? I had few friends in the world. My own flesh and blood had denied me. I was forsaken.

Lord Baldwin finally spoke, changing the subject. "I did wonder why you yourself did not make more of an effort to travel to England to claim your throne, but I see the reason now," he said, pointing at my swollen belly. "You are to have a child soon, no?"

"Yes, I must remain in Argentan until the birth. It is a sore cross to bear in this most urgent hour, but perhaps it is for the best. My children are my greatest security."

"Are the princes still in Anjou then?" he asked.

"Yes, it is the only safe place for them, for if Stephen got his hands on them, I shudder to think what he might do." Indeed, even as I said this, an image appeared in my mind of my boys lain on a table, an apple stuffed in each of their mouths, and Stephen sharpening his knife.

"And will Count Geoffrey invade Normandy again? We hear rumors."

"I hope daily to hear that he is coming north, but only time will tell. He has garnered the support of the duke of Aquitaine, which is something. To tell the truth, Lord Baldwin, I have been in a deep depression for the past several months, but your coming fills my heart with joy. It is a comfort to know that there are some men in England who still value loyalty."

"Always, my lady," he said, smiling broadly. "Now, give me a commission! What would you have me do?"

"Ride to Angers and speak with Count Geoffrey. He can command you better than I. Tell him that our child is coming soon. You may pass the night with us and take such provisions as you need. I will send a few knights with you."

"Thank you, Your Highness," he said, rising to leave.

As he began to walk away, I called, "Lord Baldwin!"

"Yes?" he said, turning to face me.

"Tell my sons that I miss them and want nothing so much as to hold them in my arms, but I shall not stop fighting for their inheritance."

"Yes, my lady," he replied, and left the room.

"Well, that was a matter of exceeding interest," Drogo commented, rising to his feet. "Do you really think he is a good one?"

"His father Richard certainly was. He was a faithful servant of King Henry. Let us hope the same is true with the son. I am sure he thinks that I can give him more than Stephen, though considering that he presently has next to nothing, that should not be hard."

"Do you think he is right about Earl Robert?" the knight asked, extending his hand to help me to my feet.

"It seems too good to hope so. I would never have thought it within Robert's character to support Stephen in the first place, so long have they mistrusted each other. Perhaps I never really knew him, but only saw what I wished to see. We must assume that he is heart and soul for Stephen. I maintain what I said earlier: we make Normandy our chief aim, so long as we will never surrender our right to England or acknowledge that traitor as king."

We turned and walked toward the same door out of which Lord Baldwin had lately departed.

"I was wondering, what about Queen Adeliza—that is, the former queen? Have you heard where she stands?" he inquired.

"She had the good sense to make for Wilton Abbey and stay out of this mess. I admit that at the present, monastic life does seem rather appealing: no wars, no betrayals—just contemplation and the work of the Lord. But no, I must be about the chase. It is my lot."

As he opened the door for me, I felt the babe inside me kick. It seemed it was as eager to leave Argentan as I was.

As the time for my child to be born grew near, I was most afeared. Little wonder there, for the birth of Geoffrey had almost killed me. A woman does not forget a thing like that, and it weighed upon my mind in those final weeks. My one comfort was that I had two sons already born who could carry on our line if I were to go the way of all flesh. Yet with only their father to defend them, their chances seemed poor indeed, for as much as the Norman lords may have hated me, they hated my husband far more.

In the end, there was no need to fear. The birth was as smooth as I could have hoped, and in the space of a few hours I held my third boy in my arms: sweet William. On account of him, I had been held in check at a time when I could least afford it, but when I was finally given the chance to meet him, all of that seemed to fade away. In the space of three years, I had brought forth three princes, fulfilling my father's wish. If only that had been enough! As it turned out, there was no manner of sacrifice sufficient to win over those who were determined to hate me.

I wrote to Count Geoffrey informing him that he had another son. He replied that he was riding north with an army of two thousand men. Here was some good news, and not a moment too soon! Our ally, Robert de Tosny, had been taken prisoner by Earl Waleran Beaumont, whom Stephen had assigned to defend the East of Normandy. Here I remembered my doubts about Waleran's change of character.

Fortunately, for all his many faults, my husband at least seemed a match for Waleran. He gained Carrouges and the region around Sées, then pressed as far as Lisieux. He burned much of that town to the ground, including its cathedral, before Waleran arrived and forced him to fall back. The next thing I knew, he wrote that he was trapped near Le Sap and badly in need of aid.

"My wife, I beg you, bid Count William gather such men as he can and march with all haste to our position!" he pleaded with me.

I did not need to be told twice. Indeed, ever since I had given birth, I had been eager to see something other than the walls of Argentan Castle and to contribute something real to our cause. True, my husband had not asked for me to accompany the men to his position, but after talking it over with the count, we both agreed that it would be good for our forces to see me in person and know for whom they were fighting. I hated to leave my new son so soon after his entry into the world, but I knew Adela would take as much care with him as if he was her own flesh and blood. I set to work at once, sending messengers to all the surrounding country. Between the count and myself, we were able to assemble some five hundred fighting men. I allowed myself to be just a little proud of this feat achieved in a short amount of time.

It was less than a day's ride to where my husband was camped. I rode with my knights beside me, sending messengers ahead to ensure that we would not be entering a trap. I had set out bravely, but as we grew closer to our destination, the fear inside me increased. After all, I had never been directly involved in a war before, even in such a minor way.

By the time we reached the camp, it was a lamentable sight. There were some tents set up in the middle of a small forest, but most of the men and goods were simply scattered beneath the trees, exposed to the elements. Everywhere, men seemed to lie about in a rather sorry state, some looking more green than white and all of them looking as if they had been half eaten by fleas. A cart passed by carrying at least ten corpses, and I had to cover my nose due to the stench. As I walked on a bit, the ground dipped down toward a small creek, and to my great dismay I saw men squatting in the water, emptying the contents of their bowels as they groaned in pain.

"Disease has infected this camp," Drogo whispered to me. "Those bodies you saw were not killed by the sword."

I made no reply, for I feared that if I continued discussing the matter I would vomit. Even as the thought passed through my mind, the flap of a nearby tent was pulled back and I saw inside a wood table covered in blood. A man who I guessed to be a surgeon dumped a pail of water on it to clean it off, and the red liquid ran off the edges and fell to the ground.

"Excuse me, Drogo," I said, looking away. "I need to step aside for a moment."

"Of course. I will wait here," he replied.

I walked quickly behind the tent where I would not be seen. I took deep breaths in and out, hoping that it would help to settle my stomach. Then I heard flies buzzing and turned to my right to see a pile of severed limbs lying on the ground—remnants of the surgeon's work. Well, that was my limit. I turned and emptied the contents of my stomach on the ground. I remained bent over for a moment, my hands pressed against my knees.

Why did I ever think this was a good idea? I thought. *This is madness. What if I become sick as well? What if I pass on the disease to my son?!* A new wave of fear passed through me, but then I reasoned that I could wait for a few days before returning to Argentan. In any case, whatever was infecting the men was likely due to their poor condition. Grimbald had said as much to me once—that disease could pass through food or drink, or among those who lived in filth. I told myself this, but it did not completely remove my fears.

When I had finally recovered a bit, I walked back to join my knight, who was still standing there faithfully.

"That is Count Geoffrey's tent over there," he said, pointing. "Are you well, my lady? You look a bit pale."

"I am fine," I declared. "Thank you, Drogo. I will just speak to my husband."

I made my way over to the tent he had indicated, avoiding a few dogs that were beset with mange. I entered to find Count Geoffrey alone and lying on a pallet, his armor cast aside. One of his feet was heavily wrapped.

"Thank God you've come!" he said, struggling to raise himself up a bit. "How many are with you?"

"More than are with you, by the looks of it," I replied. "There cannot be more than a few hundred men here!"

"Many of them fell near Lisieux. We escaped that only to be struck with dysentery. I must have lost a hundred men a day since I came to this God forsaken place!" he complained.

"Is there anything that can be done?" I asked, stepping nearer.

"Well, if I knew that, then I would hardly be lying here, now would I?!"

His face had wrinkled into a kind of scowl as his nostrils expanded and contracted. Even under the difficult circumstances, I felt there was no reason for him to respond in such a manner, especially given all I had accomplished for him. I found I was not very sad that he was in bodily pain.

"There is no need to be upset," I told him calmly. "See, I have brought you five hundred more men, armed and ready to fight. Only I hope they do not all succumb to this same disease. But what is wrong with your foot?"

"I was wounded in battle!" he snapped.

I could not believe that his injury was that serious, or it would have been reported to me already. Nevertheless, and as much as I hated to admit it, I needed Count Geoffrey. Not only that, but I needed to be on good terms with him, for we were at war together. I therefore tried to play the part of a caring wife.

"May I see it?" I asked, keeping my tone as pleasant as possible.

"Why?" he asked, casting a suspicious glance my way.

"So that I can tell if it is healing, or is that too much of an imposition?"

He said nothing, but removed the cloths. The wound did not appear putrid, but I poured some wine on it anyway, which

The Forsaken Monarch

caused him to scream. I then wrapped it again, dropping to my knees on the ground to do so, for there were no chairs to be had.

"There is no sign of infection," I reported. "I think you should not walk on it for a few days."

"Not possible," he said.

"But you are not likely to move before then in any case, with so many men ill! I have been out there. It is hell on earth."

"If Earl Waleran pays us a visit, we may not have a choice."

"Yes, of course, but—"

"Empress Mathilda," he said, pounding his hand into the pallet, "thank you very much for the delivery of my men, but I beg you not to trouble yourself with matters of warfare. That is the domain of men!"

I wanted very much to share some of my more pointed thoughts with him, but after everything I had just witnessed and in light of our mutual fight for our sons' inheritance, I attempted to be gracious.

"You know I am only trying to help," I said, with the patience of Job.

"Your help is not necessary," he replied, still glaring at me. "Go back to Argentan. See to our son."

"Very well," I concluded.

I would not offer a cross word to Count Geoffrey, but neither was I about to let him avoid any consequence for his poor behavior. As I stood, I placed my hand upon his bad foot, causing him to cry out once again, then departed the tent.

Count Geoffrey did hold Le Sap for a time, but the colder weather forced him to return to Anjou, there to gather his strength for the coming year. He clung to the hope that he might be able to sway Count Theobald of Blois to his cause, for Theobald was made bitter by his younger brother's rise.

Indeed, many of the lords had been ready to declare him king when the news of Stephen's coronation arrived. While he consented to fate, no one doubted that even as he sat in Chartres, Count Theobald grew in spite by the day. My husband had already arranged a sort of truce with the count and hoped in the coming year to win his support outright.

As it so happened, Stephen was just as intent on winning over his brother. As soon as the winter broke, he came over to Normandy to make his case for the dukedom. Among those in his company were the Beaumont brothers—earls Robert and Waleran—Stephen's own son Eustace, and William of Ypres, leader of the Flemish mercenaries. Already, that captain had earned a reputation for cruelty, and I did not fault the barons of Flanders for twice denying him the comital throne.

Stephen's forces marched to Evreux, where they met Count Theobald and offered him two thousand marks of silver a year for his loyalty. Well done, Theobald: Judas was only purchased for thirty! In truth, the forces of Stephen were so great that his brother was unlikely to quarrel with him. Having won over Theobald, the usurper had the French king proclaim him the true lord of Normandy, for which he was made to kneel at Louis' feet and pay homage. Here the loyalties of Stephen were revealed: he was no Englishman, nor even a proper Norman, but simply a vassal of the French.

With the usurper busy in the East, Count Geoffrey decided that he should press north to Caen, where Earl Robert sat in his castle. He hoped that, given the opportunity, my brother might ride to his aid. I did not share in this hope, but a small part of me naturally wanted to believe that my brother might have come to his senses and remembered our bond by blood. That was a dangerous part of me though—one that might cause me to suffer further pain or act the part of a fool. I therefore did nothing to keep my husband from going, but I did not feed his hopes either.

As I foresaw, Count Geoffrey ended up disappointed. Not only did Earl Robert fail to lend his support, but my husband was blocked by Stephen's men and, unwilling to face them in open battle, he retreated to his home in the South. To make matters worse, I soon heard that Count Stephen was marching his army toward Anjou, where he intended to crush Count Geoffrey.

Oh, why had I ever permitted my husband to ride north and reveal his position! I suppose I could not have stopped him if he was set upon his course, but I could have brought some pressure to bear. Suddenly, my greatest concern was not that I might not be able to take anything from Stephen, but that he was about to take something from me. With as much money as he had stolen from the king's treasure, Stephen might have bought every able man in Christendom for his cause, and I feared what would happen were he to succeed in pressing into the small bit of Normandy we controlled, or even crossing the border into Angevin territory. My own life would be in danger as well as those of my children.

I wrote to my husband again warning him of the traitor's intention. More than all, I told him in no uncertain terms that the princes Henry and Geoffrey must be moved south, and that William and I must make our escape if it came to it.

Count Geoffrey, I have received news that the usurper, Count Stephen, is marching to the south and west with a large company of men and that he means to either ambush you or make straight for my position to seize myself or our beloved William. I am most afraid for us both, and I do not intend to remain here and wait for that foul beast to spring his trap. If we hear that they have moved south of that line that might stretch from the abbey of Bec to Lisieux, we shall both flee from this place. I have written to our household in Le Mans and ordered them to move our sons to the fortress of Angers, and I advise you to do the same. I bid you, husband, if you encounter the army of Stephen, fight him with all the strength in your being, knowing that if you should fail, there will be little standing between him and your children.

In the days before Easter, one of my spies reported to us that Stephen had indeed passed south of Lisieux and was just two days' march from Argentan. I could not wait any longer. We arranged ourselves in two bands: one led by Alexander de Bohun that would carry Prince William and Adela to the monastery of Mount Saint Michael, and another with Drogo and myself that would ride for Aquitaine. Though our ally the duke of Aquitaine had lately died on pilgrimage to Compostela, I had reason to believe they might harbor me for the time being.

I will never forget how I stood in the castle yard that morning, watching the men gather their things and mount their horses. I did not know how long we had before Stephen would arrive in Argentan: perhaps a day or two, or maybe only hours. The rising sun was not a sign of hope to me that morn. A carriage had been made ready for the transport of William, and at length Adela came out of the front gate of the castle with him lying in her arms, wrapped in a blanket. She walked over to where I was standing, and I could see that there were tears forming in her eyes even as they were in mine.

"Have no fear, my lady," she said. "You know I love Prince William as if he were my own, even as I love you like a sister. I will guard him with my life. We will make it safely to the monastery—you'll see!"

"Ever a fount of hope," I replied, then pressed my forehead against hers and held them both in my arms.

We stood there for a moment in the morning light, the fear and sadness flowing out of us in our tears.

"You had best be going," I finally said. "Here, let me take him while you climb in."

With great care, she placed him in my arms, and I looked down at his little eyes. He seemed happy: no lines of fear were written upon his brow as they were on mine. How precious was the life of that little boy! He was my sacred trust.

"The wet nurse said she prefers to ride on horseback," Adela told me, having taken her place in the carriage. "I suppose she must enjoy the wind in her hair!"

Either that or she intends to flee the company at the first sign of trouble, I thought. I told myself it was no matter, for another wet nurse could be found if necessary. Everything was a source of fear for me that morning.

"Be a good boy for Adela," I said to William. "You go to live among good people who will safeguard you. When the time is right, I promise I will see you again. I love you, William."

I leaned down and kissed his forehead, attempting to create a memory of his sweet smell, then handed him to my maid. As the carriage pulled away and slipped through the gate, I placed my hands over my heart and wept. I feared very much that the only place I would see my son again was in the hereafter. But there was truly no time to stand there and weep, for the usurper was on the prowl. Within a few minutes, I had mounted my own horse and sat waiting to depart. Drogo rode up beside me.

"I am so sorry that you were forced to part with another son," he said quietly, so that only I could hear. "There have been too many separations of late. Are we ever to be free of the cruelties of life?"

"We will have time to be philosophers later," I told him. "Come, let us flee before Count Stephen is here to join our discussion."

Within a few hours, we had passed within the relative safety of the forest and stopped for a moment by a stream that would have been pleasant in other circumstances. The trees rose high above it on either side, their branches swaying softly in the wind, and a chorus of birds was chirping. It was strange to think that such a fine day should be the source of so much misery. Didn't nature itself know of and share in my pain? Not for the first time in my life, I felt as if I was living in a kind of shadow world beside the real one.

There were many rocks down by the stream. As the knights moved to gather water and their horses also bowed down to drink, I sat on one of the larger stones and tried to keep the men from seeing that I was crying once again, for I had no desire for them to witness such a display of female sorrow. How I hated my cousin in that moment! In my mind, I saw Count Stephen snatching my infant son and ripping his small body apart. This thought only caused me to weep with greater force.

"Mother Mary, watch over him!" I prayed. "*Kýrie, eléison! Chríste eléison!*"

Suddenly, as if it were an answer to prayer, we heard a cry in the distance. The men who had bent over the water quickly rose and pulled their weapons out of their sheaths, and a few of the horses also stood upright and raised their ears. The noise was off to my left, coming from the direction of the path we had just abandoned. By instinct, I began looking around for Drogo. I saw him behind me, lowering his helm as he ran up the incline with his sword drawn.

"Who goes there?" he called. "Declare yourself!"

Some of the brush below the trees moved, and a single rider broke out, clearly out of breath. He bore the standard of Count William of Ponthieu, and I recognized him as one of the men we had left behind that morning.

"Lower your weapons!" I commanded the knights.

The messenger alighted and handed the reins to Drogo, then walked down toward me.

"Empress Mathilda," he said, "I hoped I would find you. We received word just after you left: Stephen's forces have turned back! They are not to march south after all!"

"What?!" I cried, hardly able to believe it. "Why? Did they say?"

"Apparently, they were all camped at Livarot when a dispute broke out between the Flemings and the Normans. Some men were killed, and now they say they will not fight together. They were forced to retreat, my lady. You are out of danger!"

"Oh, thank God!" I said. "Thank God, thank God, thank God!"

I dropped to my knees and gave way to the tears. Drogo bounded down and sank to my level—which was saying something for him—to embrace me. I felt very much as if I had been rescued out of the fires of hell.

"Should I tell Count William you will return?" the messenger asked.

I released Drogo and wiped the tears from my eyes.

"Yes," I replied, "and send word for my son William to be brought back as well. He shall be safe there, at least for now."

"Very good, my lady," he concluded.

Drogo helped me to my feet and we made ready to depart once again for the North. How much easier that journey would be without the phantom of death hanging over us all! As I was about to mount my steed, I reached in my satchel and pulled out the amber moth that I had placed there. For some time, it had been a source of frustration to me as much as comfort, but somehow I felt in that moment that it had helped to deliver me from danger, and I loved it again.

"You bring good fortune after all!" I whispered, kissed it, and returned it to its place.

CHAPTER TWENTY TWO

November 1166
Rouen, Normandy

I have written so much to you of my sons in their early days that it seems only right that I should record for you what took place today. You have heard of the births of my three boys—Henry, Geoffrey, and William—and the pain with which they entered this world, uncertain of their inheritance. It has been my unhappy lot to watch two of them pass from this world before their time, and now I am left with only my eldest: the boy for whom I sacrificed so much.

No boy is he now, but a man among men. Even I must bow the knee before him, for that is what happens when you give birth to the king of England. He sits upon the most powerful throne in Christendom. I did not foresee it in those dark days, when everything seemed to be lost. Indeed, I did not foresee it even when the days became brighter, but he has made a name for himself that could equal Charles the Great, by the strength of his will holding together an empire that stretches from the northern to the southern sea.

Yesterday, King Henry II came again to Rouen and sent word across the river for me to visit him. I rose from my bed as soon as the sun showed its face and made ready to depart, arriving at the castle in about the ninth hour—the same castle in which I first met Geoffrey of Anjou and gave birth to my second son. I entered the palace, where I spoke with the steward and bid him bring me to the king, but he replied only that his lord was in the middle of some delicate matter and must not be disturbed. He brought out a chair and I waited for half an hour in the entry way where I had once been shoved against the stairs by my father. Every stone of that place is filled with memory, which is part of why I usually avoid it: not all the memories are pleasant.

I was finally led up the stairs and down the passage that contains the private chambers. We entered the king's reception room—a place where I hardly set foot in the reign of my father—and I was told to have a seat while my son finished his business. As I sat there, I began to hear sounds that troubled me greatly: the distant cries of someone in great physical distress.

I rose and walked back into the passage. Hearing the sound again, I moved toward the source of the noise, which seemed to come from my old bed chamber. I had not been in there in many years, for the room was not fine enough for Queen Eleanor and she had given it over for storage. However, based on what was happening behind the closed door, someone had clearly found another use for it. I was about to lean my ear against the wall, when the door suddenly opened and the king stepped out.

The mere sight of my son is enough to set the fear of God in lesser men. He ended up quite tall, though I'm not sure how.

He certainly does not get his height from me, and his father was not exactly a giant. Yet with his long limbs and bright red hair, he is the kind of man who would be the center of attention even if he was not wearing a crown. Still, he is my son, and when my son does something naughty, I do not simply let it pass.

"Ah, mother!" he said, shutting the door before I could see anything. "You are here rather early."

"What was that noise?" I asked, an edge to my voice.

He looked back at the door and then at me. "I didn't hear anything."

"No, there was a noise, just in there," I argued, pointing toward the room whence he had come.

"Perhaps your hearing is not what it used to be," he said, stepping between myself and the door as if to make me forget it.

I crossed my arms and gave him a stern look. "I would say my hearing is better than yours, but I suspect you have some reason to deny it. That wouldn't be the papal messenger that everyone is talking about, now would it? The one who went missing?"

Ah! I had caught him out: I could see it in his face. He had the same look in his eyes that he used to get as a boy when I caught him and Geoffrey with their fingers in a pie.

"So what if it is?" he replied.

No sooner had he asked the question, than I heard a cry from inside the room that sent a chill through my bones.

"Good Lord!" I said. "What have you done to him? It sounds like they must be plucking his eyes out!"

"Nothing of the sort! They are merely scalding him a bit," he explained, as if it was a point of no consequence.

I shook my head. "And what do you hope to achieve by that? A boy of ten, perhaps eleven years, no? What could you learn from him?"

"He already gave up the man who sent him, a Master Herbert something or other. But of course, he is in the pay of—"

"Thomas Becket. Yes, I could have told you that without being scalded. What crime is this boy said to have committed?"

"He irks me," he said rather weakly. From the slight droop in his shoulders, I could tell that he knew just as much as I that it was a poor justification.

"My lord, had I cut off one of your toes every time you irked me, you would have been lame before you could walk. Now, I bid you, let this boy go. He is not the enemy."

"You cannot command me!" he whined, sounding not unlike his three-year-old self. "I am your king!"

"Yes, and I am your mother. You love your mother, don't you?"

Ah, maternal guilt! The most powerful force for good on this earth! That look of defiance gave way, and with one last roll of the eyes, he opened the door and called, "Germain! Let him be for now. We can hang him by the thumbs tomorrow." He then turned back to me and asked, "Happy?"

"Yes, thank you."

"Here, let's go into the other room," he said, closing the door. "I hate the sound of that groaning."

He led me back into the chamber I had been in earlier, which had only two chairs and a table next to the hearth. We sat and I poured some wine for both of us, then handed it to him.

"I am so glad you have come. Will you be staying long?" I asked.

"No, I make for Aumale, where I am to fix an annuity upon Count Matthew of Boulogne."

I almost spit out the sip of wine I had taken. "Why should you pay money to that weasel?"

"Because the count of Flanders demands it."

"I thought no one could command you," I replied with a smile.

"Yes, but as you know, he married Countess Marie of Boulogne."

"You mean Sister Marie, the nun whom he seized from her abbey and forced into marriage."

"She had no dowry, so it falls to me to provide him with a source of income."

He leaned back in his chair and drank deeply from his goblet. I was quite offended, for I did not see why men who stole brides should receive anything but a blow to the head. Indeed, when my second son, Geoffrey, had tried such a thing, I refused to speak to him for a few months.

"I see. And how much will we be paying the rapist?" I inquired.

"A thousand pounds a year."

"A thousand pounds a year?!"

"Yes, that is what I said."

"I do not see why he should be rewarded for such a barbarous act," I complained, shaking my head in dismay.

"The theft of wealthy brides is one of the foundations of the modern nobility."

"Yes, well ..."

Here I should mention that the woman my second son attempted to abduct was Eleanor of Aquitaine, right at the time she had been lately divorced from the French king. Yes, that is the same Eleanor who my first son married shortly thereafter—the same woman who became Queen Eleanor of England and brought all her lands into the Angevin Empire.

"I did not steal Queen Eleanor!" the king declared, showing a flash of anger. In general, my Henry is not given to rages, but when he does become angry, there is no one within a hundred leagues who doubts it. "It was your other son who tried to do that. She was eager to marry me, and why not? Who wouldn't want to be queen of this fair realm? Of course, you never liked her."

"That is not true!" I objected. Indeed, it seemed a rather harsh blow, well past anything I had earned.

"You never liked her because she got her pick of a husband and you did not."

"How could you say that?!"

"She got her divorce. You were left in misery."

"You are so far off the mark, you are in danger of shooting your own horse!" I charged, though in truth he was quite close to the mark.

He laughed loudly. "Oh, my dear mother! Have I irked you? Perhaps you wish to lock me up?"

"Fine," I said, crossing my arms firmly across my chest. "I admit that Queen Eleanor and I have not always been the best of friends. But what about you? When was the last time you saw your wife?"

"When I sent her back to England with Prince Richard. She was none too happy about it. I can assure you of that!" Here he seemed to smile, as if he delighted in causing her annoyance.

"Why did you send her away? The two of you hardly speak any more."

"She was angry that I wished to settle Aquitaine upon Prince Henry." Here he meant his eldest son.

"And she wants it for Richard?" I asked, a bit surprised.

"Yes. She would give everything to that boy if she had the chance. I don't know what she sees in him that is any better than the others."

"Well, mothers do tend to have one son who is most favored."

"Yes, we know William was yours, though you did him an ill turn by denying him Ireland."

"Do not speak of him, I beg you!" I pleaded.

He creased his brow. "Why ever not?"

My mood had shifted rather quickly, and I was feeling again the pain of loss. "I still mourn William. He wanted to marry Lady Isabel more than anything and Archbishop Thomas forbade it out of spite. You could have fought for him, but you did nothing."

The king did not respond at once, but stopped to fill both our glasses again. He then sat back and breathed deeply. "What could I have done? There was the problem of consanguinity."

I scoffed. "It would not have been difficult to get the papal dispensation. Oh, how William loved that woman! It broke his heart, I tell you. That is why he is dead now."

We had waded very deep into my own heart. At the beginning, when he was only my son's chancellor, I had loathed Thomas Becket because I thought him too worldly and hungry for the kingdom of this earth, much like several bishops I had known in former days. When he was made archbishop of Canterbury by my eldest son and then refused the marriage of my youngest son, I was given a second reason to loath Thomas Becket. To me, he was not a guardian of the Church, but a man thoroughly convinced of his own import who would stop at nothing to conserve his own power.

"I do not blame you for hating Archbishop Thomas," King Henry said, rather avoiding the issue.

"I do not hate him," I said, though it was more a lie than the truth. "That I leave to you: you who were so intent on promoting him, even though he was not fit to wear the cloth. I warned you, Henry. I warned you! And now he has excommunicated half your counselors and would have done the same to you were you not on your sick bed!"

"I was not really sick," he said, winking at me.

"Yes, a clever ruse, but he will soon be wise to your methods. Tell me, my son: what are you going to do? Remember what happened to my first husband! You do not want to place your eternal soul in danger, not to mention your kingdom."

He nodded in agreement. "I have sent John of Oxford, the dean of Salisbury, to meet with Pope Alexander and have his office restored. Then I will have him gather evidence against *Maître* Becket. Bishop Gilbert is working with me as well. None of the English bishops favor Thomas. They see through his words and judge him by his actions."

I watched as he took another drink. So many thoughts and feelings passed through me. I hated that this boy that I had raised had ended up in this position, at war with a powerful man of God, if indeed he was not a man of Satan. I longed for peace in my old age, but I suppose such things are not granted to mothers of kings. Where had I gone wrong with my sons? Had I left them alone too long? That was always my fear when I entered the fight against Stephen. I had gone to defend their inheritance, and they turned into Angevins rather than Normans. Well, perhaps Henry has a bit of the Norman about him, but there is nothing of my own mother: nothing English.

"Well, I hope you are right," I concluded, "but I bid you safeguard the integrity of the Church. It is the archbishop who is in the wrong, not the Church itself."

He bowed his head. "As always, empress mother, I shall cherish your counsel."

In his own way, I knew that he was telling me to cease giving advice. "Come here and give your mother a kiss," I said, extending my hands.

He leaned in to embrace me, then returning to his chair, I noticed a sadness in his eyes for which I could not account.

"What is it?" I asked. "Is something the matter?"

He folded his hands and stared at the floor, evidently considering whether or not to confess. This caused me to fear the worst, and I was a bit relieved when he said, "I met a woman."

"A woman?"

"Yes, at Woodstock: the fairest thing on God's green earth."

"Oh, Henry. You're not sleeping with her, are you?"

"Well, not now! I'm in Normandy!" he replied, thereby confirming that he had had her many times over.

"I wondered," I said, shaking both my head and my finger at him. "You and Queen Eleanor have always been together for the Christmas feast, but not this past year. I should have known something was amiss. You know, she told me of her suspicions."

He raised his brows. "When?"

"Last year, before your daughter was born."

"No, that must have been someone else."

"What?" I was beginning to wonder exactly how many women he had bedded.

"I only met Rosamund this year."

Rosamund: there was a name with little promise. As we spoke, I was fairly certain that half the Rosamunds in the world could be found in the arms of a bishop.

"You have too many women—just like your father," I concluded. "I do hope you can keep them all straight."

"No, Rosamund is different: I love her!" he said earnestly, gripping the arm of his chair.

"Oh, you do not!"

"Yes, I do!" he cried, rising to his feet. "I burn with passion for her!"

My, what lust does to us! I thought, staring at the absurd figure of my son, gone mad with yearning. I motioned for him to sit down.

"My lord, you spend far too much time around the queen's poets, and now their drivel fills your head!"

"Why not? Why shouldn't I have her? I am the king!" he cried, pounding his fist into the arm of the chair.

"Your wife is about to give birth as we speak. Have you forgotten her?"

"There are times when I wish I could," he muttered.

"Is that so? Well, perhaps I should write to King Louis and let him know that you wish to return his wife. Oh, wait! He has been married twice over since then, and now he has his son. He has played the game better than you."

"I should think not! I have three sons already—soon to be four—and I have Aquitaine!"

I laughed. "Your wife has Aquitaine, and should you forget her, they might be willing to forget you."

He pursed his lips and breathed heavily. "I will not give up Rosamund. She brings me more pleasure than anything in this world. Except my sons, of course."

"Yes, of course. That is why you sent Prince Richard away and denied him any inheritance. I beg you, my liege, when I am dead and gone, think more kindly of him."

"What is this?" he asked, his mood suddenly changed. "You aren't really dying, are you?"

I let out a sigh. "I am certainly not getting any younger. You may soon have to do without me."

He knelt before my chair and touched my hand. "Let me have my physician examine you."

"And what can he do about old age? I have lived through war, desolation, sickness, and heartache. I have seen enough of this earth. Very soon, death will come knocking at my door, and when it does, I shall welcome it as a friend."

He cast his gaze down at the floor, his green eyes full of sadness. "I do not want you to go."

I placed my hand on his bearded chin and raised it so that I could meet his eyes. "Even you cannot keep me here, King Henry II of England, lord of Normandy and Aquitaine. Grant me this one last freedom: give me leave to pass from this world before I have become a blundering fool."

"Someday, but not yet. We must solve this crisis with Archbishop Thomas. Then I will permit you to go your way."

I placed my hand upon his shoulder. "Would that any king had such power, my son."

Enough of the present! I must return to the past. I left off just as I learned that we were not to become the feast on which the vultures of Flanders would feed—not yet, in any case. Such a reversal of fortune requires some explanation, and we soon had it. Ever since he reached out his greedy hands to seize the royal crown of England, Count Stephen of Boulogne had relied upon William of Ypres to command the scores of Flemish mercenaries that he had purchased with my father's gold. William was an able field commander, either in spite of or because of his willingness to carry out detestable acts that would strike fear into the heart of any man. But for all his skill in battle, he possessed little of that personal charm that would win him the love of the nobility. Many of the Normans suspected him from the very beginning on account of his origin, and this only increased during Stephen's progress through Normandy.

By the time they stopped in Lisieux to gather more men, the rancor between the Normans and Flemings had caused such a strain that a breach was inevitable. They say a fight broke out over a barrel of wine, but the truth is that none of the Normans were willing to go into battle under the command of William of Ypres. Thus, they simply gathered their things and returned by the way they had come, leaving Stephen's forces in such disarray that he had to call off the march.

I have often taken comfort in the knowledge that my enemies suffered from just as many problems as myself, which could certainly be said of Stephen in that hour. Indeed, the sweetest victory is won not by one's triumph on the field of battle, but by the folly of one's adversary. Here then is another example of Stephen's folly.

Throughout that spring, Earl Robert of Gloucester was not with Stephen in the East. He remained at his castle in Caen and took no part in the usurper's affairs, to the point that he declined to attend the royal court despite being summoned more than once. Any other noble might have found the king upon their threshold the very next day, ready to do battle, but Stephen plainly feared Earl Robert, for he chose to do nothing instead of opposing him.

Yet the earl had an enemy at court: William of Ypres. Day by day, the tiresome Fleming would whisper in his master's ear, planting the seeds of suspicion. Earl Robert was not merely seeking to maintain stability in the West, he argued, but was engaged in active rebellion against the king's authority. Moreover, there were many who said that Robert was in communication with me and plotted to transfer his allegiance. We have already seen how false that rumor was, but a rumor never failed for lack of some foundation in truth.

One day, I was seated on a bench in the garden of Argentan Castle that had been planted in the yard two years earlier. It seemed quite out of place amid the stables, coops, and smithy, but it was the best I could do. William was being cared for inside the keep, and I had a moment to simply enjoy reading the scriptures amid the glories of nature, even if the chief glory I saw was a rooster. The gate opened on the far side of the yard, and I looked up to see Alexander de Bohun and his knights returning from a raid. I returned my gaze to the written word, only to be interrupted a minute later by Alexander himself, still in his riding cloak, boots, and gloves.

"Did you hear the news?" he asked, as he approached with a smile on his face.

"What news?"

"Earl Robert is claiming that Stephen tried to kill him!"

"What?!" I cried, dropping the word of the Lord. "When?"

"I don't know. He says that William of Ypres laid an ambush for him, but he got word of the conspiracy and was able to escape. Now he is charging Stephen openly, and it seems that the false king has made no attempt to deny it, for he swore an oath before his friend the archbishop of Rouen that he would never again take part in such a vile crime. Well, there's the proof!"

Good Lord! I thought. *The very worst thing Stephen could have done—and he's gone and done it. I'm not his true foe. He is his own worst enemy.*

"I cannot believe it!" I said, shaking my head. "Why would he do such a thing? Stephen is a fool indeed to alienate Earl Robert. He really sought to murder him? It has the mark of William of Ypres: his stink is all over this."

"Actually, this could work out quite well for Earl Robert," the captain replied, as if the thought had only just occurred to him. "He has Stephen by his stones now."

Not that Stephen had any to begin with, for they all belong to his wife, I mused, but kept the thought to myself.

"It is time for Count Geoffrey to strike," I agreed. "The only trouble is, when he comes into Normandy, he does more harm than good. His methods are so brutal that he has set all the people against us. I suppose it is little wonder they despise him, since that was my first instinct. This is a time for real skill of persuasion, not a fool who hacks blindly and prays he hits his foe!"

Alexander said nothing, for he was faithful to Count Geoffrey, but I gathered that he shared my concerns. Stephen had made a mistake, and there was a chance to gain control of Normandy for my sons and me. What a horrid time to be stuck with a commander who angered everyone he met! I truly wondered what was going through my brother's mind. He would rather side with a man who tried to kill him than the sister who longed to grant him everything!

Do I know my brother at all? I wondered. *Do I know anyone or anything?*

Count Geoffrey did gather some four hundred knights and enter Normandy once again, setting fire to several villages near Exmes and creating more enemies. Yet apart from the addition of Baldwin de Redvers aiding our cause in the Cotentin, our forces were no stronger than they had been the last time Count Geoffrey invaded. The major difference was that Stephen's own forces were in complete confusion. By merely harrying him in the South, my husband was able to gain a truce with Stephen, and the traitor was forced to crawl back to Rouen like a wounded animal. The French king may have proclaimed Stephen to be lord over Normandy, but the state of affairs on the ground showed otherwise.

Around this time, I received a letter from a man I had never met, but who shared a powerful connection with myself: indeed, we had shared a father. Reginald de Dunstanville, made earl of Cornwall by Stephen, was the natural son of one Sibylla Corbet, who had known King Henry I in every sense of the word. I had never made his acquaintance, for my father begat so many offspring that it would not have been possible for me to meet every one of them—a sad testament to his lack of character. Reginald had risen in the esteem of his fellow man until Stephen granted him the earldom two years earlier. He thus owed everything to the usurper, and that he was willing to write to me was proof enough of the animosity that had arisen against Stephen.

In his letter, my brother was careful not to reveal his full intent, no doubt for fear that it might fall into the wrong hands. He simply wrote that he had passed through the

Cotentin—here I recognized that he must have spoken with Baldwin de Redvers—and would soon be in Argentan. It seemed clear that he intended to forsake Stephen and join our cause, but I warned the castle guard to make preparations in case it was some sort of trick.

When I saw Reginald for the first time, I might have known he was my brother simply by the shape of his nose, the color of his eyes, and the manner of his movement. Here was the very image of our mutual father brought back to life, apart from the girth he had acquired in later years: the same black hair and thick black brows, the same broad shoulders. He rode through the castle gate on a tall brown horse with a white patch on its head like a diamond, or like the bald spot my father developed later in life.

I stood in the middle of the yard to receive the earl, with Drogo standing at my right hand and the rest of the knights directly behind me in case of trouble—not that I imagined there could be much trouble, for my half brother came alone. The earl alighted from his horse with such ease, he might have been as light as air.

"Empress Mathilda!" he cried, kneeling before me and removing his hat. "I have come to offer you my undying fealty and the true love of a brother!"

This was a relief. Although I had suspected this was the reason for his visit, one can never be entirely sure in such situations.

"Earl Reginald," I said, as he took my hand and kissed it, "your coming was most unforeseen, but I am glad of it. What brought about this change of heart?"

He stood up to his full height, which though well above my own was still no match for Drogo. The younger man looked at the knight as one might a strange tree, then shook his head slightly as if attempting to regain his line of thought.

"When Stephen came to England, he claimed that King Henry had named him as his successor, releasing the nobles from their oath," Earl Reginald explained. "Who was I to argue? I believed the man to be my rightful sovereign. But when Earl Robert did not follow for so long, and then what happened to Lord Baldwin—he is a good friend of mine, you know. When I saw the depths to which Stephen was willing to take us all, it became clear to me that he had come to power against the will of the Lord. I do not believe our father ever changed his mind. And Stephen, he has set aside the great men of the land and raised up a pack of fools in their place! The Beaumonts control everything now. Even Bishop Roger of Salisbury has found himself on the outside looking in, as they say. I could not remain in the service of Stephen. Forgive me, my lady. I should have seen the truth long ago."

He spoke earnestly, clutching his hat in his hands and often looking down at the ground. I felt I had every reason to believe him, for I knew the wicked ways of the usurper.

"I do forgive you, and I embrace you as a sister," I said. "I can see you will prove your worth. I remember once, some years ago, brother Robert said you were quite a good shot."

"I can show you," he offered, his eyes suddenly alight.

Before I could reply, he walked up to one of the knights behind me and pointed at the crossbow he was holding. When the knight obliged, Reginald quickly readied the weapon and raised it to fire.

"That cat," he said, pointing at a poor orange creature wandering past the stalls against the castle wall, some twenty paces away.

I did not have time to object. He pulled the lever and let the arrow fly. It was a direct hit. The animal let out a terrible noise, as if it was being delivered of a demon that was pulled out through its bowels. It fell to the ground, blood running through its fur. All the men clapped and cheered, though I felt rather sorry for the beast.

"Well done, sir!" Drogo cried, patting Reginald on the back.

"Yes, if we are met by a band of vicious cats, we shall know whom to call ere they claw us to death," I said. "Come, Earl Reginald! I am most eager to hear all you have to tell us."

"With pleasure, my lady," he replied, and we walked together into the castle.

As we were about to enter through the main door, I turned back just in time to see a crow land near the cat and take a nibble. I let out a sigh and thought to myself, *Shadows and dust. Shadows and dust.*

Earl Reginald did quickly prove his value to our cause. Along with Lord Baldwin and Stephen de Mandeville, he prowled across the western reaches of Normandy, striking quickly and then retreating. They did their best to make all those faithful to Stephen feel ill at ease. Yet even as the usurper set sail for England, taking with him the Beaumont twins and the rest of the nobility, I felt as if we were no closer to our final goal. We held only a small portion of Normandy, and in England Stephen's reign seemed assured.

The truce between my husband and Stephen did allow my boys to come join me in Argentan for the season of Advent, and this was a source of no little comfort. I had not seen them for almost two years, though I had spent every moment devoted to their cause. Henry was by then more than four years old and his brother Geoffrey not far behind. Young William had become more active and made sounds we all attempted to translate. Amid the gloom of those days, it was a joy to have my sons so near. I had hoped and prayed for them for so long, and though I daily feared for the state of their inheritance, it was a blessing to simply share their company. After all, it was the first time I had all three of them together. Not even my usual annoyance with their father could steal away my joy.

On Christmas Eve, as we waited for supper to be made ready, I let Adela play with the younger boys in one room while I read to Henry by the fire in the great hall. Rather, I let Henry read to me, for he was just beginning to make sense of the words on the page. Two couches had been placed near the hearth in the middle of the room, and we sat together on one of them, he resting against my shoulder and I holding the book open. There were few adornments on the stone walls, and the light red paint was peeling to reveal the yellow stone beneath, but it hardly mattered: reading with my son was the greatest magic of the season.

We had only been at it a few minutes when Drogo entered through the door before us, the look on his face one of complete surprise. He stood just across the threshold, as if he was afraid to move any further.

"What is it, Drogo?" I asked, suddenly very nervous. "You look as if you've seen a ghost."

"You have a visitor, my lady. You won't believe who it is."

"Saint Nicholas with coins!" Henry guessed.

"No, someone rather more alive," the knight replied.

I was in no mood for questions. "Enough of these games, Drogo. Just tell us!"

Before he could answer, another man came through the door still clothed for the winter weather. He threw back his hood, and when I saw his face, it almost caused my heart to stop.

"Who is that, mother?" young Henry asked.

I swallowed the lump in my throat. "That is your uncle, Henry: Earl Robert of Gloucester, ambassador from the reign of error."

There before us stood the man to whom all our thoughts had turned for the past two years: the man who, in lending his support to Stephen, had made an end of my hopes. Beneath a beard that had grown gray, I could see his lips slightly parted as he breathed heavily, either from exercise or fear. Why had he come? Had he come alone? Of all the betrayals I had experienced over the past year, his was the one that had hurt the most, and though I had attempted to bury that pain and carry on, seeing him again made me feel as if my heart had been pierced anew.

"The earl requests a private audience," Drogo explained.

I had half a mind to throw my brother out that instant, but I sensed this would be the wrong decision. After all, he would not have come unless he had some message of great import to relay. Earl Robert was a man of such power that I simply had to hear whatever he wished to say, even if I felt like punching him. There was also something in his eyes—perhaps a sense of penitence, perhaps a last trace of brotherly affection, or perhaps the skill of a man intent to deceive. I knew not, but I knew I would regret it if I did not speak to him.

"Very well, then," I said quietly. "Sir Drogo, you may leave us, but my son stays. Let Earl Robert look into the eyes of the boy he cheated out of an inheritance." As I spoke these words, I looked directly into my brother's eyes. I hoped that they would strike at his heart that had grown cold.

"As you wish," Drogo said, and then departed.

Robert and I continued to stare at one another. Without speaking, I motioned toward the couch just across from us. My brother removed his wet things, setting them down by the fire to dry, and sank into the seat with a great sigh, smoothing out his short hair. He had clearly ridden all day to reach us.

"You must be wondering why I've come," he said.

I sat a bit more upright and firmly gripped my son, pulling him close to myself.

"I have wondered a great many things concerning you," I told him. "Why you denied me, offered your loyalty to that thief even after he sought to kill you, never returned my letters, abandoned so easily the love we once held … but by all means, tell me why you've come. We can go from there."

He leaned forward and folded his hands together. He seemed to be considering every word carefully.

"I recognize the pain I have caused you, how my actions must appear," he said. "I imagine you have lived through hell these past two years."

"Do not presume to know what I have suffered, you who have been content to sit in your fortress, far from the troubles of us all!" I cried.

I was rather surprised to hear him laugh. It seemed he did not agree with my judgment. My anger increased.

"I can see that it will not do for me to circle around the point, so let me come to it directly," he continued. "I was there with the king when he died, and I was forced to stay with the body until it was shipped off to England. I was as surprised to hear of Stephen's elevation as you no doubt were. I was trying to prevent his brother from seizing the throne, only to find that it was already taken. I knew then that my choice would be vital, and I feared for England under Stephen's control. He is a man of inferior character, not fit to sit upon the throne of Saint Edward. We have both known that for years."

"Then why did you offer him your fealty?" I inquired, finding no peace in his words.

"I could see that it would do no good to fight Stephen at that time. The earls had all declared for him along with the Church, and he had the royal treasury at his command. I could not have defeated him in open battle, and wherever I went, his spies followed. I sent word to Brian fitz Count, asking if he might have heard something from you, but he had not."

"I must have sent you twenty messages!" I cried.

He nodded. "I do not doubt it, but only one or two of them actually made it to my door, and I was afraid to open them, for I knew that even those within my own household might report me, and then my lands and all my wealth would be forfeit. It took me some time to determine who among my servants was true. In the meantime, as I said, I spoke with Brian, and we both decided it was best to pledge our allegiance to Stephen, the better to win his trust. Then we might work to eat away at his support. But this is the key: when I pledged to him, I did so on the condition that he would abide by all his promises. I knew full well that he would break them within the year, and thus I would be released from my oath. It was all for show. Maud, I have spent the past two years making efforts on your behalf. My true loyalty to you has never ceased."

This struck me as hard to believe, and I scoffed openly. "If that is true, then why did you fail to inform me of your intentions? Count Geoffrey marched within ten miles of your home, but you did nothing!"

"Forgive me, but I do not trust Count Geoffrey. I think he may be your real enemy and not Stephen, for I hear nothing but complaints from those who have had the misfortune of being in his path. They say his men violate both the law and the women. Two years of fighting, and he has nothing to show for it."

Somewhat to my dismay, my brother had made a good point. I too had been frustrated with Count Geoffrey's lack of progress, and I had heard the same rumors about his behavior. I did not doubt that he made as many enemies as he defeated. However, this would never have been a problem had Robert remained faithful to me and served as my commander.

"No thanks to those of you who have been fighting for the other side!" I declared, letting go of my son and leaning forward slightly to yell at him all the better.

"I have been fighting for you the whole time!" he argued, pressing down upon his seat. "At Exeter, when Baldwin's men surrendered, Stephen was going to have them all killed. Thanks to me, he spared their lives—indeed, he let them leave and follow whatever lord they preferred. When he came here to make war on you, I did not take part. No, I remained in Caen and did nothing to help him."

"And nothing to help us."

"There you are wrong. I was working with our brother, Reginald. I entreated him to declare for you, knowing that Stephen trusted him so completely that he would not have set so many spies about him."

Again, I scoffed. "He never mentioned anything of the sort."

"Because I told him not to! Indeed, the very rumor that I might have spoken with Reginald was enough to place me in peril. No sooner had I done so, than I received several summons to court, only I knew that Stephen intended to have me arrested for treason. He sent the wolf of Ypres after me with enough men to kill me ten times over! Of course, when I was able to prove their guilt, they were forced to repent. Even so, I saw that I could no longer work in the shadows, for Stephen would have me killed either way. I waited for him to leave, and now I have come to you."

I did not reply, but simply sat there with my arms crossed, staring at my brother. I thought back on everything that had happened in the past two years. It was possible that his story could be true. Everything seemed to fit. Part of me longed to accept it—to believe that there was still goodness in the world, and that the pain I had felt could be removed. But part of me remained unwilling to believe and desperate to punish.

"Mother?" Henry suddenly said, rather meekly.

I had been so caught up in Robert's words that I had quite forgotten the child sitting beside me in silence. I looked down and saw that his eyes were rather wide. He did not seem comfortable with the discussion.

"Yes, my love?" I replied, brushing the red curls back from his face.

"May I go play with Geoffrey?"

I nodded my head. "Perhaps you had better."

He made his way out, and it was just my brother and I sitting across from each other, one set of eyes meeting the other.

"Maud, you must believe me!" he pleaded, as soon as the door was shut.

"Earl Robert, I have heard your tale, and a part of me does want to believe it, but given that you have already gone back on your word, I have no reason to think that you might not do so again. Tell me, if you have always been content to work in secret, why should you approach me now? Perhaps you have only been working for yourself."

"I come to you now because I believe that Stephen is weak. His reign is failing. He does not see it yet, but all around him the walls are crumbling and about to give way. He has gone to such trouble to promote the *Famille* Beaumont that he has become blind to the discontent of those around him. His brother, Bishop Henry, hates Waleran with the blinding heat of a thousand suns, as does Bishop Roger of Salisbury. It will not be long before one of them eats the other. And as for Stephen, he has already spent most of the money he took from the treasury to satisfy his Flemish mercenaries. We have seen what that did when he was in Normandy, with William of Ypres chasing off all the Normans. I tell you, he is making enemies on all sides, and it will not be long before they are looking to change their allegiance. That is why I dare to speak to you now, and if you will have me, I intend in the New Year to declare myself wholly your supporter. I will lead my men into battle on your behalf, I swear to you!"

His words were like a balm for my soul, yet I had been spurned so many times that I had learned to trust no one. I looked again into his eyes, searching for something—I knew not what.

"It seems too good to be true, that you could have been on my side all along," I said, tears forming in my eyes. "Robert, you cannot know how many times I prayed to God that you would keep your oath. I did not understand why you should give yourself over to your chief enemy." My voice broke and I breathed in deeply. "Robert, I loved you, and I thought you loved me. When I thought I had lost that love—"

"But now you know that you did not lose it!" he said, moving over to sit next to me. "I never betrayed you, nor did Brian, nor did any of your true friends. We are with you, and our time is coming. Stephen's reign will be at an end."

I wiped my eyes and laughed softly. "Careful! I did not say yet whether I would accept your conversion. But you have spoken with Lord Brian? He supports our cause?"

"Of course he does! He loves you too. You know that."

"You mean as his ruler—his lady."

He tilted his head slightly. "Yes, as his lady and as a woman."

"Ha!" I cried, shaking my head. "I do not think he could love me that much if he abandoned me."

"That again? For God's sake! Listen, Maud. Our father is dead now, so I will tell you plainly. Brian spoke with the king and asked for you as his wife: a mark of courage if ever there was one, for he knew he would likely be sent into poverty. I told him beforehand that he was out of his mind, and he had always been a man of such good sense, but his will was set in stone. He thought the hazard was on his part alone and that he was sparing you from harm, but he was wrong. The king said that if he did not marry the Lady Mathilda of Wallingford straight away, he would strip you of your titles and your inheritance, force you both into exile, and have you excommunicated! That is why Brian did what he did. The king forbade him to speak the truth of what happened to you out of fear that it might prevent you from giving him up. Brian was made to act as if he was indifferent to you, but he struggled to play that role. He inquired with me often about your welfare. Trust me, there is no one on earth who is more on your side than Lord Brian. You may be as certain of his loyalty as you are of mine, if not more so."

Well, those were words I did not think to ever hear! I sensed by this admission as much as anything that Earl Robert must be telling the truth. Perhaps that was what my heart wanted to believe, but it did make sense. In the space of a moment, I had come to view the past several years of my life differently. I thought I had been forsaken by the only man I ever loved, but suddenly I saw that I was not forsaken at all: indeed, Brian had remained true to me in every way he could, even as I had avoided him, scorned him, and attempted to cut him out of my life. And of course I still loved him, even as he still loved me. I could not prevent a small smile from breaking out on my face, and Robert was quick to seize on it.

"Ah, I see I should have led off with that!" my brother proclaimed. "But what say you? Do you accept my offer of fealty? I have already hazarded my own life for you, and I will do so as many times as it takes until you and your son receive back what is rightfully yours."

I shook my head and took his hands in my own. "If what you say is true, then of course, I welcome you gladly—nay, joyfully! Robert, you have no idea how happy you have made me, and not just because we have a real chance of victory now. To have every person I loved turn their back on me and break their word, to be without friends or family in this world: that is how I have felt these past two years. Do you know how much I have missed you? Every time something would happen, I would say to myself, 'I wish Robert was here. We might have laughed about that!' I see now what you have done for me. I wish I could have rewarded you earlier, but I will do so now."

"My reward will be to see England restored to its proper order."

"With your help, it shall be," I said, letting go of his hands. "But what do we do now?"

"We must wait until the moment when Stephen is weakest. He is a good enough soldier, but a poor administrator. Not much longer now, and he will have given the lords of England and Normandy a reason to rebel. And the Church has supported him on account of his brother, Bishop Henry, but already that bond is under great strain. Stephen bought the Church with promises he cannot keep. In time, he may well lose their support, and that will be our sign. I have men that can be called on to fight, and they will not fail me, they will not fail us. Have patience, sister! When the moment comes, the usurper will not know what hit him. We will make him pay for what he has done to you!"

"Honestly, Robert, as much as I may cherish the thought of revenge, my main concern is for my sons. It is for them that I fight."

"Very well spoken. Now, did I smell food when I came in?" he asked, rising from his seat.

"Yes, I think they have made something, but it's not grand. We are in the middle of a war, after all."

He nodded. "War has a way of making the smallest morsels seem like manna from heaven. Come, let us eat together! I want to meet these nephews, but then I must be away. Stephen cannot know that I was here."

"I understand," I said, rising from the couch. "Thank you for coming, Robert. You have made this the best Christmas."

He placed his arm around me. "With God's help, the next one will be even better."

CHAPTER TWENTY THREE

The return of Earl Robert of Gloucester into my life seemed to awaken my spirit. I felt a hope I had not enjoyed in years. Of course, it did not hurt that I had also learned the truth about Brian. I would have preferred a good three days' discussion on that subject, but sadly, we were in the middle of a war and it was necessary for my brother to depart before Stephen discovered his trip to Argentan.

I do remember something Robert said to me shortly before he departed: something that came almost as a revelation from God.

"When King Henry saw the courage that you and Brian displayed on behalf of one another and the sacrifice you were willing to endure, I believe it struck him with fear. The love you shared was pure, and I do not think our father understood pure love or had ever experienced it. He had known both desire and pride, but neither of those things is quite the same as love. Every thought and feeling he had was oriented to and through himself rather than given on behalf of another, and because he could not properly give, he could not properly receive. Yes, your love and courage scared him, and so he responded the only way he knew how: with brute force. He saw something that seemed to oppose him, and he had to crush it. Force was the only language he truly understood—you and I both know this. He was a man of war. Not like you, Maud. You can feel and feel deeply. Some say that is a weakness, and the pain you have endured has perhaps made it seem so, but it is also a strength. Because you feel deeply, you live more fully. You can perceive the motives of others, and while some would merely use this for their advantage, you also use it for the advantage of others. You are clever as a fox, but you can also be kind. Our father was a bull who knew only how to charge. That was his great failing."

I meditated on those words for some time after he left, turning the amber moth over in my hand as I did so. They helped me to understand both myself and my father. I had felt such a fool for loving Brian when I thought he had betrayed me, especially given that I still loved him, no matter how hard I tried to deny it. Once I learned the whole truth, I came to see that the real tragedy was not what I thought.

We had enjoyed a pure love, even as Robert said. While everyone else was off committing every conceivable form of fornication, we cared for one another deeply. Goodness, even after his apparent betrayal I had caught myself worrying about Brian: whether he was in good health, whether he was happy, *et cetera*. I could not make myself stop feeling that, as angry as I was, because I loved him so deeply: I loved him for more than what he could give me.

My father had taken that pure love and tainted it. He had ensured that any feeling I had for Brian would be wrong, sinful, adulterous! In so doing, he stole from me one of the most wonderful things I had ever enjoyed in the course of my life and caused me to spend every day in guilt. Yes, every time I thought of Brian and felt a trace of love still there, I was struck with guilt, for I was married to another. Not that I wanted to be: that was all my father's doing. Oh, how I hated him for it!

Yet Robert's words had also caused me to see that I was greater and stronger than my father, for no matter how much he had taken from me and no matter how much guilt he had heaped upon my conscience, he could not force me to become what he was. Certainly, there were days when I was in danger of turning cruel—of allowing my hatred to consume my soul. But even in my anger, the love did not die. It was still there, a flame flickering in the wind, struggling to remain alive.

If my father could not kill the hope in me, I thought, *then I'll be damned if I let Stephen do so!*

Alas, this personal revelation did not change everything: we were still in a fight to the death with the usurper. Although my brother had not yet announced his change of allegiance for very good reasons, my uncle David had declared himself faithful to me from the beginning. When Stephen returned to England after failing in Normandy, he was greeted by a message from King David of Scotland demanding that he surrender the earldom of Northumbria according to their agreement. The false king refused, believing as he did that he could defeat any invasion from the North. King David and his son, Prince Henry, at once set out to prove just how wrong the traitor was.

When the Scots crossed the River Tweed and marched south into England, they must have seemed to the people of that land every bit as foreign and barbarous as their ancestors had in the days of the Romans. I cannot vouch for the behavior of my uncle's men, for they not only seized English castles but also women, children, and the aged, forcing them into servitude and killing any who resisted. Such things are not unheard of in war, but the result was that the lords of northern England, who had long disputed with one another, united in their hatred of the Scots. Yet although Stephen did press north as far as the Tweed and forced the retreat of King David's forces, they did not meet in battle at that time.

Even as all of this was happening, those of us in Normandy were assembling for an invasion of our own. I arranged in secret to meet with both Earl Robert and Count Geoffrey at the beginning of April 1137, when there would be a break in the fighting for Lent. The difficulty lay in finding a place where we could gather without attracting attention, for if it became known that the three of us were speaking with one another, we would lose any chance of surprising Stephen when the time came. Count William Talvas knew of a hunting lodge just west of the River Orne, about a day's ride south of Caen. It was not too close to Falaise and allowed Earl Robert to claim that he was simply out stalking.

It was as I was traveling there with Count Geoffrey that I recognized just how perfect was our choice, for although we knew where the lodge was, it still took us quite some time to find it, so deep was it within the forest. I was soon less worried that Stephen's spies would discover us and more worried that Earl Robert would not. We had to wait a full day before he arrived, accompanied by a single knight. So it was Robert and his man along with myself, Count Geoffrey, Count William, and two other servants: not a large party by any means.

The lodge, as it was called, was little more than a hovel, having only a single room. There was a very small hearth, two pallets for sleeping, a small table with two chairs, a pair of chests, and two seats by the fire. I remember that the floor boards were rotten in places, and you could see through to the dirt below. I paced across them nervously as we waited for my brother's arrival, while the counts Geoffrey and William sat at the table in silence.

What is taking Robert so long? I thought. *I hope he gets here soon. It was bad enough that I had to spend the night with these men!*

"Stop that incessant pacing, wife!" ordered Count Geoffrey. "It will not bring him here any faster."

"I shall walk if I wish to," I replied.

"I'm sure there is no need to be nervous, my lady," offered William Talvas. "The messenger said he would be here by midday, and from the position of the sun, I'd say that is still half an hour away."

I was about to respond, but was cut off by my husband.

"It's no use, William. She cares far more about him than she does either of us, though I cannot think why after he has treated her so poorly."

You're one to talk, I thought.

I did not speak what I was feeling, as the two of us were not alone and I wanted to maintain the appearance of unity. In truth, I was very much in danger of loathing my husband as much as I had done in the old days, for ever since I had learned of Lord Brian's continual devotion, my husband's own words and actions appeared all the more lacking in honor. Many times, I had caught myself dwelling on memories and had been forced to tear my mind away. How could I not think of him when my husband offered me no affection? Why would I not want to cling to those memories of real love? But that was a dangerous road to take—to think of things as they might have been, or perhaps as they ought to be. It could only place my soul in peril.

Even as I was having these thoughts, there was a knock at the door and the two men rose from the table. Count William looked through a small hole in the door, then opened it to reveal the form of Earl Robert of Gloucester, who entered and greeted us each in turn.

"Empress Mathilda, Count Geoffrey, Count William. Let's make this quick."

"I'll just see myself out then," said William Talvas.

"Thank you, Count William!" I called, as he shut the lone door behind him, leaving the three of us standing there alone.

"Where do we stand?" I asked my brother, not wishing to waste time.

"Stephen is holding a council at Northampton," he said, sitting down in the chair Count William had just abandoned. "They will no doubt be celebrating his victory against the Scots."

I sat in the chair across the table from him. "They would do better to save their strength. King David tells me he will come down again this summer."

"Good. That will prevent the northern lords from riding to Stephen's aid."

"And when do you intend to renounce your fealty to Stephen?" Count Geoffrey asked, an edge to his voice.

My husband was still standing, or rather leaning back against one of the chairs by the fire, his arms crossed and his face formed into a frown. I could not help but notice that he was literally looking down on Robert.

"One thing at a time," my brother replied calmly. "We must make sure the moment is right."

"My men are getting cut down while you wait for the proper moment, Earl Robert! We must move to take Normandy as soon as possible."

Robert nodded. "I agree, but I fear for my castles in England. If we strike too soon, then Stephen will seize them one by one while we are trapped down here."

"Earl Robert is right," I said, looking back at my husband. "He knows the Norman lords better than either of us. If he says we should wait, then we must wait."

This did not sit well with Count Geoffrey. He scoffed in a manner not unlike a snort, shaking his head.

"I beg your pardon, but Earl Robert forgets his place! Tell me, my lord, do you think we are yours to command? I have been leading us here for the past two years—organizing everything."

"And rather poorly at that," he replied, the frustration beginning to show on his face.

"How dare you!" Count Geoffrey cried, stepping near my brother, his hands formed into fists.

"Please, allow Earl Robert to speak!" I argued, touching my husband's arm. The last thing I needed was for my two chief commanders to fall out with one another. Even so, if my husband thought I was going to support him against Earl Robert when he was behaving like an arse, he was about to be sorely disappointed.

"Why should I when he merely hurls abuse?" he asked, shaking himself free of me.

"Count Geoffrey, I do not mean to deny you the respect that is yours by right, but whatever you have been doing, it is clearly not working," Robert said. Geoffrey glared at him, but he continued, "The empress is no closer to the throne today than she was when Stephen first stole it from her. You are a good man and a fine commander, but you must trust my experience. I am on your side!"

My husband walked backward slowly until he leaned against the chair again, smiling crudely all the while.

"Fine, then tell us what you think we should do, since you are so wise," he replied scornfully.

My brother turned to address me. "First, we will send a deputation to Rome to speak with Pope Innocent. We will tell him that the lords have broken their oath and that Stephen lied. Then we will ask him to transfer his support to you. That will provide the moral justification for the nobles to grant their support, as well as the Church."

"He is still likely to side with Stephen, since he is favored by Cluny," I said. It was a fair concern, given the power of that monastery.

"Even so, we must try. Second, I will send word to my vassals in England to rise up against Stephen as soon as I announce my change of fealty. Third, we should see if we can work with King David as well. Fourth, I will use the money I still have from our late father to purchase such arms as we require. Fifth, we must ensure a port of entry into England for whenever we are ready to land. And finally, Count Geoffrey and I will march on Falaise and the other castles as soon as possible. We will gain control of the west of Normandy, then Count Geoffrey will remain here to conquer the East while Maud and I make for England. What say you to that?"

With each suggestion, my excitement had increased. "All excellent ideas, but I still think it may be difficult to win over the lords," I answered. After all, I knew enough about war to know nothing ever goes perfectly.

"When we begin to apply the pressure, the divisions among them will grow," he assured me. "There are men right now who merely wait for a standard to gather around: anyone other than Stephen."

I recognized that we had cut Count Geoffrey out of the discussion. I looked over to see that he was still very sore at both of us. His arms were crossed, his brow as wrinkled as a dry fruit, and his nostrils were flaring with each breath. As much as I might have liked to simply work with my brother and not have to deal with my husband, I knew that I needed him if we were to succeed. Earl Robert needed his men to defeat Stephen. I therefore tried to make him feel like his opinion mattered.

"Count Geoffrey, what do you think?" I asked, as pleasantly as I could.

"I think you are both fools to abandon Normandy before it is won!" he growled. "Earl Robert knows that the lords all have lands on both sides of the water. They will not suffer their estates to be divided, some under one lord and the rest under another. If we achieve victory in Normandy, they will forsake him in England: you'll see!"

Here the difference between myself and my husband was revealed: he considered England an inferior jewel to Normandy. While the duchy of Normandy was part of my heritage as well as my sons' and I had no intention of surrendering it, England was the land of my birth and my mother. It was a sovereign kingdom, free from any claims by the French king, and it held the first place in my heart. I knew I could never make my husband love that land as I did, so I tried something else.

"But if he gains Earl Robert's lands in England along with all of their wealth, then Stephen will simply send over an army to conquer us here," I argued. "If we are to make our case, we must do so in England."

"Then I should come with you, for you cannot win it without my help," said Count Geoffrey.

I had just about had it with his arrogance, especially when he had made such a mess of things in Normandy. "I think what Earl Robert means to say is that we cannot win with your help, for the lords of England all hate Anjou," I stated rather bluntly.

"What she says is true, Count Geoffrey," Robert agreed. "We need you here, and the empress needs to be in England."

Count Geoffrey simply shook his head and muttered, "I do not like this—not at all."

"Well, it is not your decision to make," I said. "You may be my husband, but I am the heir. The inheritance passes to our sons through me. I was the one chosen by King Henry.

Therefore, as difficult as it may be for you, I will be the one making the final decisions."

"What do you know of war?!" my husband charged. "He has been denying you in public for two years"—here he pointed at Earl Robert—"while my knights and I have been defending you, and now you welcome him back like some prodigal son and are eager to accept everything he says, simply because it is he who says it! Well, I will not stand for it! You need me more than you need him: surely you know that."

You really are a churl, aren't you? I thought, but I knew the comment would not help the situation.

"If that were true, then I would already be sitting on the throne of England," I explained. "Count Geoffrey, I am thankful for everything you have done, and for what you will do in the future. But there is no victory without Earl Robert. You must see that. Trust him as you trust me."

He shook his head and let out another snort. "I am not sure I should trust either of you, but it seems I will not win this argument. Very well. Run off to England on your fool's errand! I will stay here and fight for our sons' inheritance: the dukedom of Normandy."

The count then turned and walked out the door, perhaps hoping that he would gain a better hearing with one of the trees.

"Well, I hope you do not miss him too much when we are in England," Robert concluded.

"Tell me, brother: when Saint Jerome removed the thorn from the lion's paw, do you think the beast missed it?"

He laughed heartily. "He is your thorn in the flesh then?"

"Until death do us part."

As the cat stalks its prey, so we began to set in motion all the things Earl Robert had advised. I sent Prince Geoffrey back to

Anjou to be tutored by one Goscelin Rotonardi, the better to keep him out of danger. For the time being, I kept my other sons with me. Count Geoffrey gathered his strength for an assault against those castles in western Normandy that were still true to Stephen. Earl Robert wrote in secret to his vassals in England to let them know that the time had come.

Soon a great many things happened all at once. Two of Earl Robert's men rebelled against the false king: Geoffrey Talbot in Hereford and William fitz Alan in Shrewsbury. We might have preferred that they wait until after Robert had announced his defiance, the better to combine our efforts, but the distance made communication difficult. No doubt, Stephen saw these rebellions as solitary actions, but they were actually the opening shots in a battle that was to consume the whole of England.

In the month of May, Earl Robert of Gloucester sent to Stephen a formal declaration of *diffidatio*, which means defiance. As Brother William of Malmesbury has noted, he declared "that the king had illegally aspired to the kingdom and neglected his plighted faith to him, not to say absolutely belied it: and moreover, that he himself had acted contrary to law; who, after the oath sworn to his sister, had not blushed to do homage to another during her lifetime."[18] I am told that Stephen received the news while traveling back to London, and here we had a stroke of good fortune, for the usurper allowed the messengers to continue on to the West and inform all of Earl Robert's vassals. Thus, their rebellion gained both strength and organization, and they adopted the city of Bristol as their center of operations.

What must Stephen have been thinking at that moment? I heard he would often go about saying, "Since they have elected

---

18 William of Malmesbury. *The History of the Kings of England and of His Own Times*, The Church Historians of England, vol. III, pt. 1, trans. John Sharpe, rev. Joseph Stevenson (London: Seeleys, 1854), 393.

me king, why do they desert me? By the birth of God, I will never be called a fallen king!" Is that not the height of hypocrisy: for a traitor to complain of disloyalty? He who sows dissension will reap dissension, and the usurper was about to discover just how far he had fallen.

Meanwhile in Argentan, the summer was upon us, and a merry summer it was, for I had every hope that my fortune would soon improve. Nevertheless, something happened that sent a chill through my bones. My eldest son asked me, "Mother, can I ride on a horse with Sir Drogo?" After a fortnight of him beseeching me thus daily, I was forced to grant him a hearing on the matter. I knew well enough that Henry must one day not only ride a horse, but ride one into battle to defend his crown. However, I also knew that riders tend to fall off horses and do injury to their bodies. Some have even been killed, and given my son's small stature at the time, I was quite afraid of a hoof to the head or some such calamity.

I do not remember how I was convinced to let him go, but I was. A meadow lay just on the other side of the River Orne, and it was selected for the occasion, which meant stepping outside the city walls. There was some fear that an archer might be able to hide in the woods beyond the meadow and take out both myself and my son, all but ensuring our line would never sit on the throne of England. Drogo therefore saw to it that a guard would be placed around the site in all directions, but not so close as to alarm the young boy.

On the morning chosen for his great ride, Prince Henry was so eager, I thought he might burst. He helped Drogo brush the horse beforehand and watched as the knight fitted it with a saddle and bridle. Drogo then placed Henry on top of the massive creature and sat behind him as they made their way to the meadow, while Adela and I walked close behind. I had wanted my son to wear a helm at the very least, but there were none small enough in the armory, and there had been no time to fashion a proper one.

When we had crossed the bridge and taken our place in the field, Drogo said, "Now, young master Henry, are you ready to go fast?"

"Yes!" he cried, his eyes wide with wonder.

I stepped forward and grabbed the rein with my left hand, looking Drogo firmly in the eye. "Do you remember what I commanded, Drogo?"

"Yes, my lady. Hold on to him tightly. Don't go too fast. Avoid any uneven ground. No sudden turns. No leaping over obstacles."

"What else?" I asked, raising a brow.

He covered Henry's ears with his hands. "If any harm should befall him, I will live the rest of my life as a eunuch."

"And don't you forget it!" I said.

"What are you talking about?" Henry whined. "I want to ride!"

I took one of Henry's little hands in my own and kissed it. "Remember what I told you, my son. Do not raise your hands. Stay safely in Drogo's grip. Obey any command he gives you. Do you understand? Henry, are you paying attention?"

His gaze had wandered over somewhere in the distance. "Butterfly!" he cried. "Sir Drogo, let's chase it!"

I let go of his hand, and the two of them rode away and began making a wide circle through the grass. I pressed my hands together and held them against my mouth. "Lord, watch over them. Let no ill befall them," I whispered.

I turned and walked back to where Adela sat upon the blanket she had lain on the grass. She was holding my very worn volume of poetry by the former Duke William of Aquitaine, which she had lately begun to devour. In the few years since we had met, Adela had not only learned to read, but become truly devoted to the written word. Hardly a day went by when she did not inquire about the meaning of a word or idea, and this one was no different.

"What do you think of Aristotle?" she asked, as I knelt beside her.

"What?" I responded, for my mind was still filled with fears about my son.

"The pagan philosopher. He was a Greek, I believe."

"Right. What of him?" I asked, my eyes still fixed on Henry and Drogo.

"Have you read any of his works?"

I forced myself to look at her, although my mind was still half with my son.

"No, I have never read him. His writings are mostly lost to us, or else they are in the Greek tongue. I hear the Moors are attempting to translate them into Latin, but God only knows how long that will take."

"Yes, that is what I heard too!" she said with a smile. "Sir Drogo told me."

"Did he now?" I asked, though the matter was of little interest to me.

"Yes. Sir Drogo says the theologians cannot decide what to make of his ideas—you know, because he was a pagan. They have been debating the matter in the cathedral schools."

I laughed. "Adela, if there is one thing you can always count on, it is that theologians will debate anything and everything. It is in their nature. They can do no other."

"I suppose you are right," she concluded softly. "I do enjoy hearing all the news from Sir Drogo though. He is so very intelligent."

She cast her eyes back down at the book and I returned to watching Henry and Drogo ride. They were taking rather more turns than I would have liked, almost as if the knight did not remember my stern warning. Suddenly, I turned back to look at Adela, who I saw was gazing at the riders even as I was, the look on her face one of deep longing. She let out a soft sigh and smiled ever so slightly. However, when she noticed that my eyes were upon her, she instantly looked back at her book.

"Adela," I asked, "why were you looking at them? Is the poetry of Duke William so dull?"

"You were looking at them too," she responded quickly.

"I have been looking at them because I am afraid my son is going to fall and hit his head," I explained. "However, I am not sure why they should be so great a subject of interest to you."

"Can I not also be concerned for the prince's welfare?" she asked, although the shade of pink in her cheeks convinced me this was not the real explanation.

Yes, I was quite certain that Adela had developed a passion for my beloved knight. I suppose it should not have been a surprise, for he was precisely the type of man young women were bound to admire: strong, wealthy, and clever. Ever since that time I had mentioned his slight loss of hair, he had taken to wearing all manner of hats, which might appeal to some women. Adela's attachment to him made perfect sense. Even so, I knew I must let her tell me in her own time. Teasing would only cause her to remain silent.

"Very well, then," I said. "Don't tell me if you don't want to."

About five minutes passed in which Adela continued to look down at the book, but I suspect she was not truly reading, for I did not hear pages turning. At the end of the five minutes, she suddenly closed the book and said, "Fine, you win!"

"I win?"

"I am sorry, my lady. You know I am devoted to your service, and I have no greater love than to do you good."

The look on her face was so earnest that I had to laugh. "But even so—"

Her eyes were by this point firmly fixed on the ground, her cheeks a shade of red. "Even so, I cannot help but notice that Sir Drogo is a fine man. He is very noble, and very handsome, and he likes books even as we do."

"I'm not convinced he likes them quite as much as we do, but go on, dear," I said.

"Well …" she began, her voice trailing off. "My lady, I was wondering, has Sir Drogo ever mentioned to you whether he desires to marry?"

I looked back at the riders. Henry was smiling and waving very much against my clear command. Drogo too was looking at us and smiling.

"He has said in the past that he might like to enter the priesthood, though I think for the moment he simply enjoys what he is doing."

I turned back to look at Adela. Her countenance was quite downcast.

"The priesthood, you say? Well, that is very nice that he wishes to do the work of our Lord." However, the look in her eyes revealed that she did not find it very nice at all.

I patted her on the back. "I am not certain that he still wants to do that. People change. Perhaps he would consider marriage, but you should know that he is a good deal older than you, Adela. Indeed, I believe he must be twice your age."

"Is that so wrong?" she asked. "My father was much older than my mother. She was his third wife after the first two died."

She had a good point, and in any case, I did not want to crush her hopes.

"Oh, never mind it!" I declared. "You are right. People often marry though they are far apart in age."

She looked back at him and sighed. "He is so very nice looking, isn't he?"

I wondered if we could be viewing the same person. Certainly, I had never thought Drogo an ugly man, but I would not have placed him next to the Greek gods either. *She must be in love*, I thought. As she continued to gaze in that manner, I couldn't help but provoke her a little.

"You're imagining him without his shirt on."

"What?! I am not!" she cried, as if I had made a great assault upon her honor.

"You know, I once saw him without a shirt on."

Her eyes lit up for the space of a breath, but she quickly calmed herself.

"My lady, I think you are attempting to provoke me into making a fool of myself by demanding to know the particulars, but I shall not give you that satisfaction."

"Oh no?" I asked, attempting not to break out in laughter.

"Most certainly not! I am a good girl, and I do not allow my mind to dwell on such things."

She said this with such conviction that I started laughing, which only seemed to increase her anger. I held up my hand to ward off whatever she might say next.

"Have no fear, Adela. I do not think badly of you, and if you must know, he had to remove his shirt because William spat up on him. I think your regard for him is sweet. If you wish, I can speak to him and see if his desires have changed," I offered.

"Oh, would you, my lady?! That would be ever so wonderful! Thank you!" she said, smiling broadly.

We were then forced to discontinue our conversation, for the riders stopped right in front of us.

"Young master Henry has decided that he wishes to pursue the butterflies on foot," Drogo announced, alighting and helping Henry down after him.

"Thank God!" I proclaimed, walking over to give my son a hug.

"Sir Drogo!" Adela called. "I am reading the poetry of Duke William." Here she held it up for him to see.

"Very nice," he said. "That is just the thing for young ladies."

She rose and walked over to him. "It speaks much of the mysteries of love. I have learned so much!"

"Perhaps a bit too much for your own good," I muttered softly enough that none of them would hear.

"I want to chase butterflies!" Henry cried, interrupting the adult conversation.

"I can take him," Drogo offered, extending his hand.

"No, I am sure Adela would enjoy going with him," I said, for I desired to speak with the knight alone.

Soon Adela was leading Henry off to the far side of the meadow, and Drogo and I were sitting together on the blanket while the horse nibbled the grass. The knight lay on his side playing with a twig while I sat with my hands folded in my lap, not sure how to begin the conversation I knew I must have. In the end, I did not have to start, for Drogo did so.

"Have you heard about Stephen's march on Bristol?" he asked.

Very well. I am more than happy to talk about something different, I thought.

"I have heard that he went there and found it well defended, and that his counselors could not agree among themselves about what they should do," I replied.

He nodded. "It's a sign of weakness. He doesn't know who he can trust any more. Our efforts are bearing fruit."

"I do hope so. It's about time we had some good news from England. Have you heard about all these earldoms he has been granting? Almost all of them are to the Beaumont family, of course. To Waleran of Meulan, he gave the earldom of Worcester; to Waleran's younger brother Hugh, he gifted the earldom of Bedford on account of the young man's lack of inheritance; to Gilbert de Clare, Waleran's brother by marriage, the earldom of Pembroke; and last of all, the earldom of Derby has been created for Robert of Ferrers!"

"That will please the Beaumonts," Drogo said with a laugh. "Tell me, did he make these appointments with a knife to his neck?"

"God only knows," I answered, with a shrug of the shoulders. "I do not doubt that he sees his ability to raise up men at will as a mark of his authority, but in truth, it is proof of his weakness. When a king feels that he cannot control those below him, he must have them removed and new men set in their place, the better to obey his every word. I remember Bruno taught me that."

"Ah, Bruno!" Drogo said with a smile. "There's a name from the past!"

"And a great name too. I wish he was here with us now. He would have some good counsel. The purge has begun at the usurper's court, Drogo, and there's no telling where it will stop."

As nice as it was to discuss this subject, I knew I must return to my original purpose, no matter how awkward it might be. "Now let me ask you about something completely different: would you ever consider getting married?"

I have seldom seen the look on someone's face change so quickly. First, his eyes became wide with concern, then he broke into a laugh. "Where is this coming from?" he asked. "Is this simply the same question you ask me every five years, or do you have someone in mind?"

By instinct, my gaze fixed upon Adela off in the distance, who was bending down and picking flowers with Henry as the two of them held hands.

"It's her, isn't it?" Drogo asked.

I turned back to look at him. "I do not know what you mean."

"You think I should marry Lady Adela."

"I said no such thing!"

I had not meant to reveal this full truth to him, for if he was not interested in marriage, I did not want him to know that she was the one who had asked: it would only cause her greater sorrow to have her feelings known. Sadly, my eyes had betrayed my thoughts.

"I suspected she might be interested in me," he said.

"Ah, and here I thought you were going to make a show of humility," I replied, shaking my head as if in censure.

He rolled his eyes. "She has sought me out for conversation on multiple occasions."

"And—"

"And what?"

I shook my head again, this time in true annoyance. "And have you enjoyed her company?"

"Oh, yes!" he said. "She is a most pleasant young woman. Very pretty too: the most comely in the castle, I would say."

I had not foreseen such an answer. I never believed he would reject her in a cruel manner, but I honestly did not think the two of them could have spent enough time together to form a strong attraction. I, for one, had never noticed them having long discussions. Suddenly, I was forced to face the possibility that they might actually desire to get married. Perhaps they would want to move to his family estate in Cornwall. I might never see them again! No, I did not like this idea at all. Nevertheless, they had both served me faithfully and I cared for them, so I could hardly deny them joy. I therefore decided then and there that I must support them if marriage was what they desired, as much as it pained me to do so.

"Well, if you wish to have her as your bride, you certainly could," I said. "What family she has is very poor, but I can provide her with a dowry."

I was surprised to hear Drogo laugh. Indeed, he was laughing very hard.

"I do not see what is so funny!" I objected.

"Forgive me, my lady," he said, holding up his hand. "Lady Adela is a fine person, yes, but I do not intend to make her my wife. I am perfectly happy as I am now. It is a great privilege and joy to lead your knights, and that commands my full attention. If a time ever came when you no longer required my services, I would want to take holy orders. Indeed, that is the only reason I would ever leave."

"Oh," I said, secretly relieved and yet concerned for how this news would affect Adela. "My mistake. I thought you were fond of her."

"I am fond of her, true enough, but surely that doesn't mean I have to marry her? I am far too old for her in any case. She will find someone else: someone young who is eager to have a house full of children. With a face like hers, she will always have suitors."

"I suppose you are right," I agreed.

I glanced back at her. How happy she looked, and yet how sad she was about to become!

Adela, you poor girl, I thought. *You poor, poor girl.*

During that summer of 1138, the usurper entered the Severn Valley accompanied by Miles of Gloucester, and they were able to make rather quick work of both Hereford and Shrewsbury. At the latter, Stephen showed none of his earlier mercy, but hanged one hundred men after the castle had fallen. Even so, our friends Geoffrey Talbot and William fitz Alan were able to escape.

At the same time as this was happening, Dover Castle rose up against Stephen, according to the order sent by Earl Robert. This was a key moment, for if we were able to possess Dover and the surrounding country, we might be able to land in England by the end of the year. Thus it was vital that the garrison held against Stephen. As the false king was still in the West, his wife, my own cousin Mathilda, sent to her home county of Boulogne and called in her fleet of ships to harry the defenders. So there was fighting in both the West and the East, but the worst was about to come.

In the month of August, even as Stephen was still caught up near the Welsh border, King David of Scotland invaded Northumberland with some twenty thousand men and began his push toward the key city of York. The usurper must have felt the whole world turning against him, even as I had felt two and a half years earlier. He could not abandon the West and was therefore forced to leave the northern lords to their fate. Earl Waleran and William of Ypres had been sent back to Normandy to prevent it from falling before the forces of Earl Robert and Count Geoffrey. Thus, the battle raged on four different fronts, and things certainly looked grim for Stephen.

This news had been coming to us quickly from the island, but in the latter days of August, all fell silent. I have never quite known what to do with silence, for it holds so many possibilities. It was possible that we had been victorious on every front: Count Geoffrey and Earl Robert were pushing northeast toward Rouen, the port of Dover was held for us, the Scots had marched all the way to York, and Stephen's efforts had been frustrated in the West. However, it was equally possible that all had come to naught. I wanted to believe the best, but I feared the worst more than anything.

On Sunday the day before the Nones of September, I went to celebrate Mass as usual at the castle chapel. It was a separate building made of wood that stood near the western wall, and there was nothing grand about it. Lord Wigan had told me he intended to build a new one from stone as soon as the war was over. At the time, such a thing was hardly urgent. Yes, war brings an end to everything of beauty.

It was the feast of some saint I know not, for I remember there were flowers in the church. Is it not strange what the mind chooses to remember? When the service was completed, we all proceeded across the yard to the keep, where the midday meal was to be served in the great hall. As I entered the main door with about a dozen people right behind me, I saw Wigan the Marshal standing there in the entry way, his hands folded, apparently waiting for my arrival. It was not his wont to attend Mass: he always found some excuse to avoid it, usually involving his need to join the morning guard. It was not very Christian of him, but as he had so graciously helped to defend me for many months, I had not raised the subject—yet.

"Welcome back, Empress Mathilda!" he said, bowing his head.

"You speak as if I have just returned from pilgrimage to Compostela," I replied, "when I have only been a few steps away."

He smiled. "You must forgive me, my lady. Even a moment without your presence seems a terrible fate to your most devoted subjects."

After a quick roll of the eyes, I turned and waved those behind me on to the hall, then moved closer to the marshal to converse in greater privacy.

"You need not have been away from my presence, sir," I said softly. "The house of the Lord stands welcome to receive you, should you deem it worthy of your time."

"Ah, yes," he replied with a laugh. "How long have you been waiting to say that to me?"

"I am not your judge in such matters, Lord Wigan—only in matters of state. However, if you have half as many sins on your record as I do, perhaps you will see the benefit of it sooner or later."

Before he could respond, I felt a tap on the shoulder and turned to see Adela standing there.

"Adela! I thought you had gone into the feast."

"I stayed back to help collect the candles," she told me. "Actually, I just wanted to ask if I could speak with you for a moment."

"I was hoping to speak with the empress first," Wigan explained. "I have some news to relay."

"What news?!" I asked, suddenly very interested. "You said nothing about news."

"Far be it for me to keep you from promoting my spiritual health," he said with a smile.

"Where is the news from?" Adela asked. "Dover? York? Caen? Rome?!"

"Perhaps you would like to join me in the private room," he said, looking at me alone and pointing at the door to my right.

I looked at Adela and then back at him. "Unless it is some great secret, I do not mind if she joins me. That way, we can discuss her matter afterward."

"As you wish," he replied, then led us both through the door into the dining room.

He offered us the two more comfortable chairs by the hearth, then pulled over a wood chair for himself from the table. He turned it backward and straddled it as he might a horse, allowing his folded hands to hang over the top of the chair.

"I am afraid that the news I have to share with you is not good," he began.

At this, Adela let out a gasp, and we both looked at her. "I'm sorry!" she said.

"As I was saying," the marshal continued, "the news is not so good. My lady, it concerns your uncle, King David of Scotland—that is to say, his army. We all knew that he was pressing south toward York and that Stephen was trapped in the West. I think we suspected or at least hoped that he would make a conquest of the North. Well, something happened."

My stomach was by this point in a knot. Was he about to tell me that my uncle was dead? That my nephew was dead? Had the Scots army been destroyed? Oh, how my heart pounded!

"You know of Archbishop Thurstan of York, my lady?" he asked.

"I certainly know the name, but I have never met the man," I replied quietly, wanting very much to get to the end of his story so that I could know whom or what to mourn.

He nodded and continued. "He is quite old now. Anyway, he called together all the barons of the North—Brus, Mowbray, Lacy, Percy, Peverel, William of Aumale, and others—and he beseeched them that to fight against the Scots is a holy cause, even as those who fought the Saracens in the Holy Land, for the Scots are a cruel race without regard for Christian brotherhood and the dignity of man. He called to their minds the persons who had been carried away into slavery, the churches that had been profaned, and the towns that had been burned. He bid them fight to the death or share in the fate of those poor souls, and he pledged to them that for every Scot they killed, they were doing the work of the Lord."

"How dreadful!" Adela interrupted.

"Quite, although I cannot blame them too much, my lady," he said. "We have all heard of the terrible acts that were committed."

I nodded but said nothing, for there was nothing I could do about it. I relied on my uncle to control his own men.

Lord Wigan continued, "Archbishop Thurstan's true act of genius was not the speech, but the device that he employed for the battle. There is a tradition among the men of Italy that when they ride off to war, they do so accompanied by a *caroccio*: a holy altar born upon a cart with the standard of the city flying over it. The archbishop took such a cart and placed upon it a pyx containing the consecrated body of our Lord, along with a pole on which flew the banners of York, Ripon, and Beverly. The nobles were drawn up around it, with the lesser knights further out, and the common men on all sides. They pledged that they would all give their lives before they allowed the standard to be taken."

Oh, let this tale end soon! I thought, but still I remained silent.

"Now, the thing you must know about the Scots is that they give their bloody work to the men of Galloway, who are as fierce as the day is long. They go into battle without any armor at all, heads shaven, bodies painted, lifting their spears into the air and slicing their enemies to bits. Such a fearful sight they must have been as they came charging down the ridge with cries of "*Albani! Albani!*" Sadly, the resolve of those from York was just as fierce, and their armor was far better. The *Galwedi* persevered for a time, though so run through with arrows that they resembled—oh, what is the name of that beast?"

"A thorny pig?" I asked, hoping to speed the process along.

"No, that's not it," he commented, "but it is like that." He thought for long enough that I was on the brink of despair, then declared, "Hedgehog! Just like a hedgehog."

"How awful!" cried Adela.

"Yes, and what happened next?" I asked him.

He sighed deeply. "King David was eager to join the fight, but his barons believed the battle was lost at that point, and they forced him back upon his horse that they might retreat. That was when the king's son, Prince Henry, ashamed to see the cowardice of the barons, rode alone into the English line, slaying many before he too was forced to fall back. For the next few days, the English chased the Scots across the moor as they attempted to retreat north. I'm afraid there is no question of them advancing into England now, my lady—none at all."

I closed my eyes and buried my face in my hands. I breathed in and out deeply, allowing his words to take their full effect. I felt very much as if I had been punched in my belly. After a moment, I looked up again.

"And the losses?" I asked, afraid to know the answer.

Lord Wigan did not reply, but merely pursed his lips.

"Tell me!" I ordered.

"Ten thousand dead or missing, my lady, about half the Scots army," he said softly.

I returned my face to my hands, for there were tears forming in my eyes, and I didn't want him to see them. Adela reached over and rubbed my upper back, attempting to comfort me, but there was little comfort to be had after such news.

"King David did at least maintain those lands he held before, so that is something," I heard the marshal say. "Earl Robert's vassals in the West are also safe, as far as I know. But I am sorry to say that Dover Castle has also fallen to the usurper. The queen's navy made swift work of that."

"She is not the queen!" I cried, raising my head to face him. "She will never be queen in the eyes of God!"

"Of course, my lady. Please forgive me!" he begged.

I closed my eyes and shook my head. "It is not your fault, Lord Wigan. You have always helped me. I think I must simply be alone now, unless you have some other tragedy to report."

He shook his head no and rose to leave at once, shutting the door behind him. Adela reached into a pocket in her gown and pulled out a cloth, which she used to dab my eyes. I took it from her and wiped my nose, then let out a long sigh.

"This may take a while to recover from," I muttered.

She nodded. "Naturally. Would you like to wait to speak about the other thing until later?"

"Oh, dear! I forgot about that. No, go ahead. What is it?"

"I was just wondering if you had a chance to speak with Sir Drogo about the matter we discussed."

It had been a good while since the subject was last raised and I had received Drogo's answer, but every time I had tried to inform Adela, something had interrupted us or I had simply lost the will to give her the bad news. It was wrong of me, of course, to delay for so long. I had simply wished to avoid spoiling what had been a happier month. However, given that the day had already ended up in tears, I decided to go ahead and break it to her.

"Adela, I am so sorry, but Drogo is not interested in marriage at the present time."

"Oh," she said, staring down at her lap.

"I wish I could have given you better news, but it seems it is not the day for that. Is there anything I can do?"

"No," she replied, shaking her head. "In any case, it was probably too much to hope for. He is a person far superior to myself."

"That is not true," I said, placing my arm around her shoulder. "He is a man of good standing with good character, true enough, but you have many things in your favor as well. One day someone will recognize that."

"Perhaps if I had done something differently—"

"No, I'll have none of that!" I declared. "There was never anything wrong with you. I told you, he wants to be a priest someday. He cannot do that with a wife. That is all there is to it."

"I do not see why," she said softly, her eyes looking suspiciously moist. "Why can a person not love God and love a human being? What is so wrong about that?"

"There is nothing wrong with that," I said, rubbing her shoulders gently. "Love is not a sin, but God calls us to different tasks, and we cannot do them all at once."

She nodded. "I suppose you are right. To speak the truth, I am not sure how much I was actually in love with him."

"You don't have to say that—"

"No, it's true! You see, ever since I was a little girl, I had this dream—a fantasy, really. I imagined that one day I would meet a handsome knight who would rescue me and take me away to live with him in a nice house somewhere with a table full of delicious foods. It is silly, I know."

"It is not silly at all!" I assured her.

"You see, we were in such a bad way when I was young—my family. We struggled to grow food. Often, we would go without. And I had not met any knights then, so I assumed they were all noble and virtuous. As it turns out, some of them are better than others."

"That is all too true."

She laughed softly and wiped her eyes. "Did you ever desire something like that?"

"To be rescued by a knight?"

"Maybe, or something like that."

I looked into her eyes that were filled with deep sadness. I decided to share a little gift with her.

"Actually, I was in love with a knight once, and he was in love with me."

"Really?!" she cried, her eyes suddenly alight.

"Yes, some years ago. It did not last very long, and nothing came of it."

"Was it anyone I know?"

"No, you have never met him."

"He's still alive though?"

"I am not going to tell you who it is, you sneak!" I cried, and we both smiled.

"So it was not Drogo then?"

"Certainly not! When we met, he was already a man and I was still a girl. He seemed very much like an older brother, and that is how I still feel about him. For his part, he looks out for me as he would a younger sister."

"How wonderful!" she said. "That is a shame though that you did not get your knight, though I suppose that Count Geoffrey is a knight."

"Yes, well, we return to the point about not all knights being particularly virtuous," I replied, rolling my eyes. "But there is still hope for you, Adela. You are not royal, and you have no family members who wish to force you into a less than desirable marriage. It is true that the very greatest men may refuse you on account of your lack of nobility, but many others would see your friendship with me as an advantage for them. I dare say you may be as free to choose a husband as any woman on this earth, but I bid you hold out for a man who truly deserves you. I don't want you to end up in my situation."

"So you think I may find my knight then?" she said, smiling weakly.

"I am certain of it," I said, embracing her.

Unwilling to be left out of our defeat, Earl Robert and Count Geoffrey laid siege to Falaise for just over a fortnight that autumn, but failed to take it. Without that castle, our hold over the West of Normandy was still not complete, and after only a month of fighting, Count Geoffrey returned to Anjou, which I had by that point decided was the best place for him. Oh, what a devastation! We had failed in all our aims: no progress had been made in Normandy, none in Kent, and none in Northumberland. Despite the presence of Earl Robert of Gloucester in our camp and the help of his vassals, we were no closer to defeating Stephen and regaining control of Normandy and England for me and my sons.

I could think of only one potential ally on whom I had not yet called, and for good reason. Although we had been friendly in the past, I hated to draw her into the fighting. Nevertheless, I sat down one day at the desk in my bed chamber to write a letter and entreat her assistance. It was a sign of how desperate I felt. As I sat there scribbling on the parchment, Adela walked in and placed a hand on my shoulder, leaning in to see what I was writing.

"Who is that for, my lady?"

"I am writing to the former Queen Adeliza, who is lately made the wife of William D'Aubigny."

"She is married again? I thought she wished to remain in the abbey."

"Apparently not," I said, dipping my pen in the ink. "They have made their home at Arundel Castle: the one gifted to her by my father."

"Do you think she can help you?"

I turned my head to look at her. "I doubt it, for her new husband is Stephen's man through and through. But given that we have tried everything else—"

"Of course. I never met the former queen. Is she a good sort of person?"

"Oh, yes! She is far kinder than myself. Sadly, wars are not kind to those who are kind. She may wish she had stayed in the cloister."

"Well, I am sure she will try to help you if she can."

"Would that God might help me! I think He has forgotten that I am here." I gazed up at the ceiling and pressed my hands together. "Please, Lord, let me see England again, and not merely from behind some prison wall! I am an exile from my own kingdom, Adela, and I hate it!"

I scribbled a few more lines before she interrupted.

"I have never seen England. Is it a fair country?"

"In the summer, yes. In the winter, not so much, but it is a fine place nevertheless. I was born there, you know."

"Not in Normandy?"

"Oh no!" I said, turning to face her again. "I was born by the River Thames. Perhaps one day I will sail up those waters again."

"You will, my lady," she told me, patting my shoulder. "I am sure you will."

CHAPTER TWENTY FOUR

Here I must speak of Bishop Henry of Winchester, born of the House of Blois, abbot of Glastonbury, younger brother of the false king. Since he was first brought to England by my father, King Henry, he had passed from strength to strength: an abbot at age twenty-eight, a powerful bishop at age thirty-one, king maker at age thirty-seven. As the year 1138 came to a close, he was ready at forty years of age to ascend to the grandest seat of them all: the archbishopric of Canterbury. How proud my aunt Adela must have been to see all her desires for her son fulfilled!

Whatever they might have thought of his brother Stephen, there were few men who doubted Bishop Henry's abilities. He had proven his worth both to the Church and the king. He was a man of great learning and greater skill. There was no one more fit to become the leading churchman in England, and as the man who had ensured his brother's place upon the throne, you might even have said it was owed to him. Indeed, I have no doubt that Bishop Henry believed that to be the case.

Herein lay the trouble, for although he may have sat at his brother's right hand in the very beginning, Bishop Henry had lately been surmounted by the Beaumonts and their allies. I have seldom seen a clan so hungry for power and so willing to strike at anyone in their way. Stephen had already given Waleran of Meulan his own daughter, Mathilda, as a bride. She was just three years old when they were wed, but she died the next year. Brief as it was, the marriage had shown how eager the usurper was to reward the Beaumonts. I believe it was largely due to their influence that a rift opened between the false king and his brother, although one might likewise say it would have been impossible for Stephen to follow through on all the promises he had made to the Church without compromising his own reign.

I am not sure how much the common man knew of this divide between the houses of Beaumont and Blois, or at least between Earl Waleran and Bishop Henry, but I was well aware of the situation. Even so, I did not imagine as the Advent season came upon us and a council was to be held at Westminster that the usurper would appoint anyone but his brother to be archbishop of Canterbury. As much as I hated him, I did not believe him to be completely lacking in sense.

I therefore gave the matter little thought and chose to enjoy those days with my boys. Although we had made few efforts to decorate the winter before, I was determined to make the year 1138 different. We may have been in the middle of a war, but we would be jolly! I ordered that boughs be brought in from trees in the nearby forest and used to decorate the window sills in the great hall and the hearth. Adela and I then shaped stars and flowers out of red and gold cloth and I called the boys to help place them among the greens. Last of all, we arranged about a dozen candles on the hearth, some taller and some shorter.

I held William in my arms and began to light the candles to the right, while Adela held Henry's hand and did the same with those on the left. My young William was by that point two and a half years old and getting heavier by the day. Nevertheless, I held him on my hip and clung to him tightly with my right hand as I moved the flame from one candle to the next.

"*Mama*, it's pretty!" he cried.

"Yes, see how the flame dances and sparkles?" I said. "Just don't be placing your fingers in it, William. *Mama* does not want you to burn yourself."

I kissed him gently on the forehead and sniffed his brown hair. Odd as it may seem, my young sons always had a special smell, and I treasured it. However, Henry noticed what I had done and objected.

"Why are you smelling William?" he asked. "He stinks of *merde!*"

"Henry!" Adela and I both cried at the same time.

"Forgive me, my lady. You go first," Adela offered, bowing her head.

Still holding William, I set down the candle I was holding and walked over to Henry, bending down to his eye level. He was tall for a boy just into his sixth year, but I hoped to keep my head above his for at least another six or seven.

"Where on earth did you hear that word?" I asked. "Do you even know what it means?"

Henry placed his hands on his hips. "*Papa* uses it all the time, and I know what it means!"

I fought the desire to roll my eyes. Of course he would have heard it from Count Geoffrey.

"Then you should know better than to use it, and do not take that tone with me, young man!" I commanded. "Also, you speak the Norman tongue when you're with me."

"*Papa* says the French speech is better!" he declared. "He says English are peasants and knaves."

I had never received such cutting words from the mouth of my son, although they were not actually from my son. He was merely repeating what my husband had told him.

"English and Norman are not the same—oh, never mind it. Henry, I don't know what has gotten into you, but I'll see that it gets out! You must learn to respect the people you are going to rule. Your father has never been to England. He is just prejudiced against anyone different from himself."

"But—" he began.

"No buts!" I told him. "Please, you make me sad. Do not say such awful things!"

There was a slight change in his face. He was no longer defiant, but defeated—struck down by the power of maternal guilt.

"What do you say, Henry?" Adela asked.

Henry cast his eyes down toward his shoes and pressed one foot against the other. I recognized that he was stalling for time.

"Henry—" Adela prompted again.

He lifted his head and looked straight into my eyes.

"I am sorry, mother," he said softly. "I should not have said that."

Choosing his moment perfectly, William reached out and patted his brother on the head.

"Yes, I agree," I said with a laugh. "All is forgiven."

The three of us embraced and Adela came from behind to join. As we were all holding and kissing one another, there was a knock at the door. I let go of the boys and walked over, pulling on the handle and swinging it open. There stood Drogo, looking as if he was about to burst out laughing.

"What's put you in such a jolly mood?" I asked.

He said nothing, but beckoned with one finger. I moved to join him in the entry way, leaving Adela and the boys to finish with the candles.

"You'll never guess what's happened. Oh, it's too delicious!" he said, shaking his head.

"Right you are. I cannot guess, so tell me," I replied, folding my arms.

He nodded and brought himself under control. "You know they were holding the council at Westminster to fill the see of Canterbury, which has been vacant for two years."

"Yes, everyone knows this," I said, my patience wearing thin.

"But did you also know that since the bishopric of London has been empty, Bishop Henry of Winchester has been overseeing the diocese?"

"Why are you boring me with this information?" I asked.

"I'm coming to it," he assured me. "On Christmas Eve, Bishop Henry traveled to Saint Paul's Cathedral for the ordination of several deacons. It must have been joyous for those men to confirm their calling at the time of year when we celebrate the birth of our Lord, but alas, it was not to be a time of joy for Bishop Henry!"

"No!" I cried, placing a hand over my mouth, so astonished was I.

"Yes, indeed!" Drogo confirmed. "Bishop Henry was in the middle of performing the service when a messenger arrived, having run there from Westminster. To the great surprise of the crowd, he announced that Abbot Theobald of Bec had been elected as archbishop of Canterbury, denying Bishop Henry the thing he so coveted. Now, you might think that, being a most serene man of the cloth, Bishop Henry would have moved on from this interruption and completed the service, accepting the will of the Lord."

"You mean he didn't?" I asked in wonder.

Drogo laughed. "Certainly not! He marched out in a fury, sensing how he had been tricked, for they waited until he was gone to take the vote. How do you like that?! After everything he has done for his brother, this is the thanks he gets! I wouldn't be surprised if he hated him now, although he probably hates Waleran and the rest of the Beaumonts most of all. This is surely their doing. Well, anything that sets them against each other is good for us!"

"Yes, I agree. We cannot possibly know how this will turn out, but an enemy rent asunder is better than a whole one, and no mistake!"

I reached out and hugged him.

"Happy Christmas, Drogo," I said softly.

"Happy Christmas, my empress," he replied, patting me on the back.

Thus were the ambitions of Bishop Henry frustrated, for the usurper had ensured that the most powerful spiritual lord in England was one he could control. And who was the great patron of Theobald of Bec who had made his case to the king? None other than Earl Waleran, leader of the Beaumonts and quickly becoming the most powerful lord on either side of the Channel.

Oh, foolish Stephen! Why did he allow the Beaumonts to rule him? Why did he place his fate in the hands of lesser men? Because having been abandoned by Earl Robert and others, he began to fear a traitor behind every corner. He would grope after rumors and lash out like a cornered beast. We have already seen how he feared his own flesh and blood. Now, his attention was turned toward another powerful family: that of Bishop Roger of Salisbury.

During the reign of King Henry, Bishop Roger of Salisbury was considered the second most powerful man in the kingdom, to the extent that whenever the king was detained in Normandy, it was Bishop Roger who would act as his regent. He was the chief justiciar in all but name, having control over all the sheriffs. What was more, his bastard son—also named Roger—had become chancellor of the realm, and he had two nephews in high positions within the English church: Bishop Alexander of Lincoln and Bishop Nigel of Ely. His family therefore held sway over the chancellery and the exchequer, which could not have sat well with the Beaumonts. Thus, the twins Waleran and Robert, along with their friend Count Alan of Brittany, began to spread rumors that Bishop Roger and his kin were about to forsake Stephen for our side.

I can see why Stephen found it difficult to trust Bishop Roger of Salisbury, who was always a sly one and never missed an opportunity to advance his own interests. His morals were lax, as the name of his mistress was known to all, and he certainly suffered from avarice. I understand that in those days he used to ride around with a large company of knights, and his household was equal in size to that of the king. He owned several castles that, should he have turned traitor, might have been difficult to overthrow. He certainly had more money than Stephen, who had spent all his treasury appeasing the barons, and Bishop Roger had taken to spending this wealth on both armor and weapons. Most suspicious indeed!

However, I was not then nor was I ever in league with Bishop Roger and his kin. From the very beginning, the bishop served one person above all else, and that was himself. I suspect he fortified his castles out of fear of the Beaumonts or simply to impress the outside world and prove his worth. It was to be his undoing.

The following June, in the year of our Lord 1139, I received a letter from my brother Robert, who was always the first to receive news from England.

Most esteemed Empress Mathilda, my beloved sister, I write to you with news that should fill you with cheer once you understand its significance. About two weeks ago, Stephen was holding a great feast at his court in Oxford, and many of the knights of Bishop Roger were there. A brawl started between the factions of the Beaumonts and Bishop Roger. You will remember how I told you of their hatred for one another. Stephen is claiming that the bishop's men started it, but we need not doubt the truth. Count Alan and the rest have had it in for Bishop Roger for some time. There were many wounded and possibly a few killed—reports differ—and the false king charged Bishop Roger's men with disturbing the peace.

Stephen then summoned Bishop Roger and his two nephews—bishops Alexander and Nigel—to come before him. I am told that Bishop Roger attempted to avoid appearing, saying that, "I shall be as useful at court as a colt in battle," but in the end he had no choice. Both Roger and Alexander came before the usurper, but Bishop Nigel was nowhere to be found.

As it turned out, it was Nigel who was the wise one, for having tricked them into appearing, Stephen arrested the two bishops and threw them in jail, saying he would not release them until they surrendered all their castles and repented of their deeds. This was in violation of his promise not to arrest those who came into his presence under the king's surety, but as we know well enough, Stephen is more than willing to break his promises.

Poor Bishop Nigel fled to the castle of Devises, home to Bishop Roger's concubine of long standing, Mathilda of Ramsbury. I met her once, and she was rather more plump than I foresaw, though such a detail is neither here nor there. As soon as the usurper learned that Nigel was at Devises, he sent the wolf of Flanders to retrieve him, which is to say that he brought a large force and placed the castle under siege. Yet Devises is one of the strongest castles in England, a massive stone fortress unlikely to fall quickly. Stephen also knew that he was already courting the wrath of the Church by arresting the bishops, for he had pledged that they and all their possessions would be subject to ecclesiastical justice rather than the crown. Therefore, it was in his interest to end the controversy with all haste.

When the wolf of Flanders was not instantly victorious, Stephen placed both Bishop Roger of Salisbury and his son, Chancellor Roger, in fetters and brought them before the walls of Devises Castle. Can you believe it? In a loud voice, Stephen cried out that he would starve Bishop Roger and hang Chancellor Roger before their eyes if the castle was not surrendered.

For his part, Bishop Nigel apparently said nothing, but the lady Mathilda was so distraught at the fate of her lover and son that she gave up the fight on behalf of them both. By the end of the month, Stephen had seized all the castles belonging to the three bishops—Salisbury, Sherborne, Malmesbury, Devises, Newark, and Sleaford—and stripped the men of their secular offices, allowing them only to maintain their sees. This is where things stand at the present time. I will write to you with any news.

By the by, do thank my nephew for the letter he sent me in his own hand, which showed all the marks of a future king in the making. Tell him I shall return to Argentan as soon as I can to see how he is doing with the new sword I had made for him. You must not fear to let him fight, for the sooner he can do so, the safer you are. Yours faithfully, Robert fitz Roy.

The end of Robert's letter filled me with pride to hear him speak of my son in such a way. Henry certainly showed skill at everything he did: so much so that I was no longer quite as afraid of him participating in sports. However, I also wanted him to become a man of letters. I considered sending him to Anjou so he could share a tutor with his brother Geoffrey, but in the end I felt that if I was going to depart for England soon—as I dearly hoped I would—then I should spend my final days on the Continent in the company of both Henry and William.

As for the bulk of Robert's letter that told of Stephen's dealings with Bishop Roger of Salisbury and his kin, it seemed utterly incredible. Did the usurper really feel so bold in his position that he did not fear abusing three of the greatest princes of the English Church?

The advantages for Stephen were clear: he continued the purge of all those who disagreed with him and was able to install his own men in both the great offices of state and the local shires; he gained direct control over fortresses that would be of great value if we were to invade; and he seized forty thousand marks of silver and other treasures from the castles. This latter point was of particular import, for it allowed Stephen to arrange for his eldest son, Eustace, to marry the daughter of King Louis VII of France. It also gave him more gold with which to buy the loyalty of the barons.

The disadvantages of Stephen's decision were just as plain. It was the Church that put him in his position of authority, but by going after three such powerful bishops, Stephen had revealed himself to be no friend of the spiritual elite. Indeed, he had broken the oaths he made to them when he first became king. And who was most angry about the arrest of the bishops? Why, Bishop Henry of Winchester, of course! He took it upon himself to become the defender of the Church.

Very soon after I received his letter, I was able to travel with my boys to stay with Robert at the castle of Caen. I had not stayed there since I was a young woman just returned from the empire. To go there with my two sons was a real pleasure. They had quickly grown to love their uncle Robert. I was only sad that none of Robert's own children were there. I was not sure where they were staying, but I gathered it was somewhere deep in Wales, far from the fighting. In addition, they were not all in the same place.

We lived daily in the hope that we might be able to cross the Channel and land upon England's shore. Indeed, that was part of the reason I had moved to Caen, for it was far closer to the sea. One evening, as the sun was setting, my brother and I stood upon the western wall of the castle, our eyes pointed in the same direction where our thoughts lay.

"Didn't I tell you this would happen? Didn't I tell you?!" he said suddenly.

"Tell me what?" I asked in confusion.

"That the lords and the Church would turn against Stephen—that he would make too many enemies!"

"Ah, yes. Cassandra herself must envy your foresight," I jested, referring to the ancient prophetess.

"I tell you, the noose is tightening! Our time is near!" he cried. "Bishop Henry has called his brother to a council to answer for his actions. He may have lost out on becoming an archbishop, but he had himself made papal legate, so he still holds the primacy in England."

"That sly fox," I said, shaking my head in wonder. "I truly cannot understand why Stephen would turn against his brother. You know him better than I. Is he really that obtuse?"

"Knowledge is one thing and wisdom another, but introduce enough stress, and even the wisest person might be thrown off course. However, I think what we are seeing now is the true weakness that our cousin has always possessed. He can lead a siege, but he cannot lead a kingdom. He has no knowledge of the chancellery and lacks respect among the nobles. He has little experience of government and does not know how to play these men one against the other."

We stood for a moment staring out into the West, where the sky had turned bright orange and red, and the sun was dipping out of sight. A question entered my mind, but I was somewhat afraid to know the honest answer. Nevertheless, I felt it necessary to ask.

"What about me?" I inquired of him. "Do I have the ability to lead men? Do I possess those skills?"

"I think you have had to learn them from a very young age," he said, without a moment's pause.

"A consort is not the same as a sovereign."

"Granted, but have no fear, sister," he told me, patting my hands that lay clasped upon the stone bricks. "I will help you, as will many others. As soon as young Henry comes of age, he can fill the breach. He can be the leader England needs. And you must never forget that you have one advantage that Stephen can never match: you are a Briton. That may not matter to the lords in Normandy, but you will find it helps you with the common man, and it is the common man who must face down the rain of arrows."

This was a point I had not fully considered. Yes, Stephen was not born in England nor was he raised there, but that was not unusual for a Norman lord. Since the great conquest of my grandfather William, the kings of England had spent as much time in Normandy as they had in their kingdom, and why not? It was the land of their ancestors. But I was half Briton through my mother, and a member of the old royal line at that. I was born in England and spent my childhood there. In my soul, I felt more English than Norman, probably on account of my mother's influence. That was no help with the Norman barons, but perhaps Robert was correct: perhaps the common people of England would feel I was one of their own.

"I hope you are right, but what now?" I asked. "You say Stephen is called to this council. Will he appear?"

"He will send a representative and seek to influence the proceedings. I am not sure how far gone Bishop Henry is—I mean, how deep the breach between him and his brother is. It seems hard to believe that he would report the case to Rome, for that might be viewed as treason. My guess is that Stephen will survive, but there is a growing discontent among the bishops. In time, we can win them over to our side. If I am wrong and Bishop Henry intends to deny his brother, then we may be able to depart for England before winter. The difficulty lies in finding a place to land. Stephen has seized all my castles except for Bristol, and sailing around Land's End this time of year ... let's just say I'd rather not."

"There I may have a solution!" I proclaimed.

He raised his brows. "Oh really?"

"I heard back from Lady Adeliza. She desires to help us in any way she can, but of course her husband is a great supporter of Stephen. She tells me that, should I ever find myself in England, I would be welcome at Arundel Castle, for that estate is hers by right, and she does not think that Stephen could fault her too harshly for offering hospitality to a relative through marriage."

Robert smiled and shook his head in wonder. "She really said that? Then she must know you are looking for a port, for Arundel is right near the coast. It can withstand a siege if need be."

"Yes, well, let us hope there is no such need. But what do you think? It is a kind offer, no?"

"Very kind," he agreed, nodding his head. "Indeed, I wonder that she is willing to stick her neck out for us when she has little to gain."

"Women always like to help other women, Robert, particularly those who have done them a good turn," I said with a smile.

"I suppose you are right. There is some further news. Miles of Gloucester may be wavering in his support, or so I was told by one of my men in Bristol."

"Truly?! That is good news indeed! If we could win him to our cause … but perhaps I am wrong to hope."

"I think not. The tide is turning, as they say. I will see if I can get word to Lord Brian—tell him to make ready in case we are able to travel there. I know Lord Baldwin is willing to do his part, for he is keen to recover his lands."

I had barely heard the words that came after "Lord Brian." Ever since Robert had informed me that Brian still cared for me—indeed, that he had loved me all those years since we were torn apart—I had thought about him not just every day, but probably every hour. Naturally, I knew that his feelings did not make things any less impossible: there was still no chance of us being together, or not any that I could possibly consider in my position. But simply to be in his presence again and know that this person I had loved for so long still loved me seemed a prize to be treasured, and though I had spoken of it to no one, the possibility of seeing him had only increased my desire to get to England sooner rather than later. Yes, I felt a bit guilty about it, but it was the truth.

As I had missed Robert's point, I decided to change the subject. "It's a pity that Pope Innocent couldn't see the merit of our case. If he had decided in our favor—"

"Do not concern yourself with that now. The Holy Father has no desire to become involved in this matter. He simply sided with the man who was already on the throne. If we can overthrow Stephen, then Rome will hearken to our call. The pope has enough enemies already: he will not make another one for a simple matter of principle."

"For shame, brother!" I said, smiling and shaking my head. "I see your opinion of Rome is somewhat worse than mine."

"Yes, but you have been there. You have seen its glories. You have allowed it to seduce you."

"I think I have suffered a great deal more on account of Rome than you ever have! I have far more reason for annoyance. But let us speak no more of such things. We will wait to hear the council's decision, then if God wills it, we will set sail for Arundel ere the frost has arrived. I shall hate to leave my boys, but this is no time for sentiment."

"Excellent!" he said, clapping his hands.

Even as he smiled at me, I thought of something else: something I had been hiding in the darkest part of my soul for some time. I had been wanting to ask this question ever since Robert had come back to me—indeed, ever since Stephen had been gifted the crown. Although it struck my heart with fear to even consider it, I knew I must speak my query at one point or another, and it seemed best to do so before departing for England. I therefore took a deep breath and proceeded.

"One thing though, Robert."

"Yes?"

"I have been meaning to ask you this, only I was afraid to—that is, I am afraid to know the answer."

"Well, let's have out with it then!"

I nodded my head. "Very well. You were there with the late king before he died?"

"Yes, every painful hour of it. They said it was the lampreys that did him in, but I think not. He was sick before he ate them."

"Be that as it may, in those final days, when you and the archbishop and the other lords were with him, did he ever say anything about the succession?"

Robert looked deep into my eyes. I felt as if he was reading my soul.

"You want to know if he released the lords from their oath of fealty? If he appointed Stephen?"

"Yes," I whispered.

"Well, it is certainly true that he was angry with you, and that Stephen had been rising in the royal favor for some time, and that many of the lords begrudged having to make the oath to you in the first place."

"Oh God …" I muttered, looking away.

He placed his hand on mine. "But Maud—"

"Yes?" I replied, turning my eyes toward him.

"He never said anything of the sort. He told me to travel to Caen and take the money out of the treasury, and then to give it to you as soon as you arrived. He wanted the throne for Prince Henry. That was his true desire. When a man is dying, he thinks less of vengeance and more of reconciliation. You can ask any of us who were there, and if they are being honest, they will tell you the same thing. Those who are saying that the king changed his mind—they were never there! They are lying to us all. You must know that!"

"You're sure there was nothing that might have led them to believe—"

"No."

I gave a sigh of relief and a few tears dropped from my eyes. "Thank you, brother. You have no idea how many times I have worried about that in the dark hours of the night. I often doubt myself in those moments."

"Do not doubt again!" he commanded. "Do not doubt that you will sit on England's throne, for I will commit my every waking moment to it!"

"Let us hope you are given the chance to do so," I concluded.

As the last days of summer were upon us, we sent Baldwin de Redvers to Wareham, where he hoped to seize Corfe Castle

The Forsaken Monarch

and thus gain custody of the port. He succeeded in his first aim, but Stephen's men were wise to his presence. They surrounded the castle and did not allow him to leave. Little did they know that Wareham was not our object at all. Had we gained it, so much the better, but the chief aim was to create confusion among our enemies. As Stephen arrived in Winchester and sent his representatives to Bishop Henry's council, his mind must have been in Wareham as much as it was in the old capital city.

As Earl Robert had foreseen, Stephen's allies were able to bend the council to their own ends. Archbishop Hugh of Rouen declared that no bishop should be in possession of a castle, for that was a mark of worldly pride and not fit for a prince of the Church. Here his intent was clear, for even as Bishop Roger of Salisbury had loved his castles, so Bishop Henry of Winchester set great store by his own estates. This was not a defense of Stephen so much as an assault upon the usurper's brother. Bishop Henry vowed to appeal to Rome, and he gained no little support from the other English bishops, who feared what actions the king might take against themselves. Stephen countered this with his own threat, vowing to banish any man who left England in violation of his wishes—that is, who went to speak with the Holy Father.

Had I not known better, I might have thought that Stephen was trying to see how far he could push his brother before he would attempt something desperate. As it turned out, we had the answer soon enough. In the first week of September 1139, I was sitting on a bench just beneath one of the windows in the upper passage of the castle keep. I had asked for it to be placed there, for I enjoyed reading with the sunlight upon me. There was a sound of someone rounding the corner, and I looked up from the page to see my brother walking toward me.

"Well met, Robert," I said, smiling at him.

"Well met indeed!" he replied.

I noticed that he had a sealed letter in his hand.

"Where is that from?" I asked, pointing at it.

"This, my lady," he said, holding it out to me, "is from the bishop of Winchester."

My eyes grew wide. "God be praised," I whispered.

I took the letter from his hand and set my book aside. I then moved toward the end of the bench and patted at the space to my right. He sat down next to me as I broke the seal and opened the letter. My heart was beating strongly and my hands shook ever so slightly.

"You go ahead first, then tell me what it says," Robert instructed.

I nodded and began to read.

To Her Most Serene Highness, the Empress Mathilda, Countess of Anjou—

You no doubt take as much surprise in receiving this letter as I did in writing it, but the state of affairs here in England is such that we must all consider how best to preserve the welfare of this kingdom. When I gave my fealty to King Stephen, it was with the assurance that he would do everything in his power to safeguard and promote the interests of our Holy Church, and he swore before Almighty God that he would not violate this sacred oath. Yet these past months have seen such grievous injury done to the practice of true Christianity that my conscience begs me to seek the support of Your Highness, for I can no longer own that all the actions of the king are in line with the will of God and the laws of the land. He has fallen under the control of most vile counselors who have made him their cuckold and wrought destruction upon this, our kingdom. Such a fearful rebellion has sprung up here that England is likely to repeat those days spoken about in scripture, when "every man did that which was good in his eyes."[19] *Now as then, a Deborah may suffice. Therefore, in light of the respect due to your person, I think it only right that you should be welcomed upon our shores, according to the will of the late King Henry, whom we all knew and loved. Only your presence here can grant safety to our beloved Church. I bid you come as soon as you can, but say not that I have sent for you, for I am already in great danger here and fear those around the king, who would gladly slit my throat and yours if they had the chance. Again, I bid you, make for England and restore us to true religion. I will ensure that you are given safe passage.—Henry, Bishop of Winchester, Abbot of Glastonbury*

When I had finished reading, I folded the letter again and held it in my lap.

"Well," said Robert, "what does he have to say for himself?"

"He wants me to come to England. He fears for the Church and thinks that I can help to 'restore true religion,' whatever that means. Also, he says I will be granted safe passage."

"And do you believe him?"

"Certainly not. That is, he may well try to make it so, but it is plain enough that he does not control the king. No, I will tell you what he is doing. Perhaps he wants to teach his brother a lesson. Perhaps he thinks that my presence there will make him more powerful, for if Stephen must fight for the love of the Church, so much the better for the bishops. I suppose it is just possible that he hates his brother so much, he would subvert his reign as a form of vengeance. However, I think it more likely that he does not so much want me to be queen

---

[19] The reference is to Judges 17:6 and 21:25.

as he wants to make his brother miserable: to strengthen the Church, and by extension, himself."

Robert placed his hand on mine. "Either way, this is our chance. Stephen is causing all men to flee from him. He has never been weaker. Leave Normandy to Count Geoffrey. We make for England."

And so it was that on the fifth day before the Kalends of October, in the year of our Lord 1139, I rose from my bed at the castle of Caen and was dressed by Adela. I handed my things to Drogo that he might ready my horse. I slipped into the chamber where my boys were sleeping and stood there for a moment watching them. God only knew when I would see them again. As I kissed their foreheads, I felt a twinge of guilt, but then I remembered that I was doing it all for them.

I made my way down the stairs and through the front gate into the yard, where over a hundred men waited with horses at the ready: Earl Robert, Drogo, Guy de Sablé, and the rest of the knights. Lady Mabel of Gloucester, my brother's wife, elected to come as well, though I deemed it unwise, not wanting any harm to befall her. This was not a true invasion party, but one meant to avoid detection. I mounted my steed and blew one last kiss toward the castle keep, then we set off for the coast. That was such a strange ride: one moment I was filled with excitement that I was finally returning, the next with fear that Stephen might seize me, and the next with sorrow to be parted from my boys. We reached the port by midday and climbed into the small vessels, none of which were likely to attract much attention, for they were no larger than fishing boats.

As we raised the anchor and pushed off into the water, I felt a rush of fear coursing through me as my actions seemed to become fully real. I turned to look back at the land I was leaving behind—a land where I might have dwelled in peace, had I been willing to surrender to fate. For just a moment, I doubted my choice. Then I felt a tap on my shoulder. It was Drogo.

"Remember, Empress Mathilda, 'Let us hold fast the confession of our hope without wavering …'"

I smiled and nodded. "'… for he who promised is faithful.'"

"Never forget that," he said.

I walked up to the bow, where Earl Robert stood with his arms resting upon the rail, hands folded, gazing forward at the meeting of sea and sky. I stood next to him, sharing in the same view. The wind was blowing gently, caressing my face and moving my veil ever so slightly.

"I am betting everything on you, Robert," I told him. "Do not let me down."

"Do you see that—there in the distance?" he asked, pointing ahead.

I strained to try to make out some distant figure, but I had no idea what he meant. "I see nothing."

"Yes, but beyond that nothing there is England! For as long as it takes, as far as it takes us, we will fight for that sacred ground," he promised, placing a hand upon my shoulder. "We will not rest until it is won."

Even as he walked away, I continued looking off to the north, a smile forming upon my face. The waves continued to lap against the stem, and I could hear the distant call of gulls.

"England," I whispered.

I hope you have enjoyed *The Forsaken Monarch*, the second of three planned volumes in the *Chronicle of Maud* series. I welcome reviews on sites such as Amazon and Goodreads. You can follow me on Twitter @AmyMantravadi, on my Facebook pages /chronicleofmaud and /amymantravadi, and on the official series website, www.chronicleofmaud.com. If you like reading essays on theological topics, you can also check out my blog, www.amymantravadi.com. Thanks again for reading!

Grace and peace,

Amy Mantravadi

CPSIA information can be obtained
at www.ICGtesting.com
Printed in the USA
LVHW011033110322
713034LV00001B/116